# The Coigreach

## A Novel

R.J. Erskine

 For information contact Stray Voltage Press, *strayvoltagepress@gmail.com* or visit website *strayvoltagepress.com*

Cover photograph by Mark Siragusa. Cover design by Chris Herron. Thanks to Hannah Gregus for graphic art and Pam Bartlett, Kym Ogden, Mark Siragusa, and Miss Constance for creative insight and editing.

Special thanks to Derek Peterson for his information and stewardship of Allerton Park.

Erskine, Ronald,
      The Coigreach / RJ Erskine.
      "A Stray Voltage Press book"
      ISBN 978-0-9971873-7-3

Printed in Lansing, MI, U.S.A.
Written only with genuine human intelligence and creativity.

# The Coigreach

## R.J. Erskine

*To John and Ineke – and a vanishing way of farming*

**Also by R. J. Erskine**

*Casting Demons Into Swine (2017)*

*Prometheus Scorned (2020)*

*Ghosts of Lost Dreams (2023)*

**Coigreach** — noun (Scots Gaelic) *m.* (*genitive and plural **coigrich***)

1. stranger, alien, or foreigner


Better to meet a bear robbed of her cubs than a fool in his folly— *Proverbs*

# LEGEND

1- Mansion

2- Gate House

3- House of the Golden Buddhas

4- Fu Dog garden

5- Gorilla Statue

6- Bear Statue

7- Goldfish Pond

8- Walled Garden

9- Greenhouse

10- Formal Garden

11- Winters Farm

12- Lost Garden

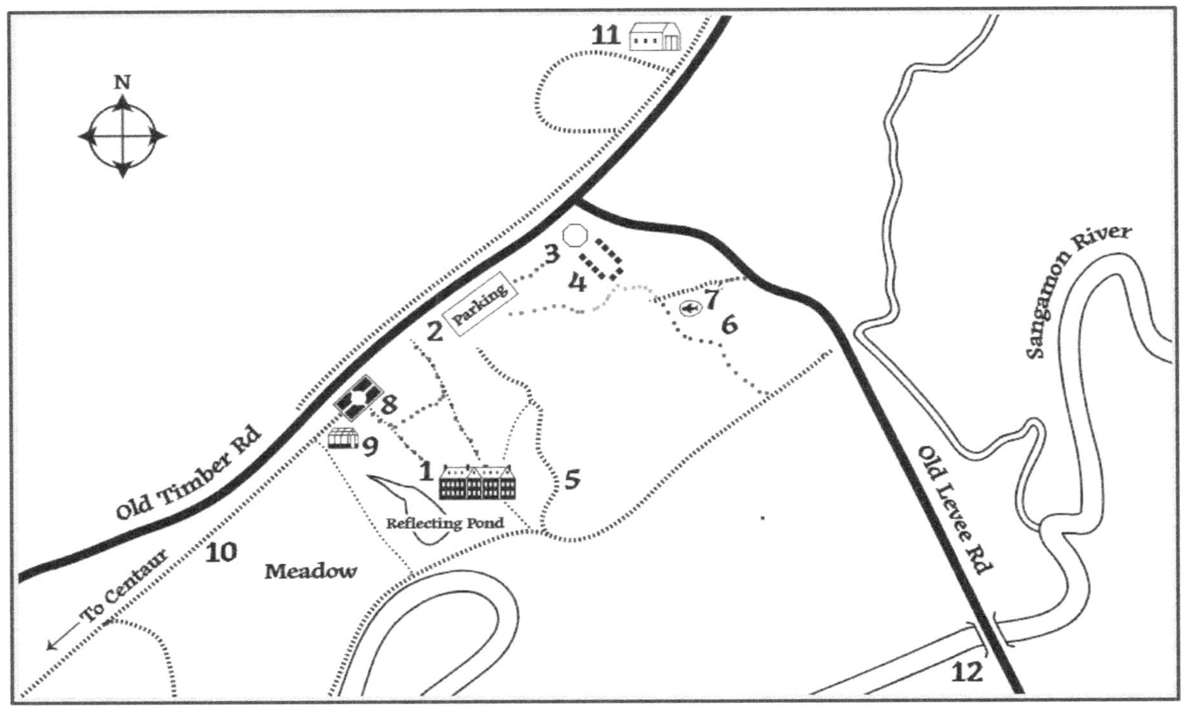

N
11
Sangamon River
3
4
7
6
Parking
2
8
9
1
Reflecting Pond
5
Old Timber Rd
To Centaur
10
Meadow
Old Levee Rd
12

# PROLOGUE

Fillan, Gaelic for 'little wolf', crossed the Irish Sea in the eighth century to help banish paganism from the wild realm of Alba. He built a stone priory along a river near Tyndrum, at a site with a still pool along the bank. When the saint immersed those who suffered from demons of madness into the pool, they were cured and gained sound mind and spirit.

Fillan's deeds, especially his powers with animals, were known throughout the Highlands. When first plowing the land by the river to plant crops, a great wolf attacked his oxen and killed one of them. Fillan placed a *geis* upon the wolf, forcing the creature to be harnessed. The spellbound wolf helped Fillan finish the field work and later, pulled cartloads of stones to construct the priory.

Soon after, Fillan visited the nearby village of Killin, where the locals were terrified by an enormous wild boar with tusks as sharp as swords. Fillan set off with his hound and tracked the brute in the deep forests by Loch Tay, at the feet of brooding Ben Lawers. More than once he found human remains, with body and limbs torn apart.

One evening, as twilight seeped through the forest, the dog caught a scent. Chasing after his hound, Fillan came upon the boar, rooting under a rowan tree. Turning his massive head, the beast cast evil red eyes on him. The boar charged, scything tree saplings with its tusks to clear the way. Fillan held his ground and raised his wooden club. With a single blow to the skull, he felled his wicked foe, striking so fiercely that the stout oak broke in half. Thus, Fillan purged the terror of Killin.

The saint then built a mill to harness the River Dochart in in the village. Here, he healed the infirmed by calling upon the spirits within several stones. Collected from the river, each stone resembled body parts that needed healing. As his reputation grew, pilgrims traveled many miles to Glen Dochart.

After Fillan's death, successive abbots of his priory continued the traditions of the *Culdees*—hallowed men and women from Ireland, who like Fillan, migrated to Scotland in the eighth century. The abbots led simple lives, secluded from lay communities, following the life of their patron saint— meditation and service emphasized over material comfort. Each of the saint's relics were protected by the *deòradh*, hereditary keepers who closely collaborated with the priory. Abhorred and persecuted by the Roman Church, the keepers upheld the *Culdee* tradition by preserving the relics and applying their powers for the common good. Over time, the *deòradh* dwindled in number, and the knowledge of their relics forgotten, as the Celtic church succumbed to the power of Rome.

Chronicles of Inchaffray Abbey

# Planning

# CHAPTER 1

Valerie Farwell believed in punctuality and disdained those who didn't. Biding her time, she took in the view through the large window, watching the sun sink over the meadow, skimming orange light off the pond in front of the mansion. Now in her second year as the Director of Allerton Park and Retreat Center, she had learned rank has its privileges—such as subordinates who could be delegated to finish unwanted tasks—one of whom stood to her right. Ashley Plambeck, the Assistant Director of Events and Planning, read Val's agitation from her posture, and stood silently in the paneled room.

Standing behind her desk, Val's mind wandered away from the office. Sapphire eyes, framed by shoulder-length chestnut hair and a broad mouth, tracked along the terraced lawn in front of the brick mansion, modeled after an English manor. When needing to clear her thoughts, she often left her office to pass through the wide hall, enter the solarium on the right, then out the French doors. Once outside, a paved walk led by a small pool with colorful Koi, carved sphinxes on either side, then down ten steps and onto the lower-level terrace by the pond.

A crushed-gravel walkway paralleled the brick wall that divided the upper and lower terraces. If she continued left, the walkway reached the far edge of the pond, then descended as a footpath towards the Sangamon River. More often, Val chose right, following the walkway under a shaded stand of trees, which ended at the formal gardens, a quarter mile distant.

Val smiled inwardly. How many other jobs in this world, let alone at the university, offered such *noblesse oblige*? Autonomy and authority to manage an old estate—her own petty fiefdom that was once the home of a fabulously wealthy patron of the arts—with uncommon interests. She managed a staff who tended to mundane tasks and a budget with ample discretionary funds, thirty minutes away from campus. The arrangement suited her well.

Val left her pastoral daydream behind and tapped a pen on the desk. "Leave it to artists to arrive for a meeting on their own time."

"For sure," the younger woman agreed, then checked her watch.

Off to her left, a sturdy man with curly sienna hair touched with grey, added, "Especially when one of them is a dean. They're pretty much God on Earth when it comes to their own turf at the university." Carl Lipinski spoke in his typical fashion, half-weary from seeing it all before.

Val rarely saw Carl smile; a personal cloud seemed to hover over him wherever he went. But he ran a tight ship as the grounds and maintenance manager for the entire park. Her eyes settled upon his work clothes, dark blue, trim, clean, and suitable for a Sears catalog. "I met Dean Duffey when we first planned this upcoming event. I think he was late then, as well." She frowned. "I hope this isn't a preview of the level of help we're going to get for this project."

Carl grunted. Voices carried through the hallway leading from the north entrance of the mansion. Val's receptionist, Jenny, engaged the visitors in a brief discussion, followed by steps echoing off the hardwood floor of the hall. Two men appeared at the office doorway. One was ruddy-faced with a trimmed white beard, navy blue blazer and khaki pants. The younger man was taller, his angular features topped by a mat of unkempt sandy hair, wearing a tailored white cotton shirt and rust-hued corduroys over suede oxfords.

Donald Duffey, Dean of the College of Fine and Applied Arts, greeted his host with gusto. "Valerie! Good to see you again." He appraised the scenic backdrop. "As always, I'm envious of the splendid view from your office."

Val wondered if the 'hail fellow, well met' manner of entrance was a prerequisite for being a dean, an academic position more aligned with politics than scholarship, after all. "Welcome to my humble space, Dean Duffey." Her eyes shared a mutual glimpse with his companion.

"Humble?" The Dean feigned surprise. "Here you stand where Allerton himself probably lingered and admired the majesty of his estate."

"And a true visionary he was," Ellington Rose added. "Glad to see you, Valerie, and thanks for meeting with us again."

Val replied, "Likewise Ellington, no problem, especially since you're the ones who travelled to the edge of the university empire. I think you remember my Assistant Director, Ashley, from the last meeting?"

Both visitors smiled in assent. Val noted a leather satchel crooked under Ellington's arm and gestured towards the far wall. "This is Carl Lipinski, my right-hand man for maintenance…buildings, grounds, even at times, security. I thought it's about time to bring him in for planning."

Ellington raised an eyebrow. "Security?"

Val waved a hand airily. "The usual kids partying at night, sometimes minor graffiti and vandalism."

"Not the sculptures and other installations, I hope. Some of them are priceless. And I've arranged a few special works for the event in October, on loan from the Art Institute in Chicago and private collections." Ellington stepped towards Carl. "Great to meet you, Carl. Nice to know you have our back."

The groundskeeper regarded Ellington's outstretched hand with discomfort but shook it anyway.

Dean Duffey cut in. "I'm sure that"—he glanced at Carl and pointed—"Mr. Lipinski, was it?" Carl nodded silently, face frozen in a grimace. "I'm sure Mr. Lipinski will have things in good order. Besides, Valerie, I think you're going to be pleased to hear what we've conjured up for the big celebration."

Settling into her leather chair, Ashley shifting behind her, Val offered a hand to a pair of armchairs in front of the desk. "Please have a seat." Carl settled in a wooden chair along the wall.

The Dean took a seat and crossed one leg over the other before speaking. "You'll recall, when we recruited Ellington onto our faculty last year, I charged him to leverage his notoriety in ceramic sculpture to improve awareness of our university assets like Allerton Park. When we met in my office a couple months ago, we were targeting something wrapped around the sixtieth anniversary of Laredo Taft's installation of the *Alma Mater* sculpture on campus."

He turned to his companion. "Ellington, if you would please bring us up to date on some of the developments and opportunities. Your thoughts might give Valerie an idea what she may need for the event's logistics."

Ellington laid the satchel onto his lap, snapped open the flap, and pulled out several photos. "As Dean Duffey stated, we intend to have a celebration of our School of Art and Design's connection with Laredo Taft." He faced Carl. "He remains one the best-known sculptors from Illinois, especially those from the turn of the century."

He took a color photo of the *Alma Mater* situated at the university entrance and gave it to Val, who studied it for a few moments, passed it to Ashley, who then gave it to Carl. "That remarkable piece was presented at a ceremony in 1929 and is an icon of the entire university. Many other of Taft's works are placed throughout the state and nation."

Ellington glanced at four other photos in his hand and again offered them to Val. "On one occasion, he was commissioned to add sculptural features to the buildings for the 1893 Columbian Exposition in Chicago, but a shortage of skilled artisans threatened his deadline to finish in time. He approached Daniel Burnham, the chief architect, and asked if he could employ female assistants to finish the work; some of them were his students at the Art Institute."

Ellington looked pointedly at Val. "Mind you this was the late Victorian era, when women were not considered to be the equal of men on many fronts, including sculpture."

Val and Ashley bristled in unison. Noting their tenor, the sculptor added quickly, "Reputedly, Burnham told Taft, hire anyone, even white rabbits, if they'll do the work." Ellington glanced at Carl, who was scrutinizing the first photo of the series. "To give you an idea of the scope of the work, you're looking at the Horticultural Building. They had little more than a year to complete the figures all about the outside." Carl nodded with appreciation.

"So, as a bit of a joke, these gifted female artists became known from then on as The White Rabbits. After the Exposition, they continued to pursue their creative passion in sculpture and became well known in their own right."

Ellington paused while Val, Ashley, and Carl sifted through the remaining photos. "The last photos are of small pieces sculpted by three of these women. Bessie Potter Vonnoh's *In Grecian Draperies*, a stunning teapot from Carol Brooks MacNeil, and a bronze casting of Janet Scudder's *Frog Fountain*." Ellington eagerly leaned forward in his chair. "I've arranged to have these three pieces loaned for display at our celebration in October." He gave a smug look. "It took a little bit of cashing in some chips for previous favors."

After passing the last photo, Val asked, "Where are they coming from?"

"The Vonnoh, from the Art Institute, the teapot from an acquaintance's private collection, and the frog, from the Metropolitan Museum of Art."

Dean Duffey cleared his throat. "Chicago, New York, the cream of the art world comes to Robert Allerton Park."

Carl stacked the photos and got up from his chair to hand them back to Ellington. "Are you meaning to have these things here at the park? Where would we show them? Here in the mansion?"

Ellington spread his hands. "Why not? Given the amount of light and the size of the place, we could arrange for each piece to be displayed in a separate room, here on the ground floor, with pictures and artist statements from Taft and the White Rabbits posted along the hall. I would first offer a talk on the history of Taft and the others. The guests could then loiter over cocktails and *hor d'oeuvres*. Perhaps followed by an outdoor buffet and a stroll through the gardens."

Val asked, "How many people are you talking about?"

Ellington shrugged. "A few dozen...plus a handful of university representatives. Keep it exclusive." He glanced at the Dean. "And premium priced for the donors."

Val's face puckered. "We'd have to find a place to squeeze them in for this seminar of yours."

Carl rubbed the back of his neck. "I imagine the frog and teapot are worth a bit of money."

Ellington smiled benignly. "More than I would want to pay."

"What about insurance? Are you willing to pay someone to stay overnight here to watch them?"

Dean Duffey held up a hand. "Good questions but give Ellington a chance to tell you the news about the money...uh, let's call them funds." He looked at Ellington expectantly.

The sculptor took off his round tortoise-shell glasses and rubbed a spot on a lens with a cloth pulled from his pocket. "We've been able to secure an endowment, the Harold and Barbara Feinman Endowment for Excellence in Sculpture. The intent of this endowment is to support continuing education to the public, faculty scholarship, and educational opportunities for students."

"Quite a coup on the part of Ellington to garner this support, I must say," the Dean added.

Ellington placed his glasses back on. "Thank you, Dean Duffey. The endowment will cover the funds needed to exhibit the special pieces. As for the food service and other amenities, we'll invite select attendees, mostly alumni, who..."

"Will want to be charter members of the Friends of Laredo Taft to support the College of Fine Arts," the Dean interjected. "We think this setting, linked with the Taft anniversary, will be the perfect place for the inaugural event. After all, there is a wonderful collection of sculpture and ceramic works throughout this park."

Val glanced at Carl, who had worked himself into a scowl. "We're honored, and I agree this would certainly draw the attention of the right kind of…influential people to our facility. One of our long-term goals is to expand the use of this park beyond the usual weddings and academic conferences. We want to become a go-to destination for diverse events." She inhaled then exhaled a deep breath. "Still, that's a lot to plan for and get ready."

Ellington studied her. "True. But for the education and scholarship portion of the endowment, I have further good news. Remember when I took the faculty position, you had asked me to initiate an artist-in-residence program here at the park."

"Meaning you'll have time to start this in the near future?"

"This summer no less. The endowment will fund a grad student internship, to serve as my understudy. The park will receive compensation for any overnight housing I might need, as well as any remodeling for the studio."

Val thought. That would help the bottom line of the budget. "I'm impressed, you've certainly scored"—she regarded the Dean—"quite a coup indeed."

Ellington gave a winsome smile. "Spring semester is almost over, and we've a big event to plan and prepare for. I'm thinking of starting to remodel the shop by the first of July and be in production soon after."

"Well, I guess we'd better get started." Taking an administrative posture, Val looked at her assistant director. "Think you can help me oversee this?"

Ashley 's face faintly betrayed her sense of unequal burden. "I'll do my best."

Facing the artist again, Val asked, "How much space are we talking about?"

Ellington pursed his lips and looked out the window. All eyes were on him as he mapped out the needs within his mind.

"A shop to mix plaster and make molds, supply room, studio…I'd say the size of a decent high school chemistry lab…plus a storeroom with shelves, an office…," He nodded. "That should about do it." Holding up his hand, he added, "Almost forgot, a kiln. But we'll plan for firing outdoors."

Facing Carl, Val declared, "There's a lot of unused space in the back side of the greenhouse. I think that would be the perfect place."

Carl knit his brow. "I wouldn't say it's unused, we store parts and pieces for our equipment back there."

She waved her hand in dismissal. "I'm sure you can find more room in the old shed on the other side of the road. Seems to me all sorts of flotsam and jetsam gets dumped over there and in the lot behind it." Looking about the room, Val announced, "We've got a plan. Carl, I know you and the boys will want to jump in on this and lend a hand."

"Sure thing," Carl said with little enthusiasm.

Ellington returned the photos back to his satchel. "Oh, after we get the studio in order, I would please like to arrange a tour of the sculptures and gardens of the park…to get a feel for the place and decide which of the installations we might want to highlight for the guests to see." He closed the clasp on his satchel and peered at Val. "As a bonus during my study here, I could try to refurbish some of the sculptures." He grew pensive. "Those cast in ceramic or limestone at least."

Exchanging a smile, Val said, "Pick a time and date, and I'll give you a personal tour."

Standing up from his chair, Ellington slipped his satchel over his shoulder. "Great. We're going to have a full summer ahead of us."

# CHAPTER 2

Impressed by the makeover, Val said, "It seems your studio is coming together."

Ellington assessed the disarray around them. "The plaster shop is still a work in progress, but I've got the mixer and sink set up. I'm still building bins for plaster storage and trim disposal. We should be ready to go by the end of the week...still, I don't know where the past six weeks has gone." Dust and grime blemished his jeans and tan work shirt, sleeves rolled up to his elbows.

Her eyes skimmed his strong hands and taut forearms—he had washed them before joining her. "I'm glad I could pull you away from your work." Val gave him a half humorous glance. "I'd like to give you a tour of one of the more curious places in this old estate and need advice on something that is right up your alley."

"What do you have in mind?"

She peered into a large box of edged hand tools with wood handles. She picked out a foot-long utensil that looked like a miniature hoe. "What kind of medieval gadget is this?"

He smiled. "A woodcarver's shave hook...handy for carving and shaping plaster molds." She poked around the box with the hook. "This is an odd assortment."

"Be careful you don't grab a fettling knife on the wrong end. It's sharp on the edges and the point."

Val put the hook back in the box. After a pause, she replied to his query. "I think the best way to plan for what I have in mind, is by you coming along and seeing for yourself." She made to leave the studio then halted; her attention drawn to a sketch pad on a table. The likeness of a dark-haired woman returned her gaze. As she reached out to the drawing, she asked, "May I?"

Ellington gestured, "Suit yourself."

Val thumbed through the pages, noting the common theme. The woman sat wearing a dress—the fabric more a thin veil than of substance. "She's certainly captivating. Someone you know?"

He shook his head. "Just one of the student models we hire out for the studio classes. I'm kicking around ideas for my sculpture for the Taft event. Maybe a study of the White Rabbits as subjects themselves."

"Intriguing," she said.

Ellington appraised the proportion of her jawline, neck, and shoulders with a sculptor's point of view. "You'd make a good model yourself."

Val faced him with a thin smile. "I'll think about it." Releasing the sketchbook, she once again headed for the door. "It's time for the tour, don't you think?"

They followed a path leading to the east side of the park. The earth had spun past midsummer only two weeks before, giving the sun plenty of heat to spare. The nearby Sangamon flood plain lent an adhesive layer to the humid air. Content to let the cicadas hold the conversation for a spell, the duo strolled along a grassy lane, lined on both sides by woven walls of green vines.

Val asked, "And your room in the Gate House is comfortable enough?"

"It's a fine old building, with lots of character. You said it once served as the residence for the head gardener and his family?"

"Yes, only a short walk to the gardens for them."

"Nice job, if you can get it."

"I'm curious. How did you end up with the name Ellington?

It's a bit unusual."

He peeked at her from the corner of his eye. "Jazz music."

She halted. "Jazz music?"

Lifting his hands and lowering his head, he replied, "My parents loved swing era jazz. So, my brother was named Hawkins, as in Coleman Hawkins the saxophonist, my sister Holiday, as in Billie Holiday…"

"And your namesake was Duke Ellington."

"Bingo."

"You and your siblings could have made a trio."

"Our family admired the music, didn't have the talent to play it."

"That's a shame, think of the promotional opportunities."

"Well on the bright side, we listened to a lot of good music when growing up. I acquired my parents record collection and" —he grinned with a slight swagger—"their vintage Zenith stereo console. It's a great piece of Mid-Century furniture to boot."

Val arched her brow. "You're a multi-talented artist, I see." They continued their trek between the vines.

Ellington gazed at the splash of sunlight framed by the end of the allée. "What a unique structure. Some sort of shrine?"

She gestured with her hand. "Our first stop."

They closed in on the white tower, a fifteen-foot-wide octagon, with a covered terrace on the second level. Vines sprawled over the first story, cut back from four sets of steps that led to a low concrete platform. Each stair set marked an opposite quadrant of the octagon. The nearest one rose to a golden figure in an alcove, hands lifted, open palms facing outwards.

Nearing the end of the shaded path, Val focused on the placid Asian face. "I believe Mr. Allerton named this tower the House of the Golden Buddhas, for a pair of Siamese-styled icons…"

"Pair?"

She turned to him. "There's another on the opposite side. Both were carved from teak wood, reputedly made in Bangkok, from prototypes at a nearby temple."

"Teak shipped from Bangkok? It seems Mr. Allerton had expensive tastes."

Her mouth curled into a half-smile. "And eclectic tastes at that. Contrast this Asian style to the classical pieces such as Adam, and the Three Graces, in the formal gardens."

Ellington gave her a sidewise glance. "If you ignore those ghastly Anglo-Chinese musicians I stumbled upon on the far side of the flower gardens."

"Wait until we turn the corner of this vine walk." Reaching the end of the lane, she pointed to the right.

Ellington halted before a long, cloistered lawn, lined by tall spruce trees, stretching away from the tower. The swooping boughs of the trees slanted to a row of six-foot pillars on either side of the manicured lawn, ten per side, each crowned by a two-foot ceramic creature. On the far end, nearly a hundred yards away, the lawn gave way to a path into the woods. One more figure sat on a pillar to each side of the portal, holding a strategic view of the garden and Buddha house.

Eyes drifting along the figures to the left, then returning to those on the right, Ellington whistled softly. "This is a phantasmal space, fitting for a monastery. Linear formality, framed within a rustic estate, itself an oasis in an ocean of corn and soybeans."

He sauntered to the first column on his right, scrutinizing the ceramic figure above. The creature sat like a dog, cloaked in a deep blue glaze. Large white eyes with black pupils, deep set under arched eyelids, glared at him with impish spite. The upper lip, curling across the entire face, cast a sinister smile. A row of flat white teeth lined the upper and lower jaw, with two large tusks curling from the upper corners of the mouth.

Ellington slowly circled the figure. "These look like some sort of Fu Dog. Were they cast in China? How did Allerton conjure up such a setting, let alone this collection of blue gargoyles?"

Val came by his side, regarding the haughty gaze of the creature. "I can't answer your second question, but you are right. This is commonly called the Fu Dog Garden, and yes, they originated from China." She canvassed the garden in a half-turn. "Twenty-two in all."

Torn between a deeper study of the Fu Dog in front of him, and the desire to review the entire array, Ellington approached the second, then the third pillar. "Whoever crafted these took the glaze work to the next level. If I'm not mistaken, they added crushed lapis-lazuli"—he turned to Val—"the blue semi-precious stone, to add the blue tint. The luster is nothing short of spectacular."

Ellington stepped back and scanned several statues from a wider perspective. "They're all a bit different from one another, the ears, postures, facial expressions, as if custom made. Who was the sculptor?"

Val strolled past him, continuing down the colonnade. "No one knows, or exactly where in China they came from. Mr. Allerton is said to have acquired them from various art dealers throughout the world and had this garden designed to accommodate the collection. The installations were completed in 1932. Although it has gone through some modifications."

Ellington trailed her, his eyes fixated on each Fu Dog that he passed. "These look as if they were molded and cast as hollow figures. I can't imagine the exceptional care and expense to have these shipped to such a remote location, during the Great Depression no less."

"Mr. Allerton had, as I suggested…unlimited resources to pull this off. His father was at one time one of the biggest landowners in Illinois." Val swayed in front of the last pair of figures and tilted her head. "The curious thing about them is that they were always purchased and delivered in pairs." She pointed. "You see, the face of one is different than the opposite one, a sort of duality."

"Which means?"

"Even though their posture seems like a dog's, they're actually models of Chinese watcher lions, or *shishi*, with origins based on older Buddhist traditions."

Ellington grunted. "Well matched with the theme of the

shrine on the other end."

"Traditionally, one lion has an orb under a front paw, representing the male and material presence, the female would have a cub under her paw, portraying spiritual elements. Together they would protect the house, or other places"—she looked about them—"such as a garden, from outside threats. Not just other people but evil spirits as well."

Ellington grinned. "Allerton must have had a superstitious streak to have so many. Maybe he wanted to feel safe while walking in the woods."

She laughed. "Who knows?"

"You hold a fair bit of knowledge about art in your own right, I see."

"I got my degree in art history, with a concentration in Asian studies, before my first job as an assistant curator in Cleveland. When the park director position came open here two years ago, I saw it as a perfect fit." Her eyes withdrew from the present. "I've always admired how sculptors contrive substance out of organic matter—metal, clay, stone. It adds a third dimension that painting lacks. As if your hands extract life itself out of clay."

Ellington considered her comment. "That's rather biblical. Good sculptors do more than imitate life…they capture it. Beyond the physical form, we try to evoke a sense of melding the subject's spirit into the clay as well." He gestured to the Fu Dogs around them, adding lightly, "Perhaps there's a…what did you call them? A *shishi* locked inside each of their hollow bodies."

"Like caged zoo animals? That's sad. Makes sculptors sound more like jailers than artists." Val lingered on her thoughts. "Which brings me to a special project that might interest you as a sculptor…and ceramicist."

They walked side by side back to the Buddhist shrine, Ellington scanning each figure as they passed. "Okay, you win. What's this special project?"

"For starters, it'll take someone such as yourself with expertise in ceramic molding and modeling." She let her comment sink in to stoke his interest. "When we first set up your sabbatical, you offered to touch up some of the statuary here at the park."

"True."

"What projects have you already lined up for this year?"

Ellington pressed his lips and squinted, gathering his thoughts. "I'm working on a multi-piece installation for a large, juried exhibit in Chicago this coming winter. I'll model and mold the pieces here, but most of the kiln firing will be done back on campus. And I'll be supervising the advanced sculpture studio class on Mondays each week this fall. I intend to come here for creative retreats the rest of the week."

"That's a lot of coming and going between here and Urbana."

"Don't you do that every day?"

"It's a fun"—she smiled—"and fast ride on open roads."

"Ahh... Of course, your red Beamer I see parked by the mansion." He scrutinized her. "That's a premium road machine."

Val returned his gaze. "Like Mr. Allerton, I have expensive tastes."

And I suppose a salary to match, Ellington thought.

Val said, "Still, there are some nights, because of weather and such, that I stay in a room in the mansion."

"As I get more immersed into my work, I'll probably take advantage of staying in the Gate House more often."

"What of your wife and son…Julie and Sean wasn't it?"

"Yes. Sean is almost seventeen. I'll be there for weekends, and his school events as needed." He waved his hand past his face at a flitting mosquito. "Oh, I almost forgot, my graduate assistant, Kim Okuma, will help with the prep work here for me—mixing plaster, glazes, tending the kiln."

"Sounds like grunt work."

He smiled snidely. "Welcome to being a grad assistant. I like to think of it as an apprenticeship. All the great artists had them, like Michaelangelo."

Val bit her lower lip. "And had a bit of an ego to match, no doubt." She paused. "Will she need a place to stay overnight at times?"

Ellington knotted his brow. "I'll place a couch in my office, like I do on campus, for what I call crash-naps. She'd be welcome to use it."

Val registered his response. "We can always arrange a room in the Evergreen Lodge."

Ellington looked at her with a face masked as a question mark.

"The motel-type building we passed on the south end of the public parking lot," she explained.

They stopped at the last Fu Dog before reaching the white tower. "As you can see, some of the figures are showing their age. The glaze is cracking and chipping…it gets worse with each passing winter. Sadly, it's a low priority on our budget."

Ellington stepped up on the concrete curb that surrounded the pillar. As he continued to evaluate the statue, Val added, "My special request during your stay is to refurbish some of the pieces, hopefully in time for the Taft event in October. There are a couple alumni who, as art patrons, are particularly interested in the Fu Dogs. I hope to show them what an investment in loving care could achieve."

Ellington gave her a side eye. "So as to jump-start funding for a restoration of all the statues, no doubt." He reached up to touch a leg of the Fu Dog. "If I have to recast some of the pieces, like the ear on this one, it will take time to set molds…and trying to match the glaze with the rest of the figure will be tricky." He stepped back onto the lawn. "Which two are you wanting to start with?"

Valerie pointed to the two watchers by the path to the woods. "They're the showcase of the garden, the way they're separated from the others."

Once again, his trained eyes scanned the specimens. "They do have unusual postures. the way they face one another…and more curves and detail. Considering I have to put the finishing touches on my shop, and Lord knows what it'll take to track down the right kind of material for the glaze and the plaster…"

She asked, "Can you do it in time?"

He glanced to the far end of the lawn, then meditated with lids half shut. His pale blue eyes popped wide behind his glasses. "The biggest hurdle will be to research how to match the original glaze"—he jerked a thumb to a Fu Dog behind him—"like replacing the lips on this Fu Dog here to match the rest of his face." Shaking his head, he muttered, "That will take time. Then trying to make the molds proportional to the other elements of each statue. The sooner we start the better."

Val narrowed her eyes. "I wonder…"

"About?"

She made a gesture of dismissal with her hand. "Nothing, really."

Ellington coaxed her. "Go on."

"If I have to, I'll personally see to it that Carl and his crew will help you anyway they can."

"Dammit! If Laredo Taft and his White Rabbits finished the facades and sculptures for an entire building in under a year, we can make a pair of Fu Dogs look good as new by the end of October." He rubbed his jaw. "I'll make a case to the Dean to dump more of my teaching duties on somebody else."

Val reflected on his off-hand remark. "I suppose you have to set priorities. I'll work with Carl and his crew to pull the first two figures down and deliver them to the studio next week."

Ellington held up a hand. "Whoa. No use for us to go there yet. They're better off and more secure right where they are. Let me work out the other preparations before we take them to the studio." He regarded her thoughtfully. "I'll start by getting Kim to experiment with different glaze mixtures on small tiles. Let's not waste time and material until I get it right."

She shrugged. "Not a problem."

They left the garden as they had entered, passing in front of the House of the Golden Buddhas and returning through the vine walk. The late afternoon sun touched the treetops, shining onto brilliant blue faces, staring blandly at the shade-speckled lawn.

# Arrival

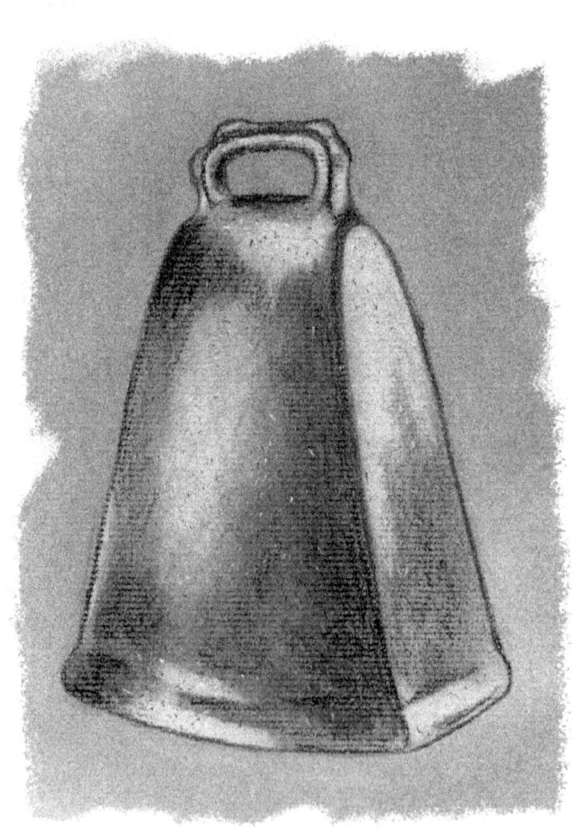

Throughout the Highlands, the common folk gave the *deòradh* of St. Fillan not only food and shelter, but tidings and guidance. It was said every burn, glen, *creag*, and *loch* whispered into their ears, and much was known to them—from the schemes of clan chieftains to the needs of humble croft dwellers, from Glen Dochart to Ben Nevis. The *deòradh* often used their insight to resolve local disputes, and when called upon, subside peril. Though few in number, the *deòradh* were the threads who spanned  the unseen web of Highland life.


— Chronicles of Inchaffray Abbey

# CHAPTER 3

A breeze brushed the hair of the sleek cattle—grazing under a blue sky dotted with clouds of white popcorn—while angry tails swished away flies over well-rounded back ends. Ailsa Winters eyed the black cows, wondering why flies and heat seemed to be at their worst in August, even though the days were creeping ever shorter.

Ailsa knew hot, sunny afternoons such as this were numbered. The clock was ticking, the harvest loomed before winter's deadline. She returned her gaze to her husband, Norm, surrounded by tightly-packed bales—at least on a third of the hayfield. The rest of the hay lay scattered waiting for the baler to scoop it up, bundle it with twine, and spew the bales back onto the ground.

Norm had been tinkering with the John Deere 24T baler for at least two hours…still dead in the water. The last three bales behind him looked like decks of cards scrambled in a loose pile. She dwelled on the first rule of farming. Equipment only breaks down when you run it, and the more you run it, the more it breaks down. From three-hundred yards away she guessed it was the knotter again. Damn baler must be at least fifteen years old by now. She sighed. Newer models cost a king's ransom.

Ailsa hoped Laverne could get it figured out; she'd been out there with Norm for half an hour. If he got to baling yet this afternoon, the hay still had to be loaded on the wagon and piled in the barn. Rain was in the forecast for tomorrow evening, the last thing they needed with most of the second cutting still lying exposed. Weather had a way of conspiring with machinery to make a disagreeable situation worse, like the well pump motor giving out during a snowstorm three years ago. She thought, all this and the corn and pumpkins are just around the corner.

She and Norm always seemed to be one step behind chores lately, ever since their daughter, Rae Ellen, got her nursing degree and moved to Rockford with her husband.

Shifting her view towards the cornfield, Ailsa flattened her hand over her brow like a visor. The lower leaves of the corn had touches of yellow; it wouldn't be long. At least the yield might push a hundred and twenty an acre. After last year's drought, they barely made seventy, forcing them to burn some of their savings to pay off the fertilizer bill and buy this year's seed.

Ailsa turned at the sound of the 4230-tractor revving up to see farmer, tractor, and baler resume their slow progress, with Skipper, their black lab, leading the way. Soon after, a red and white F-150, with a truck topper over the bed, zigzagged between bales across the field. The driver drew even with Ailsa, cut the engine, and a pair of hazel eyes set between a freckled nose and wavy strawberry blond hair peered from the cab.

Looking a bit too short given the size of her truck, Laverne Conway leaned a sturdy forearm on the window frame. "Wasn't that a kick in the ass for making hay on such a nice day."

Ailsa smiled. "If the hay doesn't get done before it rains, Norm will feel he got kicked in a worse place than his rear end."

Laverne laughed. "You don't say." She leaned back on her seat, a hand resting on the steering wheel. "We really ought to rebuild the knotter this winter. You know, a bit of prevention rather than a band-aid when you're using the damn thing."

"Seems like we're using band-aids and baling twine more and more to keep things pieced together around here." Her tanned face creased. "Patience is a virtue, I suppose."

"You should get yourself some newer equipment."

"Which means we'd need more loan money from the bank. Interest rates being what they are, no thanks."

The younger woman placed a pair of mirrored sunglasses

on her wide nose and surveyed the steady progress of tractor and baler. "Just saying. At least it won't be as miserably hot to chuck the bales onto the wagon this cutting like it was in June."

Ailsa shrugged. "Send us your bill."

"We'll work something out." Laverne turned the ignition. "Right now, Junior Mackey's Dodge is waiting for brake rotors. That's assuming the dealership got them delivered by now. See ya."

Ailsa lifted a hand and twisted a wave. The truck sped across the farm lot and cut left, heading for the Old State Road. Ailsa watched as the truck then turned at the intersection, heading east and back to town. Rubbing her mildly arthritic hands, she held Laverne as a lifesaver when it came to machinery repairs. Her nimble hands and sharp mind made all the difference at times like this. Ailsa looked at the cows again; their collective mass drifted towards the shade of an expansive white oak.

She and Norm had passed the half-century mark on life's odometer. Time was moving on. Some extra help would be a godsend, but no one seemed to want to tend cows anymore. Younger folk wanted to farm from inside an air-conditioned tractor cab. Maybe the cows needed to be sold, and soybeans grown instead of hay and pumpkins, like everyone else caught up in the sweeping tide. Fence row to fence row, making them commodity gamblers more than farmers. That would mean a new combine and heads, more loans…the cycle never ended.

Ailsa sensed the wind was changing direction. It smelled of rain coming within twenty-four hours. Closing her weathered slate-toned eyes, she caught the scent of the warm air. She frowned. Uncertainty was riding the wind along with the rain.

# CHAPTER 4

Twenty-one years old, and Devyn Lawers had never seen such land, and an untethered horizon unraveling about him in all directions. He had lived his entire life in a valley isolated by brooding ridges, traveling only to visit his grandparents, who scratched a living in Allegheny coal country. His International Scout was a tiny vessel on a concrete trade route, sailing through endless rows of corn and soybeans—the only landmarks being small towns huddled about grain elevators and water towers. A loose archipelago of farmhouses, marked by clusters of trees, dotted the vast green ocean.

Devyn had passed into Illinois an hour ago, and the day was well into afternoon. He hoped to find a campsite near the Mississippi before nightfall. Scanning the flat land and infinite sky through his windshield, he wondered if he had entered an alien world. The tidy Amish farms in Pennsylvania, with silos queued one after another like dominos, now seemed ridiculously small—carved out between woodlots, streams, and hills, with farmsteads measured in acres, not sections. Horse-drawn machinery and tractors were nothing more than toys compared to the enormous machines chugging their way across the verdant expanse of Illinois. Even the grain elevators, hovering over the old rail line paralleling the interstate, looked as if they could store more grain than the entire shelled corn crop raised in the valley. He struggled to comprehend the scale of it all.

Devyn's thoughts settled on his roots and the gifts he was given the day before. Trisha, his mom, had stuffed three brown shopping bags of dry goods and a cooler full of sandwiches, figuring it would sustain him for most of the trip. Dr. Malcolm, the local veterinarian, gave him two hundred in cash, and a set of new tires, telling Devyn, "At least you should be able to drive Lucille all the way to Colorado without running out of gas." Sophie Macnab, farmer and employer, gave him a pair of Carhartt coveralls, and a matching pullover hat, knowing he was bound to need them for working outdoors. And Sophie's daughter, Lily—Devyn thought of her braided dark hair often—a prolonged kiss and close hug, as much a suggestion to return home as a goodbye.

Devyn's gaze shifted from the scenery to the luster of the deep-yellow paint job on the hood of Lucille. He never knew why Dr. Malcolm named his old Scout this way, but his mentor had been attached to it. After Dr. Malcolm wrecked the Scout while on a call, the insurance company totaled the aged vehicle. Dr. Malcolm and Jim, the body shop owner, somehow arranged for Devyn to take on the Scout as his apprenticeship project in Jim's shop. After nearly three years of rubbing, sanding, painting, welding, and searching for parts in all sorts of salvage yards, Lucille was as good as new. As long as the engine and transmission held on, anyway.

Devyn made his way past Champaign-Urbana and headed west towards Decatur. Stretching his back, he said to himself. "Next rest stop I'm going to take a break."

Lost in thought, he calculated the miles that lay before him and the gas he would need to get there. Or more importantly, would his money hold out until he got to Denver. His calculations carried him over the next twenty miles from town, until a sharp pop burst from the underside of the Scout. Lucille lurched and leaned to one side.

"Damn it!" Fighting the wheel to maintain balance and direction, Devyn skidded to the shoulder as the Scout limped along with rhythmic thuds. Lucille came to rest, and Devyn turned off the engine, cautiously opening his door between passing vehicles. He walked around the hood to survey Lucille.

Suspicion became reality, a flat right rear tire…and no spare. "Shit, that's a piece of work, especially on a tire with less than a thousand miles on it."

Taking a few slow breaths to lower his adrenalin, Devyn looked about him. He squinted at the afternoon sun to read a large green sign with white letters and an arrow a hundred yards ahead—Monticello, exit 22.

His hair waved about his skull as a semi roared past him, shaking the Scout in its air draft. Devyn glanced at the tire again, thinking, safer to sort things out at a quieter place than here.

With one last look at the three-legged posture of the Scout, Devyn got back in the driver's seat and started the engine. "Hold tight, Lucille, we're in for a slow, rough ride." He turned on his flashers and nursed the Scout along the shoulder, trying to hug the far-right side. He winced with each bump, hoping the rubber wouldn't completely shred and leave the wheel bare on the pavement. Passing vehicles flew past him; occasionally the drivers were kind enough to swing over to the far lane. The exit ramp approached slowly, but Devyn didn't dare push his luck beyond a walking pace.

Lucille finally eased up the incline. At the top of the ramp, a sign marked Monticello was to the left. He crossed the road to the far shoulder, only to have a pickup come up from behind and lean on the horn. Devyn watched the pickup drive by and speed across the bridge. "Asshole." He smiled faintly. "I guess I have Lily to thank for that part of my vocabulary."

Devyn limped Lucille across the bridge and came up to a four-way stop sign. Waiting for all traffic to clear, he crossed the intersection, still riding on the shoulder, A large thump wrenched the Scout, followed by a sickening screech. Devyn stopped. The tire had come to the end of its limits.

He turned off the engine to think things through. He realized he had few options, especially as a stranger far away from home.

# CHAPTER 5

Laverne Conway drove east on the old state road, straight as an arrow and flat as a pancake. She kept pace with traffic on the interstate over to her left. A half mile to her right, tall hardwoods fenced in the Sangamon—a linear arboretum in the expanse of corn and beans.

Earl Scruggs was picking with his three-finger style on the banjo, playing with his sons and Vassar Clements on the cassette deck. She remembered the night when she heard Vassar play his fiddle in the old Virginia Theater in Champaign. Man, he could play like no other. She went to the show with some high school friends—a trip to the big city for wide-eyed small-town girls. Her parents would have thrown a fit had they known where she went. Laverne figured they probably found out later, but they never mentioned it. After the show, she knew right then and there she was born to be a fiddle player. She mused. I guess my life followed a different road.

She wondered how Norm was getting along with his hay. He and Ailsa would be hard pressed to get all the bales in before the rain tomorrow. Despite grumbling and groaning over the chores, they refused to let their cattle go. The two of them were living monuments to a way of farming that was past its prime. Animal husbandry as a way of life, not just a business. The world was changing around them—bigger and faster machines and bigger and fewer farms.

Laverne spotted a bright yellow vehicle almost a mile up the road, near the interstate exit. Drawing within a quarter mile, she could hardly believe her eyes. "Holy God, it's an old Scout!" As she eased up to the stop sign, she gaped at the curious vehicle, slumped on the shoulder, listing to the right side. She made the turn and pulled in behind the relic. Cutting the engine of her Ford, she mumbled, "Haven't seen one of those in a while, let alone bright yellow. I'll bet the paint job wasn't factory stock." One quick look was all she needed to evaluate the problem.

A young man, with dishwater blond hair in a ponytail, brushed back from a lean face, squatted by the right rear wheel of the Scout. As Laverne got out of her truck, he sprang to his feet, calmly peering at her with deep set, dark eyes. He was a bit shy of six feet, his wiry arms suggested agility and strength.

"Nice way to spend a lazy summer day," Laverne called out as she approached him.

"Not if I'm trying get somewhere yet today," Devyn replied.

Laverne drew even with the shot tire and shook her head. "Where did it go out?"

Devyn took in his visitor, a bit shorter than him, dressed in a tee shirt and jeans, which fit her well. "Back on the highway, just before the exit."

"You limped this three-legged mule here on a blown tire?" She bent over to get a better look. "Hope you didn't bend a rim."

"I took it real slow."

"This tire looks brand new, that sucks. Bit of bad luck I'd say." Laverne straightened up and looked at him squarely. "Got a spare?"

Devyn lowered his head. "No."

"Where ya heading?"

"I was thinking Colorado"—he squinted at the late afternoon sun—"I want to see the mountains."

Straightening her neck as if to get a wider perspective of him, she asked, "Dude, going a thousand miles without a spare tire? Where's home?"

"Pennsylvania."

Her eyes brimmed with humor and disbelief. Pondering for

a moment, she said, "Well you aren't going to make any more progress on your flight of fancy today. I can arrange for a tow to get your yellow canary to my shop for a tire. It's only a mile towards town." She walked about the rear end of Lucille.

"You're a mechanic?"

"Why, don't I look like one?"

Devyn blushed. "I meant that I didn't expect a mechanic to be the first one to stop by."

She laughed. "Your lucky day...other than your tire problem." Laverne gave the young man a once over. "Seeing how you're a man of means by no means, I think I can get someone I know to tow your rig for twenty bucks." Laverne pinned her eyes on his blank stare. "You do know the song by Roger Miller, don't you?"

"No…"

Shaking her head, she gestured towards her pickup. "Come along, Mr. King of the Road, hop into my truck. Luis is off Lord knows where getting some piece for his welding, and I have a brake job waiting for me in the shop." She held out a hand. "Eleanor Laverne Conway, at your service. But you better damn well call me Laverne."

Devyn shook her hand tentatively. "Devyn. Devyn Lawers is my name."

"Get any personal gear you may need for the night, Mr. Lawers. We'll find a place for you to hole up."

Devyn looked out from the screened porch on the backside of Laverne's modest brick ranch house. A long, shaded yard sloped to the Sangamon, its muddy banks patched together with tangled roots of sweet gum and maples. Given the width of the unhurried current, he had mistakenly called it a creek from his perspective of what a river should be.

Joined by Luis, Laverne's husband, the trio finished off an extra-large pepperoni and onion pizza. Devyn hadn't realized how hungry he was. Laverne had previously placed Devyn's ice packs in her freezer, and perishables in the fridge, commenting, "Not sure about your car, but you could about feed an elephant on your trip."

He washed the pizza down with a can of Budweiser, even though Laverne was skeptical his age was twenty-one. Late summer crickets chirped around the outside of the porch, a katydid tapped out three short blips repeatedly, an obsessed telegraph operator who only knew Morse code for the letter "s". Laverne's grey tabby cats, Socket and Bolt, sat in front of the screen, watching for night critters in the dwindling light.

Laverne popped open a new can for herself. "Talk about surprises, I didn't figure you to be the type who did auto body work. Although your color choice on the Scout is about one shade less than obnoxious."

Luis chuckled.

"I like bold colors," Devyn replied.

"Never would have guessed." She regarded the younger man. "You said you wanted to see mountains in Colorado. Aren't there mountains in Pennsylvania?"

"They're nice enough I guess. But I want to see what snow looks like on the high peaks, even in summer."

"Yeah, but you may change your mind with winter coming," Luis said.

Devyn watched one of the cats slink onto its belly, shadow stalking something outside the porch. Noting his interest, Laverne said, "Those two marshmallows can only manage to catch the occasional grasshopper." She took a sip from her can. "What did your family think of this road adventure? You ever go on a trip this long before, or on a family vacation out west?"

"It's just me and my mom at home. I don't have any brothers or sisters." He shrugged. "I guess she figures I'll do alright. It was time to give each other some space from living together." He pictured his mom's cottage, having painted the outside for her before he left—a rich red brown. "I plan to call her once a week to let her know I'm okay. She even said to call collect."

"Don't you think you should call soon, so she'll know you

made it this far?"

He fidgeted. "I'll find a phone booth tomorrow."

Giving him a petulant look, Laverne said, "You can use our phone, free of charge. You strike me as the type who wouldn't say much anyway." She nodded to Luis. "Kind of like this one. Besides, you need to save your money for whatever else might break down on that old Scout."

She got up, went inside and returned with two more beers, handing one to Luis. "So, what else did you do at home other than paint cars?"

"Worked on a dairy farm for a summer. And I rode around with Dr. Malcolm, a farm vet, now and then."

"You know your way around cattle, then?"

"A little bit."

Laverne nursed her beer, thinking about Norm and Ailsa.

Devyn broke her train of thought. "Have you been a mechanic long?"

"Since I was old enough to drive. Dad taught me how to turn a wrench when I was seven."

"You run the shop with him then?"

"He's got a bad back, had to let it go." She glanced at Luis. "My partner and I decided to buy him out and give it a go. Conway's Garage, been in town for over forty years."

Luis added, "Gotta love a woman who knows how to hold her own in the demolition derby."

Smiling at her husband, Laverne replied, "Yeah, and I keep the old man around 'cuz he's a handy welder, and a good pinochle partner." She studied Devyn. "You ever play pinochle?"

"Once in a while. Can't say I've played much lately."

Darkness had fallen, and a moth flitted about the screens, trying to find a way to the light within the porch—much to the interest of the cats.

Laverne got up again, but this time came back with a fiddle and bow. "Would you mind hearing a little music?"

Devyn looked at her with wide eyes. "Do you play?"

"As with you and cows, a little bit." Setting the fiddle under her chin she spun out an easy reel, soft and quiet, almost mournful. Devyn couldn't help but watch her hands, gliding over the strings. To hear the sound in such a personal setting was something he had never experienced. She played for the better part of a half hour. Then lifting her chin, she set the fiddle gently onto her lap.

Devyn said, "That was beautiful."

"It helps me end my day," she said nonchalantly, as if anyone could pick up the instrument and play.

"How long have you played?"

"Forever," Luis offered. "But I can't get her to play in front of audiences."

She gave her husband a baleful glance. "I don't know. Thirteen, fourteen years or so. I took some lessons in Champaign for two or three years. I stay with bluegrass mostly."

Nightfall gathered about them. "We can put you up for the night in the spare bedroom if you like, you might find it more comfortable than the backseat of your Scout."

"I'd be fine with my sleeping bag on the porch here, it's so quiet."

"Suit yourself, at least the screens will keep you from being eaten alive by the bloodsuckers." Devyn looked alarmed. Her laughter rolled across the lawn and all the way to the river. "Mosquitoes, they're thicker than cold honey around the river lowlands. You don't have them back home?"

"No, not really."

She pushed out of her chair. "Got a full day tomorrow, know a good diner for breakfast in town. Then we'll get you on the road."

The night sounds outside the porch were both familiar and unknown to Devyn as he drifted into sleep. The cats stayed on the porch to curl up on his sleeping bag in the cool air.

# CHAPTER 6

Devyn rubbed a coffee mug between his hands, not having sipped or spoken for over a minute. While sopping up egg yolk from her plate with a slice of rye toast, Laverne noted Devyn's point of interest out the window. "I did my best to find a decent used tire. One that might last 'til you get out west. It was a good deal, only fifteen thousand miles of wear. The price sure beat the hell out of getting a new one."

He grunted in response.

She sensed where his mind was dwelling and leaned across the table to catch his attention. "Kind of blew up your travel budget wider than a four-buckle overshoe, I imagine…no pun intended."

Devyn returned his stream of thought back to the diner. "Yeah. Don't think it adds up. I was thinking I might have to find work for a short spell to get some cash. Perhaps at an auto body shop if I'm lucky."

Laverne sat back in her chair and picked up her mug. "You can try Stan Ryder's shop on the other side of town. Don't think he's looking for help right now. I'm afraid we aren't either. More likely you could find something in a bigger town like Decatur or Champaign. We're kind of halfway between the two. Might even be able to find a room to rent on a short-term lease."

He stared out the window again. The idea of returning to Pennsylvania weighed on him like a stone. What would the folks at home think?  He hadn't even made it halfway.

"Finish your coffee, I got this." Laverne stood up, grabbed the check and went to the counter.

Devyn watched her go. He thought of Lily, who shared the same confident stride in her jeans. Now, at the low point of his short adventure, he realized he missed her company.

Laverne returned with a newspaper in hand and slid back on her seat. "Sometimes the bigger outfits like ADM in Decatur or the Kraft plant in Champaign advertise in our local rag's help-wanted section." She made to push the newspaper across the table but hesitated as she saw the headline. "Damn! Looks like the machine shed at the Grover's farm south of town got busted into and tools ripped off."

Devyn asked, "What did they lose?"

"It doesn't say. Third one in about a month around here. Bastards. Tools are people's livelihood. If I find anyone in my shop, I'll take a little target practice with my .38."

Devyn's eyes grew into saucers. "You have a gun?"

She laughed. "What? Are you wondering if a"—she added a sardonic tone to her voice—"*girl* would know how to fire a gun?"

Devyn's face shaded red.

She spun the paper and slid it to him. "I gotta get the brakes finished on the Dodge. Just hang out. I told Lula at the counter you might be here a few minutes to look through the paper." Laverne got up. "Good luck. You got my number if you get in a jam."

Devyn watched her go out the door and head for her pickup. The truck shot into reverse, then drove away. Loneliness fell upon him. His grand scheme seemed to be ill-planned, he had no money, and he was in an alien land. All this by the second day after leaving home. He studied the newsprint lying in front of him—*The Piatt County Journal Republican*. He wasn't even sure how to pronounce the county name.

He thumbed through the pages of the local news, mostly school events, public works projects, marriages, and obituaries. When he reached the ads, he couldn't help but look through the sales of used cars. What would it be like to have the money to buy one, rehab the body and paint, then sell it for a little cash?

He scanned the brief help-wanted section. Sales jobs, office staff, truck drivers, house painters, and pizza delivery—nothing related to auto repairs. Devyn wondered if he should heed Laverne's advice and go searching in a bigger town. At least Decatur was in the same direction as Colorado, going back to Champaign was losing ground.

He noticed Lula leaning on her elbows across the counter, her flinty look prodding the young longhair to move on. The sinking feeling of isolation returned. He was about to fold up the paper when a five-line ad caught his eye.

**Help wanted for farm work. Experience with operating machinery and tending cattle preferred. Compensation negotiated on willingness to work and versatility of talents. Housing provided on property. Contact the Winters Farm, Old Timber Road, Monticello.**

Devyn's pulse quickened. It seemed too good to be true. He reread the ad then checked the date on the top of the paper to make sure it was still current. Had someone already taken the job? His mind wrangled over the best way to find the location of the farm. The choice was obvious. He waited for Lula to leave the counter to tend to a customer and slipped the sheet with the help-wanted section under his shirt.

Nearly trotting out the door to his Scout, he started the engine, wheeled out of the parking lot and drove back to Laverne's shop. Leaving the driver's door open, he left Lucille and entered the garage. The familiar scent of grease and oil hung in the air, as a fast-rhythmed country tune echoed all around the grimy cinder block walls. Laverne had her back to him, hair tamed under a baseball cap, peering at a wheel of a Dodge pickup hoisted on a lift.

Devyn called out loud enough to prevail over the radio. "I think I found something."

Startled, the mechanic pivoted and replied, "Is that so."

He handed her the paper. "Do you know the Winters Farm?"

Puzzled, she took the sheet.

"It's a small ad near the bottom," he instructed.

She read the ad, her eyes narrowing. "Yeah, I know them. They didn't tell me they were advertising for a helper." Returning the paper to him, she added, "Still, they could sure use the extra pair of hands."

She scrawled an improvised map on a small spiral notepad she lifted out of her shirt pocket. Using her pen as a pointer, she said, "The Old Timber Road cuts south from the state road leading west of town. Their farmstead is on the right, after you make the turn. Only farm on the road before you get to the entrance of the estate." She paused to look at him. "Kind of a …unique sort of place."

"The Winters Farm?"

Grinning, Laverne replied, "Well, that, too. But more so the old estate." She looked at him pensively. "What do you know about beef cattle and corn combines if you spent most of your time in an auto body shop back home?"

"I've milked cows before. I also ran tractors and hay balers some."

"Well, their Angus are big critters, who think differently than your pampered dairy cows back home."

Devyn smiled, "I'm good with animals." He turned to leave.

"Good luck." Laverne watched the yellow, four-wheeled-wonder drive away. She thought. If things work out, it'd be a stroke of luck for Norm and Ailsa…and lemonade from a lemon for the kid.

# CHAPTER 7

Ailsa paused to wipe her brow, as the last of the bales rode up the elevator to the hay mow. Two tons of grabbing, hoisting, and setting bales on the chain drive.

Norm's head appeared in the hay door by the top of the elevator. "Is that it?"

"Yeah, the first wagon is empty. We've got the other one to unload. Might as well come down and get some water while I switch wagons with the old twenty."

Norm surveyed the hay field from his high perch. "Guessing we have about eight acres to load yet, that's close to seven hundred bales still on the ground. I hope we can get most of them in the barn before it rains. I'll tell you what, it didn't help having the baler breakdown yesterday."

Or any other day, Ailsa thought. Wavy dark hair pulled back with a clasp, arms covered with green specks and dust, she caught her breath, thankful for a steady morning breeze from the east. Her bones told her the pressure was dropping. Knowing she and Norm weren't getting any younger, the thought of lifting, loading and stacking seven more wagon loads of forty-five-pound bales made her wince.

Needing to take her mind off the hay, she regarded the pumpkin patch on the far side of the barn. Four acres and over a hundred thousand pounds of green globes, brushed lightly in orange. Grasshoppers flagged potential mates, hovered in the air with black wings, then dropped back among the vines.

Her back stiff from lifting hay, Ailsa wondered if they would be able to hire anyone this fall to help load the pumpkins on the truck. Then off they'd go by the ten-ton load to the Libby's plant in Morton, seventy-five miles away. Ailsa and Norm's contract didn't make them rich, but it was a steady market, more than she could say about cattle or corn.

Her husband bellowed from somewhere up in the barn. "Ail. Got them all stacked, I'll be right down."

She reflexively raised a hand to acknowledge the news. A cloud shadow briefly crossed the farmstead, but it wasn't the change in light that caught her attention. Looking towards the old state road leading from town, she saw only brushy trees, goldenrod, dilapidated utility poles, and prairie grass lining the abandoned railroad right of way.

An unseen vehicle was approaching, no more than a whisper carried by the wind. Yet she knew the traveler would turn onto the Old Timber Road, then come to the farm. She waited, first hearing the pitch of an engine, followed by a splash of yellow at the intersection. An old Scout slowed to a stop, hesitated, then turned left. Ailsa muttered, "I think our visitor has arrived." The Scout rolled along the narrow pavement, the driver clearly unsure of his location. Skipper trotting at her side, Ailsa made for the farmhouse to meet her new guest.

The vehicle stopped at the end of the farm lane, engine idling. After another half-minute delay, the wheels turned onto the crushed limestone and approached the farmer. Arms crossed, Ailsa stood passively. The Scout parked about fifty feet shy of her, the engine sputtered off, and the door opened to reveal a young man who might have just become an adult.

He was sturdy, but moved more catlike than bullish, lending a feeling of calm confidence. Cocoa-colored eyes, set in a long face, appraised the farm before lighting on his host. The newcomer closed about half the distance between them. "Hello, is this the Winters Farm?"

Ailsa replied, "Yes, you found us. Can I help you?" Skipper, hackles up, growled deep within his chest.

The visitor regarded the dog and lowered his hand, palm open. He kept his gaze fixed on the dog's eyes. "My name is Devyn Lawers, I was told you might need some hired help."

"By whom?"

"Laverne Conway…a mechanic in town."

"I know her. How is it you do as well? You don't seem to be from anywhere nearby."

Hearing what he mistook to be a faint Irish accent, Devyn delayed his reply for a few beats. "No, ma'am. I'm not. I'm from Pennsylvania."

"That's a long way from home." She watched Skipper with care as he neared Devyn. With each step the dog seemed to relax a bit more. "What are you doing in Piatt County, Illinois?"

"I meant to reach Colorado, I've never been this far west." He glanced over his shoulder at Lucille. "But I got a flat tire and I need to work so I can afford to go on." Skipper was next to Devyn, wagging his tail. He was rewarded by a scratch between the ears.

Ailsa took note as the dog relaxed his stance as if he knew Devyn his entire life. Restoring her focus, she asked, "How did Laverne know you might be able to work here?"

Devyn reached into his back pocket and pulled out a sheet of newspaper, unfolded it, and followed the text with his finger. "This ad was in your local paper, says here you're looking for someone with farm experience, especially with cattle." He looked back at his surprised host. "I've worked with cattle a good deal, fairly handy with machinery repairs and auto body work, too."

"The ad was in this week's paper?"

"Yes, ma'am. *The Piatt County Journal-Republican.* Has yesterday's date on it, I believe."

Ailsa studied Devyn with the shrewd eyes of a woman who perceived character particularly well. "Have you had any run-ins with the law?"

He lowered his head. "Back in high school, I got caught spraying graffiti on some county vehicles." He glanced back to her. "But I did my community service milking cows and feeding calves at the county farm. Dr. Malcolm, the local vet, says I've got a special way with cattle."

"Well, spraying paint where it doesn't belong isn't the worse thing in the world."

Devyn added in a helpful voice. "It's just that I like to work with colors."

She gave the Scout a once over. "I wouldn't have guessed. You do the body work on your Scout?"

"Yes, ma'am."

"You can stop the yes ma'am nonsense, Devyn. My name is Ailsa, Ailsa Winters, although my husband, Norm, takes a liking to shorten my name to Ail. Too much for him to put two syllables together, I guess. And we have Black Angus, and Angus aren't a bunch of dairy queens. They've got a mind of their own and will eat you if you get in their way, or worse, if you get between them and their calf."

Devyn recalled his encounters with bulls. "I know when and how to get out of the way."

She looked over at the machine shed. "I think Norm is puttering around with the tractor hitch for the wagon. You ever help make hay?"

"During the last three summers at a small farm."

"They have cattle?"

"Dairy goats mostly."

Ailsa failed to hide a wry smile. "Goats?" She nodded her head in the direction of the machine shed. "Why don't you go introduce yourself to Norm and see what he thinks."

"Yes, ma'am." She raised an eyebrow. Devyn corrected himself. "I'll do that, Ailsa."

"Oh, can I see the newspaper ad, please?"

He handed over the sheet. Turning, he made for the shed, with the dog lightly keeping pace.

She watched the procession and wondered. What will Norm think of the yellow Scout? Searching for the ad, she read it and checked the date at the top of the page. Twice. Sure enough, she had placed the ad but paid to run it for four weeks back in May and early June, hoping to snare a high school kid for a summer job. The ad ran two and a half months ago, hadn't been printed since—she made a habit of scanning the paper front to back every week over coffee. She glanced away from the paper and watched Devyn about to enter the machine shed. Something about the young traveler suggested there was more than mere coincidence at play.

Devyn entered the shop through an open overhead door, three times as wide as Lucille, and nearly three times his height. Dwight Yoakam sang a sad ballad from a radio on the workbench to his right. Various sockets and wrenches lay about on the surface, glistening under a fluorescent shop light suspended with baling twine on either end. The workbench was bookended by an air compressor tank on the near side, and acetylene tanks and welding gear on the far side.

Devyn stopped short to gape at a bright green machine resting before him. A square cockpit with wide windows all around towered above. From there, Devyn reckoned the driver to be a lord of the manor, riding a huge, mechanical beast rather than a horse. The machine was armed with eight green teeth to the front, each the length of his body, spaced like open fingers in a hand. Nowhere back home did such a monster roam through the fields of the valley.

As Devyn circled about the combine, he came upon a tractor that dwarfed the one at the Macnab farm, and an eight-row planter, both colored in John Deere green. A noise behind the tractor caught his attention, and the dog trotted over to the source, tail wagging.

"Dammit, not now, Skipper. I've got to finish this."

Devyn skirted about the rear tire of the tractor to see a middle-aged man in blue grey coveralls and a yellow baseball cap, with a winged ear of corn flying over the green visor. In his hands was a grease gun.

The farmer's brown eyes latched onto Devyn, his narrow somber face wrinkled in a scowl. "Well, who and what in the name of heaven and earth do we have here?" Skipper returned to Devyn's side, thinking he had a better chance for a scratch between the ears from the newcomer. His canine intuition proved to be correct.

"I'm Devyn Lawers, and I'm looking for work. I saw your note in the want ads."

Norm rubbed the space between his lower lip and chin, not realizing he left behind a spot of grease. "Ail must have placed the ad again, at least we got our money's worth this go around." He studied Devyn, his bushy eyebrows lending a touch of gravity. "Not too many folks looking for work on a farm these days. I thought placing an ad in the paper was a waste of time in the first place. Especially in a farm town, everyone knows we're here and what we do."

The farmer pointed at Devyn with his grease gun. "You ever work on a farm?"

"Yes, sir."

"Doing what?"

"Milking cows, feeding calves, making hay, helping with veterinary work."

"Black and whites, huh? Well, ours are all black and got more of an attitude." The older man laid the grease gun onto the bed of a hay wagon.. Wiping his hands with a dull red rag pulled from a pocket, he asked, "What do you know about machinery?"

Devyn shrugged. "A little, but I can learn. I know a good deal about body work and repair."

"Can you weld?"

"Some. I rebuilt and painted my car from the ground up."

Norm's eyebrows lifted. "Follow me." He led Devyn and Skipper towards the back of the machine shed and into a smaller room with a garage door on the far side. He flipped the light switch. "Ever seen anything like it?"

Devyn neared the car, noting the tired coat of paint and missing fenders. "Is that a Model A?"

Norm perked up at the young man's knowledge of a car built years before his time. "You know about those, do you?"

"Someone in my hometown had one, red and tan. Drove it in parades." Devyn touched the canvas roof. "What year is it?"

"Nineteen and thirty-one, the last year they made 'em. Supposed to have yellow wheel spokes and trim, along with a dark indigo blue body…think you could work on that?"

Devyn relished the possibility. "Original colors?"

"As best as we can. The engine needs a little care, but it'll start." Norm looked upon the antique. "When can you start?"

Devyn turned to face him. "Today will suit."

"Let's make the most of this opportunity. Limber yourself up for tossing hay bales today." He leaned to scrutinize Devyn closely. "Ail tell you anything about housing?"

"No, sir."

"Humph. We've got an apartment above our garage, give you one-hundred eighty per week, with a day off a week. I'll throw in a tank of gas each week from the farm tank for whatever it is you drive."

"A '76 International Harvester Scout."

Norm looked at him with disdain. "We don't have any use for that brand around here. At least for our machinery. And the gas assumes you aren't prone to driving around after drinking. We'll include the room and Ail will make sure you get fed properly each day. Where you from?"

"Pennsylvania."

The farmer reflected on Devyn's response, grunted, and gestured at the Ford. "If you stay around through the fall, we might talk about your potential winter project."

Devyn arranged his sparse belongings, mostly clothes, in his new place. Ailsa loaned him some old kitchenware. The apartment was a one-room square, with a separate bathroom in one corner, and a bed, dresser, easy chair, kitchen table, microwave, small refrigerator, sink, and counter. He was given vegetable soup in a thermos from Ailsa, to top off his still uneaten sandwiches.

Considering how unsettling the last two days had been, it was more than he could have hoped. A large picture window faced southeast, towards the road in front of the farm. The second story offered a fresh perspective; his mom's simple cottage had but one floor.

He stood outside the simple structure in the gathering dark, scanning the wide scope of the horizon, the view unblocked by hulking ridges. The cooling air caressed his tired muscles—a reminder of the sixteen tons of hay loaded and stacked in the hay mow. Much of the day he helped Norm pile bales on the wagons while Ailsa drove the tractor. If a bale missed the wagon and fell to the ground, Devyn would jump off, grab the bale by the twine and toss it onto the wagon. He then had to trot to catch up and hop back on the flat bed.

Despite the day's toil, Devyn felt fortunate to be where he stood. A sense of belonging came upon him as he worked the bales, a familiar connection with the sun, wind, and sky. His curiosity was rising about the Angus cattle—dark bodies lurking in the pasture—catching sight of them as he rode by in the hay wagon. Ailsa said he'd get his chance to meet them the next morning.

The smell of rain filled his nostrils, as soft drops tapped the ground around him. He reentered his new temporary home.

No more than a mile away, a dull luster hung onto the white walls of the House of the Golden Buddhas as the veil of rain obscured the Fu Dogs—except their bulging eyes, white stones in dark pools, blankly staring ahead—save two pairs which rotated to look towards the farmstead to the west of the garden.

Night crept from the woods and across the estate—bringing cricket chirps, katydid chants, and solemn calls of owls.

# Immersion

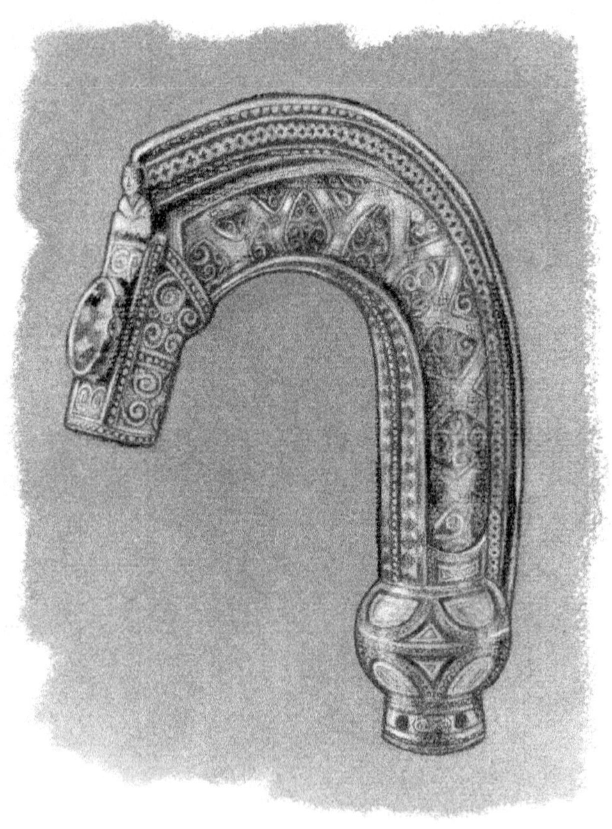

The five holy relics of St. Fillan were placed in the care of five *deòradh, or diors*, one for each relic, charged to protect the article, its lore, and knowledge of its unique power, which many believed was drawn by connecting with the elements about them. Succession for each of the five keepers was hereditary, represented primarily by Clan *Mac-a-nab,* as Glen Dochart lay in their ancestral realm. But as time passed, the weakness of human nature, abetted by religious and civil strife, deeply challenged the *deòradh* to uphold their mission.


— Chronicles of Inchaffray Abbey

# CHAPTER 8

The sun pushed its way over the treetops and into the hazy sky. Extending an arm, Norm Winters sighted how many of his thick fingers lay between the horizon and the orange orb—all four and space for two more. "An hour and a half of sunlight already gone. We still have to get the cows in the pen for Doc."

Devyn angled behind Norm to get a similar bearing. Narrowing his eyes, he asked, "How do you know it's been an hour and a half since sunrise?"

Norm glanced at his young companion and continued his way to the house. "Hold your arm out at full length and see how many fingers on your hand can fit between the sun and the horizon"—he held up his forefinger and wagged it—"fifteen minutes for each finger. Same holds for the other end of the day."

Devyn held back, Skipper staying by his side. He laid the edge of a hand on the other. Satisfied with his new knowledge, he followed Norm, stepping onto a covered porch that ran the length of the back side of the house. The wooden screen door reluctantly let go of the jamb, and Devyn entered a small mud room, furnished with a simple oak bench along one wall, and several hooks on the other. Coats and jackets of all sizes and colors covered the wall.

There being no visible hook remaining, Norm settled his hat on the top of a coat, removed his shoes, and opened a half-panel door with frosted glass. Skipper brushed by into the kitchen as Devyn paused to untie his Red Wings.

Sunbeams burst through a pair of windows over the kitchen sink, causing cherries and apples to blush on green-lined wallpaper on the opposite side of the room.

"You can wash your hands at the sink, Devyn," Ailsa greeted. "Thought I'd start our day with scrambled eggs with cheese, chocolate muffins and some fresh muskmelon."

Devyn admired the spread on the table, his first home-cooked meal in three days. "Thank you, I appreciate your hospitality."

"Welcome is the best dish in the kitchen." Ailsa lifted a carafe with a white plastic lid. "Do you drink coffee?"

"Yes, with cream please."

She pointed to a small white ceramic pitcher. "The cream is there, butter for the muffins is in the covered dish. Get yourself a tassie from the cupboard and have yourself a seat."

Devyn gave her a baffled look.  "I'm sorry, a tassie?"

"She means a mug, that's her old country speaking," Norm said.

Ailsa set the food on the table. Glancing at Devyn with humor, she said, "Och, Norm, don't be such a dafty."

Devyn ate in near silence, keenly homing in on Ailsa's speech as she and Norm estimated the date when the corn would be ready to harvest, depending on the weather, worried if the hay inventory in the barn would be enough to feed the cattle though the winter, and complained about a leaky valve on the Ritchie waterer that needed to be fixed. On the latter point, Ailsa reminded Norm freezing nights weren't far off.

Ailsa turned to Devyn. "You'll get a chance to show us your cattle skills today. Doc Haskell is coming by for the fall cow work."

"Is he your veterinarian?"

"Yup, a good one," Norm said.

"What does he do?"

Ailsa replied, "Oh, pregnancy checks, vaccinations, and the like. We'll set up the chute in the barn."

Sipping the last of his coffee, Devyn brought up a nagging

topic from his mind. "Your farm is a little different than most others around here. You're surrounded by trees on two sides. I imagine you're not far from the river."

Ailsa took a long look at Devyn. "You have a good sense of your surroundings, I see."

"Laverne mentioned there's an old estate nearby. Does anyone still live there?"

Husband and wife glanced at each other. Ailsa held her tongue for a slow count of three. "That would be the Allerton estate, named after a gentleman who lived there some time ago. It's a park and conference center owned by the university now."

"He gifted the entire place, along with hundreds of acres of farmland to the university," Norm added.

Devyn laid his coffee mug on the table. "Is it open to the public?"

"Yes, though we've got plenty of other things to do today."

Ailsa offered, "I can take you on a guided tour some day after supper." Her eyes crimped from a gentle smile. "Some of the…unusual features of the gardens could use a little introduction." She cocked her head as if listening. "I believe Doc is nearly here; you better get the cows closed in."

Philo T. Haskell, D.V.M., watched the cow parade wander into the holding pen. Enjoying a Marlboro, he pegged the wide-backed bodies as they bounced on sturdy legs. He reckoned, good genetics and the quietest group of cattle in my entire practice. His sage-toned eyes settled on Ailsa through half-framed, black horn-rimmed glasses. She had a calming effect on the animals. Norm was a good cattleman, but she knew how to move cattle without getting their dander up like no other, not an easy trick with Angus.

He shifted his attention to the young man walking by Ailsa's side, moving among the cattle with confidence and ease. One might think he had worked cattle his entire life, brief as it was. Ailsa said he had stopped by the farm looking for work, a wandering cowboy…without the gear and horse. The young man's muscles flexed like coiled springs, which got Doc to thinking his help might be handy on other farm visits—especially those where the cattle were ornerier than Ailsa's.

Norm walked up behind the last cow and managed to heave the steel rail gate shut behind her. Doc Haskell took a last puff, dropped the butt, and squished the remains on the ground. He picked up a cooler and a red, plastic milk crate, stuffed with a large jug with a pump handle top, sleeves, needles, and syringes. Shuffling in black rubber boots and white coveralls across the fresh straw, he asked in a slow pace that hinted of origins farther south. "Do you folks still have the little card table to set up my gear?"

Norm nodded. "Over on the other side of the shed. I'll get it."

"I'd appreciate that."

Ailsa met the vet at the front of the squeeze chute with a pad of paper. "Looks like thirty-one today, Doc." One of the cows in the pen mooed in a low voice in response to a calf bawling in the lot outside the shed. Ailsa regarded the cows. "They'll be in as much a hurry as we are to get this over with, on account of getting back to their calves."

Doc rubbed his grizzled hair, flat-topped, precisely one inch high. "You haven't taken to weaning the calves yet?"

"No, I don't like to have them go through too much all at once. We'll wean their babies off later."

Doc regarded the six-hundred pound-plus 'babies'. "I imagine they'll tip the scales nicely."

"Better than last year with the drought."

Devyn had come up by Ailsa's side, his hands running over the metal of the squeeze chute. He stopped to grasp the handle for the head catch. He gave Doc a sideways glance.

"Who's your new helper?" the older man asked.

Ailsa gestured a hand to Devyn. "Doc Haskell, this is Devyn Lawers. He started with us yesterday. Came here from Pennsylvania."

Devyn said in a quiet voice, "Pleased to meet you."

Doc leaned back as if to observe the young man in his entirety. "Pennsylvania? Why, hell fire, you're sure a long stretch from home. How'd you end up in Piatt County?"

"I was on my way out west and got a flat tire on the interstate near Monticello. I found a want ad in the local paper."

Doc grimaced with empathy over Devyn's response. "Seems like the planets must be aligned this week. Not every day you get farm hands falling out of the proverbial sky, Ailsa. A stroke of luck, I'd say."

Ailsa glanced at Devyn, wondering how much luck was involved.

"I gather you worked with cattle before, son?"

"Milked dairy cows. I learned some about sick cows from the local vet. I went out on calls with him."

Doc seemed pleased. "Mind yourself this morning. These black beauties" —he pointed at the cows in the pen—"know the drill here, but they can turn on you, and they're a lot tougher than Holsteins."

Norm appeared with the table, unfolded the legs and set it on the right side of the chute. Doc measured his progress. "Well, we sure have enough help today." Regarding Devyn, he asked, "You ever give any shots while riding around with the vet in Pennsylvania?"

"Yes, I did."

"In that case, you're going to be our vaccine shooter. I'll load up the dose syringe and set the dial. It'll give two cc's for each pull of the trigger, like a caulking gun. I'll show you where to jab the cow in the neck muscle when her head is caught. One quick pop and squeeze. Think you can do that?"

"Yes, Doc, I can."

"In the meantime, Norm, I'll let you work the head catch, Ailsa, you and Devyn stand on the other side, he gives the shot, you pour the wormer along her back." He paused to unfurl a plastic sleeve from his coverall pocket. "And don't go jabbing and pouring until I'm done with the preg check. Okay?" He looked directly at Devyn. "I don't want them getting sassy from their shot and vent their anger out on me with those quick hind feet. My knees are getting too old to get whacked."

Doc walked slowly to the back of the chute and pulled on a two by six oak board leaning across the entrance to the chute. "First one coming up." The lead cow of the bunch entered the chute, ears wide and nostrils flared. She thrust her head through the open end, Norm pulled the lever to catch her neck before the shoulders, the panels slid shut like a yoke. Head outside the front end of the chute, and shoulders unable to pass through the narrowed gap between the panels, the cow shuffled momentarily, then stood still. Norm pulled another handle, gently squeezing the sides of the chute against her body.

Devyn was in awe of the contraption, a cage for catching cows. The feral eyes of the Angus startled him. Her firm body, a wall of muscle straining against the chute, caused him to reconsider the relative frailty of Holsteins. Ailsa sensed his trepidation. "It holds them in place while we work with them. It's the only way you can handle twelve hundred pounds of anxiety." She smiled. "They won't stand in a tie stall and chew their cud while Doc palpates them like a dairy cow would."

Doc squeezed through an opening between the end of the chute and the holding pen, inserting himself in front of the next cow in line.  He reached his sleeved arm into the rear of the cow, and pronounced, "Pregnant about three months."

Ailsa glanced at Devyn then rolled her eyes to the cow. "Okay, Devyn, give her the vaccine." Devyn stepped cautiously up to the cow's neck. "Do it quick, don't hesitate," Ailsa coached. "They have thick hides so do it like you mean it."

Devyn reached out and stuck the needle in the cow, pulling on the trigger at the same time. The cow snorted at the brief insult and leaned against the head gate as if trying to push her way through. Ailsa poured an oily liquid along the cow's spine. "This will go through their skin and deworm them."

Norm called out, "Clear!". He released the handle as the front panels swung open, the indignant cow paced away towards the calves.

Norm reset the head gate. "Ready for the next one, Doc."

One by one, the cows entered the chute, tolerated the

unwanted attention to varying degrees then hurriedly left to mingle with the herd. There remained one last cow, a younger animal, having completed her first summer with a calf. She paced along the perimeter of the holding pen, seeking to exploit small spaces between fence panels to escape.

Doc appraised her attitude, wondering if she might even try to leap over as a means to flee. "The last one is often trouble, thinking they've been left behind by the herd. They get in this predicament because they're wary of the chute to begin with, only to wind up alone and more anxious."

He signaled to Devyn. "I need you to get in the holding pen with me. Then, we'll slowly walk on either side of her towards the chute. This way, with the two of us, she can't keep circling around the pen. We're going to take this nice and easy and let her walk in on her own time."

Devyn walked to the back of the pen and slipped over the steel rails of the panel. Despite his age, Doc deftly followed suit. "Easy does it," Doc said. "Hold your arms out steady and talk calmly to her."

Ears and eyes alert, the cow walked rapidly to the chute entrance, lined with a six-foot-high slatted board fence. She stopped to sniff the ground leading within.

"Hold up, son. Give her time to figure this out. And don't get right behind her, stay a little to the side so she can see you." Doc paused, then took a couple small steps. The beast inched forward, then wavered. Veterinarian and cow played a slow-moving game of cat and mouse; he applying pressure forward to gain a step, she then forcing him to halt until she was ready to go further.

At last, she entered the chute, and gaining sight of the herd through the portal between the front panels, bolted for freedom. Norm threw all his weight in pulling the handle down and caught her shoulders just before she escaped. The cow, realizing she was caught, banged against the sides of the chute, shaking the ton of steel as if in a minor earthquake.

The cow snorted and swung her head, wiggling her body, until Norm squeezed the panels to keep her in place. Doc slid behind her and gently raised her tail to palpate her. As he stepped back and called out, "Pregnant," a hind foot lashed out behind and narrowly missed him, clanging the steel of the chute. Removing his sleeve, he stepped away from the cow. "Don't you have some breeding index for attitude? Hope her calves won't act like her."

Ailsa quickly poured the wormer along the back and turned to Devyn. The young man stood in place, spellbound by the wild eyes targeting him as he approached her neck. The cow flung her head in his direction, making him falter.

"Get her done, son. Don't hold back," Doc ordered.

Poised for her reaction, Devyn plunged the needle into the cow's neck and pulled the trigger. She jumped and bellowed, whipping her head in his direction.

"Clear," yelled Norm as he widened the chute and opened the front panel. The Angus shoved her way through the front and pranced to the rest of the herd, then stopped twenty feet away.

Doc murmured, "Christ Almighty, she's turning on us."

A mad scramble of human bodies climbed the wooden fence or hid on the far side of the chute. But the angry cow had but one target, the one who stuck her in the neck with the needle.

Devyn bounded towards the fence behind the chute, desperately reaching out to the top board. A blow that might have been from a car rammed the back of his thigh and lifted him three feet off the ground. Sailing through the air, his body slammed onto the wooden slats. Struggling to gain his bearings, he draped an arm over the top rail and set a toe on the lowest one.

"Don't move, Devyn! Just freeze!" Ailsa stood to his right a few feet away. "If you move, you'll attract her attention."

Hanging on the fence, heart racing, his body in shock from the collision, Devyn peeked back to see the livid beast fifteen feet behind him. Bobbing her head and glaring at him with coal-black eyes the size of eight balls, she took a step closer, sizing up another lunge.

Devyn took a deep breath and the world about him went out of focus. He heard Ailsa's voice, but she seemed muffled and distant. His mind cut off all other input as he set his breathing to mimic the cow's, matching each of her breaths with his. Their eyes locked, and a surge of energy ran through his body, as he dared her to charge. The cow wavered, and snorting in disgust, pivoted and bolted from the shed to rejoin the herd.

Devyn released his body, his arms and legs turning to rubber as he set himself back onto the straw. Ailsa was the first by his side, followed closely by Doc. She asked, "Are you okay?"

Devyn leaned against the fence, rubbing his shoulder and chest. "Yeah, I think so."

"Are you sure?"

He managed a weak smile. "I didn't know a cow could do that."

Doc exclaimed, "Hell fire, son, that girl tossed you several feet in the air like a circus acrobat." He gently grasped the young man's shoulder. "You don't feel any tingling or numbness in your arms or legs, do you?"

Devyn shook his head. "Just a sore spot on my back."

"Let's go get some ice on it," Ailsa said.

Norm joined them. "Good thing she was the last one. I'd better keep an eye out for her at weaning." He looked at the herd, walking in single file out to the pasture. "Guess I should go close them in." He left, Skipper at his heels, to shut the gate.

Clucking and shaking his head, Doc gathered his gear. "I'll say this, you keep a cool head under fire, son. I might call upon you for day help in the near future."

Ailsa surveyed Devyn. There was more to him than met the eye.

Norm popped open a can of Pabst Blue Ribbon, stretched on the grey fabric of his armchair, and rested his head against the back. "Glad to have the cows and hay all set for the year."

Ailsa raised her eyes in the subdued light of the living room. Skipper lay by her feet, stretched out on a red-toned braided rug. "And most of all, knowing Devyn is okay."

Norm nodded. "Amen to that. Even so, it's good to get it done before combining the corn and hauling the pumpkins."

"Another harvest season"—she set her handwork down—"another season of machinery problems and fickle weather."

Her husband glanced at the dark green yarn in her lap. "Another sweater for the grandkids?"

"Got one made, I'll do another before Christmas. This one's for Devyn. He could use some warm clothes."

"He did pitch in with the cattle today in fine fashion." Norm rubbed the stiffness out of the back of his neck. "I'll tell you what, I thought June Bug was going to take a piece out of him." He sat upright to turn to her. "I was kind of surprised she blew out of the chute and went after him the way she did. Were you distracted after we let her loose?"

Ailsa stuck out her lower lip. "I felt her negative energy when she entered the chute. I let my guard down, I was more focused on nudging Devyn to give the shot."

Norm asked with alarm. "You knew she was going to be trouble?"

Ailsa stared into the middle distance of lost thought. "I didn't expect her to go the full measure the way she did."

Settling back on his chair, Norm mused, "Damn good thing you rebounded in time to call her off before she hurt the lad."

Resuming her knitting, she replied, "I tried to cast her away, but I couldn't get hold of her mind."

Norm glanced at her. "He might have got badly hurt."

"The reason I couldn't get a hold on her was because Devyn had already put a *geis* on her."

Her husband absorbed her comment. "You're telling me that he might have the…touch?"

The needles clacked in her fingers. "Yes, and then some."

Devyn slouched on a stump of an ancient maple. The heartwood had rotted out, but the wall of the stump was wide enough for Devyn to sit. Norm had said the tree came down during a severe storm back when he was in high school in 1963. "Same day a tornado tracked across the entire county south of town." What little he knew of tornadoes was based on movies and news clips on TV. He shuddered at the thought of a storm that could blow apart a house or a barn in seconds. What would keep a tornado from ripping hundreds of miles across such flat land as this? The ridges back home would beat back such a demon…or so he hoped.

Devyn turned to view the setting sun. Eyes on the horizon, he spaced his fingers to guess the time before sunset. Two fingers, about a half hour. Devyn hardly believed he arrived on the farm only three days ago. So many new experiences flooded his mind, the terrain, the farm, the beef cattle. Ailsa had given him an odd look after the angry cow backed off from him. As if she wondered how he had managed to cast the animal away. As yet, he was still unsure of how he invoked this power. This wasn't the first time, but for now, he thought to be more careful around others—at least around here—where folks didn't know about him.

Devyn leaned back, listening to the evensong of the birds, enjoying the mild air with a sense of pride in a day's labor done. A pair of crows rested on the peak of the farmhouse roof and called out. They flapped their wings but remained in place, watching the young man on the stump.

Devyn looked at the narrow cut of sky between the tree limbs hanging over the Old Timber Road, as it reached past the farm and through the woods. As his mind wandered into the mysteries of the estate beyond, cool air settled around him. He was taken aback when a man, dressed in a buttoned-white-cotton shirt rolled at the elbows, and khaki pants, emerged from under the trees.

The figure strolled on the road at a deliberate pace, taking time to admire the plants that lined the pavement. He had a thick shock of black hair streaked with silver, combed back away from his face, and parted in the middle of the scalp. A walking stick tapped in rhythm each time he stepped with his left foot but didn't serve as an aid for stability.

The stranger drew abreast of Devyn, who felt inclined to rise to his feet as a show of respect. Resting his arms on the white rail fence between the farmstead and the road, the visitor said, "Such a splendid evening for a walk, wouldn't you say?"

Devyn faced the man before him. Brown eyes, the right one narrowed as if aiming a rifle, gazed at the young man through tortoise shell glasses, set squarely on a wide nose. Despite the man's intense focus, he held an amused posture. "What's a young chap like you doing, sitting by the road?"

The sound and accent of the visitor's voice was crisp and a bit formal compared to Ailsa and Norm. "Just enjoying the peace and quiet of the farm after a long day."

The man raised his left eyebrow a bit more. "Smashing. Do you work on the farm?"

"Yes, I started a few days ago."

Placing both hands on the top of his stick, the visitor nodded. "Farmwork is honest and virtuous labor. I know this place well. The Winters family has farmed here for several generations. Ailsa and Norm are good people, stewards of the land and the natural resources around them."

Surprised at the hiker's familiarity with the farm couple, Devyn assumed he was talking to a neighbor. "You've lived around here for a while then, too?"

"In a manner of speaking, yes. I've been attached to this place for many years." The man looked about him. "Allerton Park is special…, a sanctuary of purity from the devices of humans." He turned to regard Devyn. "Have you explored the grounds yet?"

"No, but I'd like to."

His acquaintance burst with eagerness. "By all means, you must. I'm convinced you'll find it rewarding to do so."

Devyn looked upon his visitor with subtle skepticism.

The older man reset his stick in the right hand and as he

continued his walk, remarked, "Evening is the best time to wander through there, the light is magical. Cheers."

Devyn stood and watched him go and tried to make sense of it all.

"Thought I'd get some fresh air and I caught sight of you over here."

Devyn spun about at the sound of Ailsa's calm voice. "I was just talking to one of your neighbors walking along the road."

Her eyes examined Devyn. "Oh, aye? Which neighbor was that? Not too many places within easy walking distance of here."

Devyn leaned back to view the road. "The older man with the walking stick, right up…" His eyes searched for the hiker, no longer visible. "He must have been walking fast."

Ailsa stretched her body to scan the scene for herself. A chill brushed the hair on the back of her neck, despite seeing nothing out of the ordinary. "What did he look like?"

Devyn described the passerby, adding, "He said he knew you and Norm well. Said you were good folk."

"Well, that's nice to hear. But I'm at a loss as to who you're talking about. From your account of his looks, I can't think of anyone who lives nearby."

The young man tried to support his case. "He had an accent, like an Englishman."

She shrugged. "No matter. Come on in the house, I made a spice-orange cake. It's Norm's favorite. He had a mind to celebrate the last cutting of hay."

# CHAPTER 9

Valerie surveyed the studio in a three-sixty sweep, chestnut hair brushing her shoulders with each twist of the neck. Sunshine slanted through the panes above, filling the space with pleasant light. A sapphire necklace, cut in an exquisite teardrop and set in woven gold strands, nearly reached the point of her white V-neck pullover. Ellington stretched his attention between the gem and their conversation. The gem was winning out.

"It seems you're ready to go, do you have enough space?" Val asked.

The sculptor, in a blue work shirt and brown denim pants, looked away from the pendant and scrunched his face. "This will do fine. As you saw, the plaster shop in the back room, including the mixer, scales, plaster wheel, and work bench, are all good to go. The back door will make it easy to unload supplies from the parking area. And the utility sink held over from the greenhouse is exactly what we need to mix the plaster and clean up."

"And you'll use this front room for your modeling and casting?"

Ellington turned his gaze upward. "We couldn't have asked for better light. This old greenhouse is perfect for natural shading. We also cleared out an area out back for a small kiln, plenty big for the size of the objects we'll be firing."

"You sure turned this place around fast. Though…it could get awfully warm, greenhouses tend to do that, you know."

"We can vent the panes, or work in the evenings if needed."

Ellington nodded to a young, black-haired woman by his side. "Kim is becoming a great ceramic artist in her own right. Her help will be critical to stay on schedule for the Taft event. She has a knack for experimenting with different mixes of plaster."

Leaning against the workbench, Kim Okuma smiled. "Thank you, Ellington. I like the vibe of working on an old estate. This should make a great creative space."

Her mentor looked amused. "You might say, she's a modern-day version of a White Rabbit, and me a Laredo Taft."

The young woman flicked her eyes to him, a subtle signal of chagrin that didn't go unnoticed on Val's part.

Ellington gestured to Carl and a younger man in the corner of the studio—both dressed in grey tee shirts with a pocket, blue pants, and steel-toed shoes. "And I can't say enough to Carl and…"

"Trent," the younger man added.

"Carl and Trent for getting the plumbing and wiring done. They even widened the door from the plaster shop to the car lot so we could haul the larger equipment in."

Val glanced at Carl and his assistant. "Not surprised, I've never known a job Carl and his crew can't resolve." She pondered while looking at Ellington. "Have you come up with a design for your own installation for the event? I'm dying to know what it might be."

He gave her a half-smile. "I'm finishing the sketches, I'll run it by you soon. I'd very much like to get your opinion."

Carl sliced through the mutual flattery. "I've got some concerns."

Val asked, "Such as?"

"Are we at a point yet where we need to take the Fu Dogs down from their pillars? The first two that you are going to repair?"

Val regarded Ellington. "What do you think?"

The sculptor relayed the question to his assistant with a glance. Kim tightened her oval face. "We need to fire some small clay pieces with different glazes, to see how they turn out. We could also use a little more storage space before we start taking in something the size of Fu Dogs."

"The shop boss has spoken," Ellington said playfully. "It might be tricky to match colors to the original glaze, so given the deadline in October, we'll get on it. I'll start by sketching and taking photos of the garden."

Val asked Carl, "What about storage space in the shed across the road?"

Carl acted as if he'd been pinched. "We keep spare doors and other building materials there. Some machinery parts as well. It's going to take a good amount of effort and time to sort through all of it. Not sure there's any place to stash it."

Val made a face. "Find a home for it. You can have a yard sale for all I care."

Ellington spoke up. "We only need a few shelves to store lumber for mold boards and larger tools. Kim can help rummage and clean up the area we need." His assistant widened her eyes in surprise.

"Done," Val said. "Which comes back to my question, when should we start?"

"We'll let Carl know when we need the help," Ellington replied. "I'm thinking later this week."

Carl rubbed his scalp with thick fingers. "Which brings me to another question. Once we move them, where are the Fu Dogs going to be repaired? Here in the studio?"

Val and Ellington shared glances. She said, "Where else? This is where the work is going to be done."

"It's that"—Carl surveyed the glass walls and ceiling—"well, given the value of these dogs, this isn't the most secure building."

Val asked, "What do you mean?"

"Stealing one of these dogs from a pillar in the garden would take a bunch of people and gear." Carl jerked his thumb. "We put a new deadbolt in the backdoor to the plaster shop, but"—he swept a hand in a wide arc—"being an old greenhouse and all this glass, wouldn't take much to get in here.

Even for the amateurs who've been stealing tools from barns around here."

"How likely is that to happen here in the park?"

"Well, boss, you know we've had vandals on occasion. I don't worry about the artworks that'll be in the mansion for the October event, with the alarms and all. But given the wiring in this old structure, it would be a stretch to set up a security system in a timely manner."

"What would be timely manner?"

"At least a month. We would need to wire in a new subpanel. Might even have to get the power company involved to hook up a new mast to the power line."

Val exhaled with resignation. "What do you think?" She aimed her question to Ellington.

He removed his glasses and nibbled on one of the temples. "Does anyone else besides the folks in this room know about our plans to refurbish the Fu Dogs?"

Pressing her lips, she shook her head. "Other than our park crew and my assistants, Ashley, and Jenny…they're all sound. What about your end? Administrators like Dean Duffey love to trumpet the accomplishments of the university. After all, your recruitment to the university and residency here at the park was well reported."

After glancing at Kim, Ellington said. "I don't think anyone on campus knows specifically about this project, we haven't mentioned it. Not even to my wife. Julie's learned to pay no mind, beyond cursory interest, in my various works. She knows what it's like when I'm immersed in a project."

Taking account of the counter space, he said, "I imagine the blue Fus weigh on the heavy side." He regarded Carl. "Making it hard to walk out the door and carry them."

Carl said, "We're guessing well over a hundred pounds."

Val considered the evidence and nodded to Carl. "We don't have time to delay. Let's get this started. Have Charlie keep a lookout on this building a little more carefully during his evening rounds."

Ellington raised an eyebrow. "Charlie?"

"He and his wife live in the old gardener's house further down the road, the House in the Woods. Near the trailhead to the Centaur."

"Centaur?"

"A life-sized bronze of a Centaur in the agonal throes of death, called appropriately enough, *Death of the Last Centaur*. It's a rare bronze casting of the original plaster mold by Bourdelle."

"Emile Bourdelle?" Ellington's interest sharpened.

"Yes, it's likely the most valuable piece on the entire estate."

Kim looked at her in near disbelief. "An installation of that value out in the middle of a woods. That's twisted."

The park director held the young woman's eyes with a cutting gaze. "You'd have to discuss that choice with Mr. Allerton, who's no longer available, having died some years ago. There are other equally twisted, as you would say, features on these grounds. As a budding sculptor, you should take time to study them." A sly smile passed over her lips as she glanced at the couch in the office. "Perhaps not during the night if you choose to stay here. They might disturb your sleep."

# CHAPTER 10

The humidity swelled as morning expanded into day, straining Kim Okuma to finish her task in the poorly ventilated space. By the meager light of a small window and a pair of ceramic pull-chain fixtures, she managed to assemble the rough wood shelves. The collection of dust and cobwebs hinted the place hadn't been swept for a long time. But the concrete floor appeared to be dry and the room was just across the narrow road from the plaster shop—convenient for a grad assistant who had to lug things back and forth for her mentor.

Kim chafed at how each day El found new chores for her, giving her the sense she would never catch up. She had her own project to work on if she wanted to graduate in the spring, still needing to draw rough sketches for her committee's approval. She had learned three things about her advisor. First, he often took on too many projects. Second, when he took on too much, he often dumped some of his load on her. And third, at times, he showed a childish streak.

The meeting earlier in the morning had left a bad taste in her mouth. It wasn't El's scattered thought process, or Carl's grumpiness—he and his crew had cleared the fourteen-by-twelve-foot room for Kim within an hour after the meeting. Something deeper nagged at her. Kim felt as if Valerie held a demeaning tone towards her, of which El was oblivious.

Tugging up the bottom of her tee shirt to wipe her brow, Kim checked out her daylong effort of cleaning and arranging.

Time to go back to town, shower, hit the bars with her pals and forget life's problems.

Her eyes fell upon a door in the back of the room, with an old brass doorknob and plate, the latter with a hole sized for a skeleton key. She had been too absorbed in her work to pay much heed earlier, and she assumed it was locked. The light blue door stood out from the drab grey walls, and Kim paused to admire the arched fluted panel.

Kim crossed the room to gain a better look. "I wonder…," She reached out to the doorknob. Holding her breath, she twisted it, and the latch gave way. Pushing on the door with one hand while holding the knob in the other, she nudged the door from the tacky jamb and peered into a room the size of a large closet. Dull light passed through a dusty window to her right. As her eyes adjusted to the dim space, they fell upon the only object in the room. "Dear God!" A two-foot figure lay on its side, with a pair of large white eyes glaring at the intruder.

After climbing three low steps, Carl Lipinski continued at a brisk clip on the crushed stone path. Sunlight streamed through the trees from his left, dappling the walkway with the mellow tones of late afternoon. The weekly staff meeting in Val's office had produced a list of the typical marching orders.

Val seemed a bit on the anxious side, more so than usual. The deadline for the big event was slowly creeping towards them, and there was still a lot to prepare. For one thing, the sculptor was always requesting one modification or another in his studio. Carl and his crew had cleaned out a room in the maintenance shed, and now there was some flap that the front greenhouse door to the studio wouldn't lock properly. Carl decided to take a quick look before calling it a day.

On top of that, there was the hemming and hawing over those goofy blue dogs in the garden and their new facelift. The damn things weighed more than enough and were six feet off the ground. He didn't want to even think about one falling and breaking while moving them.

A blue jay chattered in the branches overhead as he neared the end of the path. Carl stopped shy of the tall columns before entering the brick-walled garden. It occurred to him that he needed to inspect the Fu Dogs, to figure out the hauling logistics. He was already thinking to wrap the statues in moving blankets for transport. On the other hand, finding a suitable place for the new arrivals in the studio—before lugging them over from the garden—should be the first priority.

His thoughts were disrupted by a flash of red through the trees to his right. Carl eyed Val's red BMW barreling down the drive from the manor as she left for the day. "That woman sure lives high on the hog."

Entering the Walled Garden, he passed the lounging maiden and exited through the west portal. Carl stopped to watch Ellington and his grad student leave the greenhouse. Oblivious to the grounds manager's presence, the couple chatted as they crossed by the front of the building. The young woman seemed to smile at much of what her mentor said. Carl bristled and thought, professors and their fawning students.

As he turned the corner for the parking lot, Ellington spotted him. "Ah, Carl. How are you?"

"Good enough, thanks."

"Kim and I were talking about a surprise that she found in the shed."

Carl pursed his lips. "I thought we had the room well cleaned up for you."

The sculptor's eyes gleamed. "Get this. A Fu Dog. A little worse for wear, but of all the places to find such a thing."

"Where was it?"

Kim piped in. "In a little cell on the other side of the old blue door on the back wall."

"I had no idea anything was in there. I never heard of any missing Fu Dogs." Carl regarded the pair with disbelief. "Is it going to be of any use?"

Ellington exclaimed, "Absolutely! We can use it as a model to experiment with glazes and making plaster molds."

Carl weighed his response. "If you say so. Where is it now?"

Ellington smiled. "We took the liberty of giving it a ride on our hand truck over to the studio. It's resting comfortably on the floor."

Relieved to have one less chore, Carl nodded. "Well, it's a mystery to me. Good luck with it."

Shaking his head, Carl continued to the greenhouse. Growing shadows from nearby trees dimmed the path. He paused, jangled his key ring, and went to unlock the studio door. The door wasn't fully latched shut, let alone locked. Huffing at the lack of security, he entered the studio and flipped the light switch on the wall.

A bewildering array of hand tools, containers and wooden boards lay scattered about the counter space. Bits and chunks of plaster and brown clay littered the floor. Several directional lamps stood on pedestals, arranged in corners to focus on a divan in the center of the room. The sofa lacked a backrest, with two rolled cushions on either end. Fixated on the sofa amid all the dust and chaos, Carl nearly stumbled over a tall wooden easel, covered with a blue sheet. Curious, he gently lifted the fabric to peek underneath.

After drifting his eyes over the pencil sketch, he then gauged the line of sight between easel and divan. The subject was a woman, drawn from the back. Sitting sideways, her legs crossed towards the right side of the divan, she rested an arm on the round cushion to the left. Her head was turned to look over her right shoulder, but her face lacked detail. Her curves accentuated her beauty, more so because she was nude but for a wrap around her lower torso and hips. Dark hair draped along her shoulders. "Well, well. What have we here?" Carl let the sheet fall back over the drawing. His face brimmed with smugness. "Looks like there's a bit of extra credit going on between teacher and student."

# CHAPTER 11

Sitting in the passenger seat, Devyn looked out the side window. His first ride in a VW bus, mustard-yellow with a white top, complete with raucous engine sounds rattling his ears. Ailsa explained that Laverne had rousted up the vehicle on the cheap from a "guy she knew." Norm then tore out the back seats, changing the camper van to a delivery vehicle. Ailsa surmised her husband's true motive was to protect the bed of his F-150 from the parts he hauled from the equipment dealer.

The Old Timber Road was full of bumps where ancient maple and oak roots heaved the pavement—each jolt reminding Devyn the VW's suspension was tired.

Ailsa, solid forearm resting across the steering wheel, gave him a long glance. Her face bore the same calm and patience Devyn had known with Sophie Macnab. But Ailsa's gaze was more deep-seated, as if feeling out what he was thinking. She said, "Thought you might like a brief tour of the estate. I've noted your curiosity with the place, and a curious place it is."

"Was this some rich person's land?"

"Something like that. Fifteen hundred acres of woods and prairie along the river and even more of prime central Illinois farmland."

"Who used to own all this?"

"Robert Allerton was his name, left all of this to the university back in 1945." The VW banged over a pothole.

Devyn recalled hearing the name of the park from the English hiker. "Did you know him?"

Amused with his miscalculation of her age and timeline, she replied, "No, that was a few years before I married Norm. His grandfather, then afterwards his dad, leased the farm from Mr. Allerton for a period of time. His dad then bought the place after the university acquired the estate. Mr. Allerton had granted him the rights of first refusal. Norm's dad considered selling the place as he got older, but Norm and I decided to come back and help farm."

"Mr. Allerton must have been loaded."

She laughed softly. "You could say that. His father invested in land, banks, the stockyards, and other holdings in Chicago back in the last century. The family roots supposedly went back to the *Mayflower*."

"You mean the pilgrim boat?"

"So, they say. Old money."

"And Mr. Allerton built his estate way out here?"

"He wanted his own version of a country manor he'd seen in England as a young man. Took some doing getting all the materials here." She caught his eye. "We're talking horse drawn wagons hauling lumber, bricks, windows, even the furniture from the nearby railroad."

Devyn reflected on the two-bedroom cottage where he grew up with his mom. "That's a crazy way to spend time and money."

"The wealthy can afford to follow their mad passions…or as one might describe them in polite society, eccentric." She shrugged. "Yet, it's a treasure in its own right, if for nothing else, the natural area wrapped around the river." Glancing at Devyn again, she added, "And the collection of sculptures."

Ailsa pulled into a parking area bordered by tall trees. She opened her door and slid out of her seat, beckoning him to follow. Feet crunching on packed gravel, she headed towards a path that paralleled the road. She gestured leftwards. "Up that formal lane and through the trees you can see Mr. Allerton's mansion." The evening sun touched the red brick of the second story and white dormers set in the roof.

Devyn asked, "Does anyone live there now?"

"No. It holds the administrative offices for the park. Guests can stay in some of the rooms."

"Ever been inside yourself?"

"Once, to look around the first floor. It's mostly used for weddings and university-related events."

As they walked along the flat gravel path, a tall brick wall joined them to their right. Soon after they crossed a second walkway. To their left, the path bisected a shady lawn, lined by a trimmed hedge, and meandered back to the mansion. To their right, the path passed between a pair of twenty-foot, white fluted pillars, topped by bronze maidens, cast in gossamer garments.

Beyond the entrance between the columns, a sculpture of a reclining nude woman sat on a pedestal. Ailsa led Devyn by extending her arm. "This way."

The figure reposed at the center of a brick-walled garden, which was divided into equal quadrants of clipped privet in geometric patterns. In the center circle, the young woman, sculpted from white limestone, reclined on one hand, holding a long scarf sweeping over her head with the other.

Devyn beheld the geometric symmetry of the garden. Eyeing the woman's erotic posture, he said. "Mr. Allerton didn't seem afraid to exhibit the human body."

She raised an eyebrow. "Do you find that odd?"

He admired the colors cast from the setting sun on the white stone. "No, there's natural beauty in this."

Ailsa smiled. "You might say Mr. Allerton was a passionate naturalist. In terms of flora and fauna and his…sensual partiality for some of his art." She turned to catch his eye. "Although some of the figures around here are more savage than romantic."

He regarded her keenly. "How so?"

Continuing through the garden, she replied, "You'll have to be the judge."

They exited the garden from the only other portal on the west end. A one-story greenhouse stood on their right, to their left and across a small garden, a wide meadow stretched over several acres. The path led beyond the green house to another geometric layout of hedges, then though a tunnel of arborvitae. In the distance, framed by the green walls, another figure posed on a pedestal, at least two hundred yards away.

Ailsa drew even with the greenhouse, while a cicada screeched from a nearby linden in the dwindling light. "This is a good landmark to help your bearings. The gardens run parallel with the road, on a line from northeast to southwest. The road ends at the Sun Singer on the far end."

"Sun Singer?"

"A large statue that's about a mile up the road. Some folks consider it to be the centerpiece of the estate. You can do your own exploring later, but if you leave the greenhouse and go beyond those tall arborvitae along the path"—she motioned to the setting sun—"you'll then pass a row of miniature musicians right before the Sunken Garden. From there, you enter the woods. Stay on the path and you'll come across the Centaur and eventually, the Sun Singer." She made sure to catch his attention. "There's also a loop along the river. Remember, it returns in the direction of the mansion."

Long shadows stretching over the meadow reminded Ailsa of the time. "There's one last thing you should see before dark." She regarded the greenhouse. "Looks as if this place has been spruced up a bit. It's been empty for a while." Peering through the windows, she said, "Some kind of workshop. That's new."

They retraced their steps through the walled garden, across the gravel parking area and entered a long path lined by vines wrapped about ten-foot trellises. The path ended near a two-story tower of painted white wood.

"The House of the Golden Buddhas," Ailsa said as they drew closer.

Devyn noted the trellised platform, framed by vines, on the second level. "Is there a way to get up there to look around?"

"There's a spiral staircase on the inside; you enter it on the backside away from the garden. You can climb it if you wish later, but for now we should take a stroll in the garden."

Devyn turned to see a long, narrow lawn stretching away from the tower. To his surprise, glossy blue creatures flanked the lawn on either side. "What are these things? Their color is fantastic," he said in a half-whisper. He approached the first statue with near reverence as the last rays of sun peeked through the woods to highlight its face. The figure returned his stare. Devyn found the expression of the creature both menacing and comical, but compelling, nonetheless.

Ailsa stood three paces behind him. "That is a Fu Dog, some call them lion dogs, or Chinese watcher lions. They're believed to protect people in buildings and gardens from harm brought about by others, as well as evil spirits."

Devyn faced her. "You mean like ghosts?"

"Perhaps."

"Why out here in the garden? Why not close to the mansion?"

"In Asian legend, the placement of these lions relative to the flow of the spirits was critical. Whether or not that was important for Mr. Allerton, or if it affected his choosing of this spot and setting, I can't say."

Ailsa walked to the center of the lawn. "Come here to gain the full perspective, Devyn. Here in the midst of the garden, I get a better sense of the Fu Dog's vigilance, wondering at times if it's imagined or not."

He followed her onto the center of the manicured grass.

She said, "I like to stand here and listen to the sounds of the evening woods. It's best to close your eyes to focus."

Devyn shut his eyes, leery of her purpose. Her soft voice touched his ears. "Breathe in and out slowly, pausing between each breath. Concentrate on the sounds around you."

Devyn descended through his senses as if peeling an onion, first the brash calls of a katydid and a nighthawk overhead, then the trilling song of a robin, the gentle beat of crickets, and a sad moan of a mourning dove. Deeper still, the swells of the wind, brushing the spruce limbs. He felt the breeze descend onto him from the treetops, flow by him and through the garden, then into the woods beyond.

Ailsa's voice brought him back to the present. "This estate, and especially this garden, helps me reset my outlook on life. Perhaps it'll do the same for you."

Devyn opened his eyes and took one last deep breath. Gazing at the far end of the lawn, he asked, "Where does the path between those last two Fu Dogs go?"

"To visions of the natural order of things."

"What does that mean?"

"Some things on this estate are better seen in daylight. Which by the way, is about gone. Time to head back to the VW." Ailsa turned and made for the vine walkway by the Buddha house. As he tagged along, she read his mind and pointed to the statue overlooking the lawn. "That's the Hari-Hara, a Hindu god, who destroys evil and removes darkness from our path to enlightenment."

Devyn regarded the white limestone figure watching them from an alcove in the tower.

"Why is he missing his hands? Vandalism?"

"No. Mr. Allerton had it cast from the original museum piece in Cambodia that was over a thousand years old."

"How do you know so much about this place, and these far away gods?"

Her eyes glinted in the failing light. "I keep an open mind. I come here often to clear my head and regain perspective on what's important in life." She pondered. A lesson he will need to learn.

Devyn paused, taking one last look at the dark tunnel of trees beyond the pair of sentries at the far end. He felt a deep connection and sense of being. A different type of connection than when he spent time with Lily back home. Hustling to catch up with Ailsa, he entered the vine arbor, unaware two sets of white eyes rolled under stern brows, tracking each step in tandem as he left.

# CHAPTER 12

Devyn sat in the green John Deere 4320, or what Norm called the 'old twenty'. Norm's preferred tractor for planting and plowing was the larger 4450 four-wheel drive, leaving the 'old twenty' to do the grunt work—pulling hay wagons, plowing snow in the barnyard, and feeding the cows. Devyn slipped the tractor in gear and tugged three bunk feeders, each one hitched behind the other. Eager cattle trotted across the pasture for their breakfast of corn meal, vitamins and minerals. Norm said the feed kept them in good body condition. Devyn thought it made them look fat, at least compared to dairy cows.

Devyn stopped the tractor and cut the engine. Stepping down from the cab, he unhitched the first trailer as the cows scrambled for position. Latecomers and those lower on the pecking order ambled around the rear to get to the other side.

The cattle ignored Devyn as he checked to see they were all hungry, alert, and not lame. Their glossy haircoats still glimmered from the overnight dew. He paused to absorb the scene, equal parts content animals, sunshine, and green pasture.

A pair of crows by the tree line shared their morning gossip, answered by a third, farther in the woods. The soft crimson sun inched above the horizon, gradually shrinking and changing to a pale lemon glaze. Devyn enjoyed the moment.

Leaving the cows and feeders behind, he returned to the cab, kicked the clutch to the floor, and started the diesel. As the tractor lurched ahead, he squinted at the growing sunlight. The

Fu Dogs roosted on their pedestals in that direction, not far from the farm. His mind couldn't let go of their iridescent color and grotesque faces. Ceramic sirens coaxing him to return to their watchful court. When he found the chance, he would visit the shrine again. Still pondering Ailsa's cryptic response, he was determined to venture past the dual sentries and into the woods.

Ailsa spread a beige sheet over the cord and plunked a clothespin onto the taut white line. She draped the matching fitted sheet over the line while reaching for another clothespin. Her eyes caught Devyn, sitting in the 'old twenty' and staring towards the woods. She sensed his affinity to the estate yesterday evening. Well into the night, she kept thinking to herself. How, or perhaps more vexing, why did he end up here on our farm?

A string of random events had brought him here. His trip out west that led through Piatt County, the flat tire, and Laverne's timely help. Ailsa had yet to fathom the errant newspaper ad.

Working here but three weeks and the cattle behaved around him as if he had worked on the farm all his life. Even Norm, the eternal curmudgeon, remarked he'd never had such good help with the animals.

Ailsa pondered over her own arrival on the Winters Farm. Was it really twenty-eight years ago? Had there been connecting dots to bring her here, as with Devyn?

She was finishing nursing school in Halifax, Nova Scotia, having just turned twenty. Her family lived on simple means in a small fishing village north of the city and she made ends meet by working part time as a barmaid. Her physical agility and quick wit made her popular with sailors, locals and fishermen alike. Despite frequent offers, Ailsa knew when to draw the line and keep herself out of reach. Until the day when a tall, handsome sailor with eyes the color of soft leather, on leave from a "tin can" in the U.S. Navy, sat at a table and cast a warm smile her way.

There was no turning back. She spent the night with him in a small motel, avoiding probation by sneaking into the women's dormitory before sunrise. After his ship left port the letters arrived, sometimes once a week, sometimes several at a time if he had been at sea. But always the same message; he would come back for her one day.

A year later she found Norm Winters waiting in the lounge of a doctor's office where she had taken a job. He held out a ring in his hand. For her answer, Ailsa hugged and kissed him passionately. She loved him still.

The following summer, Norm, newly discharged from the navy, made the trip to Nova Scotia with his parents for the wedding. Gaelic was spoken at the service, the predominant language among the elders of the village.

After the wedding, Ewan, Ailsa's father, implored her to consider staying near home. Her mother had passed when Ailsa was a teenager, and her father recognized the value of her bright mind and insight. But she made the case her brother was now old enough to work on the boat and her younger sister to tend to the house and their small flock of sheep. Ailsa's departure would allow them to share their father's sparse assets when he passed on. While growing up, Ailsa's family only ever had a single milk cow for butter and cream, yet she felt an unexpected attachment with the Angus on the Winters's farm.

Rae Ellen was born the next year after Norm and Ailsa settled into the old farmhouse, and once her daughter turned four, Ailsa made a point to go home to visit Grandfather Ewan every July. Rae Ellen loved the small village and hearing the elder's stories of life on the sea.

The last summer Ewan was alive, he gave his daughter a small, rectangular bronze box, that had been her mother's, and before her, her mother's mother from Ayrshire. Her craggy-faced father simply said, "Yer maw wanted you tae hae this when old enough. She kent yer warm closeness wi' all the beasties. My aging bones tell me it's time for yer new chapter in life, be it as it may hyne awa from home." She teared up while he hugged her and whispered, "Lang may yer lum reek."

Ailsa returned her thoughts to Devyn daydreaming on the tractor. What new chapter will he add to her life…and his?

# CHAPTER 13

Devyn and Ailsa sized up the fence line of what Ailsa called the fall pasture. Several posts listed at an angle and needed to be replaced. The cows were grazing in the summer pasture, giving them a chance to mend the fence without interference. A flash of color caught their eyes, and a teal two-door sedan peeled off the road and onto the farm.

Ailsa's face softened. "Here comes trouble," she uttered and walked towards the house. Devyn followed, eyeballing the car. He figured the hardtop to be an early '60s Chevy Impala.

The visitor waited in her vehicle until they almost reached the house, then tapped the horn to startle them. Ailsa shook her head. "Laverne tends to be direct at times."

Laverne got out of the car and placed each hand in a rear pocket of her jeans. "Well, howdy. What's going on at the Winters Farm today?"

Ailsa drew up in front of her. "Time to wean the calves and move the cows to the fall pasture. Just making sure the fence is sound to avoid any unwanted rodeos."

"Where's Norm?"

"He went to get a roll of woven wire from the Farm and Fleet. Once he takes off on those runs, he'll get distracted with all sorts of other things we need." She nodded to Devyn. "Besides, I have someone who can dig postholes a good deal faster."

Laverne gave Devyn a look over. "Well, it seems your hired hand is learning the ropes."

Devyn lowered his chin but kept his eyes on her. Ailsa replied, "He's been a welcome addition."

The younger woman pointed to the Chevy. "How do you like my pride and joy?" She smiled slyly. "Other than my hubby, at least on days when he makes himself useful."

Devyn studied the Impala. "Nice ride, is it a '62?"

Laverne sauntered around the car, expecting Devyn to follow suit. "Close, '61. I got this baby from my dad when I graduated high school ten years ago. Had only 33,000 miles. You might think of it as his bonus to entice me to work at the shop."

Devyn asked eagerly. "Is it an SS?"

Laverne rolled out an easy laugh. "I wish. Those are awfully hard to find." She looked upon the well-polished machine. "It does alright, 348 with three hundred and five horsepower."

The young man longed for the days when cars, made years before he got his license, were designed for style—complete with whitewalls and two-tone trim. He bent over and placed his hands on his knees. "I don't like those paint blisters at the bottom of this door. I'm thinking there's rust under there."

Laverne frowned as she neared the passenger door to take a closer look.

Devyn took another circuit around the car. "The left rear quarter panel could use a little touchup as well. I think Norm has all the tools and painting gear I'd need in his shop."

Ailsa chimed in. "With what he spends on that Model A, he better."

Devyn finished his tour. "Depending on my workload here on the farm, I could get it done in two to three weeks."

Ailsa said, "What he means to say is a few weeks after the harvest is over."

Laverne held up a hand. "Hold on, Mr. Picasso. You did a fine job with the old Scout, but I gotta know how good you are with a paint gun before I'd let you near this crown jewel."

He caressed the hood with a hand. "Norm is wanting me to paint the fenders of his Model A."

"Great, we'll see how that goes first."

He prodded Laverne with a wily grin. "Unless you would like me to trick it out in a different color."

Laverne observed the Scout parked by the garage. "You keep your box of crayon colors to yourself." Turning to Ailsa, she asked, "How's Rae Ellen doing?"

Ailsa tilted her head. "Fair enough. We won't see much of them now that her oldest is in school. Between both her and Tom working and running around for the kids, I don't know when they find the time to get things done as it is."

"Kind of like farming," the younger woman noted. She explained to Devyn. "Rae Ellen and I were classmates in high school, class of '79. She was the first friend I took for a ride in this machine. I'll tell you this" —she looked upon the car with pride—"we had more than a few good times in this old beauty."

Ailsa rolled her eyes.

Laverne said, "Now that you've been introduced, I'll bring it back later when you're more likely to have the time and I might…might let you take a spin. Assuming you're not out in Colorado by then."

After a lull in the conversation, Devyn said, "I better go dig the holes for those fence posts. Norm should be back with the fencing soon."

Aisla nodded in approval. "Sounds like a plan."

Watching the young man head for the barn, Skipper in tow, Laverne said, "Figuring it's Tuesday evening, I imagine you and Norm are going to the Wagon Wheel for supper and local gossip."

"You got that right."

"Are you going to bring your young apprentice along?"

Ailsa contemplated Laverne's naming of Devyn as her apprentice. Interesting choice of words. "He wants to take a walk to the estate this evening."

"Well, he'll miss out on a good slice of Piatt County culture, if the usual gang is there." Laverne made a face at her. "And I think on Tuesdays, a slice of decent lemon meringue pie."

Ailsa studied the distant woods. "I guess I'm the one that put the bee in his bonnet. Gave him a tour of the place the other day."

"I think he needs to unwind on a Saturday night in the big city."

"You mean Champaign?"

"Hell, yeah. PBR and fish sandwiches at the Deluxe. He'll get plenty of learning about the estate while playing pinochle."

"From Grandpa Billy, no doubt?"

"The sage of Allerton Park."

Ailsa gave her a wide smile. "And of fabled songs and farfetched stories."

# CHAPTER 14

Devyn walked along the Old Timber Road, shined to a polished black from a thundershower that rolled by earlier. He was spellbound as the menacing clouds gathered on the western horizon before rushing across the open land—black dragons spreading their wings in a sky without boundaries.

Devyn came upon the far corner of the pasture. Looking over the high-tensile fence, he sensed the herd's tranquility, damp bodies lolling in the cool grass. Dripping leaves, tinted in the colors of the evening sun, chattered in the woods.

The image of the dark-eyed man, who strolled by the farm under similar circumstances, crossed Devyn's mind. It was the visitor who implied an evening walk through the gardens would be rewarding. Strangely, the hiker hadn't come by the farm since. Where did he live? How was he linked to the estate? Devyn considered the possibilities as he neared the towering pillars on either side of the pavement.

He studied the figures atop the pedestals. Blank eyes stared from impassive stone faces. Standing proudly in algae-stained fluted robes, the statues lacked arms below the elbows, lending a bleak appearance. They seemed to be apathetic watchers for the park entrance, at least compared to the Fu Dogs.

Having passed the columns, he soon saw the white Buddha house on his left, partly obscured by a narrow line of trees. A small trail cut through the brush and over a shallow ditch to the garden.

Devyn pushed wet branches away from his face and made his way to the backside of the Buddha house. He guessed a half hour of sunlight remained. Even so, the drooping limbs of the spruce trees to his right amplified the growing shadows.

He went around the octagon to the right, to find a golden buddha basking in the evening sun. Its open hands looked as if the figure was shoving something in midair. Following the direction of the Buddha's long fingers, he raised his head to the terrace above. That would be a good place to start, he thought.

Retracing his steps, Devyn entered the stairwell. The metal treads echoed in the narrow space as he spiraled upwards, until he emerged at the center of a concrete platform. White wrought-iron columns supported an eight-sided pitched roof. Matching ironwork served as a rail along the outer edge, with a masonry bench set before each of the four cardinal directions of the compass. Devyn slowly walked the perimeter of the keep, halting to observe the Fu Dogs, who crouched below.

From this vista, Devyn better appreciated the perfect symmetry of the two lines of pillars. His eyes were drawn to each of the blue creatures, glaring at their partner on the opposite column—the faces of those to the left as yet lit by the sun, those to the right in shadow. A line, stretching through the length of the garden, split the space into halves of light and shade. He sat down on a bench, closed his eyes and felt the cool texture of the stone underneath.

Devyn once again embraced the sounds of the garden as Ailsa had guided him before. Eyes still shut, he could see the breeze sweeping along the lawn as easily as water in a stream. The current seemed to lift him off the bench, giving him a sense of floating over the tranquil garden. He came to rest at the mid-point between the Hari-Hara and the two pillars at the end, suspended in a place with no sense of the outside world.

A blurry vision of a human, moving through a dark landscape, appeared in his mind. He concentrated to bring the figure into focus. It was a woman with long hair, running through a woods. She often halted behind a tree trunk, pausing to search for something…or someone. She didn't remain in place for long, shifting through the shadows and trees. Never resting for more than a few moments. Always looking away from Devyn so he couldn't fully see her face. She moved with agile but urgent grace, as if her bare feet glided over the forest floor.

Alarmed crows called from the woods, shattering Devyn's trance. Startled, he felt himself falling and popped open his eyes—only to find he was still grounded on the bench. Thinking he had meditated for a long while, he was surprised to see the sun was nearly unmoved from when he climbed the steps. He pushed himself from the bench and eased down the stairs, finding his way to the front platform, before the Hari-Hara.

Still puzzled by his dream of the restless woman, the young man tried to unravel the meaning of the garden's design. Why did Allerton choose Chinese lion dogs? Why not some other fearsome animal like dragons? If the figures guarded against evil spirits, was there a geometric pattern for their placement that he was missing? Was this open space aligned with some sort of constellation or planet above? Burial grounds?

Descending the three steps from the platform onto the lawn, Devyn meandered along the gallery of Fu Dogs. As with a painting, each pair of eyes appeared to track his progress until he came abreast of the next pair—drawing him along within a visual relay with steady traction—away from the Buddha house and towards the sentries at the end of the lawn.

Devyn halted before the last pair, gatekeepers to the wood path. Beyond the pillars, warm sunshine dissolved into chill shade as the path curved under the tall trees to the left. He stepped forward through the exit. With each step, his feet felt as if they gained weight, his stride shorter. He took a deep breath and looked to the sky. A pale blue slit among the canopy reset his poise, and he continued along the filtered light.

Anemic grass covered the packed earth, dotted with an occasional maple leaf. A slight breeze wavered through the treetops, and as Devyn came around the bend, a small grey bird scurried from the underbrush to seek the safety of a branch. Not knowing what to expect, he walked in measured steps, senses alert. The path descended a slope, which leveled on the banks of a small pond. The trail then lifted away from the basin and continued for a hundred paces. As he reached the top of a knoll, Devyn came face to face with a pair of life-sized figures, intertwined in a deathly struggle.

A massive bear, raised on hind legs, was crushing a hapless human like a ragdoll, feet in the air. The man, wearing only a headband, crude necklace and a loincloth, vainly struggled to free himself from long claws tearing his back. Open jaws with bared teeth readied for a savage bite. The fury within the eyes of the bear towards the dying man was palpable. The man limply hung in the creature's grasp; a crude-handled knife jammed in the bear's massive upper chest gave no salvation— tied to a hide belt on his waist hung the body of a small bear cub.

Dwindling light, coupled with the site's isolation, pried unwanted visions from Devyn's imagination. The violence before him conveyed him into an age when feral beasts terrorized humans. He circled the mortal conflict. The bear riveted on the one who killed her cub—ruthless revenge for a callous act.

A disquieting vibration buzzed within Devyn's ears. The horror before him was no longer confined to lost history but seeping into the present. He couldn't avert his gaze from the bear's eyes, who glared at Devyn, no longer heeding the listless hunter. Drawn towards the pedestal, Devyn reached out to touch the bronzed arm of the doomed man, surprised to find it warm to the touch. The heat conducted up his arm and through his shoulder, as if casting his muscle and bone to metal.

He recoiled and stumbled onto the damp earth. Gasping, the young man looked up at the towering beast in near panic. The rays of the setting sun transformed the bear's eyes to vile red medallions—latched onto the trivial being who lay on the ground. Devyn scrambled to his feet, hurrying back on the path to the garden, looking over his shoulder for a last peek at the bronze predator. Mind rattled, he imagined he saw the figure turn its thick neck toward him. Devyn broke into a dead run, nearly tripping over a root by the pond.

He escaped the dusky woods to enter the welcoming haven of the grassy lawn. Devyn relaxed in the light, slowing his pace to a jog, and halting in front of the Hari-Hara to catch his breath. He listened intently for any sounds from the woods but heard nothing save a few crickets, a nervous robin and the trill of a wood thrush. He scanned between the pillars on the far side of the garden, afraid of what he might see rounding the curve of the foot path. All remained quiet and still. The Fu Dogs by the exit seemed to stare back at him, counseling him to remain calm.

Devyn's pulse and respiration slowed as he became more aware of the peace about him. Taking note of the deepening shadows across the garden, he opted to return to the farm without further delay. Even though it was a short hike, nightfall came early in the woods. He passed the Buddha house and found his way over the brushy ditch and onto the road. The pavement assured him all was well. By the time he returned to the farm, he felt somewhat embarrassed that he'd fallen in the cracks between delusion and reality.

She had reached the third year of her graduate program and Kim Okuma anticipated finishing in the spring. Teaching undergrads and her own coursework consumed her first two years. Finally, she had time for her thesis project, a ceramic installation to be submitted in a juried exhibition in March.

She had learned much of the chemistry and techniques of ceramics and mold design from Ellington. But when he was buried in a task, he essentially locked himself in his studio for days at a time. If his efforts didn't go as planned, he had a habit of abandoning his creation—often smashing the plaster and clay to pieces and starting over. Kim wondered how his wife dealt with his mood swings.

She spent three days a week at the studio, to help Ellington prepare for the Taft event at the mansion. As the summer waned and the deadline for the event drew nearer, she found she had less and less time for her own project. Ellington had become more uptight, over the water to plaster ratios, chemical mixes for glazes, neatness of the studio—even though he devised most of the chaos—inventory of supplies, and now, this project to repair the Fu Dogs. His obsession with the blue figures seemed to grow with each new day.

Kim regarded the 'rescued' Fu Dog, sitting on its haunches, staring in a unsettling fashion at her. Every time she walked by it, she got the feeling the thing was leering at her. She didn't like being alone with the creature, especially as evening approached.

Getting the last of the compounds readied for the next day—and Ellington's next attempt to match the blue glaze with a practice ceramic piece—she quickly tidied up the studio, aware all the time the Fu Dog was lurking from behind.

Relieved to be done, Kim took one last look at the unwanted guest, walked out of the front of the greenhouse, and turned the key several times before the door locked. "Damn latch won't hold." Placing the door key into her purse, she fished around for the keys to her tan VW Rabbit.

The evening sun burnished the path between the walls of arborvitae, framing the solitary statue in the distance. She recalled the previous conversation with Valerie, and her snide remarks about odd sculptures in the woods.

She turned the corner and made for the parking area at the backside of the building. She felt a vague urgency to reach her car. Perhaps it was because the days were getting shorter. Or was it that bug-eyed creature in the studio?

Kim opened the door and tossed her purse onto the passenger seat. She got behind the wheel and shut the door, making sure to push the lock button. The engine came to life and she drove down the narrow lane with the light of day fading behind her. She made a note to finish her work before dark from now on, even if she had to get started earlier in the day.

# CHAPTER 15

The setting sun finished the day's canvas with an artistic flair, spraying vermilion and marigold across the sky. Norm and Ailsa admired the canvas, goblet in hand, lazing within cushioned lawn chairs on the porch. Skipper snoozed between them on the worn grey floor.

Norm took a sip. "This year's batch needs more citrus."

Ailsa frowned. "Don't be daffy. I added the usual orange and lemon. I think it's fine."

"Maybe a little more sugar then."

"Your root beer candies are in the dish on the side table. Get your sugar fix with one of those."

Norm sighed and regarded the cattle in the pasture. Half the herd had already nestled onto the grass for the night. "It felt odd not seeing the Brinkmans at the Wagon Wheel tonight. It's still hard to believe they moved to Arizona."

"Well, after they sold their farm to the Richters they didn't want to live through another Illinois winter. All the same"— Ailsa enjoyed a taste of wine—"the supper club is thinning out. That makes three couples gone over the last three years."

Norm shook his head. "I'll tell you what, if this keeps going on, the whole town will dry up and blow away. Aren't near as many folks in the doughnut shop having coffee in the morning, either. Bigger farms, fewer farmers, less business for shops in town."

Ailsa mused. "Fewer kids in schools, too. I hear Saybrook-

Arrowsmith consolidated with Gibson City."

Skipper abruptly stood up, moaning and wagging his tail. Ailsa squinted to see what captured the dog's interest. No surprise, Devyn was walking on the road passing the near end of the pasture. "Looks like our farm hand is coming back from his evening stroll."

Norm grunted. "Why'd you get him all bothered over that old place anyway? Some of the grounds have seen better days."

Ailsa tracked Devyn's progress as she thought. Maybe…maybe not. The young man entered through the gap in the fence and onto the farmyard. Skipper scurried off the porch to greet him.

"Why don't you come on over and have some wine with us?" Ailsa called out. "Go right on in and get yourself a blue glass from the cabinet, the one with the leaded-glass panes."

Devyn returned with a goblet in hand; he discreetly regarded the wine bottle on the side table.

"Our house wine," she smiled as she took the vessel from his hands. Devyn kept his eyes on her as she poured honey-colored nectar into his glass. Motioning to the young man to take his wine, she refilled Norm's as well.

"Have a seat." Ailsa offered him a chair.

Devyn sank onto the soft cushions. She looked at him expectantly, waiting for an evaluation. Lifting the glass, he tilted it back and took a small taste. Smooth, sweet silk ran over his tongue, though the sweetness was subtle and played a far second to the taste of spicy flowers. Devyn drew his head back and studied his goblet, then tried another sip. He glowed as the elixir reached his belly, his mind letting go of worldly cares after a third swallow.

"Have it figured out?" Ailsa asked in a soft voice.

"I know this taste," Devyn peered into his goblet.

"Smell it. Use all your senses."

He shut his eyes and inhaled, nose over the wine. Bright yellow flashed across his inner eyelids. He blurted, "Dandelions! I smell and see dandelions in spring."

His comment prompted Norm to take another drink from

his glass. Shooting a side glance at his wife, he judged, "I still think the previous year's batch was a bit more of my style."

Ailsa gazed upwards, puffed her cheeks and exhaled in exasperation.

Devyn asked, "You make wine from dandelions?"

She said, "The same flowers that are as bright as your Scout."

Devyn relaxed in his seat, his hand idling through Skipper's neck. "How was supper at the Wagon Wheel?"

"Not as many folks as usual. Same old baked chicken dinner for me. Mashed potatoes, coleslaw, corn, and gravy," Norm replied.

Devyn thought. Sounds good to me. He reflected on the peanut butter and jelly sandwich he ate before his hike.

"You should join us next week," Ailsa suggested.

"I felt an urge to check out the gardens, I guess."

"Did you see anything of interest?"

He replied in a pensive voice. "Those sad-looking, armless statues by the park entrance."

She cocked an eyebrow while refilling his glass. "And did your tour include the Fu Dogs again?"

He hesitated. "Yeah…I wanted to spend more time there. I climbed the steps of the Buddha house to get a better view."

Topping off her glass as well, she glanced at the young man. "Anything else provide any…interest for you?"

"Not much." The tenor in his voice didn't match his casual words.

"You didn't happen to come across something unusual, perhaps even disturbing to see?"

He blanched, aware that evasive answers wouldn't ward off her inquiry—unlike his mother. "Yes, I, uh…did." The sips of wine were becoming progressively smoother. "I found a statue of a bear killing a hunter."

Ailsa and Norm remained silent, patient priests waiting for a confession.

"Being alone with it in the woods makes it seem more real…and frightening. Why would somebody make such a thing?"

"Because they wanted to make a statue of their nightmares, that's why." Norm snorted.

Ailsa tried to tamp down her husband's reply. Reclining back on her chair, she said in a soothing manner. "It can be shocking to see for the first time."

"I felt as if…"—Devyn looked away, then back to her—"it was as if…"

"Go on," Ailsa prompted.

"I felt as if the bear was coming alive."

"Powerful art often collides with people's emotions. There are certain areas of the estate that have…how shall we say…a spectral quality to them."

He gave her an odd look. "What do you mean?"

"A strong spiritual presence. For those who can sense such things." She noted his subtle reaction to her statement.

Venus took center stage to the west. Crickets chimed in under the porch.

Ailsa asked, "Tell me about your roots, Devyn. Who are your people?"

"I only know my mom and her family. Never knew my dad."

"That must have been hard on her and you."

He shrugged. "We did alright. I made my way through high school and got my training in autobody work. I took a part time job on a small farm, too. The place with the goats I told you about. The Macnab place, run by Sophie Macnab and her daughter, Lily."

"Macnab? An old Highland name. And your name, was it from your mom's family then?"

"Yeah. My Grandpa and Grandma Lawers. He was a coal miner in west Pennsylvania. All their sons, too. My mom left them to get away for a better life." He stopped to think about her. Living from paycheck to paycheck as a waitress. "She didn't make it too far though."

"And you don't know much about their ancestors?"

"The family settled there a generation or two before

Grandpa. He's dead and gone from the black lung."

"Mining is a hard life." Ailsa looked into the distance, gathering her thoughts. "Lawers. There's a Ben Lawers, which means Mount Lawers in Gaelic, near Loch Tay and the town of Killin in Scotland." She glanced at him. "I imagine you never heard about that place from your family."

"I didn't hear much of anything about my family. My mom didn't seem to know…or care."

"Perhaps it's all a coincidence." Ailsa sipped her wine. "And you got hooked up with the Macnab farm because…"

"Doctor Malcolm. The veterinarian who took me out on farm calls. He introduced me to Sophie."

Norm added, "Which reminds me. Doc Haskell asked if he could put you on his payroll next week, at least for a day. He could use some help on a larger cow-calf herd south of town. It'll be your chance to spend time with a farm vet in a different part of the world. You might learn a trick or two about cows you didn't learn in Pennsylvania."

"That'd be okay by me." Devyn got up from his chair. "I think I'm going to settle in for the night." He set his glass on the side table. "Thank you for the wine."

Ailsa looked at him with pensive eyes. "My father used to say, a blate cat mak's a proud mouse."

The young man turned to her.

She clarified, "Be mindful not fearful, Devyn. Sleep well."

Despite Ailsa's kind wish, a phantom troubled Devyn's sleep, stalking his dreams through a shadowy woods. He woke up, disoriented and dry mouthed. Getting out of bed, he drank a glass of water and calmed himself by looking out the open window. A half-moon washed the farmyard in tarnished silver. The air was heavy and still. It was that quiet time before dawn when even the crickets and other night callers had retired for the night. He stood in the dark silence of his room, secure in his obscurity and thinking of how the bear statue had rattled him. He convinced himself his mind had played tricks on his senses. Yet, gazing in the direction of the estate, he felt something seductive about the place…an unseen but tangible presence. He knew his appetite to visit the estate was far from over, despite the oddities within.

# CHAPTER 16

Ellington Rose stepped back from the easel and shifted his eyes from the sketch to the clay figure on the worktable. A scowl lined the sculptor's face—the figure's posture wasn't evolving into what he intended. He returned his gaze to the subject of his work, who reclined before him. The late afternoon light streamed into the greenhouse, giving a warm luster to her skin. He needed to change the angle of his perspective, to better highlight the shadowing of her limbs. Something more dynamic.

She faced away from him, dark hair reaching down her neck. Leaning to one side, she rested her thighs on top of one another, knees bent, calves trailing off along the sofa. She propped herself with an open hand, exposing a well-defined shoulder from under a loose fabric that covered the rest of her torso and hips.

Rarely did Ellington work with a model who held a posture so naturally. He looked at the preliminary sketch again, put down his putty knife and approached her. Hearing his footsteps, she asked, "Is everything okay?"

"Well enough. I need to adjust your posture. Something better to capture a natural setting, more symbolic of this estate, and less the banality of a salon." He took a breath, trying to stay focused on his work. "We need to start from scratch, different than you tilting to the side."

"Tilting? Makes it sound like I've been drugged."

Deep in thought, Ellington barely heard her. "I can't decide if you should lean farther or straighten your back."

Sitting up, she bundled her hair with both hands and pulled it over the back of her neck. "Will this help with your decision?"

"Shoulders such as yours have such a classical look. When cast in the final piece, they'll be admired,"—he smiled playfully—"and envied for their form and beauty." He frowned. "Though I know of no ceramic that will capture their essence under light such as this."

Releasing her hair, she turned her head and shoulder to let her eyes rest on his. "My, you're not only a sculptor, but a bard."

"As an artist, I try to portray…and enhance what I see. I have to say, you're far more patient than most models I work with. Young students who can't seem to sit still for long."

"I've had practice. It's how I helped pay the bills when I was in school."

"I'm sure you were a popular subject."

She spun on her rear end and reached for a flowered robe hanging next to the table. Lowering her feet onto the concrete floor, she released the shroud from her grasp and quickly put on the robe, tying the belt at her waist. "I think it's time for the model to take a break…to stretch and flex her muscles."

Padding across the hard surface as silent as a cat, she wavered in front of a large workbench. The Fu Dog sat on its hind legs, white eyes staring back at the visitor.

Val caressed the blue head then let her hand drift down the peculiar, braided mane along the back of the skull. She mused. This would make a nice color for my next Beamer, perhaps a convertible to boot. "I assume this is the piece that was found in the shed?"

"Yes, kind of a quirky mascot for the studio, isn't it? I've grown fond of it." His eyes came to rest on the sapphire necklace suspended between her collarbones.

Noting the center of his attention, she smirked. "Perhaps the artist should take a breather as well. So, he can better stay tuned in with his work."

# CHAPTER 17

"Kind of skimpy leg room, considering the size of this bus." Laverne peered at Devyn between the front seats of Luis's Chevy Blazer. "For that matter, not much of a smooth ride, either." She glanced at her husband. "I think you need some new shocks."

Her husband grunted. "Know a good mechanic?"

Devyn reflected. No doubt who does most of the talking in this pair. Sitting sideways, he stretched his leg across the back seat. Country tunes played on the stereo at low volume, as much to fill space as to listen to music.

They were on the old state highway to Champaign. Ailsa all but insisted Devyn could use a night in a campus town to, as she said, "open up his eyes." Through the side window, he scanned an old wooden elevator with faded paint and a tin roof, a listless giant looming over a crossroads with a handful of houses and a gas station.

Laverne faced Devyn, laying an arm on the console. "As I recall, you know how to play pinochle. Am I right?"

Devyn regarded her with a cryptic smile. She had a habit of puckering her lips and widening her eyes after asking a question. A flannel shirt-wearing cat ready to pounce on a dumb response.

"A little, I guess. Dr. Malcolm taught me how to play."

"The veterinary who taught you about cows in the hills of Pennsyltucky?"

Devyn absorbed her poke at his home. "He went to vet school here in Champaign."

"No shit. How about that, Luis? One of our very own Illini." She leaned back to look through the windshield. "With four of us, we can play on teams this evening, instead of the usual cutthroat three-way with Grandpa Billy." Laverne turned back again. "You'll be my partner. Luis always messes up playing the trump suit, and I want to give Grandpa Billy"—she took on a cunning look—"old jabber mouth that he is, a good thumping. Better not let me down young partner."

Devyn settled on the back of his seat.

She asked, "Was he any good?"

"Who?"

"Who else, Einstein? The vet when he played pinochle."

"Yeah, but his girlfriend usually beat him."

Laverne arched her eyebrows. "What did she do for a living?"

"Kind of a detective…for insurance companies."

"How'd she get hitched up with a cow doctor way up in the hills and hollows?"

"They worked together on some barn fire investigations."

"Barn fires…as in arsons?"

Devyn's face tightened and nodded. "Yeah, they were horrible."

Laverne and Luis looked at one another.

Stymied on how to pick up the pieces of a soured conversation, Laverne turned up the music. Head nodding to the slow rhythm of the ballad, she said, "There you go, one of my favorite cowboy singers, Don Williams." She peeked over her shoulder. "You do know about Don Williams, don't you?"

Devyn scrunched his face and shook his head.

She sat back in her seat. "Well, relax and enjoy."

Leaving the Blazer parked on a side street, the couple led Devyn through campus town, weaving their way through throngs of distracted college kids. Devyn was surprised by the level of kinetic energy about him—laughing, yelling, music blaring through open bar doors. He felt like an alien on a strange planet, nearly everyone his age, or younger. More than once, he furtively tracked a young woman that passed him by. Several returned his interest with a smile.

Luis led them through a door of a dumpy, narrow, one-story building, with *Deluxe* painted in white letters on the front windows. Inside, the noise was no less chaotic than out on the street, but the air was thicker—a warm haze of cigarette smoke and fried oil, with an aroma of fish and onions. Small tables and chairs were scattered wherever they could fit as an informal dining area near the front. Beyond the bar, gangs of players from all walks of life smacked billiard balls with cue sticks. Plywood covered the two pool tables closest to the front door.

Laverne inhaled deeply. "Fish night at The Deluxe." She turned to Devyn. "No place like it on earth."

He was inclined to agree. "What's with the boards on the pool tables?"

"Most of the eating gets done on this end of the place. Keeps the numbnuts from slopping their food all over the felt. This place is a pool hall by trade, except during the feeding frenzy on Friday and Saturday nights."

Luis pointed to a table over by the wall, occupied by a grey-haired man dressed in a tan sport jacket and jeans. "Billy got us a table over there."

"Come on, partner. Let the games begin," Laverne called to Devyn over her shoulder as she headed for the table.

Laverne grabbed a seat and motioned to him to sit opposite, with the older man placed to his left. He had a full mane of grey hair, streaked with strands of white, held in a shoulder-length ponytail. A trimmed beard, same hue as his hair, reached low enough to cover his throat. Ebony eyes, set under full eyebrows, bore into Devyn. "Howdy-do, young man. I'm Grandpa Billy."

"I'm Devyn. Pleased to meet you."

Billy turned to his left. "Hear that, Laverne? Pleased to meet me without knowing anything about me."

She replied, "He'll learn."

Luis settled in the chair to Devyn's right.

Pulling a small spiral notepad and pencil from his jacket pocket, Billy said, "So, we're going with teams tonight, are we? You're thinking, Laverne, that a young mind is sharper than an old one, I see." A box appeared in Billy's hand; opening it, he pulled out a deck of blue cards. His gnarled hands smoothly side-shuffled the deck several times, divided the cards into two packets, then riffled the packets, releasing them in a tidy stack on the table. Devyn watched the entire process with wonder.

"What do you say we get a hand in before dinner?" Billy asked. He dealt the deck, three cards at a time, around the table. Laverne winced when she looked at her choices. "I'm going to pass on the bid."

Luis showed faux sadness for his mate. "I'll open at twenty."

Billy hooted, "Not a good start for you, is it missy?"

All eyes turned to Devyn. Without raising his eyes from his cards, he said, "Twenty-five."

Laverne coughed. "What are you going so high for? It's going to be on you if we don't make the tricks and get set."

Devyn glimpsed up at her and smiled.

Billy studied Devyn closely. "That's a bold move, I'll go twenty-seven."

Laverne sat back, arms folded and watched the bid return to Luis. "Pass."

"Thirty," Devyn said without hesitation.

The old man rubbed his whiskers. His eyes flitting between Devyn and his hand.

Laverne pressed for action. "Come on, Billy. Time's a wasting."

"Thirty-one."

"Thirty-three."

Laverne laughed. "He's pushing your buttons, old man."

Frowning, the elder mumbled, "Let's see if you'll go all the way to thirty-five. Thirty-four."

"Thirty-six."

"Damn, dude, are you crazy?" Laverne glared at her partner with disbelief. "Did I not give you a clue about the less-than-desirable nature of my hand?"

Billy shifted his eyes around the table. "Alright, the bid is all yours."

Laverne scanned her hand. "What's trump?"

"Clubs," replied Devyn. She shrugged, selected three cards and passed them across the table. Devyn slid them into his hand, picked three other cards and slid them back to her.

Billy licked his lips in a wet smile. "Let's see what the young buck has for a meld." His smile curdled as the cards were laid out. "Jeeezus," he exclaimed. Luis stared at the cards with a stone face.

After the hand played out, Laverne leaned over to supervise the scorekeeping. "Make sure you write that down, Billy. We scored forty-seven in case you can't count that high."

A middle-aged woman, wearing jeans and a loose tee shirt, printed with the head of a snarling lion and captioned, '*May I help you?*' hustled to their table. "Fish?"

Laverne held up four fingers.

"White-wheat-rye-bun?" slurred as one word.

"Two white, two wheat…and three baskets of onion rings."

Luis eyed his wife. "Three? Billy doesn't eat those anymore on account of his gall bladder."

Appraising Devyn, she jerked a thumb across the table. "I'm sure *Flaco*, the card shark over there, can knock them down."

The waitress asked impatiently, "Beer?"

Laverne replied, "Three PBRs and a…" She regarded Devyn.

He asked, "Have anything on tap?"

The server replied with disgust. "Only bottles."

Laverne intervened. "Four PBRs." As the server edged to the next table, Laverne explained to her teammate. "Tradition is held close here. And whatever you do, don't ask for tartar sauce, or she'll kick your ass out the door and tell you to go get a fish fillet at McDonald's."

"Or worse," Luis added.

The pinochle game continued, Laverne and Devyn reached a hundred and fifty in five hands. Billy sat back in near shock, glumly sipping his beer. The food arrived, giving him a chance to recover.

Devyn bit into his sandwich, nearly burning his mouth on the hot battered cod. It was the best fish between two pieces of white bread he ever had. "How do they do this? This is incredible."

Laverne wiped her mouth with a paper napkin and took a swig of beer. "Not bad, huh?"

"I mean, this is Illinois, nowhere near an ocean."

"If you're going to have one thing on the menu, you better get it right."

Grandpa Billy munched on his sandwich. "Never changed for all the years I've been coming here." He looked at Devyn. "How many years you think that's been?"

Devyn snatched an onion ring. "A few, I guess."

"Almost twenty. Moved here in town back in '70. That's when I got married to my second wife."

"I liked her better than number three," Laverne declared.

"Me, too," added Luis.

Grandpa Billy swatted the air as if batting away a gnat. "Water under the bridge." He gazed at the younger man. "These two kibitzers told me you work out on the Winters's place."

"Yes, sir, I do."

"Do you like working on a farm?"

Devyn nodded while chewing.

"Get over to the old estate much? It's just up the road."

"I like to walk through the gardens when I have time. The woods remind me of home."

"Ever been through the Fu Dog Garden?"

Devyn paused from sipping his bottle. "I have."

Billy tapped the table with a finger. "Well, here's something you didn't know, I worked on the estate for many years. Started there as a young man, about when I was your age."

Laverne glanced at Luis. "Better flag down the lioness for another round, this is going to take a while."

Unfazed, Grandpa Billy went on. "Hired at twenty years of age in 1930. I'll tell you what, it was during the big crash and the Depression you know. CCC didn't exist then, jobs were scarce and that bum Hoover was still in office. Thank God for Mr. Robert, a lot of folks got by thanks to him."

Laverne's voice hinted of tedium. "And this is related to the Fu Dogs, how?"

"Like I was saying, tried my hand at barnstorming for a living when I left school at sixteen. I made good money." He touched his misshapen nose. "Had a bit of a rough landing in a cornfield one day, broke a couple ribs, an arm, and my jaw. Healed up well enough though."

"Too bad the latter one did," Laverne quipped.

"My sponsor couldn't afford another plane, but my uncle was a gardener at the Allerton estate. He got me a job there."

Billy's eyes gleamed like glowing embers. "I helped build and landscape the Fu Dog Garden, '32 I think it was. When the statues arrived, it was me, Ted and Cliff Whitsapple, and Herb Bunyon, the grounds manager back then"—Billy paused to stroke his beard—"before I took over in '55."

He pointed at Devyn, who listened with rapt attention. "There was no denying Mister Robert was mighty particular about the placement of those Fu Dogs. I dare say they were his most favorite prize. They only ever arrived in pairs and had to be placed so they exactly faced one another across the lawn. He was damn particular about that."

"Where'd the statues come from Billy?" Luis inquired.

The old man furrowed his brow. "Not sure I ever heard Mr. Robert say. He was a bit vague on that. China, I think."

Laverne said, "Imagine having that much money to haul a bunch of garden ornaments all the way from China."

Ignoring her, Grandpa Billy homed in on Devyn's genuine interest. "One day, he spent an entire afternoon staking out the dimensions and exact midline from the white tower with those Buddha gods to the end of the garden. He set the last two pillars on the far end, after using some math to figure out the spacing between each Fu Dog on the sides."

Grandpa Billy took a swig from his new bottle. "When those last two dogs arrived, numbers twenty-one and two he called them, we placed them with great care. He stood there and watched us the entire time. Well, he didn't like them, and said they were all wrong. So, he had them packed up and sent off" —Grandpa Billy became distant for a few moments—"as a donation to central campus, I believe. The next two Fu Dogs were more to Mr. Robert's liking. I remember he winked and smiled at us, telling us they would protect the gardens from wild things in the woods." The grey head nodded in reminiscence. "Had his quirks, he did, partially deaf, too, but Mister Robert was a good and kind man."

A half-smile twisted Laverne's lip. "As I recall, those dogs are looking in at the garden and not out to the woods they're supposed to be watching. I figure the wild things can sneak up on them from the rear."

Grandpa Billy looked at Devyn from the corner of an eye and whispered, "Some people believe the garden is haunted."

Devyn soaked up Billy's words like a sponge.

Devyn ate a second sandwich, but no extra order of onion rings. During the ride home, he digested both the meal and Grandpa Billy's take on Allerton Park. Despite the shock of the bear during his last visit, he now had all the more reason to return.

Laverne was as pleased with the evening as Devyn, perhaps more so. For the first time in a while, Grandpa Billy was on the losing end of the night's pinochle match. And what an ass-whooping it was. Confounded by his misfortune, Billy routinely shifted his eyes between his hand, the cards on the table and the calm young man to his right. Maybe the kid learned a thing or two about  how to play cards from that vet's girlfriend after all.

# CHAPTER 18

Ellington's mind wandered from the solarium and through the floor-to-ceiling windows to consider the pond and meadow beyond. He speculated. If I were Allerton, I would have placed an installation on the far side of the pond, perfectly framed by the gap in the trees.

Leaving his creative musings outside, he scanned the room. Coffee cups, water glasses, and glass bowls with mints littered the conference table. The gist of the current pitch was how to leverage the unique nature of Taft and the White Rabbits— the event now had a name— as an exclusive opportunity for generous alumni to support their alma mater.

Jim Kramer, Chair of the School of Art and Design, piped up, "What if we establish donor levels, you know gold, silver, bronze?"

Ashley asked, "Besides their names on a plaque, what else could we offer?"

"Recognition could happen at a champagne brunch. We need to make sure to keep the glasses full," Dean Duffey chuckled. "Nothing like friendly spirits to encourage open check books."

Val asked. "Now we're getting into catering. How many people are we talking about?"

Ashley gestured to outdoors. "We could set up a pavilion on the old music lawn on the south terrace. Like we do for wedding receptions."

"And hope for good weather," Carl groused from the end of the table.

The university development rep poured coffee from a white carafe into a foam cup. "This needs to be a truly special donor experience, not just an exclusive...but a memorable affair. Perhaps..."

Ellington's thoughts drifted away again. Over in the meadow, a small tractor pulled a mowing deck across swales of grass. At times, the sculptor wished for a simpler life, where garden chores were the main issues of the day. His daydream unraveled when he realized Val was asking him a question. He recovered by saying, "Sorry, I was kicking around donor experience possibilities. Could you please repeat your idea?"

Val looked at him with exaggerated patience. "Jim suggested that your scholarship of Taft and the White Rabbits would make a great opening seminar on their history and works."

Ellington replied, "Sounds good."

"Then after mingling around the donated installations with refreshments, we'll follow up with a workshop."

"Workshop? Where?"

"Why not in the studio?" Val leaned forward, laying her arms on the table. "Maybe you can have models or molds premade, to demonstrate the step-by-step process of ceramic sculpture."

The ceramicist sat back in his chair and meditated briefly. "Hmmm. You're talking about a hands-on affair. Reminds me of a grade school art class, only with plaster instead of fingerpaints."

Jim chided, "Now, Ellington, it wouldn't be any worse than a studio class with first year undergrads." He grinned. "You wouldn't have to grade them."

Ellington laughed. "Well, there's that to be thankful for." He looked around the table. "How many are we talking about?"

The entire group exchanged glances. Ashley offered, "Forty...ish."

Dean Duffey exclaimed, "I like it. Not only the works but the inner workings of a sculptor's mind. What better way to connect with Laredo Taft's genius?"

Ellington feigned humility. "You honor me by comparing my efforts with Laredo Taft, Dean Duffey. But I will certainly give it my best effort. If nothing else, we'll make sure to hand out aprons and gloves." He added in a mischievous tone. "I imagine this crowd will have upscale tastes in apparel."

His eyes drifted towards Val as the dialogue took a different tack. The sapphire shimmered in the light from the windows, dangling above the neckline of a stylish cashmere sweater. I'm sure she'll be up for the task as far as dress code that day, he thought. He pulled away from the charm in time to see her eyes dart at him and hear Jim's voice. "I seem to remember you mentioning a pair of alumni from Chicago who are anxious to attend, something to do with their interest in the Fu Dogs?"

Val replied, "Yes, Ellington and his grad assistant are taking this on. We hope to spruce up two of the figures in time for the event." She returned her gaze to Ellington. "It's going as planned, is it not?"

The artist shrugged. "We're still experimenting with glaze colors and materials for patching, but we have plenty of time."

Val smiled politely. "This would mean a lot to them. Apparently, they got married in the Fu Dog Garden."

"Here's an idea." Jim said. "We can offer the gold donors an opportunity to adopt a Fu Dog and offer them the chance to name their adoptee. Then we'll send them updates when their"—he wiggled air quotes with his fingers—"pet undergoes rehab."

Carl subtly shook his head and bit his lip. He pondered inwardly. Honestly? Names for statues of blue dogs?

The meeting adjourned, and the room slowly emptied. Ellington lingered, looking out the windows at the sunlight shimmering on the reflecting pond.

"It's a captivating scene. Mr. Allerton must have enjoyed it considerably." Ellington turned to see Val had remained seated across the table from him. "No doubt admiring the beauty of all four seasons."

She looked at him, her face asking a question without speaking.

He said, "I would like one more session in the studio with you."

She leaned back and give a tired look. "I thought you were satisfied with the last go around."

Ellington reached in his satchel and passed her a sketch on a large piece of drawing paper. "I am, but here's a new pose that might be better. I think it grasps the motif of the natural beauty of this estate better than a salon setting. Less formal, more…untamed."

Studying the details of his work, she marveled at seeing her likeness so well presented.

Rubbing his jawbone, he said, "I'd like to try this perspective. As you can see, I believe it's an upgrade to better match your modeling talent."

She folded her arms. "I've got a lot on my plate."

"I want to put all of my creative energies into this one. Think of the sculptures in this park. Think of them as traces of the models who posed for the artists. Their essence captured in the moment and preserved long after they're gone from this earth."

"Your dangling a bit of immortality as bait, how clever." Tapping her fingers on crossed arms, she replied, "Alright, but I can't stress enough the importance of finishing the Fu Dog work."

He grinned. "I'll have the first pair of those blue puppies groomed, bathed and wearing diamond collars for the big day." He collected the sketch back from her hands. "You won't regret this."

She dwelled on his comment and thought. Oh, don't worry, I won't. In fact, I think it'll be quite advantageous for me in more ways than one.

# CHAPTER 19

Devyn sat in Doc Haskell's pickup, surveying his host's split-level house. The lower level served as a veterinary clinic. Philo T. Haskell, D.V.M., embossed beneath a logo of a snake wrapped on a staff, overlaid with the letter 'V', marked a sign by the driveway.

"I hope you're good with egg salad sandwiches. That's one of my go-to choices for lunch on the road. Marge chops up pickles and celery into the mix."

Devyn nodded. "That's fine, thank-you." Reflecting on the veterinary logo, he asked, "Did you go to vet school here in Illinois like Dr. Malcolm?"

Doc Haskell glanced in both directions and pulled his truck onto the road. "Yes, sir, University of Illinois class of 1959." He chuckled. "That was a few years before you came into being, and before our mutual friend Dr. Cromarty was even old enough for school. Then here he goes and ends up practicing where you live, and now you're here. Who knew?"

Devyn bristled, unsure why a flat tire was part of fate's cosmic plan. "Did you grow up in Illinois?"

Doc added emphasis to his reply. "*Southern* Illinois, a town called Olney. You know what makes Olney special?"

The young man waited for the answer, not having a clue why Olney was special. As the silence stretched longer, he replied, "No, Doc, I don't."

"White squirrels."

Devyn thought he was being pulled into a joke. Doc's dead pan face spoke otherwise. "You mean their fur is really all white?"

"As I live and breathe. Only place in the world where they naturally live. They're full-time residents of the town." Doc swung a right turn onto another road. "Albinos with pink eyes. They're special to the place, no one is allowed to take them anywhere else. Like a trade secret."

"Can't say I ever saw a white squirrel."

"You'll have to get yourself down to Olney to see one."

The truck picked up speed as it left town. Doc rolled down his window and hung his elbow on the door. The hairs on his forearm vibrated in the whistling air. Shaking his head, Doc said, "Young Dr. Malcolm. The world was his oyster, he couldn't wait to be an animal doctor."

"Did you know him while he was in school, then?"

"Yes sir, he did his senior externship with me." The vet's eyes left the road to study Devyn. "He came out for some extra time when he had a free Saturday." Pausing, he smiled slyly. "Now that I think about it, he came during the week sometimes as well. I imagine he figured his time with me served as an alternative education to the classroom. And he always seemed to be playing in a softball league during the summer. Not sure all those distractions helped his grades any."

Devyn gazed at the rows of yellowing crops flying by his window, interrupted only by crossroads—narrow, straight, eight-foot-deep canyons—walled in by corn on either side. "Where are all the silos and barns on the farms around here? They seem so empty."

Doc glanced at his young companion and sighed. "You say it's mostly dairy farming back where you're from?"

"Yes, most farmers make a living milking cows."

"Holsteins?"

"For the most part."

A trace of remorse crept into the older man's voice. "I always liked working with dairy cows. It was my preference.

You know which Illinois county was number one for dairy farms when I got out of school?"

Devyn had caught on to the riddle game. "No, Doc, I don't."

"Right next door, in McClean County. You know how many are left?"

"No, Doc, I don't."

"Two. Just two…" He pressed his lips and let out a long breath through his nose.

Devyn kept quiet, judging the older man was lost in thought.

"I'll tell you what, I'm happy Malcolm found his place in life. He got to reach for his dream and I admire what he's done, not being from a farm." Doc grinned broadly. "He sure was on a steep learning curve while riding around with me. Had to learn a thing or two about practice."

"You mean about the cows?"

"There's more to being a vet than healing animals. You have to learn the art of practice." He gestured at Devyn to make a point. "More than half of being a good vet is about your people skills, most of the rest is your clinical skills, and the last bit is dumb luck."

Devyn grinned.

"You know what our friend Malcolm told me one day while driving about, don't you?"

"No, Doc, I don't."

"Well, he told me that he couldn't wait to get out of school because he's fixing to be his own boss and own a practice, like me. You know what I told him, don't you?"

"No, Doc, I don't."

"Well, hellfire. I said, young man, anyone who walks into your office with a sick pet or calls you to their farm is going to be your boss. That's the God's truth."

Devyn absorbed the lesson as the truck rolled through a small town. Parts of the main street were familiar with home—gas station, diner, fire house. Others were foreign—flat land running right up to the edges of town, water tower, large grain elevator. Passing an auto body shop, he saw a banged-up Chevy and guessed how he would repair it.

They passed a yard sale, crammed within a two-car garage. Doc shook his head. "Not much at that place, always selling baby clothes and toys. I imagine they have a bunch of kids."

About a mile down the road, Doc pointed at another yard sale. "Those folks there are always selling armchairs and sofas. You might think they have a warehouse instead of a double-wide. Maybe they've had a few relatives pass on."

Devyn looked upon the furniture showroom scattered about the lawn. "Do you stop at yard sales often?"

"Hell, yes. That's what makes Thursdays worth living."

"You seem to cover a lot of miles," Devyn said.

"Farms are fewer and farther between these days. Most of my calls are in Piatt and southern McClean County. Although after the cattle work, we're going on down to Arcola to see a friend of yours." Amused by the puzzled look on the young man's face, Doc added, "An Amish place, Levi S. Diener, it'll make you feel at home."

"You mean with horses and buggies?"

Doc shrugged. "Old Order, probably had roots in Pennsylvania some time ago." After halting at a stop sign, surrounded by corn and beans, they continued.

Doc reached for a pack of Marlboros on the dash, tapped one out, and pressed the lighter button. He held the glowing coil to the end of his cigarette. Puffing out a cloud of smoke, he said, "As I recall, Malcolm got married soon after he graduated, or maybe a little before. A real pretty gal." He inhaled another drag. "She was from up near Chicago, like him. But what little I knew of her, she didn't seem to be the type to want to live in farm country. Wonder how that worked out."

Devyn sagged in his seat. "She left him and went back to Chicago."

Doc swiveled his head. "Divorced?"

"Yeah. He didn't talk about it much."

"That's a crying shame. Is he doing alright?"

"Yeah. I think so."

The pickup followed a jog in the road to the east, then once again south. Doc let out a whoop. "There we go, I knew this gang would be open for business."

A modest two-story house, with white siding and black shutters, sat under a few trees. The house was about two-hundred feet off the road, with a concrete driveway leading to an attached garage. The entire length of the driveway was lined on both sides with small tables covered with clothes, picture frames, toys, tools, canning jars and random flotsam and jetsam.

"Kind of our local flea market. It's a little out of our way, but you want to get here early before it gets picked over." Doc slowed his truck down to a crawl and parked on the grassy berm behind a tired-looking brown Dodge minivan. Peering through his glasses at the wares on the tables, he muttered, "Looks like we got ourselves an entire church rummage sale lined up for our shopping convenience." He threw open his door and made for the nearest table. He looked over his shoulder at Devyn, who remained in his seat. "Come on, son, who knows what you'll find here?"

Devyn discovered that Dr. Philo Haskell not only had a reputation as a sound veterinarian, but also as a cagey patron of yard bazaars. Saying "Good morning" to the vendors, he was greeted in kind by several of the women who sat behind the tables, planted in lawn chairs on the grass.

A middle-aged brunette behind the third table to the right called out, "I've got another batch of clothes from Toby's closet, Doc. Hasn't been able to squeeze his big ass into them for half a lifetime but they should cover a fit guy like you just fine."

A redhead sitting behind the next table in line voiced, "You know it. The only thing that Mike can raise these days is his pant size." Laughter spilled across the merchant's tables.

Doc stood in front of the brunette. "Let's have a look-see at your wares today, Charlene." He plundered through a pile of men's pants, stopping to pull out a pair of lime-green knee length shorts. "What have we got here?"

Charlene replied, "Oh, Toby got those when we went to Florida a while back. You might want to look at this one as well." She pulled out a pair of grey shorts with yellow flowers.

Doc stretched them across the waistband to get the full view. "My, my, those are bright."

"Light weight for summer, I know you're always looking for something to keep you cool under those coveralls."

Doc held the second pair of shorts in his hands. He turned to Devyn who had arrived beside him. "What do you think? They seem to be in good shape."

Devyn's first impulse was to laugh out loud at the gaudy fabric. "Who's your helper today, Doc?" Charlene asked.

"This is Mr. Devyn Lawers. He's working at the Winters's place near Monticello. I'm taking him along as an extra set of hands today."

Giving Devyn the once over, Charlene said. "Hmmm. May be hard to find something in his size today. Clothes are always in demand for young bucks like him. They get passed as hand me downs to younger brothers until they're plain worn out." She nodded across the driveway. "You might try Mary over there; I think her youngest boy left home for the Army."

Diving deeper into the mound, Doc yanked out a pair of red-brown pants. "Hell fire, these chinos don't have any wear on them."

Charlene sighed. "Doesn't matter how new they are if the old man can't fit in them."

Doc smiled. "How much for the two pairs of shorts and these pants?"

"Four dollars for the pants and two-fifty a piece for the shorts."

"It's September. Can't wear these shorts until next year. Marge says I have too much in my closet already." He gave Charlene a hard look. "How about eight?"

Charlene rolled her eyes. "How's a girl supposed to get by if I can't make a buck selling clothes?"

Doc held up a pair of plaid polyester pants dotted with white golf balls. "Three bucks," she said flatly.

"Ten for the whole lot."

Devyn wandered further along, leaving the hagglers to work things out. Reaching the end of the line, he returned along the other side. He spied on Doc, who had moved on to another vendor—an armful of clothes in tow.

"Hello, young man."

Startled, Devyn glanced right to see a pair of keen eyes fixed on him. "Hello."

An elderly woman, with a thick mane of silver hair, laid out a hand to show the wares on a small table between them. Spidery fingers sifted through stacks of old books and magazines and settled on a wooden box. Opening the box, she pulled out a lantern and set it on the table.

Surprised by the artifact, Devyn asked, "Does this work? Looks kind of old."

"Of course, it's a simple device. Uses kerosene or lantern oil. All the clips and the ratchet to raise and lower the wick are in good order." She encouraged him with an open palm. "Pick it up and take a look."

The foot-tall lantern felt solid in his hands, while the red-glassed globe softly reflected the daylight. He flipped the wire bail over the top and gently swung the lantern back and forth by his side.

The woman's eyes glimmered. "That's it, just like the brakemen on the old trains. This one's marked, came from the P. & L.E." He looked at her with an empty glance. She added, "Pittsburgh and Lake Erie."

He set the lantern down. "I already have a flashlight." Thinking of the lanterns he saw Amish farmers use in their barns, he ran his fingers over the globe. "Wouldn't it give out more light if the glass was clear?"

"Red was used as a warning. Color changes how we see and think of things, does it not?" Nodding subtly, her eyes narrowed. "But I think you already know that don't you?"

Devyn jerked his head up and leaned back to take a look at the merchant. She stood placidly, dressed in a printed cotton dress of white and yellow flowers. "Five dollars," she said.

He hesitated.

She persisted. "I sense you'll find this to be useful in the near future."

Devyn's fingertips poked at the brass clips. For reasons he couldn't explain, he couldn't pull his hand away from the simple gadget. He pulled the cash out of his jeans and paid her.

She nodded. "A wise choice." She placed the lantern back in the box and handed it to him. "Remember, you need to put fuel in it at least an hour before lighting to allow the wick to soak."

"Thanks." He sauntered on his way, glancing over his shoulder. Her eyes followed him, her face wrinkled with a knowing smile.

Doc nearly bumped into him. "There you are." He shoved a black hooded sweatshirt onto Devyn's chest. "This is for you."

Devyn grasped the sweatshirt. "Thank-you."

"Winter is right around the corner; sweatshirts are great for wearing over other layers." The older man regarded the curio under Devyn's arm. "What you got there?" Devyn gave him the box for inspection. Doc opened the lid and whistled lightly. "This looks to be the real deal. I think it's an old Dietz Vesta railroad lantern. Worth a pretty penny." He scanned the tables. "Where'd you get it?"

Devyn turned to locate the woman. "Huh. She was right over there…" He looked in vain. "She must have stepped away from her table for a bit."

"Pay no mind. We've got to go make a living after buying all these bargains."

As they made for the pickup, Devyn asked, "What did you end up paying for those plaid golf pants?"

"Two-fifty."

Devyn smiled within. *Priceless.*

The morning passed quickly. After pulling over by the side of the road for a quick lunch, Doc said, "Now that we got the big job done for the day, time for a little reminder of the folks back home."

Arriving at the Diener farm, they entered the barn to tend to a Standardbred in obvious discomfort. Devyn watched Doc examine the horse. Peering at his thermometer, the vet said gruffly, "Nearly a hundred-four, he's got himself a good fever."

Levi S. set his hands on his hips. "Hasn't wanted to eat much the last day or so."

Doc flipped his wrist three times to shake down the thermometer. "I imagine not." He homed in on the horse's head for a closer look.

Devyn discreetly sized up the farmer, who held the horse with a lead rope clipped to a halter. Black pants with suspenders, blue cotton shirt and brimmed straw hat with a black band, not much different than the folks back home.

Doc gently palpated a puffy swelling, nearly the size of a pear, bulging from the inside corner of the horse's lower jaw. He asked, "How long has he had the snotty nose, Levi?"

The farmer replied, "Two days."

Doc turned about. "Devyn, will you get me a twelve-cc syringe with a sixteen-gauge needle please? The sixteens have grey caps on them."

After rummaging in Doc's grip, Devyn gave him the items. Doc took a closer look at the horse's neck. His fingers twirled a thread that was knotted in the skin over the jugular. "If I didn't know any better"—Doc lowered his chin to gaze at Levi S. over the top rim of his glasses—"I should think this looks like a horsehair suture to tie off the vein after you bled him a bit."

The farmer looked at his feet. "Thought it might help to remove the fever poison."

Devyn's eyes flared at the comment.

Doc threaded the needle hub onto the syringe and pulled off the cap with his teeth. "Got a good hold of him, Levi?"

The farmer's strong hands gripped the rope tighter. "*Ja.*"

Clamping the swelling between thumb and fingers, the horse jerked its head as Doc eased the needle through the skin. A thick, opaque fluid filled the syringe as he pulled the plunger back. Removing the syringe and needle, he held the specimen for all to see. "Abscess. What we have here is a case of strangles, kind of like strep throat for horses."

Levi S. nodded. "I thought that might be the case. Will we need to give him penicillin?"

Doc paused to poke the mass again. "Not yet. Got a soft spot here, I think it's ready to bust out." He faced his protégé. "Devyn, would you pop open the compartment on the top right side of the grip? You'll find sterile scalpels, individually wrapped. May I have one, along with an alcohol-soaked cotton swab? Oh. And a pack of my number eight surgery gloves."

While Devyn was retrieving the supplies, Doc explained. "Strangles is caused by strep bacteria, Levi. These germs can't survive in the barn yard, so they survive by being spread from one horse to the next."

The farmer scratched the back of his head. "I don't believe I have any other horses with this problem."

"Infected horses don't need to be showing signs to carry it to others. Has he…"— Doc pointed to the horse—"what is his name?"

"Jake."

"Where has Jake been the last three to seven days?"

Levi S. twisted his mouth. "Took him shopping in Arcola Tuesday last and Sunday church."

"Did you tie him up on a common rail?"

"I surely did."

"Were your children giving water to the horses while at church?"

"That's part of what they're supposed to do."

"Did they share buckets between animals?"

The farmer nodded. "*Ja.*"

The vet offered his hand. "There you go. You're going to have to keep Jake away from your other horses, and don't share any buckets, or anything else between them."

"Can it spread to us folk, Doctor?"

"Not likely but wash your hands. After we drain the abscess you'll need to flush it out with tamed iodine until the wound starts to heal. Make sure you wash your hands after you do this." He gave the farmer a stern look. "With soap…every damn time."

Doc stretched the gloves over his coarse hands then collected the scalpel and alcohol pad from Devyn.

Levi S. asked, "How long will this go on?"

"He should stop shedding the strep in a month's time."

Worry gripped the farmer's face. "A whole month?"

"If he spreads it to your other horses, especially the draft horses with fall field work season about upon us, you won't be able to work them because of the pain in their throats. An ounce of prevention is worth a pound of cure, Levi."

The farmer remained stoic.

As Doc neared the horse, its nostrils flared and ears perked up. He cautioned his client. "I don't think he liked the needle earlier. Hold on Levi, he may jump a bit more when I lance the abscess." The horse wheeled and jerked its head away.

Frustrated with the moving target, Doc stepped back and griped, "You need a better hold than that, Levi."

Unnoticed from behind, Devyn subtly laid his hand on the horse and stroked its back. The animal relaxed and didn't flinch once as Doc tended to his patient.

The afternoon sun dipped across the sky, stretching shadows from lonely trees across the fields. Doc slowed his truck to a crawl as he came upon a railroad crossing. The hum of grasshoppers rose from the milkweed, Queen Anne's lace, and goldenrod that stretched along the railbed as far as Devyn could see. Doc leaned out of his window, eyes searching the ground as his truck rested on the top of the grade. The truck lurched as he shifted to park and opened his door, leaving Devyn mystified in his seat.

The brushed shine on the steel rails told Devyn the line was frequently used. His eyes tracked the rails into the distance, to the point where they seemed to join into a single line. Faintly visible in the shimmering heat waves, he saw a pinpoint of light.

The older man bent over the crossing, intent on something caught between a rail and the pavement. "Hell fire. It's jammed in there." He straightened up and stuck his head back through the open door. "Hand me that hemostat sitting on the top of the dash, will you, son?"

Taking another quick look along the rails, Devyn handed Doc the tool, who returned to his task. Devyn watched with growing concern as the light in the distance gained in brightness, now more of a small spot than a speck.

"There you go." Doc stood up and triumphantly pinched a stainless-steel object between thumb and forefinger. Getting back in his seat, he held the prize in his open palm for Devyn's inspection. "What do you know, a nine-sixteenths socket. Looks like a Craftsman, too." Pleased with his new treasure, Doc leisurely put the pickup into drive and eased off the rails. "Always like to check these crossings for tools and the like. You'd be amazed at the stuff you can find that's tumbled off folk's vehicles and farm machinery. Got a coffee can's worth of machine screws and nuts at home. My best prize was a grain shovel a couple years back…in good shape, too."

The pickup rolled down the far side of the grade and picked up speed. Devyn didn't say a word. His last view down the line was of a light now the size of a pellet reaching out to him along the rails.

Devyn peeked at the lantern, wondering why he gave in to the woman's sales pitch so readily. The red glass, brass and steel had a strange appeal of its own.

# CHAPTER 20

Ellington's hand wiggled over the sketch pad; pencil nearly floating in air. His eyes bounced between Val and his work, then settled to study the diagram. He remained lost in thought for a full two minutes. Flipping to the next page, he circled a few paces to his right for a new perspective and started again. Valerie had kept count; he was on his eighth rendition.

Sitting on a wooden table, she dangled her legs over the edge, arms braced on either side, palms flat on the tabletop. She posed by leaning slightly forward, head turned just enough to peer over her right shoulder. She seemed to be disregarding a vista from a ledge, casting a beguiling gaze instead to casual observers.

Val tried to defuse his intensity. "You don't have to be so maniacal about this. You should come up for air once in a while."

He straightened his torso, raised his arms, and stretched in his grey track suit. Relaxing by holding the pad by his side, he took a breath. "I can get wrapped up in a study of form like this. Especially when the subject is so"—he smiled glibly—"intriguing."

Valerie furrowed her brow. "Intriguing, sounds like you're analyzing a puzzle."

Shaking his head, he grinned. "No. Intriguing from a sense of depth of beauty." Her eyes studied the artist, seeking to uncover his intent.

Ellington reexamined the sketch on the top sheet of the pad. Nodding, he flipped though the previous sheets, taking time to scan each one. He stopped to stare at the next to the last page.

Valerie asked, "Something not right?"

Looking up, he turned the pad over so she could see the drawing. "I believe quite the opposite." He let her take in the lines and shadows. "I'll give you this one when I'm done."

"To hang in my office, no doubt."

Ellington raised an eyebrow. "That might be a little provocative for visitors."

"Better than you taking it home for your living room, I should think"

His eyes flared as he blushed.

She laughed lightly as she placed her feet on the ground and grabbed her robe. "A little humor. Although I imagine your wife has seen other works of yours that include nudity."

"True, but with models who sat in a more professional setting."

Tying her robe, she acted surprised. "Isn't this a professional setting? Or is it because you're still dressed in your jogging clothes? Seems to me there wouldn't be much variation in the model's attire."

He watched the fabric settle over the curves of her body. "This sculpture will be among my finest. Perhaps it could be a permanent installation here at the estate."

She looked up through the greenhouse panes; the sun was squeezing between the seams in grey clouds. "Hmmm, the first piece in a series from our artists in residence program."

She spun about on the balls of her feet and approached the snarling Fu Dog. "Where are we on *this* project? Are you ready for the first pair in the garden to be repaired?"

"We're getting close. Kim and I have been tinkering with different plaster ratios. I think we've about hit on one suitable for the plaster molds needed to press the clay."

"I admit, the Fus are complex, multi-faceted pieces."

He chuckled, "Kim is a little weirded out with it being in the studio. I wonder what she'll think when we make the replicate."

"Replicate?"

"Of course, copied from this one. Both of them will become placeholders in the garden while we remove the originals for repair."

Val paused to consider his logic…and an unexpected opportunity. "So, you think you can actually copy such a piece?"

"Within reason. We're still working to perfect the glaze."

Val folded her arms. "So, what about the glaze?"

"We're struggling to find something that will match the texture and color of the original figures. There's something about them that's difficult to imitate. I want the renovations to be invisible to the casual observer. Especially given their unique history, and the occasion for their revival."

Valerie placed her hand on the creature, fixated on the blue gleam. She turned to face him. "Time is running out."

"What worries me is the different modes of light and shadow that occur over the course of day in the garden. It's hard to catch all the possibilities within this studio."

She paused to think. "I understand the Vonnoh is arriving from the Art Institute next week. May I assume you're handling the arrangements?"

"Absolutely. And the other pieces will be coming in the week after. I will personally see to the installations for all three."

She gave him a look of skepticism. "And you still have to organize the supporting material, as well as slides for the presentation?"

Ellington tapped the pad in his hand. "I'll take care of the artwork. As to the ancillary stuff like slides, photos and descriptors…those are good tasks for a grad student."

Hand remaining on the Fu Dog, Val said, "Maybe a little more effort on this project, and a little less on the study of nude models. Keep me informed." She entered the office to change her clothes, closing the door behind her.

Ellington remained in the studio well after Val returned to the mansion. He posted the sketches along the wall, in an array of perspectives for inspiration. Shaping tool in hand, he carved and scraped the clay, holding her image in his mind. The late afternoon sun crept behind the trees, then sank further to the horizon. Soon after, the crickets began their chorus, and a half-moon blossomed in the twilight overhead.

Kneading and shaping, kneading and shaping again, he didn't stop but for sporadic bites of an apple, a cheese sandwich, and an occasional sip of water. The figurine steadily awakened with each press and shave of the clay—his hands driven by his relentless muse.

When Ellington finally set his tools down, the moon had set, leaving only the studio to illuminate the nearby gardens—a bubble of light in the vast darkness of the estate.  His senses depleted, he stretched his back and stepped away to survey the figure. He had done it, unlocking her essence—or as she had said in her office, "immortalized" —in a mixture of confident body language and knowing smile.

Ellington cleaned the clay off his hands with a rag and rubbed his weary eyes. Taking one more look upon her, he felt there was something missing, a small detail that would be the icing on the cake. He scrutinized the figurine then scanned the sketches draped about the studio again. He closed his eyes and pictured her, sitting on the table, the outside light glowing on her and shining upon…

The sculptor laughed, not from exhaustion, but from an epiphany. The perfect touch to the piece, and her approach to life. The delirium subsided.  There was much to do; the firing and glazing would be done by week's end.

# CHAPTER 21

Norm held the invoice in one hand, coffee mug in the other. "Getting to be it's hardly worth fixing the old Chevy tandem."

Laverne sat across the kitchen table, helping herself to a piece of apple spice cake. "Fair amount of labor for differentials you know. The real hit is on the parts, they're going through the roof. Your ring gear and side bearing were shot. Consider yourself lucky I found them in time for the harvest season."

"Yeah, but this makes me wonder if combining corn pays."

"You've gotten more than ten years out of that puppy." She took a bite of cake. "Hauling four-hundred bushels of grain every trip you take to the river elevator."

"And don't forget tons and tons of pumpkins to the canning plant," Ailsa added.

Norm set the sheet down on the table, too distracted to eat. Devyn sliced an ample piece of cake for himself. Ailsa smiled subtly, admiring the young man's candid appetite. Norm sipped his coffee. "Can't afford to repair it and can't afford not to. Everything is getting bigger. I see more and more semi-tractor rigs at the elevator with each passing year."

"With bigger loads, you'd make fewer trips between the farm and the river," Ailsa said.

Her husband scowled. "That's overkill for the number of acres we till. We would have to sell the cattle and plow under the hay field and pasture to afford it."

Devyn held his fork in midair.

Ailsa countered, "Or we could save on the gas and get a wagon with a team of horses."

"There you go, no differentials to fix on a wagon," Laverne added cheerfully. Devyn shrugged and continued eating.

"All I'm saying is farming has changed these past ten years. Seems like we're racing against the neighbors more than time and the weather anymore."

Ailsa pondered over her tea. "It's true, not as much sense of a community as there once was, it feels more…competitive."

Laverne weighed in. "I remember when I was a kid hanging out on your farm with Rae Ellen. If you had a breakdown in the field, or some other problem, others were willing to stop what they were doing and lend a hand."

"We're in the big push now, fence row to fence row, corn and beans. Except no more fences, livestock are all gone." Norm finally grabbed a piece of cake. "As are the gamebirds I used to hunt as a kid."

"Kind of like the buffalo before the farms came along," Laverne said.

Speaking his thoughts out loud, a distant look veiled Norm's eyes. "It was potatoes, eggs, and strawberries that saved our farm during the Depression. Grandpa and Uncle Herman grew strawberries in three fields of a half-acre each. The first one had young, growing plants, the second one had two-year plants, to sell large fruit for fresh markets. Plants in their third year were smaller, the soil a little worn, we used those berries for canning mostly. Uncle Herman sold the berries in town from the back of his truck like a moonshiner. People still found money somehow for produce."

Norm shifted his gaze back to the kitchen table. "Folks thought Herman made deliveries to Jane Foster, the young widow, more than he needed to. It wasn't only the strawberries that were freshly picked."

"Norm!" Ailsa chided.

"Grandpa said corn prices crashed to a nickel a bushel. Hell, it was better to shovel it into the wood stove for heat than sell it." He shook his head. "He showed me old newspaper pictures of dairy farmers dumping their milk."

Devyn asked with alarm. "Why would they do that?"

Norm shook his head. "No markets, people didn't have the money because of no jobs." He leaned closer to his younger companion. "But people have to eat, so they'll scrimp and save, barter, whatever it takes to put eggs, potatoes, and produce on the table. Folks can't much eat dried field corn."

Devyn weighed Norm's words. "All these fields filled with rows of corn and soybeans. It must be empty looking in the winter."

Ailsa thought of winter on the farm. More than the cold and snow she dreaded the fierce winds—razors roaring over the flat land and scraping the earth into a torrent of silt. A torrent no longer checked by prairie grass and forsaken hedges of Osage Oranges. On the worst days, she had to pull the shades down over her windows and tape the edges to keep the dust out of their old house. Some days it was hard to see outside, the air obscured in a light brown cloak.

To settle her mind, she looked out the window to the cattle, content on the perennial green island of the pasture. She knew all their names…and personalities. Each fall, with the harvest safe in the drying bins, she took pleasure watching the cows glean the grain from the corn field, getting fat and fertilizing the soil. After marrying Norm, it was the cattle herd that swayed her to return with him to live on the farm. If they ever sold the cows, she would be disconnected from "her warm closeness with beasties," as her father had put it.

Her train of thought was broken as Norm said, "Here, Devyn, fetch me that lantern from the counter. I'll teach you how the thing works."

Laverne glanced at Ailsa. "Looks like Doc is teaching Devyn how to collect useless things that take up space. The man can't park his truck in his garage, on account of all the unwanted belongings of Piatt County being stuffed in there." She helped herself to another sliver of cake and set her eyes on Devyn.

"More to the point, Grandpa Billy wants a pinochle rematch, says he's got a strategy all figured out."

Ailsa commented, "Always full of ideas, that one. Billy is a three-way light bulb on a two-way switch."

# CHAPTER 22

Buoyed by the crisp morning air, Ellington jogged the entire length of the Old Timber Road, from the Sun Singer to the old state road then back to the Gate House. He was mildly amused to see an older farm couple near the park entrance, a modern version of *American Gothic*.

After a quick breakfast of yogurt and a banana, and still dressed in tracksuit and running shoes, he picked up a satchel and slung it over his right shoulder. Stepping outside, he strode along the walkway to the mansion. It had been a week since he last saw Valerie. This was the day; his sublime creation was complete. *Carpe diem.*

Ellington glanced to his right, scanning the narrow path that led to the walled garden. He thought, I hope Kim is arriving soon, we've got a lot to do today. Coming to the end of the arbor by the old stable, Ellington halted to consider his strategy. He well knew what would be on Val's mind at their meeting. Despite his pride over what hung in his satchel, the nagging problem of the Fu Dog's repair remained. Lately, it seemed Val's interest for them had grown into an obsession that far outweighed the other preparations for the Taft event.

He decided a brief detour through the Fu Dog Garden was in order. Perhaps he might catch a missed detail in the magic light of early morning. He was especially keen to study the pair of Fus at the end, they were the stars of the show, after all. He glanced at his watch, there was time if he hustled.

Hesitating to gain his bearings, he squinted into the rising sun above the visitor parking lot. A one-story building Val called the Evergreen Lodge—though Ellington deemed Evergreen Motel would better describe the structure's design—stood between him and the woods. During his initial tour, she led him on a path loop from the Fu Dog Garden to the parking lot, exiting somewhere behind the lodge. Thinking it would make a nice short cut, Ellington angled across the lot towards the far side.

Passing the lodge, he found a wide gap in the waist-high brush that bordered the lawn. Pleased with his discovery, he followed the path into the woods. The trail curved to the left and tracked along the crest of a small rise, with a gully to his right. On the opposite side of the ravine, the rear face of the mansion emerged through breaks in the trees, a couple hundred yards away. The manor topped a flat knoll, fully exposed under the sunshine and dominating the landscape—a castle on a hill.

Gazing around the woods, Ellington tried to replay his walk with Val. I didn't notice the view of the manor last time, he thought. He continued, and after a slight bend, the track climbed up a small rise. Upon reaching the crown, he came to an abrupt stop, confronted by stark brutality. By way of expertise and subject, the bronze group casting stunned the sculptor. "Jesus, Mary, and Joseph!"

A six-foot male gorilla grasped a woman under a massive, patina-stained arm. In full stride, the beast clutched a head-sized rock in his opposite hand. The ape's posture reeked of defiance. Feral eyes glared at the artist as he circled the work, the brute's stature made more fearsome by a foot-tall platform.

The ill-fated woman, feet dragging on the ground, chest pressed against the beast's, struggled in vain to free herself. She was naked but for a loincloth decorated with shells, a headband clipped with a bone to hold a ponytail, and a large round amulet hanging from her waist.

Ellington could feel the tread of the ape's feet thumping on the ground and hear the groans of anguish from the woman's mouth. Her plight had little impact on her captor, who was solely focused on what lay before him. Ellington stepped back from the assault, overtaken by sadness for the victim. What had driven the beast to such violence? What would be her fate?

He marveled at how the sculptor displayed such dynamic realism, especially for the woman. He noted an inscription at the base of the casting. "My God, it's a Frémiet. How in all the world did this wind up on a dirt trail in the middle of a woods?" Ellington returned to reality and checked the time. "Damn. I'm running late."

He looked about the woods, thinking if he stayed on the path, keeping the mansion in sight, he might find a way across the ditch and up the far embankment. He descended along the trail, glancing back uneasily at the brutal abduction. Relieved to see the figures still frozen on the pedestal, he carried on, the weight of the satchel now fatiguing his shoulder.

On reaching level ground, Ellington came upon a junction. To his left, the trail widened, leading away from the mansion between an embankment and a wooded plain. He chose to go right and soon crossed a marshy spring on a makeshift foot bridge, surrounded by bright green pachysandra. He then faced a steep incline up the bluff, hindered by the weight of the satchel. Grasping small tree trunks for balance as he climbed, he reached a low, mortared stone wall bordering the south terrace of the mansion. Scrambling over the barrier, he strode across the manicured lawn and made for the wide doors of the west entrance.

Ellington muttered, "Only ten minutes behind. Not bad for taking the wrong path." He had failed in his mission to evaluate the Fu Dogs but had found a spectacular and unexpected work of art. On the balance, a great exchange. *Carpe Diem.*

"I call her *Blue Desire.*"

Val sat behind her desk and examined the seventeen-inch statuette, gleaming in a mosaic of Cerulean and royal blue. The figure sat at ease, leaning forward on a rugged grey-green outcrop, legs crossed at the ankles, dangling over the edge. She murmured, "Your talent is exquisite."

"I thought of casting her in bronze. But it's all about the colors after all."

Tracing her fingertips over the swells and dips of the blue image, she wondered. Is this how he truly sees me, or did he add an artistic slant? The lively eyes of the miniature woman invoked Val to explore the curves of her ceramic body—a magnetism that pulled her into the indigo glaze, and as much, to see herself within. She asked, "Did you name the piece to suggest desire on the part of the viewer? The figure? Or…the artist?"

Ellington beamed. "Beauty is in the eye of the beholder." He looked at his creation with care. "There's one small feature I need to add as yet. I'll save it for the unveiling at the Taft event."

Val glanced up at him as he hovered over her desk, then back at the statue. Despite the obvious personal connection to the figure, her boost in self-esteem mixed with a sense of exposure and vulnerability. "Has anyone else"—her eyes lingered on his—"seen this yet?"

The sculptor shook his head. "Your viewing is the public debut." He shrugged. "Other than Kim, who helped with the kiln work."

She showed her displeasure with his answer.

He assured her. "No worries. She's drawn and sculpted plenty of nudes in her studio work before."

Val leaned back in her chair, regarding the blue siren with a last, long look. It's a captivating piece, she thought. "This effort seems to be well in hand. What about the more…complex project?"

"Ah, yes, that." Ellington sighed as he draped a fine velvet cloth over the statue and wrapped it several times. "I'm perfecting a suitable filler to blend in with the cracks and chips."

She gestured at the now more modestly clad figure on the desk. "You create something so lovely, as a study in blue no less, and you can't come up with any ideas for the Fu Dogs?"

"Oh, I'm chock-full of ideas, but I always end up with discolored scars wherever I apply it to the ceramic test material. I'm enriching antique art here, not fabricating a Frankenstein monster."

Valerie smirked at his description. "We only have a month until crunch time, considering I would like to get at least a pair of the statues in place for the Taft event." She glanced at her watch. "Why don't you take the lady in blue back to the studio, and I'll try to stop by during my lunch break. See if we can't have a small planning session."

He half-smiled. "Maybe I can talk you into modeling for another piece. You have an innate talent you know."

She brushed him away with her hand. "I'll see you in a bit."

Ellington picked up his showpiece. He paused. "I have to ask, the gorilla I saw on the way here…"

"Because you took the wrong path," she reminded him.

He let out an exaggerated breath. "Indeed. What's an original casting by Emmanuel Frémiet doing out in the elements, lost from the world?"

She gave him a shallow smile. "No idea. It was there when I started here. Carl has implied to me this park has been a lost and found for university oddities for some time."

"You being the art historian, I thought you might know. Strange…I was more aware of his Joan of Arc and Napoleonic pieces." Grimacing as he placed *Blue Desire* back in his satchel, Ellington said, "It's not right."

"There's another one you know."

"What?"

"Another Frémiet. A little farther out in the woods. A bear mauling a stone age hunter."

Ellington failed to hide his disbelief. "Their feral and unsettling themes aside, I still say they belong in a more civilized setting."

She eyed him placidly. "Given their feral and…unsettling feral themes as you describe them, maybe they're better off where they're at."

"I'll see you later."

Watching him leave, Val mulled over her effigy. During the past few days, she had pondered over his earlier comments in the studio about replicating the Fu Dogs. She needed to convince him of her strong support for that idea. More importantly, how to use his talent as an unwitting participant in her plan. Val smiled at the thought of the blue siren in his satchel. Was she an art installation or an idol? If the latter, she would tap into that weakness.

"I think you're striving for too much perfection. I can hardly see the seam where you placed the resin."

Ellington admired Valerie's backside as she bent to study the Fu Dog.

"Ellington?"

He awoke from his pipedream. "I'm sorry, I was thinking of another possible option for the crack by the ear."

Hand on one hip as she leaned against the workbench, she rolled her eyes. "I think you're overdoing this."

"It looks worse in brighter light"–he pointed to the glazed ceiling of the greenhouse—"especially outdoor sunlight."

She remained silent and roamed her eyes about the studio. "I have a plan B."

"And what would that be?"

"It was yours, actually. Rather than repair, how about replicating the originals in the garden like you suggested you wanted to try on this one?"

The sculptor's eyes widened. "That's a major project, especially given their age and value."

"I have faith in your ceramic skills. It's one of the reasons I pushed to have you here as the artist in residence." She mocked him in a playful voice. "There's more to you than your good looks."

Basking in the moment, Ellington took off his glasses and nibbled on the bent end of a temple. He studied the wildly emotive face with oversized eyes and teeth. "I'll cast a copy of

146

this poor, forgotten Fu Dog as a dry run. Probably from three or more molds…depending on which elements will be better to break down into smaller parts. I'll lubricate its surface to help ensure we won't damage the glaze when removing the plaster. Then press the clay into the molds and…" An eager shine swept across his face. "The glaze of the new Fus would be uniform and have no defects."

"I realize it's more involved and might push your limits." She walked across the studio to stand in front of the wood table where she had posed, pulling the velvet shroud off her likeness with a flick of her wrist. *Blue Desire* smiled at her, uninhibited by her exposure. Caressing the figure's graceful back while keeping her eyes on his, she said, "But not impossible for someone with such insight."

# CHAPTER 23

On the first and third Tuesdays of each month, Ailsa drove to Mahomet for lunch with a pair of longtime friends. Norm told Devyn such outings helped her cope with the isolation of farm life, "chatting with women of like lifestyle and mindset." He confided to the younger man, "A good marriage needs some personal space. When you get to be my age, and if lucky enough to land one like Ailsa, you'll need to find a way to muddle through the mundane together." He made his point by peering at Devyn with a hard-nosed face. "Flash in a pan romance wears thin over the years."

Choosing to brown bag his lunch outdoors, Devyn left Norm to further refine his philosophy on marital bliss over grilled cheese sandwiches and soup. He made his way to the estate but avoided the Fu Dogs. The image of the bear and hunter still pressed upon him. He would return sometime, when his uneasiness subsided, preferably in the light of day.

He figured a bench in the open sunlight inside the Walled Garden would be more uplifting. As he walked past the picnic area the scent and sight of bright leaves, scattered in the dappled shade of the woodlot, cleared his head. The changing seasons reminded him of home and reconnected him to the natural world.

Nearing the sea maidens on their tall pillars, he was curious to see an older couple by the path, resting under a tree to his left. Taking a closer look, he recognized the hiker who had stopped by the farm to chat during his evening walk. Beside him, a woman of about his age sat with her back against the trunk, reading a book.

The man smiled warmly at Devyn. As before, he wore a white collared shirt and khaki pants. "Good day, young man. It seems we've switched roles. You're the sojourner, and I'm the one resting at home."

Devyn raised a hand in a lazy wave. "I guess we both think the park is a good place to sit for a spell."

The dark-haired woman looked up from her book with surprise. "Why yes, it's a good place to read a book. Nothing but the sound of the breeze and birds." She spoke with a foreign accent. Devyn thought it may have been German. She returned to her reading.

Feeling awkward after infringing on the couple's space, Devyn nodded and proceeded on his walk.

"Lovely place for a picnic, the Walled Garden. Say hello to the girl with a scarf for me. She has chosen her spot to sunbathe well. I hope you enjoy her company."

The young man froze and looked back, stunned by the man's insight of his lunch venue. "Thank-you. I like the peace it offers."

"As do all well-tended gardens."

The woman glanced at him again, her round face and broad nose crinkled in confusion. "Pardon me. Did you say something?"

Devyn gestured, "I was just saying to your…"

She looked about her. "Saying to my what?"

Devyn stuttered, "S-s-sorry to bother you." He walked along the path at a brisk pace, glancing back once more. The man shook his head and waved.

Devyn entered the walled garden, choosing to rest on a white stone bench in front of the sitting girl, his eyes attracted to her lithe, nimble figure. Bright marigolds ringed her pedestal, trembling lightly in the breeze.

He examined the limbs and face of the statue, wondering what it would take to try his hand at sculpture. Was it like molding the curves on a fender of Norm's Model A with body filler? Her heavy eyelids and downcast head showed indifference to Devyn's presence. Unlike the Fu Dogs, who seemed to intensely watch his every move. As had the bear, he reminded himself. Devyn shuddered despite the pleasant sunshine.

As he ate his sandwich, he peered out the garden entrance in the direction of the couple by the tree. They were out of view, but Devyn knew they were there, especially the man. For reasons he couldn't understand, Devyn sensed a familiar bond with him, as if he'd known him for a long time. How was this possible if he'd only arrived to work on the farm less than two months ago? He was resolved to find out more about the elusive visitor from Ailsa and Norm. Or perhaps better yet, Grandpa Billy, tapping into the elder's long history at the estate.

Devyn returned to his contemplation of the girl with the scarf. There were so many unknown layers to this estate, of which he was only starting to realize.

Pressed to get back for a meeting in her office, Val left Ellington in the greenhouse to pore over his molds and plaster. How to go about gaining permission to replace the pair of original Fu Dogs?. The university was a morass of administrative deliberation not known for quick decision making. The timing of the Taft showcase couldn't have been better, adding a bit of purpose and urgency for approval—if she could keep Ellington on track given his distractions. A small seam widened within her mind. Why stop with only one pair? If he could manage to create high-quality replicates, this could turn into a stroke of good fortune. Especially if she attracted the interest of donors with deep pockets. She was determined to plug all the rabbit holes that led him to irrelevant side projects. From this point forward, his work needed to center on the Fu Dogs.

Deep in thought, Val swiftly covered the short distance between the greenhouse and the west entrance to the Walled Garden. Walking along the perimeter to the south entrance, she was unaware of the young man, sitting on a bench by the bathing girl statue. She left the garden and towering sea maidens behind, heading along the hedged path back to the mansion—unaware of her surroundings, except for a glimpse to her right. An older woman, dressed in a sweater, dark-colored pants, and clogs, sat alone reading a book, her back propped by the trunk of a sturdy linden tree. Feeling a chill under the tree's shade, Val wrapped her arms around her chest. She thought, personally, I would have picked a more comfortable place to read.

# CHAPTER 24

"My knees are telling me a low-pressure system is coming."

Perched on ladders on either side of a six-foot pedestal, Carl and Trent glanced at one another. Carl replied, "With all due respect for your arthritis, Charlie, I don't think the forecast agrees with yours. Pay attention while easing this thing down onto the pillar. It's hard enough working on these ladders the way the wind has picked up."

Charlie tapped the hydraulic lever to even the bucket on the skid steer with the top of the column.

"Now tilt it a bit towards us," Carl called out. The bucket angled forward, "Easy! Not so fast!" He held up his hand. "Stop there."

Carl and Trent grabbed a pair of straps that wrapped around a blanket-covered bundle. "We'll pull this puppy on top of the pillar, then lift it onto its feet." Carl leaned back to look at Charlie. "When I tell you, back the bucket out about a foot, then raise it. You got it?"

Charlie waved a hand. "Yeah, yeah. I know the drill."

Carl and Trent grunted as they slid the bottom of the bundle slowly onto the pillar. "Okay, Charlie, easy does it." The mass swayed to a vertical position onto the column.

Out of breath, Carl nodded. "Alright, Trent, take off the straps and I'll unwrap the blanket." As the shroud lowered, the surly eyes of a Fu Dog stared at its captors. Carl shoved the blue figure to better square its base with the crown of the column.

"That should do it." He pushed his hand at Charlie. "Move the Bobcat back." Glancing at Trent, he said, "Tilt it toward you a bit, so I can squeeze some of this silicone underneath to hold it in place until we mortar it. Then we'll squeeze some goo under your side."

After climbing down the step ladder, Carl paced a few steps towards the Buddha shrine and turned to gain a perspective of their effort. Hands on hips, he studied the identical pair of Fu Dogs which now marked the entrance to the woods. He regarded the previous occupants, resting on the lawn next to the pillars.

Trent came by his side. "They look aligned with each other to me."

Carl frowned. "Can't see much difference from the old ones. Other than that they don't have any cracks and are identical to one another. Still a waste of time if you ask me."

"I always thought their faces made them look more like jack-o-lanterns than mean-looking lion dogs," Trent scoffed.

Carl folded his step ladder. "At least we're shipshape and ready to go in time for the big event. We'll mortar them in place next week, we've got more important things to do until then." He took a last look at the new additions. "With their weight, they aren't going anywhere soon."

"It'd sure suck for the lawn party if Charlie is right about the rain."

"It'd sure be nice if Charlie wouldn't gripe about his aches and pains so much." Carl pointed to the figures on the grass. "Come on, let's get these two old ones loaded up on the skid steer and back to the studio."

"I would have thought the tent would be striped in orange and blue, as opposed to burnt orange and maize yellow," Ellington remarked as they neared the pavilion, its fabric billowing in the breeze.

Val watched the crew sent from central campus, setting up tables and chairs under Ashley's supervision. "Where's your sense of seasonal colors in this lovely autumnal setting?"

"I should have guessed with all the pumpkins and corn shocks lined up by the entrance." He added in a mocking tone. "A prefect harvest time theme. Better than balloons, I suppose."

She gave him a dirty look. "It's a throwback to the agricultural roots of this estate, past and present. Besides, it's all about setting up visual appeal. You, as a sculptor, should know better than most."

Rebounding from the jibe, he said, "Well, the decorations can double down for Halloween afterwards." Looking across the terrace at the mansion, he added, "Great venue for a costume party. I think I would come as"—he paused, then snapped his fingers—"oh, yes, a rampaging gorilla."

She responded with a prim smile.

They strolled towards the front of the pavilion, where rested a dais furnished with a podium and side table. She pointed to the table. "That's where we'll place your blue lady, hidden with a drape until we have the dramatic unveiling."

Ellington replied, "Excellent."

Val made a gesture of gratitude. "Your piece deserves front and center. After the brunch, we'll have the usual lineup of administrators thanking everyone for attending, then I'll give a brief introduction about you and the artist in residency program"—she smiled with a hint of sarcasm—"with plenty of thanks to the donors of the program of course."

"Of course."

"Then it'll be your turn to talk about the inspiration of your piece, followed by its unveiling."

He rested his chin on his fist. "Discuss the inspiration of the piece, interesting."

Val narrowed her eyes. "I'm thinking in terms of Taft and the White Rabbits."

"Of course."

She nodded towards the mansion. "Then inside for a seminar on the White Rabbits and a tour of their installations in the central hall. After that, I thought it might be fun to visit the Fu Dog Garden. It'll be interesting to see if anyone notices the temporary pair."

"Temporary, yes, but eventually permanent."

"Our little secret for now. I'm still working out how to approach that detail with the university. The bottom line will be to showcase your skills as a ceramic sculptor." Something caught Val's attention over his shoulder. "Excuse me for a minute." She hustled over to talk to Ashley.

Ellington reflected on her plans. He made a point to go visit the Fu Dog Garden to see how the new arrivals were faring. Would their quality hold up under public scrutiny in the light of day? What if he had overlooked a small detail?

Val returned by his side. "Sorry for that, a crisis about where to set up the buffet line. We're still organizing the layout." She pinched her lower lip. "Where were we? Oh yes, after the review of the Fu Dogs, a short coffee and bakery break, then we'll go to the studio for your workshop. How's that going?"

"Kim will have things cleaned up and pieces in various stages of completion arranged in a series."

"Good." Val looked at her watch. "I've got to get back to my office. I imagine you have some things to catch up on as well."

Ellington held up his forefinger. "Just one last question."

Val arched an eyebrow.

"What will happen to the originals when I'm done using them to make plaster molds? They are, after all, valuable pieces of art."

"I originally thought to archive them in storage at the university. In case we need a replacement after a severe storm and the like." She sighed. "But they'll likely get forgotten. A public auction has crossed my mind. Probably would generate a fair amount of interest among collectors, especially alumni. I haven't had time to think about that detail."

Jenny appeared by the French doors of the solarium. "Ms. Farwell, there's a phone call for you."

Val turned to leave. "I need to go." She dallied as if in thought. Eyeing him over her shoulder, she said, "Perhaps I'll stop by the studio tomorrow so we can plan for the original Fu Dog's future."

He watched her as she glided by tables and chairs, making her way to the open French doors of the solarium.

Water, the element of healing, purification, gardens, and travel. Also, the most simple and basic need for cattle. Not so simple when it was frozen, or so Devyn thought while helping Norm repair the float valve on the stock tank. The Ritchie kept water from freezing during the baleful days of ice and snow. If the present gusts, buffeting them as they worked, hinted at what was in store when the temperatures were fifty degrees colder, Devyn figured the heated tank was a must. But the 'goddam valve'—as Norm named it—wouldn't shut the water off when the float reached the upper limit. Water kept flowing, making a mudhole around the tank.

The late afternoon sun peeked through the dull clouds, but there were no obstacles checking the wind, knifing through the open fields. Devyn wondered how far the wind had traveled to get here. The next county, Mississippi River, Kansas? Back home the brawny ridges scraped the clouds and tamed the wind.

Devyn looked out across the pasture, a rippling sea of green grass. The cows—fattened on the lush growth brought about by cool autumn rains—had their backs to the gusts. Despite the stiff breeze, it was a day of grazing bliss, no flies, dry hair and hide, and relaxed cud chewing.

Channel-lock in hand, Devyn tried to meld with the pastoral tranquility. But a haze of foreboding weighed on his mind, as if the placid animals floating on the green landscape were an illusion, nothing more than wallpaper covering a hidden crack in the woods beyond. The hectic chorus of crows, from the direction of the estate, drew his eyes away from the cows.

The crows had been restless for much of the day, at times two or three cawing to one another, at times an uproar of many voices, all clamoring for attention simultaneously. Their voices were fragmented into turmoil, not cohesive, such as when a red-tailed hawk was close.

Closing his eyes, he meditated on the Fu Dog Garden, seeking the calm green lawn and ordered lines of bright blue statues. Instead, desolate grey light, tilted pillars, and figures covered in leprous lichen—some of which lay broken on the ground—plagued his vision. Specters of gruesome beasts with frightful voices roamed the rundown garden, sifting in and out of the surrounding landscape, scarred with leafless trees.

"You with me here, son?" Norm's voice yanked him back to the farm. "I said, can you hand me the channel-locks?"

Devyn obliged, but the crows kept harping, something had changed in the estate, a strangeness in the woods. He didn't fully understand why, but he was being called…called to intervene. But intervene with what? And why him?

# CHAPTER 25

Val savored an indulgent stretch on the table, her entire body free of tension. Laying on her back, hair tussled, she let her mind transcend through the glass panes above. A mesh of grey, spongy clouds, pierced with pinholes of sunlight, streamed lazily across the sky. Tree branches vibrated in the wind, wiggling fingers shedding yellow and red leaves.

Her white fleece sweater was pulled up to her armpits, her legs wrapped around Ellington's torso. Both were naked from the waist down and joined at the hips.

Ellington's feet were planted on the studio floor, forearms propped on either side of her waist. Head pillowed on her belly, he inhaled then exhaled deliberately, catching the subtle scent of lavender body lotion. She ran her fingers across his scalp, raking furrows in his sandy mop. With dove-like calm, she said, "Now you know what it's like to make love to her."

He lifted his head. "Her?"

Valerie arched her neck to look at the nearby workbench. The blue nymph sat leaning over the ledge, hands by her side, watching their entire act with serene forbearance. Valerie rubbed the back of his thighs with her heels. "Maybe that's why you created her, to bring your fantasies to life."

He replied in a roguish voice, "Perhaps I should design another with a different pose, to see what might come alive then."

She turned to face him, running a hand along his cheek. "I like you without the glasses. Makes you look so much more"—she laid her hand on a shoulder—"primitive."

He buried his face in her navel and growled.

Twirling his hair between her fingers, Valerie rolled her head sideways and spotted a Fu Dog, glaring with disapproval at them with those strange bulging eyes. Its partner observed her from the opposite side of the room. "This pair of Fus are the ones that Carl and his crew brought in from the garden, correct?"

Face still planted in her abdomen, Ellington replied in a muffled voice, "Correct."

"I hope the copies of these two come out as well as the first one you made."

He looked up at her. "You mean the replica of the one we found in the shed?"

"Yes, the pair of substitutes installed at the end of the garden."

Glancing at the nearest figure, he said, "These will be better. I like the way their plaster molds turned out."

Val rose to rest on her elbows. "What? You already made plaster molds from them? That was quick."

Smiling, he said, "You doubted my skills? That first Fu we replicated was a bit of a learning curve. Now, we have the plaster ratio, glaze mixture, and everything else down pat."

She returned his gaze. "That means you could…"

"Press ceramic clay into the molds, release the clay after it's set, fuse the clay parts together, trim the slag…and *voilà*, a new blue Fu…ready for baking in the kiln." Ellington gently pushed away from her body and stood. "Your replacement plan was a good idea."

"Can you copy these originals and replace the temps in time for this weekend's event?"

A faint smirk lined his face. "We do have a few other pressing matters to attend to, not the least of which is the workshop that you suggested." Sensing her disappointment, he added, " Next week would be possible, and then after that we can just roll through the entire lot in the garden if you like."

Her eyebrows lifted an inch. "What are you saying?"

"If it helps, think Jello. Once I have the molds, if I can make two, I can easily make four."

She sat up. "Four?"

"Why not? Or better yet for diversity's sake, once I get each of the new pairs from Carl, I'll replicate them. Eventually, we'll fill the whole garden with newly minted clones."

"You mean the whole collection will be like brand new?"

"Not *like* brand new, brand new."

Val ran some quick math in her head. "Could you have this done by the time your residency is finished in late spring?"

"If you arrange the supplies for me, I don't see any problem with that." He regarded the nearest Fu Dog again. "You're going to have a truckload of vintage pieces. Have any ideas yet on how to best utilize that asset?"

Val laid her arms around his waist. "I've been in touch with the university. I was told they'll get back to me. I suggested a sale as a fundraiser for Allerton Park and offered to inventory and archive the pieces."

"Sale? That's sad. The separation of the Fus from one another sounds like some sort of diaspora. "

She pulled him closer and kissed him, then ran a hand down his thigh. "Perhaps I can help keep you focused on the replacements, with what we'll call…dynamic modeling?"

"Perhaps I should cast a new figurine, which I will call *Blue Muse*."

Val peeked over his shoulder at the blue vixen with the agreeable smile, thinking, this is going better than I expected.

# Entropy

The best known of Fillan's relics were —

***The Quigrich-*** St. Fillan's crozier, the most hallowed of the saint's relics, who kept it with him at all times. He relied on the staff to search for lost or stolen cattle. Even if astray among the most rugged crags and glens, the beasts would be drawn by the staff's power. If the cattle were stolen, no reiver dared to obstruct his errand.

***The Bernane-*** A bronze bell, designed as those for pastured cattle. St. Fillan used this to dispel demons of madness, by striking the bell in rhythm, followed by immersion of the afflicted into the Holy Pool. For more severe cases, the possessed were then staked to the ground with the *Bernane* placed on their forehead until their deliriums ceased. In later years, if away from the monastery, and the *Dior-a-Bhearnain* needed the bell for healing, he didn't fetch it, but rather summoned the bell, which sailed to him on the wind.

***The Mayne-*** The bones of St. Fillan's left forearm. At the end of each day, Fillan returned to his humble dwelling to meditate and write. A curious disciple once peeked through a chink in the wall of Fillan's dark cell and saw the fingers of the saint's left arm glow to give light for writing. Pride overcame the intruder, who bragged to others what he had witnessed. Fillan, angry to have his power revealed, set a crane to peck out the eye of the trespasser. Fillan's followers pleaded for mercy, and after the foolish novice begged forgiveness, Fillan restored his sight by touching him with his divine left hand.

Chronicles of Inchaffray Abbey

162

# CHAPTER 26

A drizzle sifted from the drab, gunmetal clouds, flattening daylight onto the ground as it fell. Ailsa had roasted a chicken and made hotchpotch—turnips, potatoes, carrots, and onions, boiled and mashed with butter. Applesauce spice cake with cream cheese frosting rounded out the meal. Devyn felt obliged to clean the dishes in tribute for the feast, silently affirming he had eaten much better since arriving on the farm than at home.

A dampness crept through the walls of the old farmhouse, prompting Norm to fire up the wood stove insert in the fireplace. Satisfied with the growing heat, he settled in his armchair, turned on a lamp, and picked up the *Journal Republican*.

Clearing the table, Ailsa said, "No better time than the first drafty evening of the fall to bring out a little spring sunshine. Devyn, why don't you stay a bit, and we'll share a wee dram by the fire?"

Scouring a pot, Devyn asked, "You mean a drink?"

"Perfect for nights like these. I've still got a bit of last year's vintage." Ailsa opened the basement door and vanished down the narrow stairs. The clunk of shoes on wooden steps preceded her return to the kitchen. In her hands were two narrow wine bottles. Setting the bottles on the counter, she reached for three goblets.

Dishes done, Devyn dried his hands. "Is that the dandelion wine again?"

Fishing a corkscrew out of a drawer, Ailsa drilled open a bottle. "It's a soothing end to a long day."

He kept a close watch on her hands as she poured the wine into each glass. She held one up to the light, brought it to her nose and sniffed. Taking a small sip, she nodded, "That will do." Motioning to the young man to take a glass, she carried one to Norm. He reached up and took the stem of his glass without looking. "Thanks, Ail."

"Have a seat." Ailsa gestured to a couch while she sat in a blue quilted armchair.

Devyn sank in the soft cushions, covered in the same material as Ailsa's chair. His host looked at him expectantly, waiting for an evaluation. Lifting his hand tenuously, he tilted the glass back and let the wine seep into his mouth. Devyn drew his head back and studied his goblet, then tried another taste. After a third sip, his body relaxed and his mind let go of worldly cares.

Tasting his wine, Norm judged, "I still think last year's batch was a bit more of my style."

Ailsa pursed her lips. "It's had more time to mellow."

"Humph." He ruffled his paper and dove into an article by the local extension agronomist.

Devyn drained his glass without conscious intent. He studied a framed print hanging on the wall above the fireplace. A rag tag band of bearded warriors, barefooted and clad in tartans, knelt on the ground before a robed figure, his arms spread wide, bearing an ornate cross in one hand. Devyn was drawn into the scene, feeling the cleric's hold over what looked to be little more than a host of cutthroats.

"Maurice, Abbot of Inchaffray Abbey, at the battle of Bannockburn."

Devyn shifted his gaze to her.

"He's blessing the Scots before their advance against a much larger and better equipped English army."

Devyn returned to the print. "Did it help?"

"Hard to say." Ailsa got out of her seat to fetch the open and closed bottles of wine, plus corkscrew, while she kept talking. "It was King Robert's greatest victory over the English. Against all odds, or so it was thought at the time."

"It looks like it happened long ago."

"Almost seven-hundred years."

"Do the Scots still remember this battle?"

Smiling as she refilled all three glasses, she replied. "Very much so."

As Ailsa regained her throne, she regarded the scene. "That's Robert the Bruce in the background, on the horse. He was adamant that the abbot not only bless his army but do so with a silver reliquary"— she glanced at Devyn—"that's a box used to carry holy relics, that held the left arm-bones of St. Fillan, one of the most beloved saints of Scotland." She paused to enjoy her wine. "Especially in the Highlands."

"You mean the place you were talking about earlier?"

"Yes, he settled not far from Loch Tay and the River Dochart." Sitting back, Ailsa's eyes shimmered in the firelight. "Legend has it the good abbot, afraid of losing the holy relic should the English prevail, left the saint's arm back at the monastery for safekeeping and brought the empty reliquary." She smiled slyly. "It was the safe bet. King Robert then caused near panic among the brothers as he demanded they open the box so he could touch the bones, believing they would impart strength into his arms for battle."

Ailsa showed a sad face. "Those poor monks, caught between a rock and a hard place, had no choice but to open the box upon the king's command…only to find the bones to be miraculously in place."

Norm grunted, "I heard more believable tales from drunk shipmates when on shore leave. And I'll tell you what, they were whoppers."

Unfazed, Devyn studied the subdued ranks of fierce men, heeding the fervent holy man, and pondered how parts of an old skeleton held such sway over them.

Norm peeked over the top of the newspaper. "What ever supposedly happened to the bones, anyway?"

Ailsa took a deep breath and sighed. "They were lost over

time, probably when the monasteries were sacked during the ravages of the Reformation. As were many saint's relics."

Devyn shuddered. "Awful lot of trouble for an arm bone from a dead guy. It's kind of creepy."

She eyed the young man with patience. "There were other relics of Fillan's, including his staff, the Quigrich, and bell, the Bernane."

"I suppose they were lost, too?"

Ailsa leaned forward to refill Devyn's glass again. "It's a bit of a story. Each of the relics was in the care of what were called Dewars, translated from Gaelic *dior*, or keepers. Some did their task well, into the 1800s in the case of the Quigrich and Bernane." She nodded pensively. "They rest in the Scottish museum in Edinburgh now. The others were lost over time. As were the bones, called the Mayne, from treachery on the part of the Macnabs. It was said Arnold Macnab sold it to a curiosity collector for six silver crowns. A regular Judas."

Devyn tried to make sense of the tales. "How do you know all of this?"

"My family came from overseas to Canada a long time ago, during the Highland clearances. The stories were passed down over generations. The Dewars were more than token keepers, the relics were believed to impart special powers of healing and animal charms, the same powers Fillan was said to possess."

Both Norm and Skipper were snoring under the influence of wine and a warm stove. Ailsa drained the last drops from the first bottle into her goblet, then opened the second bottle. She remained attentive to the needs of Devyn's empty glass.

"You see, Devyn. We share a common thread in life. Both of us have traveled far from home. In the old tongue, you and I are called a *Coigreach*…a stranger, or alien in a new land."

Devyn mused over the term. "It's sounds sinister."

Ailsa smiled. "Not so, Fillan himself was a *Coigreach* among the Highlands. And he is revered to this day."

Head swimming with the bright glaze of dandelions, Devyn imagined the figures on the wall turned to stare at him. A multitude of faces from many years ago, now more attentive to him than the impending strife of battle. Ailsa's voice drew further away, gently prodding him about his previous experiences with animals. Hypnotized by the heady riot of a spring day coursing through his veins, Devyn opened his mind and tongue to Ailsa's questions.

"Have animals always seemed to be attracted to you?"

Devyn replied, "I didn't have to do much to have other people's pets or farm animals like me, it just happened. Dairy farmers, and even Dr. Malcolm, were surprised I was never kicked while milking a cow—even a nervous, recently calved heifer.

"And you repulsed June Bug, our young cow, when she charged you after leaving the chute. Have you done something like that before?" Devyn recalled his experience with a psychotic bull, rampaging loose in a barnyard, that he cast away while saving others from harm. He smiled, thinking of how the bull fled over fields and through fences, a harem of agitated heifers and cows at his heels.

She paused to gain inertia for her next question. "Has anyone ever been hurt from your…"—leaning forward, she stared at the young man with serene eyes—"shall we call it, changing an animal's actions?"

He retracted on the couch; his face grew solemn. "I made a swarm of crows scold and peck a bully who was stalking my girlfriend, Lily. It happened on her mom's farm. They chased him away." Devyn paused to think of his old flame. "I caught him trying to force himself on her."

Ailsa knew there was a deeper crevice. "Anything else?"

Lowering his eyes, his voice barely carried over the snoring duet and the crackling wood in the stove. "Heifers. Bred Holstein heifers. In an old barn during a thunderstorm. I urged Dr. Malcolm's dog to stampede heifers in a barn. I didn't see it coming…their wildness, they trampled and killed a man…a very evil man."

Ailsa's eyes glowed like embers in the dull light of the room. "We must be careful how we use our unusual gifts. It's all about balance."

As Devyn woke the next morning, he remembered little of the previous evening, save for a good meal, Scottish warriors above the fireplace, and Ailsa telling him a story of the bones of an old saint…and the taste of dandelion wine.

As he stepped outside soon after dawn, he once again heard fretful crows in the distance, coming from the direction of the estate. He needed to go there; he knew the balance of the place had been upended.

# CHAPTER 27

Kim watched her advisor dart about the studio, overcome by 'creative genius fever,' or so she named the malady. During these bouts, Ellington was unresponsive to conversation, barely aware of those around him, and irritable if prodded with too many questions. Depeche Mode was the usual music of choice. This afternoon, the synthetic beat was echoing throughout the studio.

The blue woman sat on her ledge, exposed and naked on a table under the inquisitor's spotlight. Circling around her, pencil in hand and sketchbook in the other, Ellington would stop to peer closely, scratch pencil on paper, then continue his revolutions around the table.

Kim yelled over the music. "What are you doing now? Is this part of your workshop demo?" She got no reply. "Would you like anything else before I call it a day?" He only mumbled while drawing on his pad. "Alright then, I'll take that as a no." She collected her gear to go leave. Pausing, she considered letting him know that she planned to stay on campus tomorrow to catch up on her own needs. She recalibrated her thinking. Better not, now is not the time.

Letting out a long breath, Kim headed for the front door of the greenhouse.

"Before you go, I need you to weigh and mix a double batch of each of the glazes we used for the first Fu Dog replicate."

"I cleaned up the shop an hour ago."

He peered at her through his glasses. "I want to try my hand at copying the Fus from the garden."

Kim glanced at the two figures poised on a counter across the room and cursed under her breath. Why was he fooling around with those little gremlins just days before the Taft event?

Her advisor added, "Just weigh the different materials out for me. I'll mix and dissolve them later."

Her shoulders sagged. "I thought we were keeping the workshop simple. You know, all those coffee mugs you had me cast the last two weeks. The visitors custom glaze them, we bisque and fire them afterwards, then send their special creation to their home as a souvenir gift. End of story."

"Please," he added in a kind voice.

She nodded and put down her purse and car keys. Looking at the figurine, she knew who the model was. Yeah, he's got the fever bad; this isn't going to end well, she thought. "Okay, you're the boss."

As she shuffled her tired feet to the plaster shop, he called out. "Oh, is there any leftover pizza still in the fridge?"

"I don't think so."

Ellington's face soured. "Hmmm. I better go pick something up in town. How about if I get a couple subs?" He smiled pedantically. "You'll be here a while."

Resigned to her fate, Kim replied, "Sure."

Ellington left through the back door. Kim turned the volume of the boombox down and looked about the studio. A twinge of vulnerability shaded her thinking as she realized both Fu Dogs and the blue woman were all positioned to watch her. Finding the combined attention unsettling, she approached the Fu Dogs and using all her weight, shoved each of them a half turn to face the wall. Satisfied, she entered the shop to conjure up the glazes.

Ellington barged into the shop, carrying a paper bag in his hand. "Dinner is served. Found a six pack of Heinekens to help wash things down. Who knew such culture existed in Monticello?" He halted to look at his grad student, hands stained in multiple colors and reds streaks in her jet-black hair. "My, you look like you were bathing in it. Wash up and come in the studio to eat."

Kim followed him to the front room and sat on a stool next to him by a large counter. Shoving some tools out of the way, Ellington opened the bag and handed her a foil-wrapped sub. "I got roast beef for you, knowing it's your favorite."

As she pulled the foil apart, Kim felt her hunger rise. "Thanks."

Opening a bottle and handing one to her, Ellington said, "I probably won't get to pressing clay into one of the Fu Dog molds this evening after all. I decided to finish sketching and carving a crude model of the statuette first. Nonetheless, thanks for having the glazes good to go." He opened another bottle and took a long swig. "That's the ticket."

Kim held her sandwich with two hands and took a bite. Enjoying warm roast beef, tomato, and mayo, she chomped another mouthful and shifted her eyes across the studio. She stopped chewing and swallowed. The Fu Dogs still crouched on the far counter but were once again facing away from the wall and grinning at her with their frozen eager smiles.

Ellington took notice as she nearly slid off her stool. "Are you okay?"

Startled, she rubbed her forehead. "I'm feeling exhausted. I'll take my sub along for the ride home."

He considered her mood change. "Are you okay to drive?"

She nodded. "Yeah."

Okay, whatever you think best." He reached in the paper bag. "I almost forgot, I got a bag of chips for you, too. Take it along. But better leave the beer." He grinned, "Don't worry, it won't go to waste."

# CHAPTER 28

Devyn left the road to tramp over the ditch and into the Fu Dog Garden. Chatty chickadees gossiped in a spruce tree to his right. He ambled past the west face of the Buddha house, glancing at the golden buddha gleaming in the warm pastel colors of evening. Despite the buddha's open embrace, the air cooled as he rounded the corner. He reeled back on seeing a figure sitting on the concrete steps, admiring the view of the garden. Once again, he found himself in the presence of the visitor with the dark-rimmed glasses.

Without looking his way, the man remarked in a casual voice, "This chap behind me makes good company for contemplating this space, don't you think?"

Keeping three arms-lengths distance between them, Devyn was at a loss for words. His eyes crawled to the white Hari-Hara towering over the man's back—missing arms, stony face, vacant eyes—wondering how such a stark figure could be good company.

The older man turned his head, a smile creasing his face. "So much to observe. You can spend hours here and not see everything...changes in shadows, shifting breezes, sounds marking the time of day. It's the small details that matter." He nodded to the line of trees behind the pillars to the right. "This was once an open meadow. Robert had those spruces planted when the garden was established. *Picea abies*, such lovely drooping boughs, especially when they tremble on the evening breeze such as now."

At a loss of what to do or say, Devyn remained still.

His voice tinged with remorse, the older man said, "They're getting on in years. Robert loved the trees on his estate, was always eager to know more about them. My wife and I helped him with that. My favorites are the *Tilia*." He noted the young man's silent question. "Lindens. Some call them basswoods."

Devyn studied the face of his companion. It conferred a depth of wisdom, similar to Ailsa's. "Are you one of the groundskeepers here?"

Chuckling, the man replied, "After a fashion, yes."

The shade from the spruces crept across the lawn, reaching to extinguish the light reflecting off the Fu Dogs to the left.

The seated visitor turned to regard the impassive statue. "Do you know our friend here is the joining of two eastern deities? Hara, life itself, and Hari, life's decay. A balance, you see, the natural flow of things. On the one hand we exist, on the other we age and decay into the next. When we intervene with the natural cycle, disorder and chaos ensues."

Pensive dark eyes gazed at the younger man. "You're in touch with that balance, aren't you?" The man's voice seemed to echo across the garden.

Confounded by the stranger's insight, Devyn answered, "I've never experienced a place like this before."

"Indeed, I'd be surprised if you had." The man studied the far end of the lawn. "Those Fu Dogs by the path to the woods, the two watchdogs, I call them. I believe their color looks a little off, don't you think? You might consider taking a closer look."

Vague uncertainty settled upon Devyn as he pondered the proposition, as if clouds had obscured the setting sun. Glancing back at the man, who nodded approvingly in return, Devyn walked slowly across the length of the lawn. Approaching the pillars, he examined the blue figures, resting on their haunches. Shadow edged across their faces, masking their detail, but something was different from before. Their eyes lacked awareness, staring ahead, indifferent to his presence.

Unsure of his analysis, he pivoted to call out to his mentor for advice. Only the Hari-Hara returned his gaze across the lawn. Scanning the entirety of the garden, Devyn realized he was alone.

Puzzled, Devyn remained for a minute to take a longer look at both of the watchers. Returning towards the Buddha house, he reviewed each Fu Dog to his right as the last rays of sun streaked their faces. Unlike the pair on the end, their eyes seemingly tracked him as he walked by. Thinking it might offer a visual clue, Devyn sat on the steps previously occupied by the older man. The Fu Dogs offered little more than their perpetual mocking smiles.

A pair of crows disrupted his meditation, scolding something from the direction of the river. Perhaps an owl coming to life for the evening hunt. The crows didn't relent and were soon joined by others. The ruckus reminded him sunset had passed. He rose from the steps and stretched, then remained still. Something had moved under the spruces on the near side of the garden.

Devyn peered into the deepening twilight, his pulse quickening. Whatever it was, the shadow crouched behind a trunk and was much larger than a racoon or possum. Wishing he had brought his flashlight, he took a tepid step towards the creature. The phantom bounded away, vanishing farther into the woods.

Pausing a moment to catch his breath, Devyn returned to the farm without delay, his mind tumbling over his encounters with the dark-eyed man and obscure watcher.

As he paced across the farmyard, he stopped in his tracks. Like a vine snaking through the trees, the wind carried a cry from the direction of the estate. Knowing nightfall played tricks with sound in the woods, Devyn believed the call came from as far away as the river. The voice rang out a second time, deeper and more resonant. Hair standing on end, he stared into the spreading darkness. Turning towards his apartment, he spied Alisa by the kitchen window and waved with an uneasy smile.

As Devyn reached his apartment door, the deep bellow replayed, but fainter. Whatever it was, the creature was covering distance with speed. He entered the stairwell of his apartment and locked the door behind him. It was then his mind pieced together what he had seen under the trees. Although nothing more than a fleeting moment of clarity, Devyn realized the phantom had fled on two legs, not four. It was a woman, the same woman he had seen in his previous dream.

# CHAPTER 29

Sipping her tea, Ailsa watched the walls of the barn and machine shed fading from red to dull garnet. Norm preferred green paint on his machinery and red paint on his buildings. From the kitchen window, she could see the pasture and the woods beyond. She had enjoyed this vista from the first day she moved to the farm. Black cows on green grass with a background of leafy trees—a perpetually changing canvas with the seasons.

It was a quiet evening. Norm and the dog were out in the machine shed tinkering with the combine. She stood by the window, half-open to let the house breathe a little. The scent of moist earth releasing heat into the cool twilight sifted through the open sash.

She pressed the mug between her sturdy hands, letting the warmth of the tea spread to her palms, needing a break to collect her thoughts on the farming life. There won't be many calm evenings like this soon. The corn is drying fast.

She reflexively swung her gaze towards the barn. Devyn had tossed some hay in the feeders. The change in seasons meant the cows needed to adjust to a new ration that relied less on the pasture. He was making his way to the house. Laverne was due any minute now, taking him for another fish fry at the Deluxe.

Ailsa stepped outside. As Devyn got in earshot, she called out, "It seems Grandpa Billy is finally going to get his pinochle rematch."

The young man nodded. "I don't think he liked losing last time. It was a one-sided affair."

"How was your visit to the park yesterday evening?" Anticipating his answer, she asked anyway. "Where did you go?"

Devyn hesitated. "The Fu Dogs again."

Ailsa remained silent, prompting the young man to reveal his thoughts. "I can't explain it, but there's something that doesn't seem right there."

She narrowed her eyes. "How so?"

Avoiding her gaze, he said quietly, "The man with the glasses was there, sitting on the steps of the Buddha house. It was like" —Devyn rubbed his forehead and looked at her— "he knew I was coming and waiting for me."

"What did he say to you? Did he give you his name?"

"No. He talked about how Mr. Allerton planted spruce trees and liked to know what trees he had on his estate. Then he said something about his favorite tree being a linden, he used fancy science words to describe them."

Ailsa tilted her head. "Science words?"

"Yeah, Latin or Greek or something like that. The kind of words Dr. Malcolm would use to name bacteria and such." Devyn shrugged. "He told me a pair of Fu Dogs were off color. They were blue like the others. I had no idea what he was talking about, so I walked to the end of the garden to take a look. When I turned back to ask him to explain, he was gone."

"Gone?"

"Yeah. Without saying goodbye. He's kind of a strange that way."

She offered a smile in return. "Have you seen him anywhere else?"

Devyn deliberated. "Yeah, when I had lunch over in the walled garden. He was sitting under a tree with a lady while she read a book."

"Reading a book?" A Chevy Blazer rolled into the drive. She said, "Looks like your ride is here."

Watching the Blazer drive away a few minutes later, Ailsa felt ill at ease with Devyn's story. Something jogged her memory from Devyn's description of the garden visitor, and his interest in trees. Ailsa rested on a chair on the porch and meditated. Her thoughts wormed their way to a key word. Linden.

# CHAPTER 30

Glaring at Devyn with suspicion, Grandpa Billy nursed his beer. He and Luis had lost a second game to the young man and Laverne. Hadn't even scored fifty points before the two of them blew past a hundred and fifty. Worst of all, he and Luis got set on their last bid. Grandpa Billy knew a thing or two about turning a sleight of hand but couldn't figure out the kid's gimmick. There had to be one, he couldn't be that lucky.

The older man weighed in on Devyn's identity. "Lawers? Don't know anyone with that name around here."

Laverne told him patiently. "He's from Pennsylvania, you know."

"Never been there. Been to Chicago when the City of New Orleans used to be running. I was a young man then, had me a high time. I went up to the Tip Top Tap in the Allerton Hotel, no less. Met a dame, let me tell you about the time I had that night."

"Spare us, *amigo*." Luis said.

Grandpa Billy watched a red-haired woman pass by their table, taking note of Devyn's interest. "Wouldn't blame you if you wanted to go introduce yourself."

Laverne showed her disdain. "You're offering advice on romance, now? Hope it's better than your pinochle."

"Young sailors are easily distracted when mermaids are swimming about."

"This comes from one who has flirted with disaster in all sorts of iffy relationships."

Grandpa Billy retorted, "Sometimes you have to keep trolling to land the big catch."

"Not if the women in your life were more like Loretta Lynn."

Grandpa Billy stewed over her comment, missing the connection.

She paused and gave him a cagey smile. "Guess you don't remember her singing…'there's no use spending time with a girl if you got a woman who knows how to make a man feel like a man.' Luis smiled sheepishly.

Grandpa Billy knew when to give up. He changed his tack and asked Devyn, "Have you had a chance to visit the estate again? You remember what I told you before, don't you?"

Devyn replied, "Yes, sir."

"What have you seen?"

"Different parts of the garden. Made it all the way to the Centaur statue during one walk."

Billy made a face. "That's a depressing thing to see. Seen the Fu Dogs again?"

Devyn nodded.

"I told you there's something special about the place. Mr. Robert sure thought so."

Reluctantly, Devyn said, "I also saw the bear statue."

Grandpa Billy raised a single bushy eyebrow. "So, you took a walk into the woods. They aren't tidy and manicured like the gardens."

"That statue is kind of creepy," Devyn said. "I didn't like being there alone with it. Seems out of place with the precise gardens Allerton created elsewhere in the estate."

"That's because he had nothing to do with it."

Startled by the comment, Devyn asked, "How? He…he didn't know someone put a bear statue on his own property?"

"Well, he might have heard about it, but he'd already donated the estate to the university in '45 by the time those two creatures arrived."

"You mean the bear and the hunter?"

Grandpa Billy rolled an empty bottle in his hand. "This is going to take another round. Be on the lookout the next time the barmaid comes by, Luis." Delight swept over Billy's craggy face. "You saw the bear, did you also run across the gorilla, too?"

Devyn's blank face answered the question.

"Two bronze statues, in the same neck of the woods. The bear mauling a hunter, the gorilla carrying away a naked woman under his arm. The King Kong of Allerton Park."

"Give us a break, Billy," Laverne groaned.

Billy waved a hand at his critic. "If you think about it, in both of those statues, the humans are getting the short end of the stick. They came to the estate in the mid '50s as I recall. Something to do with that famous sculptor…" He paused to sift through his memory. "The one who made the Alma Mater on the corner of Wright and Green…Taft. He owned both the gorilla and bear. Folks said some Frenchman made them."

The older man leaned to set his arms on the table to further hold Devyn's attention. "Here's the crazy thing. Those two beasts were never meant to be on the Allerton grounds to begin with. After Taft died, they were accidentally shipped with his actual art donations to the university. Supposedly, the family found out and wanted them back. Well, it seems no one knew where they went. Got lost. The university is a complicated place, you know."

Billy paused as if winded from his fervor. "I guess there was a lot of hemming and hawing and turning over all the sofa cushions looking for the things, until finally, I believe after the missus passed away, the Taft family decided to give up and donate them."

A refreshed bottle of PBR ended up in the storyteller's hands. "And do you know where those statues had been all the while?"

Devyn shook his head. "No sir, I don't."

Grandpa Billy let out a cackle that carried halfway across the noisy billiard hall. "Right there on the estate, behind the work shed, across the road from the greenhouse. Those of us who worked there knew about them, but no one ever told us folks were searching for them."

Grandpa Billy took a long belt from his bottle. "Those ugly things were there for years, gathering weeds, until one day, the grounds crew decided to have a little fun, kind of a Halloween prank. We dragged them onto a dump truck with the help of a front-end loader." He pointed at Devyn. "Mind you those were heavy sons-of-bitches. Then we drove up the service lane that cuts off the Old Levee Road by the river and hauled those beasts on top of a couple of small rises. We figured they'd enjoy a nice view of the mansion from their new home. Maybe scare anyone looking out at the woods from an upper story window. I think they're standing where we placed them to this day. Although they're set on concrete platforms now."

Devyn summed up the tale. "So, the bear and the gorilla were never meant to be on the estate."

"Nope. Not part of Mr. Allerton's plan, just showed up behind the old storage shop."

"Maybe they walked to Allerton Park all the way from Champaign," Laverne declared as she picked up the deck to shuffle.

Billy furrowed his brow. "Some folks find them a bit unsettling, you know. They say the nearby woods are haunted because the mansion sits on a bluff that was an old burial mound."

Devyn dwelled on the thought of revisiting the bear, and if he didn't lose his nerve, seek out the gorilla.

After breakfast, Ailsa left Norm and Devyn to fend for themselves and the chores. She set off to take a hike on the estate. Although curious about Devyn's account of his last visit to the Fu Dog Garden, she was more focused on his encounter with the stranger. She walked along the Old Timber Road until she reached the parking lot, then continued through the picnic grove and onto the path leading to the Walled Garden. She slowed her pace, for it was the trees about her that held her interest. Searching overhead, she scanned the leaves, not to admire the seasonal colors, but to study the shapes.

Meandering along the path, her eyes set upon her potential find. A wide tree with deeply furrowed bark towered above her. Its smooth-barked branches spread out twenty feet from the trunk, full of yellowing heart-shaped, serrated leaves. Ailsa stopped to admire the magnificent breadth of the monarch.

She strolled to the base of the trunk, looking carefully among the grass and leaf litter. Circling the tree, she used her boot to scrape at the ground. She felt something firm under her sole. Crouching, she swept the leaves from a small area with her hand and saw a glint of bronze. Tugging away overgrown sod and moss with both hands, she cleared a foot long plaque, lying flat in the earth.

Ailsa pulled a penknife from her jeans pocket and scraped away remnants of soil from the inscription and tried to make sense of it all.

G. NEVILLE JONES
1903-1970
PROFESSOR OF BOTANY AND OUTSTANDING
AUTHORITY ON THE FLORA OF ILLINOIS
HE STUDIED AND COMPILED INFORMATION
ON THE PLANTS OF ALLERTON PARK
FOR MORE THAN TWENTY YEARS

Even though considerable time had passed, it was what she had expected and remembered. Tapping on the plaque with her knife, it resonated with a hollow pulse. Alisa sat back on her haunches, thinking of Devyn. Looking up at the massive linden tree above, she thought. How can this be? And why Devyn?

183

# CHAPTER 31

Kim dug out her back door key from her jeans pocket. Four days before the studio tour, and there was a shitload of things to get ready. A gust of wind pushed against her back, whipping her hair across her cheeks. As she flipped the deadbolt, the door blew open, and the wind ransacked the plaster shop, scattering dust and paper sheets alike. "Nice touch, more cleaning."

Gathering her courage, Kim cracked open the door of the studio and took a timid peek. She was relieved to see the Fu Dogs weren't lurking on the counters. On the other hand, the studio was more unruly than the shop. She silently lashed out at her advisor. Give me a fucking break, El. Did you forget what's going on here at the end of the week?

Annoyance escalated to anger as she stewed over his lack of support...and presence. Returning to the shop, she set about cleaning up the plaster and washing off the counter. She tossed assorted tools, caked in dried plaster, into a bucket in the sink, which she then half-filled with water. Globs of plaster dotted the floor, requiring a scraper to dislodge them. All the while a small detail nagged her. Where had El put those Fu Dogs? He seemed so eager to want them around. Three hours passed before the shop was presentable.

Needing to rest, she went to El's office in search of a ginger ale. Despite sunbeams streaming into the space, Kim felt cheerless, shambling through the mess laying around her. She popped a can from the fridge and took a deep swallow. She spun about at the sound of scratches within the studio. "Nothing more than leaves scattering across the greenhouse roof," she told herself. The scratching returned.

Heart pounding, Kim steadied herself. Her eyes settled upon an oddity; two wooden crates rested on the floor by the storeroom. "What are those doing there?"

A faint noise came from one of the crates. Great, some critter snuck into the greenhouse and got trapped, she thought. Kim's hand reached for a large rubber mallet El used to take apart molds, and with catlike steps, padded over to the crate. Not knowing what sort of creature might be within, under, or behind the wooden cube, she reached out and unlatched the clasp. Hammer raised above her head, she lifted the top with a rapid pull.

She gasped. "What the hell?" A Fu Dog lay on its side, nestled in straw. Kim leaned closer to study the figure. Small defects and cracks marred the demonic face and front limbs. "I thought he was going to display these for the workshop," she muttered.

She looked at the second crate, wondering if it held the matching statue. "What's going on here?" At the sound of her voice the Fu Dog rolled its head and blinked its eyes to gape at her with its cryptic face. Dumbstruck, Kim dropped the ginger ale, bathing the blue figure in a fizzy shower. She slammed the lid shut. Trembling, she shuffled backwards, unable to process what she saw.

"Curiosity killed the cat."

Kim flinched, pivoted on her feet, and gripped the mallet in one motion. "Dear God, El! You scared the bejeezus out of me!"

Puzzled, he stared at her, leaning against the doorframe of the greenhouse, wind whipping his pant legs. "Surprised with what's wrapped up for the Christmas tree this year?"

Kim scanned her mentor from head to toe. He looked like he hadn't slept well the night before. "I don't understand. Why are the Fus in the crates? Did you place them in there while I was gone yesterday?"

Bracing himself with a hand on the door jamb, he sensed her unease and beheld her for a few moments, saying nothing.

She regarded the disorder about her and said, "I don't know what went on, but you've created a big mess to clean up. You do remember we have the tour through here in four days?"

Ellington smiled. "You seem a little frazzled. Something wrong?"

Kim eyeballed the crate behind her. "I thought you were going to display the Fus to explain the remodeling plans for the installations in the garden…to help attain funding from potential donors."

He took on a paternal posture. "Not to worry. It seems Val has worked out something with the university. Besides, the clay for casting replicas is already pressed and drying in their respective plaster molds."

Ellington took a couple steps towards her. "Honestly, your complexion looks like you've seen a ghost. Let me show you how I divided their features into four separate molds to fuse together into the whole figure."

She backed off holding up her hands. "I'm good, no need."

"Why not learn something? The postures in this pair were more challenging to cast than the Fu Dog you found in the shed." He unlatched the second crate.

Kim held back from closing the distance between them.

"What are you afraid of? It won't bite. Go ahead, take a look."

Kim twisted away.

"What's the matter with you?"

"Too much weird shit going on here. I need to clear my head and take a break. Maybe I breathed too much dust when I cleaned the shop." She bolted out the front door and set off towards the arborvitae-lined path to her right.

"Good God! Where do you think you're going?" Ellington ran after her as far as the door.

Kim didn't look back, hustling away from the greenhouse in a fast walk.

Tired and at his wit's end over her behavior, Ellington returned inside to take stock of the studio. She was right, he had let things go a bit too far. "Well,"—he looked at his watch—"I guess I could pitch in and clean up."

Walking into his office, he opened the minifridge but found only cans of soda pop. He scowled, then regarded the lower drawer of a cabinet. His found a two-pack of iced, strawberry Pop-Tarts and a package of cheese crackers with peanut butter. Returning to the fridge, he grabbed a can of ginger ale and slumped onto his desk chair. Ellington ate his snack, then washed it down with the soda. Sated, he contemplated what yet needed to be done by the end of the week. He closed his eyes and fell asleep.

Ellington lurched upright, as his head slid off the back of the chair. Rubbing a crick in his neck, he looked at the wall clock. Damn! An hour and a half sleeping in this miserable seat? He pushed himself up, mouth dry and tasting of peanut butter.

The sculptor shuffled out of his office and grimaced at the sight of the studio. I've got no energy to do this until morning, he reasoned. He wondered if Kim had returned while he was napping…another loose end that needed to be tied up. With a last look about the room, he perceived motion in a windowpane by the door. A face glowed in the light of the studio—a woman's face, measuring the sculptor with stoic curiosity.

Ellington paced to the door and stepped outside. He peered into the dusk-shrouded gardens. "Hello? Is anyone out there?" She was nowhere to be seen. "Hello?" Doubting his sleep-deprived mind, he rubbed his eyes, pulled the door behind him and thought, it's been a long day. I need something real to eat.

He turned off the lights and shuffled through the plaster shop, apathetic to the order brought about by his grad assistant's heroic efforts. Weaving his way to the back door, he shut and locked it, noting Kim's VW Rabbit was missing. "Damn!"

He left the greenhouse behind to take the short walk to his Gate House quarters. "I'll get up early. Got a lot to do."

As Ellington walked away, the wind teased open the front greenhouse door. A leaf blew into the room, gently scraping the floor, accompanied by soft scratches on wood and creaking hinges.

# CHAPTER 32

"The fact is…they bounded across the road like they had springs on their paws, right over the hood of my truck."

"Charlie, better go see your eye doctor again. I think your bifocals need fixing," Trent quipped.

The older man wagged a finger at his critic. "You younger bucks think you got it all figured out. I'm old enough to remember when there were bobcats around here, and I know what I saw. You wouldn't be so cocky if you came face to face with one."

"If you say so."

Carl intervened. "You say you saw two of them? Are you sure they weren't coyotes? They're more likely to travel in pairs."

"No dammit, I know what a goddam coyote looks like, and they don't look like no bobcat. Plain as day in my headlights, their big white eyes looking at me. Big fangs and cat paws."

"And where did you say you saw them?"

"Last night, while driving on my rounds before calling it a day. Right where the Old Timber Road splits between the Sun Singer lane and the 4-H camp."

Trent grunted. "Probably going to stretch the tale into a pair of cougars next."

Carl said, "Maybe they've been travelling along the cover of the river. Doesn't matter, they're no threat to livestock." He gestured. "Let's get these pallets off the truck."

Ellington tromped up the road from the Gate House, refreshed from an early jog about the park. Approaching the rear of the studio, he was surprised to find Carl and his crew stacking pallets by the back door. "What are you guys doing here?"

Carl scratched his head. "Well sir, it seems we're both in the dark about this."

Ellington pointed at the pallets. "Why are they here? We're trying to tidy up for the event."

"Boss lady says they're for shipping a couple of Fu Dogs. My guess would be it's the same pair we hauled from the garden to your studio a while back. She told us they're going to the art museum in Chicago for some special show."

"Chicago?"

"Yeah, you folks sure swap these dog statues around a lot."

Ellington was speechless. Carl kept filling him in. "Movers are coming towards the end of next week. They'll finish packing to their specs, take pictures, and set up a manifest. I guess for insurance. We're leaving the pallets here so they can load the crates onto them."

Ellington ambled around the pallets and peeked into the plaster shop. "Have you moved the crates, yet?"

Carl and his crew exchanged glances. "Well, no. Not since last week when we boxed up those blue Fus exactly how you wanted them. We've got too much on our plate to be monkeying around with those damn things all the time."

Ellington left Carl behind, hurried through the shop, and opened the door to the studio. He sighed in relief. The crates remained where they stood the night before.

Carl edged up behind him. "I thought you were going to repair those things, Mr. Rose. Personally, I didn't see much difference between those old ones and the new ones we placed in the garden. I wish Ms. Farwell would make up her mind on what she wants. They're not easy to carry around, you know. What between the weight, easily busted if dropped…"

Ellington looked at Carl, barely hearing a word he said. "Next week you say?"

"You mean when the movers arrive?"

The sculptor's eyes flared. "Yes, dammit!"

"That's the order from on high. I believe Friday morning."

Spinning about in a daze, Ellington left the crew without saying another word, went into his office and shut the door.

Leaning on the door jamb between the shop and studio, Charlie dismissed the drama by shaking his head. "Lots of crazy things going on around here." He glanced towards the open back door. "Time to go."

Val spoke in an exasperated tone. "What are you talking about?"

Ashley did her best to calmly deflect her boss's shock. "Like I said, the trash dumpster was lying on its side when I arrived this morning. Paper, plastic and food scraps were dragged all over the back lot by the kitchen."

"How in the hell did that happen?"

Asheley shrugged. "I don't know. A raccoon, maybe?"

Val was incredulous. "Are you kidding, me? Raccoons? Knock over a dumpster of that size? A whole platoon of them couldn't do that." She threw her hands into the air. "Unbelievable."

Regaining her composure, Val murmured, "Sounds more like a bunch of high school kids pulling off an early Halloween prank." She looked out her window to the reflecting pond. "Why was there so much garbage in the dumpster anyway?"

"We had the Biochemistry Department retreat earlier this week, and trash collection isn't until tomorrow, being Thursday." Ashley suggested, "It was perfect timing, I guess. Lots of food scraps."

Val shook her head and reflected silently. Perfect timing? For whom? "Where's Carl? Please tell him I want that cleaned up, pronto. Drag in the kitchen staff to help, if you have to…and figure out a way it doesn't get knocked over again."

"I'm on it." Ashley turned to leave, but Val thwarted her exit.

"Have you got the wind ensemble performance all set?"

"Yes, they'll play for a half hour during the mimosa social, then another hour during brunch."

Valerie nodded in approval. "And this cost got added to the ticket price for the event?"

Ashley smiled. "That and whatever else I could think of to pad into it."

The women fell silent, puzzled to hear footsteps pacing down the hallway. Out of breath, Ellington thrust his head through the door. Right from the get-go, Val felt uneasy with his entrance. The usually whimsical, spectacled eyes had become ominous. He said flatly, "We need to talk."

Glancing at the younger woman, Val spoke in a cool voice. "Ashley give us a couple minutes, will you? Run the food delivery plan by Jenny and make sure the kitchen crew is prepared for storage. And get a hold of Carl."

Ashley gave Ellington a weak smile as she left the room, relieved to have things to do somewhere else. "Close the door please." Val called after her. Facing the sculptor, she asked in a soft voice, "Is this something that really can't wait?"

Ellington acted as if the fingernails on his right hand held great interest. "When I was growing up in Chicago, I liked to watch the shell game tricksters in my neighborhood practice their art." He switched his gaze to her with no touch of humor in his eyes. "Somehow, the bean was never under the cup that the mark chose."

Val strained to find meaning in his words. "Where is this going?"

"I thought the original Fu Dogs were going to university archives for storage. After I finished recasting them."

She studied him before replying. "That was the original plan."

"Indeed. I just found out the plan now includes an all-expenses-paid trip to Chicago instead." He paused. "Leaving late next week. What's the rush? What if I need to remake one of their plaster molds?"

Val knitted her brow, wondering how he came by such information. "Deeper pockets up there. We could hold a fundraiser auction at the Art Institute. That would be an ideal foster home for them until we sent up the rest."

He leaned his hands onto her desk. "Sounds like a noble cause. But I doubt that's the real one."

"What are you talking about?"

He gave her a half-smile. "Oh, I think you know very well." Stepping back from the desk and folding his arms, he said, "I got to thinking. When we first started on the Fu Dog project it was all about a pair of alumni who had a special, and supposedly nostalgic interest in repairing the statues. Big donors, you told me. I suspect their donations are linked to a special private sale side-stepping the need for an auction."

"This is making no sense."

He laughed. "Oh, please. In reality, who would ever miss the originals? Most folks won't even know they exist. And like previous escapades with sculptures around here, out of sight is out of mind within the university system."

Ellington looked out the window. "Yeah, the gardens will remain, folks will walk by the Fu Dogs, take pictures and gawk. But few if any, would ever know the difference between the replicas or originals."

Val appealed to him with clasped hands. "That's because you did such a great job."

He peered at her with eyes wide. "I did, didn't I? And you're probably getting a tidy sum on behalf of my creative effort." He nodded. "That's fine. I want my cut from this private arrangement."

Her eyes hardened. "What? Are you implying I'm selling them for personal gain?" He remained silent, staring at her. She added, "They're in less than mint condition from enduring a half century of Illinois weather. They might not be worth what you think."

Cleaning his glasses with a small cloth tugged from his pocket, Ellington gave her a pedantic look. "Then again, we both know it's not only the condition, but the rarity of an art piece, or in this case, a matching pair that drives the value. But most importantly, you need a buyer with a strong interest to acquire them. I've been doing a little homework"—the glasses returned to the artist's nose—"concerning the Van Teeswaters with my contacts in the Chicago art community. Nice couple, elegant homes in Chicago's Gold Coast, London, Toulouse…apparently they're well-traveled art dealers in the global market. They often attend Sotheby's auctions and the like. I doubt they would have movers pack old Fu Dogs and shipped to the Windy City only to put them by their front door to protect the house against evil spirits."

Val fidgeted but stayed silent.

Ellington dialed his voice to a more conciliatory tone. "Those Fu Dogs are rare pieces. Lord knows I've never seen a glaze like it, that iridescent blue. There's something more than crushed lapis lazuli mixed in." He opened his arms, hands out and palms up. "You leave me no choice but to suggest we split the…donation. Fifty-fifty."

"Twenty percent…consider it a consignment sale with me as the agent. Plus, your free rent at the Gate House and all the supplies that were generously provided."

Ellington surveyed her office at a leisurely pace. "But inasmuch as you are an art historian, you must have a good bead on their value. I wonder what the university might think if the director of this park was found to be embezzling some of its assets to the highest bidder."

Her mouth opened with a wicked grin. "I wonder what your wife would think if she knew the real story behind *Blue Desire*. Nice touch with the miniature necklace and stone you contrived for her that mimics my pendant, by the way." She laid a hand

across her chest. "I can still feel your groping hands toying with it."

Ellington wavered; his face flushed.

She pushed the verbal knife deeper. "Maybe you should make a second figure, a self-study of the sculptor. Make sure to include a wedding ring that matches yours, along with an erect phallus."

He stiffened but paused before speaking quietly. "You greedy, back-stabbing bitch."

She deflected his riposte airily. "I think my modeling time and how shall we say…extra benefits provided to you along with five grand are more than enough compensation."

He gave her a withering gaze. "I suppose you had this figured to play me from the start? Selecting me as the artist in residence…"—he checked his temper to finish a thought—"Perhaps you even jumped on board with this whole Laredo Taft event as a sham to arrange the art sale. It's funny how you were the one to suggest replicating rather than repairing the Fus. Always vague on the details about their future after their replacement."

Val's lips smiled, but not her eyes. "It's not all bad, think of what you'll gain after this event. A leading scholar regarding the Taft and the White Rabbits. I imagine the demand and value for your works will grow considerably."

"You have no idea what it means to pour your heart and soul into a creation, do you?" He made to leave.

Her lilting voice followed him. "Remember, I'll forever be sitting on the ledge with the darling little necklace dangling over my body, smiling at you."

Ellington pulled the door open. "We'll see how long your sense of humor lasts." He walked down the hall, greeting Jenny and Ashley amicably as he went out the door. As he strolled by the red BMW parked close by, Ellington thought, time for her lesson in playing shell games…and little project in the studio.

# CHAPTER 33

This was one of those days when Carl Lipinski felt every one of his forty-eight years on life's odometer. The chilly morning reminded him winter wasn't far away—the annual endurance test for those who often worked outdoors.

The day started well enough. Entering the park on the Old Levee Road, he took time to admire the stately trees lining the entrance. As he neared the small bridge arching over the Sangamon, he spied a couple of crows pecking at something on the ground. Carl drove closer, prompting the birds to hop to the shoulder, then fly onto a nearby branch, protesting their interrupted meal.

Carl parked his light blue Silverado on the bridge. The head and torso of a doe lay on the road, its front legs stretched across the pavement. He sighed, "Not the first impression we want for visitors when they arrive on Saturday."

Easing out of his pickup, Carl wondered how anyone could be travelling on this narrow, bumpy lane fast enough to strike a deer—unless it was a really dumb deer. As he drew near, Carl changed his thinking. He was mildly surprised to see the hind quarters of the animal were missing after the rib cage. He cast his eyes about the immediate area but couldn't find other remains. Coyotes didn't waste any time scavenging this one, he thought.

He studied the doe's position relative to the road. Maybe it wasn't hit by a car after all but got hunted down by coyotes or

a pack of dogs. Carl took a more careful look beyond the doe. A crude swath of flattened grass and goldenrod led into the woods. He grabbed the carcass by the front legs and leaning backwards, dragged it off the road. Returning to his truck, Carl mulled over the possibilities but couldn't come up with a firm solution to the puzzle.

The pumpkins had ripened, their undersides were no longer green and when Norm cut into a few with his knife, the flesh was deep orange. Time for the buff-colored globes to take the ride to the Libby's plant. Devyn regarded the six-acre pumpkin patch with trepidation. Norm had figured on about fifteen tons of pumpkins per acre. The thought of loading tens of thousands of pounds of basketball-sized fruit into the high bed of the C-65 tandem seemed overwhelming. He was relieved to find out Norm had other ideas than picking up all those pumpkins like bales of hay.

After using a snowplow-shaped blade to push the pumpkins into quarter-mile windrows, Norm attached a side attachment to the old twenty that reminded Devyn of the elevator used to carry bales into the haymow. Norm then drove the old twenty along the windrows, with Ailsa keeping pace driving the tandem, scooping up pumpkins, which then scooted up the conveyor belt on the ramp and onto the truck. Devyn's job was to grab the fugitives that rolled back onto the ground and reload them onto the belt. He figured about one in twenty had to be chased down and reloaded, but it was better than doing them all.

It took a half day to harvest and deliver a truck load to the plant. Hoping to get the entire crop delivered before corn combining, Norm was trying to make two runs to Morton a day. Sitting at the kitchen table with Devyn, Ailsa watched the tandem lurch out of the farm lane and struggle to gain speed on the road. They munched on grilled cheese sandwiches and a mug of vegetable beef soup.

"I believe we had a good yield for the pumpkins this year," Ailsa said.

Devyn replied, "They're a funny color compared to the pumpkins I know."

"They're not your typical Jack O' Lanterns, they're a special variety with more flesh for canning. Not so thin walled."

Devyn reminisced over his younger years. "I guess Halloween isn't all that far away. Time for trick-or-treating, and ghosts and goblins."

Ailsa peered at him, holding her mug with two hands. "Indeed." She set her mug down. "Have you seen the man with the glasses since we last talked about him?"

He shook his head. "No. Have you figured out who he is?"

"I have a possibility. Someone I haven't seen around these parts for some time."

"What's his name?"

"Mr. Jones. I should say Professor Jones. He was a friend of Mr. Allerton's."

Devyn gave her a strange look. "I thought you said Mr. Allerton left here many years ago."

"Well, yes. But Mr. Jones knew him before he left Illinois. He was a botanist at the university who helped identify the trees within the estate, which Mr. Allerton was keen on knowing."

Devyn needed a few moments to absorb Ailsa's words. "Did you say, he *was* a botanist?"

Ailsa gazed at Devyn with a somber face. "I did."

"Like he's dead or a ghost or something?"

"I confess, I'm having trouble with what to make of it."

"How long ago did he pass away?"

"Nearly twenty years ago. Perhaps you've met someone who happens to look like him."

Devyn pondered the botanist's baffling appearances. "I don't think so. He's trying to tell me something…something about the Fu Dogs."

Ailsa was impressed with the young man's poise. "Such as?"

"I'm trying to figure that out."

Ailsa shared his sense of a disturbance in the equilibrium of the estate. Yet she couldn't fathom why G. Neville Jones was reaching out to Devyn, and only Devyn.

# CHAPTER 34

A stiff wind lingered overnight, littering the gardens with leaves and twigs. Ellington made his way through the picnic grove between the Gate House and the studio. He had slept fitfully, his mood soured by the unsettled weather, the upcoming event, Kim's odd mood swings, and most of all, his quarrel with Valerie. Despite his lack of sleep, he walked the path with vigor, ignoring the Sea Maidens, exposed in the mellow glow of dawn. Maybe a morning jog around the Sun Singer would do him well. But first, he had to tend to his new obsession.

Reaching the greenhouse, he found the door entirely open, flattened along the outside wall. "What the hell?" Ellington fumed over the erratic door latch. He remembered leaving through the back door yesterday evening. When he returned a few hours later to shut off the kiln, he never went inside. An alarming thought crossed his mind. What if Carl's concern about local hooligans was valid?

He rushed through the studio and the plaster shop, swerving between counters and debris. Fingers trembling, he flipped the deadbolt, then wrenched the back door open. Anxious eyes checked the kiln thermometer as he grabbed a pair of gloves—well below two-hundred degrees—all he needed to know to unlatch the kiln door. Elation swept through his body as the heavy portal swung open. "Blessed Jesus!"

Ellington lightly tested the surface of the figure with his finger. Lukewarm to the touch. He scooped it within his hands as if holding a young kitten. A silly grin spread across his face as he critiqued the statuette from different angles. "Oh, you fabulous vixen. All you need is a little glaze and your final firing…and you'll the belle of the ball." He shut the kiln door and cradled his prize back to the studio, enjoying a brief period of gloating.

Ellington glanced at the wall clock, time for his morning jolt of caffeine. Gently resting the unfinished piece on a table, he entered his office and froze. Anger seeped through his veins. "This place is trashed. Who was in here?"

He set up the coffee maker and moments later, the sound of water gurgling through the grounds honed his edginess. He mumbled, "Only two days until the event." Looking upon his newest creation again, he couldn't stop smiling. There she was, basking in the growing light of day. "Don't worry, there's plenty of time for you."

Bending over the small fridge to get some half and half, he thought some cold fried chicken would make a nice breakfast. He halted with the door open. The box of chicken was gone, along with a small tub of coleslaw and the cream. "What've you been up to, Kim?" he grumbled. Scanning the walls, he realized his jogging pants and jacket weren't hanging where he usually left them. Ellington began to doubt the mental stability of his grad assistant.

He knew what had to be done…swallow his pride and apologize. No matter how erratic her recent behavior, he needed her to arrange and oversee the workshop. Picking up the receiver from the desk phone, he punched the numbers to her apartment. The line rang several times before switching to a message machine. Twirling the phone cord while waiting for the beep, he beseeched, "Hi Kim. I wanted to say how sorry I am for losing my cool. I confess to being a bit surly as of late. This whole Taft exhibit is wearing on me more than I thought. Please call me in the studio. I should be here most of the day. I could use your help." He paused to think if there was anything else to say. "Please," he added, then hung up.

Grabbing a handmade mug from his desktop, he poured coffee to nearly overflowing, sipped carefully, and strolled out to the studio to plan his workflow. His eyes fell upon the pair of crates. "That's job number one." Taking his mug, he returned to the plaster shop. He approached a white sheet draped over a counter. Yanking the cloth away, the ceramicist halted to admire his work.

Several large pieces of plaster, reminding him of three-dimensional parts of a Fu Dog puzzle, lay in front of him. "These will do fine. Time to press in the clay."

It was simple plan. Use the plaster molds to cast new copies of original Fu Dogs from the garden, and after glazing and firing, switch them with the ones in the crates that Valerie was arranging to ship to Chicago. He had faith in his ability to create top-notch reproductions. Even if they were discovered to not be the originals upon inspection, what would happen? Valerie and her patrons could hardly claim foul over stolen property.

Ellington smiled inwardly. You'll make a good mark for this version of the shell game, my dear. He frowned. What would he do with the originals once he made the switch? No matter, it would take a few days to complete the copies, especially with the Taft event coming up. He had plenty of time to finish them before the end of next week. The best part was while he fused and cut the slag off the replicants in plain view during the next two days, he would be making the case it was all part of the workshop demonstration. Form follows function, after all.

For inspiration, he left the plaster shop, entered the studio and walked over to the crates. "Let's remind myself how to keep my eye on the prize." Ellington lifted the lid of one of the wooden boxes. Blood drained from his face as he propped the lid against the wall. "Holy Mother of God!" He scrambled to lift the lid of the other crate only to find the same outcome.

Nearly dizzy from shock, Ellington took a breath, then steamed to his office and picked up the phone. Sinking back onto his chair, he hesitated, then set the receiver back in the cradle. "It's hard not to admire your cunning, even if you are a conniving swindler."

A small smirk grew into a snicker, then outright laughter. Looking at the disarray in his office, Ellington said in a soft voice, "I've got better things to do with my time right now. I'll call her after another coffee"—he cast his eyes upon the figurine he collected from the kiln earlier—"and a little work on my special addition to Saturday's program."

# CHAPTER 35

Carl's luck continued on a downward slide the next morning. He had a hunch that yesterday's mysteries of upended dumpsters and roadkill deer were small potatoes compared to what now lay in store for him. Leaving the machine shop, he tramped into the teeth of the wind, summoned by the boss lady's phone call—he didn't even have time to turn on the coffee maker—bidding him to her office ASAP. Some sort of problem with the pavilion, caused by the blustery overnight weather, or so she thought.

He turned onto the sidewalk by the Gate House, heading for the mansion. Eyes slanting towards the brick residence as he paced by, the grounds manager considered how life had been more complicated ever since the 'artist in residence' had set up shop. Let alone the big event piling onto his normal tasks. The whole affair had become a full-on pain in the ass. He hoped tomorrow's forecast still called for a calm sunny day.

As he converged on the mansion, his interest was piqued on seeing soil scattered onto the sidewalk. A bed of mums lay crushed on the ground, their bright bronze and yellow heads soiled and bruised. Carl surveyed his surroundings. A matching array of flowers further along the path was also upended. "Now what?"

Several plants were uprooted, not just trampled. No deer hoof prints marked the wet earth. He mulled over the possibilities. "Sure as hell wasn't a groundhog." For now, Carl discounted teen vandals; experience suggested statues and structures such as the Buddha house were their preferred targets. He forged ahead, wondering if the string of unusual episodes shared a connection.

As he climbed the steps to the upper terrace, his russet eyes grew into half-dollars. "Holy hell, what went on here?" The autumn-toned pavilion was intact. But many of the tables and chairs, which yesterday afternoon were in neat rows and files, were overturned. A giant hand seemed to have shoved the setting aside with no more effort than a child swatting doll house furniture. White tablecloths draped the wreckage, some ripped and torn. Carl's eyes latched onto Val, standing by the front dais with Ashley and the head chef.

Striding along the outer perimeter, Carl closed the distance to the group. He was still more than fifty feet away when Val's voice came into range, stressed at a high pitch. "How could these tables possibly blow over? Aren't they solid enough?"

Carl couldn't hear the rebuttals from Ashley or the chef but lively gesturing and pointing hands said it all. Valerie screamed, "Two days before the event and look at this…"—she waved her extended arm in a half-circle about her—"this disaster." Her angry gaze fell upon the unruffled grounds manager. "There you are! How do *you* explain all of this?"

Carl sucked in a breath and exhaled to help measure his response. "Those are solid wood-surfaced eight-footers, should have stayed right in place during the wind last night." He glanced upwards. "The pavilion itself didn't suffer any, hard to figure what went on down here."

"Well, barring a bunch of gremlins, I'd bet some local delinquents thought to spoil our party. I imagine neither Charlie nor anyone else saw something suspicious last night?"

"Given the wind, I can't imagine anyone would have been out for a fun scamper in the park."

Val clamped her hands onto her hips. "Well, get Trent and Charlie up here. Pronto! And round up the garden crew as well. This is going to be an all-hands-on-deck job!"

Carl grimaced. *Not including the other jobs that are on our list today,* he thought.

The French door of the solarium opened, and Jenny stuck her head out. "Ms. Farwell. Professor Rose is on the phone."

Valerie rolled her eyes and sighed. "I'm a little wrapped up in other problems right now, Jenny."

"I told him that, but he was a bit…pushy. Says it's urgent."

Doubting the veracity of Ellington's opinion, Valerie eyeballed Carl, relaying her expectation for quick action, and left for her office.

Carl and Ashley glanced at each other in a mutual moment of respite. He ambled through the pavilion, absorbing the chaos of tangled cloth and furniture. Squatting, he wedged his hands under an overturned table, setting it back on its legs. Taking a closer look at a crumpled tablecloth, he ran a hand underneath the fabric. Four parallel gashes tore through the cotton, two feet long from the edge to the center.

Curious, he moved to another upended table, righted it, and again took notice of the tablecloth, which had the same four linear tears as before. He couldn't picture a device that would rip material in such a way. "Someone went to a lot of trouble to pull this off," he muttered. He scanned across the pond to the meadow, then looked back at the solarium entrance, calculating the direction of the wind. The tent was protected by the high walls of the mansion. An orange glimmer on the walk between the sphynxes drew his interest.

He took a few steps and bent over to look at his find. "Lord Almighty, life is full of surprises today." At his feet lay the head of an orange and white koi, staring with a glassy eye. A second half-eaten carcass lay on the other side of the pond. "Damn raccoons." Carl walked carefully along the edge of the pond, finding no telltale tracks.

He stewed over the details of this new find but was cut short when Val burst through the solarium door, leaving it open in her wake. Marching with a full head of steam, she blew past Carl, went down the steps to the lower terrace, and veered towards the path leading to the Walled Garden.

She shot a fiery glance at Carl over her shoulder. "The Fu Dogs have been stolen."

"What? The new ones we placed in the garden at the beginning of the week?"

"No, dammit. The ones in the greenhouse, that were to be shipped next week."

Carl fell in step behind her, hustling to keep pace.

# CHAPTER 36

Devyn squeezed the pump handle, lifting gasoline vapors into his nostrils. The splashing sound of fuel in the tank, deep within the grain truck, grounded his thinking. A simple act of normalcy in an otherwise off-kilter world. In the far woods, crows volleyed cries of alarm to one another. After a period of calm, the chatter began again from a new location. Whatever was agitating the birds was on the move.

"You're looking played out," Norm said. "When you're running loads to the bins, make sure to keep your mind right and fuel up from the gasoline tank. The C-65 isn't a tractor, and its V-8 doesn't like diesel." Norm trudged to the machine shop, calling over his shoulder, "When you're done with that, check the air pressure in all the tires, including the wagons. Then grease the axles."

The noise in the woods faded away, but Devyn's senses remained on full alert. He regarded the wall of trees on the farm's edge. Despite a sense of growing dread of the place, he knew he had to return. His mission was simple enough, but the plan was filled with uncertainty and complicated by a rise in the number of people flowing about the estate—Ailsa had mentioned an upcoming reception at the mansion. Daylight would be more comforting but he needed to avoid attracting attention. The best time for his sortie would be under the cover of darkness.

Deep in his bones, the young man knew working after nightfall would demand extra caution. Devyn smiled as he remembered previous nighttime escapades when still in school—brightening public property with fresh coats of paint.

Some might consider it vandalism; Dr. Malcolm joked his artistic efforts showed civic pride. Yet the present situation was more risky and any misjudgment on his part could be perilous. The click of the pump handle brought his mind back to the farm.

Replacing the gas cap, he climbed inside the cab and drove to the machine shed. Shutting off the truck's engine, he kept his mind distracted by finishing Norm's to-do list.

Black moccasins with white stitching, pumping rapidly on the garden path—the kinetic flashes of Val's footwear interrupted Carl's concentration. She was oblivious to the strong breeze as they approached the Sea Maidens, wearing only a loose-fitting sweater, knitted in a design resembling a Rubik's cube, and dark slacks. He maintained formation about two steps behind and to her left.

Assuming he was in earshot, Val spoke in a voice that was cooler than the air. "I told you guys to keep an eye out for intruders. Did you ever get around to fixing that front door latch of the greenhouse?"

Carl thought to respond that regardless of the door latch, the dead bolt he'd installed worked fine…if someone remembered to use their key to lock it. He chose silence instead.

She resumed her rant. "I don't trust him. He's up to something. This is his way of getting back at me."

Carl mentally gambled who she might be talking about…the jackpot reel settled on Ellington's face.

Val cut the corner by the sunbathing girl, heading for the west exit of the Walled Garden, and talking to herself. Her footspeed had increased.

The greenhouse door was open. Ellington held a pail full of wooden-handled tools. In his other hand, he clutched a pair of sculpting chisels. His posture spoke of defeat, the color in his eyes washed out. "I still have this mess to clean up yet."

Carl confirmed the artist's opinion with one quick scan.

Valerie came out swinging. "What did you do with them? Did you think you could hide them like some naughty child?"

Ellington regained some of his pluck. "Me? May I remind you the Taft event is in two days? You think I have time for this bullshit? And where would one hide, let alone haul away, a pair of hundred-pound-plus ceramic pieces? You think I'd carry them around like a clay flowerpot?"

"What about your grad student? She could help get them onto a cart."

Ellington gestured at Carl but kept his eyes on Val. "You're the one with all the hired muscle. They brought them here, am I right?"

"You're a lying asshole!"

Carl held up a hand. "Calm down you two." He looked at Ellington. "Was the door to the greenhouse locked when you arrived this morning?"

He sank his shoulders. "Well, no."

"Who was here last before this morning?"

Ellington's face tensed. "I was. I worked into the evening. I could have sworn I left out the back door."

"Idiot!" Val spat out.

Carl examined the door handle, running his thick fingers along the jamb. "Doesn't look like it's been jimmied." He shifted his gaze to the crates across the studio. "Is that where you saw those blue dogs last?"

"I haven't moved them since you placed them there."

"When did you last see them?"

Ellington emptied his hands onto a countertop, then shifted his stance to lean against the table. "I don't know…two days ago maybe."

"Anyone else with you at the time?"

The disheveled sculptor paused. "Kim. I don't think she appreciated them being in the studio all that much."

Val blurted. "And why isn't she here now? Shouldn't she be helping to get the workshop ready?"

"She worked hard to clean the plaster shop the other night. I told her to take some time off."

"Seriously? Nice timing."

"If you don't mind," Carl said, squeezing by Val to take a closer look at the crates. "Were these clasps locked when you last saw them?"

Ellington was slow to answer. "No."

Carl turned with surprise. "You didn't ever lock them?"

"Didn't think we needed to."

Val snorted with disdain.

Carl studied the inside of each crate. He bent over to pick up an empty ginger ale can from the nearest one. Puzzled from his find, he asked, "What are those square blocks of tile in the bottom?"

The sculptor scratched the side of his head. "That's the wild thing, the Fu Dogs are gone without their bases."

"You mean someone sawed them off?"

"I have no idea how anyone could do that."

Carl rubbed a finger over the top of one of the bases. "Don't see any cracks or chips as if they were broken. Maybe they sliced through some sort of caulk that held them in place."

In a rare slip of her composure, Val's jaw sagged. "W-what? Broken? You're telling me they were smashed?"

Carl held up both hands. "Not saying that at all. Perhaps we should call the sheriff's office."

Visibly shaken, Val braced herself with a hand on a small table. "That's the last thing I need. Not only do we have to reset the pavilion, but the Dean's office called. He wants to stop by tomorrow afternoon for a pre-event inspection."

Carl said, "I was just thinking we should report it."

Ellington agreed lightheartedly. "That's a smashing idea, no pun intended." He shot a side-eye at Val. "Don't you think we should let university archives know about this? Afterall, they were making all the arrangements for the"—Ellington acted as if searching for the right word—"transfer of the Fu Dogs to Chicago, were they not? I'll be happy to call them if you like."

Val gave him an icy stare. "We'll wait until after the event. We might get this sorted out by then."

Carl pouted. "I don't think we should do that."

She snapped back. "I'll do the thinking here."

"If you say so." Carl shrugged and made for the door. "I guess I'll round up the crew and go reorganize the pavilion, then." Val and Ellington stayed in place as he left.

Walking away on the path, Carl listened as the pair of squawking jays inside the greenhouse exploded into a shouting match. He grumbled, "They sound like a married couple squabbling over stuff at a divorce hearing."

The artist's words echoed in his mind. Where would someone carry, then stash two heavy ceramics pieces, presumably in such a way not to bust them? That the trail was now two days old worried him.

Frustrated, and under a deadline, he'd find the time to investigate the Fu Dog Garden later, once the pavilion was in order. One other detail nagged him. The inner surface of the crate lids had what looked to be deep scratches, marring the wood in parallel lines. Carl thought an overnight vigil of the pavilion tomorrow night might be needed. He would recruit Trent to help…and tell him to bring his rifle.

Ellington finally found the time in the afternoon to mix different salts and materials in large bowls with reckless abandon. With aching arms and back, he paused to review his latest batches of glaze. This will have to do. He ran some quick calculations through his head. There was still enough time…if he began the firing right away. He'd have to return at midnight to turn off the kiln, allowing the piece to cool for inspection in the late morning. He was confident she would make a splendid splash at her unveiling.

# CHAPTER 37

Devyn picked his way through the clammy brush towards the Fu Dog Garden. A brief squall had pelted him earlier, soon after he left the farm. His sweatshirt was wet, despite the refuge he took from the lashing wind behind one of the columns at the estate entrance.

He paused behind the cover of the Buddha house. An aura of peril hung over the damp garden. Waiting for a long minute, he searched for any movement in the spruce trees behind the pillars. He started at a sound from the woods, then assured himself it was nothing more than an errant branch swept by the wind. Perhaps even a small creature foraging nearby, secure in knowing the rain was over.

The setting sun dappled the lawn in gilded light, enshrining the Fu Dogs on their pedestals, blue coats glistening after the shower. Stepping forward onto the wet grass, Devyn advanced down the length of the lawn. drawn toward the two watchers by the portal to the woods.

Unlike their peers along the colonnade, whose cunning eyes appeared to track his steps, the watchers stared blankly ahead, sullen and lacking emotion. Perplexed by their indifference, Devyn's thoughts drifted to the path beyond the pillars. Tree branches shimmered in the breeze, and the steady tap of fluid crystals, dripping from wet leaves, resonated through the woods with a serene rhythm. He closed his eyes briefly to recapture his poise and awareness.

Devyn scrutinized one of the sentries. The figure's bland attitude lacked vitality. As twilight trickled through the woods, its face seemed to recede—diminishing into a listless wraith, its color dissolving into obscurity.

He reached into his pocket for a small flashlight. Flicking on the beam, he studied both of the apathetic watchers. They seemed out of synch with each other. "I don't believe it. Why didn't I notice this before?" he blurted. Feeling foolish at uncovering the obvious, Devyn realized the pair was identical—both posing with heads facing over their left shoulder—and not a mirror image of each other.

Confused, he cast his beam on the nearest figure in line. It cast an austere gaze over its right shoulder. Spinning about, he examined its partner across the lawn. The pose differed but more notably, it faced him over its left shoulder. Devyn whispered, "They're alike but opposite, like matching bookends." He repeated his inquiry on the next pair and found the same result. All along the line to the Buddha house, each pair looked across the lawn in the same opposite fashion. He glanced again at the pair on the far end. They don't belong here, he thought.

A stillness settled over the garden as the light dimmed, washing the trees in shades of dull pewter. Devyn gazed upon the Hari-Hara. The statue seemed to shrink in size, as if it was sliding further away.

A crow settled upon a nearby bough of a spruce, croaking as it swayed in the breeze. The noise distracted Devyn and he swept the light towards the bird. Something caught his eye, a reflection hidden among the branches behind the tree. Startled, he aimed the beam and stared in disbelief. A pair of human eyes blinked at the light.

Recovering his wits, he appraised the woman, about his age and height with long dark hair and brown eyes. She half crouched behind the trunk of the tree, eyeing him with a blend of suspicion and interest. She appeared to be wearing a lightweight jacket. Taking measured breaths, neither of them moved nor spoke.

"Hello," he said tentatively. "I'm Devyn." He redirected the light away from her face and more on the tree trunk in front of her. She remained silent. "What's your name?"

He took a relaxed step toward her. "Are you in need of help?" The woman leaned back in response, her eyes intent on the young man. He said, "No need to worry." He tapped his chest. "I'm Devyn...Devyn Lawers, I work over at the Winters place." He pointed towards the farmstead.

Her eyes flicked in the same direction, then returned to him.

"Are you sure you're alright?" Her body language remained withdrawn, her voice silent. Bewildered by her lack of a response, Devyn made to leave the garden. The woman broke into a monologue, of which he didn't understand a single word. Halting, he asked, "Are you lost? Do you need some help?"

She touched her collarbone. "Boree. Boree."

"Is that your name?" He placed a hand on his chest. "Devyn." Gesturing to her, he added, "Boree."

Her eyes softened. "Boree."

Devyn nodded. "Okay, we're on a roll. Do you live nearby?"

She spoke again, punctuated with frequent motions and glances in the direction of the woods.

Devyn shrugged with a helpful look, lost as to what to do. She repeated her message, using many of the same words as before, as far as Davyn could tell. He also detected an urgency in her voice.

From the direction of the river, a crow cawed four times. The garden companion flapped its wings and relayed the message. The distant bird called out again, joined soon after by a third.

Devyn knew the avian dialogue was a warning. The nature of the garden had changed, no longer secure, but foreboding. A gust of wind rattled the branches overhead, sending the crow off his perch. It sailed along the wood path, calling in alarm with a growing number of its peers.

The woman cried out in fear. Signaling to Devyn to follow, she yelled in the unmistakable tone of a command. She pleaded with him in despair then spun about and raced off in the direction of the parking lot.

Devyn cried out, "What's the matter?" Filled with uneasiness, he watched her vanish among the trees with the agility of a deer. "Wait! Stop! Where are you going?"

A low, raspy bark came from the woods to his left. Devyn shined the flashlight down the path. His beam diffused in the gloom under the trees. To his horror, the ominous sound repeated, seemingly coming from along the trail. Unable to peel his eyes away from the oncoming force, Devyn backpedaled slowly.

The bark amplified to a low bellow, rapidly closing the distance between them. The crow reappeared, flying towards the far end of the garden, cawing repeatedly. Unsure if it was a trick of the mind or ears, Devyn heard a thumping rhythm echo all about him. He whirled about and fled towards the House of the Golden Buddhas.

Deep huffing grunts boomed from behind, shaking the ground under his feet. He sensed the beast had nearly reached the garden, perhaps rounding the last curve before the entrance.

Devyn bounded up onto the concrete platform of the shrine, halting as he drew even with a golden Buddha. He pressed himself against the wall, trembling as hideous snorts carried across the length of the lawn. A half-moon pushed free of the clouds, blending ashen light into the dusk of nightfall.

Terror gripped Devyn as a dark, hulking shape came into view, ambling through the far end of the garden. Snuffling and grunting, the creature stopped, crouched, and sniffed the base of a pedestal, then lifted its head to catch a scent in the wind.

Aware of his exposure in the dull light, Devyn shrank into the alcove behind the Buddha. The moon, free of any clouds, colored the creature in charcoal satin. It advanced to the next pedestal and once again sniffed about the base.

Devyn erased the notion of outpacing the beast by running back to the farm. The brush and gathering dark would prove to be more of a hindrance for the prey than the hunter. Back against the wall, he slowly slid to the far side of the shrine and came upon the spiral staircase. The dilemma was frightening, climbing to the platform above and hoping the creature remained searching the ground, or becoming trapped with only one way out. He laid a hand on the rail of the staircase and silently went up the stairs, feeling for each metal tread with his feet.

With a final step, he grasped the outer rail and gained the terrace. Sinking behind the ironwork, he peeked through the vines to watch as the figure cantered between the Fu Dogs, grunting, sniffing, bearing towards the shrine, one pedestal at a time. Devyn reeled back, ice gripping his spine. He recognized the shape of the beast…it was a gorilla.

The squall ripped across the farm, battering the farmhouse with horizontal rain. Norm watched the rain strike and blur the kitchen window. "Might have known this was coming the way the wind was blowing from the south today. I imagine the temperature will drop once the front blows through."

Ailsa sipped her tea, looking out across the farmyard through the comfort of the glazed storm door. She replied in an absent tone, "Into the dark and drublie days…as Dunbar would say." She turned to join her husband by the kitchen table. Laying a hand on his shoulder, she said, "Devyn didn't have much appetite for supper." She paused, then asked, "Did he strike you as being more quiet than normal today?"

Her husband stuck a forkful of apple pie in his mouth. "I can't say that he did. Hard to tell with him, sometimes he's for chatting, more times he's not." He aimed his fork at the plate in front of him. "I don't know why he wouldn't want some of this pie. This is as good as it gets."

"Cortlands and Ida Reds make the best combination." Ailsa knew a thing or two about her husband. Norm would be on his deathbed before ever turning down a fruit pie. As she settled across the table from him, she steered back to her line of thinking. "I can't explain it, but I had a feeling his mind was somewhere else than here. During supper, his eyes seemed to be looking through me, not at me."

Norm jabbed another piece of apple. "He was a little asleep at the wheel today. I had to remind him several times to stay on task when lubing the fittings with the grease gun. Not sure he didn't overfill a couple. Good thing we weren't moving cattle through a chute."

Ailsa became lost in thought. The rain abruptly ended. Skipper got up from the floor and braced himself by the back door, hair standing on end. Her eyes wandered to the dog, whose chest now rumbled with a low growl. The pair looked at one another, as Skipper barked repeatedly in a threatening voice.

Norm said, "Must be some sort of critter in the barn yard."

Ailsa got up from the table and opened the door. She stepped out onto the porch, watching Skipper sprint across the yard. The air smelled fresh and raw from the rain.

Ailsa peered across the barn lot but failed to see anything unusual. A bank of clouds slid over the sinking sun, dimming her view of the pasture as the sounds of bawling and thumping hooves carried across the distance. The cattle were moving, and in a hurry, towards the shed. "Norm, get your .22, there might be some coyotes running the cattle for sport."

The farmer took one last bite of pie and got up from the table. "It'd be a dumb ass coyote that'd try to mess with an Angus."

"Just the same, something has got them worked up."

"They're just spooked by the weather."

Ailsa watched as the cows huddled within the shed, bawling and circling. Norm came by her side.

She shifted her gaze back to the pasture and caught a glimpse of movement. "There!"

"I don't see anything," Norm groused.

An obscure shape lumbered across the field. "Damn it. Right there."

"Looks like some sort of a large rock."

"That's no rock!"

"Well, I don't think—"

"Fire a damn round!"

Norm aimed and squeezed the trigger. The loud crack of the report made Ailsa blink. She pointed. "Over there!"

Norm fired another round. A deep roar carried across the field. He peered into the dusk. "What was that?"

Ailsa tried to resight the target but was unable to find it. After a few seconds, Skipper ceased his frenetic barking. Frustrated, she said, "That was a bit of a shot in the dark. I guess we better hold off with the shooting, the cattle are upset enough." She walked towards the shed, talking to the cows in a soothing voice.

Ailsa leaned on a fence post. "Norm, get a bale or two of hay to toss over the fence, that'll help distract them." She spoke to the cows in a quiet monotone, staring into their anxious eyes. The circling subsided, their ears drooped. "That's it, girls, everything is alright."

As Norm lugged a pair of bales to feed the cows, Alisa meandered to the pasture fence. She stopped, listened, and centered on her breathing. She paused to regard the garage apartment window. No light shone from within. He's likely trekked over to the estate again, she thought.

Ailsa closed her eyes and searched for life shadows while invoking the Fu Dog Garden in her mind. Something pushed back against her and cloaked her vision. Despite the hazy contact, she perceived enough to realize Devyn was not alone.

# CHAPTER 38

Devyn crouched behind the ironwork, his body tight as a drum. The gorilla bounded through the garden, often reaching to grasp a pillar, then swinging its massive bulk through the air. The beast homed in on the Buddha house, grunting and huffing in an obscene cadence. Devyn sized up his stalker, superhuman muscles bulged across its torso and neck. More disheartening, long arms vaulted its body across the garden at a speed that far eclipsed what he could hope to run.

Heart pounding, Devyn shrank lower, bewildered by the madness closing in on him, and mortified by his lack of options.

The snap of a branch pulled Devyn's attention to the spruce trees to his right. A fleeting shadow sprang from one droopy bough to another. The figure floated on the limb, nearly level with the terrace. A second specter surfaced just above the first. Devyn stared in disbelief as their large eyes opened and closed like shutters of a camera—focusing entirely on him.

The gorilla had ceased its rampage, its only sounds now muted grunts. Devyn leaned forward to peer through the vines again. The fiend turned its sloped head to the Buddha house, pausing to assess the structure. Devyn took a deep breath, knowing his best chance was to release his terror and cast a *geis* to subdue the beast. He stood up to reveal himself and gazed upon the gorilla, concentrating his entire consciousness into an unwavering stare.

Hateful red eyes returned his gaze with impunity. A flash of white heat split Devyn's skull, forcing him to recoil. Eardrums throbbing with pain, he staggered into the inner rail, barely able to keep himself from tumbling down the stairwell, He gasped for air as he fended off a wave of nausea. Disoriented, he gripped the ironwork and turned his head—to see his foe pound his chest and shout in triumph.

Devyn's vulnerability now exposed, the ape veered towards the white tower. Still grasping the rail, Devyn sized up the wide girth of the creature, giving him a sliver of hope—the beast might be too large to fit up the narrow spiral stairs, or at the very least, do so with great difficulty. But a quick glimpse of the massive arms and hands sank his morale. The brute could easily scramble up the structure's side and over the railing.

Grunting and hooting, the lurching figure hopped onto the tower platform near the Hari-Hara. Devyn's tongue swelled in his dry mouth, while a fist drummed the wall below. Unnoticed by him, and the gorilla, the shadows abandoned the trees and slinked along the ground. They crept behind a Fu Dog pillar, then peered around opposite corners.

With a scream that shattered the garden, the gorilla grabbed a support column and thrust upward. Thrashing through the vines, the brute quickly scaled the wall. Savage eyes leered at Devyn over the ironwork. Steadying himself on the handrail, Devyn side-kicked the dreadful apparition with the heel of his boot.

The beast flinched but held onto the outer ironwork with one hand, swaying the entire structure while its body dangled in mid-air. The gorilla recovered and twisted its torso to grasp the wrought iron with both hands.

Devyn scrambled down the spiral staircase, just as the beast sprang onto the terrace. Nearly losing his footing in the poor light, he crouched half-way down the shaft. A brawny arm reached down, vainly grabbing at its prey.

The gorilla squatted by the opening, awkwardly pushing one leg, then trying to force the other into the tight space. Unable to fathom the stairs, and too large to squeeze between the stairwell walls and steps, the enraged beast wrenched the iron staircase violently, forcing Devyn to cling to it for dear life.

The gorilla stopped to glare at Devyn, baring his large canines under curled lips. Shaking the staircase one more time, it stomped about the terrace, picked up a concrete bench with ease, and tossed it onto the lawn below. A quiet lull ensued, broken moments later as the structure swayed to the sound of snapping vines. Devyn realized the monster was dropping to the ground for a new assault on the staircase—from the bottom. Alarmed, he clambered up the narrow steps and back onto the terrace.

A small cloud drifted over the moon, and the stalkers behind the column sprang across the lawn, covering the distance to the shrine in three bounds. One of them swatted the gorilla on the rear end, causing it to lash out with a massive fist. His assailant leapt away unscathed, while its partner blindsided the beast with a slashing paw.

The gorilla lashed out with the force of a sledgehammer, only to whiff air. The cat and mouse ballet repeated for three more rounds until, with a thunderous howl, the titan hustled to the end of the garden. Swiping at his heels, his assailants gave pursuit well into the woods.

Moonlight returned to the garden as the acrobats trotted across the lawn, their eyes focused on Devyn. He tensed, wondering if he was their next target. As they drew close, they appeared to be bobcats, at least in size and behavior.

They stopped twenty feet in front of the shrine, sat on their haunches, and gazed up at him. Their features were undeniable—facial expressions, large ears, and oversized heads. The young man exclaimed in a stifled voice. "Fu Dogs!" Under the silver light, their bodies shone as if cast in sable fur.

Devyn's mind wavered between elation and disbelief. He leaned over the terrace rail, unable to decide what to do. The creatures licked their paws, then arched their backs to gain all fours. They jumped onto the platform below, sat back on their hind paws, and scratched the walls as would naughty housecats on a cushioned chair. Taking one last glance at Devyn, they returned to the cover of the spruces.

Devyn listened for a period of time. There was no sound other than the night chirpers and the breeze. He looked upon the lawn, still processing what happened and debating the risks of staying in place or descending the stairs. Perhaps the most disturbing trait of the gorilla—even more than its brutality—was its ability to fend off Devyn's mind meld. Despite this shock, he dwelled on the foreign woman. Who was she? Where was she from? Did she find someplace safe, out of reach from the gorilla? There was little doubt she was familiar with the monster—a disturbing thought in itself.

Finding his courage, Devyn clicked the flashlight on and fled the Buddha house. On reaching the road, he ran the entire length of the journey back to his apartment.

# CHAPTER 39

Ailsa poured herself another cup of coffee. Leaning against the back of her chair, she thought of the harvest. The most critical time of year and the most stressful, for their marriage and the farm. A year's worth of loans for fertilizer, seeds, crop treatments, fuel, machinery repairs, all boiled down to a few days of combining. The weather could be cruel, especially if rain came and didn't leave. Getting the grain at the right moisture so they weren't docked at the elevator, hauling the grain to the river, betting on the day you put in a contract bid. More often as of late, the price barely paid all the bills.

Devyn left his work boots by the door and padded into the kitchen, Skipper by his side. Ailsa regarded his bloodshot eyes. It doesn't look like he slept much last night, she thought. Stirring cream in her coffee, she casually asked, "Did you get the hay fed, then?"

He went to the sink to wash his hands. "Yes, all done."

"All of them come up to the bunk with a good appetite?"

"Yes, all of them."

"Glad to hear it, they were worked up last night."

Devyn turned about, soap still on his hands, failing to mask his surprise. "I don't remember that."

"No? Just after sunset." She glanced at her husband across the table. "I think that was about the timing of things, wouldn't you agree, Norm?"

Her husband cut a piece of waffle, loaded with butter and syrup, and poked it with his fork. "Yup, after the rain let up."

Devyn hurriedly rinsed off and dried his hands, taking his place at the table.

Norm said, "You sure look like you could use some coffee."

The younger man nodded as Norm passed him the pot. "Thank you."

Norm finished his waffle and slurped his brew. Putting his mug down, he looked out the window. "Forecast calls for dry weather well into next week. I'd like to start combining the corn tomorrow."

Devyn enjoyed his first sip of morning joe, a habit Dr. Malcolm had helped cultivate.

Norm looked at him sternly. "Once we get going on harvesting, it's a non-stop flight. That means long days and nights. There won't be much free time for strolls in the park."

Devyn nodded. "Sure. Whatever it takes."

"You can drive the grain truck. You'll be the shuttle between the combine and our grain elevator."

"What about when I'm away from the field? Where will you empty the combine bin?"

"I'll load the wagons. Ailsa will tow them around with the old twenty." Norm got up from the table and grabbed his plate. "It'll be balls to the wall until we're done. We only get so much of a window with the weather, and it's damn fickle enough as it is." Rinsing his plate in the sink, he left the kitchen to gather his coveralls and cap.

Ailsa watched him go, then glanced at Devyn. Passing the waffles, she suggested, "You should have something to eat."

Devyn spiked a waffle onto his plate. She held the serving plate steady. "Take another, you'll burn it off. Strikes me you were a little light on supper last night."

He scraped a thick pat of butter over his waffles. She offered a small pitcher of syrup to him. "You look as if you had a hard night. Not feeling well?"

He shrugged. "I'm feeling okay."

"Can't believe you missed the cows carrying on so. There was a wee set-to in the pasture, not far from your quarters. If nothing else, I would have thought the rain and wind might grab your attention."

Chewing on his waffles, he explained, "Maybe the weather made me kind of sleepy." His eyes shifted to the window as a flight of crows cawed noisily unseen in the distance.

She noted his diversion. "The birds have been agitated as of late. I wonder what's ailing them so."

Devyn washed a mouthful of waffles down with a sip from his mug. "I think they don't like something that's going on over in the estate."

She raised an eyebrow. "How so?"

Hesitant to reply, Devyn said nonchalantly. "I don't know, I have a feeling."

She thought. He saw something last night, and he's frightened. "I'd hold off going back over there for a bit. Norm can get mighty cranky during harvest. Especially when things break down…and they will. Maybe it's just as well, the big public event is taking place over there tomorrow."

Devyn cupped his mug between his hands and stared at his coffee. As if weighing his words, he spoke without shifting his eyes to her. "I was in the Fu Dog Garden yesterday."

Her eyes bore into him. "When was this?"

Devyn's body language signaled his unease as he strained to find an answer. "Right after the rain, about the same time you said the cattle were frightened." He lifted his eyes to meet hers. Her serene gaze urged him on.

He paled as he recalled the scene. "I don't understand how, but I saw a pair of Fu Dogs chase away a gorilla from the garden."

She started. "Fu Dogs? Gorilla?"

"I was hiding on the terrace of the Buddha house. The gorilla was coming after me. They attacked him."

"You're sure it was a gorilla?"

"I looked into its face." He paused to collect himself. "I couldn't force it away with my mind. That's never happened to me before."

Ailsa pressed her lips to check an immediate response of alarm. She looked out the window at the sunshine to offset the pall settling over the kitchen. "I can't get a sense of why this happened." She regarded Devyn. "Can you?"

He shook his head. "Not sure, but I think the folks at the estate might have swapped some real Fu Dogs for fakes."

Surprised, she asked, "What? Which ones were swapped?"

"The pair at the end of the garden. They don't match the others."

She rehashed his response and thought, this could lead to trouble…deep, dark trouble. "I knew your curiosity would lead you back there. As I said, it's best you stay clear until I figure this out." Sensing a missing piece in his story, Ailsa asked in a kind voice, "Did you see any other creatures?"

Devyn stammered. "Th-there was a woman, hiding in the trees. She spoke a strange language."

"A woman? What did she look like?"

"It was hard to see her in the dark. I think she knew of the gorilla. She was afraid and ran way before it came into the garden."

Ailsa sat in silence, her face set in stone.

Needing to clear his head, Devyn rose from the table, carried his plate to the sink and washed it. "I better go see what Norm wants me to do today." He smiled wanly. "We don't want him to get crankier." Skipper got up from under the table and followed at his heels.

Ailsa closed her eyes to meditate over Devyn's encounter. What had he stumbled onto there? Or was it better described as who had he unearthed? She let out a long sigh. All of this on top of the harvest.

Along the road, the sumac berries were already drying into rust, seemingly bleeding their red color into the leaves. Ailsa turned her thoughts from the changing seasons to Devyn. He was pulling the feed wagons behind the old twenty while the cows ambled behind him. A smile twisted her lips. A motorized Pied Piper leading the animals with a tractor rather than a flute. One thing about the young man, not once had he missed a chore…or left a gate open.

A pair of crows cried out to each other south of the farm. The black heralds had been at it all morning.

Devyn left the tractor to unhook the wagons, his bovine following surged about him, eager for their meal. He reached out to scratch the tailhead of one of the cows. Ailsa did a doubletake. My God, even June Bug will let him rub her now. Two months on the farm and his touch with animals still surprised her. Devyn briefly bonded with the placid cow, then returned to the tractor cab. Shooting a glance across the pasture, his eyes met Ailsa's.

Try as she might all morning to gather in the substance of what lurked in the woods, her visions were little more than vague shapes and blurry figures. She would keep a close tab on Devyn's whereabouts for the rest of the day—after she returned from her walk.

Carl spent most of the morning running and jumping to Val's bidding. To describe her attitude as frantic would be an understatement. The pavilion was back in order; most of the final details revolved about food service, music, name tags, decorations, and seating arrangements—minor problems that thankfully didn't involve him. However, a major aggravation still irked him, the unexplained theft of sculptures.

The grounds manager took off his red visored cap, IH patch sewn on the front, and rubbed his scalp. He resigned himself to the idea of a night patrol, and Trent and Charlie earning a little overtime pay from his budget. He gave them the afternoon off to collect themselves, or in Charlie's case, probably a long nap.

Carl sauntered away from the pavilion to the far side of the upper terrace, seeking a little-used path near the low brick wall. The trail sloped down, away from the bluff where the mansion stood, and towards the service road that paralleled the river. As he crossed a small wooden footbridge, a bed of overgrown pachysandra in the moist ditch caught his eye. Fugitives from the gardens that found a new patch to their liking, he figured.

Continuing along the path for fifty yards, he came to a fork—one path bearing left and uphill to the gorilla statue, the other, and wider trail, tracking ahead on level ground. Choosing the latter, his work boots shuffled through dying leaves scattered on the packed gravel.

He treaded on firm ground, to his left a small embankment, to his right, tall sycamores and maples thrived in the rich soil of the Sangamon's flood plain. In the spring, their trunks would be stained with watermarks, as much as three feet high, and parts of the path he now took would be under water.

The peak fall colors and the sound of chickadees and woodpeckers relieved Carl's morning stress. Blue sky prevailed overhead, making him believe the forecast for clear weather the next day was real. Thank God.

After about a half mile, he spotted the junction with the Old Levee Road. He paused to reset his bearings. To his left, a small path wound its way up the embankment, to eventually reach a flat clearing with the bear and hunter. Ellington came to mind as he thought of the odd statues. Artists.

Carl continued to the small gate where the service lane ended on the Old Levee Road. Still bothered by the deer he had previously found on the way to work; he took a right and walked the short distance to the bridge. Half expecting to smell the remains or hear buzzing flies, he searched through the brush where he had left the carcass. It was gone.

"I give up." Carl wheeled slowly in a full circle, studying the woods. His eyes settled onto the pavement. A brick-red stain discolored the right lane of the road and smeared the asphalt for twenty yards beyond the gate. Carl followed the trail until he came across a mangled hoof and the head of the doe.

He muttered. "Why would coyotes drag the carcass nearly fifty yards before finishing off the remains?" Perplexed, Carl continued north. He came upon a footpath to his left that led to the goldfish pond. Wanting to complete his circuit through the Fu Dog Garden, he descended into the basin. The pond was little more than a bog, covered with bright green duckweed. The low-lying ground was slippery, and while watching his footsteps to avoid the stickier spots, Carl spotted tracks in the mud. He bent over to examine the imprints. "What in the hell is this?"

Tracing his fingers along the edge of the tracks, his eyes narrowed. They were easily the size of a coyote's, a large coyote, or dog. He straightened up to gain a wider perspective, troubled by seeing something unknown in all his years of hunting. The tracks seemed to be catlike. A large cat, the size of a bobcat, at least. "Damn. That old coot was right."

Hastening his pace, Carl left the pond. He followed a curve fifty yards distant and passed the pillars topped by the substitute Fu Dogs. He halted to look at the collection of snarling, bug-eyed faces all about him. They peered defiantly at him from their pedestals. He shook his head. "I don't get it."

He made for the House of the Golden Buddhas, all the while as the armless stone figure gazed at him with blank eyes. Better go get some grub, it'll be a long night. He reminded himself to bring his hip flask—topped off with Red Breast to ward off the chill. He stopped short half-way across the lawn. "What in the bloody hell is going on here?"

He hastily walked to the tower, distrusting what he saw. A cement bench from the terrace lay on the ground, one corner sunk several inches in the moist soil. Clipped green leaves lay scattered on the lawn all around him. Carl looked up at the terrace. The vines along the near face dangled in the air, torn away from the terrace ironwork. The grounds keeper fumed at the desecration of the structure. He would have to get the skid steer to pull the bench out of sight this afternoon. Lifting it back onto the terrace would have to wait for another day.

Fit to be tied, Carl stormed past a gold Buddha, checking to ensure it wasn't damaged. Once again, he stopped in surprise. Much of the wood and paint near the alcove was frayed by deep linear scratches. Disturbingly, they were similar to what he observed in the pavilion earlier. "Goddam high school punks. There'll be hell to pay for whoever did this," he muttered. Carl weighed in his mind that his shotgun might be better suited than whiskey for the night watch.

After running errands in town, Ailsa took a detour past the farm on the Old Timber Road and entered the estate in her VW bus. She parked in the visitor lot, foregoing a hike to the Fu Dog Garden, in lieu of a path into the woods behind the Evergreen Lodge. The parking area was more crowded than normal. Perhaps related to the event tomorrow, she thought.

Alone on the path, she listened attentively to the sounds about her, eyes searching for any clues…clues that were vague at best. Nothing seemed to be out of the ordinary for a midday stroll among the colorful trees. Still, she felt a tension—a coiled spring compressing tighter within her torso.

She soon reached a rise along the trail, tracking on the crest of a shallow ravine. The mansion came into view on her right. Climbing up a last small knoll, she entered a clearing and gasped. It was vacant, save for a circular concrete pedestal. Ailsa forced herself to remain calm. Around her the birds sang under the sunshine of a lovely fall day.

Ailsa looked in the direction of the mansion. Her inner spring tightened as she considered her current discovery in light of the planned social gathering tomorrow. She surveyed her location once more, then headed back to her vehicle. "Enter the fray, we must." She halted. Was it only the gorilla that was running rampant?

# CHAPTER 40

Kim drove her Rabbit between the armless charioteers. As she drew abreast of the Gatehouse, she reminded herself returning to the studio was against her better judgement. Thinking of the awkward rendezvous, she could feel her stomach tying in knots. Was her advisor on the verge of exhaustion? Or had she witnessed an unhinged side that he masked for the past two and a half years? She clenched the steering wheel, knowing she needed to hold the line for seven more months. Ellington's reference was crucial for applying for a residency at the Archie Bray Foundation. Seven months of the current state of affairs would be hard—but the change of scenery in Montana would be worth it.

The car lurched as she downshifted and wheeled into the parking lot behind the shop. Turning off the ignition and resetting herself, she got out of the car. She walked to the back door and twisted the knob. It was locked. Maybe he went through the front door, she reasoned.

Kim inserted her key and pushed the door open. The shop was cool and dark, little had changed from the day before. Kim called out tenuously, "Ellington, are you here? Ellington?" She treaded with nimble steps through the shop and peered into the studio. Despite the clutter, she welcomed the solitude with a sigh of relief.

A tremor pulsed down her spine as she took stock of what lay before her. Something didn't feel right. Frustration coiled into anger within. "Honestly, El, this late in the day, and with the event on tap for tomorrow?" She prioritized the bedlam around her. "Maybe I'll get more done without him here anyway."

Setting her jacket on a counter, she reached for the light switch, then froze. The wooden crates still sat by the office door, but their lids were fully open, leaning against the wall behind them. Kim edged towards the crates, pulse quickening, drawn by morbid curiosity. Stretching on her toes to keep her distance, her shoulders relaxed as she saw nothing but empty space. She looked about the studio, the quiet now becoming unnerving. "This is getting a little too weird."

Crossing the room, she pushed the play button on the stereo. Her spirits lifted as David Byrne chanted *Psycho Killer*, prompting her to grab a handful of misplaced tools. Prancing and bobbing her head to the beat, she yanked open a drawer and dropped the tools into place.

Yeah, I can set up the workstations and supplies for the visitors and get out before he gets back, she thought. Maybe he'll figure out it was me…or whoever else might wander in.

Devyn stretched his arm to the west and sized up the distance between the horizon and the sun—four fingers, an hour until sunset. Lumpy clouds, dusted with saffron, hung above the orange orb. The evening air was cooling, coaxing him to zip up his hoodie. He reached into a sweatshirt pocket to make sure of his flashlight; a twenty-five-foot lariat with a snap release coiled about his shoulder. His left hand held the lantern. He examined the device—its light could be the final clue that he was making the right decision.

Knowing Norm and Ailsa were glued to the TV and the evening news, Devyn strolled to the machine shed without haste. He entered through the open, cavernous door. The monstrous combine lay in waiting, anxious to wreak havoc with its steel jaws on the unsuspecting corn.

Devyn entered a small side room full of hand tools pegged on a wall and garden tools braced in a row along the opposite side. He marveled at Norm's unfailing tidiness and organization. Even his tool room floor lacked dust and grime. Maybe the Navy taught him that, he thought.

Resting his hand on the posthole-digging bar, he set the lantern down and lifted the six-foot iron with both hands to test his arm strength. Satisfied, Devyn lowered the bar, balancing it in one hand, retrieved the lantern and left the room.

He chose to exit the machine shed by the small side door, out of sight from the house. He walked around the far side of the old corn crib and set off at a good clip along the Old Timber Road, making for the House of the Golden Buddhas. There he would rest and wait, hiding until twilight. Timing was everything. Burdened by his gear, he would have preferred driving his Scout, but a bright yellow vehicle parked by the road or in the lot would attract unwanted attention.

He came to a dead stop at the park entrance. A cold hand gripped his soul as feral cries echoed through the woods—not from the direction of the Fu Dogs, but from farther along the Old Timber Road. Steeling himself, he hurried to his destination.

Bone weary from cleaning and organizing, Kim caught her reflection in a panel of windows, prompting her to comb her tussled hair between fingers. She thought, I can hardly wait to see what I look like in front of a mirror. Her stomach complained from working into the dinner hour, prompting her to wrap it up and go find something to eat. Hands on hips of her dusty jeans, she relaxed to take one last survey of the studio. "You owe me, El."

Making her way around an obstacle course of ceramics, she exited the greenhouse door, pulled out a key and locked the deadbolt. As the bolt clicked, a loud ruckus drew her attention. Peering towards the arborvitae-lined path, she was startled to see the top half of a plant bend over, snap in half and tumble onto the ground. Moments later, a dark shape flew through the air, smashed through the opposite wall of plants, and into the garden behind them.

The tops along the line of evergreens violently swayed in an oncoming wave towards the greenhouse. Kim gulped as she saw a massive creature hurdle over the far wall of the garden, followed by terrifying noises echoing along the road. The changing pitch of the howls made it clear the beast was making haste in her direction.

Kim doubted she could reach her car before the beast got there first. Her fingers fumbled with the key as she hurried to reopen the deadbolt. She jumped inside, then slammed and locked the door. Feeling threatened in the open space of the greenhouse, she ran to the shop, shut the door and used all her weight to shove a barrel full of plaster scraps against it. She then sprinted to the back door, her nervous hands struggling to turn the latch. The creature sounded to be just outside. The dead bolt clicked. On the verge of hyperventilating, Kim scanned the shop and scrambled under a table.

A snuffling sound circled the back door jamb, then without warning, three rapid blows slammed the door—beating the metal with such force the bolt rattled violently against the faceplate. The young woman cowered, afraid to look at the door. The room went silent, save for Kim's whimpered breathing. A heavy thump on the roof fractured her moment of calm, followed by dreadful steps scrambling overhead with surprising speed. She hunkered down as the entire room vibrated from the sounds.

Glass crashed onto the greenhouse floor. Fighting the urge to scream, she chanted softly, "Dear God, dear God, dear God." Harsh screams blasted from the studio, coupled with the sounds of unknown objects banging off the walls. Kim cringed into a ball, praying the monster wouldn't surge through the shop door.

# CHAPTER 41

The setting sun reflected off the pond, a finishing touch for the decorations on the south lawn. Planters of mums lined the steps to the upper terrace, offset by orange and yellow mums in blue vases, centered on tables draped with cream-colored linen tablecloths. The dais was set at the west end of the pavilion to provide a view of the meadow and pond as the backdrop for speakers. Best of all, tomorrow's forecast called for a sunny day.

Lively banter echoed across the south lawn, lifted by the finality of the arrangements and jazz circulating in the air from a portable stereo. Ellington mingled with Dean Duffey and Jim Kramer, gin and tonics in hand. His eyes tracked Val, bustling about the tables and dais with Ashley and a squadron of staff. She would occasionally cast a furtive glance his way. They had remained in an uneasy truce while in the public space, so far at least.

Ellington scanned the stone wall bordering the far end of the terrace lawn, already shaded from the trees at the edge of the bluff. He had hid a satchel on the far side of the wall, to be retrieved at the right moment. Waiting impatiently, he watched the pageantry under the pavilion as daylight slowly waned.

Only half in-tune with the conversation between the Dean and Jim, Ellington's eyes once again settled on Val. There she was in all her glory, the queen bee in command as always, dark hair flowing over her shoulders as she gestured with her hands. A flash of sunlight played off her chest, the necklace gleamed briefly. A sense of loss came over him, wondering if he should give up on his scheme. Perhaps this was a step too far…even for her.

Below the bluff and beyond the woods, the river flowed into the shadows of the fading day. Ellington waited, mulling over his decision. Twilight would soon arrive.

# CHAPTER 42

Devyn held the lantern at shoulder level to examine the Fu Dog. Under the red glow, a constellation of violet flecks sparkled throughout the glaze. It struck him that the figure glistened like polished amethyst only under red light, not when illuminated with his flashlight. Devyn walked to the next statue in line to find the same effect, the lantern mutated the figure into a violet gemstone.

He paced along several more columns, enthralled with his seemingly magical power to transform each Fu Dog. As he paused to contemplate the meaning of his find, a shadow flickered in the corner of his eye. He scanned the edge of the garden, sensing their presence more than seeing them—crouching under the spruce limbs. Watching, listening…and waiting.

Devyn neared the far end of the lawn. Standing before the two identical figures, he again lifted his lantern. The red light had little effect, their glaze no more than an anemic bruise of drab blue and red. "That's what you're trying to tell me, Mr. Jones. It's all about their color," he muttered. An unsettling chill caused him to pull his hoodie up over his head. Devyn now knew his plan of action was the right one.

Setting down the lantern, he unwound the lariat. Making a loop with the clasp, he tossed the lariat over the head of the Fu Dog to his right and snagged the loop around the neck. The imperious creature, face frozen in a snarl, eyed him with crazed eyes—as if daring the upstart human to continue. Devyn stayed the course. Gaining consent from an absurd imposter mattered little to him.

Devyn hoisted the digging bar off the ground and balanced the steel between his hands. Raising the bar even with his shoulder, he thrust at the space between the figure's base and concrete pedestal. The figure scarcely tottered. He pulled his arms back, then lunged with more force and viciously speared his target again. Dime-sized splinters showered the air as metal striking stone shattered the garden.

Devyn hesitated amid the clamor, realizing the piercing sound was likely carrying over a fair portion of the estate. He gritted his teeth and struck again, committed to his task. Each heave of the chiseled blade chewed deeper under the Fu Dog. The figure tilted towards him.

Ears still ringing, Devyn paused to listen, pleased to hear quiet settle back onto the garden again. He wedged the blade between ceramic and stone, then forced the steel deep under the base. He reached up with both hands to the far end of the bar and suspended himself off the ground. The statue wobbled an inch but no more. He repeated the jabbing and hanging motion again. Perhaps gaining another inch. Frustrated by the figure's resistance, Devyn's ire towards the mocking face drove him to grab the lariat. Wrapping the rope around his waist, then taking hold with both hands, he leaned back and pulled with all his weight. The creature wavered but didn't topple over.

Devyn focused all his energy for the next jerk. He halted as he pulled the rope taut. Nightfall had crept from the woods, nibbling away at the last dim light in the open garden. Devyn had no time to waste.

Standing by his truck in the parking lot, Carl said, "Charlie, I want you to patrol the roads in the old pickup every thirty minutes. That also includes the Allerton and Old Levee roads."

"What do I do between each run?"

Carl replied, "I don't know, figure it out, bring a thermos of coffee and take a break in between."

The older man frowned as dusk fell upon the trio. "Are we going to be at this all night?"

"Not sure. That's why I gave you the afternoon off to go home for a siesta. So, we'll be awake with eyes open. And keep your two-way handy."

Charlie muttered indistinctly but unmistakably in protest.

Carl glanced at Trent, who cradled a .22 in his arms. "Got that thing loaded and safety on?"

The younger man gave a grim smile. "Yeah."

"Flashlight?"

"Yeah."

Nodding in approval, Carl gently picked up his Remington twenty gauge from the seat of his pickup and loaded five shells into the magazine—alternating shot with slugs.

Trent gestured across the lot towards the mansion. "What are you thinking might happen over there?"

"Hopefully nothing, but if it does, I doubt it'll be possums or racoons." Carl took one last look at Charlie. "Stay alert, Pops. Trent and I are going on a hike around the estate. I'm thinking we'll start by having a look-see around the perimeter of the pavilion."

Carl and Trent approached the Gate House. All the windows were dark. Carl thought, I wonder if that sculptor is over at the mansion with the rest of the party, or in his studio?

Turning onto the path leading to the manor, Carl held up his hand for Trent to stop. Cocking his head, he asked, "Did you hear something?"

Breathing slowly and remaining in place, Trent shook his head. "No."

The pair resumed their trek but halted again after a few more steps. "Over there! Towards the Buddha house. Listen!"

Trent's face wrinkled. "What did it sound like?"

"Like a hammering noise."

"I still don't hear anything."

With an edge in his voice, Carl said, "Just shut up and listen, damn it!" His persistence paid off. A harsh clang carried across the parking area.

Carl smiled. "I think we found our elusive creature." Assuming his companion would follow, Carl marched off with quick, sharp steps. "Let's go through the vine walk. As we near the garden, make sure you're ready."

Trent clasped his rifle tighter, thinking, ready for what?

The evening news was little changed from the day before, politicians wrangling, reporters covering the aftermath of the earthquake near San Francisco, and investigators trying to piece together why an explosion killed so many workers in a chemical plant in Texas. Aisla decided to get some fresh air to rid herself of the constant downfall of humanity. At least the forecast was favorable to combine the corn.

She stepped onto the back porch, wrapping her sweater tighter against the evening chill. Skipper wandered out with her, trotted onto the lawn to lift his leg on a boxwood bordering the porch rail, and returned ready to call it a day.

Astute eyes, hardened by many years of farming, set upon the cows in the pasture—solid black matter melting into the dusky light. Ailsa admired their simple life, no politics or thoughts of impending disasters or wars to clutter their minds. Eat grass, chew their cud, stay with the herd and keep a look out for their calves.

Turning her gaze to the window above the garage, Ailsa raised her eyebrows on seeing the unlit glass. "So…," she whispered. "He got a bigger head start than I thought." She turned and looked beyond the road and rough meadow. A slight breeze freshened her face, carrying sound from the woods. She stood still, ears tuned with the diligence of a cat.

A shape, little more than dark matter wrapped in power and rancor, emerged in her mind. It prowled among the ancient, white-barked sycamores, not far from the river. Ailsa's neck hair stood on end.

She followed Skipper through the back door as he burst into the house. Norm sat at the kitchen table, a piece of cake and mug of tea before him. "You look like you're heading for a fire."

Ailsa glanced at him. "Of a sort." She pulled open a cabinet drawer to grab a flashlight, jacket, and keys to her VW bus.

"Something I should know?"

She shook her head. "Just trying to keep Devyn from getting into trouble."

# CHAPTER 43

Ellington's eye followed Val, looking trim in her brown leather jacket and jeans. She was holding court by the podium, next to a small table—a modest artifact destined to play a leading role in tomorrow's performance.

The ceramicist pondered the fate of the shrouded figure resting on the table. If he could get it back in his hands. His first thought was to heave it down the slope and into the woods, a forlorn figure abandoned on the forest floor. Better yet, toss it in the river, to let it sink into the mud. His lip curled as he pictured the sitting woman's smile smeared in slime, beguiling only fish, snails, and other bottom dwellers.

Ellington reconsidered his motives. Why should he let her betrayal push him into childish revenge? He took pride in his work, but he needed to erase the sinister smile, knowing that as long as it existed—even if eroding in the river—it would trouble his mind. Perhaps it needed to be pulverized back into blue dust and scattered to the wind.

Ellington was so removed from reality he failed to notice Jim and the Dean as they meandered about the terrace. Engrossed in an animated conversation, the pair approached the stone wall. Ellington regarded them with growing anxiety as they debated a proposal before the university faculty senate, on the merits of foreign language requirements for graduation.

His superiors halted on the edge of the terrace a few feet away from where he had stashed his satchel. They carried on, gesturing and overlooking the wooded slope. Ellington winced, a half turn and brief glance down and to their right would bring discovery, shame and ridicule, or worse. He hardly breathed, his mind spinning to conjure up an excuse should they find the leather pack.

"Donald! James!" Val called out. "What are you doing over there? Don't want you stumbling over the wall in the dark. Let's go to the solarium and enjoy some convivial time over another cocktail."

The Dean winked and nudged the department chair with an elbow. "And maybe one for the road as well." Chuckling, they spun about and joined the others towards the open French doors.

Waiting to fall in behind the other guests, Val asked, "Ashley, would you please have the kitchen provide some pretzels, cheese, and the like? Best not to let them drink on an empty stomach with a half-hour ride back home." She pointed to the dais. "And have someone take the stereo inside, please."

"Will do." Going against the grain of the group's current, Ashley headed for the door on the far side of the mansion.

Val took one more survey of the preparations. Carl better keep it together tonight, or we're screwed, she thought. She had arranged to stay for the night—a second-story room with a view of the terrace lawn and the meadow. Another set of eyes from a higher vantage point wouldn't hurt. She let out a sigh and thought. What a day, I could use a stiff one myself.

Straightening her jacket, she zigzagged around the tables, pleased to let things be, if only until tomorrow. She caught sight of Ellington loitering on the far side of the pavilion. "You waiting for something?"

He shrugged. "No. Just wanted to take in the evening air for a minute."

Suspicious, she shook her head and left to join the party. A worn voice crackled over her two-way radio. "Valerie, are you there?"

Grasping the device from a clip on her waist, she muttered, "Yes. What's up?"

"Valerie, please come in, this is Carl."

She gave the radio a dirty look and pressed the button. "I know who you are, Carl. Only you, Charlie and I have a radio."

A pause ensued. "Trent and I heard some strange noises."

"What kind of noises? Where?"

"Like striking metal on stone. Over towards the Fu Dog Garden."

"Fu Dogs! I knew it. Well, get the hell over there, for Christ's sake."

"We're already on our way, going down the vine path to the Buddha house as we speak."

Val pressed her lips and tapped the radio. "I'll head over there. I'll follow the footpath that cuts from the back of the mansion to the far side of the Evergreen Lodge. It'll save time."

"Ten four."

Val looked at the warm light coming from the mansion windows with a tinge of regret. The martini would have to wait. With one more baleful glance at Ellington, she left the terrace and clicked on a small flashlight pulled from her jacket pocket. Passing the kitchen, she neared a pair of brick pillars that once marked the stable entrance. Her beam scanned the woods. She found a path, little more than a narrow breach in the brush, and descended a series of steps. The track bridged a shallow ditch with side-by-side planks, then led up and to the left. As she climbed the rise on the opposite side of the ravine, sharp clangs echoed among the trees.

Her lips curled into a dry smile. I don't know how, Ellington, but I know your involved. Following her light, she rustled through the leaves and made for the garden, unaware of a pair of bright red orbs watching her from a small rise farther in the woods.

Valerie was gone, the stereo recovered for indoors. All was quiet, but Ellington delayed two full minutes to ensure he wouldn't be disturbed. Intrigued to see Val leave in haste and in the opposite direction from the rest of the party, he speculated what was in play. The radio babble was beyond earshot, save for Val speaking about Fu Dogs.

She's up to something. He wanted to follow her but held back. He reached over the stone wall and carefully picked up his bundle. Casting a furtive glance at the mansion, he made for the pavilion.

Once under the canopy, Ellington silently critiqued the décor. Nice job, although orange ribbons on blue flower vases are a bit gauche. Relying on the dim light cast from the mansion windows, he moved carefully so as not to stumble over any chairs or tables—or worse, knock something over. He stepped up onto the dais and neared the shrouded figure on the side pedestal. Reaching into his satchel, he extracted a penlight and clenched it between his teeth. He lifted the cloth with a flair, pausing to let out a breath of sad admiration. Val was a stunning model.

Ellington removed *Blue Desire* gently and set it on the podium, replacing it with a figurine he gathered from his satchel. Penlight now in hand, he directed the beam on the new arrival, then rotated the pedestal to an angle that would best affect the audience. Surprise unveiling indeed, he mused. Elegantly draping the cloth over the new piece, and placing *Blue Desire* in his pack, he looked in the direction where Val had entered the woods. He mumbled, "Must be some sort of path over there."

He took two steps, turned his light off and halted. A couple of high school-age kids, probably kitchen staff, stepped out the back door for a break. Self-absorbed, giggling, they lit up a joint and shared tokes.

Ellington shrank back into the shadows as the faint scent of pot wafted across the gravel lot. He thought. They should bake some brownies for the garden party tomorrow. That'd lighten things up. Despite the humor, he frowned. The smokers could hang there for a while. To follow Val on her path, he'd need to walk out in the open, and under bright coach lamps on the pillars. He balanced the pros and cons of going back to his apartment in the Gate House. On the plus side, he could drop off the figure, and its weight, then head for the Fu Dogs. But the Gate House could only be reached by walking in front of the solarium. From the noise level, it seemed the French doors were wide open. Ellington fidgeted with the penlight between his fingers. Better to stay out of sight and out of mind regarding his absence.

There was another possibility…the path that descended from the bluff, close to where he hid the satchel. He was unsure of its exact track, but remembered it went by the gorilla installation and back towards the Fu Dog Garden…or was it the parking lot? More than a month had passed since he had unwittingly wandered on the trail, but he recalled the path cut in the general direction he wanted to go.

Ellington noted the gathering dusk in the woods. The penlight would offer only minimal guidance, not the best way to follow a foot trail in the dark. He remembered the trail sloped down from the stone wall and crossed a small bridge over a ditch with bright green ground cover—an easy enough landmark to find his way. He slipped away from the pavilion and the teens and crept over the stone wall. He found the narrow path twisting past the trunk of a maple and heading downhill.

Ellington followed the muddy track, his balance encumbered by the weight of the satchel clinging to his hip.

# CHAPTER 44

Carl and Trent came to a standstill at the end of the path. Silence had returned to the garden. A waxing moon, two days short of full, crawled through the treetops across the lawn. Careful not to attract any attention in the dim light, they peered around the cover of the vines to survey the manicured lawn. All seemed to be in order, although the near side pillars blocked their view of the far end.

Signaling Trent with a forefinger to his lips, Carl motioned the younger man to follow. They slid along the shadowy space between the spruces and the backside of the columns, firearms at the ready, safety on. Reaching the first pillar, Carl held up his hand and flicked his fingers at Trent to join him. Hugging the cold concrete and leaning around the corner, the hunters witnessed a surreal scene.

Under the soft, red glow of a kerosene lantern, a hooded figure, most likely a young man, had a rope wrapped around his waist. The other end circled about the neck of a Fu Dog, set on a pedestal next to the garden exit. The sound of his panting carried across the lawn; the vandal was clearly giving everything he had to topple the statue.

Carl waved his hand to return to the back side of the garden. A scramble of rustling limbs and breaking twigs erupted from the nearest tree. Startled, Trent brandished his rifle and clicked off the safety. Before he could finish his next breath, the creature shimmied up the evergreen and threatened them with a soft hiss. Trent tried to sight his target, holding his gun with trembling hands. Carl laid a firm hand on the barrel and pushed it down. With a quick knifing gesture, he got his message across, then squatted, pointing at Trent to do the same.

Peering through a narrow space before the next pillar, they saw the intruder had ceased his effort. Face tinted in eerie crimson, he looked towards the commotion in the tree. Carl and Trent didn't move. They waited, their beathing tense and shallow. Carl exhaled as the red-hued figure resumed his tug of war with the Fu Dog.

Wanting to close the distance before revealing themselves, Carl straightened and gingerly treaded in the shadows between spruces and columns. Trent cast one more anxious glance to the tree top and trailed his boss. Coming abreast with the last pillar, the older man beckoned Trent. They stepped out onto the lawn just as the roped statue teetered over. With a sickening crack, the Fu Dog broke its neck on the curb at the pillar's base.

Huffing and puffing, Devyn relaxed, regarding the severed head, staring at him in shock from the violent act. His elation dampened as two men, with guns pointed at him, emerged from the darkness to his right.

Carl's face was set in stone. "What in the hell do you think you're doing, asshole?"

Still catching his wind, Devyn withdrew into complacent silence, boldly returning Carl's gaze.

Carl looked at the carnage wrought by the young man. A second Fu Dog, broken in half, lay in the grass between the pillars. The figure snarled in defiance, though impotently given its current predicament.

The ire of the grounds manager rose to near boiling. "How dare you, you little son of a bitch? I've a mind to tan your hide right here and now."

Trent gloated over the older man's shoulder. "We should give him a whipping from here 'til Sunday."

"How many more were you going to destroy this evening? You have any idea what these things are worth?" Carl clenched his teeth, trying hard not to resort to physical violence. "Let alone all the work that goes into making them." He noted the digging bar propped up against a pillar. "Steel bar, rope, lanterns…What other toys have we brought along to play with tonight? Any weapons?"

Devyn reached into his sweatshirt pocket.

"Freeze!" Carl aimed his barrel at Devyn but restrained himself from loading the chamber.

"Only a flashlight." Devyn held up one hand while the other eased the device out of his pocket.

Trent motioned the barrel of his rifle to the ground. "You drop it right there."

Devyn complied, then regarded the statues on the ground. "I'm truly sorry for this, but these two had to go. We have to restore the balance of this garden."

Carl and Trent exchanged glances. "What did you say?" Carl asked, his voice rising an octave as he spoke. "What's with the red light from the lantern. Is this some sort of satanic ritual?"

Trent appraised Devyn from head to toe. "Seems to me, this little man has got faulty wiring in his brain. Maybe we should call the guys in the white jackets along with the sheriff."

"If I had my way, the sheriff would be too good for him," Carl replied. "I suppose you were also…balancing the furniture in the pavilion the other night as well."

Devyn looked puzzled. "I don't know what you're talking about."

Looking back along the length of the garden, Cal set a trap. "And you also did a little remodeling in the Buddha house as well. Impressive effort, although I don't think you're man enough to have done it alone."

Devyn's voice faltered at the thought of the gorilla's assault. "Buddha house?"

Carl and Trent laughed in unison, without mirth. "Get this one, boss. Catch him in plain sight and he denies he did anything."

"I told you I didn't have anything to do with a pavilion, or the Buddha house." Devyn pointed to the disgraced Fu Dogs at his feet. "These fakes had to be removed. We need to let the others come back."

The smugness in Carl's face ebbed. How did he know these two dogs weren't originals? He had insider information…and possibly help. Carl's sobriety sharpened from a new complication. Repeated grunts, or barks, resonated from the woods.

Wild-eyed, Trent turned to look towards the source of the noise. "What the hell was that?"

The deep, staccato woofing called out again. Carl's tone of voice betrayed his unease as he tried to calm the younger man. "Nothing to be concerned with. Probably a whitetail buck in rut." It was an empty explanation, and they both knew it.

Devyn's eyes gleamed in the red light. "There are violent monsters in these woods, you must help me force them back to where they came from." He gestured to the empty pillars. "The guardians keep them there."

Shotgun at the ready, Carl screwed his face into a knot. "What are you talking about?"

"We have to let the watchers return."

Trent stepped away from the madman. "This is getting too fucking weird, Carl."

A strained voice on Carl's radio broke the silence. "Carl, are you out there?"

Keeping his eye on Devyn, he hoisted his radio and pushed the button to respond. "Right here waiting for you in the Fu Dog Garden, Valerie. We caught some nutjob pulling the statues off the pillars. He broke two of them. We got him, and he isn't going anywhere."

"I'm on the path between the back of the mansion and the parking lot. I hear some strange animal sounds. I think it's following me." Val's voice lacked her usual bravado.

Carl glanced at Trent as he replied. "You say you're on the path that leads from near the kitchen past the Evergreen Lodge?"

Fear tinged her reply. "Yes, please come find me, I've got my flashlight."

"Okay, I'll take the path that cuts from the end of the garden to the parking lot. Wave your light through the trees so I can see you." Thinking a bit, he instructed Trent. "You wait here with this moron, while I go find Ms. Farwell."

"What if he tries to get away?"

Carl lowered his eyes to Trent's .22. "That's a simple option, I should think."

Worn out from his struggle with the fake statues, Devyn slumped onto the ground, sitting with crossed legs. "I have no reason to go anywhere. I have to help the keepers return."

"Shut your mouth," Trent ordered. "And stay right there."

Smiling, Devyn gazed at his adversary with placid eyes.

"Carl, are you coming? I think whatever is out there is getting closer. Please hurry."

"On my way." He replied into his radio. "Meet me at the end of your path by the parking lot." He turned on his flashlight and double-timed his pace through the exit, taking the trail that split to the right.

Trent's eyes wandered from his prisoner as the barking grunts called out again, closer to the garden than before.

Aware of his guard's unease, coupled with the loaded rifle in his hands, Devyn relaxed, not wanting to add to the crisis. His eyes followed the Fu Dog line to his left, basking in pale moonlight—their ludicrous eyes ogling across the lawn. The same sort of eyes which spied on him from under the spruces. Two pairs, side by side, blinking from the shadows.

Kim had never been so scared in her life. She couldn't make any sense of it. Still under the table, shivering from frayed nerves and adrenalin, she took a deep breath, held it, then exhaled. She repeated her exercise twice. She had lost all sense of time.

The terror had been like a funnel cloud or severe thunderstorm. Loud, violent, unseen—but over in a short space of time. Whatever ransacked the studio left as suddenly as it

252

came. Glancing at her watch, she waited for ten minutes. She half-smiled. What was so special about ten more minutes to ensure the marauder was gone? Because it obeyed the law of even numbers?

She sat in the dark room, with only dim light eking through the small window, thinking things over. She struggled over who to contact. The police? Estate staff? Maybe Ellington would be the best choice. Who would believe her with this bullshit story?

The time passed and Kim stood up and stretched to release her knotted muscles. Fighting her reluctance to do so, she crept over to the studio door, pulled away the bin, and silently twisted the knob. Opening the door a few inches, she peeked around the jamb. "Holy shit!"

Not a single piece of furniture, including the counters, remained on its legs. Broken glass was scattered throughout, and a gaping hole in the greenhouse roof looked out at the evening sky. The outside door was still closed and latched.

She backpedaled to the shop and closed the door behind her, unable to process what she saw. She would call Ellington. Not from here—she didn't want to go in the studio to call from his office. She crossed the shop with caution, unlatched and opened the back door, and looked about. After waiting to listen, she ran to her car, happy she had the habit of leaving it unlocked.

The engine coughed to life. She kept the headlights off until she got up to speed. Driving with a vengeance, she raced past the pillared entrance to the park.

# CHAPTER 45

Carl scanned the woods with his beam. "Ms. Farwell? Ms. Farwell, you out there?" Distracted by the rustle of leaves as he walked, he held up every few steps to listen. Other than his breathing, there was no other sound of life. He reached the end of the trail and gathered his thoughts in the open space of the parking lot. Val should have exited from her path and been in plain view by now. His uneasiness grew—an expanding balloon ready to burst.

Lights from the kitchen and service area of the mansion were visible in the distance. Carl held his position, ears tuned for any sound of footsteps among the brush. Maybe she strayed off the trail in the dark. One hand balancing his shotgun, the other sweeping the flashlight at waist level, he called out again, amplifying his voice. "Ms. Farwell?" He reached for his radio and repeated his plea, in case she was out of earshot. He was met with silence.

His head swerved to the sound of thrashing vegetation. Perhaps a hundred yards away. I must have flushed a buck from his hiding spot with all the shouting, he thought. Waving the beam towards the noise, he yelled, "Ms. Farwell? This is Carl, I'm over here."

Fearing Val may have fallen or injured herself, he decided to cross the parking lot and backtrack on the other path to find her. He barely took his first steps when a savage roar thundered through the trees. The shrill scream that followed was more dreadful. Keeping his grip on the light, Carl pumped the twenty-gauge to chamber a round. "Ms. Farwell, are you alright?"

A pitiful voice, more whimper than shout, replied, "Please help me…no, no. He-e-e-lp!" The voice trailed away with surprising speed, amid the sounds of snapping brush.

Carl had no choice but to leave the path, over uneven ground with the extra liability of a loaded shotgun. He followed his instincts, heading towards Val's last cry. Feet advancing in measured steps, senses wired from adrenalin, Carl twitched with each new shadow.

He climbed up a small knoll overlooking the gulley and the mansion beyond, then stopped to listen. Faint moans and sounds of a struggle came from his left. Staying on the crest of the ravine, he closed in on the turmoil.

Carl came upon a clearing of sorts…brush and saplings lay flattened on the ground in a small circle. A crude track cut through the woods, as if a small steam roller crushed all in its wake. It was plain to see the stems were freshly broken.

The grounds manager deliberately pushed the trigger safety off and raised his flashlight and shotgun to shoulder level. Twice he inhaled deeply through his nostrils and exhaled through his mouth. He tried to stay focused, as the invisible cord between hunter and prey tightened with each slow step. Thankfully, he was able to step out of the brush and onto a trail. He darted his eyes to either side. The track of ripped vegetation seemed to end where he stood. He realized he had chanced upon the trail loop between the parking lot to his left and the gorilla to his right. He chose the latter.

Carl paced evenly along the path, his confidence steadied by the firm footing underneath his hunting boots. He soon approached the small rise to see the gorilla poised on its pedestal, frozen in bronzed stride with the struggling woman in his grasp. Although preferring to remain undetected, a sense of duty steeled his spine. He spoke into the radio. "Ms. Farwell? Can you hear me? Please, I'm close by." Only a faint shimmer of dried leaves replied. *Dear God, Valerie, where are you?*

Carl took advantage of his elevation to shine the light in a full circle. He waited for several minutes. Hearing nothing, and fearing the worst, Carl grit his teeth. Better get Charlie to call for help. Calling out one last time, the grounds keeper retreated from the rise to follow the path back to the parking lot.

Trent's nerves and trigger finger grew twitchier with each new sound and passing minute. It wasn't so much the calm, cavalier attitude of the hoodlum sitting on the ground—nor Carl's distant pleas to find Ms. Farwell—but the disturbing animal noises that surrounded him. Holding his rifle in both hands, his eyes and gun barrel swiveled between the malignant sounds and his captive.

For his part, Devyn rested his back against a pillar, watching the moonlight creep across the ground to reach the toppled Fu Dogs. A deep growl punctured the woods. Devyn glanced at his sentry. "There are things going on around us that you and your boss can't control, you know. I might be able to help."

"Shut up, asshole!" Trent aimed the .22 at Devyn to make his point. "I don't need you to be cooking up a bunch of mumbo jumbo bullshit. Keep your fucking trap shut."

Shrugging, Devyn closed his eyes, knowing the keepers had crept closer, now under the nearest spruce to his left. He felt their hesitation, but something was holding them back.

Carl's voice rang out from the far reaches of the woods again, futilely seeking the park director. Devyn needed to come up with a plan. A calm voice interrupted his thoughts, speaking from the direction of the Buddha house.

"A most unusual night. Pleasant enough with the moonlight, but things seem out of sorts, don't they?"

Trent wheeled about to find Ailsa standing in the center of the lawn, hands open and out to her sides. He stammered, "Wh-wh-where did you come from?"

"Easy with the gun, Trent. It's me, Ailsa, from the farm down the road."

"Why are you here?"

Ailsa took a couple small steps forward. "To help get things right. I see my young apprentice"—she gave a disapproving look at Devyn—"has been a little busy this evening."

"Yeah, well he's gone and busted up some valuable statues, and made a mess of things over by the mansion as well. Carl is out in the woods fetching Ms. Farwell as we speak."

Ailsa's eyes lifted past the garden as a guttural scream came from the woods. She nudged closer to Trent. "I fear if we don't take care of this situation soon, we may be too late."

"You stop right there!"

Ailsa slowed her pace. "Nothing bad is going to happen here, Trent. You know me, why don't you lower the gun?"

The young man wet his lips. "I mean it. Keep your distance."

"Okay. Just relax." She held up her hands, gazing at Devyn. "Out looking for some…friends of yours?"

Devyn felt her probing his mind, her eyes searing through his. He mumbled, "They need to go back where they belong."

"Indeed." Her right hand reached across her body and lifted a cord from around her neck. A bronze medallion dangled beneath her hand. "To do that, we need to clear the air, and the woods around us." She closed her eyes in brief meditation, then dug her heel into the lawn, shearing off a piece of turf.

"You see, Devyn, you have to connect with the spirits by melding with their original elements." She crouched to grab the divot. "For creatures of clay, the earth from which they're made."

Trent stared at her with eyes wide open. "What are you doing with that dirt? Put it back down!"

Ailsa gave Trent a fleeting smile, then redirected her gaze to the woods beyond. Her sturdy hand crumbled the clod of earth. She then rubbed some of the soil onto the talisman between her fingers. Speaking in a language Devyn didn't understand, she tightened her grip on the charm. The moonlight dimmed and a gust of wind blew through the length of the lawn, causing the trees around them to moan and sway.

An invisible cold hand pushed against Devyn's chest. The air and trees then settled and the garden regained its silver glow under the moon.

Ailsa smiled, her hair in disarray from the wind. Glancing to the shadows below the trees, she called out. "Time to return to where you belong, my friends."

Face contorted with fear, Trent pivoted at the sound of padded paws rushing into the garden. He squeezed his trigger, and the crack of the rifle shattered the silent garden.

# CHAPTER 46

Ellington paused at the bottom of the knoll, unsure of his location. He tried to retrace the previous walk in his mind. But that had been in daylight and his meager penlight wasn't much help. He recalled following a series of right-hand turns from the parking lot, which had brought him to his present location. He reasoned in a half-voice, "If I do the opposite and veer left at each fork instead, I'll reach the parking area." There was only one way to find out.

The ceramicist, still doggedly hoisting the parcel across his shoulder, wound his way through wide tree trunks. Relying on the light's timid glow, he avoided roots and stones as his shoes tramped along a carpet of discarded leaves. He came upon the wooden bridge, ten feet across, crossing the pachysandra-filled ditch. The familiar feature eased some of his misgivings.

As he aimed his beam to glance at the plants, Ellington's toe caught a seam between the far end of a bridge plank and the path. He tumbled onto the soft earth. Upon impact, the penlight flew from his hand and splashed into the furrow.

Humbled more than injured, Ellington gained his hands and knees and spied the light glowing from the ooze. His hands searched the ground about him, and finding a small branch, he poked at the light, trying to flip it out of the mire. After several attempts, the tacky soup relented, and the device popped onto the ground in front of him. Ellington grabbed a handful of leaves and rubbed it, gaining little except smearing mud over the device.

Letting go of his pride, he rubbed the light on the side of his pants. He gained his feet only to have the beam sputter erratically. Ellington scolded, "You can do better than that." He tapped the light on the heel of his palm, which steadied the glow. Satisfied, he renewed his hike. The light flickered after three steps. Having to thump the penlight at regular intervals, he meandered under expanding moonlight. "I'm not going to get anywhere fast at this rate."

Ellington finally prevailed over the device to get a steady glow. He realized his constant tinkering had caused him to leave the ditch farther behind than planned. Taking stock of his surroundings, he noted the path had widened to a trail, large enough for a car and firmed by limestone gravel pressed into the earth. "Can't say I remember this, but it does seem to be a main drag." He looked overhead at the narrow cut of open sky between arching branches. "At least for out here."

Wanting to avoid another pratfall, Ellington chose to remain on the more solid, straighter, and level trail. He sped up his gait. A wooded plain bordered the trail to his right, and a low but steep embankment to his left. He passed under the silhouettes of several massive sycamores, their ghostly white bark looming out of the dark.

Despite the ease of the hike, doubt dragged on Ellington's mind. He reckoned he was now a solid half mile beyond the footbridge; the path to the gorilla should have cut off to the left by now. "It seems I ended up on more of a service road than a foot trail," he thought out loud.

Ellington paused again to survey his surroundings; his penlight diminished by a film of dirt on the lens. He had two options, go all the way back to the ditch, and try to find the trail he had sought in the first place...or the easier choice, forge ahead. At least he his current bearing would likely lead to a landmark, perhaps a building or paved road. The rising moon wedged itself between the treetops directly above the lane. Compared to the shadows all around him, heading under the silver beacon appealed to his instincts. Still mumbling over the unreliable light, he proceeded ahead.

As he rounded a bend, a shriek cleaved the silence of the woods. His body tensed. It was followed by a scream of distress—from a female voice.

Heart pounding in his chest, Ellington tried to make out the direction of the sound. It came from behind and to his left, but the embankment masked the range. A second scream, more abrupt than the first, cried out.

"My God, that sounds like Valerie!" Ellington idled in place briefly, then opened into a jog along the lane, the pinpoint light waving up and down in synch with his pumping arms. Nearly stumbling twice, he came upon a split in the lane. Ahead, a gate marked a rough intersection with a road. To his left, a wide path rose over the embankment. He spoke out loud to bolster his relief. "At last, contact with civilization."

His first impulse was to make for the road. "With the moonlight, I could cover a couple miles quickly on the even surface. Even without my running shoes." He hesitated, unsure of the road's direction, and reassessed the path to the left.

The ache of the satchel on Ellington's shoulder gave a subtle reminder that running in ambiguous moonlight, even if he chose the right direction, may be more than he bargained for. He clambered up the knoll, and following the trail, soon reached a clearing on the summit.

Catching his breath, he was surprised to see a curious artifact. A round concrete pedestal, lacking any other feature. Drawing closer, Ellington squinted at the oddity, speculating on its purpose. "Someone needs to commission an installation for this setting." A sly smile spread across his face. "At last, the perfect place to lighten my load."

Reaching in his satchel, he lifted the figurine and cradled it within his arms. "A fitting venue for your beauty, my dear." Ellington gave *Blue Desire* a feathery kiss, bent over, then took two steps back. The smiling, sultry nude posed front and center on the oversized stage, illuminated in moonlight. The sculptor clapped his hands. "Bravo. Your most provocative performance to date. Bravo!" Ellington exalted in his choice of venue. "Farewell, two-faced Medusa."

A feral snarl, resonating with spite and power, shook the clearing. Dumbfounded, Ellington spun about to face his critic but was denied the opportunity to respond to its hostile opinion.

# CHAPTER 47

Carl figured his inability to track Val's assailant beyond the gorilla statue could only mean the fiend…, or fiends, had fled deeper into the woods. If the direction of the escape headed towards the parking lot and mansion, the possibility of someone seeing a vehicle used for the abduction was in play. Or they might have gone towards the river. Whoever it was, they seemed to have knowledge of the area.

His mind whirling from so many unexplained clues, he teetered on the absurd notion the park director had vanished into thin air. He raised his walkie-talkie. "Charlie, come in." Already on pins and needles, he shouted, "Damn it, Charlie! Where are you?"

A groggy voice replied. "I'm here, I'm here. What's the big rush?"

"Haven't you been listening? Let me guess, you turned down the volume on your radio."

"Well, I was driving back and forth all around the estate, wasting gas like you told me to. I must have drifted off while parked by the greenhouse."

"Get your ass to the nearest phone and call the sheriff's station. Now!"

"What?"

"I said call the sheriff."

"About what?"

"Just do it. Tell them to meet us at the public parking area, it's an emergency. Possible kidnapping."

"What? Who...How?"

"Get to the goddam phone."

"What's going on?"

"I said now, goddam it." Carl replaced his radio in his belt, having little patience for further banter with the older man. He reached the parking lot, keeping his shotgun ready. A report, sounding like a .22, rang out from his right. Carl double-timed across the lot and entered the vine walk. He couldn't clear his head from a disturbing vision—Val deep in the woods, or by the river, being ravaged in lonely terror.

Despair weighing on his shoulders, the grounds manager left the walled vines, turned past the Buddha house and came upon the milky light of the lawn. There were now three figures at the far end, two standing, one sitting hunched on the ground. Slowing to a walk, Carl once again released the safety on his twenty gauge. As he drew near, he saw Trent crouched on the ground, the young troublemaker leaning on one of the pillars, and that the new arrival was a woman—her face hidden in shadow.

The whereabouts of Trent's .22 was unknown. Carl treaded carefully. "Everyone remain where you are."

The woman turned slowly. "Easy there, Carl. It's me, Ailsa Winters."

"Ailsa? What in the hell are you doing here?"

"I came to help."

Still wary, Carl gazed at Devyn. "Yeah, well we caught that farmhand of yours vandalizing the statues."

Aisla glanced at Devyn, then reset her eyes on Carl. "Oh? Which ones?" She pointed to the top of the pillars. "Those?" She swept her hand to the ground behind her. "Or these?"

Carl shifted his gaze to the columns. Incredibly, two Fu Dogs snarled defiantly from their perch. The ransacked figures still remained broken on the ground. He backpedaled, not believing his senses. "How did this...?" Narrowing his eyes, he asked, "What sort of game are you playing here?"

Ailsa swept an open hand in a welcoming gesture. "You'd make me feel a whole lot better if you'd stop brandishing your shotgun our way. There's nothing to fear here."

Carl aimed his beam at his assistant's face. "Trent. What the hell happened? Where'd they get these two other blue statues from? How'd they lift them?"

The younger man sat, arms wrapped about his knees, rocking back and forth. His colorless face reflecting a ghostly alabaster sheen in the light. His rifle lay on the grass several feet away.

"Trent. Do you hear me?"

Trent stuttered in a barely audible voice. "Th-those things…ca-came out of the trees. Ran right over me. Their big eyes…"

Carl lowered his gun and spoke gently. "Did these two overpower you? No shame if they did."

Trent looked at him with petrified eyes. "Out of the trees. Running on all fours."

"Thank goodness he's a poor shot," Devyn said.

Carl spun towards the young man. "How would you like a mouthful of birdshot?"

Dismayed with his lack of tact, Ailsa gave Devyn a sidelong glance. She calmly said, "Carl, I know it's hard to believe and accept. But the heart of the matter is that everything is back in order. You don't have to worry anymore."

Carl glared at her. "The hell I don't. Ms. Farwell is missing out in the woods. I think some creep attacked her."

Ailsa raised her eyebrows. "Attacked. What makes you think that?"

"She called me on the radio." Overcome by the unexplained, he paused to gather his wits. "I heard her scream out there, I tried to track her, but…" He shifted his focus to Devyn. "That one there"—Carl then pointed at Ailsa—"and maybe you, too, are part of something here. Believe you me, we're going to get to the bottom of this."

Ailsa closed her eyes, took two deep breaths, then popped them open. "We have no time to waste, though I worry we might be too late." She nodded to the portal between the pillars. "Come on, Devyn."

"Hold on. That kid isn't going anywhere. Sheriff deputies are on their way. We need to work this out with the law."

"Carl, you need to believe me. We may yet save Ms. Farwell."

Carl raised his gun again. "Nope."

Resigned, Ailsa folded her arms. "I fear for her, from something far worse than you can imagine."

"Oh, really? I think this little shit is involved somehow."

Ailsa's eyes hardened. "And how would that be? Wasn't he standing here with you when the radio call came in? And all the while with Trent while you were stumbling around in the woods?"

"Maybe he had some sort of accomplice."

The matron rolled her eyes in disgust. "Carl, when are you going to get it through your head there are other possibilities." She paused to gaze at the sentinel Fu Dogs proudly peering over the garden. "Highly unlikely possibilities, I'll grant you."

Carl looked down upon Trent, shivering on the ground. He pondered. What the hell is going on here? He considered another option within his mind. Val and Ellington were having an honest dust up the last time he'd seen them together.

Disconnected gears meshed inside Carl's head. Was it the sculptor who told the delinquent about the fake Fu Dogs? Ellington had an obvious interest in them. Between him and the kid, they could have orchestrated a lot of the recent mayhem together. Where was Professor Ellington Rose at this moment, artist in residence who liked to make statues of naked women?

# CHAPTER 48

Wispy fog crept from the banks of the Sangamon, circling tree trunks as it snaked across the flood plain. The rising sun had yet to dispel dawn's chill, but the search party was good to go. Carl, Trent, a handful of sheriff's deputies, and local volunteers converged at the parking lot on the Old Levee Road, on the opposite bank of the river from the mansion. After a frantic phone conversation with Ashley overnight, Carl agreed to keep the workings of the search party discreet, as best he could. The Taft event was still on, and a veneer of normalcy would be best.

Carl hoped the State Police forensic team, arriving later in the morning, got the message to park on the far side of the river as well. If the press found out what was going on, all bets were off. There are some things in life you can't control.

The volunteers split into teams to search three sections of the estate— one each on the paths and woods along the north and south banks of the river, and the third in the woods bordered by the mansion, the Old Timber Road, and the north bank of the river. Charlie was assigned to park by the river bridge to direct any latecomers and deflect any curious gawkers. If anyone asked, he was to tell them it was a training exercise for search dogs.

Carl and Trent crossed the bridge with their team and hiked away from the river. After reaching the crossroad near the Buddha house, Carl spaced the trackers twenty yards apart along the roadside. Once complete, the line stretched along the

Old Timber Road from the estate entrance  to the Gate House. With three blasts of a whistle, the entire line advanced, returning towards the north bank of the river. Avoiding the mansion, the team rolled past the parking lot and Fu Dog Garden, becoming more deliberate when they reached the woods.

Carl purposely centered himself in the formation, along with the canine teams. Boots scraped and scuffed through leaves, as the dogs tugged on their leashes to gather a scent. He peered at the sun, a faint orange disk in the murky air. Visibility could have been better. Then again, he wasn't sure of his desire to see what might lie before him.

As he picked his way around a maple, a shrill whistle came from his right. "Over, here!" Carl perked up on the hope of finding a clue. He jogged towards a volunteer with a bright orange hunting cap and jacket.

Pointing to the ground, the man said, "Right there, Carl."

Carl's eyes fell upon a woman's white blouse, torn and twisted with a dark bra, trampled into the bed of mud and leaves.

A deputy bent over to pick up the tattered garment. Carl grabbed his shoulder and said tersely, "Let it be. Could be evidence."

The volunteer gaped at Carl. "You think it's her clothes?"

Carl grimaced, grappling to remember what Val wore the last time he saw her. "Could be." The grounds manager looked about the scene. His shoulders sagged as he spotted the trail of flattened brush he had followed the night before, just a few feet away. "Son of a bitch, I missed this last night." He clicked the button on his two-way. "We need the dogs over here to get a scent. About a hundred yards south of the public parking lot, nearly even with the mansion."

"Roger that."

As others gathered about, Carl studied the forest floor. He drifted towards the rough-hewn path of crushed saplings and retraced his steps from the night before. Reaching the crest of a small rise, he peered towards the gully at the bottom. Halfway down the slope, he spied an object hanging from a small branch.

He moved closer and inhaled sharply. A woman's brown leather jacket. Val's jacket, nearly ripped in two. Carl closed his eyes, the noise from the search parties and excited dogs drifted from his mind. Nausea crept through his body. She's a goner, he thought. He clenched his teeth. Gotta find that son of a bitch sculptor.

A frantic young man bounded through the trees. "Mr. Lipinski! Mr. Lipinski!"

"Over here," Carl yelled.

The runner reached him, his eyes wild. Out of breath, he blurted, "Our team found a body. Close to the river, down this slope and about two hundred yards away."

Carl grabbed the youth by the shoulders. "Is it a woman? A dark-haired woman? Answer me!"

"No, no", the younger man said defensively. "It's a man. With long hair and…"

"Speak up."

"Naked. Looks like he was slashed and torn apart and…."

The older man shook the messenger violently. "I said speak up, dammit!"

"His…one of his legs is missing, like it was chewed off."

A nearby deputy subconsciously unlatched his holster. A lively buzz circled about the search team, as several of them broke away to go look for themselves, including the canine teams. Following after, Carl said, "Show me the way, kid."

Trent called out, "Hey! We didn't finish our search all the way to the end of the perimeter."

Carl waved a hand at him. "Gather up who you can and do what you can. Spread them farther apart if you have to. I have enough on my hands for now."

# Balance

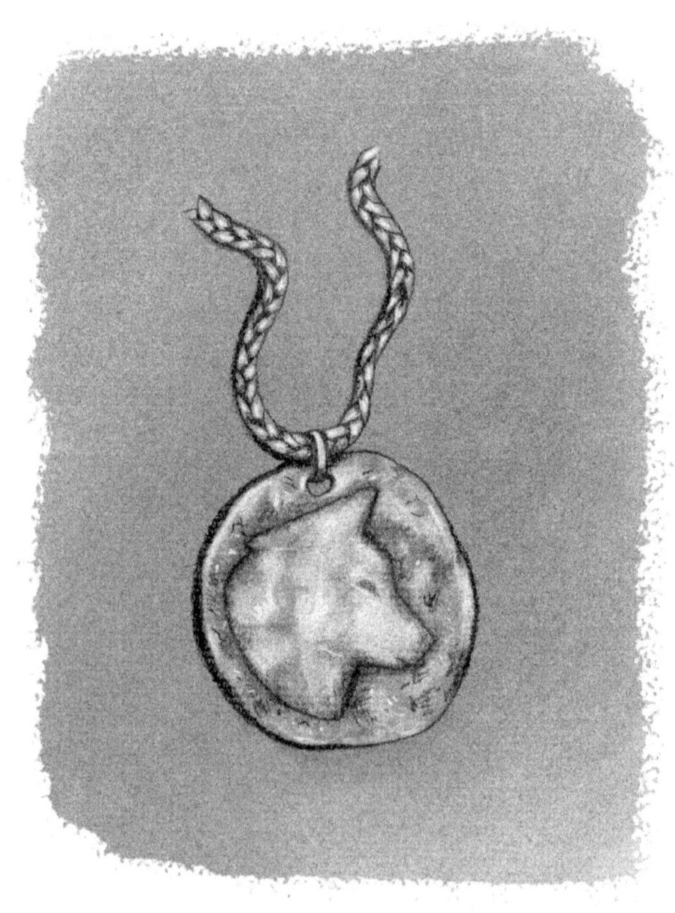

The remaining relics of St. Fillan were also in the care of the *deòradh*, though the nature and fate of these relics is less certain than the others.

***The Messer*** - It is feared this relic was destroyed, most likely during the rampant zealotry of the reformation during the 16th and 17th centuries. Many hold forth that the Messer was the manuscript of scripture Fillan wrote using the light from his left hand, the ink of which would illuminate in the dark.

***The Fergy-*** The least known of the relics, its origin and substance forgotten over time. The hereditary *Dior-a-Fairge* had a croft at Auchlyne in Glen Dochart and kept the relic in a nearby chapel, *Caibel-na-Fairge*, before the 'dark and drublie' days of the Highland clearances and iron-fisted English rule. It was said the Fergy was the most mystical of St. Fillan's relics. Yet, the physical nature and the powers the relic may have bestowed upon the saint, or in what fashion he used it, have passed from memory of the living.

Chronicles of Inchaffray Abbey

# CHAPTER 49

Sunshine warmly embraced the 'Celebration of Laredo Taft and The Roots of Women in Midwestern Sculpture'—as the event was now named— with a vibrant flourish. Despite the perfect weather, Ashley Plambeck's anxiety was through the roof. Dean Duffey, splendid as a peacock in an Illini orange jacket, blue tie, black slacks and hundred-dollar shoes, mingled with guests on one side of the pavilion. Jim Kramer, who offset the team colors with a dark blue sports jacket, orange tie, and khakis, worked the far side. The brunch was drawing to a close, the chocolate mousse torte served, and the program was due to begin. The pair of administrators meandered ominously ever closer to the dais where she stood.

As she scanned the agenda, two problems confronted her— Valerie and Ellington. Her boss was on tap to emcee the program. The sculptor was the program.

She expected the artist to be casually late, but Valerie? The one who micromanaged everything? Not a chance. Ashley allowed herself a glimmer of a smile. The mousse had been her personal choice, far better than Valerie's ice cream on a brownie.

There was something terribly wrong. Carl, Piatt County Sheriff by his side, visited her earlier in the day. The grounds manager was haggard, and his baggy eyes lacked sleep. With the help of the law and other volunteers, they were scouring the estate, most notably along the river.

Not knowing what the search would uncover, Carl had suggested keeping things under wraps until more details emerged. He seemed especially keen on any possible contact with Professor Rose in the vicinity of the mansion the prior evening. Ashley pondered what sparked Carl's new-found interest in him.

The Dean, drawing ever closer to the front of the gathering, glanced at Ashley. Smiling and shaking hands, his eye contact with her was a far cry from warm and gracious. Chewing her lower lip, Ashley scanned the brochure, elbows resting on the podium. She needed to fabricate a plan, and fast. Lying to her superiors and an audience of well-heeled donors wasn't her forte.

The Dean managed to clear the last of his glad-handing, converged with Jim at the steps leading to the dais, and walked across the small stage. "Any word on the whereabouts of those two?"

Ashley replied meekly. "No. I don't know what happened to them."

Dean Duffey viewed the audience. "They're going to get restless soon. We need to get started."

"We can have you unveil the work by Professor Rose." Ashley gestured towards the hooded sculpture on the small table behind the podium. "Then we can buy some time by saying there's been a small change in the order of the schedule. Perhaps a stroll through the mansion to view the White Rabbit pieces. After that, a tour of the studio, to demonstrate the value of having an artist in residence."

The older man responded with an icy glare.

Ashley wilted. "It's the best I can do. We could say Valerie is sick, and I'm standing in for her."

"And"—the Dean turned to fix his wrath on Jim, casting responsibility for the no-show ceramicist on his supervisor—"how do we make do without the artist?" He paused, thinking of the potential donations flitting away by the time the day was over. "Alright. I'll give the usual welcome speech"—he jerked his thumb at the hidden figure—"then I'll unveil the statuette and we'll wing it from there."

The Dean brought the program to order, providing charm, wit, and stature. While he talked, Ashley solidified a plan, but she needed to get to a phone. She stepped to the podium after an exuberant introduction provided by the Dean, seasoned with remorse over the untimely illness of Ms. Farwell.

As a wave of uncertainty flooded her mind, the young woman fought to keep her voice from cracking. She offered a brief history of the event, praise for the great sculptor, Laredo Taft, and gratitude for Professor Rose's installation that would now be unveiled to celebrate the occasion.

Gaining confidence with each passing minute, Ashley approached the small table and gestured to the Dean to slip the navy-blue velvet off the figure.

A collective murmur buzzed from the audience, Ashley blanched, and a puzzled look crossed Dean Duffey's face.

A blue, nude woman, with legs crossed and looking over her shoulder, sat on the hood of a red sports car. The figure had a small necklace with a tiny sapphire pendant and a dollar sign engraved on her back. Her defiant expression had a hint of cruelty. In large letters, scrawled on the base, were two words. *All Mine.*

A smattering of tentative applause ensued.

Kim opened an eye to peek at the phone by her bed, wishing it would disappear. Eight rings and counting. She rolled her head on the pillow, waiting for the obnoxious sound to end. Ten rings and counting. I shouldn't have turned off the answering machine, she thought. It's him, the last person I want to talk to on this planet. Twelve rings and counting. Scowling, she sat up, ready to tell her advisor to fuck off once and for all.

"What do you want, now?"

A sterile silence ensued, followed by a tremulous female voice. "Is this Kim Okuma?"

Kim relaxed her shoulders. "Yeah, sorry, I thought you were someone else."

"Kim, this is Ashley Plambeck here at Allerton Park. You might remember, I'm Ms. Farwell's Assistant Director."

Running a hand through the bird's nest, which was once straight hair, she replied. "And?"

Again, there was a pause at the other end. "I have a favor to ask of you…a huge favor. Something strange is going on over here…"

Kim grunted, thinking, tell me about it.

"We've finished the brunch this morning in the pavilion, you know for the Laredo Taft event."

The grad student rubbed her drowsy eyelids, wondering if Ellington had pushed Ashley to make the call. "Yeah."

"It's weird, neither Valerie nor Ellington have shown up. We can't track them down anywhere. I even called Ellington's wife. She's super worried."

Here we go, Kim thought to herself. El has finally managed to get himself caught in an affair that's going to go public. "I suppose you checked the studio?"

"Twice. Carl and the crew have been searching for him. The sheriff is also involved. Apparently, the greenhouse was vandalized."

Reminded of her horror, Kim paled and slumped against her headboard. Half-awake as she tried to take it all in, she asked, "Sheriff? What do you want from me? I haven't seen Ellington for a couple days."

"Do you think you could give his seminar about the White Rabbits? Maybe even a tour of the shop and studio? I understand the university sent a crew to clean the place up a bit."

Good luck with that, she thought. "I had an awfully long night."

"Please?"

"A long night with poor sleep…*very* poor sleep."

"We have some big donors here, plus the Dean and the Art School Director…we need to buy time while we keep looking for Valerie and Ellington."

Kim wondered if someone should check the airport for flights to Acapulco for the absconded duo.

"We'll see that you get an honorarium…a most gracious honorarium."

Kim considered the offer. If she played her cards well, she might be able to cash in her chips for a change in advisors to finish her degree "Okay, I'll do it."

She could feel the relief through the wires. "Thank you! Thank you! Uh…can you be here in under an hour?"

The bedraggled grad student squinted at her alarm clock. Ten o'clock, an ungodly time to be calling her this particular morning. "With the drive from town, let's make it more on the long side of an hour."

"Perfect, come right up and park by the manor entrance. We already have the slide set ready to go in the room. We'll keep an eye out for you."

The line clicked off. Kim hung up the receiver and scrambled out from under her sheets. "I better make it a quick shower and grab a burger on the road." She smiled to herself. No doubt the slides were ready to go, I was the one who did the research, made them, and put them into the carousel. The life of a grad student—same as it ever was.

A diesel-fuming giant shook Devyn from his catatonic slumber. Sunshine streamed through his window. His stomach grumbled, it was well past breakfast time. He got up, put on some clothes, and grabbed his sweatshirt.

Hurrying down the stairway, he popped outside to confront the green combine idling thirty feet away. Norm and Ailsa were conversing in the farmhouse yard. Still groggy, Devyn straggled over to join them. Skipper heralded his arrival with unnecessary barking.

Norm wheeled about and took a long, hard look at the young man from under his John Deere cap. "I figured you'd get the message. A combine idling by your window makes a nice alarm clock, doesn't it?"

Devyn rubbed his face. "Sorry, I guess I slept in this morning."

Norm gestured to the machine shed. "Well, go get the tandem and get ready to follow me to the field. Your beauty rest is over. We have corn to harvest. I can't imagine what you were up to last night."

Devyn shifted his eyes to Ailsa. She called out as the young man turned to obey Norm. "Hold on a minute, Devyn." She went in the house and returned with a packet wrapped in wax paper and a thermos in her hands. "A couple of egg sandwiches and coffee. Take them along with you."

Devyn reached out, his grateful eyes shifted between his benefactor and inquisitor. "Thank you. On my way." He loped to the shed with quick strides.

Norm grumbled, "He's spending too much of his time over on the estate."

Ailsa hugged her husband. "I wouldn't worry about that. I'm confident he's had his fill of the place for a while." She gripped him tighter. "You make damn sure to be careful and don't you"—she nodded towards Devyn—"or let him, do anything foolish around the machinery. Dangerous enough as it is."

# CHAPTER 50

It was bound to happen. After a flotilla of state police vehicles descended onto the estate, leaks from the county sheriff's office flowed to *The Journal Republican*. The story quickly got picked up by the AP and Chicago papers, and a deluge of reporters flooded Piatt County. For two weeks, Monticello was choked with cameras, sound bites, and unwanted gapers.

Footage and photos of divers dragging the Sangamon River, the local courthouse, the missing couple, the park entrance and mansion, and even the Fu Dog Garden set the scene as reporters taped reels for the five o'clock news.

The remains of a white male, medium build, likely in his mid-twenties, and reportedly found without clothes, still remained unidentified, despite intensive forensic analysis. Foul play was suspected. Charlie fanned the fires of speculation during interviews regarding the victim's demise. He gave accounts of how vagrants used to camp on the estate, especially when the nearby rail line was running. He proposed the victim fell prey to cougars—now upgraded from bobcats—after witnessing them himself while patrolling the estate.

Tips and sightings bombarded the police; few were founded in fact. With each passing day, the trail of evidence grew colder, as did the weather.

Ashley Plambeck gazed out the office window in the mansion. Watching an occasional snow flurry flit by, she took stock of her exhaustion. The university administration deemed her to be best suited as the new interim park director. She equated interim as meaning, "Don't rock the boat and make sure the lights get turned on and off each day."

Her appointment also filled a void, to serve as a stopgap for the PR shitstorm swirling about the estate. The phone rang constantly, and reporters often stalked outside the mansion, waiting for her to appear when she left the building.

Ashley slumped in the large armchair behind the desk, Val's desk, her mind rambling in all directions. She thought of Ellington's wife, Julie, badgered by reporters outside her home, while driving her son to school, shopping…

The conjecture and rumors based on 'reliable sources' kept on coming. Perhaps it was a love affair gone **awry**—complete with a murder-suicide—or a mysterious stalker, now dead in the woods. Others believed there had been various attacks from a bear, a pack of feral dogs, or perhaps the most outlandish possibility, testimonials of strange lights in the sky during the night of the disappearance. Ashley sighed, alien abduction would have its benefits, if nothing else to leave all this behind.

She was profoundly sorry for Val. She could be hard-driven and a task master. But she was supportive and generous. Ashley forced the darker possibilities of Val's fate from her mind. She had tried her best to show optimism and reach out to Val's family, living near Milwaukee. They were in shock.

The university, to demonstrate collective remorse over the missing employees, suspended the artist in residence program. Ashley suspected Dean Duffey suggested the closure, probably because the fund-raising event didn't come close to meeting the expectations. She wondered what the Van Teeswaters, who commissioned the installation, thought of the *All Mine* sculpture, unveiled in their honor at the brunch. She was still perplexed by the last minute change from the original statuette.

Thank God for Kim, who was willing, and paid well, to navigate the dismantling of the ceramic studio, and get the material returned to campus.

Ashley looked out the window, across the pond, and to the woods on the far side of the meadow. Her perspective of the estate had changed. The flowers, manicured gardens, and whimsical statues had lost their innocence. The statues seemed to judge her now whenever she walked by, studies of silent ridicule in bronze and stone. Even the warm opulence of the mansion had become unsettling. She couldn't shake off a feeling of isolation and vulnerability. As the days shortened, she made a point of leaving for home while daylight remained.

# CHAPTER 51

Norm stooped within the interior of his '31 Model A coupe. The deep blue body, detached from the chassis, rested off the ground on a mishmash of sawhorses and oak boards. Cramped in the tight space, screwdriver in hand, he fumbled to align a machine screw with a hole in the windshield hinge. Devyn and Laverne were stationed outside, even with the firewall. They held the framed windshield in place, tilting the top end towards Norm.

Adjusting his trouble light, Norm muttered, "Hard to see if the holes line up in here." He glanced at Devyn. "Lower your side a bit more, it's not fitting right." Devyn eased his end as ordered. Satisfied, Norm twisted his screwdriver furiously to drive home the screw.

Laverne winked at Devyn. "Thank God for magnetic screwdrivers, be a real bitch to have those little bastards fall below." Norm ignored her comment. She added, "I wonder if it was a three-person job to attach a windshield on Henry Ford's assembly line in Dearborn? They'd be doing this while the bodies were rolling on the line. How about it, Norm, think you could do this on a moving target?"

"Just keep your tongue and the windshield still until I drive in a second screw."

Devyn and Laverne grinned at one another.

Letting out a breath, Norm finished the second fastener. "That'll hold her in place, you can let go. I can get the rest of the screws in on my own now."

Devyn gently swung the bottom of the windshield, now hinged on top. "This opens over the hood to let in air under the windshield? It seems backwards."

"Pretty cool, huh?" Laverne replied. "Although, back then most folks wouldn't drive these things over thirty-five."

"Is there a windshield wiper?"

Norm pointed to the top of the windshield. "Got to hook it up. Runs on a vacuum line off the intake manifold."

Devyn stepped back to admire the machine. "How do you know so much about this old car. Do you have a manual?"

Norm gave him a stern look. "Manual? Who needs them?" He aimed his screwdriver in the direction of the farm machinery. "The same goes for those. All the money spent and they give you instructions that are worth no more than tits on a boar. They'll tell you everything but what you want to know."

Devyn recoiled from the tirade. He glanced to the other side of the garage, where four tires with straw-yellow wire wheels supported the naked chassis and engine. "It'll be a sweet ride when it's all put back together."

"Well. Since you got those fenders painted, we're about ready to start sorting things out. Body isn't too heavy, but we'll need Ailsa to help lift it into place." He peered at Devyn. "After we finish running corn to the river."

Norm fished out another screw from his pocket and went to work.

Laverne and Devyn walked across the shop to look at the four fenders, painted gloss black. She gave a low whistle. "Is this your handiwork?"

Devyn reached out to trace his fingers over the closest fender. "Yeah."

"You've got some talent, dude."

"It took me a lot of practice over three years. I learned how to use the paint gun on a few totaled wrecks at the body shop. You need to sweep the sprayer at the right pace and distance from the surface, so the paint flows and spreads. Too fast or far away, you don't cover well. Too close or slow, the paint sags." He sighed. "If that happens, you have to sand it all down and start over. Took me two tries on the hood of my Scout."

"You've got the touch."

"Colors brighten a dull world."

Norm joined them. "Perhaps I'll let you brighten up the old twenty."

Laverne poked Devyn's shoulder. "Look at you. Painter and pinochle player." She let go an easy laugh. "Grandpa Billy was beside himself with the last whupping you gave him. He's wanting a rematch."

Norm left to find the windshield wiper blade, while Laverne and Devyn strolled out of the garage. Laverne tilted her head and asked, "How about cashing in my chips for a touch up on my Chevy? It's getting near time to mothball it for the winter."

His eyes opened like a kid under a Christmas tree. "I'm down on that."

She stuck her thumb in a side pocket of her jeans. "I'll drive it over sometime." She gestured back to the garage with a head roll. "It seems you've gotten a bit settled here with the old man. Still kind of odd how you ended up here. Makes me think." She gave him a winking smile. "Which I try not to do too often."

Ailsa appeared on the back porch of the house. "You're done with Norm's hobby car?"

Laverne replied, "Yup. And the grain truck is back with the spring repaired. It's all ready to make the runs to the elevator again."

"Well, come in and have a coffee and apple spice cake."

"Sounds like a plan."

As they entered the kitchen, Laverne said, "Hey, did you hear Piatt County made the news again? It seems there were sightings of our own local Bigfoot running about earlier in the month. It was seen in the woods near the Allerton Road. Big as a gorilla somebody said, but you know how people exaggerate."

Devyn exchanged a glance with Ailsa and stayed silent.

# Chapter 52

Valerie and Ellington remained missing. The sum of the evidence amounted to torn clothes, barefoot human prints in the mud by the river, and—despite thorough searches of missing person records—an unidentified body. For this effort. two days' worth of helicopter fuel was spent, many law officers collected overtime, and a volunteer sprained an ankle.

A new lead arose when a second set of clothes, torn and blood-stained, and a broken pair of eyeglasses, were found two hundred yards from where the body was discovered. Professor Rose's wife identified the articles to be his. Yet, this only added uncertainty to the case. She had previously testified the body found in the woods was not her husband's.

The state police questioned all the employees of Allerton Park, Ellington's wife, Julie Rose, his colleagues—including Dean Duffey and Director Kramer—their neighbors in Urbana, and finally, Norm, Aisla and—due to Carl's insistence—Devyn. There were financial and insurance records to pore over, and past relationships for both Ellington and Valerie. All these paths dead-ended until a deputy patrolling along the Old Levee Road spotted a woman wearing a grey jogging outfit and—what he described later as a barefoot hippie-type with long hair—running across the bridge and vanishing by the river.

Search parties once again rallied in the parking lot by the Lost Garden. Carl was among them, eager to pounce on the trail. The dogs arrived before sunset but failed to make a hit. After an hour of stumbling and cursing through the brush in twilight, the sheriff called off the search until the next day.

A light blue Chevy pickup remained in the parking lot after all had left. Carl refused to give up. Shotgun in hand, flashlight sweeping the ground, he first traced the circular hiking trail that looped back to the parking area. He then made his way along the bank of the river. Walking cautiously; he tuned his ears for any unusual sounds. The going was slow, twigs swept across his face, roots and small stones snagged his boots.

He came upon a massive sycamore, its bleached trunk nearly a yard wide. Random leaves still sprinkled the branches, yellow platters spotted with brown decay. His eyes caught an unexpected find by the base of the trunk. A small mound of ash lay on the ground. Fresh, damp leaves had been scraped away in a wide arc, exposing bare earth below the fire site. Carl crouched to lay his hand onto the cinders. They weren't warm, nor were they wet. Someone had lit a fire since the rain a few days ago. He glanced away from the tree and saw what seemed to be the remains of a rabbit—furry hind feet, entrails, and a long-eared head,

Cat-like footsteps stalked Carl from behind. A twig cracked to his left, alerting him to pivot, just as a blow fell upon his shoulder. A second strike crashed onto the back of his skull, shooting flashes of light through his eyes, which then faded to black.

Carl's eyes opened to see a blurry moon directly overhead. He was flat on his back, the scent of dried leaves in his nostrils. His lower neck and shoulder ached; the back of his head throbbed. After taking several long breaths, the moon came into focus, framed by sparse branches. His skin felt clammy.

Groaning, he rolled onto his side, then dragged himself onto all fours. He paused to fight off a wave of nausea. The trees about him were cast in patches of grey and silver. He grasped a fallen log and steadied himself to gain a seat on the moss-covered bark.

Searching the small clearing with anxiety, he heard or saw nothing beyond the sighing of the breeze through the limbs above. It occurred to him his hands were empty, no gun, no light. Shivering, Carl realized his vest was missing. He thought. Sweet Jesus, where did that go?

His got back on all fours to scramble the leaf litter with his hands. He had no idea if his shotgun was nearby. If it was, it wouldn't matter if the gun was fifteen or a hundred feet away in the pallid light. The flashlight was the bigger loss. A distressing thought crossed his mind. In near panic, he tamped his pants pocket then his rear pocket with his hand. He still had his pickup keys and wallet. He sat still, shivering and thinking.

One thing he knew, he must have been lying on the ground for at least an hour, judging by how far the moon had inched across the sky. He needed to get moving and to his truck, the cold was boring through his body. Gaining his feet, Carl looked about and guessed the direction of the river. From there, he could follow the footpath to the parking lot. He shuffled his feet forward and almost fell over as his toe caught a firm branch lying among the decaying leaves. Carl bent over and stiffly picked up the branch.

The bough had no side twigs, was six feet long and two inches in diameter. It would make a good staff to prop him along in the dark. He paused as his hand ran over a knob on the top end, wondering if the staff had also served as a club.

Carl willed himself to go on, his stagger gradually becoming more even, though his pace remained slow. The thought of his pickup, heater turned on full, kept him going. With gratitude for the little victories in life, he came to the parking lot. Never had he appreciated his Chevy as he did now. Oozing his sore body into the cab, he shut the door. With the heater fan blasting at high speed, he settled back in the seat to collect his thoughts, then remembered his wife. He mumbled, "Damn. Marlene is probably fit to be tied with worry."

# Chapter 53

The news frenzy reignited after the grounds manager, Mr. Carl Lipinski, age forty-eight, was assaulted while patrolling Allerton Park. For a third time, a search for a perpetrator ensued, and for a third time, puzzled law enforcement officials came up empty handed. Convinced a violent felon was in the area, citizens were urged to lock their doors and be wary of strangers. Interviews with local residents suggested some sort of cult, living off the land, had injured Mr. Lipinski, and abducted the missing park director and sculptor. One local resident was quoted as saying, "Well, you might expect these sorts of things given the types of statues in that place."

Feeding the cows that evening, Devyn wondered how they could thrive in the sharp wind knifing across the open fields. Dairy cows in Pennsylvania were housed in warm barns during this kind of weather. Over supper, Ailsa explained as long as they had a windbreak and a place to stay dry, they'd be fine. "Angus are just like that." Her catchall response to describe the black cattle's toughness, ability to wear down fences, and ornery disposition near their calves.

Earlier in the day, Devyn went with Norm to deliver a load of corn to Havana and got his first look at the barges lined up by the elevators on the muddy Illinois. Gazing out the windshield, he realized how vast and wide the prairie could be, now that it was swept clean of corn and beans. In his mind, the combines were giant vacuum cleaners, churning in a cloud of dust, leaving behind a threadbare carpet of stubble on the brown earth. Acres and acres of brown earth, rising and dipping between green ribbons of drainage ditches and creeks.

Ailsa, Norm and Devyn enjoyed the comfort of the fireplace, sipping dandelion wine while Skipper stretched across a braided rug by their feet. Norm had the *Journal Republican* stretched wide, both elbows set on an armrest of his chair. "Says here they still haven't found the wild woman over on the estate. You'd think they'd had got her by now. I'll bet she's connected with the missing people and the mysterious dead body. People are calling them the Sangamon Sasquatches. I'll tell you what, Allerton Park is sure getting lots of mileage from the press." He lowered the paper just enough to peer at Devyn. "It is a peculiar place after all, and I got better things to do with my time."

"Be thankful we have such a peaceful place of beauty right next door to our farm," Ailsa chided. "And it serves as a great windbreak for the cows, which by the way, were tended well this fall." She purposedly looked at Devyn so Norm could get the hint.

Norm nodded. "You did right by us on that score young man." Setting the paper onto his lap, he said, "Perhaps you'll be wanting to stay to help me finish the rest of the Model A this winter. An extra set of hands would come in handy around here."

The farmer pushed himself out of his chair. "Getting late. I want to get up in time to hear Orien Samuelson tomorrow. He's going to talk about grain futures. That'll give me a look-see into when I should take the next couple loads over to the river." The farmer left the room and ambled up the stairs. Skipper thumped his tail on the floor as a salute.

His wife watched him go. "A man of few words, but you can translate his comments into a job offer for next year"— her eyes drifted to Devyn—"if it suits you."

She poured a refill into both of their wine goblets. The crackling log and wine encouraged a silent spell.

"I know you've been curious about it," Ailsa said. Devyn gave her a puzzled look. "You know what I mean." She lifted the circular medallion from under her sweater, unclasped the braided leather cord from her neck and offered it to him.

Devyn reached out tentatively. "Go on," she prodded.

The piece was nearly as wide as his palm. He rubbed the bronze and studied the worn wolf's head on the front surface. "It looks like some sort of antique necklace."

"It's more than a necklace, it's an amulet, a charm to protect one from harm. She regarded the print on the wall of the Abbot of Inchaffray blessing the Scots horde. "It's the last, and perhaps the most powerful, of Fillan's relics, Devyn. The Fergy."

He gazed at the scene with awe, as the cleric extolled the rag-tattered host. "The Highlands must be a wonderful, mystical place."

She smiled. "You could say that."

He puckered his brow. "How'd you get this?"

"It was my mother's."

"That would make you one of the keepers."

"Aye. The *dior ab'fergy*...Dewar of the Fergy."

He examined the piece within his hand more closely.

"Make a fist while holding it," she suggested.

As Devyn gripped tighter, the talisman evoked a sensation of grabbing a hot pan out of the oven. Startled, he popped his hand open and dropped the medallion.

Ailsa reached over to collect the Fergy from the floor. "The capacities of this relic are not to be taken lightly."

"But how did you make the Fu Dogs return to their pedestals?"

"They were eager, but I had to empower them to do so. Of course, you primed their return by clearing the space."

"I don't understand."

The older woman eyed Devyn intently. "Strange, in all my years here, I've never felt a disturbance like that in the estate, or anywhere else, before. Was it because of the attempted theft, your presence…or both that stirred things up?"

A chill hand grasped his neck, despite the glow of the fire. "What about the gorilla? Why was it running around? Was the bear roaming the woods as well?"

She remained quiet and sipped her wine. "The Fergy touches the spirit world. I sensed chaos when the watchers were taken from their pillars. Once they returned and reset the balance, I placed a *geis* upon the bear and gorilla. It took all my power to force them back to the spirit world where they came from…with the guardians help." A shadow of sadness passed over her face. "I felt great rage… and agony before they relented, however."

Moments later, Ailsa said, "If you decide to stay a while, there's a great deal more than farming to learn. I believe you would make an excellent apprentice." She held her goblet up to admire the flickering light through the blue glass, then gave him a sharp look. "Although you'll need to understand the fine line between confidence and over-stepping the boundaries." Waiting for effect, she added, "On a lighter note, I understand you're off to the Deluxe tomorrow evening."

"Yeah, another round of pinochle and fried fish."

"And a heavy dose of Grandpa Billy's wisdom, no doubt."

"No doubt."

Sleep was touching Devyn. "I guess I better get myself to bed as well."

"That's a mutual need." As he stood up, she asked, "Did you ever see Professor Jones again?"

He shook his head. "Haven't been on the estate for a while, I imagine he's still around."

She smiled. "I should think he is. You might say he has a lasting presence."

Devyn walked across the barnyard, pulling his sweatshirt tighter against the cold wind. Something caught the corner of his eye in the shadows of the machine shed. An apparition with long dark hair peered around the corner of the structure. Her face seemed to glow in the chalky light of the mercury vapor light. She returned his smile.

# Epilogue

Spring emerged in Allerton Park—summoning a riot of Dutchman's Britches, Bluebells, and Mayapples in the woods, and an orderly procession of perennials in the gardens. The change in seasons also brought a change in personnel. Trent quit soon after the search parties gave up on the missing director and sculptor. He moved to Decatur after landing a job at ADM. Charlie retired and spent his winters with Edna in Phoenix. Ashley, after serving as interim director for six months, transferred to a position in university admissions on campus. Other than the manor staff, only Carl Lipinski remained, continuing his role as Assistant Director of Facilities and Maintenance.

With the start of the growing season, there was much to do, including the training of new employees. Yet, Carl found himself strolling through the wooded paths of the estate more frequently than he'd ever done before. Perhaps it was penance for not rescuing Val on that terrible evening. Others might describe it as an obsession.

The groundskeeper often went through the Fu Dog Garden, looking upon the blue figures, as if they held a secret he needed to solve. The pair at the end of the garden drew his attention in particular. Mocking eyes returned his gaze, posed as bookends on opposite pillars. His mind tumbled the events of that night over and over, but his linear thinking rejected the most likely option.

Many times, he walked by the bear and the gorilla searching the nearby paths, thinking he would find a lost clue. On some afternoons, he would hike the length of the twisted trail along the Sangamon or cross the bridge and wander the Lost Garden.

Perhaps it was Carl's search for what he expected that kept him from seeing the unexpected. Had he scrutinized the gorilla and bear more carefully, he might have noted peculiar details. The woman, her hair still in a ponytail, lacked any other attire, the sole exception was a necklace, with a teardrop-shaped stone cast upon her bronze chest. As for the dying hunter, arms futilely struggling against the bear, the ring finger of his left hand was cast with a burnished bronze ring. A few feet away from the struggle, buried in the dirt and leaf debris on the forest floor, *Blue Desire* lay on her side, smiling eternally at the tortured and nearsighted eyes of the hunter.

The warm evenings of spring brought Devyn Lawers back to the estate, who visited the formal gardens more frequently. He often ate lunch while sitting in the Walled Garden, looking upon the Girl with a Scarf, basking in the sunshine after a lonely winter's vigil. As time would allow, he would take the garden path to the Sunken Garden and back, absorbing the geometric designs and floral beds—inspiration for the mural he planned for the barn on the Winters Farm, a concession on the part of Norm for Devyn to remain.

In the evenings, after supper, he would go outside, carrying what he called a 'bedtime snack', and make a surreptitious detour to the barn. There, he met a long-haired woman, speaking to her while she ate. Taken aback with how quickly she had learned basic English, they sometimes would talk well after dark.

Sitting on the porch, Ailsa Winters watched her cattle as they enjoyed the lush, spring pasture. Sensing Devyn's company, she thought, accidents happen for a reason.

# Bibliography


Bock, Kay J. 1998. Majestic Allerton-The Story of the Creation of an Oasis on the Prairie. University of Illinois Foundation, University of Illinois, Urbana-Champaign, Illinois, U. S. A.

Frith, Donald E. 1985. Mold Making for Ceramics. Krause Publications, Iola, Wisconsin, U.S.A.

Holtz, Maureen. 2021. Robert Allerton-His Parks and Legacies. Arcadia Publishing, Charleston, South Carolina, U.S.A.

Nelson, Glenn C. 1960. Ceramics. Holt, Rinehart, and Winston, Inc. New York, New York.

Scheinman, Muriel. 1995. A Guide to Art at the University of Illinois. Board of Trustees of the University of Illinois. University of Illinois Press, Urbana and Chicago, Illinois, U.S.A.

Tranter, Nigel. 1996. The Bruce Trilogy. Coronet Books, Hodder and Stoughton, London, U.K.

# Author's Notes

I've had a long, and grateful relationship with Robert Allerton Park. It is, as Kay Bock described, an oasis on the prairie, and a place I often visited while a student at the University of Illinois. Upon graduation, my late wife, Margaret, and I were married in The Sunken Garden on a calm and sunny June day.

No matter what your taste in art, the setting and installations in Allerton Park are unique. The figures blend formal and feral themes which evoke whimsical, as well as disturbing terrifying impressions. The change in seasons refreshes the 'canvas background' for the sculptures—the view of the Centaur, Sun Singer, Fu Dogs, etc. are different, but equally captivating throughout the year.

Laredo Taft's legacy as a sculptor for the university, the state of Illinois, and throughout the Midwest, was known to me. However, the history of the gorilla and bear, reputedly lost orphans from the Taft estate for many years, and their unplanned appearance at Allerton Park, opened up ideas for a fictional mayhem. I just needed to conjure up the characters; the setting at Allerton Park provided plenty of material for a suspense plot.

Some years before this novel was conceived, I came across the legends of St. Fillan while visiting the village of Killin, Perthshire, Scotland. A small museum provided information as to the saint's exploits and his relics. Nearby, one can visit the original site of Fillan's shelter and monastery, including the river pool that he used for healing. As to the *diors* (or dewars), I first encountered their role in Scottish history in the trilogy written by Nigel Tranter. The stunning scenery of the southern Highlands, and the colorful tales of St. Fillan and the *diors* further fostered my imagination.

Finally, I was aware of both the contributions to plant identification, and the tragic accident (while driving to

Allerton Park from Champaign) of G. Neville Jones from Margaret. She took a course in taxonomic botany as an undergraduate at the University of Illinois. G. Neville Jones's widow, Almut Gitter Jones, a botanist herself, was the instructor of the course. Allerton Park was often used as an outdoor laboratory for the class. Based on Almut's accounts during class, Margaret was led to believe since G. Neville Jones was on friendly terms with Robert Allerton, his remains are buried in the park, the only person for which this was allowed. G. Neville Jones's plaque still rests in the grounds under a linden tree, not far from the Walled Garden. Whether or not G. Neville Jones's remains are actually buried in the park, based on secondhand accounts to the author, I will leave to the reader's imagination.

And finally, while recently visiting Allerton Park, I couldn't tell the difference between the old and new.

https://allerton.illinois.edu/can-you-find-the-new-fu-dogs/

# MURDER
# OUTSIDE
# THE BOX

## SARALYN RICHARD

PALM CIRCLE PRESS

**Other Books by Saralyn Richard**

The Detective Parrott Mystery Series
*Murder in the One Percent*
*A Palette for Love and Murder*
*Crystal Blue Murder*
*Murder Outside the Box*

*A Murder of Principal*
*Bad Blood Sisters*
*Naughty Nana*

*This book is dedicated to my brother,
Nathan Jack Jacobson, with love.*

"'Hope is the thing with feathers –
That perches in the soul –
And sings the tune without the words –
And never stops – at all -"

—

*Emily Dickinson*

# CHAPTER ONE

Late summer had painted the Brandywine Valley green, and dawn was coming up orange, but this early Monday morning in August ushered in the blues—the baby blues.

Detective Parrott dropped the spoon into his unfinished oatmeal and dashed toward the east-facing windows, the phone glued to his ear. "Can you repeat that?" How come the phone had worked way better in his one-bedroom bungalow, but it cut out every few seconds in this expensive house in West Chester?

"Sorry to call at the crack of dawn, but I wonder if you could come to Bucolia right away. T.J. and Kate's cottage." More than a year had gone by since Detective Parrott had spoken with Caroline Campbell, but the urgency in her voice was contagious.

Parrott squinted at the streaks of orange peeking over the horizon. In most precincts residents would call the station to report a problem, but in privileged Brandywine Valley, some residents had Parrott's private number. And they used it.

Not that he begrudged anything when it came to the Campbells. Caro and John E. had helped in several investigations, including the death of Caro's cousin, Preston Phillips. T.J. and Kate were the caretakers of the land, sometimes doubling as wait staff. They lived on the property and were more like family than employees.

"On my way. I'm assuming it's not an emergency, or you would have called 9-1-1."

Caro chuckled in that delicate way she had of acknowledging irony, but not mirth. "Not exactly an emergency. You were the first person who came to mind when Kate called me a few minutes ago. There's an abandoned baby on the back porch of their house. The baby's half-asleep in a box, whining, and she didn't know what to do."

"That's a crime scene. Don't touch anything if you can help it," Parrott said, already plopping his bowl and spoon in the sink and filling his thermos with coffee to go.

"Okay. Come to the cottage. I'm there now. We're in the back."

Parrott decided not to wake Tonya, who was upstairs in the primary bedroom suite and most likely wouldn't hear him leaving. He closed the fertility article he'd been reading on his computer and deleted it from the browser's history. He then scribbled a note saying he was going in early. He decided against giving her details.

The drive from West Chester to the Campbell place was forty minutes. Parrott missed being able to get from home to work in a fast fifteen, but the new house was spacious and comfortable, and it made Tonya happy, so he couldn't complain.

Through the car's open windows, the dry early morning air whipped against his mustache and the sides of his head, hinting at cooler fall temperatures to come in the next few weeks. The dashboard thermometer registered sixty-nine degrees. No danger of a baby's freezing.

Babies left on doorsteps had been a thing back in the day, before Parrott was born, even. Dorothy in *The Wizard of Oz* had been left outside Auntie Em's and Uncle Henry's house. He'd heard about babies left at orphanages, churches, banks. Even on a train. Mostly white babies, but he hesitated to stereotype the kind of mother who would abandon her infant in this way.

Having never experienced a case with an abandoned baby, Parrott's mind churned with questions and bits of relevant legislation and protocol. The Pennsylvania Safe Haven law popped into his head, though it only applied to babies left at designated public places—not private homes. As he drove, he speed-dialed EMS to meet him there. They would transport the baby to the hospital for a medical exam and observation. Violet, the sister of Lucretia, who worked at the police station, answered. When he explained the situation, she said, "Oh, my! We've got an idle unit. We'll be rolling in sixty seconds."

Later he'd call his contact at child welfare to arrange for a foster placement, but first he needed to assess things on his own. Who in Brandywine Valley would leave a baby on a doorstep, and why at a caretaker's cottage, instead of one of the big mansions?

All victims evoked his sympathy, but a helpless baby with a mysterious past and a complicated future stimulated his protective nature with a strength that surprised even him.

Caro was a smart lady, and she'd lived through a police investigation in her own home. So had Kate and T.J. Surely, they would respect the crime scene and keep it intact. Then again, a live baby needed feeding and changing, and it wouldn't patiently wait for a police detective.

Parrott's GPS said twenty more minutes to destination. He used the magnetic flasher on the roof of his car to get there in ten. Something in his gut told him to hurry, and then a second call came in from Caro.

"The baby's screaming. What should we do?"

Parrott repeated his admonition about not touching anything, especially the box. "If you have to pick up the baby, use disposable gloves." He raised his windows and stepped on the gas. "Hang on, little baby. One way or another, I'll find out your story."

# CHAPTER TWO

Kate Bath paced from the driveway to the sidewalk leading to her back porch, where Caro sat next to the box containing the baby. *Where is T.J.?* Her heart pounded the refrain into her ears, while she searched for any sign of her husband.

The detective Caro had summoned would be here any minute, and a bad feeling was brewing in Kate's mind, growing stronger and more bitter. She clenched her hands in a knot to keep them from picking up the infant. Maybe she shouldn't have called Caro without talking with T.J. He and Lucy, their golden retriever, had gone out early, as usual, and when she'd seen the box on the steps, and found the sleeping baby inside, she hadn't known what to do.

She'd texted T.J. and when she hadn't heard back, she'd called him, but the call had gone straight to voicemail. She thought about jumping in her SUV and driving around the property, but most likely he and Lucy had gone off-road in the Polaris, and she wouldn't be able to get to him by car. She also was afraid to touch the baby or the box, and she couldn't leave it alone on the steps. What if its scent attracted a hungry animal?

Kate ached to scoop up the baby and bring it inside, but something held her back. The pink-and-yellow sleeping bundle couldn't be real. If she touched it, it might disappear. A strange paralysis took hold of her, threatening to rob her of common sense.

If the infant woke up and started to cry, for sure she would have to pick it up. She'd ask for forgiveness later.

While she waited for the arrival of Caro and Detective Parrott of the West Brandywine Police, a disturbing chill set her nerves on edge. What cosmic convergence of circumstances had brought this precious little being to her doorstep? Kate was torn between wanting to protect the infant and knowing she would be expected to do the right thing. *If only T.J. were here….*

The crunch of tires on the driveway interrupted her thoughts. Whatever would come of it, someone had arrived, probably Caro. The drama was underway, and she only had a small part.

# CHAPTER THREE

Parrott pulled his Toyota onto the gravel driveway behind a Chevrolet SUV and a Mercedes. He tried to imagine how a birth mother might approach this house without being noticed. Would the gravel have made noise? Were there tire tracks or footprints?

A thirtyish round-shouldered woman with fluffy light-brown hair and hooded eyes hurried toward him. He remembered having interviewed her briefly after Preston Phillips' death a few years before.

"Detective Parrott? I'm Kate Bath. I'll take you to the baby. I wasn't sure what to do with it."

Parrott nodded and fell into step. The word "it" stood out in his mind. Of course, no one could tell the baby's gender without peeking. "C'mon, let's take care of the baby first, and then I have some questions." The duo headed toward the back of the brick cottage, shielded from the driveway by a row of sycamores. The porch had likely been dark when the box was plunked down.

As he approached the wailing baby in the box, he was struck by the tableau. Caro eclipsed his view of the makeshift cradle. She paced across the entrance to the house, arms crossed. "I wouldn't let Kate pick up the baby," she said over the repetitive sobs. "She didn't have gloves."

The sun had risen enough to illuminate the scene, so when Parrott peered into the cardboard box, he could make out a purple-faced infant, wrapped in a yellow blanket trimmed with embroidered ducks, and screaming its head off. Girl or boy, the baby looked to be no more than a few days old.

Kate inserted herself between Caro and Parrott and leaned over, about to grab one of the bottles of milk by the baby's feet. "I can't stand the crying. I'm going to feed it."

"No, stop! Don't touch that bottle. We don't know what's in it." Bottles of milk were good news from one standpoint. Someone had thought to provide for the baby before leaving it, and the

bottles might provide evidence down the road, but right now, Parrott needed to take care of getting the baby to the hospital. Only medical professionals would know whether the baby was healthy and whether the milk was safe.

Parrott turned to Kate. "What time was it when you discovered the baby here on the porch?"

She hesitated, looking skyward, as if to measure time by the sun. "I'd guess about six. I'd showered and poured myself a cup of coffee. The weather's so nice, I was going to drink it here on the porch."

"Was your husband with you when you came out here at six?"

Kate swallowed. "T.J. wasn't here—still isn't. The door banged when he and the dog went out to work about five o'clock. They hop on the Polaris and head for wherever they're needed."

Parrott could hardly believe his luck. Assuming T.J. hadn't stumbled over the box on his way out, it hadn't been there at five a.m. The window of time in which the baby could have been left on the porch was narrowed to an hour.

He voice-texted a quick message to his colleague, Officer Randy Barton, to ask if any reports had come in about strange cars or people in the area over the last few hours, or whether any of the hospitals in the area had reported a missing baby.

Parrott had more questions, but first he needed to call child protective services. Technically, the baby was automatically under the custody of the Commonwealth of Pennsylvania, but the Chester County Child Youth organization needed to formalize the responsibility by starting paperwork and meeting the baby at the hospital. They would place the baby in foster care. In less than two minutes, Parrott reached his colleague and made those arrangements.

Still keeping an eye on the now-hiccuping baby, he turned to matters within his own bailiwick. He pulled several pairs of latex gloves from his pocket and handed them out. "Let's take this little one inside. We can talk better there, while we wait for EMS."

Kate took a step back but remained hunched over the box, as if a magnet held her there. "Would it be okay if I went to the hospital with the baby? I want to make sure it gets there safely."

Caro patted Kate on the shoulder. "I'm sure EMS will take good care of the baby. They're prepared for things like this, right, detective?"

Parrott nodded. He used his cellphone to snap photos of the baby, the porch, the area around the steps. The cottage sat on the edge of a massive field about a quarter-mile from the Campbell mansion. The nearest neighbor otherwise was more than a mile away, unless wildlife counted.

Donning gloves, Parrott lifted the box. He guessed its weight to be less than fifteen pounds, the tiny infant perhaps six. Kate opened the screen door wide, ushering Parrott and Caro inside.

A dog barked outside in the distance, and Kate uttered a cry. "That's Lucy. She and T.J. must be coming." She scurried down the steps to meet them.

The floor plan of the cottage reminded Parrott of the house he and Tonya had recently sold. The aroma of fresh-baked bread permeated the air, although no loaves were visible. A single space served as kitchen, dining area, and family room. He set the fidgety baby on the uncluttered kitchen table. Now exhausted, the baby squirmed and opened its eyes for a few seconds but closed them again.

Kate rushed through the back door, shouting over her shoulder to her husband behind her. "—and here's the box with the baby in it."

Lucy bolted through the door and sprang toward the table, long tail wagging, and pushed her nose over the edge to sniff. T.J., on the other hand, took his time entering the house. A dark-haired man of about forty with a brooding expression, he glanced at the box before acknowledging Caro and the detective with nods. "Looks like I missed a lot of excitement this morning, eh?"

Parrott shifted his attention to T.J. "What time did you leave the house this morning?"

"Around five, like every morning. I like to feed the horses before sunup, while things are quiet and cool."

"Did you see this box on the back porch when you left?"

T.J. looked at him like he was crazy. "'Course not. I wouldn't've gone. The box definitely wasn't here then."

"Did you see or hear anything unusual around the porch or in the vicinity?" Parrott asked, wondering about the man's attitude.

T.J. walked around the kitchen almost in circles, his hands clasped behind his back. "Nope, nada, nothing."

Parrott's internal radar bleeped over T.J.'s responses—the man was uncomfortable having a baby, his boss, or a police detective there, or maybe all three.

"Have any of you touched the baby, the box, or anything in it?"

"I might have, not intentionally." Kate clasped her hands. "It was still dark, and I had to figure out what was inside the box. I've fought the impulse to pick the baby up and hold it ever since."

Parrott looked at Caro, who shook her head. "I don't think so."

"Okay," Parrott said. "I'll just need your fingerprints to exclude them." He peered into the box. Two bottles of milk by the baby's bundled feet could become important clues. In addition to carrying fingerprints, if they contained breast milk, there might be DNA.

"Do any of you know a reason someone might leave a baby here on this porch?" Parrott looked from one to another.

No one replied for at least a minute, unless T.J.'s, "Nah," counted.

Finally, Kate broke the awkward silence. "Maybe someone who knows us knows we don't have kids. Maybe that person thinks we'd be good parents."

"Jeez, Kate. Don't start getting attached to a stranger's baby, for God sakes." T.J. covered his ears and stormed out the back door, letting the screen slam behind him.

Caro's eyes met Parrott's. Whatever was going on between Kate and T.J., Parrott had a job to do, and now, he needed to focus on the baby, who had startled when the screen door slammed, and now began to fuss. Kate leaned over toward the box, humming a lullaby.

"Listen," Parrott said, addressing Kate. "Can you find a suitable piece of clothing or small blanket that we can wrap the baby in? Something to use as a diaper, too. I need to bag what it's wearing now, so this will be temporary—until the baby gets to the hospital."

"Sure. Be right back." Kate leaped into action. She returned with a box of onesies, a soft muslin cloth, and some safety pins.

"I bought this for my cousin's baby gift, but this little one needs it more."

"I wish I could be of help, but I don't know much about babies," Caro said.

Parrott remembered from previous dealings that she and John E. had no children. He'd never paused to wonder why, maybe because their child-bearing years were long past when he met them.

"On the other hand, Kate, you're a natural." Caro made way for Kate, who spread out a large bath towel on the table next to the box. Kate headed for the sink, where she ran the hot water until the temperature was suitable, and she filled the bowl.

"I'm the oldest of five. I've known how to care for babies since I was four years old." Kate headed for the infant, whose cries sounded more like soft smacks. "This baby's either hungry or thirsty. See how she's smacking her lips?"

"She?" Caro asked. "How do you know it's a girl?"

"Just a feeling. Can I pick her up now?" Kate appealed to Parrott, her eyes moist.

Parrott checked to make sure she was wearing the disposable gloves. "I'll lift the baby and lay it on the towel. You can undress the baby and then lift it up, so I can bag everything it's currently wearing."

Kate nodded, putting on the gloves. "It's a shame to take her out of such a cute outfit to dress her in this. I wish I had something prettier to put her in."

Parrott wasn't thinking about the baby's clothes. He itched to know who had left this baby, and, more importantly, why.

# CHAPTER FOUR

While Kate glommed onto the fussy infant, Parrott grew wistful about his own desire to have children. He and Tonya had moved to a large house in West Chester with hopes of filling the bedrooms. After a major breakthrough in her PTSD therapy, Tonya had declared herself ready for motherhood.

While visiting him in the hospital after his serious brush with fentanyl, courtesy of a deranged killer, Tonya had informed Parrott that she would need his help to decorate the nursery of the new house. Believing that Tonya was pregnant, Parrott had practically leaped from his hospital bed to waltz his wife around the tiny room. So happy was their celebration, and so crushing several days later, when Tonya's period arrived late.

Now, he returned his attention to the kitchen table, ready to lift Baby Doe from its makeshift crib. "Here you go, little one," he said, thinking about the ironies of life.

"Be sure to support its head," Kate said, staring into Parrott's face. "Babies' necks can't support the weight of their heads. Why don't you let me pick her up?"

Parrott knew that much about infants, but Kate seemed so eager to care for this baby, and now that she wore gloves, he didn't see how it would hurt for her to transfer the baby to the blanket. He nodded and stepped back, so she could pick up the baby, blanket and all.

While she did so, he extracted from his jacket the sealable paper bags he'd brought to secure the evidence. As Kate lifted the baby, he caught a whiff of baby scent—powder mixed with something earthier, but not unpleasant.

Caro stood behind Kate and Parrott, whispering nonsense syllables, as if to make herself feel useful. "Such a sweetie," she said, as Kate laid the baby on the towel.

The baby couldn't have been more cooperative. Its only sounds now were a series of endearing grunts.

"The baby might make a fuss when the cool air hits its body," Kate said.

"If so, we'll deal with it." Parrott was glad to have the two women assisting, especially since he'd never experienced a case with a baby. He knew the protocols, but applying them to someone so helpless gave him pause. He was concentrating on whatever little gems of evidence that might be in the baby's clothes or blanket. Hair, skin, spit-up, even urine or feces might help in identifying the baby's origins. Anything found within the confines of the box was fair game for forensics. Somewhere there would be parents to match up to this little bundle, and Parrott would do all he could to find them.

As it was, Caro and Kate were transfixed by the drama unfolding on the kitchen table. Kate's gloved fingers worked the ends of the blanket loose, exposing arms and legs, hands and feet. The baby's eyes fluttered open, and it took in a big breath as it flung its arms upward in a startle reflex. But it didn't cry.

Under the blanket, the baby wore a t-shirt and short onesie, also yellow with ducks. Parrott didn't know much about baby clothes, but the elaborate embroidery on the outfit and blanket probably cost a pretty penny.

Kate opened the snaps at the bottom of the onesie, lifted it and the T-shirt over the baby's head, and set the baby back down on the table. An inch-long umbilical stump was still present, resembling a piece of rawhide. The edges were ragged and pink. Kate opened the plastic tabs on the diaper. As she pulled the diaper's front open, revealing a soft pile of yellow poop that smelled more like sweat than feces, loud sighs erupted in stereo.

"You were right," Caro said. "She's a girl. She's a beautiful baby. Look at those tiny toes."

The little body was perfect, all parts present and accounted for, and not a mark anywhere, except for a tiny scratch on her neck. Parrott took photos front and back, as well as closeups of her head, face, and umbilical cord. Though used to snapping photos in his work, this time new feelings of connection rose in him and bubbled over. *Where are this baby's parents, and how could they dump her like this?*

"What's going to happen to her once EMS gets here?" Kate's tremulous voice betrayed deep feelings, and Parrott thought of T.J.'s admonition before he'd left the house. Kate had definitely become attached.

"They will assess her and take her to the hospital. There she'll get a complete medical exam. Then protective services will work on a foster placement for her."

Kate clasped the naked baby to her chest and closed her eyes, ignoring the baby's dirty bottom. Parrott slid the bundle of diaper, onesie, and blanket to the side.

Caro took a step closer to help Kate with cleaning and dressing the baby. Now she placed a hand on Kate's wrist and squeezed.

"Do you think—I mean, would it be possible for T.J. and me to be the foster parents? Maybe she was left here for a reason."

Hearing the hope in Kate's voice, Parrott chose his words carefully. "That's not usually how it works. Family members get first priority, and if none can be found, then the best placement is made through the foster system." He was ready, now, to wrap up his evidence bundles. "You and T.J. would need to apply and be approved, and, even then, no guarantees."

Parrott continued to bag the baby's clothing, saving the yellow blanket for last. While he lifted and folded the blanket to fit into the bag, Parrott's mind was on the speed with which the woman had bonded with a stranger's baby.

Kate's face paled, her eyes widened, and she uttered a loud sob, as she clasped the little one in the crook of her arm.

Oh, no, Parrott thought. She's not going to give up the baby easily. "Listen, Kate. We need to—"

Kate wasn't listening. She was staring at the bundle of evidence in his arms and pointing with her free hand. "The blanket," she said. "The baby's blanket is full of blood."

# CHAPTER FIVE

Quick, let me check for any signs of a wound." Parrott had taken photos of the baby and hadn't seen anything but a tiny scratch on the neck, but that was before anyone had noticed a five-inch stripe of blood on the baby blanket. How had he missed seeing that swath of red when Kate was undressing the baby?

Kate's initial assessment that the blanket was full of blood was an exaggeration. The blanket wasn't soaked. The wide patch of brick-colored material adhered to the blanket, tacky and thick, but not seeping through to the inside. Parrott's heart pulsed with the possibilities. The blood might have come from the baby, or, more likely, the mother. The blood was an ironic gift for him as an investigator. It would help to tell the story of who had left this baby and why.

"No corresponding wounds on the baby, except for the umbilical cord, which is dry. If that had bled, it would've stained the front of the blanket, not the back." Parrott handed the baby back to Kate, who, singing a tune, re-dressed the baby in the makeshift outfit. The baby stared at the sound.

Caro's eyes met Parrott's. She probably shared his growing concern about Kate's immediate attachment to the baby.

Kate had brought over a wicker basket with a wide handle. Now that the baby was dressed and swaddled, it was time to set her into the basket, but Kate's reluctance to do so was written all over her face. "Can I just hold her until the authorities arrive? Babies need cuddling, and this one especially. Poor thing, hasn't got a proper mommy around to do the job."

A twinge of compassion filled Parrott's throat. Before he could respond, Caro said, "I don't see how that could hurt anything, as long as you understand the need to let her go when the time comes. Legally, the baby belongs to the Commonwealth of Pennsylvania. Isn't that right, detective?"

The back door whooshed open, and T.J. walked in without the dog, followed by a woman wearing a navy jumpsuit, a neon orange backpack, and a nametag saying, Brittany. Behind them a jump-suited man rolled a stretcher fifty times too big for Baby Doe. An infant car seat had been installed on it, unusual and sad to behold. The sun had risen, and the fragrance of fresh-cut grass clung to T.J.'s work clothes. When T.J. saw Kate, rocking the baby in the crook of her arm, his eyebrows merged in a scowl, and his lips drew inward.

Brittany stopped in front of Parrott and thrust her chin out. "Detective Parrott? You called EMS?"

Kate's body tensed, but she remained silent. Her gaze followed T.J. as he stomped toward the back of the house.

Parrott explained the situation with the baby. "She was left in this box with two bottles of milk approximately an hour ago. We haven't fed her. All we've done is remove her clothes and change her diaper."

Brittany had pulled a clipboard from beneath the stretcher and was writing notes on a form. Parrot knew that form, so he called on Caro to provide the needed names and addresses. "I live here at Bucolia, and this is the home of Mr. and Mrs. T.J. Bath. Mrs. Bath, Kate, is holding the baby."

Parrott nodded. At this point, his nerves were snapping. "Once you transport the baby to the hospital, the people from the county will show up to take charge of her placement." He was eager for EMS to take the baby to the hospital, where professionals could examine and care for her, so he could get started on what he needed to do.

Brittany asked Kate to place the baby on the stretcher. Kate complied but remained standing behind the baby's head, where she could observe the EMS procedures. As soon as she put the baby down, the infant's face scrunched up, and she started to whine. Within seconds whining turned to wailing.

"Can I pick her up again?" Kate asked. "Maybe we should give her one of the bottles from the box."

Brittany shot a glance at Parrott. While the baby continued to cry, Brittany did a quick check for temperature, blood pressure, heart rate, and oxygenation rate. "Everything checks out fine."

She turned to Kate and said, "Until we know exactly what's in the bottles, we can't use them. We'll take the milk with us and have the contents analyzed in the lab. The staff on the neo-natal floor will have something appropriate to feed the baby."

Parrott pulled Brittany aside to ask if he could take samples from each of the bottles. He'd brought empty vials with him, along with the paper evidence bags.

"Sure. As long as we follow protocols and document everything, I have no problem with it." She slipped on the latex gloves Parrott handed her and assisted with the delicate transfer.

Parrott sealed each of the tubes and labeled them with the date, time, and his name. He fixed similar labels to the bottoms of the two bottles that were being taken to the hospital. "I'd like to get these back, along with any other materials related to the infant, if possible."

"I'll let them know at the hospital. Anything else?" Brittany was already securing the squirming baby into the infant seat that hooked onto the stretcher.

Parrott signed paperwork transferring custody of the baby to EMS. As soon as he finished, Brittany signaled to her partner, who started rolling the stretcher out of the house, down the porch steps, and toward the side of the house.

Kate collapsed into a chair, muttering. "I didn't realize how much I've missed by not having a baby." Caro pulled up a chair and sat next to her, putting an arm around Kate's shoulder.

When EMS left with the baby, the room was silent, and tension hung in the air, as if Kate's heart had fled her body and couldn't find its way back. T.J. emerged from the back of the house, a hand towel draped around the back of his neck. He looked around, and when his eyes landed on Kate, hunched over the kitchen table, with Caro patting her back, he pivoted as if to return to where he came from.

"Come sit down," Parrott said. "I have several questions to ask you and Kate."

"Should I leave the three of you, then?" Caro asked. "I don't need to be here—unless you want me to."

Parrott nodded, grateful that he didn't even have to ask. Some of the questions were personal. The Baths might not feel free to

answer in front of their employer, no matter how friendly the relationship.

Caro gathered her keys and cellphone, gave Kate a quick hug, patted T.J. on the shoulder, and shook Parrott's hand before exiting through the screen door. T.J. still paced around the room, eyes fixed on the floor. Though his behavior was strange, Parrott judged it to be more annoyance with Kate than anything else. He pulled a chair away from the table where Kate sat and stared at T.J. until the farm hand caught the message and sat.

Parrott sat across from T.J. and cater-corner from Kate. "I have some personal, but necessary questions for the two of you." He tapped his phone app to jot notes. He started with each of their full names, dates of birth, places of birth, date and place of their wedding five years ago, when T.J. was thirty-one and Kate was twenty-one.

"Do you have any children?" Knowing that the baby on the porch had raised emotions in both of them, Parrott watched their faces closely.

"Nah," said T.J., his tanned, hairy arms crossed over his middle and glancing at Kate. "We never wanted kids, did we?"

Kate's no was softer, more wistful. Her freckled complexion, ponytail, and casual work clothes fit in with her circumstances, but Parrott detected a more genteel upbringing behind her exterior.

"How about outside of the marriage. Any kids for either of you?"

Kate shook her head and looked away. T.J. smirked. "Not that I know of." Parrott couldn't imagine two married people more different in personality and attitude, and he wondered whether the baby on the porch had brought out this rift, or whether it had been there.

Shifting subjects, Parrott asked how long the couple had been working for the Campbells.

T.J. leaned back in his chair, gripping the edge of the table with both hands. "I've been out here at Bucolia since before we were married." He glanced at Kate. "Maybe six years? Other people owned the farm, the name of Paul. The Campbells bought the farm, tore down the big house and built a new one. About five years ago."

The groundskeepers' cottage showed signs of needing some updating. Parrott estimated its construction as being in the 1960s. "Why'd the Pauls leave?"

"Aged out, I guess. This kind of living don't always appeal to people in their eighties and nineties. Sometimes their kids pressure them to move to retirement homes."

"So, the Campbells bought the farm and kept you on?" Brandywine Valley was full of owners and workers whose ties to the land were generational. That was part of what made the community unique, and also what sometimes made Parrott feel more of an outsider.

"Yeah. Not to brag or anything, but there aren't that many guys like me who know how to take care of these gentleman farms. I know every square inch of this acreage."

Parrott turned to Kate, whose lack of contribution to this conversation reminded Parrott of a mountain peak shrouded by clouds. "You seem to have a good relationship with Mrs. Campbell. What has been your experience living and working at Bucolia?"

"We've got a good life out here," Kate said. "Clean, healthy. Always something to do. Sometimes a little isolated, but otherwise, fine, and occasionally I get to New York to visit a museum or see a play. The Campbells treat us well. They're remodeling our house, starting next month. I got to pick out all new appliances."

T.J. leaned his chair forward and set his elbows on the table. "Yeah. The Campbells don't have kids mucking around in our business, telling us what to do. We got more of a say in how stuff goes down."

Because T.J. and Kate seemed more relaxed now, Parrott hated to raise the next question, but he needed to wrap up this interview and get on with the case. "I want you to think hard about this, both of you. Is there anyone in either of your families or among your friends or acquaintances, who might have had a baby recently? Anyone who might have been desperate enough to leave the baby on your back porch?"

"I can't think of anyone," T.J. said, rubbing the back of his neck with the towel. "Can you, Kate?"

"Not off the top of my head." Kate stood in place and crossed her arms over her waist. "My cousin's having a baby soon, but she

lives out of state. But I know where I would start if I were in your shoes, detective."

"Where is that?" Parrott asked, used to people who offered suggestions.

"I'd start trying to find out whose blood's on the back of that baby blanket. Whoever it is, I'll bet they didn't willingly separate from that precious baby."

# CHAPTER SIX

This was one of those times Parrott wished he could clone himself, or that he worked for a larger police department. He had at least five tasks he needed to do right away, including transporting the baby's clothing and box to the lab at Chesco, the Chester County Forensics Services. But first, he wanted to follow a hunch he had about the blood on the blanket.

He'd left the Baths' cottage after questioning T.J. and Kate, dissatisfied with both his questions and their answers. He'd gotten as much as he could from them, considering they were in the same room at the same time. Once he'd pursued other avenues, he would double back to talk to each of them separately.

He placed the evidence in the trunk of his car but didn't leave right away. An idea germinated about how to proceed next. By now it was eight-thirty, and Chief Schrik would likely be in his office. Parrott's call went through on the first ring.

"'Morning, Parrott. You out in the field today?" Schrik had to pass Parrott's office on the way to his own, so his question was rhetorical.

Parrott filled him in on the situation with the baby. "Between EMS and child protective services, she's being cared for." He went on to describe the evidence he'd collected and the interview with the Baths.

Schrik's reaction was loud and swift. "An abandoned baby. Whaddya know? We haven't had one of those here for the past twenty-two years. Hard to believe, really, since this community is a perfect place for someone to leave a baby—isolated and wealthy. If I were going to drop off a baby outside of safe haven places, I'd choose a rich family."

"Well, the groundskeepers' cottage isn't exactly the lap of luxury, Chief. Anyway, there's something else you need to know." Parrott explained about the blood on the blanket. "We know someone dropped the baby off at the porch between five and five-thirty. I want to jump on a search before the trail gets cold."

"Okay." Schrik softened his tone. "That bumps things up in a hurry. What do you have in mind?"

"I texted Officer Barton about any reports that might've come in. Didn't hear back. Maybe he could check with all the area hospitals. I want to scour the area, preferably by air. See if I can find anything suspicious."

"Sure. No problem, except Barton called off this morning. Said he'll be in around noon." The chief's teeth clicked against the paper clip he used to remind himself not to smoke.

Parrott took a deep breath before plunging forward. "I know a guy in Brandywine who owns a Sikorsky S76B. He's got a landing pad and storage on site at his farm in Coatesville. Whenever I see him, he offers to take me up, free of charge."

"A civilian? You know how I feel about mixing police business with social relationships. And no comment about the kind of people you're hanging out with these days."

Parrott cringed. He hated Schrik's insinuations about the leap in economic status Parrott had made since he and Tonya were given a largesse. "Not a social relationship—just an acquaintance. The guy likes any excuse to take it up, and I know we can cover ground faster this way."

"Okay, Parrott. I trust your judgment. Be safe and keep me posted on what you find." Another line rang in the background as the chief hung up.

❇ ❇ ❇

Within the hour, Parrott was sitting in the cockpit of a sleek whirlybird for the first time ever, his ears buzzing from the spinning rotor blades, despite the headset he wore. His stomach lurched from the fuel smell and the vibrating engine, but he welcomed the experience.

Lew Grossman glanced at him and grinned. "How's that for a smooth take-off? This baby might be the handiest, most versatile means of transportation in the universe."

While appreciating Grossman's excitement, Parrott tried to block out the dizzy, nauseating sensations. *So this is what Tonya experienced every day as a Navy helicopter pilot in Afghanistan.*

As the helicopter ascended, it stabilized, and Parrott could manage looking down. He took deep breaths and pointed Lew in the direction of the Campbell farm.

"What are we looking for when we get there?" Lew asked. His voice, coming through the headphones, trumped the mechanical noise. Parrott had been intentionally vague about the mission, only explaining the need to use the Campbell farm as a central point of reference, and to fly in a grid from there.

"Anything unusual or out of place. Somebody in harm's way. Something that doesn't make sense. I can't be more specific." Parrott gulped air, and after several times, his gut calmed down.

"Okay. We're going to use the infrared sensor synced with the GPS on my cellphone." He set the hand-held device in the cup holder between them. "I bought it to track animals for game management, but it works just as well on humans. We'll be flying at about eight hundred feet and a hundred seventy-five knots. Hard to see something as small as a human being from that height." Lew's habit of elbowing Parrott with every detail was annoying, but it was a small price to pay for the valuable service. *Let the guy enjoy himself a little.*

The wind created by the rotor blades whipped against the sides of the aircraft, sweeping away Parrott's discomfort and muffling any conversation, even through the headsets. Beginning to enjoy the ride, Parrott gripped a map of Brandywine Valley on his lap. Many of the farms looked identical to one another from the air, so the map's detail was essential. Parrott had marked Bucolia and the groundskeepers' cottage, and he had drawn a grid around that spot in a ten-mile radius.

The 'copter had no sooner reached its altitude, than Grossman's cellphone flashed and beeped. "Probably a deer. The sensor detects body heat and motion. Sends a signal to the GPS on the phone. Remarkable device, eh? Never steers me wrong, but let's fly lower and see what it's showing us."

Sure enough, as they lowered altitude and hovered over the area marked by the GPS, a pair of deer darted through the wooded area below.

Parrott appreciated the assistance offered by the infrared technology, but at the same time, he didn't want to be distracted

by every animal in Brandywine Valley. "How about we ignore the cellphone until we get to ground zero, which I've marked on this map?"

"Okay, bud. I know Brandywine Valley like I know the floor plan of my home. Last month I took an aerial photographer around Chester County and Wilmington for a spread in *Delaware Today*. Whatever you're looking for, if it's here, we're gonna find it." Grossman grinned and jabbed Parrott in the ribs.

Within minutes, the helicopter reached Bucolia. The farm acreage, the mansion, and the various outbuildings, including the stable and horse paddock, looked different from above, smaller and more ordinary. Huge expanses contracted to squares on a board game. Grossman hovered over the Baths' cottage to make sure that was the correct starting point. Once Parrott confirmed, the pilot lifted and thrust forward into a strategic flying pattern composed of twenty-one-mile squares.

"If you see anything of interest, just tell me, and we'll drop lower to get a better look. We can go forward, backward, or laterally—whatever suits your purpose."

"Thanks, man," Parrott said, his eyes glued on the ground below. Occasionally, he glanced at the map to orient himself. All he could see at first were the tops of trees, rooftops, vehicles, and dots that were probably horses. The land was green and textured in places that indicated gardens or riding trails. The sensors flashed with a greater intensity than before.

"Horses. We don't have to follow up on those fast flashes, unless you want to. They're probably stables or paddocks full of horses. We get a lot of those out here." Grossman pushed his sunglasses up on his nose. "I'm guessing you're looking for a single person in an unlikely spot."

Disappointed that the air search was proving more complicated than expected, Parrott gazed at the ground, hoping to find anything that would lead him to the baby's mother. "That's true. I didn't think—"

"Don't let the flashes discourage you. Overall, things are pretty quiet out here in the country. If we were closer to Philadelphia, this sensor'd be jumping all over the place."

They passed the Hill Girt Farm near Chadds Ford, where a tributary of Brandywine Creek flowed. Later they passed the Weymouth family residence and outbuildings. There were swimming pools, porches, gazebos, and ornamental gardens.

At one point, as they flew over the Brandywine Creek behind the farm adjacent to the Campbells, the sensor started flashing "Uh-oh. Something's down there, but the signal's weak. Let's take a look," he said, pointing at the dark dot.

As Grossman drew closer, a steep embankment grew larger and more distinct. The precipitous drop-off would make the topography nearly impossible for an animal or human to climb. Next to the creek were industrial railroad tracks, and next to the tracks was an elongated speck, whitish against the dark landscape. Whatever caused the signal to beep caused icy flips in Parrott's gut. "Can we land? I'd like to take a closer look."

"I need to find a clearing. Let's check things out while I hover. I can get close to the ground this way." Grossman manipulated the controls using his hands and feet with an expertise that reminded Parrott of a quarterback, coordinating a strategic play.

Several hundred feet from the tracks on the same side of the creek, lay a hayfield, freshly mowed from its end-of-summer harvest. Grossman landed the helicopter and opened the doors. Parrott removed his headset and seatbelt. The sweet smell of hay enveloped him as he leapt from the vehicle. On another day and a different kind of errand, particularly if Tonya were with him, he might have been tempted to lie down in the field and inhale the fragrance.

Grossman held the infrared in one hand, the cellphone in the other. "C'mon. The signal is coming from the north." Both men took off at a sprint, but they couldn't go as fast as Parrott wanted to, because the devices needed to lead them.

Details about the vista registered with Parrott. A large willow tree, its branches dropping almost to the ground in a fountain-like profusion. The sun on the top of his head, toasting it lightly, until a breeze cooled the air. He'd pay attention later. Now he darted ahead to where the embankment ended in a ledge. He yelled over his shoulder to Grossman. "I'm going down there."

He slid down the grassy slope, about fifteen feet. His heart pounded as he scrambled over the tracks in search of whatever was causing the infrared to beep. Hopefully he'd find a person, someone tied to an abandoned baby girl.

# CHAPTER SEVEN

Below the embankment, Parrott gained his bearings and checked to make sure his cellphone was still in his pocket. He shouted at Lew Grossman, who had caught up to Parrott and was peering over the drop. "Sit tight. I'm going to look around. Be back in a few." Parrott noted the time before crossing the railroad tracks, where he'd seen the light-colored speck from the air.

He followed the path beside the creek, brushing past wild shrubs. Struck by the lush, quiet landscape, Parrott was alone with only the burbling of the creek and the beating of his heart. No animals, not even birds, so who or what had transmitted the infrared signal? About three hundred yards from where he'd left Grossman, the path took a turn to the south, opening a new vista. Here the train tracks curved away from the creek, and the embankment above formed a promontory.

Parrott ran across the uneven ground, scanning the landscape for anything out of the ordinary. He stopped short at a pile of river stones. Off-white in color, the formation of stones may have been what he'd seen from the helicopter and thought was a person.

Disappointed, he maneuvered around the rocks and kept looking ahead, trying to shake the feeling that he was immersed in an elusive video game quest. A jog around some weeds led to what looked like a woman lying face-down.

Parrott checked the time on his cellphone. Fourteen minutes had passed since he'd left Grossman. Judging by his sprinting speed on the uneven topography, he was about a mile west of where the Sikorsky had landed. He did a quick three-sixty scan for anyone who might be nearby, and then he rushed toward the woman, fearing the worst.

The ground near her head was dark red, presumably from blood. Long tresses, matted together, might have been blonde before the back of the head had been shot. The arms were spread out, palms

down, and the head lolled in an unnatural position. The coagulated blood glistened in the morning sun, still fresh and attracting flies.

She'd been a young woman, long-legged and fit. Perhaps she'd been shot in the back of the head, while running. He hoped she hadn't seen it coming, hadn't felt a thing.

Parrott scoped the area again, gun drawn, looking for a killer, following protocol.

Seeing and hearing nothing, he returned to the body. He flirted with the idea that this might be the mother of the abandoned infant, but he wouldn't allow himself to make that leap without evidence.

He was approximately three miles northwest of the Campbells' farm, a mile from where the helicopter had landed. He dropped a pin to himself on his cellphone and let Google Maps identify the latitude and longitude. He texted it to Schrik and the people at the county lab. Then he called Grossman to describe what he had found and where.

Grossman's voice faded in and out. "Did you measure the body's warmth? Must be a recent kill, or the infrared wouldn't have picked up a signal. That's why it was so faint."

Impatience eclipsed Parrott's interest in the infrared monitor, which had now served its purpose. Plus, he was annoyed by Grossman's telling him how to do his job. "That's the coroner's job. With no signs of life, all I could do now would be to disrupt the evidence."

Grossman launched into a long-winded explanation about the valley's one-lane roads, railroad tracks, and the creek's twists and turns. "I won't be able to get much closer, but an ambulance could go out to the back of the Mooney property. You want me to send 'em?"

"Nah. I've got the forensic guys from Chesco coming out. I appreciate the offer, but I don't want to hold you up anymore." Parrott clipped his words. "Not so fast," Grossman said. "I'm not gonna leave you out in the boonies with no transportation. Whoever shot your victim could still be around. I'm going to stand by until your people get there. Call and let me know."

Parrott clicked off. He hated to inconvenience the guy, but he didn't have the time to argue. The baby abandonment case had

taken a back seat to a murder, and the need to open an investigation was urgent.

Chief Schrik answered the phone on the first ring. "I got your location. Whatcha got?"

"A young female, shot in the back of the head. Back acreage of the Mooney farm by the creek."

Schrik's chair creaked. "Not far from the Campbells. Maybe she's tied to the baby on the porch. Have you called the coroner and forensics yet?"

"No. I sent them my location but called you first. There's got to be a way to get here by car, but right now I can't see any roads. Grossman's parked south of here, fifteen feet higher." As he talked, Parrott waved insects from the body without touching. He hoped the team would get here before vultures or other critters started to pay attention.

Another phone line rang at the station. Schrik paused a few seconds before replying. "Yeah, I'm looking at the map. You can get in through Strasburg Road. I'll call and get Chesco out there. I'll come out, too. Barton's still out, and you'll need a ride back, won't you?"

Parrott didn't know what to think. To his knowledge, Schrik had never left the station to check out a crime scene before. "I'm good. Grossman's still here, or I can probably hitch a ride with Jerry or Maria, whoever comes out from the county."

"Nonsense. There's nothing drastic going on here this morning, and my legs could use a little stretching. I'll stop at Mooney's first, so you don't have to. Besides, it's not every day that we've got a baby *and* a dead woman."

"Okay, Chief. I'll tell Grossman to head on back. I'll see you when you get here." Parrott called to dispatch the helicopter pilot, thanking him for all his help.

"Nope. I'm not leaving until your people have feet on the ground. I'm comfortable here. When Chesco gets there, I'll do a flyover. Who knows? Maybe I'll see something useful."

Parrott wasn't used to having somebody watch over him like this. He doubted he was in any more danger, being alone in the farmland, than Grossman was, but the guy had a good point about

taking in an aerial view. "Not a bad idea. If there's a killer on foot, your infrared might pick him up." He agreed to keep in touch.

While he waited, Parrott busied himself observing the scene, looking for signs of how the woman had arrived in this remote setting, who had come here with her, and whether there had been a struggle. The warm sun bathed her with light. Using his phone, he photographed the body from every angle he could without moving or even touching her. She wore a light-colored print dress, now partly stained reddish-brown. Her bare legs were tanned, and her platform-sandals-shod feet were splayed by her fall to the ground. On one wrist was a bright yellow string bracelet with a smiley face charm.

Parrott paced the area around the body. There was no road, no tire tracks, no footprints—hers or anyone else's. The bullet and its casing were out there somewhere, unless the shooter got them both. He eyed the ledge above and imagined the trajectory that the body might have followed if it had been shot and dropped below. Not only was it possible, but close examination of the path the body might have taken as it rolled down the incline showed crushed grass tinted with brown.

While he waited for his team to arrive, Parrott watched everything from the rough ground to the bright horizon, and pondering the circumstances that might have brought a young woman—not much more than a girl, really—to being killed in this remote, quiet landscape.

The swath of blood on the baby blanket popped into his mind. *That's right—if this turns out to be the baby's mother, and her blood is on the blanket, she might not have been killed after leaving the baby.* That meant someone else, maybe the killer, delivered the baby to the Baths' cottage after the mother's death. Whatever the story was, Parrott's batteries were charged, and he was ready to find out.

# CHAPTER EIGHT

The Chesco dream team—Maria Rodriguez, Chief Coroner; Jerry Fite, head of forensics; and a third person Parrott didn't recognize; appeared on a distant footpath near the mouth of the creek, followed by a plodding, paper-clip-chewing Chief Schrik. Maria and Jerry were the county's heavy-hitters, both experienced and professional.

Parrott jogged to meet them as they navigated the rugged terrain. He shook hands with each one, and guided Schrik by the elbow as he stepped closer to the creek. "Where'd you park?"

"On the grounds behind Mooney's outbuildings. I stopped to notify Mooney about the body on his property first. He gave his okay, but I wouldn't be surprised if he comes down to rubberneck while we're here."

The group approached the woman's body with a silence born of respect. They formed a semi-circle, keeping about six feet away. Maria, as coroner, would be the first to examine her, but first everyone looked to Parrott to explain whatever he knew about the situation.

Parrott drew a long breath. "An infant girl was abandoned by an unknown party on the porch of the caretakers of the Campbell farm at approximately five-thirty this morning. There was blood on the baby's blanket. After the baby was transported to the hospital, I began a helicopter search with a local pilot. The woman's body gave off a weak signal to his infrared sensor, leading us here." He pointed to the berm. "Crush marks and what might be blood suggest the possibility that the woman was shot up there and the body rolled down the slope."

Parrott made eye contact with Maria. "In addition to the usual info, I'm hoping to learn whether this is the mother of the abandoned baby."

Maria nodded, and she gloved up before crouching next to the woman's body. She wore a navy-blue jumpsuit to protect her clothes. As both coroner and a licensed physician, she started

in examining the body and estimating the time of death. Parrott enjoyed working with Maria, because her zeal for uncovering information matched his own.

Although the woman exhibited no signs of life, Maria listened through her stethoscope for a heartbeat. Next, she lowered the woman's bikini panties and took her temperature with a rectal thermometer. Careful not to touch or move the body unnecessarily, she examined the back of the skull. Parrott had already looked. Besides copious amounts of drying blood, there was a bullet hole, possibly a .38. Maria stepped back and motioned for Jerry and his assistant, also clad in jumpsuits, to take over gathering evidence. She would do more once the body was taken to the morgue.

While the forensics team bagged the woman's hands and feet, Schrik stared, as if he'd never witnessed such a scene. Cases could be won or lost based on the accuracy of on-the-scene forensics, so his steady gaze probably reflected serious interest, but he remained hands-off.

Parrott stepped away to call Grossman back. Now that Schrik was here, Parrott wouldn't need to fly back by helicopter. "I appreciate all your help. Without you, I might be slogging through the countryside for days."

Grossman reported no unusual activity but promised to scour the area one more time on his way back.

Parrott disconnected while the forensics team was turning the dead woman over onto an unzipped body bag. Her front was as bloody and damaged as her back. The bullet that had ripped into the back of her head had been high-powered enough to blow off most of her face. Bile rose in Parrott's throat, and he walked over to Schrik in a fruitless attempt to ease his nausea. No matter how many dead bodies he'd seen ravaged by violence, each time the anger and bitterness brought an overwhelming reaction.

Schrik, too, had to turn away. He muttered something about her being too young to die and wandered toward the sycamore tree.

Parrott, despite the bilious clump in his chest, forced himself to watch. The woman's dress was bloody and dirty, ripped at the bodice, exposing part of a braless breast. From his spot, about fifteen feet away, it was impossible to tell whether the woman had

recently given birth. Anyway, Maria would give him a thorough report once she gave the body a full examination.

The cotton dress was loose at the waist, but now twisted around the woman's hips and thighs. The platform shoes featured four-inch heels. Without them, Parrott estimated the corpse's height at five-seven. Not that Parrott was a fashion expert, but the dress and shoes didn't appear to have been anything special. The baby's outfit and matching blanket had been more expensive-looking.

Bright coral nail polish covered the toenails and fingernails. No wedding ring, no jewelry except for the string bracelet, adorned the woman's body. Whatever had brought her to Brandywine Valley, she looked as out of place here on the back acreage of the Mooney farm as that sweet baby girl had been on the Baths' back porch, wrapped in a bloody blanket.

While the Chesco dream team zipped the victim's body in a protective polyurethane bag, Parrott strode to where Schrik was leaning against the tree. He bent to peer at Schrik's ashen face. "You okay, Chief?"

"Yeah. I'll be all right. Not used to seeing bodies up front and personal anymore. Somehow the photos take some of the sting out. You ready to go?"

"Sure. Give me a minute with Jerry. If he can meet us at my car, back at Grossman's place, I can transfer custody of the evidence from the baby." Parrott made the arrangements and met Schrik at the edge of the grass where he entered the scene.

The sun was overhead, and Parrott thought of all that had happened since Caro Campbell's early morning call. Schrik trudged next to him, apparently lost in thought. As they settled into Schrik's silver Lexus, the chief said, "I don't guess you're up for a late lunch."

Parrott shook his head. "Not at all."

Schrik started the car. "Me neither. Let's go to your car then."

# CHAPTER NINE

Schrik dropped Parrott off at his car, which he'd parked in front of Lew Grossman's helicopter hangar. The plight of the infant and the demise of the young woman preyed on his mind.

Jerry met Parrott while the others wrapped up the crime scene, and they transferred chain of custody of the baby's clothes, box, and vials of milk. Jerry would analyze them at the county forensics lab. A dozen ideas clamored for dominance in Parrott's mind. Who were these victims, and what were their stories? But before he did anything else, he needed to talk to Grossman.

As if on cue, the pilot's aircraft appeared overhead in the distance and whirred its way toward the landing pad a quarter-mile from Parrott's Toyota. It had been almost five hours since he and Grossman had taken off on their trek. Parrott jogged to where the 'copter was blowing hot wind in his face. Grossman cut the engine and removed his headphones.

"Glad you're still here, Parrott," the pilot said, as he stepped out onto the tarmac. "I ran a new grid over the ten-mile area that centered at the creek, where you found the body. The infrared beeped several times, but when I homed in on the signal, it was an animal, equestrian, farm hand—what you'd expect out here."

Before Parrott could thank Grossman and set off for the Mooney property, his phone beeped with a text from Tonya. Parrott almost never accepted phone calls when he was out in the field, and he and Tonya had a mutual understanding about not interrupting the other's day. Something told him he'd better read the message. Ever since Tonya's PTSD diagnosis, an unexpected beep from her set Parrott on edge.

"Excuse me a minute," he said to Grossman, and walked down the tarmac.

*Dr. Goldstone's office called to remind you to stop by to give him a sample. Love u.*

Producing sperm in a jar for the fertility doctor was the last thing Parrott wanted to do, but he also didn't want to debate over it now. He texted back, *How late is office open?*

*Till five, but receptionist said if you get there by six, someone can let you in.*

*OK, I'll try. Probably late for dinner.* Parrott's neck tightened from all the disparate issues, vying for priority. A cloak of stress wrapped around him whenever the topic of baby-making came up.

Parrott put away his phone. He needed to yank his mind back to the task at hand. He returned to Grossman, who was inspecting a mark on the door of the helicopter. "Thanks again for all—"

"Wait a minute. I'm not finished," Grossman said. "I think you ought to go back to that promontory above the body. I hovered over that area for a good ten minutes, trying to get close enough to pick up something useful. I didn't land, didn't want to do anything to mess up the scene. Looked to me like there might have been some kind of activity up there recently—maybe tire tracks. There's a copse of bushes, too, and something shiny lying on the ground past them, right near the ledge. That's all I could see."

The thought of something shiny lit up Parrott's brain. It could be a bullet casing, a hair ornament, or something else connected to the dead woman. Parrott had planned to go there as soon as he left Grossman's, but now the pull surged through him like a magnet. He copied the location from Grossman's GPS, thanked the man again, and took off in his car, windows down.

The late summer day filled his car with warm whooshes as he barreled through the quiet landscape. He gripped the steering wheel as if he were in a tight race. One thing he knew about evidence. It didn't like to wait around. If it was there, he needed to seize it while he could.

About two minutes before reaching his destination, he raised the windows and called Schrik. Maybe the chief had news about the baby. "I'm going back to the top of the embankment above where the body was found. Grossman thinks he spotted tire tracks up there."

"No problem. Let me know what you find." The chief's voice boomed through the cellphone. "I'm back at the office now, and

Barton's SUV is in the parking space. Hopefully, he's already calling hospitals."

Parrott clicked off and lowered the windows again, as he slowed and pulled off Strasburg Road onto a narrow two-lane street that served several farms. He drove to where the road intersected with a one-lane path to the Mooney estate, where a sign said, *Moonglow*. The path sprawled like a nest of pythons, toward the main house, split off into a circuitous route to the barn and stable, and then slithered to the back lot. A little further, a fork in the path led in one direction to the lower level where the creek was. That was the route Schrik and the forensics team had taken.

Parrott stayed on the path leading to the promontory, based on the GPS directions from Grossman. As he drove, he examined the area for signs of previous activity. The fact that there had been no rain for the past week would make it hard to discern tire tracks, but if Grossman had seen them from above, he should be able to see them, too.

There was only one route to the promontory by car, and this was it, an unpaved path in the middle of nowhere. Once he traveled past the outbuildings, the path became even narrower and soon it ended. His GPS said he was only two-tenths of a mile from the ledge.

Parrott jumped out of his car and started on foot. Grossman had mentioned tire tracks, and Parrott didn't want to contaminate the scene.

The uneven ground inclined gradually. The grass hadn't been mowed recently, and it tickled his ankles through his socks, as he walked. A hawk circled overhead, and Parrott passed several trees and shrubs that probably housed other birds and critters, but he forced himself to look down, where faint indentations in the grass had caught his eye. Were these the tracks Grossman had referred to?

Parrott opened the magnifier on his cellphone and held it about two feet from the ground. He couldn't be sure, but he thought these were tire tracks. He walked a few feet on one side of the marks. Finding no corresponding tracks there, he walked a few feet on the other side. *Bingo!* There was another stripe of indented grass. Even though they didn't show up well, Parrott photographed the

treads. He walked alongside the tire marks, which coincided with the directions his GPS was giving him.

Picking up the pace, he sprinted toward the ledge, and the closer he got, the deeper the marks grew. Finally, he came to the promontory, which was covered with patches of grass, pebbles, dirt, and bushes. There the tire tracks circled to the west, creating deeper ruts. A vehicle had obviously driven here recently, turned, and driven away. Parrott photographed the tread marks and measured the distance between the center of one and the center of the other—just over eighty-two inches. He'd figure out later which cars had wheelbases that wide.

Happy with the finding, Parrott turned his attention to whatever other clues might be found on this deserted piece of land, specifically the "something shiny" Grossman had mentioned. What he hoped for was the bullet casing that would match the bullet fired into the back of the woman's head. Of course, there was no guarantee that he would recover that bullet, considering the exit wound to her face. Still, Parrott would consider the casing a valuable piece of evidence.

He strode to the drop-off, aligning himself with the now-deserted area where the body had been discovered. Marked with stakes and crime scene tape, the rectangle drew his attention. Working backwards, he imagined the force and trajectory that would have landed her there. He crouched at the spot where he guessed she had stood when she was shot.

Lightly brushing the ground, Parrott found nothing of significance. The greenery was thick in patches, especially around the bushes Grossman had described. He lowered himself to hands and knees. Inch by inch, he combed through the terrain in an imaginary grid pattern similar to the one Grossman had used to search from the sky.

Aside from an anthill and a thorny weed that dug into his knee, he didn't find anything of interest, but he pushed on. Entering the area closest to the edge, Parrott found something shiny. He sat up on his knees and photographed it. He pulled the latex gloves and bag from his pocket. With gloved fingers he lifted a shiny silver toe ring and turned it in the afternoon sunlight.

Parrott bagged the small, filigreed ring and sealed the bag before putting it in his back pocket. The tire tracks, the ring, the blood on the slope, and the location of the body had gone a long way toward supporting Parrott's theory about the way the killing had gone down, but he wasn't entirely satisfied yet.

Back on hands and knees, Parrott patted the ground around him, moving to the right, to the left, and backward. A breeze cooled the back of his head and neck, while the rocky ground caused sporadic shots of discomfort through his knees, his palms, and the tops of his shoes. He was about to give up, when his hand brushed against something small and hard, buried in a large tuft of grass. Still wearing the glove, he photographed it and lifted the object into the light, as he had done with the ring. What caught the daylight in a mellow glow was a slim, five-inch switchblade, sprung and ready to use.

# CHAPTER TEN

Parrott bagged the knife and the toe ring and secured them in his locked glove compartment. His stomach rumbled. Too many hours had passed since the half-eaten bowl of oatmeal this morning. He pulled into a Wawa for a pit stop and a ten-inch hoagie on his way to the station. The smell of the tender roast beef and cheddar cheese nearly knocked him over. He debated buying two.

The clock over the checkout counter said three-forty-five, so he passed on the second sandwich and added a Snickers bar instead. His grandmother had rewarded him with a Snickers on special occasions, and today he'd earned one. He'd planned to wait till he got to the station, but his mouth watered so much that he bought a tall black coffee and picnicked in his car.

Back at the station, Parrott parked between Schrik's Lexus and Officer Barton's SUV. Glad that both were there, he retrieved the toe ring and knife from his glove compartment and hustled into the station, stopping first to lock the evidence in the station's safe. He'd deliver it to Jerry on his way home.

Parrott then headed for Randy Barton's small office at the front end of the hallway, next to the kitchenette. Barton was leaning back in his chair, eyes closed, phone receiver mashed against his ear. Parrott knocked on the doorframe, and Barton's eyes flew open. He stood and waved Parrott into the office, pointing to the single chair in front of him, and holding his index finger in the "one-minute" signal.

The room smelled faintly of tobacco, and Parrott wondered whether Barton had taken up smoking. He hoped not, since Chief Schrik, having kicked the habit, had strong opinions about cigarettes on the premises. Parrott lowered himself into the metal chair, taking in details while he waited. The officer looked every bit of his fifty-two years. Whiskers dotted his face and neck, and his eyelids threatened to close again any second. Whatever caused

him to take the morning off must have butt-kicked him but good. Parrott considered himself a friend, but not close enough to ask.

"—And that's the last one? Okay, thanks much." Barton scribbled something on the paper in front of him and hung up. "Hey, Parrott. I hear I missed a lot of excitement this morning. Sorry not to have been able to help out more." He handed the chart he'd been writing on across the desk.

Scratchy handwriting filled boxes, and doodles decorated the margins. "This the list of female births?" Parrott ran his finger down the eight listings. One column held the date of delivery. The others showed the hospital, hospital location, mother's name, date of discharge, and address. One of the rows had the words *twin girls* in the right margin. "Did you go to all five of the hospitals in the county?"

"Yep. I talked to the records people in person. This last one was born today, so probably not relevant. That's why they called me just now. They wanted to make sure the list was complete. I've got the data from each hospital on email. This is my own creation." Barton managed a fleeting smile.

"Thanks, man. Have any of these eight babies have been reported missing?"

"Nothing's come through that I know of, but I'll keep checking." Barton took the chart back from Parrott and set it inside a manila folder.

Parrott stood. He wanted to get to Schrik's office before the chief left for the day.

Barton also stood. "Care to fill me in on the case?"

"Sure, but not right now. I've got a million things to do, and Tonya needs me to make a stop on the way home. How about we talk in the morning?"

The officer threw his hands in the air. "Okay, okay, busy person. I can't keep up with you these days."

Parrott stopped in his tracks. He hated the implication that he was marginalizing Barton. The officer had both age and experience on Parrott, and Parrott's speedy rise to the position of detective must chafe. He returned to his seat. "I'm not trying to keep you in the dark, man. All I know so far is a baby left on a back porch is now at Brandywine Hospital. A dead woman, shot in the back of

the head, was found on the back acreage of Stuart Mooney's farm. I can't confirm a connection at this point."

"No ID?"

"That would be too easy," Parrott said, chuckling. He leaned back and scratched his head. "I've talked to the couple who found the baby. I didn't get much, but I'll go back. I need to interview Mr. Mooney, too. Right now, I'm waiting for reports from Maria and Jerry at Chesco."

"We'll figure it all out, Parrott. We always do." Barton gripped the edge of his desk. "Funny, though."

"What's funny?" Parrott asked.

"Why would someone leave a baby at the doorstep of a groundskeeper's cottage when the Campbells' house was right there? You'd think they'd want the child to be raised by somebody rich."

Parrott headed for the door. "Agreed. When you're finished checking out the eight babies, maybe you could run background on T.J. and Kate Bath. I assume T.J. is a nickname. Perhaps there's a connection between them and the baby."

"Yeah. What's the old saying? If it's not about money, it's gotta be about sex, politics, or religion."

# CHAPTER ELEVEN

Time was getting away from Parrott with so much on his mind, and as he drove west toward the fertility clinic, the descending sun shot glaring rays at his windshield. He pulled down the visor and squinted. It would be dark before he got to Chesco and then home.

He'd only been there once before. Dr. Goldstone, a genial man with graying temples, a New York accent, and a soothing manner, had reassured them with explanations of modern treatments and encouraging statistics. "If you get to that point," he'd said. "Right now let's assume you are two healthy young people, and you won't end up needing my services after all."

Parrott had exhaled from the reprieve. As much as he wanted to be a father, he wasn't eager to embark on a regimen of tightly controlled scientific experiments involving strangers in what should be private marital moments. But Tonya had a different mindset. She'd put off trying to get pregnant while she dealt with PTSD, and now that her therapist and she had pronounced herself ready, she didn't want to waste more time. She and Parrott both were approaching their twenty-ninth birthdays, and she was determined to have her first baby before she turned thirty.

As he turned into the parking lot for the fertility clinic, he thought about the mental paradigm shift that occurred when a couple stopped preventing birth and started promoting birth. The image of the baby in the yellow duck-decorated outfit floated before his eyes, and he wondered about the person who had left her on a groundskeeper's porch.

Following instructions, Parrott parked in the back, opposite a green door with an electronic combination lock. He grabbed his evidence from the glove compartment and secured it in his jacket pockets before jumping out and locking his car. His assigned combination was 1-4-3, code for the number of letters in "I love you." Dr. Goldstone had explained the back entrance was a means of providing privacy and a measure of comfort for prospective

fathers, who might appreciate not being scrutinized by the female patients in the waiting room at the front of the office.

As soon as he gained access to the inside hallway, the green sign saying, "Gentlemen Only," drew him to the small bathroom. Soft music and a piney smell greeted him inside, where sterile plastic containers, packets of alcohol wipes, and instructions for collecting sperm sat on a small table. Fine-tip markers and labels stood ready for accurate identification. When he was finished, he was to carry the specimen to the counter at the end of the hall, where someone from the lab would log it in. Everything, it seemed, had been ordained, except for putting him in the mood for producing the sample. That was entirely up to him.

Parrott conjured the image of Tonya and invited her into the Gentlemen Only bathroom. He did what he needed to do. Afterwards, he toted his labeled specimen jar into the hallway and headed for the lab counter, where he deposited the jar into the hands of a receptionist, who placed it in a mini-refrigerator.

Voices emanated from the room beyond the counter, and Dr. Goldstone emerged, a briefcase in one hand and his car fob in the other. "Goodnight, Julia. I'll see you in the morning."

Seeing Parrott, he freed his right hand for a warm shake. "Hello, detective. Your wife told me you might not make it before we closed." An empathetic smile creased the skin around his eyes. "Once upon a time, I was in your shoes. I remember the experience."

A little uncomfortable with the intimacy, Parrott nodded, but shifted back into detective mode. "Actually, I have a question for you, doctor, on another topic altogether."

"Sure. Would you like to sit down in my office?" Goldstone pointed across the hall.

"Not necessary. I imagine you've delivered a lot of babies, right?" When the man nodded, Parrott went on. "Can you take a look at this newborn baby's umbilical cord and give me your thoughts?" Parrott opened his cellphone photos and scrolled to the ones of the baby's middle.

Dr. Goldstone set his briefcase on the floor and put his fob in his pocket. He leaned his back against the wall and gazed at the photos for a while. "Well, it doesn't look like the typical umbilical

stump. It's usually about yay long." His thumb and forefinger demonstrated a one- or two-inch measurement. "Usually the edge has been cut with a scissors and placed in a yellow plastic clamp. Looks a little like a hairpin. The whole thing dries up and falls off about forty-eight to seventy-two hours after the procedure."

Parrott asked, "What does it mean that there is no clamp in this case? Also, the edge is jagged and a little red."

The doctor raised an eyebrow. "I noticed that, of course. I couldn't say for certain, especially if I didn't know how much time had elapsed post-partum, but most likely the umbilicus would be slightly infected if it's red. It might have been tied off with a string or a shoelace, instead of a surgical scissors."

Parrott's mind raced with thoughts about the abandoned infant. "Would that mean—"

Goldstone's eyes met Parrott's. "It most likely would indicate that the baby had not been born in a hospital or under medical supervision, such as by a midwife. Professionals would have the right equipment."

An annoying twinge bothered Parrott. There were many things he didn't know about babies. As he put away his cellphone, Goldstone cleared his throat.

"Something else?" Parrott asked.

"Well, since I know your occupation, I'm guessing these photos belong to an unidentified newborn. The only way to identify the baby would be DNA. If you have the afterbirth or any tissue from the mother, that tissue will give you the best answers."

A piece slipped into place in Parrott's evolving picture of his new case. He was more determined than ever to find out this foundling's origins.

# CHAPTER TWELVE

The west-bound traffic on Highway 30 slowed Parrott's trek to the Chester County building in West Chester. In the few minutes that he'd been inside the fertility clinic, the sun had dived into the horizon, leaving streaks of varying shades of blue and gray in its wake. He didn't mind the driving. The day had been chock-full of activity, and the car's motion helped him process.

Caro, the Baths, the baby, the EMTs, Grossman, the dead woman, the forensics team, the promontory, the list of female births, and the fertility clinic—all provided bits of information that might or might not fit together into patterns in the coming days and weeks.

First thing tomorrow he needed to see Judge Manetti to approve warrants for testing the DNA of the dead woman and the live baby. Meanwhile, he could gather information from Chesco.

The county building was modern, brick, and full of windows. No matter what time of the day or night, there were always lights on in some of the offices. Parrott eyed the window on the first floor, occupied by the morgue and its adjoining offices. Stripes of light spilled through the blinds, which had been lowered, but not closed. Death never took a break, not at night, not on weekends, not on holidays.

Parrott had good relationships with both coroners and most people in the forensics lab, but the Chief Coroner, Maria Rodriguez, and Forensics Director, Jerry Fite, were especially close colleagues and friends. Both had done him favors in the past, like ignoring time protocols and pushing for quick answers. He crossed his fingers that one or both were still in the building.

He started with forensics. He wanted to get the toe ring and switchblade into custody with the other items related to the dead woman. Jerry was packing a briefcase, preparing to leave for the day, when Parrott entered.

Greeting the detective with an eyeroll and a toothy grin, Jerry said, "Well, I almost made it out of the office for the day." He set his briefcase on a chair and invited Parrott to sit across from him. "I'm actually glad you came in when you did. I have a bit of news for you—actually, could be important news."

"Tell me." Parrott set the two bags of evidence on the desk in front of him, where Jerry could see them. "I can use important news right now."

"Okay, but it looks like you have important news for me, too. I'll go first." Jerry leaned back in his chair, his eyes shining. "When we returned to the lab, I went to the morgue to fingerprint the victim. I sent you a copy of the prints. They should be in your inbox. Then I got started with the material from the baby, specifically the stains on the baby blanket. The Kastle-Meyer test showed a peroxidase reaction of hemoglobin."

"So it is human blood." Parrott had expected as much, but it was good to have that confirmed.

"Unless we had a false positive, which I doubt." Jerry laced his fingers and stretched his hands behind his neck. "I then ran an ABO typing test to individualize the sample. The blood on the blanket tested positive for type AB blood, the rarest type, as you know."

From an investigator's standpoint that was good news. Less than six percent of the world's population had AB blood. "Go on."

"Next, I ran an Rh typing test. The Rh factor was present."

Rh negative blood in the AB category would have been even rarer, with less than one percent of the AB population having no Rh cell surface protein on their blood, but Parrott was good to go with the AB+ result. His thoughts jumped from the baby blanket to the blood oozing from the woman's body.

"I know what you're thinking, and Maria and I were on the same wavelength. Maria's preliminary assessment of the woman's body revealed that she had recently given birth. She gave me a blood sample from the woman's body."

Parrott gulped a breath and held it. A post-partum mother and an established connection with the abandoned infant would make both investigations more targeted, more precise.

"I ran the same tests on that sample. Same results."

Parrott huffed and reached across the desk to shake Jerry's hand.

Jerry gripped tightly but tilted his head in warning. "Don't forget there's a margin of error in these presumptive tests. You can leap, but not too high."

Parrott understood the caution, but a two-time result of AB+ blood was convincing enough for him right now. "I get it. I'm going to proceed with caution on the assumption that the baby's blanket had contact with the dead woman, but I can't assume that the dead woman is her mother." He rose and paced to the door and back. "I'm hoping we can do DNA testing right away, as soon as I can get the warrants. That connection is vital to this investigation."

"I knew you would think so," Jerry said. "I'll order it the minute you have the warrants. Planning to use hair from the woman and a sample of the feces from the baby's diaper. Maybe the breast milk sample, too."

"Thanks, Jerry." Parrott returned to the chair. "You're the best ever."

Jerry's smile revealed a dimple in his left cheek. "You're not bad, yourself. Now can I go home?"

Returning the grin, Parrott slid the two evidence bags across the desk. "Not like you need permission from me, but I do have one more favor—"

"Log in this new evidence? Sure thing." As he began the process of labeling the new evidence, Jerry glanced at Parrott and said, "You know, I think this is the most evidence I've ever seen you turn over in any one day."

# CHAPTER THIRTEEN

The lightness in Parrott's mood after leaving Jerry's office had little to do with shedding the two evidence bags and everything to do with the information about the blood type match. Despite what he'd said to Jerry, his heart flipped with the likelihood that the post-partum woman was the mother of the baby.

He almost flew down the stairway to the coroner's office. Maria exited the office as Parrott approached the door, and they nearly collided.

"Oomph. Sorry, I didn't see you." Maria was wearing most likely her third wardrobe change of the day, a navy skirt and a powder blue tank and sweater. Even with six-inch heels, she was a foot shorter than Parrott.

Parrott stepped back, trying to minimize the clumsy near-contact. "Entirely my fault. I wasn't paying attention." Heat rushed to his face. "You're obviously leaving for the day."

"Yes, I'm meeting my husband for dinner. I can give you a couple of minutes if you'd like. I sent you a preliminary report by email."

"That's okay then. I don't want to delay you." Everyone had worked a long day, and he looked forward to relaxing with Tonya and their pet cockatiel Horace.

"You sure? If I know you, you have a million questions about this dead woman, and, although I don't have a million answers yet, I do have a few." She dug into her handbag for her ID badge to swipe access back into the office.

"No, how about I walk you to your car? You can brief me on the way."

Maria put her badge away and led the way to the exit. "Okay, I don't have much. The TOD, based on body temperature and weather conditions is approximately five a.m. with a half-hour margin of error on either side. The woman had given birth recently—no episiotomy or stitches, but obvious signs of stretching, trauma,

and discharge in the vaginal area. The muscle tone of the belly is also consistent with recent pregnancy."

Parrott opened and held the exterior door open, and the two stepped into the evening air. The neighborhood was dark and quiet, the art gallery and breakfast restaurant across the street having closed hours ago. "How recent do you think the birth was?" Parrott couldn't estimate the age of the infant, except that Dr. Goldstone had mentioned the umbilical stump's forty-eight to seventy-two hours.

"Not long—maybe a day or two or three. Her breasts were leaking, but not engorged. Typically, the hospital gives non-breast-feeding mothers a hormone shot to dry up their milk, but we aren't able to evaluate whether she received the shot at this point."

Maria fobbed the door of her Jeep Cherokee, and Parrott opened it. "Anything else I should know before I read the report?"

"Not all that much. Lots of scratches and bruises, some scars, no tatts, tan lines. The gunshot wound in the back of the head is most likely the cause of death, but we won't be positive about that until toxicology comes back."

"You have a guess as to her age?"

"Somewhere between eighteen and twenty-two, I'd say, but—" Maria scooted onto the seat of the jeep and swung her legs in. "I don't want to sound insensitive or disrespectful, but this isn't the body of an innocent young woman. Not the kind we normally see in these parts."

"Because she had a baby, you mean?" Parrott asked.

"No, more than that." Maria fixed her skirt and started her engine. "The nail polish and the fashionable clothing and shoes paint one picture, but multiple scars from cuts and burns paint another. You know the old saying about a girl having been around the block? I can't help thinking that about her. Please keep that between you and me."

"Of course," Parrott said, stunned. This was the first time Maria had ever described a victim in anything other than objective terms. Maria's professionalism was impeccable, so there must be empirical evidence that had prompted her opinion. "Thanks for the info. Have a good evening."

Maria took off, and Parrott called Tonya to say he'd be home in fifteen minutes or less. As he drove, he thought about all the things he hoped for, little and big. He hoped the sample he'd produced at the fertility clinic would turn out fine. He hoped he'd be able to learn the truth about the woman's death. Most of all, he hoped the infant girl in the yellow embroidered outfit would survive her shaky beginnings and enjoy a good life.

# CHAPTER FOURTEEN

The gigantic house in West Chester lacked the coziness of the one-bedroom bungalow where Parrott and Tonya had started out their married life. True, they had a swimming pool and an in-house gym now, thanks to the multi-million dollar gift from their friend, Elle Carmichael, but all their basic needs had been met in the smaller place, and Parrott had loved being "tucked in" with Tonya and Horace. Here, the spacious rooms and high ceilings gave him a cold shiver as he entered, even though the rooms were comfortable temperature-wise.

Horace was having a difficult adjustment, too. The fifteen-foot ceilings in the kitchen and family room were a particular bother for the bird, whose cage and tiny play area in the other house were his kingdom. Horace had already hurt himself a few times by flying into the tall windows, and the vet had suggested keeping him in his cage for most of the day, for a few more weeks, until he acclimated.

Tonya was nowhere in sight, so Parrott strode straight to the bird's cage. "How's the best bird in the universe?" He opened the door and extended a finger for Horace to hop onto.

"Welcome home," the bird squawked, as he jumped to Parrott's shoulder and nuzzled his neck. Horace had been a gift from Tonya before she deployed to Afghanistan. He and Parrott had kept each other company for a long time now, and Parrott regarded him with amusement and affection.

"Where's your mama?" Parrott asked. The aroma of chicken and dumplings grabbed his attention, and he sauntered to the stove, where a foil-wrapped aluminum pan sat, still warm. His mother had been over and dropped it off—he was positive.

"One-two, one-two." Horace's vocabulary required no further explanation. Tonya was downstairs in the gym, working out.

Parrott set the bird back in his cage and closed the door. On his way to the basement, he passed several sealed cardboard boxes marked, "Ollie," on the floor next to the sofa. More evidence that

his mother had been here. He took off his jacket and folded it over a chair.

Dashing down the stairs to the basement, Parrott had a random thought. Tonya had known he'd be home, and she typically didn't work out in the evenings. Not that he had a problem with having to find her, but he wondered what might have happened to break her pattern.

When he entered the gym, Tonya was standing by the parallel bars, lifting a ten-pound weight with her "bad" arm. She wore a sports bra, tight-fitting sweatpants, and ballet slippers. Her eyes were closed, and she whispered, "One, two, one, two," as she bent her arm at the elbow. He hated to stop her reverie.

"Hi, honey. Mind if I join you?" Parrott lowered himself onto a large fitness ball opposite her.

Tonya's eyes flew open, and she set down the weight. She straddled the ball behind Parrott and encircled his waist with her arms. "I didn't hear you come in. I'm so glad you're home."

She lifted herself high enough to kiss his neck, and he pulled her around for a mouth kiss. Finally, Parrott knew he was home, right here, sitting on an exercise ball.

"Hungry? Your mother brought dinner."

"Right now I'm very hungry," Parrott said.

"Which kind?"

"Both." Parrott took his wife by the hands and led her to the slant board, which, at this moment, looked big enough for two.

A half hour later, Tonya asked, "Now do you want to satisfy your other hunger? We've got chicken and dumplings upstairs."

When they emerged into the open space that was kitchen, breakfast room, and Horace's room, the bird cawed, "One two, one two." Laughing, Tonya opened the refrigerator. "Do you want a drink while I heat up this dinner?"

Parrott hesitated. "Not really. Maybe I'll cut up a salad." While he gathered the ingredients, he asked Tonya about her day.

"Nothing special," she said. "I had a Zoom session with Alice this morning."

Alice was Tonya's therapist at the VA hospital. "How'd it go?"

"Fine. Good. Then I stopped at the library to check out the new release shelves. Ed Aymar has a new thriller out. And I met a

woman who lives at the end of the *cul de sac*. Lorraine Franklin. Her husband Will went to Syracuse a couple of years before us. She seems like a good person."

Parrott was delighted that Tonya was meeting people in the neighborhood. Maybe she really had conquered the worst of the PTSD. "Why don't you invite them over for drinks and dinner by the pool? I can barbecue, but we'd better do it soon. This warm weather won't last much longer."

"That sounds great, but are you sure you won't be tied up in some big case or another? You left out of here so early this morning, I thought, *Uh-oh*."

Guilt tapped against Parrott's heart. He had good intentions, but the truth was, when he had a case going, his home schedule was erratic. And as of this morning, he had a case going. He poured bleu cheese dressing over the salad and tossed it before carrying it to the table. "You're right, baby. My work isn't compatible with a social life a lot of the time, and I'm sorry for that."

"You know you can quit anytime, Ollie. You don't have to turn yourself inside out every time someone in Brandywine Valley goes batshit crazy. After that fentanyl incident, I don't know how you have the nerve to keep doing this." The timer buzzed, and Tonya removed the pan from the oven and carried it to the table.

"We've had this talk. I can't see myself retiring at age twenty-nine. I haven't worked hard all my life—in school and at West Brandywine—to sit on my rear and act like the idle rich. That's not me. I have a talent, and I need to use it." The words sounded abrupt, even to his own ears, and he knew he should walk it back. "That said, I want us to have a normal life, and if you want to make friends with these neighbors, I'm in. Invite them for Saturday night or Sunday, and I'll make it my business to be here." Parrott thought of the dead woman and the little baby and hoped this was a promise he could keep.

While they dined on Cora's famous chicken and dumplings and Parrott's salad, they discussed everything from Dr. Goldstone to decorating plans for the house. After a while, they landed on the topic of the boxes on the floor marked, "Ollie."

"My mother's probably divesting herself of my keepsakes, now that we've got room in our house to store them. Let's just put them in the basement."

"Maybe we should open them and see what's inside. I'm not a believer in keeping junk. If there's meaningful stuff in them, let's get it out in the open."

An imaginary hand gripped the back of Parrott's neck, sending cold waves down his spine. "I—uh—I might not be ready to open those boxes quite yet."

Tonya reached across the table to take Parrott's hand in her own. "Why, Ollie? What do you think might be in the boxes?"

Parrott swallowed hard. He found it way easier to confront other people's problems and sorrows than his own. "Not what I think. What I know. There's a bunch of things in those boxes that relate to my cousin Bo. I might not be ready to sort through those things."

Tonya's eyes filled with sympathetic tears. She had also known losses. "Bo's been gone for three years now. Maybe the best way to honor his memory would be to unpack and remember the good times, instead of keeping them locked up in a box?"

"Good point, except that I'm still torturing myself over the fact that Bo was killed by a cop." Parrott's normally smooth baritone came out like a growl. "Even though he was 'collateral damage,' I can't help thinking that could've been me. I could've been the one who killed my cousin."

"O-kay," Tonya said, as she rounded the table to put her arms around her husband's neck. "Looks like I'm not the only person in this household with PTSD."

# CHAPTER FIFTEEN

A recurring "cop dream" fractured Parrott's sleep and woke him. He stared at the electric blue light of his alarm clock—5:14. This dream featured hand and ankle cuffs that prevented Parrott from defusing a bomb set in a baby's nursery. The nightmares had begun after Parrott was poisoned with fentanyl, and they showed no sign of letting up. He swung his legs out of bed, trying to decide whether to get up or return to the nightmare. Finally giving up on any amount of quality rest, he set up his laptop at the breakfast table instead of in his spacious new home office. Having an office would take some getting used to. He might as well put the wakefulness toward something productive.

He tiptoed around the kitchen so as not to wake Tonya, even though their bedroom was upstairs and down a long hall. His preset Keurig Duo had already brewed a pot of black coffee and was keeping it warm. He filled the large mug, a souvenir from their honeymoon cruise. In the old house, Parrott would have removed the cover from Horace's cage and let the little guy keep him company at the table. But now, until he became accustomed to the new environment, Horace needed to stay in his cage. Between that and Tonya's sleeping in, Parrott felt like a solitary castaway on a very big island.

Exhausted, he'd gone to bed without opening the Chesco report containing the dead woman's prints. Now he needed to put together the warrants for Judge Manetti and run the prints through AFIS, the automated fingerprint system. While the database did its magic, Parrott fixed some fried eggs and bacon and refilled his mug. Parrott loved the sizzles and the smells of a kitchen at breakfast time. Many times, this scene might be the only warm and cozy part of a long day.

By the time he'd eaten and cleaned up the kitchen, the fingerprint report was in. He crossed his fingers mentally before opening the link. The brevity of the report sent his heart to his feet, even before he read the words. No match.

Parrott recalled his remark to Randy Barton yesterday. Nothing was ever easy, investigating Brandywine Valley cases. It was if the fates enjoyed messing with the process. AFIS searched billions of records, but unless the prints came from someone who had been fingerprinted—a person of interest, a convicted criminal, a public servant—he or she wouldn't be identified. When prints didn't talk, DNA would be the next step, but DNA took longer and cost more.

Since he was at the computer, Parrott looked up criminal records for Stuart Mooney, Kate Bath, and T.J. (Thomas John) Bath. He didn't expect to find anything much, not because the Brandywine people were clean, but because they rarely got caught. So when T.J. Bath lit up with a simple assault from a bar brawl ten years ago, Parrott was surprised. Ruled a third-degree misdemeanor, Bath had been sentenced to a year of probation. Parrott wondered whether Caro or John E. knew their handyman had been convicted of a crime. The Campbells hadn't hired him—he'd worked for the previous owners.

No criminal records on any of the others. County tax rolls showed Mooney as having purchased his property, Moonglow, nineteen years ago. A quick check of Mooney's driver's license revealed his current age to be fifty-nine. Forty was relatively young to be able to afford a large property in Brandywine, but Mooney's scotch company had produced generational wealth, not uncommon in this area.

Not being a connoisseur of scotch, himself, Parrott took a few moments to read up on the product. As with other alcoholic beverages, there were a wide range of brands, production processes, flavors, and a snobbery, in this case, in favor of scotch produced in Scotland. Moonglow's high quality taste evidently came from Scottish barley, peat, barrels, and tannins, and it enjoyed a fine reputation among the Scottish-derived drinks. The company held no presence in the United States, beyond having its product imported and distributed here.

Stuart Mooney, in fact, maintained his primary residence in Edinburgh and had dual citizenship. He'd married an American heiress, Constance Flynn, and raised his two children, Catherine and Steven, in the Philadelphia area. A public figure, Mooney was featured in dozens of photographs on the internet, some

with dignitaries, some with his wife. A few photos included his daughter, now an adult.

Parrott could find no photos of Mooney's son, which raised a possible red flag. There could be innumerable reasons for the son of an extremely successful businessman to be out of the family's social picture, most of them innocent, but Steven Mooney had snagged Parrott's interest.

Of course, the Mooney family as a whole could be entirely irrelevant to the abandonment of the baby, and even the body of the young woman. The proximity to the former and the location of the latter could be pure coincidence, in which case, Parrott would soon lose interest in them. But his gut wouldn't let them off the hook yet.

His mind turned to the plight of the baby. He wondered whether she had spent the night in the hospital, or whether she'd been placed her in a home already. The demand for adoptable newborn babies had grown in recent years. Placing her would be easy, a perfect little baby with all her fingers and toes. The memory of her umbilical stump, ragged and slightly red, gave him a twinge and reminded him of something he needed to tell Randy Barton.

By now, Parrott had downed the second mug of coffee, and his nerves were jumping, ready to start the day. At almost six-thirty, he wouldn't wake Barton if he sent a text message to halt the post-partum investigation of babies born in area hospitals. They could always resume that later, if need be, but for now Parrott felt reasonably sure this baby hadn't been delivered by a professional. Barton's time could be put to better use. Parrott sent a second text with the photos of the tire tracks from the promontory. *Can you check on what kind of vehicle could leave treads like these, eighty-two inches apart?*

What really had Parrott's mind buzzing, though, was the possible connection between the dead woman by the creek and the baby on the porch. The AB+ blood from the woman and on the blanket was a strong clue, but Parrott needed more. Waiting for DNA results was nerve-wracking, but the police contact at child protective services, Monica Bell, should be able to find out whether the baby had Type AB+ blood.

He put in a call to Monica's office, expecting to get voicemail and leave a message, but evidently she was an early riser, too. "How may I help you?" she asked, wasting no words.

Parrott gave her his badge number and the details of the child abandonment. "I'd appreciate any information you can give me about the infant's condition, how old she is, but I'm especially interested in her blood type."

"Stand by. I'll call you back."

Parrott didn't mind the abruptness. He understood how swamped the personnel in the system were, and he could also do without niceties. Before he could plan his next steps, his cellphone rang.

"Detective Parrott? Monica Bell." Traffic noises punctuated the background. "Your infant is doing well. She's in a temporary placement in Philadelphia. She was approximately three days old when brought into the hospital, and her blood type is B positive."

"Ohhh," Parrott said, his hopes falling like a pair of worn-out suspenders.

"Why so dismayed, detective? Were you expecting something different?"

A little embarrassed at being so transparent, Parrott explained that he was trying to match the baby to a possible mother with type AB+.

"An AB mother can have a B daughter. Doesn't prove the relationship, but doesn't rule it out, either." A car honked, and Ms. Bell uttered a grunt. "Anything else I can help with?"

Armed with this bit of information, which Parrott would double-check with someone in the medical field, he was in a hurry to disconnect, too. His day was off to a productive start.

# CHAPTER SIXTEEN

Leaving a note for Tonya, Parrott filled his thermos with coffee, grabbed his briefcase, and headed for his car. Now that Parrott lived in West Chester, stopping by Chesco on his way into the station was convenient. He wouldn't wear out his welcome, but when he had an active case with forensic evidence, Jerry never seemed to mind his dropping by in person, especially if accompanied by coffee and a bagel.

Of course, the evidence in question had arrived there less than twenty-four hours before, so Parrott didn't expect much in the way of reports. In fact, he wasn't sure whether Jerry would be on duty this early after late hours the day before.

He was glad, then, to find Jerry—not only at work behind the wall of glass in the lab, but also examining the toe ring and the switchblade Parrott had brought in yesterday evening. Jerry was covered from head to toe in protective garb, including latex and plastic. He wore magnifying glasses, gloves, and a mask covering his nose and mouth, and he used pincers to handle the objects.

Parrott stayed on the lobby side of the glass wall but held the tray from Dunkin Donuts aloft. Jerry pointed to the outside counter. "Be with you in a minute. I'm almost finished here."

Parrott set the coffee and bagel down but passed on taking the single seat at the small table in the outer office. Instead, he walked back and forth, concentrating on his memory of the promontory, where he'd discovered the tire tracks, the toe ring, and the knife. He hoped Jerry could connect the latter two objects to the dead woman.

Jerry secured the evidence, stripped off his outer garments, and exited the clean room. He rubbed his hands together as he reached for the tall cup of coffee Parrott had brought. "Just what I need to get my engine in gear this morning. Thanks." He walked around the counter to sit at the table.

Parrott perched on the edge of the chair and waited. Jerry would reveal what he could in his own time. His jolly voice boded well.

"Okay, buddy, I've got some news for ya." Jerry stood to retrieve the bag with the bagel from the counter. "Hey, cinnamon-raisin, my favorite." He broke off a piece and popped it in his mouth, dry. "The knife had plenty of good prints, none of them wiped. I compared them to the prints from the vic in th'morgue. They match."

Parrott huffed. Prints of the killer would be better news, but at least he had a proven connection between the knife and the dead woman, and he could factor in the location. "No other prints on the knife? How about blood?"

"Nope, no blood. Just the vic's fingerprints. Begs the question of how she was planning to use the thing, but that's your bailiwick, not mine."

Parrott was thinking the same thing. "Maybe she was suspicious of the person who killed her, and she had it ready to protect herself, when he blew away the back of her head."

"Well, as I always say, conjecture is your world. Data is mine." Jerry took another bite and chewed, washing it down with coffee. "Now, about the toe ring. Measures four and a half centimeters in circumference. The dead lady's second toe, left foot, measures four on the nose—er, on the toe. Her other phalanges are wider than that, so if she wore the ring, it was on the second."

"And the extra half-centimeter might have been enough to cause the ring to slip off before she rolled down the hill." Parrott pictured a violent skirmish involving a knife, a gun, a toe ring, and a vehicle with an eighty-two-inch track width. More details would need to fall into place before he'd have a good enough image, but he was on his way. "Have you got anything else for me this morning?"

"Nope, not yet. Waiting on the DNA to come back. Maria and I are betting it's the vic's blood on the baby blanket and the vic turns out to be the baby's mother."

"I won't bet against you on those," Parrott said. "Well, let me get out of your way. I know you've got plenty other cases to work on, and I appreciate the quick service."

"No problem," Jerry said, standing and waving his empty food bag "Thanks for the wake-up food."

Parrott had left his own wake-up food in his car, a blueberry muffin to go with the coffee in his thermos. He took a swig of coffee, which had cooled a little, but still filled the car with a bittersweet aroma and went down like warm honey as he drove to Judge Manetti's house, where he was expected. Within a few minutes, he had the DNA warrants in hand, ready to go.

Arriving at the station, Parrott carried in  the cardboard tray and a bag containing coffees and muffins for Schrik, Barton, and Lucretia, the dispatcher. After the long day yesterday and almost no sleep, he felt like playing Santa Claus. Generosity had always been his way of perking up.

When he got to work, though, neither Barton nor Schrik was there. Lucretia was thrilled with her breakfast. She told Parrott she'd put the others' in the breakroom fridge. The two men could use the microwave whenever they came in.

Parrott headed up the stairs to his office, mulling over possible reasons Randy Barton would be out again this morning. Schrik, he didn't concern himself with. The chief made his own hours, often coming in late and staying late. But Barton's pattern was different—reliable, prompt. He'd never come in late two days in a row. Of course, a personal emergency could derail anyone's work schedule, but cops made their livings noticing patterns, so a broken pattern stuck out like a summer snowflake.

When he got to his office, another broken pattern hit him in the face. A manila envelope was taped to the door by its unsealed flap. Inside was a list of vehicles with an eighty-two-inch track width. The single sheet of paper had been printed from an internet site at 7:04 this morning, a little more than a half hour after Parrott had texted Barton with the tire-track photos. There was no note, no signature, nothing to identify the person who'd taped the envelope to the door, except it could only be one person.

Parrott glanced at the paper. All the vehicles listed were trucks and SUVs. The burning question was not about automobiles. It was about Randy Barton. At the risk of being over-sensitive, Parrott could think of only one reason for Barton to submit such a cursory list in such an uncommunicative way. Barton must be resentful. Maybe he thought Parrott had no business ordering him around. None of this passive-aggressiveness had existed between

them before the multi-million-dollar gift had completely altered Parrott's world. *Damn it.*

Parrott checked the text he had sent at six-thirty, calling him off investigating the hospital births and asking him to check out car track widths. Parrott's text had not been overly solicitous—he hadn't used the word, "please,"—but it hadn't been rude either. Parrott and Barton had worked together three years now, and they texted each other like this all the time.

The acid from this morning's caffeine had crept high into Parrott's throat. He unlocked his door and strode to the desk, tossing the envelope and its flimsy contents there, and opening the blinds to let in the morning light. His window overlooked the parking lot and a children's playground, currently empty.

Schrik's Lexus was pulling into the chief's parking spot. Parrott forced himself to sit at his desk. He skimmed over the page Barton had left. A thought germinated, while he waited for Schrik's footsteps in the hallway. He pulled out his cellphone and searched for the track width measurement on a 2015 Ford Explorer. The answer filled him with a dreadful satisfaction. The track width he was looking for matched that of Officer Barton's personal vehicle.

# CHAPTER SEVENTEEN

Chief Schrik rapped on the frame of Parrott's open door, and Parrott motioned him in. "Lucretia told me you brought breakfast. Thoughtful of you."

"No problem," Parrott said. "Have a seat?"

Schrik lowered himself into the guest chair opposite Parrott, sending a whiff of minty aftershave across the space between them. "Anything new to report?"

Parrott reviewed the information about the blood type and fingerprint matches. "We've got tire tracks and a toe ring in the wings, as well, but right now I'm waiting for a DNA report."

Schrik grimaced, an expression that could mean annoyance or impatience. Schrik was on the record for hating modern-day dependence on time-consuming and expensive DNA tests. "Did you see the list of local births that Barton collected?"

"Yeah, he did quick work on that. The only thing is, I don't think this baby was delivered professionally." Parrott explained what Dr. Goldstone had told him about the baby's umbilical cord. "Statistically, a woman who delivered in a hospital would be less likely to turn around and abandon the baby. Anyway, for now I'm following the theory that this baby wasn't born in a hospital."

"Does Barton know? I thought he was going to follow up on the list."

Parrott chose his words carefully. To Parrott's knowledge, the chief never talked about Barton or Parrott behind their backs, a practice which Parrott appreciated. "I told him. Apparently, he came in this morning, at least for a short time. I'd asked him to check on tire track widths, and he taped this to my door." He held up the sheet of paper for Schrik to see.

"He must've swung by on his way out of town. He's taking a personal day today." Schrik rose and headed toward the door. "Oh, by the way, I ran missing persons reports for the baby and the woman. I sent you the results, but nothing jumped out at me. You can take a look later on. What's next for you today?"

Parrott would be glad to review the missing persons, but mostly he wondered why Barton would come in late yesterday and be out all day today. He kept his mouth shut. Personal days were few, and employees didn't have to give reasons. "I need to circle back to Mooney and the Baths. Speaking of Mooney, any idea why his son doesn't appear in any society photos with the family?"

Schrik covered his eyes with a hand. "Steven, if I remember correctly, wanted to be a cop when he was a kid. Mooney used to bring him into the station once in a while. He brought toys for the underprivileged at Christmas time. Good-looking kid, but something wrong with him—a speech impediment maybe. I haven't thought about him in years."

Another thing Parrott appreciated about Schrik was the connection to the community. Having served here for more than three decades, he knew things about the residents. When Parrott tried to project himself into the future, still working crime in Brandywine Valley, he couldn't imagine he would have the same kinds of relationships. Then again, sometimes change brought surprises.

Schrik was halfway out the door when he turned back. "One more thing, I just remembered. Mooney's wife is related somehow to one of the working families in the area. It would be a long shot, but if she's related to the couple on the Campbells' farm, that would be something." Walking away toward his office next door, he said, "Keep me posted."

Parrott picked up a pen and a legal pad from his bottom desk drawer. He drew three columns down the middle of the page and labeled the tops with the names of his next witnesses, Stuart Mooney and T.J. and Kate Bath. His plan for this morning was to interview each of them separately, but he liked to write out his questions and fix them in his mind first.

He started with T.J. *Are you in any way related to Stuart Mooney or his wife, Constance Mooney?* Before he could get to the next questions, which he intended to encompass T.J.'s vehicles and gun usage, Parrott's cellphone rang. Dr. Goldstone's name flashed, and Parrott jumped to answer, wondering what the fertility specialist wanted.

"Mr. Parrott?"

The doctor's voice sent prickles through Parrott's body, and his reply came out as a croak. "Yes? Dr. Goldstone?"

"Yes. Have I caught you at a good time? I won't keep you, but I wanted to chat about the sample you submitted yesterday."

A clump of worry formed behind Parrott's eyes. Goldstone wouldn't be calling him if everything was all right. "Go ahead.".

"Let me start with a question. Have you been ill in the last six months? Have you been out of the country, or have you had Covid by any chance?"

"No. I completed that survey in your office during our initial visit. I told you then I've been healthy."

"So you did. Has anything unusual happened to you in the last six months? A traffic accident, a hard fall, a sports incident? Anything like that?"

The worry clump ignited into a fireball. "Nothing like that, but I was exposed to fentanyl last July in a work-related incident. Why? What's wrong with my sample?"

The doctor's voice became softer, slower. "You didn't list the fentanyl exposure on your questionnaire. I didn't know that."

Parrott gripped the phone. "I guess I forgot." Muted voices and phones ringing in the background heightened Parrott's anxiety. "What's the problem?"

"I'm sorry to tell you. The sample you produced had low sperm motility. Sometimes this can be a temporary condition—such as after an accident or an illness. Fentanyl exposure might be to blame. I've seen some research about that, but I need to read more about it. In any case, you and Tonya shouldn't begin fertility treatment until we check you out further."

When had the room become suffocatingly hot? Parrott undid his tie and opened the top buttons of his shirt, fanning himself with the legal pad. "Have you told this to Tonya?"

"No, I wanted to call you first—out of courtesy. Remember, I told you I've been in your shoes. Let me emphasize this is an obstacle, but not insurmountable. Modern medicine has many options for infertile couples. You appear healthy and fit otherwise, but I'd like to start you on an over-the-counter dietary supplement called D-Aspartic Acid, or D-AA. After two weeks of eating healthy, getting enough sleep and exercise, and this daily

supplement, we'll retest and go from there. Would that be okay with you?"

Parrott gulped air and let it out. He'd been hesitant to go to a fertility doctor to begin with. He'd wanted to keep the baby-making process private, between him and Tonya and Mother Nature. Now he realized they could never go back. Their road to having a family might involve other people, treatments, procedures, and heaven knew what else. And it was all his fault. "Sure. I'll take the supplement. And please let me be the one to tell Tonya."

"I thought you'd feel that way," Dr. Goldstone said. "Let's make an appointment for both of you to come in after you've been on the supplement for two weeks. Feel free to call me if I can answer any questions in the meantime. I'm optimistic we can make a difference in your situation."

Parrott disconnected and sat for several minutes with eyes closed and his head in his hands. He felt sure the fentanyl exposure was responsible for this blow to his manhood. As a football player and a police officer, he'd never shirked physical risks, but infertility was a huge gut punch.

Tonya might be distraught by this news, and she would most likely question Parrott for continuing to work in a dangerous profession. As close as they were, Parrott always feared bringing up unpleasant topics that might trigger her PTSD. He would have to find the best way to tell her, and that would be hard.

Right now, he decided to concentrate on the interview questions. In the space of one phone call, Parrott's case had become easier and less perilous than talking to his wife.

# CHAPTER EIGHTEEN

Parrott decided to have a face-to-face with Stuart Mooney first. Normally, a resident of such stature in the community would require an appointment, rather than dropping in, and Parrott wanted to show respect. On the other hand, he preferred a more spontaneous interview, where Mooney wouldn't have time to prepare careful answers. The crime scene on Mooney's lower acreage gave Parrott a good reason to drop in unannounced. Parrott could update Mooney on the current status of the investigation. He hoped he wouldn't be too early, but Brandywine folks were generally early risers.

Within fifteen minutes, he turned onto the path to the front of the elegant residence. Three stories tall and ten windows wide, the white brick-and-wood house had a long porch and Corinthian columns for decoration. An assortment of Chinese cabbages, pumpkins, and gourds graced the ledges next to the stairs to the front door. He checked the crease in his pants, tucked in his starched shirt, and tightened the knot in his tie, as he rang the doorbell.

A tall, slim middle-aged woman, wearing tortoise-shell glasses and a green dress, answered the door. Parrott badged her and asked to speak with Mr. Mooney.

Stepping aside to allow him entrance, the woman introduced herself as Mr. Mooney's assistant, Jade. "You can wait in the library," she said, "the first room on the right. Mr. Mooney is taking a business call, but I'm sure he would like to speak with you."

Mooney's library could have been called a museum. Shelves of books were interspersed with glass cabinets and framed photos regaling Mooney's scotch whiskey company's history and successes over the years. Parrott had tasted Moonglow scotch before, but never realized its owner lived in Brandywine, or that the name of this house was a match for the company name. He couldn't help being a bit impressed.

The mammoth room smelled of furniture polish, cigars, and old money. Strolling around, Parrott took in a photo of a short, balding

man of about thirty, wearing a tuxedo, holding a lowball glass. The second President Bush, similarly dressed, had an arm thrown over the man's shoulder. Presumably Mooney's. Parrott leaned over one of the glass cases, careful not to leave fingerprints. This case held an assortment of bottles and labels, as well as handwritten testimonials from famous people, including A-list actors and rock stars.

"Do you enjoy scotch, detective?" The middle-aged man attached to a seductive voice had entered the room without warning and appeared at Parrott's side, dressed formally for eight-thirty a.m. in a suit and tie. He shook Parrott's hand with a tight grip. "Stuart Mooney."

"I'm not much of a drinker," Parrott said. "Athletics department in college made sure of that."

"Too bad," the man said, leading Parrott to a sitting area near the cold fireplace. "I believe today's coaches are more lenient. We're working on an advertising project with a top-notch NFL quarterback, a big scotch fan. I know you'd recognize the name."

Parrott didn't know about that, but he had to give Mooney points for an unusual conversation starter. "Yes, well, you've probably guessed I'm here to talk about the dead body on your property. Thanks for allowing us access yesterday."

The liquor CEO undid his tie and opened the collar of his dress shirt, revealing an abundance of dark hair. If he was trying to compensate for the lack of hair on his pate, Parrott didn't care. Mooney sat forward in his chair, his eyes focused on the Persian carpet. "Dreadful. Do you have any details about whose body it is?"

"I'm afraid it's too soon for that. The woman's been taken to the county morgue. Our team has cordoned off the area with crime scene tape. We'd be appreciative if no one disturbs it."

"That won't be a problem." Mooney brushed the top of his shaved head. "We never go out there by the creek. Nobody even rides horses down there. You might worry about critters, but not people."

"I've taped up the area on the ledge above, as well. We'll do our best not to inconvenience you." Parrott crossed his leg. "I do have a few questions for you, however."

"Sure. Happy to help if I can." Mooney mirrored Parrott's posture.

"Do *you* have any idea of who the dead woman might be? Anyone who might have had a reason to be on your property?"

Mooney responded quickly. "Of course not. If I had, I would have told Chief Schrik immediately."

"Can you give me a list of everyone on the premises of this estate yesterday or night before last—names, positions, times of arrivals and departures—to the best of your knowledge?"

"Sure. It's been quiet here, except on Zoom. My assistant, Jade Bender. The housekeeper, the groundskeeper and his wife. Everybody but Jade lives on the property. I'll get her to write out the names for you. Of course, it's ludicrous to think any of my employees had anything to do with this."

"What about family members?" Parrott asked.

"My wife's out of town currently. She went to Chicago to help our daughter, who's expecting a baby any day now. I'll fly out as soon as the baby is born."

Parrott couldn't believe how many times the word *baby* had come up in these two days. He uncrossed his leg and leaned his elbows on his lap. "Congratulations. Is this your first grandchild?"

Mooney nodded. "I'm looking forward to spoiling it rotten."

"What about your son, Steven?"

"What would you like to know about Steven?" Mooney let out a heavy breath. "Steven is a wonderful young man—bright, sincere, probably too caring for his own good. He's a guy in his thirties who hasn't found himself yet. He lives in Philly, and hardly ever comes out here."

A beep on Mooney's phone provided a distraction. While Mooney checked, Parrott shifted gears. "Mr. Mooney, can you think of any reason a young woman might have been killed on your property? Any connections she might have had with you or any of your staff?"

"If I knew the poor woman's identity, I might be able to answer your question. Off the top of my head, I have no idea. Moonglow is more than fifty acres of quiet, peaceful horse country. That area out there by the creek is the quietest of all. I never would have imagined a murder on this land—never in a million years."

Mooney drummed the arm of his chair, and his eyes shifted around the library, landing everywhere but on Parrott's.

"Is there anyone who might have a grudge against you, your family, or your property? A business deal gone bad, for example?"

"Are you implying that this woman's death is a crime against me or my family? I don't see it that way. I'm sure it has nothing to do with me—just a nasty accident of geography." A muscle in Mooney's right eye twitched as he spoke.

Parrott ended the interview for now, but he would circle back another time. Whatever was bothering the scotch tycoon, Parrott intended to find out. When he was halfway out the door, he pivoted back into the room.

"By the way, Mr. Mooney, where were *you* yesterday morning between five and ten a.m.?"

"I wondered when you'd get around to asking me that. I slept late, having been up quite late the night before. Cook served me breakfast at eight-thirty, and I retired to my bedroom to shower and dress for the day. I logged onto my computer then. Ten a.m. here is three p.m. in Scotland, so I was busy communicating with my company. I was still involved with that when your chief rang my doorbell. I hope that's a satisfying enough alibi, detective."

Parrott left without commenting, though he didn't feel satisfied at all.

# CHAPTER NINETEEN

After driving around the accessible areas of Bucolia, Parrott tracked down T.J. Bath. He was ensconced in one of the outbuildings, repairing a rotary cut mower. "Sorry to interrupt, but I need to talk to you for a few minutes. I'm down by the grove of maples at the main house."

"No problem," the groundskeeper said. "How 'bout I pick you up and bring you back here? We'd have some privacy."

Parrott was all for privacy, too. T.J. showed up in the Polaris, an off-road vehicle, a few minutes later, wearing work clothes, a Phillies cap turned backwards, and dark sunglasses. Parrott climbed into the utility task vehicle, and T.J. took off down an unfamiliar bumpy path. The mid-morning sun bathed the men and the vehicle in warm golden rays, but the breeze created by the moving vehicle feathered away the heat, except for the heat in Parrott's gut. He had hard questions for T.J.

The engine's rumble cut through the serenity of the country landscape. Eager to get started, Parrott opened with a question that had been bothering him. "Hey, didn't you go by a different name when I met you at the Campbells' a few years ago?"

"Yeah. You have a good memory. I decided it was time to get rid of that juvenile nickname and be a grown-up."

T.J. parked next to a large shed that served as workshop and storage. Beyond the shed was a paddock where five horses paraded about, apparently enjoying the warm weather. The shed offered the two men a shady place to sit amid smells of gasoline and wood chips. T.J. pointed to a tool-laden table and two folding chairs. He opened a small refrigerator plugged into an extension cord plugged into an overhead light. "Want a beer? A water?"

Parrott shook his head. What he wanted was serious communication, not a good ol' boy social event. "C'mon, sit. And let's talk. Nobody can hear us but the horses."

Still wearing the shades, T.J. grinned, his teeth gleaming next to his weather-tanned complexion. "These horses don't care about

anything but eating, trotting, hunting, pooping, or mating—and not in that order."

"How 'bout taking off your sunglasses?" Parrott asked. "I like to see who I'm talking to."

T.J. made room among the tools and hardware to set down the glasses. He folded his muscular arms across his belly. "No problem. Forgot I had 'em on." He shifted in his seat. "Before we get started, I have an apology. I didn't tell you the truth yesterday when you asked if I had any kids."

Parrott raised an eyebrow. "I believe you said, 'Not that I know of.'" When someone started off admitting to a lie, how could that person be trusted to tell the truth afterwards? Still, sometimes Parrott could learn as much from the lies people told as he could from their truths.

"Yeah. I'm sorry about that. I do have a daughter. Last I knew she was living in Texas. She'd be about seventeen now. I never married her mother, and I never told Kate."

Parrott started to say, "Do you think that was wise?" but caught himself. It wouldn't do to sound judgmental. Instead, he asked, "Why not?"

"Maybe you noticed. Kate is a really refined person. She comes from a proper Philadelphia family with good education and manners. She married down when she married me." T.J. picked at a spot on his tanned forearm. "I never intended to keep it a secret, but I never found the right time to bring it up."

"Do you have contact with your daughter—or her mother?" Parrott asked.

"Not at all. We broke up before the girl was born. Her mother didn't want anything to do with me. A mutual friend told me she married and moved to Texas. I lost track completely after that." T.J. put his sunglasses back on and slid them up on the crown of his head. "I figured I'm not in her life and she's not in mine, so why upset Kate by telling her?"

"Why do you think it would upset Kate?" Parrott's mind spun this information like bitter cotton candy, trying to imagine how T.J.'s illegitimate child might impact this case. The mother, in her thirties, would be too old to be the dead woman, but the daughter, at seventeen, might not be too young. He wanted to keep T.J. talking.

T.J. stood. "Oh, c'mon. You saw how badly Kate wants a baby. Kate is still young, and her maternal instincts are flowing. That baby on the porch stirred something up in her."

Parrott thought of Tonya's maternal instincts and the bad news he had to give her this evening. "You made it clear, at least to me, that you don't want to have a baby."

"Not just, 'Don't want.' Think, 'Can't.'" T.J. began pacing, and the words came faster. "After the experience with Crystal—my former girlfriend—I didn't want any more babies that I couldn't be a father to. So I had a vasectomy. And before you ask, yes, Kate knows about that. I told her before we got married. She was okay with not having kids then."

After Parrott wrote down the little information T.J. could give him about his former girlfriend and child, he remembered what Schrik had told him about Mooney's wife's having a relative in Brandywine, Parrott asked, "Is Kate related to Constance Mooney?"

T.J. stared at Parrott, his mouth forming an "O." "How'd you find that out so soon? Never mind. You don't have to answer that." T.J. sat back down and leaned his chair back. "Kate and Connie are cousins. Another reason for me to feel inadequate. I can't give Kate the kind of life she wants. I was foolish to think I could."

Parrott steered the questioning away from T.J.'s pity party. "How did two cousins come to live on adjacent farms out here? Was it a coincidence?"

"Not exactly. There's a lot of kinfolks around Brandywine Valley, if you haven't noticed. Some are even kissing cousins." T.J. snickered. "Of course, Connie is the age of Kate's mother, so Kate is closer to Connie's kids than she is to Connie."

Parrott made a mental note to ask Kate about Steven Mooney. "Did the Mooneys have anything to do with introducing you and Kate?"

"Technically, no. I told you I worked for the Pauls before the Campbells moved here. The Pauls and the Mooneys were both in the liquor business. They were big buds. Every year at Fourth of July, they invited everyone in the valley for a huge barbecue, fireworks, dancing, a big deal. I oversaw the fireworks— purchasing, setting the stage, lighting them, and cleaning up. The Mooneys' relatives came in from out of town and stayed for the

weekend. I met Kate over the glow of dynamite, and she set off explosions in me immediately. It must have been mutual. Before she left, she'd given me her cellphone number and friended me on social media."

"How did your families feel about that?" Parrott asked.

"You mean, how did Kate's rich family feel about her associating with a poor boy like me? They tried to break us up. I was older, less educated. They had other expectations for Kate, and they worried she was setting a bad example for the four younger kids in her family. But Kate is headstrong and independent. She had romantic notions about living a clean, honest life without unnecessary frills. I loved her for it."

Parrott would follow up on the Mooney connection with Kate when he interviewed her privately. "Let's talk about yesterday morning. You told me you left the house around five, and there was no baby on the back porch. When you returned around six, the baby was there. Correct?"

T.J. nodded and shifted in his chair. Parrott continued, clearly taking charge now. "Why did you return home at six?"

"Well, I think I told you my dog Lucy and I go out to feed the horses around five a.m. Not my favorite job, but I told the Campbells I wouldn't mind helping out at the stable in the mornings, since I'm up anyway. The sun don't rise out here this time of year until after six, and I need daylight to do my other jobs."

Annoyed that answering direct questions was not T.J.'s strong suit, Parrott asked, "How long does it take to feed the horses?"

"Depends. I don't pay much attention to the clock. I'm just focused on getting the day started right."

Parrott pointed in the direction of the stable, beyond the shed where they sat. "You and Lucy don't walk over there, do you?"

"Nah. We use the Polaris, same as you and me."

"Do you always go back home around six, or was yesterday unusual?"

T.J. crossed his arms over his chest again. "That depends, too. Sometimes I circle back to eat breakfast. Sometimes I'm not hungry and keep on moving."

Frustrated not to get a simple answer to a simple question, Parrott asked again. "What made you go back home around six yesterday?"

"Sorry—you asked me that before. I thought about that same thing last night. I debated about going back home. I thought I'd grab some toast and orange juice, but it was getting light, and I had some mowing to finish. What pushed me to go back was Lucy."

"What do you mean?"

"You've seen how well-behaved Lucy is. She doesn't make a fuss when strangers come around. She takes her cues from me, and when we're out working, she's an angel."

"But yesterday?"

"After we fed the horses, Lucy started whining and carrying on something fierce. I thought Lucy might've heard something. I looked for my cellphone, and it wasn't in my pocket. So we hurried on back in the Polaris, and that's when we saw you and Kate and Caro, huddled around the baby."

Before Parrott could comment or ask another question, the beep of a text came in on his phone. "Excuse me a second," he said, glancing at the message. *Big news. Call me ASAP.* It was from Maria, the coroner.

Chills raced from sacral to lumbar to cervical vertebrae, but Parrott couldn't cut this interview short. He asked a few more questions designed to nail down what T.J., or Lucy, might have seen, heard, or smelled during that critical hour yesterday morning.

T.J.'s responses were all benign. Whether he actually didn't observe anything, or whether he was protecting someone, Parrott couldn't tell. "I have a couple more questions."

T.J. leaned forward. "Go on."

Parrott watched T.J.'s shifting brown eyes and decided to take a gamble. "I'm sure you remember giving us fingerprint samples. What if I told you your fingerprints were on the box?"

The eyes blinked, but T.J. held contact. T.J.'s face blanched, and now his eyes dilated. The question hung in the air for several seconds. "Tell you the truth, detective, I'm not sure how they could be. Maybe I touched the box when I came back for breakfast. I remember being in shock—a baby on the back porch isn't the

most common sight, and I was worried about how Kate might be affected."

"Hmm." Parrott left that thought hanging. He wanted to see if T.J. would say more without being prompted.

T.J. paused and then his eyebrows shot toward his hairline. "You don't think I put the baby there to begin with, do you? I swear I have no idea where that baby came from or who put it there."

"Calm down, man. I'm not making accusations. Just looking for information." Parrott tapped the edge of the table, hoping to mollify before he asked his next question. "When you do your work here on the farm, do you ever use any other vehicle, like that SUV I saw parked at your house?"

T.J. huffed, and the muscles around his mouth relaxed. "Not really. I always use the Polaris when I can. Saves on gas. Besides, the Trailblazer is mainly Kate's."

The explanation was plausible, but Parrott wasn't sure it was truthful. He'd need to check the Chevy's tire span, either way.

"How about guns?" Parrott asked. "Were you packing yesterday morning?"

Slamming a fist on the table, T.J. stood and began pacing. "I don't know what you're getting at. I have guns, sure. I hunt for sport, and sometimes I need a gun on the farm. I've shot a few snakes and other critters in my time. But no, I was not carrying a gun yesterday, and I'm no criminal."

Parrott held out a hand and asked T.J. to sit back down. He wasn't quite ready to end the interview, and he didn't want to end it on such a stormy note. When T.J. returned to his seat, glowering, Parrott assumed a casual tone. "I am curious about something totally unrelated, though. What can you tell me about the barroom brawl ten years ago that landed you on misdemeanor probation?"

T.J. put his head in his hands. "Oh, man. That was nothing. I'll tell you whatever you want to know, but please don't let Kate or her family find out about it."

"Another thing Kate doesn't know?"

"Right. And if Kate finds out, she'll absolutely kill me for not telling her."

Parrott wondered what other secrets T.J. was keeping.

# CHAPTER TWENTY

The sputtering of the Polaris with T.J. Bath on the way back to Parrott's car was the only sound, but the silence between the groundskeeper and the detective was not uncomfortable. Parrott had assured T.J. that he had no intention of revealing his secrets to Kate. The only way that would happen was if they came out naturally in the investigation of the case.

Bath's jaw clenched and unclenched as he drove, but Parrott had asked all the questions he'd wanted to for the time being. Now Parrott's mind jumped with the prospect of hearing what Maria had to tell him. Big news had to mean the dead woman's toxicology or DNA—or both.

Once back in his own car, Parrott called the coroner. "I can talk now. Is this a good time?"

"Where are you, Parrott? Can I call you back in twenty minutes?"

Inwardly, Parrott groaned, but it was a fact of life in this business. The people at Chesco were inundated with work, and Parrott couldn't expect their schedules to revolve around his. "Sure. I'm headed for the office now. I'll wait for your call."

Under ordinary circumstances, Parrott would have circled back to the Baths' cottage to talk to Kate, but Maria's tease about big news had seized his attention. He'd prefer to be at his desk, taking notes on whatever she had to say.

Parrott busied himself with small tasks. He "dotted his p's and q's," as his grandmother used to say. He made notes from his meeting with T.J. Bath. He checked on the exterior width and front and rear track widths of the Polaris and Chevy Trailblazer, both of which were narrower than eighty-two inches.

Phone calls lit up the panel on the station's landline, and voices drifted in from the hallway. Twenty minutes had passed several minutes ago. Parrott suppressed the urge to make a pot of coffee. He didn't want to be in the breakroom when he answered Maria's call.

He did a computer search for fentanyl and low sperm motility. There was a correlation, according to a recent study. As he looked for evidence that the condition might be temporary, his cellphone rang. Parrott swiped the answer button harder than necessary. "Hello, Maria. What've you got for me?"

Her tinkling chuckle only lasted a second. "I'm sorry to keep you waiting. I've just returned to the office from an unattended death. Took me longer than expected."

Fingernails tapped on a keyboard. "Pulling up the reports now."

Impatience fluttered inside Parrott's chest, but he waited in silence. Maria would want to read verbatim from the reports, rather than summarize or paraphrase and risk misinterpretation. She understood the importance of meticulousness.

"Okay, here we go, and you understand these are preliminary. The blood was free of infection, inflammation, high blood sugar, low blood sugar, abnormal blood cells, or toxicity, including poisons, alcohol, or drugs. Cortisol level was high, possibly from stress the body was responding to at the time of death. The stomach had emptied its contents by the time of death, suggesting that the woman had not ingested anything for at least six hours."

Fine, the woman was young and healthy and killed by gunshot wound, but Parrott didn't think this qualified as "big news." He drummed his fingers on his desk.

Maria's voice changed to a higher register. "A vaginal sore turned out to be herpes. But here's where it gets interesting. The preliminary DNA is back. The blood on the baby's blanket is a ninety-seven percent match with the dead woman's blood."

Parrott's exhale came out as a whistle. "I was hoping for that. Thanks for rushing this job. I know—"

"Hold on, Parrott. Don't thank me yet. I'm not finished. The woman's blood is on the blanket, and some of the baby's DNA is under the woman's fingernails. There's a definite connection between the woman and the baby, confirmed by DNA transfer."

Perplexed, Parrott interrupted. "Sounds like there's a 'but' coming."

"You know me so well. There's a big, incredible 'but' coming, Parrott. The woman's DNA and the baby's do not match. The woman is not the baby's mother."

# CHAPTER TWENTY-ONE

Parrott gripped the phone and stood. Had he heard Maria right? "How can that be? You told me the woman had just delivered a baby. And her DNA is on this baby's blanket."

"I know. It sounds bizarre, but DNA doesn't lie. The relationship between the woman and the baby is not maternal."

"You're right. This *is* bizarre. If the woman is not the baby's mother, then where is the baby's mother, and where is this woman's baby?" Parrott's stomach clenched.

Maria gave another small chuckle, but Parrott knew she didn't think this was funny—just strange. "Good questions to ask, detective, but you can't ask them of the DNA reports. You will have to find another way."

After making sure there were no other important details in the reports and thanking Maria again for expediting, Parrott disconnected, but held the phone to his chest. This baby and this woman were causing his temples to pound.

He strode to the breakroom for coffee, his head spinning with possibilities. Two aspirins and a thermos full of black coffee later, Parrott hovered over his desk, scribbling on a legal pad. This case resembled a logic problem like the ones his mother used to do in the crossword puzzle magazines. Before he could begin to solve the case of the abandoned baby or the murder of the woman, he needed to identify both. The old standbys of fingerprints or missing persons reports had failed to turn up anything. He'd hoped—no, if he was honest, he'd counted on—the blood on the baby blanket as matching that of the dead woman. That wish had come true. Therefore, the living baby and the dead woman were connected.

The fact that the woman had recently given birth couldn't be coincidence. Parrott drew boxes within boxes, trying to figure out a way that the preliminary DNA test could have been incorrect. Maybe the lab made a mistake, switched samples. But that wasn't realistic. DNA labs did meticulous checks and cross-checks of their work. That was one of the reasons DNA testing was so time-

consuming and expensive. Parrott drew fat question marks around the nesting boxes.

What were the possibilities? Two babies switched by accident? This was highly unlikely, since evidence from the woman's body and the baby's umbilical cord pointed to an "out-of-hospital" birth. How about two babies switched on purpose? Two women, perhaps friends or relatives, exchanged babies in order to accomplish some mutually beneficial goal. While this was certainly possible, it would be difficult to implement, since timing would be critical, and babies' arrivals were unpredictable.

Perhaps the anonymous woman found by the creek didn't know the baby in the yellow outfit was not her biological child. Maybe another party, her killer, for example, replaced her baby with the one in the yellow outfit. Within the realm of possibility, this scenario was far-fetched, too. The kidnapping of the replacement baby would surely have triggered a missing persons alert. Another dead end.

His next logical step might be to craft a careful article for the local paper. Somebody had to have seen or heard something that would help him get moving. He texted Chief Schrik to get approval. The *Daily News* had a noon deadline, so, while he waited for Schrik's response, Parrott opened his email and began a message to the news editor, a gal named Trina Hayes. *I'd appreciate it if you could get this into tomorrow's paper in print and online:*

The West Brandywine Police Department is looking for information related to a female infant, wearing a yellow outfit, left on a back porch in the Coatesville area off Strasburg Road, Monday morning between four and six o'clock. *Also, could you put in a separate mention:* The West Brandywine Police Department is asking for any information regarding the death of a young woman, who may have recently had a baby, found near Brandywine Creek in Coatesville on Monday morning.

He would hold back the detail of the yellow ducks on the baby's outfit, as well as the dead woman's apparel, as a means to confirm that anyone who replied had legitimate information. Parrott added the station's phone number and an assurance that all tips would be kept confidential.

Schrik's return text gave Parrott the go-ahead. He hit *send*, satisfied to move forward. Within seconds he received a confirmation from Trina. He was good to go, and his next stop was interviewing Kate Bath. Hoping she would be home and available now, while T.J. was out in the field, he closed his computer. On the way out, he popped a large piece of a power bar in his mouth and called it lunch.

Back at Bucolia, Parrott rapped on the door of the groundskeeper's cottage. Barks from within suggested Lucy was spending the afternoon with Kate, rather than T.J. Kate opened the door, a dishcloth in her hand, and a worried look on her face. "How's the baby?"

Parrott assured her the baby was healthy and in good hands. A minute later, he was inside, sitting on a barstool in the same room where only yesterday they had undressed the baby. Today, however, the house was awash in the aroma of home-baked bread.

Kate's light brown hair was pulled into a ponytail and held by an orange hair tie. Her face glowed with a just-washed shine, uncomplicated by makeup. "You're just in time for a sample of my Pennsylvania sourdough bread. Old family recipe."

Parrott's mouth watered as Kate cut one of the warm loaves into slices and set them on a plate next to a tub of butter and a bowl of blueberry jam. He usually passed on offers for food or drink when interviewing witnesses or suspects. He didn't want to give the wrong impression about his purpose. This time, however, whether it was Kate's sincerity or his rumbling stomach, he couldn't say no.

Kate had one of those smiles that caused the corners of her lips to turn down, instead of up. "Go ahead. Take as many as you'd like. I've got more than a dozen loaves besides this one."

"Delicious. What do you do with them all?" Parrott made a mental note to tell his mother about this. Cora, while being a phenomenal cook, was an unenthusiastic baker, and she often purchased home-made bread for her catering business.

"I sell them at the farmer's market. I have my own label, see?" She showed him a shiny gold sunburst sticker with the words, *Fresh from Kate's Kitchen*, written in calligraphy.

"I will have to buy some." He wiped his mouth with a napkin. "This could be the best bread I've ever tasted." Now Parrott would have an extra-hard time keeping this interview professional. Maybe he should have skipped the bread.

As if she'd read his mind, Kate said, "I'm glad you like it, but I know you didn't come here to chat about bread. What can I help you with? I heard there was a dead body down by the creek."

"Since you mentioned the family recipe, let's start with your family. I heard you're related to the Mooneys."

"Is that common knowledge?" Kate sat on the opposite side of the counter.

"We try to know everyone in the jurisdiction, where they come from, who their family is."

"I *am* related to Connie Mooney. We're first cousins, even though she's closer to my mother's age. I'm in between Connie's children, Catherine and Steven, age-wise."

"What can you tell me about them?"

Kate's eyebrows wrinkled, as if sorting through possible responses was difficult. "I see Connie occasionally at local events, Stuart less often. Catherine lives in Chicago, so I almost never see her."

"What about the son? Steven?" Regret lapped at Parrott's consciousness that he couldn't be straight-out honest, but questioning witnesses required a certain amount of subterfuge, no matter how many slices of warm bread they offered you.

"Steven." Kate crossed her arms and gripped her elbows. "Steven is a sweetheart. We grew up together."

"When's the last time you saw him?"

"Oh, he drops by occasionally when he's out here visiting his mom. I tease him that he comes to see Lucy, not me. Lucy is part of the litter from his former golden retrievers, Cinnamon and Becky."

*Interesting that Steven visits his mom, not dad.* "What does Steven do professionally? Does he have a family?"

Kate sighed. "Steven hasn't exactly found himself yet. He's tried his hand at a few different things—he has a degree in health informatics, the technology of medicine—but he switches jobs a

lot. It doesn't help that his father is so successful. Hard to compete with the CEO of a world-famous billion-dollar company."

Lucy nudged her mistress, and Kate patted the dog on the head. "I worry about Steven. He's never married, never had a long, serious relationship. No one talks about why, but I suspect he's on the spectrum."

"Autistic, you mean?" Parrott's cousin Bo had been diagnosed with Asperger's syndrome shortly before being killed as an innocent bystander in police action. Parrott had often wondered whether the Asperger's had anything to do with Bo's being in the wrong place at the wrong time.

"Yes, Steven is good-looking, smart, kind, but quiet. He has no trouble finding women to date. He's always got a new girlfriend, but they don't stick around long. Connie thinks it's because he doesn't go through the proper channels to meet them, but that's a different story."

"When is the last time you saw or heard from him?" Parrott asked.

"Two weeks ago. He called me for my birthday. He always remembers my birthday." Kate pulled at a strand of hair that had escaped the ponytail. "Why so many questions about Steven, anyway? You don't think he had anything to do with the baby, do you?"

Parrott looked her in the eye. "Just routine information-gathering. Is Steven close to his sister?"

Kate's lips turned downward, but this time she wasn't smiling. "Not so much. Catherine's definitely the fair-haired child. She's married, having a baby. She and Steven have nothing in common, besides genetics and growing up in the same world. Steven's always saying I'm more like a sister to him than Catherine is."

Parrott knew he'd be treading delicate ground with his next question, but he needed to ask. "I couldn't help noticing how eager and attentive you were with the baby. Are you interested in having a baby of your own?"

Kate brushed breadcrumbs into her hand and took them to the sink. After washing her hands, she turned back and gazed directly into Parrott's eyes. "Do you have any children, detective?"

Jaw clenched, he said, "Not yet."

"Well, I used to think I wasn't the maternal type. But now I might be having second thoughts."

Parrott asked a few more questions about Kate's comings and goings, routines, and visitors. Nothing about her responses stood out as much as her relationship with Steven Mooney. He would keep that information on the front burner.

# CHAPTER TWENTY-TWO

After the detective left, Kate put away the half-eaten loaf of bread and returned the butter and jam to the refrigerator. She wished she could sweep away the foreboding that hovered over her.

She had overreacted to the baby on the porch. She knew that now. She'd called attention to herself, to her childlessness. She never should have behaved so openly. Bad enough that Caro had witnessed the raw emotion she'd displayed over the infant.

Her fawning had caused T.J. to act strangely, and she'd provoked the detective's curiosity. His question today wouldn't be the last.

Now that the loaves of bread had cooled, she needed to sheathe them in the cellophane wrappers bearing her logo. She would carry the wrapped loaves to the basement refrigerator, where they would sit until tomorrow's farmer's market.

This part of the process usually brought Kate a great deal of satisfaction. She'd brought the task to completion, and she had perfect products to show for it. She twisted the shiny gold tie with a vengeance.

Kate had answered Parrott's question honestly. She had never seen herself as the mothering type. The key to the good life, she'd thought, was simplicity. She'd seen her own mother dragged down by the responsibilities of children, material things, and status in the community. Kate preferred freedom. T.J.'s having had a vasectomy gave her even more freedom. She'd never have to worry about an accidental pregnancy.

T.J. earned a good living taking care of Bucolia, and she was free to garden, bake, and even ride horses on the property. She enjoyed the wholesomeness. And when T.J. was away from the house, she usually had Lucy to keep her company. The golden retriever was always a comfort and never talked back. If she ever changed her mind about babies—well, she had plenty of time to think about what might happen.

Not until her thirty-first birthday had it hit her that soon her decision to skip motherhood might preclude her from an important life experience for good. Perhaps the Campbells' choice not to have children hadn't been as enlightened or as romantic as Kate had first thought. Everyone her age, including her cousin Catherine, was having babies. Maybe she'd better reconsider and look into adoption.

Then, about a month ago, she had made a huge mistake. One night over an intimate dinner and a bottle of wine, she'd shared her thoughts with T.J.

His reaction had been swift and strong. Red splotches had covered his face and neck, and he'd slammed a fist on the very table where Detective Parrott had just eaten her bread. "What the hell? You know I can't give you a baby, Katie. Where is this coming from?"

She'd never seen him so upset. Whether he was angry with her for reneging on their agreed-upon life plan, or whether he was upset with himself for not being able to accommodate her changing attitude, Kate wished she had never said anything. She'd tried to walk it back, but Pandora's box was mercilessly open, and her tearful pleadings did no good.

Neither of them had spoken another word about a baby until the sweet baby girl had turned up on their doorstep. And now a woman was dead, and a detective was sniffing around. Kate closed her eyes and hugged herself, trying to make the terrible, shaky feeling go away.

"God help me," she prayed. Her greatest fear was that T.J. had done something awful in order to bring her a baby, and she had complicated everything by reporting it to Caro.

# CHAPTER TWENTY-THREE

Frustrated that he was no closer to identifying the dead woman or the baby, Parrott reassessed his plan of action. There were threads he could follow. T.J. Bath's illegitimate daughter and her mother might be worth looking into. The toe ring, knife, and tire tracks might lead to something. Maybe there was a connection the woman or her killer had to Brandywine Valley that he was missing—like a horse person, an artist, an antique dealer. Any of these was as ephemeral as the afternoon clouds that dotted the sky as he drove back to the station. He needed something solid, like a name, a relative, a connection that made sense of the facts at hand.

The only way he could think of to get what he needed was to send DNA to Ancestry and 23andMe. He'd never worked a case like this, but one of his associates in the New York Police Department had. When Parrott reached his office, he called Turnitta Rayburn.

"Hey, Parrott. Long time, no see. How're things in the valley?"

Parrott grinned. Officer Rayburn hadn't been half that folksy when she was investigating the death of Blake Allmond. Allmond had maintained two residences, one in Brandywine and one in New York City, where he'd been killed. "Great, as usual. Don't tell me you're ready to give up the excitement of the Big Apple."

"Nothing like that. What's up?" Traffic sounds in the background indicated she was driving or riding in a car.

"You told me you worked with autosomal DNA at Ancestry, right?"

"Yeah, like two or three years ago. Battered guy turned up in the hospital with amnesia. No idea who he was. No prints, no priors. Ancestry was the last resort."

"Any tips about working with them? I know they're slow."

"Slow is a relative concept. They sped up the process for us. The average guy waits six weeks. But, yeah, felt like a decade when we were trying to ID our vic." A screech and a long pause

later, Turnitta continued. "Sorry, my partner's driving, and I hafta go soon. You'll like what you get back from Ancestry. You can use groups and filters to sort the data, and you can find which relatives come from the maternal or paternal side."

"Sounds complicated," Parrott said.

"Nah, not for you, Parrott. You're a genius. Anyway, you might want to submit to 23andMe, too. Doubles your chances for matching up."

Parrott signed off, glad he'd thought to call. Before he headed next door to get Schrik's blessing on sending in the DNA sequencing to the two agencies, Parrott decided to see if Randy Barton was at the station. If he was, maybe he'd like to be in on the meeting, and Parrott would have a chance to put eyes on him.

When he arrived at Barton's office, the door was closed, but the light shone through the frosted glass. Barton was shouting at someone. Parrott leaned closer, not knowing whether he should interrupt or not. He couldn't make out any words, despite the volume. Rather than interrupt, Parrott could go to the chief's office alone. Just as he pivoted to walk away, he made out the sound of a loud, "Goodbye," accompanied by a slam.

Parrott turned back and listened, waiting a decent interval before knocking.

Barton's silhouette appeared through the glass door, and he opened it wide. "Come on in." The words were friendly, but the tone was monotonal and flat, and Barton's hair looked as if he'd run a thousand fingers through its strands. "You got something new for me?"

"Sort of." Parrott remained standing, leaning against the doorframe. He explained the mismatch in DNA between the woman and the baby. "I've got to find a way to ID these two. I've about decided the best route would be the ancestry groups. Want to go with me to get Schrik's blessing on that?"

"Uh, you don't need me for that. I'm sure Schrik will okay it." Barton's eye twitched. "The only thing is, those services can't give you data unless there's a match with people who've joined, right?"

"That's right, but chances are some people in the family tree are in the database, and those people can lead to others. It's worth a shot."

"Well, you go ahead, Parrott. You're the detective, and you're young enough to understand all that DNA *fal-de-rol*. I wish you the best."

Disappointed, Parrott offered his hand. Barton hesitated for a fraction of a second before clasping it in a solid, but damp, handshake. Something had really changed in Barton's life, or in their relationship, but Parrott hardly recognized this man he'd worked with for three years.

Parrott trudged to Schrik's office by himself, filled the chief in on the need for autosomal DNA matching, and received permission to move forward. Wanting to get the process started immediately, he spent an hour on the phone with specialists at Ancestry and then at 23andMe, who worked exclusively with criminal justice cases. Parrott made arrangements for the DNA sequencing to be sent to Utah and California.

By the time he finished, he was ready to call it a day. He still faced having to tell Tonya about his low sperm count, something he dreaded more than any police task he'd ever faced.

He called to say he was coming home early, and Tonya answered the phone with a lilt in her voice. "Wonderful, Ollie. I just hung up talking to your mother. She and Herman are having a spur-of-the-moment barbecue in their back yard, in honor of the good weather. They've invited some of the neighbors, too. I told her we'd come. Hope that's okay with you."

The weight on the back of Parrott's neck lifted a little at the thought of a light-hearted evening at his mother's. The food would be good, the company would be pleasant, and he'd have a short reprieve from giving Tonya the bad news.

# CHAPTER TWENTY-FOUR

Holding hands, Parrott and Tonya strolled around Cora Parrott's path-lit walkway to the back yard, where they were greeted by an aromatic horticultural spectacle. The profusion of hydrangeas and the prolific herb garden gave off a *Better Homes & Gardens* vibe.

"Lovely," Tonya said, as she bent to sniff the delicate lavender fronds. "I'll bet you never had a garden like this back in the 'hood, did you?"

"Actually, Ma always had a garden. She's always been a good cook, and some of her best dishes were made from home-grown ingredients. We were never too poor to have carrots or squash, or chard from the back yard. We used to plant seeds from what we ate, so we could grow more food for later. Nothing wasted."

The memory triggered another, of Bo and him, laughing and picking every green tomato from his mother's plants. He'd hardly ever seen Ma so angry. "You're right, though. This garden is much fancier. All these basil plants? Soon they'll be turned into jars of pesto to be used for catering."

The walkway wound onto a paved patio, where four people sat under a broad umbrella table, strung with fairy lights, drinking mojitos, and chatting. More lights around the back of the house and the fence surrounding the patio gave a magical ambience to the gathering. Sunset would soon heighten the effect. Aromas from the covered barbecue pit hinted at charcoal-roasted ribs and chicken.

Herman spotted them first and rose to welcome them, voice booming. "Hey, Ollie and Tonya are here. Let the party begin."

Wearing a cherry-colored pant suit with a lime, red, and-navy silk scarf around her neck, Cora welcomed her son and daughter-in-law with hugs and introduced them to her neighbors, Warren and Simone Keyes, both of whom looked to be in their fifties. "Simone is a librarian, and Warren works for the company that manages the King of Prussia mall." She waved at the two empty chairs. "I've already told them all about the two of you."

"How 'bout some mojitos?" Herman asked, strutting to the outdoor bar.

"Sure," Parrott said, "but sit. I can make my own."

"Nonsense. I've pre-prepared everything. Just need to shake and pour. Tonya?"

Tonya shook her head. "I'll have a club soda with lime."

Parrott gazed at his wife, whose favorite summer drink was mojitos. She met his eyes and smiled, and his heart cracked. He could think of only one reason she would pass up the drink, and he hated to tell her she didn't have to worry about that right now.

"Do you have children?" Tonya asked the Keyeses. The next several minutes were spent hearing all about their five children and two grandchildren. Tonya engaged with the vignettes, commenting with enthusiasm in all the right places, but Parrott slipped further into a funk, worrying about the news he had to deliver later.

Cora popped in with a remark about how she wished she'd been able to have more children. "Ollie's father passed unexpectedly before we could get around to having a second baby."

Unhappy with the conversation thus far, Parrott said, "I never felt like an only child, though, because Aunt Rachel and Bo spent so much time at our house." As soon as the words left his lips, Parrott regretted bringing up another sore subject.

Herman placed the mojito and Tonya's club soda in front of them. "You have to try your mother's crab appetizer. She flew in crabs from Maryland. "What all's in this, honey, besides the baby potatoes?"

From then until the meat was ready, the six of them talked about food and drink and entertaining. It turned out that Simone had once aspired to be a chef, and her parents had sent her to Escoffier in Austin. "I was the only Black in my class, and the only woman, too. Those days nobody cared about inclusion, and I never felt comfortable. I left after one semester."

"Their loss was my gain," Warren said, patting his stomach. "Y'all will have to come over sometime for Simone's *coq au vin*. De-licious."

During dinner, Simone engaged Tonya in a discussion about the new house in West Chester. Parrott relaxed, enjoying the now-

easy chatter among people with whom he had a lot in common. It was a welcome change from having to keep up his guard all the time at work. Tonight he didn't have to be a detective, a wealthy man, or a husband with a low sperm count. He could talk sports and real estate and put off the inevitable for a couple of hours.

※ ※ ※

The drive home only lasted twelve minutes. He'd turned on the radio to their favorite jazz station, and Tonya turned the volume down low.

"Nice evening. Warren and Simone are good people, and I like Herman more each time I'm with him."

"Haha."

"What's that supposed to mean? I'm paying him a compliment."

Parrott grinned. "What's nothing times nothing? Last year this time you didn't want to be in the same zip code with Herman."

"True, but I was being short-sighted. Now I think he's a gentleman and he's head over heels for your mother."

"Just like I am for you," Parrott said, reaching across the console to take Tonya's hand.

She pressed his hand between both of hers. "I remember the first time we held hands, Ollie. Yours were warm, and mine were freezing cold. I thought I'd never let go. I still feel that way."

The burden of what he needed to share with his sweet, beautiful wife was nearly choking his windpipe. He pulled off the road and into an empty church parking lot.

"What are you doing?"

"There's something I need to tell you, and I want to do it now, before we get home." He shut off the engine and unclasped his seat belt.

Tonya turned in her seat, wide-eyed. "You're scaring me. What is it?"

"You know that sperm sample I gave to Dr. Goldstone yesterday? I got a call from the good doctor today. The sperm count is low—so is the motility. I'm so sorry—" Parrott's smooth baritone broke into a thousand jagged pieces, and it was Tonya's turn to reach for his hand and squeeze.

# CHAPTER TWENTY-FIVE

The next morning, calls came in from the articles Trina Hayes had run in *The Daily News*. Lucretia had transferred two to Parrott's voicemail before 7:30, when he'd arrived at the station. Obviously, Brandywine was an early-rising and early-reading community.

Still not hungry after the barbecue last night, Parrott had packed a honeycrisp apple and his thermos of black coffee. He plopped into his swivel chair and poured himself a cup. He took a bite of the apple and dialed into his voicemail.

The first message came at 6:03 from a female, who sounded like she was on speakerphone or holding the phone far from her mouth. "I saw in today's newspaper you're looking for information about a poor little baby and maybe its mother. I don't know if this'll help you or not, but the girl who worked for Elsa Taylor and her husband over in Unionville got pregnant and moved back to New Jersey with her mother. Rumor had it that Elsa's son might've been the father. Maybe I have an overactive imagination, but that was about eight months ago, so worth checking into. I believe the girl's name was Tessie."

The woman hung up without leaving her name or contact information, and she'd star-sixty-sevened the call to remain anonymous. Parrott didn't mind, since the tip probably amounted to gossip. Still, he started a list on a legal pad and jotted the details as the first item.

The next voicemail had come in at 6:12 from a phone number with a 484 area code. "Detective Parrott?" The shaky voice belonged to an elderly man. "You m-may not remember me, but I met you at Blake Allmond's funeral when you were investigating his m-murder. M'name's Leonard Frost. I used to live out there next to the Mooney place. M-my son's family lives there now—Frosty Groves is the estate. Anyway, my son told me that dead woman was found on Mooney's property, and I just thought I'd try and tell you to be careful when you talk to that Stuart Mooney.

He's a real stubborn Scotsman if I ever did know one. He didn't make all that money bein' a gentleman, either. If you get on his wrong side, as I once did, he can be downright mean-spirited." The caller left his phone number in case Parrott wanted details.

Before he logged that information, a live incoming call came through. His pulse sped when he saw the caller ID. "Good morning, Mrs. Campbell. How can I help you?"

"I've told you a hundred times to call me Caro."

Parrott shifted in his chair. He felt awkward addressing some of the Brandywine residents whom he'd come to know well. He usually solved the problem by avoiding referring to them by any name. "I know. I don't mean any disrespect, but I wasn't raised that way."

Caro chuckled. "I understand, and I won't push you again. Listen, I saw your blurb in today's paper about the dead woman on Mooney's property, and it reminded me of something I thought I should tell you. I met my cousin for lunch at Philter Coffee in Kennett Square last Friday. We love their spiced carrot and kale salad. While we were there, there was a young couple arguing at the next table.

"She was pregnant and large, ready to deliver any minute. She was blonde and pretty in an athletic sort of way. Not beautiful, but tanned and natural-looking. She was trying to grab the cellphone from the guy across from her. He was talking in a hushed, strained voice, as if gritting his teeth—you know? We tried to ignore them, but it was impossible. They seemed on the brink, like twigs ready to snap."

Parrott leaned forward in his chair. "Could you identify either of them?"

"I got a better look at her than at him. His back was to me. Neither of them seemed familiar. Anyway, shortly after that, she stood and threw her napkin down. Then she marched out of the restaurant in clunky platform sandals that squeaked. The man tossed some money on the table and ran out after her. I never thought about it again, not even after the baby on the Baths' porch. Not until I saw the bit about a dead woman who might have recently had a baby. Maybe that was her."

The platform sandals stuck in Parrott's mind as if super-glued. "I'm really happy you remembered this. And even happier you called. Would it be all right with you if I came to Bucolia later this morning with some photos and/or an artist? I'd like to document your descriptions of this man and woman."

"That's fine. If you have photos, why an artist?"

"The woman's face is disfigured, so all you can tell from the photos is body shape, clothing, etc."

"Okay.  I'll be home. Do you want me to call my cousin, too? She lives in Philly."

"Not right now. Let's see if we can get a sketch, and we'll go from there."

A doorbell rang in the background at Caro's end. "I have to get that. I'm the only one home. Come on over whenever you can. I'd do anything to help identify that sweet baby girl's mother."

Parrott didn't bother to tell her that the dead woman wasn't the baby's mother.

# CHAPTER TWENTY-SIX

A three-man police department couldn't afford the luxury of a police artist, but on the rare occasion one was needed, Parrott knew where to go. Elle Carmichael, partner of the deceased Blake Allmond, and benefactor to many, including Tonya and Parrott, was an artist and art teacher. In fact, Tonya had met Elle through the art therapy lessons given on site at the Allmond estate, Manderley. Tonya had formed a friendship with another student, Liz Levy, whose skills at portraiture were, according to Tonya and Elle, top-notch. Both Tonya and Liz worked part-time at Elle's Don Guanella campus, serving mentally-challenged adults through art therapy activities, so they were still in touch.

Liz had expressed an interest in diversifying into police artistry, and she'd given Tonya her contact information to give to Parrott. Sometimes that was how things worked out. An investigation required a service, and someone popped up to provide that service. Helicopter pilot, Lew Grossman, had been one example. Liz Levy, if available, would be another.

Caro's description of the couple arguing in the Kennett Square restaurant three days before his victim was found dead had his gut instincts fizzing like the contents of a shaken pop bottle. He found Liz's phone number in his contacts and pressed send, crossing his fingers that the woman would remember having made the offer.

"Hello? This is Liz. How may I help you?" The New York accent was overlain with a cheerful warmth.

Parrott introduced himself as a detective from the West Brandywine PD and mentioned Tonya.

"Of course. Tonya has told me all about you, and Elle has, too." A bird tweeted in the background, and Parrott wondered whether she had a window open or a pet bird. "Don't tell me—you have a need for a portrait artist? I've been waiting for this for a long time."

"Actually, that's exactly why I'm calling. I'm sorry for the short notice, but I wondered if you could meet me at a Brandywine residence sometime this morning?"

"Sure I can. Happens I'm off today and nothing would make me happier."

Parrott gave her Caro's address, and they agreed to meet at nine-thirty. "Do you charge by the hour, or by the drawing?"

Liz's laugh tinkled like a tiny set of chimes in a breeze. "I should ask how much you charge to give me the experience. Let's just say it's my pleasure to help you. I'll bring an easel and all the materials."

Remembering what Chief Schrik had said about working with Lew Grossman, Parrott tempered his enthusiasm. "I'm looking forward to working with you, Liz, but I need to remind you the information we share with you and the work that you do this morning is police business and therefore strictly confidential. I will need you to sign an agreement to that effect."

"I've done a lot of research on the role of a police artist, so I understand and will sign. You can trust me to keep it to myself."

Parrott disconnected and called Caro back to let her know the arrangements. "I'll plan to get there earlier, so we can go over the photographs before Liz arrives."

With little more than an hour before he'd have to leave for Bucolia, Parrott listened to the third voicemail from earlier. "Hey, Parrott. It's Jerry from Chesco. Just thought you'd like to know it was breast milk in those samples you gave me to test. The lab was able to isolate identifying cells that matched those of the dead woman. So, the breast milk came from her. Also, we got some prints from the box the baby was in. Call if you have any questions."

Before he could fully process the idea of the breast milk's having come from a woman who was not the baby's biological mother, Parrott heard familiar footsteps from the hall outside the office. Parrott jumped to the door to flag Chief Schrik down. "Do you have a minute?"

"Sure. I was going to stop in for a minute anyway." The older man's forehead was crimped with worry lines. "I've got something to tell you—may or may not be worth anything."

Parrott ushered Schrik in and offered him a chair.

Schrik set his briefcase on the floor next to Parrott's desk and sat.  "I've got a meeting in half an hour with the township

manager. I stopped for breakfast at the Little Chef. Evidently your *Daily News* bits have touched nerves."

"Yeah, I've already had two voicemails and a live call, and it's not even nine a.m."

Schrik's eyebrows entered the war zone of his forehead. "Really? Tell me."

Parrott brought him up to speed on the two voicemails and Caro's call. "Obviously, the mention of platform sandals riveted my interest. I'm going over there in a few minutes with photos and an artist." Before Schrik could question the artist, Parrott explained. "I don't know how helpful Ms. Levy will be, but she can't hurt anything, and it's worth a try."

Schrik brushed the air, as if he had more important things to worry about. "Your call about Mooney concerns me, even though I usually think anonymous calls don't amount to much. But two guys at breakfast tried to pump me about the dead body mentioned in the newspaper. They'd heard it was on Mooney's property. That launched a diatribe about Mooney."

"What about him?" Parrott asked.

"Nobody trusts the guy. Unusual for people out here. One guy works for the conservancy. He said there are rumors Mooney's been talking about selling his property to condominium developers. Supposedly Mooney's marriage is on the rocks, and the prospect of splitting all that money with the wife has put Mooney over the edge."

"Interesting," Parrott said. "Even more reason to keep our eye on Mooney."

"Yes, but it gets worse," Schrik said. "The other guy, Hank Rivers, is a plumber. He said he was working over at Mooney's place the other day, and he heard Mooney on his cellphone, raising his voice. Rivers said, 'I felt sorry for the bastard at the other end. Mooney wouldn't let him get a word in.'"

Again, Parrott thought the information to be of mild interest. The potential divorce and property sale could relate to Mooney's state of mind and motivations, but an angry phone call could be about anything.

"And then Rivers asked me—out of the blue—if I had a patrolman named Barton on staff." Schrik's hand cut a swath into the air. "Sure, I said. And you know what he said then?"

Parrott's eyes met Schrik's and waited.

"The guy Mooney was shouting at was Barton."

# CHAPTER TWENTY-SEVEN

The morning sun streamed into the living room windows of the Campbell mansion, thanks to the opened drapes and raised shades covering the south- and west-facing windows. Parrott imagined himself in a museum exhibit. The room itself was a formal work of art, with a modern white sofa, plush chairs covered in a black-and-white silk pattern, and a deep turquoise lacquered Oriental etagere, dotted with expensive-looking antiques. A Persian rug and a couple of impressionist oil paintings tied the colors together into an elegant, yet cheerful whole.

"I thought this room might offer the best light at this time of day," she said to Parrott. "I can bring in a dining room chair for Liz, and you and I can sit here. What do you think?"

"Looks perfect to me. Liz will bring an easel. You need to sit where you can watch as she sketches. I'll carry the chair in."

Before Parrott set the chair down, John E. Campbell popped his head, and then his body, into the room. He was dressed in boots and riding clothes. "Just thought I'd stop to say hello. It's been a long time."

Parrott shook the older man's hand, remembering the first time they'd met the weekend of John E's sixty-fifth birthday celebration. Although the first impression hadn't been favorable, he'd come to know and respect Caro's husband.

"I'm sorry to hear you've got another Brandywine death to solve. Happy to help you in any way, but let me get out of your way right now." John E. pecked his wife on the cheek and said, "I'm off to the stables. Be back in an hour or so."

Caro flipped on the modern floor lamp and beckoned Parrott to sit perpendicular to her in its light. "I'm not looking forward to seeing these, especially if they're bloody. Violence is not my thing."

Parrott explained how meaningful Caro's participation in identifying the body might be. "Violence shouldn't be anybody's thing. I ask you to look past the gruesome aspects of the photos.

The one hypothesis I want you to validate is whether the woman could possibly be the same woman you saw at the restaurant last Friday. Look for the details that might prove or disprove the match. In this case, you'll be looking at the woman's body, while with Liz, you'll be describing the woman's face—and as much as you can tell us about the man she was with."

Caro nodded and curled her fingers into her palm. Parrott brought up the first of a dozen photos on his cellphone. "Feel free to enlarge or reduce the sizes as we go through each of the photos."

The first photo showed the back of the woman's head. Long, blonde hair fanned out around her head, with a bullet hole in the center of her skull. Caro commented that the hair style and color were similar, if not the same, as that of the woman she had seen.

Parrott hadn't been able to make print copies of the photos yet, but maybe they were less horrifying this way. He skipped over the next few photos, which showed the badly damaged side of the victim's face, mostly covered by blood and hair. He didn't want to upset Caro with these, since there wasn't enough of a face left to make an identification.

In the next photo, the woman's back, shoulders, and upper torso, arms flung, could be seen. Caro simply shook her head at these.

When he got to the photos of the woman's lower body, he watched Caro's reaction intently. The splayed legs and feet, still wearing the platform sandals, were key. "Could these be the shoes you saw the woman in the restaurant wearing?"

Caro's eyes moved from the photo to Parrott's and back several times. "I can't be positive. I only saw them for a few seconds, as she stormed out of the café. But they caught my attention, maybe because she had such long legs, and it's unusual to see a pregnant woman in shoes like that. The platforms made her seem very tall. And her feet looked nice against the light-colored straps. I remember thinking it was late in the season to be wearing those shoes."

Hope fluttered in Parrott's mind. "Do you think these are the same shoes?"

"I can't be positive, but, yes. The shoes, the tanned legs, the blonde hair. My impressions are positive."

"How about the bright toenail polish?"

"I can't tell. All I can say is the woman I saw had well-groomed feet. I'm sure her nails were polished."

Parrott took a deep breath and let it out. "One more question— did you notice any jewelry, by any chance?"

Caro shook her head. "I wouldn't have been able to see anything that small. And, remember, I watched her walking out of the restaurant. Mostly from the side and back. I'm sorry."

Parrott started to comment, but, a glimpse through the dining room windows revealed a silver SUV parking in the circular driveway, and a pixie-ish young woman emerging from the car. "Looks like Liz is here. Let me go help her."

Liz introduced herself on the way in and shook hands with Parrott and Caro. A dimple showed in the corner of her mouth, and her effervescence was contagious. She almost skipped into the house, while Parrott followed with her easel and rolling suitcase.

Parrott carried the dining room chair into the living room, and Liz set up her materials, including a laptop. Once everything was ready, she explained to Caro how she wanted to proceed. "A lot of this type of portraiture depends on impressions. I'll ask you a lot of questions about the individual features of the person you remember. Don't worry about being exact. Just try to give me your best guess, based on the encounter you had. I'll show you samples of individual features, and you can tell me which one seems most accurate. Okay?"

Parrott was impressed with Liz's organization and process. For someone without any real police artist experience, she had the demeanor of a pro. He settled into the comfortable upholstered chair and observed the dialogue between the two women.

Liz started with the shape of the face. She pulled up a template on her laptop with various face shapes for Caro to consider, one-by-one. Caro narrowed her choice to two—round and heart-shaped, finally opting for heart-shaped. Parrott thought he could agree, since the shape of the victim's jaw in his photos was consistent with the model on Liz's computer screen. Liz drew a heart-shaped outline on the easel's pad of paper. *Off to a good start.*

Next, Liz asked Caro to describe the hair of the person she saw in the restaurant. Only after Caro threw out adjectives, like

blonde, shoulder-length, thick, layered, curled around the face, did Liz bring up templates with hair styles for Caro to match. Before drawing the hair, Liz asked questions about the woman's forehead, cheeks, and ears. Once all these were established, she drew the hair to fit around the features.

Liz used the same process for eyebrows, eye shape, eye color, eye lashes, each detail requiring a match to a template on the computer. "Tell me if something doesn't look right to you," Liz said. "We can always make changes."

Caro seemed more decisive with each choice she made, and as the drawing began to take shape, she nodded. "I never would have thought I could remember so many details about a face that I might have looked at for maybe a minute, but you're making it easy."

After Liz drew in the details of the nose, and then the mouth, including lips, teeth, gums, and tongue, and the chin and neck, she pulled out colored chalk and asked questions about complexion, make-up, eye coloring, freckles or moles, wrinkles, or any other identifying marks. She began coloring and shading the portrait, and she encouraged Caro to keep describing the woman while she watched.

The end product was a portrait of an attractive young woman with clear, tanned skin, blue-gray eyes, dark blonde hair streaked with lighter blonde highlights, skinny eyebrows, and a squarish point on the tip of the nose. The drawing was life-like, and Parrott was already thinking of several ways he could use it.

"Shall we try to get a drawing of the man?" Parrott asked. "I know you felt more confident about describing the woman."

Caro bit her lip. "We can try, but all I really saw was the back of his head. Maybe a side view as he stood to leave the restaurant."

"I'm game if you are," Liz said. She changed the screen on her laptop to show the backs of male heads. "Let's look at shape and size, shall we? Then ears and hair style."

The women continued until Liz had a rendition of a young man with thick, dark hair, medium-sized ears, broad shoulders, medium complexion, and a black polo shirt, tucked into pressed jeans. It wasn't much, but it was something.

Parrott asked Caro to describe the voices of the man and woman, as well as details about their posture and body language. At the end of the session, he had a clearer picture of the woman in his head and two drawings to use as he saw fit. He couldn't be positive that these detailed images would lead him to the dead woman, but he clutched the drawings as if they were made of gold.

# CHAPTER TWENTY-EIGHT

A heavy dread had hung over Kate ever since the baby on the porch. Delivering a dozen loaves of bread each to farmers markets in Lionville and Exton in the warm, sunny weather had given her a respite, but now the gloom was hovering again.

She wished she had never told T.J. weeks ago she wanted a child. Everything was much simpler before, and now—she couldn't be sure of how she felt about anything—babies, the future, even her husband. Everything had changed in the space of a few hours with the arrival and departure of the baby.

She'd tried to clear her mind of these thoughts, to throw herself into her regular routines. But the joy she usually gained from bread-making had disappeared. All she could feel when she kneaded the dough was the infant's warm, tender skin. The walls of their cottage closed in on her with their empty silence.

Last night when T.J. had initiated love-making, she had held back. She wasn't being fair to herself or to him. Their physical connection had always been strong and fueled by intimacy. Now the pilot light barely flickered.

Though not especially hungry, Kate couldn't remember her last meal. She opened a couple of cans of tuna fish and started dicing celery and onion to make a salad. Lucy's bark wafted in from a distance through the screen door, and when Kate looked through the window, T.J. was pulling up in the Polaris, with Lucy loping alongside.

Kate opened the door, and Lucy bounded inside, pausing to lick Kate's hand on the way to her water dish. "Is something wrong?" she asked, reading the downturn of her husband's lips. T.J. removed his hat and sunglasses, tossing them on the counter. "I'll let you answer that question." He headed for the back bathroom. "I'm going to wash up."

After refilling Lucy's bowl, Kate washed her hands and opened another can of tuna and added mayonnaise to the mix. Once in

a while, T.J. finished a job on the property and wandered in for lunch, but this time he tromped through the house like a man with an agenda. Kate toasted slices of her homemade bread for sandwiches and set out two placemats and napkins. She'd bought a couple of home-grown tomatoes at the farmer's market, so she cut one of those and arranged the slices on her favorite blue-trimmed plate.

The shower was running, which meant T.J. was finished working outside for the day. Kate wasn't sure if she was heading for a show-down, a discussion, a romantic encounter, or, Heaven help her, a confession, but she stuck to the routine of preparing food and prayed for the best.

A few minutes later, T.J. emerged, clean-shaven, his hair still wet, but combed, and smelling like Irish Spring soap. Lucy lifted her head from the rug, where she had curled up, and T.J. bent to pat her on the head. The gesture brought tears to Kate's eyes, and she turned quickly to hide them.

"I've fixed us some lunch," she said, not meeting her husband's eyes. "Would you like lemonade or a beer?"

"Why don't you put away that tuna salad for a little while. We need to talk." He plopped onto the sofa and motioned for Kate to do the same. When she did, he scooted to the corner and turned his body sideways, one knee bent in front of him, blocking himself.

Kate began to cry, why, she didn't know. T.J. pushed a box of tissues closer, and she drew several out. "I'm sorry to be crying." She blew her nose, willing herself to calm down.

"I know you're upset. After ten years I can tell when things aren't right." T.J. scooted closer and cupped his wife's chin in his hand and brushed the wetness with his thumb. "It's about the infant on the porch, right?"

Sniffing, she nodded. "So strange. Nothing's really different, but those few minutes she was here changed everything." She sneaked a glance at T.J.'s dark eyes. Were those tears forming?

"I'm sorry I can't give you a baby. When you told me you'd changed your mind, you wanted one, it broke my heart. You know I'd do anything for you, Kate."

Fear clutched her heart, and she reached for T.J.'s hand.

"I went to a clinic to see about reversing the vasectomy. I was hoping they'd made new discoveries or something."

"But they haven't, right? I did some research on the internet, too. It's been so many years since you had the surgery."

"They didn't tell me outright that it's impossible, but they calculated a success rate based on my age and the surgery I had, and they only gave me a twenty percent chance. I made an appointment for the surgery. I'll go through with it, if you want me to."

Kate scooted closer. "It's sweet of you to offer, but I saw the statistics, and the description of the surgery, and the expense. I couldn't put you through that. And who knows if I'd be fertile after all that? I'm thirty-one and never been pregnant."

"Come on over here," T.J. said, pulling his wife into his chest, her back to him. He whispered into her hair. "I didn't stop with the vasectomy clinic. I checked out other options. I've gotten myself involved now. I only want to make you happy."

Wings of panic beat against Kate's forehead. She didn't want to know what T.J. had done. Not now, and maybe not ever. Her fear that T.J. had committed two heinous crimes to make her happy crowded out the rational part of her brain. She couldn't let him say it. Saying it would make it true, and she couldn't bear that. She jumped out of his embrace and ran to the back door. "I can't talk about this right now, T.J. I'm going for a walk. Don't come after me."

The unknown fueled new tears and enough adrenaline to propel Kate through the back door with a whoosh and a slam. She was a woman with a husband she loved, but couldn't talk to, and it was all her fault.

# CHAPTER TWENTY-NINE

Armed with Liz's drawings, Parrott raced back to the station to access the National Missing and Unidentified Persons System, otherwise known as NamUs. He had used the clearinghouse last year when another unidentified body had been found in an exploded Brandywine barn. The system worked best when there were a lot of data points to match on both sides—the person reported missing, and the person reported found.

The dead woman found by the creek had given Parrott little to go by. She was nameless and faceless, until now, assuming that Caro's description and Liz's portrait were indeed of the same woman who'd been killed. Making that assumption would have been a monumental leap of logic, except for the fact that the woman Caro had seen in the local restaurant was heavily pregnant and likely wearing the same platform sandals. Liz's portrait gave Parrott several points of description to enter into the software, besides height, weight, and hair color, which he had from the coroner. NamUs would tell Parrott if someone matching the description had been reported missing. He couldn't wait to plug in the information.

But first he stopped by Surefire Graphics to run print copies of the artist's drawings. That way he wouldn't risk losing or damaging the originals when he showed them around.Hunger pangs ricocheted through Parrott's belly, reminding him that all he'd eaten today was an apple. Little Chef, the place where Schrik had eaten breakfast, was in the next block. Parrott decided to stop for some jambalaya to go.

The breakfast crowd had long gone, and there were only a few groups at tables or at the counter. Parrott placed his order and perched on a barstool to wait. One of the waiters mopped the laminate counter with a soapy rag and polished it with another. When he finished, he offered Parrott a glass of water.

Parrott declined, but, instead, withdrew the fresh copies of the drawings from his jacket pocket. "If you have a minute,

I'd like you to look at these. Recognize either of these people? Maybe customers?"

The man set his cleaning rags beneath the counter and wiped his hands on his apron. "Sure, I'll look." He studied the drawings, his eyebrows drawn into fuzzy ledges, and biting his upper lip. After a minute or so, he said, "Pretty girl. I think I'd remember that face if she'd come in here. But I don't. And the guy—you don't give me much to look at, but he looks like a lot of our customers. Can't say as I know him or don't know him, but the shape of the head, the hair looks familiar." He handed the papers back. "Your order's prob'ly ready. I'll go check."

Parrott thanked the employee and carried his warm container, complete with pungent, mouth-watering aromas, to his car. Within minutes he was sitting at his desk, digging into the spicy sausage, chicken, and shrimp, as if it would disappear any moment.

Coming up for air after consuming more than half of the take-out portion, Parrott glimpsed Officer Barton, in a slightly too-big uniform, shuffling past the open door. "Hey, Barton," Parrott said between bites. "Come on in if you have a minute."

The officer stepped inside and glanced around, as if looking for somewhere to run, causing Parrott to wince.

"I can't stay and talk, Parrott. I've been tied up with a vehicular this morning, and I've got to finish the paperwork. You know how it is." The only eye contact he made was with Parrott's food.

Still trying to engage his colleague, Parrott said, "We might've caught a break in ID'ing the woman by the creek. Caro Campbell saw a young pregnant woman on Friday at a café in Kennett Square. Wearing those platform sandals and accompanied by a male." He shoved the remains of his lunch into the paper bag and set it in the wastebasket. "You want to see the artist rendering?"

*Was that a flinch?* Parrott couldn't tell for sure, but Barton looked as if he'd sucked a lemon.

"Maybe later," Barton replied. "As I said, I've got paperwork, and I'm on deadline." He gave a wave, little more than a flick of the fingers, and moved on, less like a man on a deadline, and more like a man on tenterhooks.

Parrott recalled the story Schrik had told him about Mooney and Barton. If Barton were somehow in Mooney's pocket, that

might explain Barton's reluctance to converse with Parrott about the body found on Mooney's property. There was no point in forcing contact, but at the least, losing Barton from the investigation team meant more pressure on Parrott. At the most, if Barton and Mooney were up to no good, well, Parrott didn't want to think about the scandal that would cause. And what if Barton sabotaged Parrott's investigation by giving confidential details to Mooney? Whether that was the case or not, Barton was a friend, and Parrott could feel their connection trickling downstream, like the Brandywine Creek.

Rather than dwell on Barton, Parrott compartmentalized and logged into the missing persons site. In the United States there were currently over twenty-three thousand missing persons. He'd already run fingerprints and come up negative. Experience had taught Parrott the importance of choosing the right physical attributes to query. NamUs would work with DNA and odontology, but Parrott wanted to try for easier matches first, without involving extra work from Chesco.

Identifiers that were too broad could yield too many matches, and too narrow could result in few or no matches, so he needed to play Goldilocks and select the ones that were just right.

He began with "Caucasian" and "female." He added "pregnant." He thought to query for "Pennsylvania," but held back because he didn't want to limit himself. His victim could easily have traveled from another state. Next, Parrott entered the woman's height and weight, as provided to him by the coroner. Long, straight blonde hair would narrow the field. Caro had described the woman she saw as "light-eyed." That could mean blue, green, or gray. Parrott entered eye color as "not brown."

Hoping these elements were enough to provide a decent search, he pressed "submit." He left to get a cup of coffee from the breakroom while the software did its work. When he returned, there were more than three hundred matches. He stared at the artist rendering, wishing the subject had an observable tattoo or mole. He entered "smiley-face bracelet" and "toe ring" into the mix and drained his coffee mug while he waited.

The resulting entries numbered fifteen, a much more manageable number. Excited, Parrott pulled up the first profile,

ready to compare the missing person photo to Liz's artist rendering. Before he could do so, however, his cellphone pinged. The incoming text came from the specialist at 23andMe. It said, "Good news. We found relatives for both of the DNA samples you submitted. Emailed reports to you in separate files. Call if you have questions."

Parrott's fingers tingled as he minimized the NamUs screen and opened his email, not knowing which source would provide the best information. Whichever, Parrott's instincts told him he was getting close.

# CHAPTER THIRTY

Kate's abrupt exit from the cottage offered immediate escape from facing T.J.'s possible confession, but, even as she stomped through the fields behind Bucolia, she realized running away wouldn't provide any solutions. If T.J. had kidnapped a baby and killed the baby's mother, life as they'd known it would be over. Whether he'd done those deeds or not, how could she go back home to live with a person she suspected of evildoing? On the other hand, where else could she go?

Her father's warnings echoed in her head. "T.J.'s a nice guy, but people of our background need more than "nice" in a life partner." Ben Pritchard had high expectations for his five children, and, because Kate was the oldest, he pressured her to set the example. He hadn't disowned her, but he'd kept a distance from Kate and T.J. as a couple, and that had given Kate reason to stay away.

As the years went by, she'd felt vindicated. Her siblings had grown, and two of them had married and divorced. So much for marrying within one's background.

Kate's mother had been less judgmental of T.J., but, whenever she came to visit, she stayed at Moonglow with her sister, Connie Mooney. Her rationale was she didn't want to inconvenience her daughter and son-in-law, whereas staying with Connie would just inconvenience the servants. Kate interpreted that excuse as a stinging criticism of her and T.J. and their way of life.

Kate shoved her hands into the pockets of her jeans and trudged on. Why, oh, why had she mentioned wanting to be a mother? That conversation with her husband was beginning to feel cataclysmic, like a tornado or earthquake. Everything prior was calm and sweet and normal. Everything afterwards was twisted and wrong.

She still loved T.J. She wanted to go back home and feel his muscled arms around her. Maybe he wasn't going to confess to a crime. Maybe she should have listened to him before running out. She wanted to forget about the sweet-smelling baby in the box on her porch. She wanted to dismiss her fears that her husband, in his

deep love for her, would go to the ends of the earth to give her a baby. But she couldn't.

If she left home now, she might draw unwanted attention from that nice detective toward T.J.—or toward her. If she went back home, how could she continue to bake her bread and sleep in the bed with T.J., harboring so many doubts in her heart?

Really, what choice did she have? She couldn't, wouldn't go home to her parents. Her aunt was out of town. Her cousin Catherine was about to have a baby. Caro might, under other circumstances, be a confidante, but she could never share her fears about T.J. with his employer. Basically, she was stuck.

She was about to turn around and head back home, when she thought of someone she might be able to talk to. She pulled her cellphone from her back pocket and scrolled to Steven Mooney's number. Her cousin Steven, for all his problems communicating with others, had always been a good listener.

Kate took a deep breath and pushed Steven's number.

# CHAPTER THIRTY-ONE

Not for the first time, Parrott wondered about the people who submitted their DNA to Ancestry and 23andMe. As far as he knew, no one in his personal circle of friends or family had ever done so, and he couldn't imagine a circumstance under which he might. Maybe if he needed an organ transplant, but even then, it seemed selfish to connect with someone and immediately ask for his kidney.

He was glad, however, that more and more people of all ages were jumping on the DNA bandwagon. The search agencies provided a useful new landscape for investigators. This being his first foray into DNA database searching, Parrott buzzed, like a kid at a carnival, jumping onto the carousel, but not being able to decide which horse to climb on.

The report would show names of others whose DNA had been submitted to 23andMe with matching centimorgans, or lengths of shared DNA segments. He opened the report on the dead woman's DNA first, thinking that her connections would be many times more plentiful than those of a newborn baby.

The report referred to the dead woman as Brandywine A. He liked the initial and thought of the young woman, lying face down by the creek as Brandywine Anonymous. People connected to her were listed in numerical order, according to the percentage of match. The higher the percentage, the closer the relationship.

Parrott's hopes fell when he saw the scarcity of connections for his victim. There were no matches at fifty percent, which would indicate a parent or child. There were no matches at twenty-five percent, which would indicate a grandparent, grandchild, aunt or uncle, niece or nephew, sibling or half-sibling. Eight connections at a little over twelve percent reflected cousins, and those were all located in Texas, Louisiana, and Alabama. Nothing explained the young woman's presence in Pennsylvania.

The software gave Parrott the ability to contact these cousins, and since he had professional access, he had quicker and better

options than most people, but he bookmarked the page for later. He was eager to see any results for the infant's DNA.

He clicked on the link for Brandywine B, in this case Brandywine Baby. Parrott thought of the tiny girl's velvety skin and scrunched-up eyes. If any of her relatives turned up, Parrott would jump on that DNA train right away, so he could return her to her rightful family as soon as possible.

When the page opened, Parrott rubbed his eyes in disbelief. Brandywine Baby had twenty-five percent relatives spread out all over the country, several pages of them. How could one little baby have so many second-degree relatives? The software couldn't delineate between which relatives were on the maternal or paternal side, but the number and degree of relationships contrasted starkly with those of Brandywine A. The saying that DNA doesn't lie echoed in Parrott's head. But as an only child with four grandparents and a handful of aunts and uncles and cousins, he couldn't fathom how this little person could have three pages of second-degree connections. And these were just the ones who had signed up on 23andMe.

Parrott was pondering this irony when a text came in from Tonya. *If you have a minute, I have a quick question—not urgent.*

Alone in his office and ready to take a break, Parrott called his wife. When she answered, a whirring noise overpowered her voice.

"Sounds like a bulldozer in the background. Are you remodeling already?" Parrott asked.

The whirring stopped, and Tonya's dulcet tones filled his ear. "Guess again, detective. You're way off. Think kitchen." She laughed, and Horace chirped in the background, "Thank God. Thank God."

"Does the ear-splitting sound have anything to do with your quick question?" Parrott asked.

"In a way. I know you haven't forgotten we're having a barbecue Saturday night. I'm slicing cabbage and carrots in the food processor to make your Aunt Rachel's crunchy ramen salad. That's always a hit, and it's easy."

Parrott rubbed the side of his head. He hadn't exactly forgotten about the social engagement, but he'd put it on the back burner. "Yeah. The neighbors should like that salad fine."

"The Franklins. Lorraine and Will. They're very nice people. I can't wait for you to meet them." Horace made an unintelligible remark. "Anyway, your D-aspartic acid capsules came from Amazon today. You can start taking them tonight. But that's not why I texted. Lorraine's sister and her wife are visiting from Alabama. The sister is expecting their first baby in a few weeks. I told her she could bring them along. Okay with you?"

"Of course. Let's be gracious to our new neighbors. You don't need to ask me. You're the family social director." Parrott glanced at his computer screen, where Brandywine Baby's relatives danced before his eyes.

"—how you would feel hanging out with an expectant couple. I mean, I know it wouldn't bother you that they're gay." A spoon clanged against the metal mixing bowl. "They used a fertility clinic in Birmingham, and they're taking turns carrying babies fertilized by the same guy's sperm."

A lump formed in Parrott's throat from the double reminder that his own sperm was not up to par, but he wouldn't let it get in the way of Tonya's get-together on Saturday. Making friends, especially neighborhood friends, was a significant step toward having a normal life after her experiences in Afghanistan. "I'm good."

"Okay, fine. Just 'cause they're having a baby doesn't mean we will or won't have one. Maybe we'll learn a thing or two from them."

Parrott wasn't keen to learn anything about making babies without male partners, but he kept his voice cheery as he ended the call and turned back to 23andMe. Then it dawned on him. If a fertility clinic offered donated sperm to women without male partners, or whose partners couldn't produce viable specimens, were there limits to how many progeny could be created from sperm donations over a number of years and across geographic distances? Maybe the Brandywine Baby was fathered by a sperm donor.

# CHAPTER THIRTY-TWO

Kate listened to the phone ring and decided to disconnect. Talking to Steven Mooney on the telephone was never easy. He'd had a lot of therapy, but the pacing and intonations of his speech remained odd and sometimes difficult to decipher. Kate had learned years ago not to use idioms or sarcasm when she spoke to him, and, somehow she had managed to communicate well enough with her cousin to build a comfortable relationship. But phone conversations never went well. She decided to text instead.

Steven was book-smart and math-smart. His difficulty in communicating had hampered him in many ways, but to Kate, he was a sweet, trustworthy guy.

Kate plodded through the grass, still wondering whether she was doing the right thing to tell anyone about her marriage. She typed, *Hi, Steven. It's Kate. How're you doing?*

His response was immediate. *Fine.* Steven's clipped response was typical. Kate knew not to be offended. It was an indication of discomfort with communicating.

She forged on, as if they were having a full conversation already. *Yes. I'm doing all right.* Except my life as I know it may be falling apart as we speak. And what, if anything, could Steven do about that? *I hope I didn't catch you at a bad time.*

*Bad time? No.*

Kate smiled at her cousin's response. *I've got a problem, and you're the only person I feel comfortable talking to. I know you won't tell anyone.*

*Hmm…wait.*

While she waited, Kate sat beneath the shade of a willow, her back against the trunk and knees bent. She played with a fraying hole in her blue jeans, thinking.

*Okay, I'm here.*

Kate typed. *Somebody left a newborn baby in a box on my back porch. I don't know who put her there, or why, but I wanted to keep her.*

Kate hit send to pause the narrative for Steven, and also to swallow an imaginary stone that had risen in her throat. *I'd already been thinking about having a baby, you know.*

Steven wrote, *Sounds like somebody wanted you to have a baby. You'd be a good parent.*

*Thanks, Steven. I couldn't keep the baby. Child protective services has her. Also, the police are investigating the death of a woman who recently had a baby. You might know about it 'cause the woman's body was found on your parents' property.*

*Oh, no.*

Kate hoped she wasn't making Steven too anxious. He didn't do well with too much drama. *Well, anyway, I worry T.J. did something terrible. What if he took the baby from its mother and put it on the porch for me to find? He might have thought that was the only way to give me a baby.* Kate's own emotions rose with each word she typed. She was glad to be outside in the middle of nowhere.

Steven didn't respond for such a long while that Kate wondered if he had left the conversation. In her own distress, she'd forgotten how upsetting this might be for Steven. *Steven, are you still there?*

*Yeah.* Steven said. *Don't worry so much. T.J. is a good man.*

Tears stung Kate's eyes as she read Steven's words. *T.J. is a good man, and he loves me. The question is, does he love me so much that he would harm someone and steal her baby for me? I'm afraid to go back home and find out.*

Steven paused again. *Okay. I don't think you should leave T.J. He's a good man, and he loves you.*

*But what if he committed a crime? I don't know if I can trust him. I wish I'd never told him I wanted a baby.* Steven would understand trust. Kate was one of the few people in the world Steven trusted. She continued. *If I leave T.J., can I come stay with you?*

*Sure. Okay. But Katie, why not go home and talk to T.J.? Ask him if he put the baby there. I bet he'll say no.*

*I'm afraid to ask him. What if he says yes? And if he says no, he might be lying.*

Steven took a few minutes to reply. *Give him a chance. Go home. Talk to him. If you're still scared after that, come on. You can stay with me until things calm down.*

Steven's kind words caused the tears to spill and her nose to clog. Her emotions seemed to have spiraled out of control, like last month's fireworks—once lit, there was no turning back. She sniffled while she collected her thoughts.

*Thank you for listening. I know you're right. T.J. deserves to have a 'fair trial.' I'll go home now, and I'll call you back if I need you.*

*Try not to worry so much. Things will work out. Always do.*

Kate clicked off and put her cellphone into her pocket. She brushed the seat of her pants and huffed at the irony. Her next moves would be made exactly by the seat of her pants.

# CHAPTER THIRTY-THREE

The more Parrott thought about the long list of relatives that Brandywine Baby had on 23andMe, the more he believed it was possible she had been conceived with a sperm donor. Either that, or one or both of her parents had been an extremely fertile vagabond. He had professional access to names and contact information for the people who shared the baby's DNA, but he reminded himself that even if the baby was conceived through sperm donation, the dead woman was not the biological mother. In short, he had two separate cases that may or may not be related.

Before forging ahead with the infant's relatives, Parrott wanted to go back to the dead woman. While her 23andMe list was thin, the list of fifteen missing persons from the NamUS search was promising.

If any of their photographs resembled Liz Levy's artist rendering, he wanted to prioritize that lead. One by one, he pulled up each of the missing person matches and printed the information associated with the listing. The photographs varied from candid to professional shots, some clearer than others. Parrott didn't discriminate on this first look. He wanted to keep an open mind, especially since his victim's face had been so severely damaged. Liz's drawing might not match up exactly with a photograph, and attributes he had entered into the search fields might not be precise. For example, hair on the missing persons report might have been dyed by the time the body was found.

In other words, Parrott was looking for similarities, not mirror images. He examined the photos, holding each one next to Liz's portrait.

All of them were possible, but three stood out as more likely than the rest, based on the heart-shaped faces, the suntanned complexions, and the long, straight hair. The three missing women were Darcy Klein from Omaha, Nebraska; Trish Mackintosh from Hamilton, Montana; and Amanda Hoffman from Sulphur Springs, Texas.

Each listing had a police contact name and number, and, fortunately all three were in earlier time zones. Before he started calling, he needed a nature break. He'd pass by Barton's office, too, in case the officer would want to help in running down the baby's 23andMe relatives.

Barton's door was closed and the lights off. Not yet four p.m., it was a bit early to go off-duty, but there could be lots of legitimate reasons. Parrott took the stairs down to the dispatcher's station, where Lucretia was working a crossword puzzle.

"You happen to know where Barton is?

Lucretia filled in a word before looking up with a sideways glance and a grin. "Left about ten minutes ago. Said he had an appointment and a stop to make. Said he'd be in early tomorrow morning. You want me to page him? He couldn't've gotten very far."

"No, thanks," Parrott said, "it can wait until tomorrow." He was about to comment on Lucretia's crossword puzzle prowess when the phone rang, distracting her. He tapped her desk and returned to the second-floor breakroom, where he used the facilities and purchased two bags of salted peanuts from the vending machine.

Carrying his cache back to his desk, he mused about Barton's appointment. He still wanted to give Barton the benefit of the doubt, but Parrott couldn't forget that Barton's personal SUV's wheelbase matched the tire tracks from the promontory. More than that, Barton's evasive behavior and unusual hours were extremely out of character.

Parrott put Barton out of his mind for now and concentrated on calling the missing persons contacts. He started with the Omaha PD, where he spoke with Officer Gregory Martinez. Parrott explained the particulars of his case, describing the dead woman, but leaving out the abandoned baby. "The missing persons report on Darcy was filed three months ago. Do you have any idea how far along in pregnancy she might have been then?"

Martinez coughed into the phone, and when he talked, he sounded nasal. "Sorry, just getting over a bad cold. Darcy disappeared after a fight with her boyfriend. He wanted her to have an abortion. She refused. Parents say she'd just confirmed the pregnancy, so I'd guess first trimester."

"That doesn't line up with my victim. She delivered before she died. Thanks anyway, man. Feel better soon."

His enthusiasm having been taken down a notch, Parrott opened a bag of peanuts and dug in. He washed the salty bits down with water.

He called the number in Hamilton, Montana, where Trish Mackintosh had been reported missing five months ago. This time he was put through to a female officer. When he explained about the body discovered by the creek, she said, "Pennsylvania? I suppose our young lady could have turned up in Pennsylvania, but what are you, two thousand miles away? Clear across the country."

"I thought the same, but I need to follow every lead." Parrott described his situation and the artist rendering.

"Did you load your info into NamUS?" the officer asked. "I'd like to take a look at your portrait, maybe show it to the parents."

"Give me your number, and I'll fax it. I haven't entered anything yet. I have some other leads to follow up on first." As before, Parrott asked about the status of Trish's pregnancy at the time she went missing.

"The parents weren't sure. Trish told them she was running away with her boyfriend. She said she was pregnant, but they said she wasn't showing, and they had no proof."

Trish didn't sound like someone who might've been four months pregnant when she ran away, but he kept her on the "possible" list. He disconnected, promising to send the drawing, and looking forward to hearing back if it struck home with Trish's family.

The third missing teen was from Texas, the same state where T.J.'s illegitimate daughter lived. Probably a coincidence, but maybe a good luck omen, too. Parrott took a swig of water and called the number of the Sulphur Springs PD.

Their version of Lucretia listened to Parrott's request and hooked him up with a Sergeant Davis, a guy with a too-many-cigarettes scratchy voice. "What can I do for you, detective?"

Parrott recounted the discovery of the body by the creek. "The autopsy shows she delivered a baby recently, and your MP was pregnant. Any chance this could've been a match?" He held his breath, waiting.

A phone rang in the background, and Sergeant Davis said, "Christ, hold on a minute. I gotta put you on hold."

Butterflies jumped around in Parrott's stomach while he imagined the satisfaction of finding out that the dead woman was Amanda Hoffman. He made accordion pleats with the peanuts wrapper, and then tossed it in the wastebasket. He opened the second bag and rolled a couple of nuts in his hand before deciding he was too keyed up to eat them.

When Davis finally came back on the line, he said, "Sorry to keep you on hold. This Hoffman case is a heater. That was a related call. Except that your victim is a fatality, I'd be delighted to know you've found her."

"Agree." Parrott was curious about why the Hoffman case was causing such a ruckus, but that was none of his business at the moment. "Let me tell you what I've got." He described the body as he'd found it, the gunshot in the back of the head, the disfigurement of the face, the dress, the sandals, the nail polish.

Davis didn't interrupt, but the background sounds on his end distracted Parrott. Obviously Sulphur Springs PD had a lot more activity than West Brandywine.

Parrott went on to describe the assumed scenario of the woman's being shot on the promontory and rolling down to land near the creek, face down. "We found a silver toe ring and an open switchblade on the ledge—might be related. Oh, and the woman was wearing a smiley face string bracelet."

Sergeant Davis sucked air. "Amanda Hoffman wore a bracelet like that. Can you send me photos?"

"Sure. I've also got a portrait of a woman seen three days earlier in a cafe, wearing the same shoes. The drawing looks similar to Amanda's MP shot. Give me your number, and I'll text."

"Stand by, and I'll call you back after I look at the photos. Sounds promising."

Parrott figured it might take a while for Sulphur Springs to examine the photos, and he was too wired to sit at his desk while he waited. Grabbing his cellphone, he darted out of his office, down the stairs, and onto the playground adjacent to the parking lot. For the moment, he had the place to himself. The adult swings beckoned, and he lowered his tall frame into one of the seats. He

remembered how he and Bo used to swing together, each trying to outdo the other in terms of speed and height. He held onto the chains and walked backwards as far as he could go, then let the swing whip him through the stiff breeze. He closed his eyes and imagined he was flying.

After a few minutes of Parrott's hard pumping and leaning to and fro, a car pulled up in the parking lot, and four children tumbled out and ran to the slide and monkey bars. Not wanting to explain why a grown-up detective enjoyed swinging, he brought the equipment to an abrupt stop, nodded to the children and their mother, and strode with as much dignity as possible into the police station. And into his office.

That's when the phone buzzed, and the Sulphur Springs PD popped up on caller ID.

Parrott jammed his forefinger against the answer button. "What do you think, Davis. Do we have a match?"

# CHAPTER THIRTY-FOUR

Sergeant Davis' voice had a new lilt. "I've conferred with three other officers here, and we think your victim might be Amanda Hoffman. Can you overnight me some DNA? Also, I can tell from the photos that many of your victim's teeth were messed up by the gunshot, but I can send you dental records, and you could check against what's left of her mouth."

Parrott's blood beat against his temples with the welcome tempo that only happened when he got a break in a case. "Glad to help any way I can." Parrott took down all the particulars and gave Davis his own information.

"Now that we might have a connection," Parrott said, "let me tell you about another case that might be related." He proceeded to lay out the timeline and details about the infant who was left on the Baths' back porch. "The timing and circumstances suggest a link, but we checked the dead woman's DNA and the baby's, and they don't match,"

A loud squeak that might've been Davis' chair as he leaped to his feet echoed in Parrott's ear. "For crying out loud, Parrott. And the baby's alive, you say?"

"Alive and healthy. She's in the foster system as we speak."

"You'd better sit down, Parrott. You're not gonna believe this. I don't know how Amanda Hoffman got from Texas to Pennsylvania, or how she ended up with a bullet in her head, but I'd bet my last dollar she's your victim."

The pulse in Parrott's forehead thrummed even faster, and the vision of the infant in the yellow outfit swam before his eyes, "Tell me."

"Okay. You remember I told you this case was a heater. Amanda Hoffman isn't just any pregnant teenager. I'll give you some background. Amanda's dad owns a construction company. Her mom's a dental assistant. An only child, Amanda was brought

up with the best of everything, spoiled. She did all right in school, excelled at swimming."

So far nothing stood out as extraordinary, so Parrott leaned back and laced his fingers behind his neck.

"Amanda hit puberty and boys started coming around. She took up with the wrong crowd—drugs, alcohol, sex—she got into trouble here and there. Nothing criminal, but on the edge, if you know what I mean.

"This here's a small town, and word gets around fast, 'specially when the word is bad. The parents finally realized no amount of punishment could control her. When she graduated high school, they kicked her out. Sent her money each month to pay rent for an apartment, but she was on her own for food and clothes and gas for her car."

Parrott thought of the neighborhoods he and Tonya had grown up in, where nobody's daddy provided apartments or cars. "Okay," he said.

"Well, within a few months, Amanda had her car stolen, and pretty much went through all the money she'd earned working at Applebee's as a waitress. Too proud to go to her parents, or admit that her lifestyle wasn't working, she took up pet sitting and dog walking. Before long people were whispering about Amanda's belly. She was obviously pregnant.

"Funny thing, though. The boys had stopped hanging around. Cut off from her parents' money and working all those jobs, I guess she wasn't that popular anymore."

Parrott stood. "She must have been popular with some boy, or how'd she get pregnant?"

"That's right, Parrott. You've asked the exact right question. And people around here love to speculate, but nobody had any idea who the father of Amanda's baby was. A local mystery, you might say.

"Wasn't till after she disappeared in her ninth month that all that cleared up. All of a sudden, the phones were ringing, and our department came under pressure to find her."

"Her parents pressured you?"

"Yes, but that's not all. We started getting calls from one Sheltering Palms Fertility Clinic in Dallas. Evidently Amanda

had found a unique way to augment her income. She'd become a surrogate mother."

Parrott's heartbeat picked up again, as a major puzzle piece slid into place. *So that's why the baby's DNA didn't match. The dead woman gave birth to the baby without being the biological mother.*

# CHAPTER THIRTY-FIVE

Walking home after talking to Steven, Kate pondered what she would say to T.J. Steven was right. She needed to confront T.J. with her fears and give him a chance to explain them away if he could.

On top of everything, a certain memory nagged at her. A few years ago, when she'd first started taking her bread to the farmer's market, one of the vendors had approached her.

"Aren't you married to T.J. Bath?"

Kate had met the old woman's steely eyes. She failed to place her. "Yes. How can I help you?"

The woman cackled. "Oh, I'm not the one who needs help, honey. You are."

Kate had begged for specifics, but the woman turned away, refusing even to look at Kate. Not wanting to create a scene, Kate had dropped off her loaves and hurried away, but she hadn't forgotten. She'd looked for the woman every time she'd returned to the market, but she'd never seen her again.

Now as she traipsed through the dry grass and brush in the waning golden sunlight, she rolled down her sleeves and buttoned them at the wrist. The touch of chill in the air matched the one in her heart. Over the years, Kate convinced herself that she'd imagined the whole incident with the woman. She'd tried to forget it, but that was the problem with doubt. Once implanted into a brain, doubt could never be completely erased. It remained tucked into one lobe or another, coiled and ready to strike at a moment's notice.

Who was that mystery woman, and how did she know T.J.? How did she know anything about him that Kate, herself, didn't know? Ever since the baby on the porch, Kate had questioned her relationship with T.J.

Because T.J. was a decade older, Kate assumed he had past experiences, past loves, that were none of her business. If anything unsavory were in his past, surely he would have told her before

they were married. The Campbells wouldn't keep him employed if he were untrustworthy. If Aunt Connie had heard anything negative, she would have shared it.

Maybe she'd been naïve to put her whole heart into the relationship without asking more questions. Well, it was never too late for questions. Kate picked up the pace as she approached the cottage. Judging by the position of the sun in the western sky, T.J. would be home, waiting for her.

She would do as Steven suggested. She would ask her husband where he'd been and what he'd done on Monday morning, before she found the baby on the back porch.

If he couldn't or wouldn't provide a satisfying answer, she would take that as a sign. For the first time in her marriage, she entertained the idea of being separate from T.J. At thirty-one years old, she needed to think of her future. She straightened her spine and held her head high as she climbed the steps to the cottage, ready to do battle, if necessary.

Kate turned the doorknob to let herself into the unlocked house, expecting Lucy to come bounding to the door to greet her. What greeted her instead was a dark and quiet house—no Lucy, no T.J. A cold, clammy fear shimmied up and down her spine, counteracting her hot resolve. Something was wrong. Kate flipped on the light switch over the kitchen table. As her eyes adjusted to the showering brightness, she focused on a folded piece of lined notebook paper on the center of the table. In T.J.'s scrawl was the single word, *Kate*.

# CHAPTER THIRTY-SIX

Parrott's blood rushed through his body as if on a raft in rapid waters. The exhilaration of connecting the baby with the surrogate mother from Sulphur Springs, Texas, would last for hours. For now, however, Parrott needed to shut down his computer and head for home. He couldn't wait to tell the chief what he'd discovered, but when he walked next door on the way out, he found lights off and door locked. He would text Schrik after dinner.

Intuition prompted Parrott to stop by Barton's office on the way out. He didn't expect the patrolman to be there, especially since his hours had been so erratic of late. But the light shone through the frosted glass into the hallway, and when Parrott knocked on the door, Barton's voice responded. "Just a minute."

Parrott waited for Barton to let him in. He might have interrupted a private moment, but Parrott's thoughts were free to roam all over the possibilities.

Before Parrott could go too far in imagining, Barton opened the door, his face haggard and his hair disheveled "Working late, Parrott? Come on in."

The room reeked of sweet rolls and day-old coffee, overlain with tobacco. "I could say the same about you. I hope everything's okay with you and your family." Parrott glanced at papers strewn over Barton's desk.

"We'll be all right. Just a few bumps in the road, but everybody has those." Barton sat and drank from a half-empty bottle of water. "Well, maybe *you* don't, Parrott. Most of us don't have millions of dollars fall into our laps."

Heat rushed into Parrott's face and neck, eclipsing all the happy feelings he'd had about the call with Sulphur Springs. The multi-million-dollar gift from Elle would never stop interfering with his relationships. He sucked in a breath and let it out slowly.

He sat and leaned forward, making eye contact. "Listen, Barton. If you need money, I'd be glad to help."

"No thanks. Call me proud, but I need to work this through on my own. Might take me a while, but I'll manage." Barton swept all the papers on his desk into a single stack, tapped the bottom against the desktop, and slipped them into a folder. "Anyway, what's up? We've both got things to do, and it's closing time."

Parrott drummed his fingers on his knee, unsure how much to share with this rude colleague and former friend. If there was even a chance that Barton's SUV was the one on the promontory, or that Barton's connection to Stuart Mooney would compromise this case, Parrott needed complete discretion. He rose and stretched his back. "All I wanted was to wish you a good evening."

Normally the two of them would shake hands, but Parrott didn't extend his, and neither did Barton. As Parrott turned to leave, Barton's cellphone rang to the tune of *Rocky*.

Barton answered quickly, turning his body away from Parrott. "Thanks for getting back to me," he said into the phone. "Yes, I can have it ready for you to test drive by tomorrow morning."

Parrott turned back, straining to hear.

"I can meet you at ten a.m. at 198 Lafayette Road in West Brandywine. It's the township offices, where the police and public services are housed. There's a parking lot in front of a playground." Barton lowered his voice. "Yeah, cash only."

Parrott took his time leaving, his mind a-flurry with possibilities. If he wasn't mistaken, Barton was going to sell his SUV tomorrow morning. Parrott needed to figure out a way to stop him.

# CHAPTER THIRTY-SEVEN

Parrott took his first dose of D-aspartic acid with his evening meal, and he spent some time afterwards planning for the following day. He sat at the breakfast table with his computer, while Tonya put together a recipe for flourless chocolate cake. He was amused to watch her moving around the kitchen in her feathered lavender slippers, humming a tune.

Horace, in a rare respite from his cage, tiptoed around the perimeter of the table, muttering, "Oh, boy," in a shrill chirp. The picture of domestic tranquility was especially precious, because it was so fragile. A trigger could set Tonya into PTSD hell at any moment. But right here, right now, she was happy. Maybe they should entertain company more often.

Before he went to bed, Parrott put Horace in his cage and considered diving into one of the boxes containing mementos of his years with Bo. "Tonya, where are the boxes my mother brought over?"

"I put them on the empty shelves in the laundry room cabinets." She cocked her head and looked at him, as if he had asked her where he could find world peace. "I thought you weren't ready."

"Yeah, maybe I'm not. I was just thinking about boxes, how we use them to put things away, out of sight or out of reach. How many boxes we still have sitting in the garage, how long it will take to unpack them, and where we'll put everything once we do. I've been comfortable keeping memories of Bo packed up tight for three years, but sooner or later I need to open those boxes."

"Want to lick the bowl?" Tonya held out the remains of chocolate batter lining a mixing bowl, along with the spatula. The change of subject was probably intentional.

"Hmm…more batter than usual. Are you sure you can't scrape more into the cake pan?"

Tonya grinned, showing the gap between her front teeth. "The better to fatten you up, my love."

Parrott licked the spatula and scraped every molecule of batter from the bowl that he could. "Mmm, the neighbors are never going to go home until every speck of this cake is eaten." He smacked his lips and blew the kiss into the air, like a French chef.

While Tonya baked the cake, and Parrott helped her clean the kitchen, his thoughts turned back to boxes. He needed to run the prints Chesco found on the box Brandywine B had been left in. Now that he had a possible established link between the mother and the baby, fingerprints might be crucial to solving both cases.

He had one more task to do before retiring for the night. He needed someone to play an important role early tomorrow morning, someone not associated with any of his cases. After mentally auditioning dozens of men and women he knew, he decided to call Wren Vargas. She and Alexander, Elle's adopted nephew, had recently tied the knot, and the Parrotts had attended the wedding. Wren was the perfect actress for the part—she was young, innocent-looking, smart, and assertive.

Fortunately, Wren was available and game to help with Parrott's operation. Another bit of luck was the home safe in Parrott's new house, where he kept a considerable amount of cash. He got everything ready for the next morning and went upstairs to shower and shave.

When he finished, Tonya had already slid into bed, wearing a lavender nightgown. Parrott rolled over and reached for her hands. As he brought them to his mouth for kisses, a scent of honeysuckle lotion tickled his senses. Tonya wrapped her arms around his neck, and soon Parrott forgot about Barton, his SUV, and even the chocolate cake.

# CHAPTER THIRTY-EIGHT

Kate stood paralyzed in her kitchen, like a player in freeze tag, caught in an awkward motion. The note from T.J., sitting on the table, might have been a bomb or a ration of anthrax for all the fear it elicited in her. Reading it would probably change her life forever.

Slowly, by degrees, she broke her position and shook her arms. She didn't have to read the note right away. She poured a bottle of club soda over ice, and, as an afterthought, added a splash of scotch. The Moonglow label distracted her, and she sat on the sofa to stir her drink. She sipped and ruminated about growing up with Catherine and Steven. How different each of their paths were now.

Outside, dusk was turning to dark. The kitchen light poured over the table, where the note sat, calling her name. The scotch had gone down smoothly, more so because she rarely drank. The insides of her limbs and toes and fingers glowed with a comforting warmth. She could read the note now. She wanted to read it.

She took her drink to the kitchen table and sat in her usual chair. She reached for the folded sheet of lined paper, propped up on the napkin holder. T.J.'s handwriting, the way he wrote her name, seemed dear to her at that moment. She held the note to her chest.

Another sip later, she opened the note. It was only three lines long.

*I'm going away to think. Taking Lucy with me. There're things I haven't told you, and you deserve better. If you leave, I'll understand. Love always, T.J.*

*P.S. Told the Campbells I'd be gone for three days.*

Kate read the lines out loud, imagining T.J.'s voice. Her first impulse was to search for him. He couldn't have gone far. The little house was so quiet without him and Lucy. She couldn't bear to stay there alone.

What did he mean by "things I haven't told you"? Were her worst fears materializing? One thing Kate knew for sure--she didn't want to stay out here in the country alone, surrounded by

doubts and anxieties about her husband. Her head pounded, and her breath was short.

She texted Steven. *T.J. left and took the dog. Okay if I come stay with you for a few days?* Without waiting for a response, Kate pulled a suitcase from the top shelf of her closet. If Steven said no, she'd go to a motel. Two pairs of jeans, three tank tops, three blouses, underwear, and her purple pajamas should be enough for a few days in Philly.

She was packing toiletries in a cloth and plastic travel bag when her phone pinged with a message from Steven. *Okay.* Tossing in a couple of loaves of frozen bread to give to Steven, she debated taking T.J.'s note with her. Having already memorized it, she left it on the table.

At the last minute, Kate decided to leave a note of her own. She pulled another sheet of lined notebook paper from the desk drawer in the kitchen. Folding it and writing T.J.'s name on the outside, she wrote, *Got your note. Going away to think this through. If you want to talk, call my cell. Xxoo.*

Satisfied she was doing the right thing, Kate locked up the cottage and loaded her belongings into her car. Hopefully she could gain some insights being with her cousin. Steven, for all his social complexities, had always led a peaceful life. She was grateful to escape the source of her turmoil, but she had to be careful not to carry it with her to Steven's. Turmoil was something Steven didn't need.

# CHAPTER THIRTY-NINE

Before six the next morning, Parrott met Wren Vargas at her home in Philadelphia. He gave her the cash he'd removed from his home safe and reviewed the role she was to play later that morning. They rehearsed a few times, using different scenarios, and then Parrott went back home to West Chester to await her arrival.

Tonya had a therapy session with Alice, and then she was going to stop by Elle's. Since they'd moved, she had stopped working there on Wednesdays, but she loved to visit with Elle and the special adults who lived, learned skills, and worked on the Allmond estate.

So, Parrott and Horace had the house to themselves. Parrott set up his computer on the breakfast table. He'd already received and forwarded Amanda Hoffman's dental records to Chesco, but his mission now was to learn whatever he could about Sheltering Palms Fertility Clinic.

His first surprise was to learn that Sheltering Palms had forty locations across the country. Sulphur Springs was less than eighty miles from the closest one in Dallas, but there were four in Pennsylvania, and one only thirty-five miles from Parrott's new house in West Chester. Parrott put the address in his cellphone's GPS for later.

The corporate website had a positive vibe. Phrases like, "get your family started," "achieve your dreams," and "state-of-the-art procedures," were no doubt designed to lure the visitor. A drop-down menu expressed support and empathy for infertile couples.

Parrott's personal feelings about being infertile rose into his throat. He hoped he and Tonya wouldn't have to resort to drastic measures to have a family, but if they did, this website offered it all—hormone therapy, in vitro fertilization, sperm donation, surrogacy—a horn of plenty for the disappointed and discouraged. Infertility was big business, judging from the many locations,

resources, and treatments listed. Another menu addressed costs—interesting, but not what he was looking for now.

Parrott made a list of questions for when he visited Sheltering Palms in Philadelphia. Mostly, he wanted to know about matches of donors and surrogates, how they were handled, what protections were in place for the various stakeholders. He wondered specifically how a surrogate mother in Texas carried a baby whose DNA was linked to relatives in several Southern states and who ended up in Pennsylvania. If he could learn more about Brandywine B's origin, he believed he could get closer to Brandywine A's murder.

Parrott checked the time, eager to call Monica Bell at protective services. Monica was also an early bird, so he took a chance, even though it was not yet eight o'clock. The phone rang several times, and he was preparing to leave a voicemail when Monica answered, breathless.

"Good morning, detective. Aren't we getting an early start today?"

Parrott enjoyed Monica's chipper spirit. Many of the CPS people he'd dealt with spent more time grumbling. "Hope I didn't wake you. But I have some news worth hearing."

"Tell me." Parrott could picture Monica leaning on her elbows, pouring all her attention into whatever he might say.

"Not confirmed yet, but I believe I'm close to finding the abandoned infant's rightful parents." He explained how the DNA in the breast milk left with the baby matched that of a murder victim, who had recently given birth.

"How sad. So, the baby's mother is deceased."

"Not exactly." Parrott went on to explain how the baby's DNA did not match the mother's. "She was a surrogate mother. That's what we think. My victim was carrying a baby for someone else. I'll know more later today, if the dental records match up, but I wanted to alert you."

Monica whistled. "Unbelievable. Never in all my years has something like this happened. I'm glad you told me. If this bears out, we'll have a whole different process to follow, getting this little one back to the biological parents."

"Yes. I don't know who that is, but chances are it will be parent, not parents." Parrott hadn't planned to divulge everything yet, but the words had spilled out.

"What do you mean? Every child has two parents, right?"

Parrott said, "Of course, but in this case, the child may have been conceived with a sperm donor."

"Oh, my! A surrogate mother and a donor father? This *is* unusual." Monica giggled. "We are going to need paperwork out the wazoo to document this baby's origins before we can transfer custody. Otherwise, she will remain in our care. The foster parents have fallen in love with her."

Promising to keep in touch, Parrott hung up. Horace was stirring in his cage, so Parrott took a break from work. "'Hey, Horace. How was your nice big bowl of birdseed?"

The cockatiel squawked, "Oh, goody. Oh, goody."

*Everybody should act this happy,* Parrott thought, as he removed the soiled newspapers from the cage and replaced them with fresh ones. "Want to come out to play?" He held out a finger, and, when the bird hopped on, he ferried the bird to his shoulder.

While Parrott washed his hands, his stomach burbled, and he had a sudden urge for food. He'd eaten his normal breakfast before driving to Wren's, so what was this about? The fridge was stocked with bacon, eggs, cheese, vegetables, butter, milk, plums, and grapes, but none of these appealed for a mid-morning snack.

He opened the pantry and scanned the shelves. He finally settled on a box of graham crackers. Maybe he'd fix some more coffee and dip the crackers the way his grandmother used to do. He started for the coffee maker but stopped before putting the K-cup into the basket. For the first time in a decade, the thought of black coffee caused a disagreeable phlegm to form in his throat.

Instead of coffee, he poured himself a glass of milk. It turned out that graham crackers dipped in milk were delicious, and he ate an entire sleeve of them. Where was this drastic change in appetite coming from? Could it be the D-aspartic acid?

He fished the product information out of the box that the bottle had come in. The tiny print was full of details, but he skimmed to the "side effects" section. There it was, "Increased

appetite, stomach distress, diarrhea, increase in body fat, bouts of depression, increased aggressiveness."

Not one to jump to worst case scenarios, Parrott reminded himself that he probably wouldn't experience all of these, but the increased appetite was already kicking in after one dose.

Before he could think about the other product warnings, his cellphone buzzed with a call from Jerry at Chesco. "Hey, Parrott. Just letting you know the dental records matched. Your victim is definitely Amanda Hoffman."

Even though he was expecting that news, Parrott's brain lit up like an old-fashioned slot machine hitting the jackpot. "Wonderful, Jerry. Thanks for the info and the quick work." He disconnected and searched for the number for Sergeant Davis in Texas.

He wanted to celebrate this big breakthrough in the cases, but the truth was, knowing the identity of the victim was only a step. He had a long way to go to figure out who abandoned the baby and who killed her surrogate mother.

# CHAPTER FORTY

After fulfilling her "assignment," Wren pulled up in Parrott's driveway in a 2015 Chevy Blazer at almost eleven a.m. Parrott had been watching for her. Once she turned in from the street, he dashed outside through the single garage door, the one designated for a third vehicle.

"Pull her on in here." He waved Wren into the parking spot, pleased that everything had apparently gone according to plan.

Wren cut the engine and hopped out of the car, careful not to touch anything more than was necessary. Her strawberry-blonde hair was pulled back in a tight ponytail, and she wore an Eagles sun visor over it. Sunglasses concealed her eyes, and her beige nondescript warmup suit hung loosely.

Wren handed over the keys, and Parrott closed the overhead garage door, locking the car inside. "Why don't you come in for a minute?" Parrott asked. "I'm eager to hear."

"Okay, but just for a minute. I've got to get back soon. I promised Alexander I'd go with him to pick out some bricks he's purchasing."

Parrott ushered her into the oversized entry hall. "Can I offer you a drink—some iced tea or water?"

"No, thanks. I will use your restroom, though, if that's okay."

While Wren ducked into the powder room, Parrott closed his computer and packed it in its case. As an afterthought, he included a six-pack of power bars in case he got the munchies again any time soon. Whenever Wren was ready, he'd give her a ride back to the station, where she'd left her car.

Emerging from the powder room, Wren opened her slingbag and handed Parrott an envelope. "Didn't want to forget this. Here's the title. And here," she said, pulling out another envelope, "is your change."

Parrott opened the first envelope and glanced over the title. "How much did you pay?"

"Twelve-five. The other guy really wanted the car, but he couldn't go over ten. Made it easy for me to step in."

"You don't think Barton suspected anything?"

"Nah. He looked at me funny when I first walked up. I parked around the block. Told him I'd walked to the township office to pay my trash pickup bill. I said my car died on me, and I needed something right away. I'd just made a withdrawal from the bank so I could go used car shopping this afternoon." Her affable grin and the lilt in her voice gave a credible impression. "Anyway, after I paid him and got the title, I went into the township office and pretended to pay the bill. I think he bought it."

"I can't thank you enough," Parrott said. "C'mon. Let me drive you to your car."

"No need to thank me. Alexander's told me what good people you and Tonya are, how much you've done for Elle. This was no trouble. You can call on me anytime."

On the way from West Chester to West Brandywine, Wren chit-chatted about the new house that Alexander was building for them. "We've got an architect and a lot. My dad's involved, too. It's all very exciting."

Wren's bubbliness reminded Parrott of a bird's chirping, and he chuckled to think that she was aptly named. Her delight over her new house was contagious. He knew Elle would leave the Whitman estate, Manderley, to Alexander, but, hopefully, that transfer of property wouldn't take place for a long time.

"—get to pick out the brick, the tile, the floors, the appliances." Wren warbled on, unfazed by Parrott's silence. "Not everybody is as lucky as we are. We hope to start a family soon."

*There it was again. More talk of babies.* Parrott was starting to feel the baby blues, and he didn't want to. A firm believer that where the mind goes, the energy flows, he forced his thoughts to the 2015 Blazer he had just bought and secreted in his garage. Whether it turned out to be evidence in a murder or not, having the car safely in his possession helped him send those blues away.

# CHAPTER FORTY-ONE

When Parrott dropped Wren off at her car, it was after noon, and his stomach was giving him fits. Fortunately, Manny's street taco truck was ensconced in a shady corner under an elm tree. Parrott knew Manny through his mother's catering business, and the thought of a basket with tacos, beans, and rice, made his mouth water.

*I'd better be careful with all this eating, or I'll be looking pregnant.* He carried the foil-wrapped treasure to his car and drove around the block to the station. Barton's empty parking spot caught his eye, like a newly-missing front tooth. It would be interesting to see how and when Barton replaced his vehicle.

Before climbing the stairs to his office, Parrott stopped in to say hello to Lucretia. She was occupied with a vociferous couple, complaining about a parking ticket. Parrott caught her eye and waved, and she made a sign with her right hand, pointing upward and encircling her ear. Parrott knew what that meant. The chief had been looking for him.

Parrott purposely didn't want to tell Schrik about Barton's car. He didn't want to put his boss in the middle of his suspicions about a member of their team. Another factor was Parrott's unorthodox use of personal funds to secure the car. He wouldn't lie about the ruse, but he didn't want to broadcast what he'd done, at least for now.

He bypassed his own office to go to Schrik's but was surprised to find the door locked and the lights on behind the frosted glass panel. He guessed the chief was somewhere in the building. Shrugging, he backtracked to his own office and sat down to eat his tacos while they were still warm. Meanwhile, he was trying to decide whether to visit Moonglow or Sheltering Palms this afternoon. He was leaning toward interviewing Stuart Mooney, since he'd already driven into Philadelphia and back once today, and the day was getting away from him.

Before he took the last delectable bite, Chief Schrik rapped on the open door and popped his head inside. "Got a minute?"

Parrott closed his take-out lunch basket and slid it into the trash can before offering Schrik a chair. "Lucretia told me you were looking for me. I was out in the field this morning." A twinge of guilt flickered in Parrott's gut, although the statement wasn't false.

"Yes. I wanted to share something with you, but first, a question." Schrik cleared his throat. "Where are you with interviewing Stuart Mooney? He's lawyered up."

Parrott shook his head, although hiring lawyers was a typical practice for the ultra-rich. "I was just getting ready to swing past there when I finished my lunch."

"That's why I was looking for you." Schrik shifted his weight and crossed one leg over the other. "I got a call from a New York attorney—a guy named Price. Wanted to know if Mooney was a suspect."

"What did you tell him?" Parrott couldn't help thinking if Mooney hadn't been a suspect before, hiring a lawyer certainly put him on the list of possibles.

"I said it was too early. We're still gathering information. I asked him why Mooney would think he needs a lawyer now." Schrik grunted. "Of course, I didn't expect an answer. I hate it when these Brandywine folks think they have to insulate themselves from us—complicates everything."

"Agree. Guess I can't go by today to talk to Mooney."

"Nope. Attorney Price insists on being present for any questioning." Schrik ran his hands through the sparse strands of hair above his ears. "You know the drill."

Parrott rolled the mouse of his computer back and forth over the mouse pad, thinking. As much as he hated to bring up Barton in a discussion with Schrik, he really had to. "Mind if I close the door?" Without waiting for an answer, Parrott strode to the office door and pushed it closed. He returned to his chair and sat, elbows on the desk. "This is a tough conversation, but maybe necessary. I can't stop thinking about what you told me about Barton's possibly working for Mooney."

Schrik rubbed his eyes and his whole face. "I know. I've been thinking the same."

"I've tried to convince myself he's merely moonlighting, nothing wrong with that. Maybe he's in a jam for money." Parrott began pacing. "But why would Mooney need the services of a West Brandywine police officer? When might he have been hired, and what might he be doing for Mooney? Most of all, did Mooney or Barton have anything to do with a nineteen-year-old woman's death on the grounds of Moonglow?"

Parrott perched on the edge of his desk and made eye contact with his boss. "I don't like thinking ill of my colleague. I don't even like bringing this up with you. But we have a murder to solve—not to mention a baby abandonment case—and I'm going to have to talk to Mooney."

"I hear ya, Parrott. And I appreciate your wanting to be discreet. I'm going to have to talk to Barton, as well. Maybe there was no conflict of interest when he was first hired to work for Mooney, assuming the rumor's true, but now there sure as hell is."

Parrott was relieved to hear Schrik's intent. With Barton's car in his garage in West Chester, Parrott was already up to his eyeballs in messing with Barton.

Schrik sighed. "Listen, I trust you to deal with Mooney and his fancy attorney, but I need to jump on this thing with Barton right away. If there's even an appearance of impropriety with one of my officers, I need to be the first to know." He leaned forward, his green eyes blazing. "That means I need you to tell me every single thing you know or suspect about Barton."

Icicles swept through Parrott's body, and indigestion rose in his esophagus. "Okay, but let me preface by saying Barton's a friend, and I hope this will come to nothing." He began pacing again. "You'll remember that Barton was AWOL at the time we found the baby and the woman by the creek."

"Right," Schrik said. "That's why I went out to Moonglow. I notified Mooney and got his permission to search the property."

"Yes, and later, when Grossman took me to the promontory, we found tire tracks and other physical evidence. I measured the width span between the tires. I researched vehicles with that measurement. Barton's Chevy Blazer was one of them."

Schrik's eyebrows soared, but he remained silent.

"Afterwards, you told me about the possible connection between Barton and Mooney, and that made me really suspicious, especially because Barton continued to be absent or tardy in coming to work. When I asked him to help ID the victim, he begged off. He claimed to be busy with other things, but I started to think he was trying to avoid this case."

Parrott returned to his desk. He needed to sit to talk about this next part. "I don't imagine you're going to like what I say now." He swallowed. "Late yesterday afternoon I overheard Barton talking to someone on the phone about selling his car. He told the person to meet him at the station parking lot today at ten a.m. and to bring cash. Whether he needed money or needed to get rid of evidence, I couldn't let that deal go through."

Schrik's gaze burned through Parrott. "Go on."

"I set up a phony buyer, somebody Barton wouldn't recognize. She outbid the other offer and took possession of the car. It's locked in my garage now."

"You used your own money?" Schrik asked. "You know I can't reimburse you."

"I know. If the car turns out to hold evidence, even if not probative, I'll be satisfied I did the right thing. If not, I still own the car. I have some ideas of what I can do with it. That brings you up-to-date."

Schrik rose and shook Parrott's hand across the desk. "Thanks for your honesty and dedication to the job, Parrott. There aren't many men who would go so far with their own money. I'm not even going to ask how much."

Parrott breathed more easily. He hadn't realized how suffocating keeping this secret was. "No problem, chief. Now let's hope we don't need to use it."

# CHAPTER FORTY-TWO

Kate was more comfortable than she'd thought she'd be at Steven's spacious two-bedroom condo in the Chestnut Hill area of Philadelphia. His unit was about the same size as the cottage, but the vibe was entirely different. Steven had nine-foot ceilings, two modern bathrooms, a gourmet kitchen, and even a wine cooler, not to mention a doorman, a maintenance staff, and a housekeeper.

She'd arrived before dark the night before, and Steven was just coming home from his job at St. Paul's Episcopal Church down the block. When she asked what he did there, Steven muttered something about services. She imagined it was a volunteer job.

Steven could never have afforded such a fancy home without financial backing from his parents, but Kate wasn't judgy when it came to her cousin. She was glad he had such a nice place to live.

"Would you like me to cook something for us for dinner?" she asked, once she had unpacked her belongings in the guest room.

Steven shook his head. "Nirvana is good."

"Nirvana?" Kate wasn't sure whether he was talking about heaven or food, but her stomach burbled, and they both laughed.

"Indian restaurant across the street."

As much as Kate preferred country life, she had to admit that living in the city had its benefits. Steven hardly ever drove his SUV. He could walk to work, to eat, to shop. His boutique condo was well-situated, and the street was lively with people carrying packages, talking on cellphones, walking dogs.

"This is a real change of pace for me," she said, as Steven opened the door to the restaurant. Pungent smells of garlic and curry stung her nose, and she was overcome with mouth-watering pleasure, almost enough to make her forget why she was here.

The restaurant owner greeted Steven with effusive friendliness. He introduced himself to Kate and welcomed her, as well. "Would you like your usual table, Mr. Mooney?" he asked, as he sidled to a table at the back of the room.

Kate scooted into her seat, admiring the crisp placemat, tablecloth, and napkins in a red-and-gold color scheme. "Lovely restaurant," she said to Steven. "I can tell the owner likes you."

"I come here a lot." Steven devoted his attention to the menu, although Kate guessed he knew it by heart.

"I'm pretty sure the owner thinks I'm your girlfriend. I could tell by the way he greeted me."

"I get the vegetable samosa and the chili chicken. Everything's good."

The menu featured a wide variety of vegetarian dishes, as well as a few with chicken. "I can't tell you the last time I was in an Indian restaurant. This is so nice. I'm hungry enough to order one of everything."

"Way too much."

Kate smiled. "I was exaggerating. Actually, I think I'll order the eggplant and the chicken kabobs. And dinner is my treat, since you are generous enough to put me up in your home."

"No. There won't be a bill. I pay once at the end of the month." Steven signaled for the waiter, a middle-aged woman who might have been the owner's wife.

After they ordered, Kate tried to draw her cousin out in conversation. Years of experience had taught her how difficult that could be, but those same years had given the two of them many things in common. She started by complimenting him on his home, his neighborhood, and his job at the church. "Seems like you've got an ideal set-up here. Have you made any friends?"

Steven shrugged and stared at his placemat, exposing the thinning dark hair on his crown.

"Do you ever think about getting married, having a family?" she asked.

Another shrug and a squeezing of Steven's eyes shut told Kate this was not a viable topic, so she shifted into a safer subject— her own personal life. "Ever since I passed my thirtieth birthday, I've been re-evaluating. I thought I was completely happy being married to T.J. Dogs were easier than kids, and we had each other. But life in the country can be isolating. Every day is a lot like the last and the next, and there is nothing new."

Steven appeared to be listening, but Kate's instincts told her she was talking mainly to herself. That was okay. She needed this self-revelation. "Last Monday somebody put a precious baby girl on my back steps. She was sleeping inside a cardboard box, wearing the most adorable yellow outfit with ducks on it." She sipped from her water glass and rolled the wetness around in her mouth. "She was a gift. I wanted to keep her."

The waitress approached the table with their appetizers, pausing the conversation, but before he picked up his fork, Steven brushed at his eye. The moment passed, and the cousins dug into their vegetarian dishes.

From then on, they talked solely about the food. When appetizers and main dishes were consumed, Kate laughed. "Suddenly I'm not hungry anymore. I don't think I could eat another bite."

"Desserts are good," Steven said. "But I'm full, too." He swiped at his mouth with his napkin and slapped it down on the table. "We can go now."

"Can I leave the tip?"

"No. All taken care of." Steven stood and stretched. The hem of his polo shirt had come out of his jeans in the back, and a section of inked skin was visible.

*Oh, my. I guess there are some things I don't know about Steven.* Kate complimented the restaurant owner on the way out, and the cousins strolled back to the condo in the cool evening. The first hint of fall had arrived, and that made Kate think about Brandywine. Three days away from the cottage, Lucy, and T.J. were beginning to seem like forever.

When they returned to the condo, Steven turned the TV on and switched the channel to an action movie. Never having been much of a TV-watcher anyway, and not a fan of action movies, Kate excused herself, claiming a preference to read her latest mystery novel. She showered, put on her PJs, and climbed into bed. Before opening the book, she checked for messages from T.J., but there weren't any. Debating about whether to send one, proclaiming herself safe and sound at Steven's, she decided to hold back. Maybe tomorrow.

The next morning, Kate awoke at nine, the latest she had slept in years. Steven had left for work, and the prospect of another

entire day with no responsibility or obligation loomed like an uncharted path in an unfamiliar forest. No messages from T.J. She wondered where he was and what he and Lucy were doing.

Brewing herself a cup of coffee, Kate looked around the condo for something to do, some way to help Steven. She considered cooking one of their grandmother's dishes and freezing portions for future meals, but Steven had appeared to be content with eating out, and his freezer was already full of leftovers from restaurant meals. The housekeeper must have recently cleaned. The kitchen and bathrooms were fresh, and the carpets had been vacuumed.

A dirty clothes basket in the laundry room was overflowing, though. There were at least two loads to wash, and that would keep her busy for a while. She began sorting the whites from the colored items, and assessing which ones were permanent press.

There were enough whites for a full load, so she opened the washing machine and moved them over, one at a time, from the basket into the tub, while putting the dark-colored items on the floor. When she reached the bottom of the basket, she found something soft and flimsy. She pulled it out and uttered a cry of surprise. In her hand was a white Maidenform bra.

# CHAPTER FORTY-THREE

Saturday arrived, the day of the barbecue with the Franklins. As antsy as Parrott was to move forward on the case, he didn't want to leave all the preparation work to Tonya. Having company was a brand-new experience in their marriage and an important step for Tonya. She'd avoided social situations since being traumatized on duty in Afghanistan.

The night before, they'd drafted a to-do list and divided up the duties. Parrott would make the home-made barbecue sauce, using his mother's recipe; marinate the ribs and chicken; shuck the corn on the cob and wrap each ear in foil with butter and seasonings; set up the outdoor bar and grill; and make sure all the furniture around the pool was clean and properly arranged.

Whether from the testosterone capsules or thoughts of the barbecue—or maybe because of the murder case—Parrott had had a restless night. He finally gave up on more sleep and got out of bed at five a.m. He started for the coffee maker but held back when he imagined the acidity of his usual black coffee. He poured himself a glass of milk instead.

*Might as well start in on my preparations. These could actually be fun.* Parrott had accomplished all his tasks by the time Tonya came downstairs at seven-thirty. Barefooted and dressed in short cut-offs and a crop top, she could've been a model, despite not having touched her hair or put on makeup.

"Good morning, beautiful wife, queen of the household, and deluxe party planner." He nuzzled the back of her neck and wrapped an arm around her waist.

She yawned and reached an arm behind her head to pat his face. "You're up early."

"Couldn't sleep. I finished my list." He let go of Tonya and took the cover from Horace's cage. Horace lay on the inclined plane that doubled as exercise equipment and bed. Parrott whispered Horace's name and gave a soft whistle, as he did every morning.

Usually, Horace righted himself immediately and shrieked some greeting, full of energy. Today, he continued lying still.

Worried, Parrott opened the door of the cage and tickled the bird with a finger. "Wake up, Horace. Rise and shine."

The bird leaped into an upright position and squawked, "Gotcha." He flew out of the cage and onto Parrott's shoulder, continuing to flap his wings.

"That's it, Horace," Tonya said, leaning over to make kissing sounds at the bird. "I love a bird that wakes up ready to exercise."

"Speaking of exercise, can I interest you in a workout in the pool this morning? I need to burn off a few days' worth of calories."

"Hm, a tempting offer, but I haven't completed *my* preparations yet. My appetizers await." She led Horace to his personal bird-gym in the corner of the family room. He had just begun resuming workouts as part of acclimating to the new house, and he repeated, "Oh, boy, oh boy," about fifty times.

Tonya followed Parrott outside to the swimming pool. "You don't have to go into work today? I've been crossing my fingers."

Parrott wrapped his arms around her waist and led her to the chaise lounge, where he sat and eased her onto his lap. "Me, too. Unless something catastrophic happens, I'm yours all day and all night. You'll probably be ready to send me back to work by tomorrow morning."

"Not a chance, detective. You haven't seen the morning-after to-do list." Tonya stood. "I'd better get started on my list. And Horace's play time is just about up." She pecked him on the cheek and dashed back inside.

Parrott stripped to his BVDs and began swimming laps. A strong swimmer, he'd completed water safety instruction and served as a lifeguard when he was younger. Stretching the muscles in his limbs and spine felt great, but within a few minutes  his cellphone rang. Parrott hoisted himself out of the pool to answer. It was Schrik.

"*Good* morning, Parrott. Hope you're not planning to go into the station today. Broken water main. Township's closing operations till it's fixed. We've routed calls to Lucretia's home phone, and she'll call if anything arises."

Parrott grinned big-time. Now he could enjoy this day at home without guilt—like a person with a normal occupation. "Thanks for letting me know."

"Oh, and, Parrott," Schrik said, "when I called Barton to tell him about the water main, he sounded congested, like he had allergies or something. Told me, unless a call came in, he'd be in bed all day."

"Sorry to hear. Hope he feels better." Parrott disconnected. Prickles of annoyance eclipsed his joy at having a clear shot at a day off. He doubted that Barton had allergies. This wasn't even allergy season. *Barton's head doesn't seem to be in the job anymore, and that means more will fall on Schrik and me.*

� ✻ ✻

The aromas of barbecue, fresh-cut grass, and chlorine blended into a pleasant bouquet, as the Parrotts and their guests sat on the backyard pool patio. The air was dry and crisp, cool, but comfortable. Cicadas competed with background music, piped in through a sound system, and the fairy lights strung around the curve of the patio and the cabana lent more atmosphere.

During dinner, Lorraine and Will offered the lowdown on the neighborhood based on their experiences as the first Blacks to purchase a home there fifteen years ago. "Things have changed a lot since then, but there haven't been a lot of people moving out or in," Will said. "We're so glad to have new neighbors who look like us."

Happy to have a rare chance to kick back, Parrott drank a couple of beers and decided he could get used to this. Lorraine told vignettes about experiences their children had had, growing up there. Some disheartening, some poignant. "In the end, I think kids in every neighborhood confront prejudices and challenges. We wanted our kids to experience excellent schools and privileges we didn't have, growing up. West Chester was a good place for that." She turned to Tonya. "Are you and Ollie planning to raise a family here?"

Tonya had just put a chocolate-covered strawberry into her mouth, rendering herself unable to answer anything but an

*mmmph.* Parrott, having heard the question over Will's laughter at a story about his son's football coach, intervened. "We're working on it." Parrott wiggled his eyebrows and clasped Tonya's hand in his own.

Parrott diverted attention to Lorraine's sister, Juanita, who looked to be about eight months' pregnant. "Tell me about your baby plans. How are things in Birmingham for raising young children?"

Juanita caught the eye of her wife, Clara, before responding. "We thought long and hard about having kids. Birmingham's an okay city nowadays. We live in a good school district, and all. We both have good-paying jobs, where we don't want to take off too much time. And raising Black kids who come from a home with two mothers might be problematic—not for us, but from outside."

Clara took off her sandals and dipped her toes in the pool. "Hey, sometimes you gotta have faith in your own relationship, your own dreams. I've always wanted to be a mom. Juanita and I are going to be great parents."

Juanita rubbed her belly. "Yeah, as soon as I give birth to this one, Clara's going to be inseminated with the same father's sperm. Our kids will be half-siblings."

Glad for the turn in conversation, Parrott asked, "Mind telling me how that works? Is a fertility clinic involved?"

"Oh, yes," Juanita said. "We could never have accomplished this without Sheltering Palms. They're expensive, but so professional. So worth it. They arranged everything—the sperm donor, the IVF, and contact with our obstetrician."

Parrott perked up at Juanita's explanation. Was the beer causing him to imagine things? "Sheltering Palms? That's a national outfit, isn't it?"

Clara replied. "Yes. We got to pick our baby's father from a bank of donors from all over the nation."

"I think they do that so they don't have too many babies from the same father in the same area," Juanita said. "I wouldn't want my kids in the same kindergarten class with fifteen half-siblings." She laughed and popped a piece of ramaki into her mouth.

"Is there a limit to how many times a particular man's sperm can be used?" Parrott asked.

"Yeah," Will said. "I asked that same question. One guy could end up with hundreds of kids, if not. Not good for genetics. The donor's anonymous, so his offspring could end up marrying other offspring without knowing."

Parrott wondered about Brandywine A's parentage. Was her biological mother a partner in a gay marriage? Were her sperm donor and the surrogate who carried her chosen anonymously in the same way as Juanita's and Clara's baby's? He thought about all the relatives who had turned up in other states for her on Ancestry. The baby might have lots of relatives, but they probably wouldn't be showing up at family reunions.

The conversation poolside switched to other topics when Lorraine asked for the recipe for the crunchy ramen noodle salad, but Parrott's thoughts remained on babies—how they were conceived, how they were raised, and by whom.

After the guests left, Parrott and Tonya carried in the leftovers and the dishes. They worked side-by-side in the kitchen to clean up, congratulating each other on the success of the evening. Parrott marveled at what a perfect hostess his wife had turned out to be.

Tonya said, "You seemed mighty interested in that fertility clinic. Were you thinking we should look into that for us?"

Parrott shoved the plastic-wrapped platter of leftover chicken and ribs into the refrigerator, and he took his wife in his arms. He planted a kiss on her lips that drove everything out of his mind, except for her floral scent, the smoothness of her skin, the warmth of her hands on the back of his neck, and the flames igniting inside.

He lifted her against his upper body and carried her upstairs to the bedroom. If he hadn't been so distracted, he might have prayed for the D-aspartic acid to do its thing. But right now, in this moment, his heart was completely full.

Sunday afternoon, after Parrott and Tonya finished their after-party clean-up, Parrott turned his attention back to the case. Sheltering Palms and Stuart Mooney would have to wait—he'd never be able to arrange meetings with administrators or lawyers on a Sunday. On the other hand, Sunday might be a great day for catching T.J. Bath at home.

Tonya had curled up on the sofa with Horace on the arm rest next to her, watching her new favorite Netflix show, *The Upshaws*. "You think Kim Fields looks like me?" she asked.

"Not half as beautiful," Parrott said. Tonya's therapist had suggested watching comedy shows, and so far *The Upshaws* had been good medicine. He sat on the sofa, and Horace flitted to his shoulder. "Want to pause it for a minute?"

Tonya pressed pause and turned to face her husband. "Let me guess. You're going out to work on your case." She leaned over and kissed his cheek.

"If you mind, I won't go."

"Honey, I'm so happy you were off all day yesterday and last night, and this morning. And I've got Kim Fields to keep me company."

"Me, too," Horace chirped.

Parrott wrapped an arm around her shoulders and planted a smooch on her lips. "I won't be gone long. A couple hours at the most." He strode toward the garage before realizing Horace was still on his shoulder. "C'mon, buddy. Back into your cage."

"Oh, goody." As much as Horace liked being cage-free, he never complained about returning "home." *Maybe because we've equipped your cage with every convenience known to birds.* Parrott latched the door to the cage and whistled to the tune of *Bye Bye, Blackbird*.

He grabbed his gray heather sports jacket from the entry closet and draped it over his arm. That, on top of his collared sport shirt and slacks, would look professional enough, particularly since he

was going to Brandywine Valley, where country casual clothes were always stylish.

On the way, he ran through the topics he wanted to touch on with T.J. If he were lucky, he might be able to interview both T.J. and Kate. Now that he had an ID on Amanda Hoffman, he could use that for a new line of questions.

The Baths' cottage had no signs of life as Parrott drew up and parked his Camry. The Polaris was parked under a *porte cochere,* but neither of the other cars sat on the driveway. Parrott climbed out of his car and trod on the pavers leading to the front door. He rang the doorbell, listening for Lucy's bark, but, except for the scurrying of a pair of squirrels along a tree limb, all was silent.

Parrott circled the house to the back steps, where the baby had been found. He peered into the kitchen window. No lights were on, no visible activity. He hated that he'd apparently made a trip out here for nothing. Maybe he should knock on the Campbells' door. Surely Caro or John E. would know if the Baths were out of town.

He backtracked to the Campbell mansion and parked in the circular drive. This time when he rang the bell, a dog ran toward the door, barking wildly. Though he couldn't see the animal through the frosted glass panels, he could have sworn it was Lucy.

John E. opened the door, wearing riding clothes—boots, breeches, and an air vest. Dirt on the boots said he'd been on a morning ride. Lucy bounded outside, circling around Parrott and sniffing, before succumbing to his generous petting behind her ears.

"Detective Parrott," John E. said, with a friendliness that soothed Parrott's guilt at having disturbed on a Sunday. "What brings you here today? Anything more on the baby? Come on in."

Parrott wiped his shoes on the doormat before entering. Except for what sounded like a TV on in the family room, the house was quiet, and Caro was nowhere in sight.

"Let's go to the family room. I was just watching the news. Have a seat." John E. punched the remote control, and the only sound in the room came from Lucy, who lapped water from her bowl in the corner. "What can I do for you?"

"You've already answered one question. I knocked on the door at the Baths' house."

"Oh, yes. We're dog-sitting till tomorrow."

*Nice to have employers who'll take care of your pet.* "Do you know where they've gone?"

"T.J. didn't say, and we wouldn't ask. He almost never asks for time off, so when he does, we're glad to accommodate. And Lucy's not a bother. We've enjoyed having her around. Sit, and let me get you something to drink."

Parrott sat on the couch, where he'd interviewed suspects in the past. "No drink, thanks. I would like to pick your brain a little, though."

John E. sat opposite, and Lucy settled at his feet. "Shoot—or maybe that's an insensitive word when talking with a detective."

Smiling, despite this being the thousandth time to hear the lackluster joke, Parrott said, "I don't know how much you know about the Baths' personal lives, but I'm trying to figure out why someone would leave a baby on their particular doorstep. Their cottage is off the main path and certainly quite modest."

"Caro and I have discussed this very thing. We couldn't come up with an answer. As for knowing about their personal lives, we try not to intrude. They are good, hard-working people who appear to have a good marriage, but, obviously, no children. I don't know if that's by choice or fate."

A sound from the back of the house caused Lucy to raise her head and bark before dashing into the next room. "Hello," a feminine voice called out.

"Caro's back from riding," John E. said. He sauntered toward the kitchen, "C'mon in, honey. Detective Parrott's here."

Once again Parrott apologized for stopping by on a Sunday, but Caro waved her hand. "You're welcome here any day of the week. You know that." She kissed her husband on the cheek and they both sat opposite Parrott. Lucy stretched and retreated to a spot by the fireplace, having apparently lost interest in Parrott's interview.

"The detective is asking about T.J. and Kate. Particularly why someone would leave a baby on their steps. I told him we had this same conversation." John E. put his hands behind his head and leaned back.

Caro leaned forward. "Are you thinking the baby and the body found on our neighbor's property are linked?"

"I can't say too much at this point, but I'd appreciate anything you could tell me about either or both." Parrott shifted to the edge of his seat. "Do you know of any reason anyone would want that baby to go to the Baths?"

Caro exchanged glances with John E. "Well, the Baths have no children. We thought they didn't want any. But after witnessing the way Kate bonded with that baby, I'm not sure. I hate to judge, but her behavior was unsettling."

Parrott agreed. "How so?"

"I don't know. She seemed desperate. I've never seen her like that before."

"This may be a hard question to answer, but I have to ask—do you think either of the Baths might have said or done anything to cause someone to bring them a baby?"

John E., who'd been leaning back, straightened his posture and stared at Parrott. "You mean to kill a mother and take her baby to them? That's ridiculous. If they had, why on earth would either of them call you when they found the baby? They would have quietly kept it, adopted it through private channels."

Caro tapped her husband's knee. "Actually, neither of them *did* call the police. *I* did."

Parrott nodded.

"But that doesn't mean I think T.J. or Kate did anything illegal. I don't. I would be shocked." Caro began walking around the room. "Another thing that gnaws at me—Kate is the niece of Stuart Mooney's wife. The body on his property and the baby on hers. I hope it's mere coincidence."

Grabbing onto the opening, Parrott said, "Let's talk about Stuart Mooney, if you don't mind. How well do you know him and his wife?"

"He's a neighbor. That's about it," John E. said. "He doesn't own horses or ride, so he's not part of our social network out here."

"We had some concerns a few years ago," Caro said. "Mooney let it out that he was planning to sell off some of his acreage to a developer. Most of us support the Brandywine Conservancy, so those are fighting words to us."

Parrott was familiar with the conservancy. He'd learned about it from a case he'd solved last year, when a barn exploded from meth.

"The conservancy approached Mooney and convinced him to sell the acreage to them instead. At the last minute, Mooney pulled out of the deal altogether. Said he wanted to keep it for himself." John E. rubbed his goatee. "No one could figure out why he created such a fuss. He came off like a real jerk."

"Can either of you think of any reason he or his wife or children would have a connection with a young woman from Texas?"

Once again Caro and John E. looked at each other, and John E. shrugged. "Beats me," he said. "Mooney is from Scotland, and Connie is from Philadelphia. Maybe one of the kids?"

"The person who knows Mooney's son and daughter best is Kate," Caro said. "Have you asked her?"

"I tried. No one was home at their cottage, so I came here."

"Guess you'll have to come back tomorrow," John E. said. "T.J. said three days, and he never breaks a promise."

Parrott had no more questions for the Campbells. The interview had started and ended with T.J. and Kate, so he would come back on Monday. He shook hands with John E. and thanked him for his time. When he turned to Caro, she was standing at the doorway to the dining room, her eyebrows drawn into a single ridge and the knuckle of her index finger pressed against her lips.

"Something bothering you?" Parrott asked.

"Yes. I just thought about this. When T.J. came over to ask if we would keep Lucy for three days, he said, 'I need to take care of some business.' He didn't say 'we.' I figured Kate was going with him. Otherwise, why leave the dog here?" Worry lines merged between her eyebrows. "I just hope nothing has happened to Kate."

# CHAPTER FORTY-FIVE

First thing Monday morning, Parrott called Sheltering Palms and asked to speak with an administrator. The gatekeeping there was tighter than Parrott's belt on the last hole, which he'd had to use since taking his testosterone drug. After giving his badge number to six individuals, he connected with Abram Josephson, MBA. Mr. Josephson said, yes, he would be available for a brief meeting with Parrott at the facility in Philadelphia. They agreed upon eleven o'clock.

Parrott arrived ten minutes early and was ushered into an antiseptic-smelling outer office consisting of two chairs, an end table, and a wall-mounted tv showing PR slides for the facility. No assistant was there to welcome him—just a closed door with Josephson's name in gold and black letters.

The missing personal touch didn't bother him. He could use the time to familiarize himself with the clinic through the information on the slideshow. Perhaps he'd learn something beyond what was on the website.

At precisely eleven o'clock, a tall, thin man in a three-piece pin-stripe suit opened the door and greeted Parrott. "Sorry to keep you waiting. I hope you were comfortable." His handshake was firm and dry, quick.

"No worries," Parrott said. "I was early. Watched your videos."

"We're extremely proud of our clinics, detective. We accomplish a lot of good in the world, your unfortunate case notwithstanding. Have a seat."

Parrott lowered himself into one of the two plush upholstered chairs facing Josephson's desk, while the administrator took his place behind it. "I appreciate your availability to answer my questions. I understand how busy you are, and my case doesn't even involve your clinic."

Josephson tented his long fingers and held them over his chin. "True, but we are a national organization. What happens with one

center affects the reputation of Sheltering Palms. If I can be of help, I'm glad."

Parrott had already briefed Josephson on the facts of his case—the baby, the murder, the ID of the victim as a surrogate mother. "I understand my victim was carrying a baby whose conception was handled through your Dallas clinic—an egg from a patient and a sperm from a donor bank."

"Correct. I don't know the particulars of who the parents are. HIPAA and our stringent privacy protections would prevent me from discussing those, even if I knew."

"Of course. But speaking in generalities, can you give me an example of a scenario that fits this situation. In other words, how and why might a patient access your services for finding a sperm donor and a surrogate?" Parrott thought of Juanita and Clara and their reviews of Sheltering Palms.

"The typical example is a woman without a male partner, for whatever reason, who wishes to have a baby, but who has been unsuccessful in carrying a pregnancy to fruition. This woman could contract with us to obtain a sperm donation and a surrogate. We facilitate the matches. The surrogate is a woman who contracts with us to receive transfer of the zygote, the fertilized egg, into her uterus. The zygote may not implant the first time, but we have a high success rate for second and especially third procedures. The goal, of course, is to deliver a baby to the egg-donating woman at the end of the pregnancy."

Parrott thought of the baby in the yellow-duck outfit. Someone had gone to great extremes to bring her into existence. "How are the sperm donors and surrogates selected?"

Josephson nodded, probably expecting this question. "The processes are similar, of course, but not exact. We don't store eggs or sperm on site. Our sperm comes from an international bank. You may have heard of Cryos, the largest sperm bank in the world. We can access sperm from there or from other banks. It's shipped under heavily controlled conditions.

"It's important not to overpopulate a specific area of the world with too many sperm from the same donor. Genetic implications, you understand."

It was Parrott's turn to nod. "So, your patient chooses sperm from an available donor?"

"Yes, and there are many restrictions in place. For example, all donors go through rigorous genetic testing, reviews of family medical history and life experiences. Within the United States, we are limited to fifteen families using a single man's sperm. The geographical location of the sperm donor is far from where the patient lives. We also scrutinize the reason for donating."

"What are the most common reasons?"

Josephson leaned back and crossed leg over knee. "Money, of course. The desire to help others. Sometimes the donor is close to someone who had trouble conceiving. There are some who relish the idea of having offspring spread out over the globe. But usually the donor sees this as a relatively easy way to earn money."

Parrott remembered his less-than-pleasant experience in the bathroom of Dr. Goldstone's office. He couldn't see himself being paid for that. This whole fertility business was hard to wrap his mind around.

"The surrogate is a little different. Her location is unimportant genetically. In fact, we prefer that she live in the same region as the patient. That way the IVF transfer is convenient, and we can better monitor the pregnancy, delivery, and ultimate transfer of the baby."

"Makes total sense. But in this case, the surrogate ended up more than a thousand miles away. You mentioned a contract. Can you describe the arrangements your clinic makes with the surrogate in this contract?"

"The surrogate agrees to provide a healthy environment during the gestation period and through delivery. The requirements are simple—regular doctor checkups, good nutrition, keeping in touch. The expectation is that the surrogate will stay in the local area—the doctor checkups help with that—but we can't prevent someone from traveling between visits.

"The most sensitive requirement is that the surrogate relinquish all rights to the baby post-partum. She has no biological ties to the infant, beyond having "rented" her uterus. Her relationship to the baby, its parents, and the clinic is terminated when she delivers the baby."

Parrott could see how this final stage could be the most difficult. "So the surrogate can't change her mind, like a new mother who has agreed to give up her baby for adoption."

"That's correct. We refer our patients and surrogates to attorneys before they sign our contracts. The fertility processes are long and complicated. We want all participants to be thoroughly prepared for whatever might happen."

The irony churned in Parrott's gut. There was no way—in his murder case, or in his own desire for a child—to be thoroughly prepared. Both human nature and human biology were sometimes arbitrary and unpredictable.

"I'm sure no one foresaw what happened in this case." Even at this stage, when Parrott knew who the surrogate was and where she came from, he couldn't explain how everything had gone so wrong. "I appreciate your time and expertise."

Josephson glided around the desk. "I hope I've been helpful. The good news in your case is that the baby will soon be in the arms of her rightful parents. If not for you, that would have been impossible."

Parrott left Sheltering Palms with concerns about the baby's origin lifted from his shoulders, but new questions arising from the interview weighted his steps into the parking lot. He still had a lot of work to do.

# CHAPTER FORTY-SIX

Instead of returning to the station, Parrott drove to the Campbell property. His desire to talk with T.J. Bath had increased since learning more about the role Amanda Hoffman had accepted as surrogate. If he could establish a connection between the young woman and the Campbells' property caretaker, he'd be well on his way to understanding why the baby was left on his back steps.

T.J.'s secrets from his wife and his three-day absence from Brandywine added to Parrott's suspicions of the man. In addition, T.J.'s love child lived in Texas—where Amanda Hoffman was from.

When he arrived at the front of the Bath cottage a little after one, the Polaris was still under the *porte cochere*, but Kate's car was in the driveway, and she was bending over the open trunk, gathering something in her arms. When Parrott slammed his car door, Kate turned around, her eyes wide and her manner jumpy.

"I didn't mean to startle you," Parrott said. "Here, let me help you carry something."

Kate gave a wobbly smile. "I thought you were T.J." She refused the offer of help, although she had to set her suitcase down on the pavement in order to shut the trunk. "How is it that whenever I go anywhere, my baggage multiplies?"

"May I ask where you went?"

She hesitated before answering. "I needed a break. I stayed with my cousin in Philadelphia for a couple days."

House key in hand, Kate paused to give Parrott a head-tilting stare. "Why are you here? Is something wrong?"

"No, no. Contrary to what most people think, a visit from a cop isn't always bad news." He followed Kate into the cottage. "I was hoping to talk to T.J."

Kate's face twitched, and she squinted. "So am I. T.J. left with Lucy one day last week, and I haven't seen or heard from them since. That's why I went to Steven's—"

*So the cousin in Philadelphia is Steven Mooney. Very interesting.* "I was here at the Campbells' yesterday. Lucy is over there."

"Really? I had no idea. I'll go get her after I unpack. Did the Campbells know where T.J. was going?"

"Not to my knowledge. But they said he'd definitely be back today." Parrott looked around the combination family room and kitchen. His eyes lit on two notes, folded and propped up on the kitchen table, one marked *T.J.* and the other, *Kate*. Why two people who live in the same house had to communicate with written notes was beyond him, but he couldn't judge. He often left notes for Tonya when she was sleeping.

"Well, he's not back yet." Kate swiped at her eyes. "This is the longest we've ever gone without communicating. I hope he's okay."

Parrott had his own concerns about T.J.'s being AWOL. "Do you want to file a missing persons report? I can help you with that."

"No, the day's not over yet. Maybe he'll turn up in the next few hours."

Parrott didn't say John E. was under the impression T.J. would be back at work this morning. "Do you have any idea where he went?"

Kate shook her head. "Here's the note he left me." She picked up the note and read it before handing it to Parrott. "See what you think."

Parrott handled the note gingerly, respectful of the trust Kate had shown in letting him read it. *I'm going away to think. Taking Lucy with me. There're things I haven't told you, and you deserve better. If you leave, I'll understand. Love always, T.J.*

*P.S. Told the Campbells I'd be gone for three days.*

"Wonder why he changed his mind and left Lucy with the Campbells?" Kate meandered around the room, touching the back of the sofa, the corner of the kitchen counter. On her second circuit, she picked up the folded note with T.J.'s name on it. "I can rip this up now. My note for him in case he returned first." She tore the notebook paper into halves, fourths, eighths, sixteenths and threw the pieces in the trash can beneath the kitchen sink.

"Won't you sit, detective? I'll brew you a cup of coffee. Or how about some sourdough bread? I can take a loaf out of the freezer."

Still holding T.J.'s note, Parrott sat on one of the two chairs. "No, thanks. Come sit. I assume you recognize this as T.J.'s handwriting?"

Kate nodded.

"And the wording—sounds like something T.J. would write?"

"Yes. What are you suggesting, that someone else might have written the note?"

Parrott didn't want to alarm her, but his investigator's mind could take him far afield. "Just asking. Probably a good idea to bag the note, on the remote chance we need it later."

"You're starting to scare me. You think something's happened to T.J." It was a statement, not a question.

Parrott wasn't sure what to think. His focus was catching a murderer, and T.J.'s strange behavior made him wonder about the man's involvement in this whole baby-surrogate situation. "Let me ask you," he said. "Did you and T.J. argue before he left?"

"We never argue. We discuss." Kate's tone was the most sarcastic Parrott had ever heard. "We've come to a point in our marriage where we want different things, I think. We still love each other." She tromped to the cabinet where plastic bags were stored and brought a quart-sized one back to the table. She slid the note in and sealed it. "I'm worried. When T.J. says three days, he means it."

"Can you guess where he might've gone?"

"No clue. He's not close to anyone in his family. His friends from high school have scattered all over. The only thing I can think of is he mentioned reversing his vasectomy. Maybe he had the surgery and is recovering somewhere."

"Do you know his doctor's name? Or hospital?"

"Sorry. He didn't tell me, and I didn't ask. He wasn't sure about doing it. The chances for success aren't that good."

*Another situation for a sperm donor—I could give them a recommendation for a fertility clinic.* Parrott reminded himself that T.J. Bath was a man of many secrets—his criminal record and his daughter among them. Parrott had pledged not to reveal anything to Kate unless he had to, but Parrott's mind whirred with possibilities beyond the couple's infertility.

He extracted a business card from his pocket and handed it to Kate. "Call me as soon as T.J. comes home, or as soon as you hear anything." He'd start his own search, if T.J. didn't come home by tomorrow. "Will you be okay here?"

"Yeah," she said. "I'll go get Lucy. She'll keep me company."

Parrott turned to leave, but Kate called him back. "Don't forget this." She handed him T.J.'s handwritten note sealed in plastic. "I hope you won't need it."

# CHAPTER FORTY-SEVEN

Parrott mostly hated the fact that Stuart Mooney had lawyered up, and with a New York lawyer, no less. The barrier created by this representation was frustrating. Parrott imagined the billionaire in a political cartoon, locked inside a Fort Knox vault, singing the old ditty, "Ninety-nine bottles of scotch on the wall." The attorney would make it hard, and maybe impossible, for Parrott to get answers to the increasing number of questions he had for Mooney, but ultimately, Mooney was the one hiding in the vault.

That begged the question—what did the billionaire have to hide? The attorney could play hard ball with Parrott, refusing to let his client answer any questions, but any attorney worth the substantial retainer Mooney must have paid would understand the delicate position it would place his client in if he refused to cooperate with the police in a murder investigation.

Parrott had experience with these types of interviews. They were challenging, no doubt, but, as his grandmother used to say, "We can do hard things." If pressed, he could ask the DA to subpoena Mooney to appear before the Grand Jury. However, Mooney and his attorney could show up there with a single response—the Fifth Amendment. The whole thing was like a game of chicken.

Now back at the office, Parrott accessed the text Schrik had sent with Ethan Price's contact information. He called the attorney's office, expecting to have to suffer through insulating platitudes from receptionists and administrative assistants, announcing a twelve-name law firm, one of the names being Price. Instead, Ethan Price answered his own private line.

"Price. How may I help you?" The voice was young, polished, white. Maybe the son or grandson of the Price in the firm name, but too young to be a senior partner.

Parrott introduced himself and the West Brandywine Police Department. "I understand you represent Stuart Mooney, who lives in my jurisdiction."

The attorney took in a breath before affirming. "Please hold the line a moment."

Without waiting for Parrott to agree, Price clicked a button that transmitted soft classical music into the telephone connection. Parrott watched the seconds click by on his screen while he waited. He speculated that the attorney was either conferring with Mooney or another member of the law firm, or twiddling his thumbs while he made Parrott sweat over what might come next. *Either way, I'm not worried.*

After two minutes and thirty-seven seconds, the attorney came back on the line. "Yes, detective. Sorry to keep you waiting."

Determined to sound unruffled, Parrott took his time. "I'm investigating the murder of a woman found on the Mooney property. I'm told you wish to be present at all interviews with Mr. Mooney, and all arrangements are to go through you. I would like to set up an interview as soon as possible. I have new information since the first time I spoke with Mr. Mooney."

"What is the purpose of said interview? Is my client a suspect in this woman's murder?"

Parrott nodded at the question, which he'd fully expected. "We are nowhere near ready to make an arrest, if that's what you mean, Mr. Price. We are merely gathering information about how the murdered woman came to be on the Mooney property. If you're familiar with criminal investigations, I'm sure you understand."

Price muttered something unintelligible. "I've advised my client not to participate in any interviews at this time. He has provided you with all the information that he has about the unfortunate incident. The body on his property, he assures me, is a random accident."

Anticipating this volley, Parrott fired back with Plan B. "In that case, I ask that you and Mr. Mooney grant us permission to re-investigate the outdoor property at Moonglow, including the area by the creek, the promontory above that, and the yard surrounding the house itself."

"May I ask why? It was our understanding that your department conducted a thorough investigation of the scene last week. Certainly, any evidence you might have found then would have disappeared by now."

"I assure you that we don't want to waste our time, or your client's for that matter. We have discovered new information that gives our search a new direction—that's all."

"New information? Can you share the nature of that information?"

Parrott knew he would ask. "I'm not at liberty to discuss it at this time. When might you and your client be available to meet with me? I'm sure you are as eager as I am to bring a murderer to justice."

Price hesitated a few moments. "Let me confer with my client, and I'll call you back."

Fairly sure that Price had taken the bait, Parrott wrote down the time, 1:27. He wondered how long it would take to hear back. Mooney, and therefore his advocate, would want to know whatever information he could share. While he waited, he needed to assuage his stomach, which was chugging like a train's steam engine.

Fortunately, he had stopped at Wawa on his way back from Kate's, and a classic Italian hoagie, wrapped in foil and waxed paper, sat on his desk, emitting the delightful aromas of oregano and cucumber. He dug into the sandwich with as much gusto as if he hadn't eaten in a week. He opened the bottle of water he'd purchased at the same time. More than three days without coffee—he was sure this was a record.

Before he could finish his meal, his cell phone lit up with Ethan Price's phone number. The time was 1:43. "Parrott speaking," he said.

"Can you meet at Moonglow tomorrow morning at ten?"

"I'll be there." Parrott disconnected and finished his lunch. If he could've high-fived himself, he would have.

# CHAPTER FORTY-EIGHT

Before meeting with Stuart Mooney, Parrott wanted to have as much information as possible about Amanda Hoffman and the baby she had carried for Sheltering Palms. When he had talked to Josephson at the Philadelphia clinic, he learned that the baby would soon be transported to her biological mother. That meant Monica Bell, as the child protective services agent, would likely have updated information.

He put in a call to Monica, who answered on the first ring.

"Detective, I'm so glad you called. You won't believe it, but I had my finger on your contact number when my phone rang." Chatter in the background said Monica was in a busy place. "Thanks to the DNA, statements from Sheltering Palms and you, and the Good Lord above, we are able to give this infant the life she was meant to have. Miracles like this don't happen very often here."

Chills tickled Parrott's arms, and a wave of emotion made him think of kids he'd known who grew up "in the system." Many lucked out with loving homes, but even the best situations didn't give them the kind of belongingness and stability that Parrott, himself, had experienced. "I'm glad to play a part in finding the baby's rightful home."

Monica went on, a lilt in her voice that hadn't been there before. "The parents are flying here to pick her up—as we speak. The hearing's scheduled in Judge Solomon's courtroom for three p.m. They'll be taking her back to Texas later this evening. You can imagine how busy we are with paperwork. That's why I was going to call, to thank you, but you beat me to it."

"I wanted to ask a few questions, but now I've got a favor to ask, as well. Would it be possible for me to meet with the parents when they take possession of their baby? Out of the norm for you, I'm sure, but I think they might help me get a handle on the circumstances that led to the surrogate's death."

"I'd like to say yes, but you know what a bureaucracy this is. Let me run the idea up the chain of command. We might have to get consent from the parents, too, and they won't be here until after three o' clock. You know what? Let's risk it. Come on."

Parrott smiled. Sight unseen, he already regarded Monica as a friend. "By the way, what are the names of the baby's parents?"

"Elena and Rodolfo Hidalgo, from Fort Worth. They sound like a nice young couple. She works at American Airlines' corporate office, and he's a manager at a big health network."

It wasn't often that police detectives were able to witness happy outcomes from cases. He still didn't know who or how or why the baby was abandoned, but the satisfaction of being a part of her safe return home warmed his insides.

Parrott ended the call, grabbed his sport jacket and a pack of gum, and headed for his car. He texted Chief Schrik where he was going and set his GPS for the Department of Human Services building. Rather than turning on the radio, he lowered his windows and let the wind cool his flaming desire to talk to the baby's parents. *Elena and Rodolfo sound like a heterosexual couple. Maybe Rodolfo has a low sperm count like me.*

He unwrapped two sticks of gum and folded them into thirds before jamming them into his mouth. The sweetness of peppermint exploded on his tongue and traveled through his nose to his sinuses. At a stoplight he played origami with the inner and outer wrappers before throwing them into the compartment on his door.

Whatever the situation, Parrott felt good about the prospect of talking to Brandywine B's parents. On top of the other important questions he had, he wondered what they would name their daughter. For some strange reason, he really wanted to know.

# CHAPTER FORTY-NINE

Monica Bell looked exactly as Parrott had pictured her—fortyish, petite with thick, dark, curly hair swooping across the crown of her head, and vivid blue eyes. She had a firm handshake and smelled like lavender. "Come in, and make yourself comfortable," she said, pointing to a utilitarian chair next to her utilitarian desk.

A framed sign on the wall said, "It is easier to build strong children than it is to repair broken men." *Frederick Douglass' words could have found no better home than in this office.* The quote had also graced Parrott's Sunday school classroom.

"The case worker is on the way with the baby, and the Hidalgos are due any minute. Reminds me of tales of Robin Hood, in which all the characters meet up where the paths converge in the forest." She smiled, revealing straight, white teeth.

"Maybe I should wait in another place until the Hildalgos have a chance to—"

"That won't be necessary. Elena Hidalgo called a few minutes ago from the Uber. I asked if she and her husband would mind talking to you, and she said no. They are both very grateful and happy to assist you in any way."

Voices in the hall caused Parrott to stand, and Monica to rush to the doorway. Two young Black women dressed in jeans and button-down blouses chattered as they approached Monica's door. The taller of the two carried a bundle. "Here we are with the little princess," the shorter woman said. "Where do you want us?"

"I reserved the visitation room," Monica said. "There's not enough space for this happy party in my office." The visitation room was furnished with a square table, four chairs, a baby crib, and a rocker. Monica introduced the two case workers to Parrott and thanked them for bringing the baby. "You can put her in the crib. Her parents will be here shortly."

The tall case worker tiptoed to the crib and placed the infant in the center on her back. Before she could turn to leave, sharp

shrieks emerged from the bundle, echoing in the room. The woman giggled. "I guess she doesn't like being still. She's gonna be a mover and shaker."

"That's okay," Monica said, her voice raised over the cries. "You two can go on back to your offices. I'll handle it from here."

Parrott had crossed the room to the crib, drawn by the little person who was screaming her lungs out. "I'll hold her till the parents get here," he said. "You all have work to do, but I'll just sit here in the rocker with this little angel." He cradled her into the crook of his arm, careful to support her head and neck, and marveling at her perfect little features, the warmth of her body, and the sweet scent of baby powder. He eased himself into the rocking chair.

A few rocking motions and some baritone crooning later, the infant stopped crying and fell asleep, her tiny fingers gripping one of Parrott's. Parrott congratulated himself for managing the turnaround. Handling babies required finesse. And the movement of the rocking chair relaxed him, too. He would have to remember to get a sturdy rocker for their house when the time came.

Parrott had almost lulled himself to sleep when the Hidalgos arrived. Fanfare in the hall preceded their entrance, and the baby startled in Parrott's arms. The parents stood in the doorway to the room for about three seconds before rushing to Parrott's side.

"Our baby, our baby." Tears covered the mother's face. She reached into the hollow of Parrott's arms to lift the bundle, where she could examine the little face. "She's beautiful. Oh, my precious *mija*."

Mr. Hidalgo peered over his wife's shoulder as she nestled the infant into the crook of her elbow. Parrott vacated the chair, and Mrs. Hidalgo sat without taking her eyes from the baby. There was something almost holy about the tableau—mother and child and the man who was not connected by biology, but was ready to assume parenthood.

Monica broke the spell by inviting everyone to sit. She produced all the documents, some that had been signed in advance, and others to be signed before the baby could be released. "Under different circumstances, Sheltering Palms would handle this transfer in Texas, but since no one from there could be with us in

Pennsylvania, I'm authorized to act as their agent. The last step will be the brief hearing in Judge Solomon's court this afternoon."

The parents' eagerness was palpable. Parrott couldn't blame them. They must have panicked when the surrogate disappeared. Monica explained everything in a calm voice. "Mr. Hidalgo," she said, "you understand that although the sperm donor has relinquished his rights to the baby, you will have to initiate court proceedings to adopt her. Your name will appear on her birth certificate once the adoption is approved."

The infant had begun to squirm and make soft noises while Monica reviewed the papers. Monica lifted an insulated carry-all from the floor in the corner of the room. "Here," she said to Mr. Hidalgo. "We've packed a few necessities for you—some bottles of formula, diapers, changing supplies, and some onesies. I think she's ready for her first feeding with her mother and father. There's a microwave here if you want to warm the bottle."

Hidalgo unzipped the bag and handed a bottle of formula to his wife. "You can do the honors."

"With pleasure," she said, "but please take the cap off of the bottle and warm it for a few seconds."

Everyone chuckled at the innocence of the new parents, who would have much to get used to, even in the simplest routines. Once the bottle was heated and tested, the baby had no hesitation about latching onto the nipple. Just a week into her life, she already knew what she wanted and how to get it.

"While the baby eats, why don't we have Detective Parrott talk with you," Monica said. "You can sign the papers afterwards, when the baby is full, and your hands are free."

Parrott positioned himself to face the Hidalgos. He began by explaining what a privilege it was for him and the West Brandywine PD to play a role in returning their baby to them. "This is a story with a happy ending for you and your child. But we cannot close our police files yet. The murder of the surrogate remains unsolved, and we need your assistance to help us learn how and why she was killed."

Cooing sounds from the baby punctuated Parrott's introduction in a way that created closeness rather than distance. Everyone was there because of the infant. "I'd like to understand what motivated

the surrogate to leave Texas. Some of my questions may be personal. I hope you understand."

"Go ahead," Hidalgo said. "Elena and I will answer what we can."

"You don't need me to be here at this point," Monica said. "I'll give you some privacy, but I'll be across the hall if you need me." She closed the door when she left.

"Let's start with your experience with Sheltering Palms." Parrott had been mulling over this question all day. "You had your own eggs harvested, Mrs. Hidalgo, and contracted for a sperm donor and a surrogate to carry the baby. Is that correct?"

Elena nodded as she pulled the now-empty bottle from the baby's mouth. She placed a cloth diaper over her shoulder and placed the infant there for a burp, rocking all the while.

Parrott turned to Mr. Hidalgo and lowered his voice. "May I ask what the reason was for the sperm donor?"

Hidalgo glanced at his wife before answering with an emotionless tone of voice. "I am unable to father a child, detective. I had an injury in the service of our country before we were married. We always knew we would need assistance to have children. Sheltering Palms has been extremely helpful."

Parrott mimicked the lack of emotion as he turned to Mrs. Hidalgo. "And, if you don't mind telling me, what was the reason for the surrogate?"

A loud belch issued from the infant, causing laughter all around. "We tried IVF at Sheltering Palms with donor sperm and my eggs—twice last year. My eggs are healthy, and I became pregnant both times. But, unfortunately, once the fetus reached the second trimester, my uterus couldn't sustain the pregnancy. Both times I lost the child."

Parrott paused. "Must have been very difficult for you both."

"Our faith got us through the hard times. We kept believing someday we would have a baby, and now she's here." Mrs. Hidalgo continued to pat the infant on the back. "The IVF procedures were expensive, and my gynecologist suggested we look for a surrogate. Sheltering Palms offers that service, as well."

Remembering what he'd learned from Mr. Josephson, Parrott framed his next question. "I'm assuming your selection of a

surrogate was anonymous, like your selection of a sperm donor. However, I'm interested in what exactly you were told about the woman who carried the baby."

Mr. Hidalgo replied, while his wife busied herself with changing the baby's wet diaper, using an empty chair as a changing table. "We actually were counseled not to be concerned with the surrogate's genetic background, since she would not contribute DNA to the child. We knew her age and general health, which was excellent. She lived somewhere in Texas and passed a criminal background check. The egg harvesting, fertilization, and subsequent transfer took place at the Dallas facility. But we never saw her. We didn't even know her name. That was on purpose. To protect her and us."

Parrott continued. "Were you kept informed about the pregnancy?"

Mrs. Hidalgo, having completed the diaper change, responded. "Oh, yes. We received a report after the doctor visits each month. Everything was going well."

Leaning forward, Parrott asked, "How and when did you learn that something had gone wrong?"

Mrs. Hidalgo handed the sleeping baby to her husband, and she began to pace. "We kept track of every doctor appointment. Once we were in our ninth month, the appointments were supposed to be every week. Rodolfo and I looked forward to the emails. That second Tuesday there was no email. 'Something is wrong,' I said to Rodolfo."

"The surrogate missed her appointment." The new father whispered, so as not to wake the baby. "We called Sheltering Palms, beside ourselves."

"And what did they tell you then?" Despite himself, Parrott sat on the edge of his seat.

"They said they'd look into it and call us back. We were frightened that something terrible had happened to our baby. We were frantic, sick with worry. Finally, they called back, and that was the start of a true nightmare that just ended for us today." She kissed the now-sleeping baby on the top of the head.

"What did Sheltering Palms tell you about the surrogate?"

"They said they couldn't locate her. She'd gone missing."

Parrott was most interested in the gap—what had transpired with Amanda Hoffman between her last completed doctor appointment in Texas and her body's final destination by the Brandywine Creek—but the Hidalgos wouldn't be able to provide that.

"There is one more thing I'd like to know, if you can tell me," Parrott said.

"Anything, detective." Mr. Hidalgo turned his eyes from his wife and child to Parrott.

"What will you name the baby?"

Hidalgo's face illuminated with a toothy smile and shining eyes. "Her name is Adalia, Ada for short. It means *found*."

# CHAPTER FIFTY

By the time Parrott arrived home from Philadelphia, dinner was almost ready, and he was starved. Two chicken breasts and a rack of ribs were still left over from the barbecue, andTonya had added a green salad to the menu. She retrieved a cold beer from the refrigerator and carried that and her glass of sparkling water to the table. After kissing his wife, petting Horace, washing up, and tossing the salad, Parrott joined his wife at the dinner table.

"I hope you had a good day," he said, as he shoveled a bite of chicken into his mouth.

Tonya lifted her glass in a mock toast. "It was fine. I was invited to a baby shower for Juanita and Clara, so I drove to Kennett Square after my therapy appointment to get a gift."

"Did it upset you to shop for their baby?" Parrott asked.

"Not really. Their baby-journey hasn't been the smoothest in the world, either. I don't begrudge them."

Parrott swigged his beer, thinking what a mature and positive attitude his wife had. It could've been so much worse. "What did you buy for them?"

"I'll show you after dinner. They don't want to know the gender of the baby, so I had to get something neutral. It's really sweet."

"How was Alice?" Parrott had learned not to ask specifics about Tonya's therapy, but asking about the therapist, whom he truly admired, was perfectly fine.

"She's much better now that she's over the virus. We had a good session. She mentioned going to every other week, so we'll see." Tonya gnawed on a barbecued rib. "Change of subject—what are you planning to do with that SUV in the third garage?"

Surprised, and a little annoyed with himself for delaying, Parrott tried to rationalize. "I'll get to it soon. I've been a little distracted this week. Why, do you have plans for that space?"

"Not really. Just thinking ahead to fall. I think the previous owners kept pool equipment there during cold weather months."

"Okay. Apparently, my to-do list is not yet to-done." He made a mental note to fingerprint the car as soon as he had a few minutes, maybe later tonight.

After dinner, Parrott and Tonya did the dishes together. When they were finished, they watched Horace play with his gym in the family room, while Netflix was on in the background.

"Want to show me the baby gift you bought today?" Parrott asked.

"Sure. Let me get the box." Tonya sauntered to the entry closet where a mint-green shopping bag rested on the top shelf. "This came from Brandywine Creek Kids, a very exclusive store." She slid the box out and set it on the counter of the kitchen's island. "Good thing I didn't have them wrap it. I wanted to include a children's book with the package." She opened the box and spread the tissue paper, so Parrott could see. Inside was nestled a perfectly folded infant outfit and matching receiving blanket, yellow with embroidered ducks.

Parrott's brain lit up like a Fourth of July grand finale, and he leaped from the sofa to examine the outfit under the bright kitchen light. "Where did you say you bought this?"

Tonya gave a head-tilt and squinted at her husband. She repeated the name of the store and said, "I never thought you'd be so excited about a baby gift."

"Never mind that," Parrott said. "How much did you spend on this?"

"I think a hundred dollars. Why? Do you think it was too much?"

"Not at all. In fact, I'm so happy that you bought this." Parrott hugged his wife around the waist. "Were there any others like this in the store?"

"I don't think so, Ollie. But why? The outfit is cute, but I don't get your reaction—unless, does this have something to do with your current case at work?" She folded the tissue paper, covered the box with its lid, and returned the package in its shopping bag to the closet shelf. "Never mind. You don't have to answer that."

"Wait, don't put the package away. I want to take a photo." Parrott peppered his wife with questions. "Can you give me the

address of the shop and the name of the salesclerk?" After clicking several photos of the outfit, some enlarging the detail, he looked up the store hours on the internet—ten to seven. As soon as he left the interview with Stuart Mooney tomorrow, he would race to the doorstep of Brandywine Creek Kids.

# CHAPTER FIFTY-ONE

The next morning, Parrott was energized, despite not having coffee and not having slept well after fingerprinting Barton's SUV. Scads of fingerprints covered the steering wheel, gear shift, and door handle on the driver's side, so many that they were hard to distinguish. Those on the passenger side seat belt and door handle and in the back seat interested Parrott more. Parrott had comparative prints on file for Amanda Hoffman, T.J. and Kate Bath, Wren Vargas, and Barton, but he would need to get prints from Stuart Mooney somehow.

Also, he was eager to use Chief Schrik's new toy—a fingerprint lab at the station. Until now, all their print work had to be done by techs at Chesco. Those techs had lots of experience, and their testimony carried a lot of weight at trial, but the benefits came with a price. West Brandywine had to take its place in line with other PDs, and carrying evidence back and forth had risks. Schrik had found a grant that enabled them to carve out space and purchase equipment for their own lab, and now Parrott could run immediate tests without worrying about transporting evidence. Of course, Chesco would continue to collect evidence on-site, as they did with the body on Mooney's property, but the prints from Barton's car were a perfect chance to try the new lab.

Looking forward to interviewing Mooney with his lawyer, Parrott dressed quickly and downed a big bowl of oatmeal with raisins. He ran through the questions for Mooney. Even if the lawyer refused to let Mooney answer, Parrott wanted to get his thoughts out in the open and watch Mooney's body language for tells. Although he had no evidence for the death of the Hoffman woman that pointed directly at Mooney, Parrott wasn't feeling warm and fuzzy about excluding him from the suspect list. He wanted to know why Amanda Hoffman's body was on the Mooney property to begin with. Was it true Mooney had hired Randy Barton, and if so, why? And why did Mooney need a New York lawyer to protect him from the West Brandywine police?

Parrott also wouldn't mind knowing whether Mooney's wife Connie had filed for divorce. And what kind of relationship did Mooney's children, Catherine and Steven, have with their father? Most of this was shooting in the dark, but Parrott was digging for a possible motive. Was Mooney romantically involved with nineteen-year-old Amanda? Maybe she tricked him into thinking the baby was hers. Or maybe the young woman had extorted money from Mooney. Experience had taught Parrott that nothing was too far-fetched when it came to murder.

When Parrott pulled up to the front of Moonglow, another car was parked in the circular drive, and a man in a grey suit, carrying a briefcase, stood at the door. Parrott jumped out of his car and sprinted to the door, hoping to be admitted to the house at the same time. He introduced himself to the thirty-something man, who identified himself as Ethan Price. The lawyer was neither effusive nor unfriendly. He probably wasn't used to making house calls a hundred and fifty miles from his office.

The same woman in tortoise shell glasses as before—Jade— answered the door. Dressed in a similar green dress, this time she flinched, and her eyes shifted from Parrott to Price. "You are here to meet with Mr. Mooney," she said, her tone flat. "Come in, please."

She directed them to the library, as before. "Please be seated." She closed the exterior door and followed them into the elaborately appointed room. The two visitors exchanged glances.

Jade stood opposite their two chairs, in the center. She cleared her throat. "Unfortunately, Mr. Mooney is unable to join you for this meeting. He asked me to convey his sincere apologies, but an important matter has arisen, and he had to leave immediately."

The attorney muttered something unintelligible, but Parrott caught the words, "Son of a—." Parrott's initial reaction was similar, but he didn't comment. His mind sizzled with suspicion. Who hires an attorney and goes to all the trouble to set up an appointment, only to stand up the other two parties—unless he'd decided fleeing was his only option?

Price paced, ending up at the window. "Where did Mr. Mooney go? When will he be back?"

The woman walked to the corner of Mooney's massive desk, returning with a sealed envelope in each hand. "Mr. Mooney asked me to give these to you. He said they would explain his absence."

Parrott accepted his envelope and pocketed it gingerly, so as not to smudge any fingerprints. Price, on the other hand, opened his and began reading from a handwritten letter.

"Cripes, he's gone to Chicago. Out of my territory and yours, too, Parrott." He removed what looked like a check from the envelope, took a glimpse of the inside, and put everything back in the envelope. "Looks like my work here is done," he said.

Asking the personal assistant if she might show him to the facilities before his drive back to New York, Price waved at Parrott. Without Mooney, the two had nothing to say to one another.

Alone in the room, Parrott stole toward the desk, thinking the likelihood of finding anything was slim. Still, he hoped to pick up a clue that might explain Mooney's impulsive departure. The top of the desk was messy, as if Mooney had left in a hurry, without time to straighten up. Without a warrant, Parrott couldn't conduct a proper search, but anything left out in plain view in a room that Mooney's own employee had led him to, was fair game. Several manila folders were stacked haphazardly on the desk. Parrott scanned the tabs on the folders that he could see without touching any of them. *Attorney, bills, contacts, employee info*—nothing unusual here—then, *Hoffman, Amanda*, plain as day. Chills caused the hair to rise on his arms and the back of his neck.

In a hurry to get out of the room before the attorney and Jade returned, Parrott hustled to the entry hall. Price came out of the powder room and walked toward Parrott, while Jade followed. Parrott handed his business card to the attorney, and the two shook hands.

"Thank you for your assistance, Jade—" Parrott said to the woman.

"Jade Bender."

"Thank you, Ms. Bender. Tell Mr. Mooney we'll be in touch." In truth, Parrott had no idea when or how he might stay in touch with Mooney. The meeting was a bomb, except for two things. First, Mooney had kept a file on Amanda Hoffman. Second, Parrott was pretty sure that sitting inside his jacket pocket, he now had Mooney's fingerprints.

# CHAPTER FIFTY-TWO

The sky had clouded over while Parrott was at Moonglow, and there was a definite chill in the air. The impending autumn had left its preliminary signature on the leaves, too, apparently overnight, and a few sprinkles of moisture on the windshield caused Parrott to roll up the windows.

He removed an evidence bag from his glove compartment and transferred Mooney's note into it for safekeeping. As much as he wanted to deal with the note right away, he knew there was no rush. As long as he was out here, he could swing by the Baths' cottage to check on Kate. Having heard nothing from her last night, he assumed T.J. was still in the wind.

He parked at the front of the cottage. The Polaris and Kate's car were still the only vehicles there. By now rain was pelting his car, and thunder rolled in the distance. Parrott locked the glove compartment and dashed to the back door, even though he didn't mind getting wet. He knocked on the door, taking advantage of the small overhang to brush water from his head and face.

Kate opened the door and urged him in. "Here, let me get you a towel." Lucy loped to the spot in front of Parrott's feet and extended her head for petting. T.J. was nowhere in sight.

He stomped on the braided rug at the door and stepped inside, grateful for the aroma of bread. Loaves were lined up on the counter, and more were in the oven, according to the panel lights and the beeping of the timer.

Kate handed him a towel and scurried to the oven, where she turned off the timer and opened the door. A whoosh of warm, yeasty air passed through the room, causing Parrott's eyes to moisten and mouth to water.

Kate called over her shoulder. "Last batch. Just in time for a hot-from-the-oven sample." Parrott's appetite was in overdrive from the meds, and, remembering the luscious taste from the last time, he accepted Kate's offer. He dried his face and head, then

dabbed at his shoulders and lapels. "What would you like me to do with this towel?"

Kate pointed to the bathroom. "Why don't you wash your hands in there? You can leave the towel on the side of the bathtub." She washed her own hands in the kitchen sink and dried them before cutting into a new loaf and arranging the slices on a platter. "What do you want to drink? Black coffee, like last time?"

Parrott returned from washing his hands. He was beginning to regret having said yes to the bread. Kate was behaving as if they were at a tea party, and he'd enabled that. "No, thanks. I'll have a taste of the bread, but I can't stay. I'm mainly here to check on you. You haven't heard from T.J.?"

"Actually, he texted me a few minutes ago. He says he'll be home sometime this evening, and we need to talk."

"Did he say where he's been?"

"No. That's all he said." She buttered a slice of bread and handed it to Parrott. "I would have called you, but the text just came in at—" She opened the app on her phone. "—ten-oh-two." Kate seemed disinclined to show Parrott the text itself, and he didn't ask. "I'm sure all will be revealed. Meanwhile, detective, do you have any updates on the baby in the box?"

Parrott hesitated before replying. Aside from privacy issues, he didn't want to reveal anything that might compromise his case, and Kate was technically on the suspect list, albeit low. "I can tell you she's no longer in the custody of the State. She's been placed with her biological mother."

"Wow, that was fast work. I'm happy for the baby and the mother." The downturn of her lips and moisture in her eyes said otherwise. Turning off the oven and slapping her palms, as if to signify a job finished, she trudged to the sofa, next to where Lucy was sleeping. "Won't you sit down?"

"No, thank you. I have another appointment. I do have a question before I leave, though. Are you aware of anything going on in Chicago with your cousin Catherine Mooney, or whatever her married name is?"

"Catherine? She's due to give birth any day now, but no. I haven't heard anything. Why?"

"Seems like I'm doing a lot of keeping up with baby news these days." Parrott manufactured a chuckle, hoping it passed muster. "Thanks for the delicious bread. I'll swing back around to talk to T.J. in the next day or two."

The rain shower had ended by the time he said goodbye and walked to his car. The nip in the air reminded Parrott to step up his investigation. He still had a lot of questions. The weather was one thing, but he didn't want his case to grow cold.

# CHAPTER FIFTY-THREE

Kennett Square was busy even on a weekday, even after a rainstorm. Parrott found a parking place near Brandywine Creek Kids. On his way into the store, he passed a woman pushing a toddler in a stroller and trying to keep her preschool son from splashing in every puddle. Parrott smiled, remembering how he and Bo used to see who could kick the most water onto the other one. They'd driven their mothers crazy.

Parrott bypassed the little family and opened the door into the children's clothing store. A bell, hanging from a wide ribbon, announced his presence, but the two clerks were busy with other customers. Parrott stood in line, waiting his turn, and looking around at the neat displays. The aroma of baby powder floated around him, and he sniffed, trying to figure out the source. Finally, the woman in front of him turned sideways, exposing the view of a little one, nestled in a carrier at her middle.

Parrott imagined Tonya—or himself—wearing their sweet-smelling baby like that. This case had ignited his desire for a baby of their own, or maybe the D-aspartic acid was working overtime in him. He yanked his mind back onto the case at hand and pulled his badge to show the clerk.

The customer ahead of him completed her purchase and turned to exit. She threw her handbag into the mint green shopping bag, so she could carry both in one hand. The infant carrier certainly made shopping more convenient.

Stepping up to the counter, Parrott made eye contact with the woman whose name tag said, "Maureen." He guessed her age at around sixty, although age spots on her hands said she might be older. As discreetly as possible, he opened the case to show her his badge and asked if he could have a few minutes with her in private.

Maureen nodded and tapped the other clerk on the shoulder. "If you need me, I'll be in the back."

"Of course, Mrs. Patton," the young woman said.

The back room of the store might have measured twelve by fourteen. The walls were lined with shelves and counters, which shone, as if they'd been dusted and waxed five minutes earlier. The stock of items on the shelves ranged from thick blankets to tiny shoe boxes, and everything in between. The organization appealed to Parrott's love of structure.

A computer sat on a small table, flanked by two chairs. "Why don't we sit here? How can I help you?"

After Parrott ascertained the woman's full name and position as the store owner, he showed her the photos he'd taken of the yellow duck ensemble Tonya had purchased the day before. "I'm sure you're familiar with this product. My wife bought it here yesterday."

"Yes, it's quite popular. This is a designer going home outfit and blanket, made by Baby Dior."

"Do you sell a lot of these outfits here?"

"They fly off the shelves. In fact, I believe your wife bought the last one, but I've reordered. Is there a problem with the outfit?"

"No, ma'am. I have reason to believe someone else purchased another of these outfits here last week, and the clothes may be evidence in a case I'm investigating. Do you work here every day?"

"Oh, my. I hope nothing bad happened to one of our babies." She wrung her manicured hands. "I'm usually here, but occasionally I take time off for an appointment. Do you have a particular day in mind?"

"Possibly last Friday," Parrott said, thinking the couple may have purchased the outfit the same day Caro saw them at Philter Coffee. He scrolled on his phone to the photo of the artist sketch of Amanda Hoffman, followed by the actual photo he'd downloaded from the missing persons site. "Do you recall seeing a customer who resembled this woman? Nine months' pregnant, young, wearing platform sandals, accompanied by a dark-haired man, maybe in his twenties or thirties."

"The description rings a bell. I didn't wait on them, but I remember the platform sandals. Pregnant women don't usually wear them, especially at the end. Let me ask Gina." She walked to the doorway and stuck her head out. "Gina, could you please come here for a second when you finish what you're doing?"

While they waited for Gina, Parrott asked whether other stores in the area carried Baby Dior.

"Our arrangement with Dior is exclusive. No other store within fifty miles can stock it. The line is a best seller for us, and this particular ensemble has great appeal. It can be worn by either gender."

"Do you sell a lot of these ensembles?"

"We only stock a couple at a time. I believe we sold that one last Friday and another yesterday."

When Gina popped in a few seconds later, Maureen stepped out to mind the store. Parrott obtained Gina's full name, position, and how long she'd worked there. He showed her the two photos on his phone. "Oh, yes. I remember that couple. They didn't know the baby's gender—unusual these days—so I suggested this outfit. I wondered whether they were married—no rings. And those high shoes she had on! Squeaked when she walked. Definitely not our typical shopper."

Neon lights flashed in Parrott's brain. The clerk was the first person he'd met who'd seen Amanda Hoffman's companion face-on. "Can you describe the man? Eye color, features, any identifying marks?"

Gina bit her lip. "I don't know. I try to pay attention to my customers, but the shop was busy. Also, my focus was on the woman. Now I remember admiring her satchel, uh, shoulder bag. I remember the man didn't say much. I got the impression that the purchase was his idea, though. He's the one who paid. In fact, he pulled cash out of his pocket—no wallet or anything."

"Please close your eyes and try to remember. Anything you could tell me about this man's face would be very important."

Eyes scrunched, Gina said, "Dark hair, straight, parted on my left. Lightish eyes—not blue—maybe gray. Sort of distracted-looking. Clean-shaven. Nice-looking in a plain sort of way." She opened her eyes. "Sorry I'm not being much help."

"You *are* being helpful. Can you remember the shape of the face?"

"Not round or long. Kind of average. Maybe the hint of a double chin."

"Would you be able to recognize him if you saw him again?" Parrott asked.

"I might. I did notice his hands when he paid. No rings or other jewelry. Stubby fingers, and dark hair past his knuckles and on his wrists."

Parrott was about to wrap up this interview when something Gina said earlier snagged on the reel in his brain. "Wait a minute. Let's go back to what you said about the woman's satchel. Can you describe it in detail for me?"

"I can do better than that. I can draw it for you, if you'd like." She pulled a sheet of paper from the printer and ran to the front room to grab a pencil. As she outlined the shape of the purse, she gave a running commentary. "I've never seen one like this. The shoulder strap is clear plastic, but sturdy. You wouldn't even notice it. The bag is large enough to carry everything a girl might need, but it fits snugly under the arm." She continued to sketch the design on the bag, sunbursts with smiley faces. "Shades of beige and yellow, very subtle in color. I loved that it would go with anything."

"Can you estimate the size of it?" Parrott wondered if it might double as a diaper bag when the time came.

Gina's hands formed "L's" to demonstrate a rectangle of about twelve by fifteen inches.

This was the first Parrott had heard of a shoulder bag, and his heart pounded with the question of where it might be now. There'd been no sign of one near the body or on the promontory. Assuming she had it with her the morning she was killed, then someone either dumped it or hid it. Good information to know.

Parrott put contact information for Gina in his phone and gave her his card. "You've been very helpful. If you think of anything else—even a tiny detail—please call me. I might be in touch with you again, as well."

He walked Gina back to the cash register, and Maureen traded places with her again. Back in the little room, she folded her hands and turned to Parrott. "Anything else?"

"Yes, if you don't mind. Do you keep a record of every sale each day?"

"Oh, yes, I see where you're going. Let's look up our sales for last Friday." Maureen logged into a spreadsheet with different tabs for each day. She pinpointed last Friday's sales and ran the cursor over the columns until she found what she was looking for. "Here it is! Cash purchase made at 11:21 a.m."

"No name of the customer, then?" Parrott held his breath. That was within three days of Amanda's death.

"I would, if they paid with a credit card, but this purchase was cash."

Parrott circled around the table. Not that he suspected Maureen of lying, but he needed to see for himself. A name would have been so helpful. "Is there anything else you can remember about this couple?"

"No-o-o. As I said, I didn't wait on them, myself. Are they in any trouble?"

Parrott handed her a business card. "Please call me if you think of anything else. I guess you could assume if I'm looking for them, it probably involves some kind of trouble."

Maureen squeezed her hands together again, as if in prayer. "Well, for the sake of the newborn baby involved, I hope you can find them, and I hope they're okay."

Parrott walked past the mother, toddler, and puddle-splasher on his way out. Confidence that he was on the path of the victim, and perhaps her killer, pulsed in his veins. When he passed the rain puddle, he gave it a strong, satisfying kick.

# CHAPTER FIFTY-FOUR

When he returned to the station, Parrott entered all the fingerprints from Barton's SUV and the note from Stuart Mooney into the evidence log and secured it in a locked file cabinet in his office. He wanted to keep them away from Barton's eyes.

Then, while fresh in his mind, he made notes in the file on his computer about Gina's description of the man who bought the embroidered baby outfit. Dark hair, light eyes, a hint of a double chin, hair on the fingers and arms.

Meanwhile, he put in a call to Sheltering Palms in Dallas. Maybe someone there would help him piece together more details about what went awry with Amanda Hoffman. The best way to ask these questions would have been in person, but Dallas was too far, and the priority for this information was too low for the department to foot the bill for an out-of-state trip.

The other question mark was whether the administrator would talk to him. He'd learned from Mr. Josephson at the Philadelphia facility how strict the privacy policy was. On the other hand, the happy return of Ada Hidalgo to her parents might count for something. The only way to know was to try.

Parrott went through the same annoying rigamarole with the phone system that he'd faced when calling the Philadelphia clinic for an appointment. After listening to prompts and pushing buttons for several minutes, he finally was able to hold on for a live person. He put the call on speaker, so he could use the wait time to organize his questions.

At last a woman with a Southern twang came on the line. "Sorry to keep you waitin'. How may I direct your call?"

Parrott explained who he was and why he was calling, making it a point to mention that he had already spoken with Mr. Josephson in Philadelphia. "I'd be grateful if you'd connect me with the clinic's administrator.

"Hold on, please."

Impatient, Parrott completed his list of questions and retrieved a bottle of water from the case under his desk. He twisted the cap off and took a swig. Hunger played a sonata in his belly, but he didn't want to be chewing a power bar when someone came on the phone.

A moment later, a man's voice boomed in Parrott's ear. "Detective Parrott. Jarrett Hubbard here, administrator of the Dallas facility. Can you tell me which of our patients you're calling about?"

Parrott explained about the Hidalgo baby and the murder of the surrogate. "I have a release from them authorizing you to speak with me."

"Thanks for that. Would you mind if we took this call to Zoom? Since we're not in person, we'd like to verify your badge number, see your face, and record the session, if possible."

"Fine with me. May I have a copy of the recording?"

"Of course."

No stranger to Zoom, Parrott turned on his computer and clicked on the link sent to him by email. When the link went through, Parrott was surprised by Hubbard's appearance, so unlike that of Mr. Josephson. Hubbard was younger, fitter-looking, and Black.

Parrott assumed, by the soft chuckle, that the administrator connected equally with his appearance, though no words to that effect needed to be expressed. Parrott showed his badge and explained his connection to the case of the Hidalgo baby.

Hubbard cleared his throat and said, "We are deeply indebted to you, Parrott. The circumstances surrounding the Hidalgo baby represented a black eye for Sheltering Palms. We do our best to select only the best donors and surrogates. We vet them thoroughly, so we were frankly appalled when the surrogate went missing." Phones rang in the background, but Hubbard ignored them.

Parrott nearly choked on the *vet them thoroughly* part. "I understand. Glad to have played a part in restoring the baby to the Hidalgos." Parrott glanced at his notes. "But I still have a murder to solve, and I'm hoping you can answer some questions about Amanda Hoffman."

"No offense meant to you, detective, because we, of course, want to help you, but we obviously didn't know enough about

Ms. Hoffman, and what we do know now is, well, not very complimentary." Hubbard paused to tell someone at the door that he was on a Zoom and would be unavailable for the next hour.

Parrott needed to make it clear he wasn't seeking to exonerate Amanda Hoffman just because she was a murder victim. "Whether Amanda Hoffman was good or evil, somebody murdered her, and that person is still at large. I need the truth—even if it's ugly."

"Then the truth is what I'll give you, as much as I'm able. I never met the young woman, myself. That would have been one of our social workers."

"Fair enough. Are you familiar with the application Ms. Hoffman submitted to become a surrogate?"

"Yes, I have it right here in front of me. Also the contract she signed once we selected her to be the surrogate for the Hidalgos."

"Would it be possible for me to have copies of both documents? Also, could I meet with the person who *did* meet Hoffman in person?"

"I'll have to check with our corporate office. Personally, I have no problem, but Sheltering Palms has built its reputation on holding high standards for privacy. The fact that she's deceased may make a difference, but we may need to consider her next of kin. I'll see." Hubbard looked down at the documents and turned a few pages. "Meanwhile, what would you like to ask?"

Even though he'd prepared questions, suddenly Parrott's tongue stuck to the roof of his mouth. This was the closest he had come to knowing Amanda Hoffman so far, and questions pounded in his head with the pressure of making a first down deep in the opponent's territory. He was glad he had the list in front of him.

"Let's start with her application. What criteria did she present that met your standards for selection?"

Hubbard held up a checklist, so Parrott could see. Each item on the list had a score, and there were a lot of fives. "Age, marital status, location, general health, gynecological health, lack of bad habits like smoking, drinking, drug use. She passed two physicals—one with her own doctor and another with ours—with flying colors. Fitness—she was a competitive swimmer in high school and kept up her skills. Her driving record was flawless.

No arrests, no red flags. At the time of application, she had a job at Applebee's."

"Did she state what her motivation was to become a surrogate?"

"Yes, there's an essay here." He paused to read. "She says she saw a movie about a woman and her husband who couldn't have a baby, and she realized that was something she could do to make a difference for someone else. She was curious about childbirth and didn't mind giving up nine months of her life to try out pregnancy and delivery without having to worry about supporting and taking care of the baby. In other words, the A+ answer."

*Sounds like a lot of BS to me. I have to wonder about this place, maybe this entire industry.* "How does that compare to the typical response?"

Hubbard gave another high-pitched chuckle, almost a giggle. "Everybody, donor or surrogate, wants the money, plain and simple. Lofty, altruistic statements win points, but let's face it. There aren't many people who would disrupt their lives for a year if it weren't for the money. Only time I've seen it is when relatives step up to help.

"In the case of sperm donors, there might be some kind of genetic pride—populating the world with one's progeny, but surrogates don't even have that."

So far, Hubbard hadn't told Parrott anything surprising. "Is there anything on her application that didn't receive a high score?"

"Interesting question. Amanda was eighteen and living alone when she made application. By law, she didn't need parental approval. We asked several questions, though, about whom she could rely upon for emotional support during the pregnancy. She mentioned a former teacher, her supervisor at work, and a girlfriend who was in college, but not her parents, and she had no siblings."

"Was that all?" Parrott couldn't help feeling pity for the girl who voluntarily stepped into this baby-making factory.

Hubbard hesitated. "I'm going to be straight with you, Parrott. Once this girl went missing, we pored over this application a hundred times, trying to figure out where she might've gone, and, later, where we went wrong in choosing her. There's a certain arrogance in Hoffman's writing. An entitlement mentality, so to

speak. Here's an example. 'I've taken excellent care of my body my whole life. You won't find a smarter, healthier, or more fit person.' In the emotional support part, after naming those people, she said, 'I doubt I'll need much emotional support. I've learned to rely on myself.'"

"I see what you mean," Parrott said. He was beginning to get a picture of a young woman whose lack of stability had been hidden by a pseudo-self-confidence. "Let's talk about the timeline. How much time was it between her signing the contract to next steps, and were there any times she violated the contract along the way?"

Consulting the document, Hubbard said, "Hoffman submitted her application a little over a year ago. She was selected as a match for the Hidalgos soon after. We brought her to town for an interview and a thorough physical with our doctor last September. The IVF transfer was done in mid-November, here in Dallas, We kept her here for the first two weeks to make sure everything was going well. Then we transferred care to a doctor we work with in Sulphur Springs. He monitored her carefully for the next eight weeks, sending reports from ultrasounds and bloodwork. After the first ten weeks, Amanda was free to go about her business with monthly checkups. We have records of all her visits and reports, until the end of July. No contract violations until the big one."

"I know you pay the surrogate for her services. Can you tell me how that works?"

Hubbard tapped the documents on his desk. "Compensation is in the form of room and board expenses, plus medical, paid monthly for the period of the contract, plus a hefty "signing fee," paid at the beginning, and an even more substantial severance stipend paid after the birth and transfer to the biological parents. We pay the rent directly to the landlord. The living expense allowance is determined early on and is quite generous."

"Was there ever any contact between Amanda Hoffman and the Hidalgos?"

"Absolutely not. Neither knew the identities of the other. That is strictly enforced policy, important for many reasons, including moral, ethical, and legal ones."

Parrott thought of the yellow going home outfit purchased from Maureen's store. "Was Amanda Hoffman ever told the gender of the baby she was carrying?"

"Not unless there was a breakdown in procedures. Our doctors are permitted to share with the surrogate any medical information regarding her health or how the pregnancy is affecting that, but we intentionally suppress any information about the birth parents or the child. Our intent is to prevent any bonding between the surrogate and the fetus. We don't want anything to stand in the way of the surrogate's walking away from the baby after delivery."

"At any time did anyone from Sheltering Palms have any contact with Amanda's parents or others, for example, the people mentioned in her emotional support response?"

"I don't believe so. We would have had no reason to interact with anyone but the surrogate herself, at least until she went missing—and then, we turned the matter over to the police."

Parrott was nearing the end of the questions he'd written down, but he wasn't ready to disconnect. He sensed Mr. Hubbard still had something to tell him. He leaned into the computer screen to simulate the kind of eye contact and body language he would have used in person. "I appreciate your time and sincerity, Mr. Hubbard. I'm going to ask you a different kind of question now. You're a man of considerable knowledge and experience. Based on these, I'd like you to speculate on how and why Amanda Hoffman left Texas and ended up in Pennsylvania."

Hubbard chuckled again, and Parrott decided the administrator's vocalization came more from nerves than humor. "Well, as I said earlier, I never met this young woman. But if I had to guess, I'd say Ms. Hoffman was motivated by money. She was coming to the end of being supported by Sheltering Palms. Soon she would have to pay her own rent and expenses, and maybe she'd gotten used to having money given to her without working for it.

"As long as she carried the Hidalgo baby, she wielded a lot of power, but she knew once she had the baby and collected her final stipend, it would all be over. Maybe she was abducted or got involved with someone who convinced her to leave town while she still had control of things."

"So, you think she might've wanted to hold the baby for ransom? Something like that?"

"Not beyond the realm of possibility, is it?"

"Did she ever communicate with Sheltering Palms after she left Texas?"

"No. Who knows what she encountered en route to Pennsylvania? Nine months' pregnant and ill-equipped financially. I think she was an impulsive person who thought she could do whatever she felt like doing, regardless of contracts and medical advice. She never gave a thought to the people whose baby she was carrying. Or the consequences of her actions.

"I'm sorry if I sound insensitive, or even bitter, but, assuming she left willingly, Amanda Hoffman put a lot of really good people through a nightmare."

Parrott nodded, but the clinic's representative had also left a bad taste in his mouth. "And the chain of events that had brought her right here ended up being *her* worst nightmare, as well."

# CHAPTER FIFTY-FIVE

After talking to the administrator of the Dallas fertility clinic, Parrott received a call from Maria Rodriguez, the coroner. "Hey, Parrott. I wanted to let you know we're ready to release Hoffman's body. Does she have next of kin to receive her? Do we ship her, or what?""Good question." Parrott leaped at the chance to find out more about the victim. Release of the body would give him a good reason to contact Amanda's parents. Even though the young woman was estranged from them, they might offer valuable information. "Let me make some calls, and I'll get back to you ASAP. Meanwhile, anything new from toxicology?"

"Nothing earth-shattering. No drugs, no alcohol. Of course, TOD was early morning. Hormones consistent with being post-partum. Aside from what I told you before about her being bruised, the girl was a very healthy young woman who met with a quick, violent death."

"Any guess as to what kind of gun?" Without the bullet or casing, nailing down the weapon would be conjecture. Parrott had his own hypothesis but waited to hear Maria's.

"I'd say a .38 or .45, considering the velocity and amount of cranial matter displaced. A .22 probably wouldn't have exited, but if it did, the force wouldn't have blown the woman's face off."

"That's what I thought. A .38's a big gun to be carrying around on an everyday basis. Typically a man's gun, but not impossible for a female." Parrott's thoughts galloped through his mind like thoroughbreds.

The squeals of children from the playground outside his window reminded him of the waning afternoon. He said goodbye to Maria and punched up the number of Sgt. Davis from the Sulphur Springs PD.

When the sergeant answered, Parrott said, "Glad I caught you. We need to contact Amanda Hoffman's NOK, assuming that's her parents. Looking for contact info and any advice you might have."

"The body's ready? Sure, I can get you their phone numbers. You're not planning to fly down here, are you? Hold on a sec." Davis put the phone down while he rustled papers. He read the home and cell phone numbers to Parrott. "If you want, I can pave the way—ask them to call you instead."

"You think that's necessary?"

"Not necessary. I'm sure you're experienced with making these calls. Tricky, even in person. The parents are grievin'—understandably—but differently. The victim was apparently a daddy's girl. He spoiled her. Mom was the disciplinarian—"

A female voice interrupted the description, and Davis put Parrott on hold again. Parrott's mother had been his uni-parent, but Tonya's parents, both deceased, had been like that. Tonya often spoke of how her mother laid down the law, but her dad took her fishing.

"Sorry. We've got a situation here. What I wanted to tell you—when I went to notify the Hoffmans, they took it hard. Started yellin' at each other, big time. She blamed her husband for giving the daughter too many material things. He blamed her for giving too little emotional support. Evidently, making Amanda move out and support herself was the mother's idea. Tough love. Wouldn't be surprised if those two split up over this."

"Compounding the tragedy," Parrott said. "Anything else I should know?"

"No, I guess not. Shame you can't go in person. Good-looking parents in a nice house in a nice neighborhood. The daughter was an only child. Photos of the three of them all over the walls and everywhere. A whole bookcase of swimmin' trophies. The girl musta been good."

Not wanting to hold up Sgt. Davis any longer, Parrott thanked him and signed off. He needed to call the Hoffmans as soon as possible. Their daughter's body needed tending to, whether they opted for burial or cremation. Earlier, Davis had told him Hoffman owned a construction company, and his wife was a dental hygienist. He hoped they would both be home, but Sulphur Springs was an hour behind.

He dialed the home phone number and let it ring. Voicemail picked up after four rings. He considered hanging up, but caller

ID would leave his number, and he didn't want to appear rude. On the other hand, his was not the type of message he could leave on a machine. When the message beeped, he said, "This is Detective Parrott of the West Brandywine Police Department. I need to talk to you about an important matter. I will call back shortly."

Before he left for home, he wanted to test Stuart Mooney's note for prints, and run the prints taken from Barton's SUV through the system. T.J. Bath's note could remain bagged for now, since his prints were already in the system from his prior conviction.

Parrott took the items in question from his file cabinet, along with a print kit, and set up on the small table in the new lab. Print work was a routine, but delicate science. Parrott whipped through the spraying of Mooney's envelope and letter with ninhydrin and waited for the prints to show up in purple on the porous paper. The acrid odor stung his nasal passages and caused his eyes to water. He'd used a different process with tape to lift dusted prints from Barton's car. These had been easier to obtain, having come from a smooth, nonporous surface.

Once he had all the prints, he moved everything to a counter, where a covered microscope was set up. He had several good prints and a few partials from the envelope and the note inside. These begged the question of why a guy who was so careful as not to talk without a lawyer present would hand-write a note and put it in an envelope himself. Of course, some of the prints from the envelope might be from Jade Bender, Mooney's assistant, but presumably the ones on the paper that had been sealed inside were Mooney's.

First, Parrott examined the prints from Mooney's note. He focused on the ridges, loops, and whorls on two of these, one a thumbprint. Good, usable prints were a gift. He set these aside to check out the prints from Barton's car. Not surprisingly, there were several different prints, full and partial, some on top of others. Parrott expected at least two distinct sets, one from Barton and one from Wren Vargas, who'd stood in for him to buy the car. He was more interested in the prints that came from the passenger side of the front seat. He'd gotten a few clear ones from the seat belt and from the dashboard on that side.

Now he slid the tape with the prints from the SUV into the stage of the microscope. He adjusted the nosepiece and lenses and studied the patterns. He blinked several times and sucked in a breath. He removed the prints and substituted the ones from the paper. His heart raced, and he felt like shouting. The prints from the note and the prints from the car matched perfectly. He could now place the person who touched Mooney's note in Barton's automobile. For the moment, Parrott would consider those prints to be Mooney's.

Excited, he scanned all the prints into the computer and uploaded them to AFIS for sorting. The computer identified Barton's prints, as expected. All police officers' prints were on file in the database. Mooney's prints came back as unknown, but Parrott manually identified them as "likely" Stuart Mooney's and saved them in the evidence folder.

He'd already sprayed the back seat and trunk with luminol to look for blood traces, but there were none. He'd have to think about how to use this possible fingerprint evidence of a connection between Barton and Mooney. Even though he'd used subterfuge to purchase Barton's car, he'd done nothing illegal. Barton was selling the car, and Parrott bought it. He needed to talk to Chief Schrik in the morning. He might confront Barton with the fingerprint evidence and see how he explained it. He still lacked enough evidence for a warrant to search  Moonglow.

Before he did anything rash, he put everything away in the lab and locked the evidence in his office. He'd take it to Chesco later. He tried Amanda's parents one more time before he headed for home. He redialed the number in Sulphur Springs and waited while it rang. This time a female voice answered.

# CHAPTER FIFTY-SIX

Asking bereaved parents how they wished to take care of their daughter's remains was not high on Parrott's list of favorite tasks, but someone had to do it, and he strove to be as professional as possible. The job was made harder by having to use the telephone.

Parrott introduced himself as the detective in charge of the investigation into Amanda's death.

"Murder, you mean?" Ann Hoffman's voice sounded gravelly, possibly from grief or cigarettes or both. "My daughter didn't *die*. She was *killed*."

"Yes, ma'am. That's true, and I want to assure you and Mr. Hoffman that we are doing everything in our power to learn the truth about what happened to your daughter and bring her murderer to justice."

A sniffle caused Parrott to pause for a few seconds. "Before we continue this conversation, is Mr. Hoffman available to join us on the line?"

"Hold on. I'll get him." The receiver slammed on a hard surface, and shuffling noises filled Parrott's ear.

"Yes, Detective Parrott, is it? Like the bird? This is Ben Hoffman, and my wife Ann is on the extension. What can we do for you?" Hoffman's voice was deep and depleted, as if he'd been pulled out of bed in the midst of a nightmare. Maybe not far from the truth.

"As I told your wife, Mr. Hoffman, the West Brandywine PD is working hard to apprehend the person responsible for your daughter's death. At this point, the coroner is ready to release Amanda's body. As her next of kin, you can instruct us as to your wishes."

"Oh, God—"

"It's okay, Ann. I've been expecting this call. What are our options?"

Parrott explained they could choose cremation or burial. They could come to West Chester in person and accompany the body or the ashes back to Texas. Or they could arrange to have either transported to Texas, where they would take possession. Whichever option they chose, they would be responsible for the expenses.

Another sniffle preceded the mother's next words. "Amanda gave us many surprises during her short life. She was never very predictable. But I never expected to have to pay for her funeral." She sobbed. "Oh, this is so hard."

"Yes, ma'am. I understand—"

"How soon do you need an answer?" Hoffman asked. "Maybe we should discuss it and call you back."

Before Parrott could reply, Ann Hoffman wailed. "—made worse because she's so far away. How on earth did she end up in Pennsylvania, of all places? Can you tell me that, Detective?"

"I'd like to know that, myself," Parrott said. "Do either of you have any ideas?"

Amanda's father took over, uttering a long sigh. "I don't know how much you know about our daughter. I'm sure you've talked to members of our local police department. Amanda was a troubled girl. Not always. When she was younger, she was vivacious and funny. She was athletic and loved physical challenges."

Someone, Parrott suspected the mother, blew a nose. "When she hit puberty a new Amanda showed up. We'd raised her to be strong and independent, but this Amanda became demanding and stubborn. She began to miss practices at the school. We caught her smoking and drinking and sneaking out with boys—all the worrisome behaviors parents pray not to have to deal with. No amount of punishment had any effect on her."

"Hmmph. As if you ever disciplined her," the mother said. "I had to be the bad parent. I never had the opportunity to show her I loved her."

"Ann, the detective doesn't need to listen to recriminations. He asked if we knew why she left town, and the answer is no. If I had to guess, though, I'd say it had something to do with money."

"Why do you say that, Mr. Hoffman?" Parrott asked, thinking how easy it was to blame money, as the infertility clinic had

done, instead of taking responsibility for their parts in the young woman's actions.

Mrs. Hoffman was the one who answered. "Nothing but money motivated Amanda. She had a taste for material possessions, but when she had to pay for them herself—"

"—That's water under the bridge, Ann. Detective, if I could have my baby girl back, she'd never have to pay for another thing herself. I'd rather spoil her to death than have to bring her body back, murdered."

In an effort to keep the parents talking, Parrott said, "If you don't mind my asking, when was the last time either of you talked to Amanda?"

"We don't mind. Sgt. Davis asked us the same thing. Probably four months or so ago." Mrs. Hoffman cleared her throat. "A neighbor of mine saw Amanda at the supermarket. Said she looked pregnant. I couldn't contact her by phone. I didn't have her number. So, I went over to her apartment and sat on the steps until she straggled in one night.

"I asked her what in hell she was doing to herself. I demanded to know who the baby's father was, whether he was goin' to support her. She wouldn't tell me anything. She just said not to worry. She knew what she was doin', and she'd be okay."

Mr. Hoffman broke in. "We didn't know until she went missing that she was carrying a baby for another woman. That she was doing it for money. Arggghhh. What a crazy idea. I still can't believe it."

"Are you aware of any friends, male or female, who might've gone with Amanda? Anyone connected to Pennsylvania in any way?"

"I think Amanda broke off with all her friends and former boyfriends after she graduated from high school," Mr. Hoffman said. "For all I know, she met somebody on social media or a chat room or something. She never woulda told us anything like that."

Parrott figured he'd learned as much about Amanda as the parents could tell him. He provided them with the name and number of the Chester County morgue. "Your local funeral home can make arrangements with them. And you can call me back if you have any questions or other thoughts."

"Yeah, maybe we'd better. You don't need to listen to us argue. I hope you find whoever did this to our daughter. She wasn't perfect, but she deserved better."

Parrott hung up the phone, his heart heavy for this couple, whose lives would probably never recover from this tragedy. In a way, they'd lost their daughter long before she ended up miles away with her face blown off. The picture of Amanda he was forming in his head after talking to them had her as less of a victimized woman and more of a willful, rebellious adolescent. He was itching to find out more.

# CHAPTER FIFTY-SEVEN

T.J. had never looked more handsome than when he walked through the door and set his roller bag against the wall. Lucy bounded to him, leaping in the air and attempting to cover his face and hands with sloppy kisses. Kate, though more restrained, empathized.

Then the enormity of how much she'd missed him flooded through her like a raging current. Her head told her to stand in place, to wait for him to make the first move, but the current, now rapids, thrust her into his arms.

He enfolded her in the tightest hug imaginable. They stood together, gently swaying to a silent melody for what seemed like an hour. When they broke apart to gaze into each other's faces, tears streaked both faces. "I'm sorry," they said in unison and then laughed.

"No, I'm the one who needs to apologize," T.J. said. "I should never have left without explaining. I hope you can forgive me."

"I've been so worried. Why didn't you text or call?" The initial joy at T.J.'s homecoming already started to fray around the edges. Kate had so many questions.

"Let's sit down. This talk is way overdue." T.J. led the way to the sofa, allowing Kate to choose her seat in the corner first. He plopped on the ottoman across from her, making eye contact the whole time. "I didn't call or text because I lost my phone. No time to replace it. I was worried about you, too. I kept telling myself you're a smart, strong woman, that you could get along fine without me. Better than I could without you."

"You lost your phone?" *Hard to believe.* "Where? Where did you go? And why did you take Lucy with you, only to leave her with the Campbells? I don't understand any of it."

T.J.'s lips formed a half-smile. "So many questions all at once. Let's see." He leaned sideways onto an elbow and kicked off his desert boots. "When I left, I wasn't sure where I was going. You know how you felt when you ran out on me—you just needed to

escape. I had a lot on my mind, and my original intent was to take Lucy with me, to drive around and get my shit together. I didn't plan on staying away long—maybe just overnight.

"The baby stuff threw me into a panic. I saw how you reacted to that infant on the porch. I'd never seen you want anything so much, and that scared me. I knew I couldn't give you the one thing you really wanted, and I was terrified I would lose you."

T.J. paced around the tight space of the combined kitchen, dinette, and family room. "I told you about my vasectomy, but I never told you the whole truth about why I had it. I meant to tell you, but the time never seemed right. If things were going well, I didn't want to upset you. If things were tense, I didn't want to add to the tension."

Chills jetted through Kate's body, causing her to shudder. Whatever T.J. was trying to say, it sounded ominous. Was he ill? Did he have some kind of genetic disease he didn't want to perpetuate? He was ten years her senior. Anything might have happened before they were married, and she wouldn't have known. Her mouth dried up, and her voice sounded like paper rubbing against paper. "Tell—me—now."

T.J. sat again and took Kate's hand in both of his. "There are things about me that you don't know—I didn't tell you, because I didn't want to lose you. Before we met, I was even more impulsive. Sometimes I was a jerk, and sometimes I made mistakes."

The old fear that T.J. might have committed a crime to give her a baby crept into Kate's mind like an insidious poison. She looked away, focusing on Lucy, curled up at her feet.

"I dated a lot of girls, women—none as beautiful or smart or kind as you. There was this girl named Crystal. I liked her a lot, and she was crazy about me. We were both in our early twenties, not kids. One thing led to another, and pretty soon Crystal turned up pregnant."

Kate was speechless. She thought she knew everything important about her husband of ten years, but how naïve that was. They hadn't asked questions about each other's past relationships, and now she realized that in some ways that was a mistake.

"I wasn't ready to settle down, and I had a sense Crystal wasn't the person I wanted to spend my life with. I suggested an abortion,

offered to pay for it. I panicked and probably didn't handle myself very well. Crystal was Catholic and wouldn't consider any option but having and keeping the baby." T.J. winced, as if in pain. "We split up, and she moved to Texas. I heard through the grapevine she had a daughter. The girl would be about seventeen now."

Outside, night had wrapped itself around the cottage in the way nights in the country did, with only the moon and stars for illumination. The only light on in their single multi-purpose room was the fixture over the kitchen sink. Kate was glad for the dimness that protected her from being totally exposed. Her husband had fathered a child.

She managed to squeak out some questions. "Are you in touch with them? Are you supporting this child?"

T.J. shook his head. "Crystal didn't want anything from me. She married another guy. I told you I was kind of a bad boy back then, but all that baby stuff shook me up. I started dating other women and didn't want history to repeat itself. I didn't think I was 'father' material."

"So, you got a vasectomy to make sure you'd never get someone pregnant again." Kate choked on the word *pregnant.*

"That's about right."

"And you never told me anything about it."

"I'm sorry about that. You have a right to know. You could have married anyone. You could have married a rich guy who could give you lots of babies, and instead you've got me."

"Does it matter to you that I never wanted a rich guy or a lot of babies? That I was happy here with you?" As the words came tumbling out, Kate realized she was speaking in past tense.

"Of course, it matters. We've been very happy—at least I always thought so. But when I witnessed your reaction to the abandoned baby, I knew I needed to do something. I saw the way you looked at me, as if I were some criminal, some albatross. At first, I thought of going to Texas, taking Lucy with me. Maybe I could research Crystal's whereabouts, meet the daughter I've never known.

"Then I decided that was ridiculous. Nothing would be solved by opening that closed book. I checked into a motel, had a few drinks, and thought things over. I decided to take Lucy to the Campbells'.

I went ahead and kept the reversal surgery appointment. Not a big deal, and no guarantees that it will work."

Kate hardly knew what to say. There was something sweet about the act of faith T.J. had made in reversing the surgery, but the way he'd gone about it—running off and leaving her guessing as to his whereabouts. His actions, and maybe her own, didn't speak of a stable marriage of two people who love and communicate with each other.

"So what happened to your phone?" she asked, still suspicious.

"Don't know. I had it before the day surgery, but when I came to, it was gone. I made a big stink about it at the hospital, but they have big signs saying they're not responsible." T.J. perched on the ottoman and leaned across the gap to place his hands on Kate's shoulders. "I love you, Kate. I'd do anything in my power to make you happy. So what do you say? Can you forgive me?"

Kate hesitated. Gazing at his thick, dark hair and light eyes, she was tempted to fall into bed with him immediately and test to see if the surgery was working. But something held her back. Would a man who kept big secrets from his wife be a good father? And what other secrets might he still be holding back?

The bottom line was—Kate was afraid of her own husband.

# CHAPTER FIFTY-EIGHT

On his way home after talking to the Hoffmans and dropping off the fingerprints at Chesco, Parrott reviewed the status of his case. He'd made a lot of progress and gathered a lot of information. He had ideas about the weapon, the suspects, fingerprints, and DNA. What he didn't have yet was a motive, and without that, it was nearly impossible to create the scenario for the murder.

A few questions that kept surfacing in his mind were logistical and involved the baby. Who left the baby in the box? When? Why? One possible scenario had Amanda Hoffman leaving the baby before she was killed. Perhaps the bottles of breast milk reflected a concern for the baby's welfare after abandoning her. The yellow coming-home outfit gave the same vibe.

Dried blood on the blanket, Hoffman's blood, might have come from the delivery, or, more likely, from the violence Hoffman sustained at the time of her death. The latter suggested that the baby was put in the box after the surrogate was injured or killed.

The time of day and place raised speculation, too. Dawn in the country was a time for early risers who tended the land, the horses, or both. Hoffman's presence in Brandywine Valley at that time of day was remarkable. Was she there voluntarily? How did a nineteen-year-old from Texas even know the community existed? Beyond that, the Baths' cottage was way off the beaten path.

Parrott had pieced together a disturbing picture of Amanda Hoffman from interviewing her parents and the administrator of Sheltering Palms, as well as Caro and Gina, who had seen her briefly at Kennett Square. Evidently the nineteen-year-old had been impulsive, materialistic, self-centered. Her difficult personality might explain something that would help in solving the murder.

Parrott concluded, as he pulled into his garage, that he needed to shift focus away from Amanda Hoffman and toward the man who had accompanied her in the restaurant and store in Kennett

Square. If the young woman wasn't grounded in Brandywine Valley, perhaps he was. More importantly, he was probably still alive. Parrott was determined to find him.

※ ※ ※

After filling up on stir-fried chicken, Parrott and Tonya cleaned up the kitchen together and entertained Horace for a while. Parrott stretched out on the sofa, propped up on an elbow. His other hand played with his wife's silky hair, which had been unbraided and straightened a few hours before.

"I could stay like this all night. I haven't felt this relaxed in ages," Parrott said.

Tonya leaned back into the sofa and made eye contact. "You're entitled after a long day's work. Then I won't suggest the after-dinner activity I was thinking of."

Parrott wiggled his eyebrows. "Never too tired for *that*."

Tonya kissed him lightly on the lips. "Not what I was thinking of, although it does take place in a bedroom."

Sitting up, Parrott sighed. "Okay, tell me. I've had enough mystery-solving for one day."

"I thought maybe you'd like me to help you go through some of the boxes your mom brought over. Alice always says the hardest part of a difficult task is taking the first step, and even harder is doing that alone. Why don't we tackle the first box tonight, together?"

"You mean the Bo stuff." Parrott had been resisting even the thought of those boxes in the upstairs bedroom. His throat constricted, and he took several deep breaths. "I guess Alice is right. Avoidance isn't a positive strategy." He invited Horace to his shoulder and pulled Tonya to her feet. "Let's go."

Five boxes lined the closet floor in the fifth bedroom, each box labeled with years. Bo was three years older than Parrott, so the items inside ranged from when Parrott was two until he was in his twenties. "Do you want to go chronologically?" Tonya asked.

"No, I don't think so." Parrott rubbed his eyes. "And I don't want to start at the end, either. Let's open this one." He removed the small knife from his pocket and reached for the middle box.

"Whatever's inside will be from my teenage years. We had a lot of good times then."

Parrott slid the blade through the tape, opened the flaps, and removed the packing material. On top was a mini-photo album containing pictures of Bo and him from a day trip to Atlantic City. There was one of the cousins, hamming it up in a white wicker pushcart with a red-and-white awning. Another had them eating cotton candy. Aunt Rachel and Parrott's mom looked so young.

"We went to Atlantic City the summer before my sophomore year. Bo was starting college soon." Parrott stared at his cousin's face, searching for a sign that their time together would be cut short. "It's funny," he said. "I must've seemed like a shrimpy pest to him, but Bo never talked down to me. He never made me feel like I was out of his league."

"You two were more like brothers than cousins," Tonya said. "I remember how happy he was to meet me."

"Yeah, he told me you were a keeper. But that was much later." Parrott rummaged through the box, removing a program, cap, and ticket stubs from a Phillies game. The photo paper-clipped to the program showed Bo and Parrott wearing caps and sunglasses, leaning forward on their elbows in the nosebleed section of the stadium. He opened the program and found the pages where Bo had scored the game.

Parrott opened a souvenir from the end-of-year athletic banquet at the high school. Despite being only a freshman, Parrott had received a small trophy commemorating his record-setting number of rushing yards gained in the season. That was the year Bo was honored at the banquet, the end of his senior year. Parrott remembered how Bo had slapped him on the back. "Proud of you, cuz. I thought I was a great football player, but you outran, outcaught, and outpassed me."

Near the bottom of the box, Tonya lifted a prom picture of Bo and a buxom girl in an ice-blue satin, spaghetti-strap dress with the slit up to the top of the thigh. "Oh, ho. Who's the bimbo?"

Parrott chuckled for the first time since opening the box. "I think her name was Monique. She thought Bo hung the moon. She and her mom lived in the projects, and I think she saw my cousin as her ticket out. She had her hooks into him but good."

"He must have liked her if he took her to the prom."

"They broke up before he left for college. He said she was too crazy. She threatened him or something, and he left town for several weeks just to get away from her." Parrott rubbed his head as he thought. "Bo told me to be careful who I dated. He said, 'Sometimes a good-time girl turns out to be a nightmare.'"

Tonya swiped across his back. "Not sure how to take that, Ollie."

"You should take it as a compliment, sweetheart. You're my dream girl—always have been." He leaned over and gave his dream girl a long kiss. "And now, we've reached the bottom of this box. Let's put Horace to bed, and then ourselves."

It wasn't until much later that Parrott rolled over in bed and thought about Bo and Monique. Maybe Amanda Hoffman had been a good-time girl who turned out to be a nightmare.

# CHAPTER FIFTY-NINE

The next morning, bright and early, Parrott lifted weights in his basement gym before work. A call came in from Kate. "I hope I'm not calling too early," she said. You told me to call if I thought of anything, and I did. Think of something, I mean."

Parrott perked up. Sometimes his best information came from people who just happened to think of something. "Sure. What is it?"

"Well, first, T.J.'s back, but that's not why I'm calling. You know that box that the baby was in?" Kate sounded breathless. "The plain cardboard box?"

"Y-e-s," Parrott said, wishing she would get to the point.

"It reminded me of something, and I couldn't think of what until this morning, when I went to the basement freezer. We have shelves along one wall of the basement, and we store things there that we don't use often."

Parrott thought of his own basement storage area on the other side of the gym's wall. He, too, had boxes on shelves.

"We have four or five of those boxes—same size and weight, same sturdiness—with no markings on them anywhere. Perfect for carrying a baby, but also perfect for breakable objects, right?"

Parrott wasn't sure where Kate was going with this, but he was interested. "Right."

"So, our boxes came as Christmas presents, filled with bottles of cask-strength scotch whiskey produced by my uncle's distillery. We get a box full, twelve litre-size bottles, every year. We don't drink scotch that much, so the boxes accumulate, and we store them in the basement."

"Why wouldn't your uncle's scotch come in boxes with the Moonglow name and logo on it?" Parrott asked.

"I wondered the same thing, and I asked one time. I was told my uncle keeps plain boxes for family and special friends to distinguish the products inside. Regular customers get forty proof

scotch whiskey, while we get the full seventy proof, and we can add water to dilute according to our tastes. There's no need to advertise to us—we are swimming in scotch and receive more every Christmas. The plain boxes are fine for us."

Parrott put away his weights and bounded up the stairs to the kitchen, eager to get ready for work. "Let me ask you a question. How does the box of scotch bottles get to your house at Christmas time? Does it come directly from Scotland, or here? Is it shipped?"

Kate hesitated. "Don't misunderstand me. I'm not saying the baby's box came from my uncle's company. I just think that box might have held heavy glass items at some point."

"Of course," Parrott said. "I'd still like to know how the box comes to you."

"Well, in my case, it is hand-delivered, either by my aunt and uncle, or one of their employees. But—"

"If you don't mind, I'd like to stop by to see the boxes in your basement. In fact, if you could spare one, I'd like to take it with me for comparison purposes."

Kate uttered a soft gasp, like a balloon losing air after a long party. "Okay, but I hope you don't—"

"I promise you I'm not jumping to conclusions. I appreciate your sharing these thoughts with me. Your idea about the box is a good one."

"Well, I'm a little obsessed about that whole baby-on-the-porch incident. I still don't understand why the baby was brought to *my* house. I'd be surprised if some random person chose my house, way out here. I keep coming around to wondering who knows me, knows where I live? Who would bring me a baby out of the blue?"

*My thoughts exactly.* Parrott thanked Kate again and planned to stop by later that morning. Kate might have presented him with a gift even better than cask-grade scotch.

# CHAPTER SIXTY

P arrott showered and dressed quickly, his mind spinning with possible avenues of investigation following his conversation with Kate about the box. He packed a power bar and a thermos of milk in his car for breakfast *en route* to Brandywine. The last few days he'd been trying to exercise more and eat less, hard to do, since the testosterone medicine had turned up the volume on his appetite. Still, he didn't want to have to buy a whole new wardrobe.

At the point where he had to decide between going to the station or going to the Bath cottage, he opted for the latter. He wanted to get that box from Kate's basement before she had a chance to change her mind, or before someone like T.J. might change it for her.

He remembered Kate's fingerprints on the other box, the one with the infant inside. Now there might be a way to connect that box with the ones in the Bath basement.

At eight-fifteen when Parrott arrived at the cottage, T.J. was gone, and Kate had just started mixing the ingredients for her sourdough bread.

"I don't want to interrupt," he said, as Lucy nuzzled him, and Kate greeted him at the door. "If you'll just point me toward the basement, I'll be out of your hair in three minutes."

Kate wiped her hands on the terrycloth towel attached to her apron. "No problem. I'll show you." She ushered Parrott to the basement stairs and preceded him down. "Here are the boxes."

Even in the dim light from the overhead bulb and the fact that the boxes were pushed back on the shelf, their uniform appearance and similarity to what he remembered about the box with the baby in it were startling. "May I?" he asked, as he slid the first box out a couple of inches.

"Go ahead. It's heavy."

Parrott set the box on the floor. It had been opened and re-closed, by criss-crossing the flaps. He opened them to find eleven bottles

of scotch and a hole where the twelfth one had been. He pulled out a bottle and examined the label in the light, although he was less interested in that than in the box itself. Just as Kate had said, the bottle contained seventy-proof scotch. He didn't know how much one bottle of the strong stuff would be worth, but twelve of them made for a pretty valuable gift.

Parrott made no comment about how similar the box was to the one in evidence. "Okay if I take the bottles out and relieve you of this box?"

"Help yourself. You want a bottle of scotch, too? We have so many." Kate began emptying the box and placing the bottles on the shelf in a neat row.

"No, ma'am. I thank you, though." He accompanied her back up the stairs and said his goodbyes. He put the box in the trunk of his Camry. He wouldn't be able to drive to Chesco, where the other box was being held, until much later, but he continued to think about how this unmarked, reinforced cardboard box had been manufactured and distributed.

When he arrived at the station, Barton's parking spot was vacant again. Parrott needed to confront Barton about Mooney's fingerprints in the SUV, but he wasn't ready for that conversation yet, and Schrik needed to be involved.

The bug in Parrott's bonnet when he sat at his desk was the blood on the baby blanket. Not until yesterday did its importance stand out in Parrott's mind as a possible indicator of who put the baby on the porch. Jerry had compared the dried blood on the blanket to the dead woman's blood. Maria had verified that connection through DNA-testing. But none of that helped Parrott hypothesize whether Hoffman was killed before or after the baby was left at the Baths'.

He hadn't been ready to ask that question before, but now his own blood was pounding with the urgency to know. He checked the time—eight forty-five—not too early to try Dr. Goldstone's number.

When he had the gynecologist on the phone, he said, "I'm not calling about Tonya or me, but information about a case."

"The same one we talked about earlier? The baby's umbilical cord?" The doctor had a smile in his voice. "Happy to help."

"Thank you. I'll be brief. I have a sample of dried blood on the baby's blanket. It's already been tested and proven to have come from the deceased woman, post-partum. Here's my question. Is there a way to tell whether the blood came from the vagina during the birthing process, as opposed to from a gunshot wound or any other injury?"

A tapping sound filled the silence. Perhaps the doctor was hitting a heavy pen against his desk. "I think I understand what you're getting at, detective. You're asking a before and after question."

"That's right."

"So, my answer is quite important, and I'll explain it this way. Once a baby is born, the placenta separates from the uterine lining. We refer to this as the afterbirth. The bleeding that occurs during this event is called serous bleeding. *Serous* comes from the same root as *serum*. That blood is mixed with mucousy fluid."

Parrott sucked in a big breath. "And the blood from a head wound would be completely different, right?"

"Yes and no. Coming from the same woman, both blood samples would be the same type and have the same characteristics. But the afterbirth bleeding would contain a lower percentage of hemoglobin, red blood cells, and white blood cells, because they would be diluted by the other fluids."

Excited, Parrott thanked the doctor profusely and called the coroner's office. Maria answered on the first ring. "What's up, Parrott? You're an early bird."

"Same as you. Quick question. Do you still have blood from the baby blanket?"

"Not much. Remember, it wasn't that big a sample to begin with, and Jerry and I both used it. Why?"

Parrott explained why he wanted to know if the blood on the blanket had come from the vagina during the birthing process.

"I might be able to scrape another sample out of that blanket. Testing it is no problem. When do you need the information?" She laughed. "Never mind. I know you need it yesterday. I'll get to it as soon as I can."

"Thanks, Maria. You're a peach."

"My pleasure. If anyone near to me ever would need a detective, I'd hope they'd have someone like you. Nobody I know takes his cases to heart the way you do. *Hasta luego.*"

When he disconnected, Parrott decided to pay a visit to Chief Schrik, mostly because he didn't want to move forward with Barton without having the chief on board. As he took the chair across from Schrik, the odor of tobacco stung Parrott's nose. He couldn't help sniffing and turning his head aside. The chief had quit smoking years ago.

"No, I haven't started smoking again, if that's what you're thinking. Barton was in here not five minutes ago, and he reeked of cigarette smoke. I need to open a window or something."

"Allow me," Parrott said, as he stepped to the wall of windows overlooking the same side of the building as his own office. He unlocked the latches and flung the windows open, so a cool breeze flowed into the room. They rarely opened windows, because the building, which they shared with the township offices, discouraged interference with the year-round climate control system.

"Since when did Barton become a smoker?" Parrott asked.

"I don't ask those kinds of questions. I wish I didn't know how smoking can take over your life. Barton's been using our patrol car, taking it to and from home. We had a discussion about those arrangements."

"No indication that he's going to replace his personal car any time soon?" Parrott pictured the SUV, sitting in his single-car garage at home.

"No. I got the impression that he was looking to keep the police cruiser long-term."

"Doesn't that make you wonder? Why did he sell a perfectly serviceable SUV? A vehicle which happens to contain Stuart Mooney's fingerprints on the passenger side of the front seat."

Schrik's eyebrows almost collided with his receding hairline. "Anybody else's?"

"None pertinent to the case. However, I still have a bad feeling about those tire tracks on the promontory. Somebody with an SUV was up there with our vic when she was killed."

Schrik walked around his desk and touched Parrott's shoulder. "We've talked about this before. There are a million SUVs,

probably hundreds in Brandywine Valley. Unless you have solid evidence that can place Barton's SUV at the scene, there's no point in even talking about that. Besides, getting the car without a warrant? Highly unorthodox."

Parrott jumped to his feet, slightly offended. "Why? Wren Vargas bought the car fair and square. She gave it to me to do with as I wish. I wished to test it for fingerprints. What's illegal about that?"

"Calm down. I didn't say you did anything illegal, but you know as well as I do, if Barton were charged with murder, you'd have a heck of a time getting evidence from that car admitted into the record. It's probably a blessing that all you've found are Mooney's fingerprints. And all that proves is Mooney rode shotgun in Barton's car. So what?"

Not wanting to back down, Parrott circled the desk. "Even if you're right, which I'm not conceding, I think the car gives us leverage to get Barton to talk. C'mon, chief. Barton's been acting all weird, missing work, coming in late, smoking—and hanging out with a murder suspect who's in the wind, purportedly out of the country. Barton knows a lot more than he's telling. He's supposed to be on *our* team." He huffed. "Not to mention getting rid of a car that might link him to our murder case. I don't see how you can defend him."

Schrik perched on the edge of his desk and stared hard at Parrott. "I'm not defending him. Everything you say is true. I'm just cautioning you, Parrott. Don't lose your head over Mooney's fingerprints being in Barton's car. And don't forget—Mooney's a very rich, very powerful man. Maybe that doesn't cut any ice with you, but it does with me. If Mooney—or Barton—turns out to be our perp, let's nail 'im good, but we have to have an iron-clad case, and right now we don't."

Unmollified, Parrott crossed to the door, ready to end the meeting. "Okay. Do you want to talk to Barton, or shall I?"

Schrik bared his teeth, perhaps meaning, but failing, to smile. "You go ahead, Parrott. I trust you. But I've gotta be there."

# CHAPTER SIXTY-ONE

Fortunately, Randy Barton wasn't in his office when Parrott left Schrik. If Parrott had pushed for a meeting with Barton and Schrik while his emotions were stirred up, he might have said or done something he'd regret later. This way, he'd have a chance to chill and organize his thoughts.

While he didn't have all the information he needed, he did have suspects. Based on the remoteness of the kill site and the cottage where the baby was left, he felt certain that the killer was either familiar or hired by someone familiar with the Brandywine community. He drew boxes on the top page of a yellow legal pad.

In the first box, he wrote *Stuart Mooney*. The billionaire had opportunity to kill the young woman, although why leave her body on his property? The association with Barton raised a red flag. Mooney had access to boxes like the one the baby was found in. Hiring a lawyer and leaving the country added to the suspicion, and he probably had guns. The main thing missing was motive. Would Mooney risk everything he had to kill a young woman or have her killed? Maybe if the baby she had delivered was his or his son's, and maybe if Amanda had blackmailed him with being the father of her illegitimate baby, but the baby she carried was neither his nor hers. Parrott wished he had probable cause for a warrant to search Mooney's house. He didn't know what to look for, but his instincts told him there was something valuable there.

He couldn't rule out Randy Barton as a suspect, either. Barton had weapons, opportunity, and a clearly established connection to Mooney for whatever reason. And, of course, he had an SUV with a wheelbase the same size as the tracks. Strapped for money, Barton's behavior reflected a new nervousness. Why would Mooney hire Barton? As a long-time police officer, Barton surely understood the risks of moonlighting in a situation that might conflict with an investigation being handled by his own office. Barton's name went into the second box.

Before he could fill the third box with another suspect's name, Parrott received a call from Caro. Calls from her were never frivolous. "Good morning, Mrs. Campbell," he said, glancing at the top of his screen. "Good afternoon, I mean. How can I help you?"

Caro laughed. "Time gets away from me, too, detective. I hope you are doing well." She paused, and Parrott could hear a whirring in the background, maybe a vacuum cleaner. "I debated about calling, but decided, under the circumstances, you might want to know this bit of hearsay. I hope I'm not bothering you with something petty."

"No, no. Sometimes little things turn into big things. What's going on?"

"Just a minute. Let me close the door." A soft slam, and the whirring became a muffle. "I may have mentioned when you were here that I have a new housekeeper. Her name is Fay Nowak. She was here when you came over with the artist. She's a cousin of Josephine Wisniewski, who works for the Mooneys."

Parrott's spine tingled. Anything having to do with Mooney was high priority, even servant gossip, if that's what this was. "Okay."

"The two women talk occasionally. When I hired Fay, she asked if she could have Mondays off, so she and Josephine could meet up. I was happy to accommodate, since living out here can be so isolating. Anyway, yesterday they spent the day and night in Philadelphia with another cousin. This morning, Fay asked if she could talk to me about something."

Parrott held his breath. *Bring it on.*

"Evidently, Josephine is currently alone in that house at night. Mrs. Mooney's gone to Chicago to be with her daughter, and Mr. Mooney left town, too. 'For an extended period,' he told her. During the day, there are other servants coming and going, but at night, Josephine is the only one."

Someone knocked on the door in the background, and Caro asked him to hold on. A muted conversation ensued, and a minute later, she returned to the phone. "I'm so sorry. Anyway, Josephine told the cousin she was afraid to stay there alone at night. The past several nights she'd heard scraping noises, like someone was trying to break in."

"Surely the Mooneys have an alarm system," Parrott said.

"Yes, and the alarm was set and didn't go off. But the noises unnerve Josephine and keep her from sleeping. She said she felt like a sitting duck on a property where a woman had been killed. She's really stressed out."

"I understand," Parrott said.

"So, Fay remembered having seen you here. She knew you were a detective and wondered if you'd go over to Moonglow to look around and make sure her cousin is safe."

Parrott looked skyward and gave a silent prayer of thanks. Hadn't he just wished for an entrée into Mooney's house? But there were limits to what he could do legally. "Of course. I'd be happy to advise. I can't just show up on the doorstep and say I heard through the grapevine that you're feeling unsafe."

"That makes sense," Caro said. "What should I tell Fay?"

Parrott thought of Schrik's comment about needing an iron-clad case. "First, have her make sure all doors and windows are locked, and the alarm system is set whenever she goes out and at night. If she sees or hears something suspicious, have her call 911. Someone will be dispatched immediately. I'll drive by occasionally, as well. Let her know help is only a phone call away if she needs it."

"That's great," Caro said. "It'll be a big relief for Josephine *and* Fay. Also, for me. Thank you so much, Parrott. We're all so lucky to have you in this community." As an afterthought, she added, "I hope she doesn't have to call."

"Don't worry if she does," Parrott said. "That's what we're here for."

As he disconnected from the call, he uttered another silent prayer. *Please let Ms. Josephine call soon.*

# CHAPTER SIXTY-TWO

Parrott was famished, but he'd promised himself to eat sensibly, so even though he yearned for a pizza or a hoagie, he ran out for an albacore tuna salad from Green Street Grill. He munched on the tasty, fresh ingredients, while working at his desk, wondering why he hadn't done this more often.

As he ate, he flipped through the case photos related on his cellphone. He skipped over the ones of Amanda's gunshot wound, but he wanted to refresh his memory about the other details—the nail polish, the sandals, the smiley face bracelet, the toe ring, the open switchblade, the tire tracks. He'd come a long way since glimpsing the body from Grossman's helicopter. Now that he had a name and identity for the victim, the scene had come to life. It told a story.

Each detail added to a picture of the person who had been Amanda Hoffman. Parrott ran through them slowly, then quickly, hoping to jog something in his brain. What stood out for him now was what was missing. There was no bullet casing, no gun. Nothing pertaining to having recently had a baby—no bottles or diaper bag. No wallet or handbag—what was that word the salesclerk had used to describe Amanda's shoulder bag? No satchel.

Parrott imagined the person or persons who had been on the promontory with her. After the shooting, the killer would most likely have taken steps to clean things up, to remove whatever he or she had touched. Whatever items had been removed had the potential to complete the story. Parrott wished he could find them, but even if he didn't, he *would* find the young woman's killer.

He finished his salad and recycled the container. The legal pad with suspect boxes drew his attention again. He had already listed Mooney and Barton, as well as the reasons he suspected each of them. Now he wrote T.J. Bath's name in the third box. T.J. was dressed and out on the Campbell property early on the morning of the murder but could easily have crossed over to Mooney's without being observed. While he typically went to work in the

Polaris, Kate's SUV was parked at the cottage, and he might have taken that. His background included a prior conviction and an illegitimate daughter, both of which he'd kept secret from his wife. Could a man who kept important secrets like that be trusted to tell the truth? More importantly, T.J. might have had a motive—to take the baby from Amanda Hoffman and place it on the back steps for his wife to find. The sturdy box might even have come from his basement. T.J.'s behavior ever since had been questionable, as well.

Parrott underlined the word *motive* and turned his thoughts to Kate. Kate's desire for a child—

Before Parrott could write the "K" in the next suspect box, his cellphone rang. Maria was getting back to him already. "That was fast," he said.

"What can I say? My mother was a drill sergeant."

"Be sure to thank her for me." Parrott couldn't imagine a better coroner to work with. Not only was she fast—her work was impeccable. "What've you got?"

"I was able to eke out one more fleck of blood from the blanket. Hope you don't need more tests. I'm able to answer the question you posed. For certain, the blood on the blanket did not come from the victim's vagina as part of the afterbirth. Straight blood, no mucous, this sample came from either the gunshot wound or another wound on the woman's body." Maria's voice held that triumphant tone that announced what she deemed to be good news. Of course, one might argue that any news coming from a coroner wouldn't be good.

"That's wonderful, Maria. Thank you so much." Parrott worked at matching her enthusiasm with his own. In truth, Parrott *was* happy. Another piece had fallen into place. He was developing a hypothetical timeline in which Hoffman gave birth between twenty-four and forty-eight hours before she was killed on the promontory. Between those two events, Hoffman had produced breast milk, and apparently fed the baby. The blood on the blanket had come from a pre-mortem wound, possibly on the part of the face or head, which was subsequently obliterated. Perhaps the victim and her assailant had gotten into a violent confrontation, causing bleeding and escalating into murder. Parrott's gut told him

the baby had been at the scene of the murder at the time when Amanda's blood soiled the baby blanket. If that were the case, Amanda was not the one to transport the baby to the cottage. The person who did that, then, was most likely the murderer.

# CHAPTER SIXTY-THREE

Parrott left work early, so he could stop by Chesco with the empty box sitting in his trunk. He hoped to catch Jerry before the technician went home for the day.

"Oh, no, not another baby?" Jerry pointed to the box in Parrott's hand as he waved the detective into his tiny office. "Wanta sit?"

Parrott lowered himself into the metal chair and set the box on the floor at his feet. "No more babies, thank goodness, but I'd like to compare this to the box you have."

"Sure looks the same. C'mon back to the evidence room with me." Jerry tossed Parrott a package containing a plastic smock, gloves, booties, mask, and hairnet. He opened another package for himself.

Parrott could count on one hand the number of times he'd been allowed into the Chesco evidence room. Contamination of evidence stored there was a huge concern, so personnel were instructed to limit visitors and to take extra precautions whenever bringing someone in, including themselves. Important cases could be won or lost depending on what happened to a piece of stored evidence, and these days, with DNA-shedding, the protocols were strict.

"I don't have to go in," Parrott said. "You can take the box in without me."

"No. You might observe something I'd miss. We can tag-team it."

Parrott donned the protective garb while he explained that the box he'd brought in had held a case of liquor. "I'm not concerned about prints. I just want to see if the size, weight, and construction of the two boxes match closely enough that the evidentiary box might have come from the same source."

"Gotcha." Jerry led Parrott into the evidence room. All the items related to this case were stored in a wide locker and tagged with a case number. Inside, each item was tagged, as well. So far, the box, the baby's diaper and garments, the bloodied blanket, the empty milk bottles, the victim's toe ring, and the switchblade

resided on the shelves and floor of the locker. All were contained in sealed and labeled paper bags.

Jerry lifted the bag with the box from the floor of the locker and carried it to an evidence bench on the other side of the room. He invited Parrott to set the comparison box on the bench "Let's check out these puppies," Jerry said, handing Parrott a pair of goggles and putting another pair on, himself. He opened the resealable closure and lifted the baby's box out. He turned on the UV light, and fingerprints on both boxes appeared like magic.

"You say you aren't interested in the prints on the second box?" Jerry asked. "You can see there are quite a few."

"That's right." Parrott stared at the number of prints on the evidentiary box, grateful that UV light would protect the prints from deterioration. That box would be a treasure one day, when the case went to trial. At least he hoped so. "All I need to know now is whether these two boxes might have come from the same manufacturer. Since they're unmarked, I don't have much to go on."

Jerry pulled out an instrument that measured size to the millimeter. As he measured the various dimensions, Parrott recorded the data on his cellphone. Length, width, height for the box, and the same for the flaps matched. Then he weighed each of the boxes on a scale. Each weighed 1.247379 kilograms, or 2.75 pounds.

"Looks like a match," Parrott said. "The color matches, too."

"I have an idea," Jerry said. "You said this box held a case of scotch?" When Parrott nodded, he said, "Scotch bottles are heavy. Let's see if there are any indentations in the bottom inside."

Jerry held the lamp over the box and leaned over the edge, his face next to Parrott's. His voice took on a playful tone. "I don't think this box is big enough for the both of us."

"That's okay," Parrott said, backing away. "It's your party."

Jerry shone the UV light into the box and peered into the bottom. "Hey, did you see what the bottles looked like? Were they square?"

"Yes. Twelve of them."

"Look, the marks are faint, but you can see where the bottles sat." He moved aside so Parrott could see. "Now, let's see if the

other box has the same." Jerry bent over the evidentiary box with the light. "This one isn't as clean. There's all kind of fibers and other debris from its service as a baby cradle, but we'll ignore all that."

Jerry moved the light around for what seemed like an eternity. Finally, he stood back and whistled into his mask. "See what you think, Parrott. Unless my eyes are playing tricks on me, I'm finding those same pressure marks."

Parrott held his breath and leaned over the box with the light. "'Glory be,' as my grandma used to say. I think we've proved what we set out to prove." He slapped Jerry on the back. "I owe you big time."

Behind the goggles, Jerry's eyes crinkled. "Well, if you get a couple of bottles of that scotch for comparison purposes—"

Parrott laughed. "Sure, Jerry. No problem."

"Just kidding. You might say *I* owe *you*, Parrott. You're keeping me in business." Also a forensic photographer, Jerry unlocked a closet where his camera equipment was stored. "I'll take the pics and save them to the case file. You're planning to leave the second box here, right?"

"You bet." Parrott offered to stay and help with the photos and clean up, but Jerry shooed him out of the lab.

"Go home and tell that beautiful wife of yours that ol' Jerry says hello."

Tonya and Jerry had met a couple of years ago when Parrott called Chesco to fingerprint the bathroom at Blake Allmond's house during his post-funeral gathering. "Will do."

Parrott removed his goggles and set them down on the counter. When he left the lab, he discarded the disposable protective clothing and headed for his car. If it weren't so undignified, he might have skipped out the door. The baby's box could be tied, circumstantially, to Stuart Mooney's Christmas gifts. Parrott chuckled. For him, Christmas came early.

# CHAPTER SIXTY-FOUR

After dinner, the Parrotts took advantage of the clear, brisk night to swim in their heated pool. There wouldn't be many more evenings like this for a long while. Parrott swam laps along the length of the pool, enjoying the exercise under the fairy lights. Tonya stayed in the shallow end using weights for core strength.

"Aren't you going to swim?" Parrott asked.

"I don't want to ruin my hair. I just had it done yesterday. But you keep on. I'm enjoying the view."

After a while, they climbed out of the pool, shed their suits, and donned their long, fluffy bathrobes. Shivering and laughing, they ran into the house, where they made two cups of hot chocolate and collapsed on the family room sofa. Horace called from his cage, "Oh, boy. Oh, boy."

Parrott stirred his cocoa and took a swig. "You know, when I was a kid, I only had access to the public swimming pool. Later I lifeguarded there. I never dreamed I'd have a swimming pool at my house."

"Me, either. Or such a big, strong partner to swim with. I saw those powerful strokes, Ollie. I'll bet you burned at least a thousand calories."

"I hope you're right. That D-aspartic acid's made me hungry day and night."

Tonya scooted closer and leaned her head onto his chest. "I hope the drug's doing its job."

Parrott thought of the Hidalgos, Juanita and Clara, and everyone else who went through some process to have a baby. "I have a great idea. Why don't we go upstairs and try to find out?"

Tonya laughed that throaty laugh that spoke of more than humor. "Have you practiced that pickup line long?"

Parrott nuzzled her neck. "I'll show you a pickup line." He lifted her into his arms and waltzed toward the stairs.

❊ ❊ ❊

At precisely 2:48 a.m., Parrott's cellphone rang. He'd left it on the kitchen counter before covering Horace's cage and going upstairs. The shrill ringtone compensated for the distance and pulled him out of bed and downstairs. He answered on the third ring.

"Detective Parrott. This is Kim from the Public Safety Answering Point (PSAP). We received a 911 call from a home in your jurisdiction. Suspected break-in. We've dispatched a county sheriff's deputy, but he might need backup, and I thought you might want to go out."

The PSAP was managed by trained personnel twenty-four hours a day. If the call fit the protocols for a true emergency, they were obligated to respond with swift action. As a detective, Parrott almost never was called, but if needed, he was always willing.

Kim continued in a matter-of-fact tone. "I couldn't reach Officer Randy Barton, so I'm going up the chain of command."

Fully awake now, Parrott dashed upstairs, trying to hurry without waking Tonya. "Sure. What's the address?"

"The property's named Moonglow. Off Strasburg Road in Coatesville. Do you know it?"

"I do. Tell the officer I'll be in plain clothes." Adrenalin powered through his body. His wish to get into the Mooney estate might actually be fulfilled. Parrott grabbed the pants, shirt, socks, and shoes he kept at the front of his closet for these types of emergencies. He scooted back down the stairs, while Kim told him the details she knew—housekeeper alone in the house, loud noises upstairs near her bedroom. "She's locked herself in her room."

"Okay, we'll handle it." Parrott dressed quickly and stuffed his badge and wallet into his back pants pocket. He unlocked a cabinet in the utility room, where he kept a fully stocked duty belt, including a pistol. He needed to be prepared for whatever might happen at Moonglow.Before he moved to West Chester, he could have been there in ten or fifteen minutes, but he was a good thirty-five minutes away in normal traffic. At three a.m., however, the streets were mostly deserted. He set the magnetic roof light on his car, started the engine, and hit the accelerator

hard, knowing if he were noticed, the officer would join into the rush to the Mooney mansion.

Arriving at Moonglow in just under eighteen minutes, Parrott doused his roof lights. The sheriff's department cruiser was in the driveway, and the deputy most likely inside. The sky was charcoal turning to navy, but the full moon, combined with security lights strategically placed around the exterior of the house, cast an eerie glow on his path. On his way to the door, Parrott breathed in the acrid aroma of vegetation past its peak. He scanned the area and listened for any signs of an intruder, but aside from flickers of movement from an occasional insect or ground squirrel, all was quiet.

As he approached the front door, it eased open, and light poured out. The deputy greeted him with a hushed voice, and Parrott showed his badge. "I'm glad you could come out. We've got one very anxious woman. I had a heck of a time getting her to leave her bedroom. I had to get PSAP to patch me through to her."

"What about the alarm system? Is the house secure?" Parrott asked.

"System's on the fritz. Haven't searched yet. The housekeeper wouldn't let me till you got here." He held out a hand. "Name's Simon, last name, that is. Lady's right here beside me."

Parrott crossed the threshold, his senses turned hypervigilant and his hand near his gun. As glad as he was for a legitimate reason to be in the house, he wasn't crazy about walking into a gigantic mansion where someone felt unsafe. He glanced at the marble staircase with its carved wooden banister. With three stories and who knew how many bedrooms, the house contained many hiding places. He could understand how the housekeeper might feel uneasy being there alone.

He nodded at the pale, fragile woman in a long, gray velour bathrobe, wire-rimmed glasses pushed up to the top of her head. Her face was all eyes, darting from Simon to Parrott. Her lips pulled inward until they disappeared.

Deputy Simon introduced Parrott to Josephine Wisniewski. Parrott nodded and took charge. "You've heard noises?"

"Yes, the third time this week. The creakings keep me up at night. I'm scared somebody's lurking in the shadows."

Parrott assured her they would get to the bottom of this. "Can you tell us specifically where you've heard the noises?" He unsnapped the cover over his pistol.

Josephine wrapped her robe tighter and retied the sash. "Follow me. I can explain better in the kitchen."

Parrott put an arm out to stop her and turned to Simon. "Did you clear the kitchen?"

The deputy nodded, and Parrott allowed her to proceed. She led them through a modern kitchen, almost twice the size of Parrott's. Beyond the storage and work areas, the room extended to a breakfast counter, dining area, sitting area with a big-screen TV, and glass walls surrounding an indoor pool. In daylight, the area might have been cheery, but now, with only a single light over the sink, illuminating dark blocks of counter and appliance, the room was cold and eerie.

To the right of the pool entrance stood a set of stairs, hidden in shadows. The housekeeper pointed in that direction. "This is the servants' staircase. It takes you to the second, third, and fourth floor. I can take you."

"No," Parrott said. "You need to stay down here where you're safe." He eyed the door to the servants' stairs. "Does this door lock?"

"Yes, close it and I'll show you." Josephine moved the glasses down from the crown of her head and demonstrated the locking mechanism.

"Can someone open the locked door from the inside?"

"Only with the key."

Parrott checked to make sure there was no key in the inside of the lock and then relocked the door. "And the main staircase leads to the same floors?"

"Only to the third. To get to the fourth, you go over to the servants' stairs."

Parrott explained that he and Deputy Simon would use the main stairs and keep the servants' stairs closed off.

Josephine gave the men a detailed explanation of the upstairs layout. The second floor was where the family stayed. The third floor was for guests. The fourth floor was where she lived. The rest of the fourth floor was storage space. "The noises, they come at night. They sound like a man stumbling around the house, looking for something."

"Okay," Parrott said, ushering her to the library, where he made sure the room was empty. "You stay here and lock the door." Before he left, Parrott asked, "Ms. Wisniewski, have you noticed anything unusual in the house recently? Any sign of forced entry? Anything missing?"

The woman shook her head. "Only the noises, only at night."

He made eye contact with Deputy Simon. He was about to ask an important question, and he wanted to make sure the sheriff's representative was listening. "I understand you are alone in the house. Can you tell me when Mr. or Mrs. Mooney will return?"

"I dunno. Mrs. Mooney, she went to her daughter's for the baby's birth. An' Mr. Mooney, he didn't tell me when he comes back."

Parrott nodded. "In the indefinite absence of the owners of the house, would you like us to search for an intruder?"

"Oh, yes. Please." The petite woman clutched her elbows and rocked herself. "I'm so afraid."

"Okay," Parrott said in the calmest, steadiest voice he could muster. "We'll take a good look, and check out every room in the house, floor by floor."

Leaving Josephine in the library, Parrott turned to his colleague. "It's a big house. How do you want to do this?"

"Why don't we go floor by floor, together? You can search one side of the house, and I'll take the other. That way, if either of us needs backup, we can shout. When you've finished your half, meet me at the staircase."

"Sounds like a plan," Parrott said. He sped through his half of the first floor, which included the formal dining room, library, utility room, and back into the kitchen.

He motioned Simon to the wide curving staircase in the entry hall, brandishing a flashlight in his left hand. The other hand hovered over the duty belt, ready to draw his pistol if needed.

Ascending the stairs together, they landed on the second-floor hall. Their flashlights danced before them in a weird waltz, moving from side to side, searching for anything that moved or made noise. Occasionally the floorboards groaned under their weight. Except for the rustling of their own movements, all was quiet.

Energized and vigilant, Parrott took off to search his part of the second floor, not wanting to waste a second.

# CHAPTER SIXTY-FIVE

The second floor of Mooney's mansion consisted of four bedrooms, each having a private bathroom. The formal staircase bisected the wide hallway, and the servants' staircase was at the far end.

The primary bedroom, near the top of the stairs, was part of the wing Parrott searched. The sheer size of the boudoir told Parrott that this part of the house had been remodeled, even before he examined the modern bathroom. Houses as old as this one generally didn't have big bedrooms, although they did have sitting rooms and parlors. Parrott was sure walls had been knocked out to create this palatial suite, but he wasn't there to admire the décor. He whipped through the room, wall by wall, opening closets the sizes of rooms and shining his flashlight around them. Everything smelled fresh—a combination of lemon, mint, and sandalwood— even though the room appeared to have been unused. The king-sized four poster bed sat about eighteen inches off the floor, so he knelt to shine his light underneath. Because his purpose there was limited to the scope of investigating the 911 call, his search was limited to areas where an intruder might conceal himself.

Finding nothing, not even dust, he moved on to the bathroom. Neither the modern tub, shaped like an old-fashioned clawfoot, nor the immense glass shower stall with a marble bench and fancy double faucets and heads, could provide cover for an intruder, and none of the cabinets were big enough to hide a person.

He moved on to the other bedroom and bath in his part of the floor. Two closets held empty hangers and what looked like extra pillows and blankets folded into zippered bags on the top shelves. Another king-size bed, a foot off the floor, hid nothing underneath. Again, the room was immaculate. *There must be a whole staff of house cleaners to tend to these rooms.*

Before returning to the main staircase to meet up with Simon, Parrott made sure the second-floor entrance to the servants' staircase was locked. The two men were ready to tackle the

upper floors, where Josephine had heard the frightening noises. If someone was hiding in the house, this might be the most likely area.

On the third-floor landing, the men exchanged glances, and Parrott drew his gun. This hallway was darker and narrower with more closed doors. Parrott guessed there were five or six smaller bedrooms and three or four baths. In addition to being warmer, this level of the house had a different, almost Gothic, vibe.

Parrott pointed in the direction that matched his end on the second floor. "Meet you back here in a few minutes." He started at the door in the middle of the hallway, planning to work his way down to the end.

As he expected, the bedroom was compact compared to those on the second floor. Moonlight sifted in from around the closed draperies, but it wasn't enough, so Parrott kept his flashlight on. The double bed had a metal headboard and a thick, fluffy comforter. Parrott shone his light under the bed. No person was hiding there, but this time the floor was littered with dust bunnies. Perhaps the person assigned to clean this end didn't work as often or as thoroughly.

He flung open the closet door, and a light inside came on automatically. Except for empty hangers and boxes stored on the closet shelves, the closet was devoid of personal effects. Parrott started to close the closet door, when he did a double take. The nondescript boxes on the back shelf were the same size and shape as the abandoned baby's box.

Parrott would have loved to open the boxes and examine the contents, but he needed to stick to his purpose, searching for an intruder. He closed the closet door, checked out the adjacent bathroom, and moved on to the next bedroom on the floor.

There were two more bedrooms on his end of the third floor. He entered the first of these, still holding his breath and hovering his hand over his gun. Complacency in police work could be deadly. Parrott had only to think of last year's brush with fentanyl poisoning to remember that.

This bedroom differed from the others, because it was furnished with both a double bed and a baby crib. Perhaps the Mooneys were preparing for a visit from their unborn grandchild in Chicago,

or maybe they had other guests who brought little ones to visit Brandywine Valley. There was nothing under the crib, but the bed was another four poster, about eighteen inches off the floor. Gun in one hand, flashlight in the other, Parrott knelt and then flattened himself to look under the bed. Again, the floor was littered with dust. A baby pacifier suggested that the room had been inhabited by at least one young guest. A green plastic comb lay next to it, and a candy wrapper, and what looked like a crumpled receipt.

When he opened the walk-in closet, the light came on, and an opened carton of diapers fell off the shelf above him and crashed on the floor at his feet, spilling contents. He jumped back, but immediately sprang into the closet to search for a person who might have wanted to distract him. Several ladies' dresses hung from the rack, blocking Parrott's view of the back of the closet.

Parrott swiped them aside to examine the rear of the closet, but the only thing of interest was another unmarked cardboard box on the floor. Parrott closed the closet door and moved on to the bathroom. Here the toilet roll was empty, and the bathmat was pushed against the wall. This wing of the house was definitely due for housekeeping.

Having heard nothing from Deputy Simon, Parrott assumed things were calm on the other half of the floor. He had one more bedroom to search. The door to this room creaked, and the inside was smaller and darker than the others. In fact, the room held a musty smell, as if no one had inhabited it for a long time. A foreboding chill came over him as he pushed the door open all the way. What better place for an intruder to hide than in this remote, neglected room of the house?

He flicked on the overhead light and scanned the bookshelves, double bed, single nightstand, and low dresser in the room. A mirror over the dresser had pockmarks around its edges. Bereft of closet or attached bathroom, this room stuck out like a malformed appendage. Perhaps it had been used as an office or servant's room in the past.

While Parrott took in details, he also steeled himself to look under the bed. Of all the under-bed hiding places, this one drew his attention like metal shavings to a magnet. He fell to the floor in

a prone position at the middle of the bed, shoving his gun before him.

No person hid in the shadows, but something else grabbed his focus and sent lightning shocks through his body. He dropped his gun. At the far end, shoved beneath the headboard, lay a large satchel with a clear plastic shoulder strap. Light in color, perhaps beige and yellow, the handbag lit up Parrott's brain. He questioned whether he was imagining it. He blinked. It was still there.

Parrott wanted to crawl under the bed and grab the bag that he believed to be the one Amanda Hoffman had carried into the children's store. But he couldn't. Without a warrant he would probably render the item unusable as evidence. Nevertheless, his mind buzzed. Now he could place Amanda--or her killer--inside the Mooney mansion. His testimony to that effect would lend probable cause to his request for a warrant to search the house.

Even though it wasn't permitted, he took a photo of the shoulderbag. He couldn't wait to pay a visit to Judge Manetti for the warrant, but first he had to find the resident intruder.

# CHAPTER SIXTY-SIX

When Parrott met Deputy Simon in the middle of the third floor, he practically bounced on his feet from what he'd found under the bed. He formed a plan for how to proceed, but he couldn't interrupt the work at hand, so he kept mum.

"All right, Simon, ready to search the attic? That's where she said the noise was. One of us can guard the stairs while the other checks out the maid's room and the storage area."

"Good idea. Flip a coin?"

"Nah, I'll go." Gun in one hand, flashlight in the other, Parrott led the way up the narrow back stairs to the fourth floor. On the landing, he switched on a small overhead light. He turned right to enter Josephine's quarters.

An overwhelming raspberry smell hit him in the face, and his eyes were drawn to a plug-in fragrance near the baseboard. A shaded bedside lamp cast a circle of light onto the floor beside a twin bed. A nightstand, dresser with a TV, and an old-fashioned radiator filled the room, and a window with Venetian blinds faced what Parrott thought was the back of the house. A narrow closet door stood in the corner.

He did a cursory look in the tiny closet. The bed frame was low enough to the floor that a person couldn't slide under, so he didn't look under it. The adjoining bathroom contained a small tub with an open shower curtain around it.

Ready to leave the modest room, Parrott shone his light around the baseboards. A scuff mark on the wooden floor drew his attention, mainly because of its location in the corner. He knelt to examine it, but the raspberry smell was overwhelming him, so he exited the room, closing the door behind him.

Opposite the bedroom door was a wall of unpainted sheetrock. A cheap-looking door stood in the middle. Parrott holstered his gun in order to turn the doorknob, but the moment his hand touched the

imitation brass, a scuffling sound arrested his attention. Someone or something was moving beyond this door.

Heart pounding, he turned off the light in the vestibule. He didn't want to make himself a perfect target backlit for someone sitting in the dark attic. He drew his gun and held it ready.

Simon, possibly taking the turned-off light as a signal, clambered up the stairs behind him. Parrott turned the doorknob as quietly as possible and then shoved the door open with the barrel of his pistol. The storage area was dank and smelly. There were nooks and dark corners everywhere he turned.

Parrott found a light switch and flipped it on. The attic was full of objects—a big steamer trunk, an old desk, a few lamps, a wardrobe rack with zippered bags of clothes hanging. Shelves were built into the walls around the perimeter, spaced far enough apart that a person could roll under them to hide.

"Police. Drop your weapon and come out," Parrott shouted.

An echo reminded him of a hooting owl, mocking him. Parrott swung his pistol to the right and left, systematically covering the entire space.

Without being asked, the deputy came in behind Parrott with his gun drawn. A scratching sound came from one of the shelves straight ahead.

Parrott crouched, his heart thumping. He held his gun in front of him like a shield, hoping he wouldn't have to use it, but knowing he would if he had to. "I know you're in here," he shouted. His voice reverberated. The long shelf in front of him shaded everything beneath it. "You're surrounded," he shouted into the dark space.

Simon squatted and shone his flashlight under the shelf, and Parrott flattened himself on the floor, aiming the gun in front of him. A rustling sound attracted Parrott's gaze to the front of the area. A pair of eyes gleamed from the darkness, and Parrott gulped air. He grabbed his own flashlight and thrust it into the corner. A very frightened-looking raccoon stared back at him.

Relieved to have cornered a raccoon instead of a person, but still aware of the danger, Parrott kept his voice calm. "You secure the door. I'll clear the rest of the attic," he said to the deputy. He eased himself into an upright position and walked forward, keeping his gun at the ready.

After making sure there were no people or other animals in the attic, both men stepped outside and closed the door. Parrott let out a huge whoosh of air. "Raccoon. No wonder the housekeeper heard noises at night." He motioned to the deputy to head down the stairs to the third floor.

"Raccoons can be aggressive." Simon turned off his flashlight and holstered his gun. "She needs to get somebody to remove it."

Parrott stretched his back. "Absolutely. The county can help her with that. In the meantime, she shouldn't go back up there."

Simon brushed his palms against each other. "You think we can phone this one in now?"

"Yeah, but there's something I'd like you to do for me first."

# CHAPTER SIXTY-SEVEN

Parrott and the deputy sheriff descended the staircase much more slowly than they had ascended it. The time on Parrott's phone was 6:14. They'd been in the house more than two hours.

"What do you want me to do?" Deputy Simon asked. Age, extra bulk, and shorter legs probably caused him to huff to keep up.

Parrott paused at the top of the second floor, giving his colleague a moment to catch his breath. Before they were within earshot of the housekeeper, Parrott needed to share what he'd seen under the bed.

"You know I'm investigating the murder of a young woman whose body was found on this property, right?" Parrott made eye contact. "I can't combine that case with this 911 call, as you know."

Simon nodded and massaged the back of his neck. "Yeah. Without a warrant, yada, yada. But you saw something?"

"Yes. In the routine search for an intruder. Under a bed that was high enough off the floor to accommodate a person hiding." Parrott kept his voice steady and quiet, despite his excitement. "A distinctive shoulder bag I believe might belong to the victim. I didn't touch it, and I can't take you to see it, but I wanted you to hear about it in case I need backup later on." Parrott described the bag and its location in the third-floor bedroom.

"You got it," the deputy said. "Sounds warrant-worthy to me. Let me know if you need me to corroborate."

"Thanks, man." Parrott resumed bounding down the stairs with Deputy Simon a few steps behind. When they arrived on the first floor, they reported to the library, where they found an exhausted-looking Josephine, pacing along the wall with the windows. She flinched when they entered the room.

"Oh, I'm so glad to see you. I've been so worried." She continued to wring her hands, as if, when she stopped, her heart would cease to beat, as well. "What did you find?"

"You can relax, Ms. Wisniewski. Let's sit." Parrott led the way to the sofa and chairs. When the woman was seated, he explained that the noises she'd heard on the fourth floor could be attributed to the raccoon they'd found in the attic.

"We checked every room on every floor," Deputy Simon said. "There was no intruder—human, that is."

Parrott said, "I don't know how he got up there, but we left him shut in that attic area. Unless he leaves the same way he came in, he'll be looking for food and water. Probably best if you don't go back up there till you know he's gone."

"The county has an animal control department that can help." Simon scrolled on his cellphone. "I'll write this number down for you."

"I need to tell Mr. or Mrs. Mooney," the housekeeper said, finally unclasping her hands. "I try not to bother them, but they need to know this." She squinted through her glasses at the clock on the mantle. "Probably too early to call Chicago now. Maybe I should send a text." She withdrew a cellphone from a pocket in her robe, then replaced it. "I dunno. Will you be leaving soon?" The wire-rimmed glasses magnified her watery blue eyes, making her resemble a just-caught fish.

*She probably doesn't want to stay here alone.* "Pretty quick. What time do other employees usually arrive for work?" A twinge swept through Parrott's gut as he thought of the third-floor bedrooms that needed cleaning.

"Martha's due here by eight-thirty. Maybe Mrs. Mooney, she won't want anyone in the house until it's safe." Josephine gripped her cellphone. "I'm gonna text her now. I wanna let her talk to you if she has questions." After sending her text, she waved the officers toward the kitchen. "Let me fix you some coffee while we wait."

Before Parrott could decline the coffee, Josephine's cellphone rang. "It's the missus," she said, as she pounced on the answer button. Parrott listened intently while the housekeeper described the early morning events—the noises, the 911 call, the responders, the search, and the raccoon.

Josephine pressed her free hand against her ear, although the kitchen was quiet. "Yes, ma'am. Sorry to bother you." More

listening, and then, "Sure. You can talk to Detective Parrott." She covered the phone and whispered to Parrott. "Ms. Catherine is in labor. They're at the hospital."

Parrott glanced at the sheriff's deputy and took the phone. "Yes, Mrs. Mooney. I'm here at the house with Deputy Simon of the sheriff's office. We've conducted a thorough search of the house from top to bottom."

Mrs. Mooney's voice was so subdued. He also covered an ear in order to hear. "I can't talk long," she said, "but I want to make sure Josephine and all the rest of the staff is safe. What does my husband think?"

Chills raised the gooseflesh on the back of Parrott's neck. "Mr. Mooney?" he asked. "Isn't he there in Chicago with you?"

"No. I'm here with Catherine and her husband. I thought Stuart was taking care of things at home." She let out a long exhale, laced with exasperation. "Let me talk to Josephine again."

Parrott returned the phone to its owner, who nodded and said a few more, "Yes, ma'am's." When she disconnected, she turned to Parrott and Simon. "Mrs. Mooney says I should tell Martha to stay home. She doesn't want anyone in the house until the raccoon is gone. She told me if they don't get it out by tonight to sleep in a hotel."

Josephine made a quick call to Martha, and Simon called the animal control people. Then Parrott accompanied the housekeeper to her bedroom, so she could pack her clothes and toiletries, just in case. They returned to the kitchen, and the officers said their goodbyes, leaving Josephine to wait for the county to come out.

Three things had Parrott jazzed: the shoulder bag under the bed, the calling off of the servants, and the fact that Mooney had apparently not gone to Chicago. With the proverbial wings on his feet, Parrott was off to petition Judge Manetti for a search warrant.

# CHAPTER SIXTY-EIGHT

Kate had begun to trust her husband again. T.J. appeared to be all in with regard to baby-making, so they'd laughingly agreed to practice morning, noon, and night whenever possible. Even if they weren't successful, the renewed intimacy was breaking down the barriers between them, and Kate had a pep in her step that hadn't been there for a long time.

As for T.J., after this morning's close encounter, he'd whistled on his way out to work at five a.m. "See you at lunchtime, my love." His parting kiss was a delicious promise.

Kate and Lucy watched him go off in the Polaris. Kate was torn between starting her chores and returning to bed for a little while. A big yawn persuaded her to get more sleep. She wanted to keep herself in tiptop condition in case she was pregnant.

As she pulled the covers up to her chin, she luxuriated in the freedom she had to sleep late if she wanted, to bake and sell her bread, to maintain her small house the way she liked, without having to worry about servants' interfering with her privacy. These were the simple things in life that she had fallen in love with, as much as she had with her ruggedly handsome dark-haired, gray-eyed husband. She was already looking forward to their "afternoon delight."

Lucy rested on the floor next to her mistress, and the two fell asleep. Kate's was filled with a bizarre dream, however. She and Lucy were sitting on the edge of a creek. A large fishing pole filled her hand. Catherine and Steven showed up with poles and plopped down on either side of her. Catherine pulled up fish after fish, each one bigger than the last. Each fish had the face of a baby. Steven threaded worms on his hook and cast off further than either of the girls, but each time he reeled in a catch, his hook was weighted with a shoe, a hat, a white brassiere—never a fish. Kate, who sat in between the cousins, kept hoping for a beautiful baby-faced fish like Catherine's, but so far, she hadn't brought in anything, and time was running out.

Kate awakened with a headache. The dream slipped away from her like the ebbing tide. She remembered Steven, though, sitting next to her quietly with his baited line. She decided to text her cousin. Even if he was at work at the church, she wanted him to know she was thinking of him.

*Hey, cousin. I dreamed we were fishing, and it made me realize I hadn't thanked you properly since I got back home.*

*Hello.*

*Are you at work?*

*Yes. Taking a break.*

*T.J. came home. We are back together again.* Kate looked around the kitchen to find something to eat.

*Good.*

*Thanks for letting me stay with you.*

*No problem.*

*Let me know if you come out this way any time soon.*

*Catherine's having baby now.*

*Really? Catherine's in labor? That's exciting. You're going to be an uncle.*

*Guess so.*

The conversation had just about reached its limit, so Kate typed goodbye. Despite Steven's difficulty in communication, or perhaps because of it, she held him close to her heart. Steven didn't have a mean bone in his body. He had followed Catherine and her around like a pesky little brother when they were kids, and now that they were adults, there was nothing he wouldn't do for her. Kate hoped someday he would find someone to share his life with.

Speaking of sharing one's life, Kate checked the clock, realizing she didn't have much time to straighten up the house, feed Lucy, and prepare lunch for T.J. She jumped in the shower and washed her hair. She brushed her teeth and put on a minimum amount of makeup. She put on a pair of soft wash pants and a V-necked top with no bra. And she was barefooted.

Filling Lucy's dish with kibble and carrots, she cut extra carrots for a chef's salad. Romaine lettuce, tomatoes, Swiss cheese, hard-boiled eggs, and ham would make a good lunch.

T.J. pushed open the back door at eleven a.m. He smelled of horses and hay, but he wasn't sweaty or dirty. "How's your day been?" he asked, his eyes passing over her skimpy clothes.

"So far, so good. I texted Steven. He told me Catherine's in labor."

"That's nice. What's for lunch?"

"Chef's salad. I didn't think you'd be hungry so early."

T.J. wrapped Kate in his arms and lifted her off the kitchen floor. "I'll show you how hungry I am, and then we can eat lunch. I've got to get back to the barn pretty quick." He carried her into the bedroom, Clark Gable style, and closed the door behind him.

T.J. ended up taking his salad to go in a plastic container. When he left, Kate dedicated herself to doing laundry and straightening up the three-room cottage. She hadn't cleaned the fireplace mantle, the bric-a-brac cabinet, or the gun cabinet for a really long time, so she pulled out all the stops to make these shine.

The gun cabinet was locked, but they kept a key on a nail in the top right-hand kitchen cabinet. She unlocked the cabinet and stared at the guns inside, a rifle T.J. had received from his dad when he was a child, another rifle he preferred to use for hunting, a shotgun he took when he went trap shooting, and a .45 caliber pistol he'd inherited from an uncle. None of these was loaded. T.J. had taught her about gun safety, and she was particular about making sure the guns and ammunition were kept in separate places.

Kate began removing the guns and dusting them one by one, then replacing them in their designated spots in the cabinet. When she pulled the last one out, she noticed another gun lying on the floor of the cabinet in the back. It was a .38 caliber pistol, one she'd never seen before. She picked it up carefully, checked to make sure the safety was on, and opened the cylinder. A sharp intake of breath expressed her surprise. The unfamiliar gun was loaded.

# CHAPTER SIXTY-NINE

Despite being called out of bed at three a.m., not having had a drop of coffee, and having run up and down a four-story house, Parrott wasn't a bit tired. He was racing against time to get his probable cause affidavit and warrant to the courthouse for Judge Manetti's signature. The reason for the big rush was two-fold. He wanted to get in there to search before animal control could remove the raccoon, and before Martha, or whoever oversaw cleaning that third-floor bedroom, could remove the shoulder bag. He also wanted to keep a lid on the number of people who would know that he was searching.

The absence of both Mr. and Mrs. Mooney was convenient. The fact that Mr. Mooney hadn't gone to Chicago, as he stated in his letters to Parrott and his own attorney, sizzled in Parrott's brain. Before Parrott could deal with that, he needed to conduct a proper search of Moonglow. An added need for secrecy involved Officer Barton. Knowing Barton worked for Mooney, Parrott couldn't let any information leak through the department's channels, because that might tip Mooney off and shut down all hope of obtaining evidence from the house.

Parrott had discovered three significant pieces of evidence: the file labeled "Hoffman, Amanda" on Mooney's desk; the plain same-size, same-shape boxes as the one in which the baby was found located in the upstairs closets; and the shoulder bag believed to belong to the deceased woman, under the bed in the furthest third-floor bedroom.

He was pretty sure those would be enough to convince Manetti to authorize at least a limited-scope warrant. Mooney's wealth and stature in the community would undoubtedly protect the home from a full search, but that was okay. He put together the information and stopped by Schrik's office to clear everything before going to the courthouse.

Schrik was sitting at his desk with an unopened takeout container from Wawa. Their breakfast hoagie was a favorite of

Parrott's, and the aroma of bacon and eggs made Parrott's mouth water.

Schrik must have sensed Parrott's hunger, because he offered him a hoagie.

"No, no, I couldn't," Parrott said, though a geyser was erupting from beneath his tongue.

"Don't be silly, Parrott. I bought two, and I can't eat them both." Schrik opened the container and handed over the foil-wrapped sandwich. "Eat while it's still hot." He scooped up his own breakfast and took a large bite.

Parrott sat and gobbled a generous fourth of the sandwich at one time. "Mmm, this lives up to the hype every time." The affidavit could wait for a nutrition break.

"Sorry I didn't buy coffee. My doc says I need to cut down." Schrik chewed. "Never did drink as much as you, though. You must put away a gallon every day."

"Not anymore, Chief. I can't stand the smell or taste now. I've gone cold turkey."

"Like me and cigarettes, I guess. Can't believe I smoked for twenty plus years. Truly a nasty habit." Schrik took slower bites now. "What're you up to so early this morning?"

Parrott closed the office door and returned to finish his hoagie. He explained the three-a.m. call to Moonglow, the search, the objects, and their significance to the case. "It's looking more and more like Mooney's involved. And get this, Mooney stood me *and* his attorney up. Said he'd gone to Chicago. But when the housekeeper called Chicago to tell Mrs. Mooney about the raccoon in the attic, she didn't know anything about Mooney being in Chicago."

Schrik passed a napkin to Parrott, who dabbed at his mustache. "Another thing—the 911 call went to Barton first, but he was unavailable. Not that I'm complaining. I'm ecstatic to have gotten into the Mooney house. But where was Barton at three a.m.? The dirtier Mooney looks, the less I trust Barton."

"You're right, Parrott. We can't share any of this with Barton. In fact, I don't want you or anyone to have a conversation, even a mundane one, with him, unless I sanction it and am present. You still have his car?"

Parrott nodded, wondering how long he might have to keep it in his garage. "Oh, one more thing. Mrs. Mooney told the housekeeper that Catherine was in labor. Maybe being a new grandfather will flush out Stuart Mooney."

Schrik balled up his empty food wrapper and shot it toward the wastebasket, missing by about two inches. Sheepish, he scooted over in his chair to retrieve and dump it in. "Go ahead and get your warrant, Parrott. And keep me informed." He paused a few seconds before adding, "And regarding Barton, apply the mushroom theory—keep him in the dark and feed him BS."

Parrott thanked him for breakfast and headed for the door. Brandywine Valley was prized for its mushrooms, but Schrik's metaphor left a bad taste. Their little police department was shrinking faster than Parrott could count to three. He was glad the breakfast hoagie hadn't contained any mushrooms.

# CHAPTER SEVENTY

Judge Manetti's courtroom was practically empty, but the judge was on the bench when Parrott arrived, a few minutes after ten-thirty. Manetti had a reputation for being a stickler when it came to fine points of the law, as well as courthouse etiquette. That included not wasting time.

Knowing this, Parrott approached the clerk with his documents, preparing to wait as long as necessary to get an audience with the judge.

"The cases are moving quickly today," the clerk said. "As soon as he wraps up this one, he'll adjourn to chambers, and you can talk to him."

A few minutes later, Parrott presented his affidavit to the judge. "I can give you the background, or you can read it."

Manetti, dressed in his robe and looking stately with his black hair combed back from his forehead, twisted his thin lips into an expression somewhere between amusement and impatience. "I'll read."

He spent the next few minutes perusing the affidavit, working his mouth as he flipped pages. "Is this Stuart Mooney of Moonglow Scotch? The one with that big mansion in Brandywine Valley?"

"Yes, Your Honor. It is."

"I hope you've dotted your 'i's' and crossed your 't's.'"

"I have, Your Honor." The Mooney name, like so many others in Brandywine Valley, commanded power and respect, and Parrott understood Manetti's concern. His re-election bid next year could be affected by anything he put his name on.

"Let me get this straight," the judge said. "I understand why you need the shoulder bag and the folder on the Hoffman girl. Also the cardboard box. But tell me what makes you think there may be other evidence in any of the other bedrooms on the third floor of Mooney's house."

Parrott explained about the baby's pacifier under the bed in the room with the crib. "If I can tie that pacifier to the abandoned

newborn, I'll have a significant piece of evidence with regard to Ms. Hoffman's whereabouts when she delivered the baby and before she was killed." The judge interlineated the warrant before signing and thrusting it back into Parrott's hands. "I'm limiting the scope of your search to the two third-floor bedrooms and the library. Bring the inventory of what you find directly to my courtroom. And, Parrott, I pray to God whatever you find out will lead to the absolute truth."

Parrott flew out of the courthouse and drove back to Moonglow, armed with his hard-earned paperwork. He had already arranged for backup with the county sheriff's office if the warrant was signed, so all he had to do was text for someone to meet him there.

When he arrived at the mansion, the county's animal control van was parked on the driveway, and two men struggled to lift a bulky cage with a frantic-looking wild animal inside. The front door of the house and the back door of the van were open, and there was enough thrashing and grunting to create a fascinating drama.

Josephine stood at the door, one hand clapped to her mouth. No longer wearing her gray robe, she now had on jeans and a matching tank and sweater set in a shade of purple that made her look more refreshed than before.

Deputy Sheriff Sanders, a younger version of Simon, drove up at the same time Parrott climbed out of his car. Things were moving forward like a well-choreographed dance. Parrott filled him in on the early morning activities, assuring him that the house had been cleared. He explained the need for Sanders to sit with Ms. Wisniewski in the library while Parrott searched for evidence. The raccoon-catchers drove off with their quarry, and the two officers approached the housekeeper in tandem.

Wisps of hair had escaped her bun, and the quizzical look coming from behind the glasses brought a flash of empathy from Parrott. She had already been through a lot in the past few hours.

"I'm sorry to take you away from whatever you were doing," Parrott said. "Is there anyone else in the house?" He handed the warrant to the woman and watched while her eyes rolled over it. "The warrant authorizes me to conduct a partial search of the premises, specifically, the library and two third-floor bedrooms."

"But—the animal people just left. Maybe you should come back later."

Parrott had no intention of delaying his search, but he didn't want to frighten the woman by being overly aggressive. "No, ma'am. I need to conduct this search immediately. Deputy Sanders will stay with you in the kitchen. I'll be finished and out of here before you know it."

"Shouldn't I call Mrs. Mooney and get her permission?"

"You can let Mrs. Mooney know I'm here if you'd like, but this document comes from the court. Even if Mrs. Mooney were here, she couldn't stop me from conducting this search." He softened his approach with a smile. "You're free to use your cellphone to occupy your time while you and the deputy are in the kitchen."

She moved aside to let Parrott into the house.

"Thanks. I'll get started on the third floor and work my way down." He dashed up the stairs to the third floor and strode to the end of the hallway, where he had seen the distinctive-looking shoulder bag. Once in the room, he turned on the overhead light and dropped to the floor to peer under the bed.

His heart pounded. No one had disturbed the bag. He pulled out his cellphone and began snapping photos that showed the item in place, at the far end of the bed, under the headboard and next to the exterior wall. After he photographed the context, he moved the bed away from the wall, exposing the shoulder bag. Parrott set a dollar bill next to the bag to show its relative size.

A light coating of dust on the surface of the bag might be used to establish the time that had passed since the bag had been stashed there, so Parrott gloved up and brushed a small swath of dust away before taking a close-up shot. Many photos followed—close-ups of the handle, the sunbursts, the seams, the zipper, and several of the whole shoulder bag as it lay on the floor.

Parrott opened the bag and photographed the contents without removing any of them. He was mainly looking for a gun or other weapon inside the bag, but, finding none, he re-zipped and placed the bag inside a large paper evidence bag. He would take it back to the Chesco lab for more detailed processing.

If the shoulder bag belonged to Amanda Hoffman, as Parrott believed it did, what was it doing in this room of Stuart Mooney's

house? Did Amanda bring it here, herself? Parrott opened the bed coverings and sniffed for any lingering fragrances of cologne or perfume. He did the same in the bathroom medicine cabinet. If the bed had been slept in, someone had remade it afterwards. The sheets and blanket were smooth and well-tucked. There was no closet in the room, but Parrott checked the four drawers in the chest—all empty except for floral parchment lining paper.

Since it seemed highly unlikely that a woman would hide her own purse, Parrott was working on the theory that the shoulder bag had been stashed by someone other than Amanda Hoffman. If that were the case, was the stasher someone who lived in the house, or someone who was visiting? Josephine had told Parrott that the second-floor bedrooms were used by family, the third floor by guests.

Parrott moved on to the bedroom with the baby crib. Again, he was relieved to find it had not been cleaned since he was there, judging by the dust. He removed one of the cardboard boxes from the closet. Not heavy, the box contained an assortment of board games and crossword puzzle magazines. He removed the contents and carried the empty box to the top of the stairs. He would take it with him to compare to the abandoned baby box.

Parrott checked all the areas in the closet, the drawers, even the window ledges to make sure he wasn't overlooking something important. The license to search and seize items was a one-time-only privilege. He was thrilled to have taken possession of the shoulder bag, but he wished for more—a gun, a photograph, or something personalized with a name on it.

He dropped to the floor to look under the bed, where he had seen the baby pacifier before. There lay the dust-covered items left underneath—the candy wrapper, the pacifier, the comb, and the receipt. He used his phone to photograph the items, showing how close in proximity the other items were to the pacifier. When he'd taken several pictures, he moved the bed and took more photos under the overhead light. The pacifier drew his interest the most, because he might try to tie it to Baby Adalia.

He ignored the candy wrapper, but he examined the comb to see if there was any hair in it. Finding one, he bagged the comb. The final object was the folded piece of paper that looked like a

receipt of some kind. He unfolded the note and used the flashlight on his phone to illuminate the details.

His heart skipped a beat when he saw the printing at the top of the paper—Brandywine Creek Kids. The receipt showed a cash purchase made the previous Friday for a yellow homecoming ensemble.

# CHAPTER SEVENTY-ONE

In the library, Parrott zeroed in on Mooney's large antique roll-top desk. He hoped someone had cleaned off the top of the desk and moved the Hoffman folder to the file drawer. That way, he would have grounds to open the file drawer to look for it. And, looking, he might turn up something else of interest.

The inch-thick file, however, was sitting right on the desktop where Parrott had seen it before. Without peeking inside, he lifted the folder with all its contents and set it inside an evidence bag. He couldn't wait to get everything back to Chesco for closer examination.

Carrying his various sealed evidence bags, he returned to the library, where Josephine and Deputy Jones were seated, both scrolling on their phones. "Thank you for your assistance and patience. I'm ready to leave, just as soon as I ask you a few questions, Ms. Wisniewski."

"Need me to stay?" Jones asked. He was clearly tired of babysitting. Parrott understood.

"Not at all. Appreciate the help, though." He was eager to get on the road, too, but he couldn't pass up the opportunity to talk with the housekeeper one more time. When they were left alone in the library, he sat opposite her and leaned forward.

"Ms. Wisniewski, am I correct in saying that you are the head housekeeper here, and you live on the premises full-time?"

"Yes, that's true. I showed you where I stay, on the fourth floor."

Parrott nodded. "Yes, I remember. Now you don't work seven days a week, twenty-four hours a day, do you? Do you ever have time off?"

Josephine straightened her spine and tilted her head. "Yes, of course. My official hours are nine to five six days a week. Of course, there are times, like now, when I'm the only one in the house, and I have to do whatever is needed, no matter what time of day."

"Understood," Parrott said. "And you probably don't clean the whole house—a house this big—you probably have other people responsible for sections of it, right?"

"Of course. I am in charge of my own quarters and everything on the first floor. That is a full-time job, believe me. As soon as I finish the last room, it's time to do the first one again."

Parrott could identify. He and Tonya had only been in the new house a few months, but keeping the dust at bay had already been a challenge. "Do the Mooneys have other housekeepers to clean the second and third floors?"

"Yeah. Martha, she cleans the second floor, where the family lives. She's worked here longer than me, but she don't live in. And Franny—she cleans the third floor. Franny's been sick with the diabetes, so she hasn't been here in a couple of weeks." She clasped her hands together on her lap. "Maybe not so important, since nobody stays on the third floor unless there's company."

That accounted for the dust in the third-floor rooms. Parrott was glad to segue into the topic of company. "So, when there's company, is it part of your job, since you live in, to greet the visitors and show them to their rooms?"

"Sometimes. If I'm here when they arrive. I'm usually on the first floor, so I answer the door for Mr. and Mrs. Mooney. I did that when you came the first time."

Parrott smiled. "I remember." He leaned back and put an arm along the back of the sofa. "Have the Mooneys had company in the past few weeks, let's say three weeks?"

Josephine closed her eyes and touched her forehead, as if consulting an internal calendar. "I don't know for sure. There are usually people in and out of here, in the daytime, in the nighttime. Mr. Mooney, he has a lot of businesspeople who come in and stay. The last few weeks, Mrs. Mooney, she's been gone to Chicago. The baby gonna be born any minute now. And Mr. Mooney—he just left. I can't keep track."

"Do you remember anyone who stayed here recently with a newborn baby?" Parrott held his breath, waiting for the answer.

"A baby? There's a baby bed in one of the bedrooms on the third floor. Sometimes family or friends come with their children,

and that room gets used. We haven't had anyone with a baby in quite some time, unless they came and went on my day off."

Parrott had figured out that the day of the killing, last Monday, was most likely the day someone would have hidden Amanda Hoffman's shoulder bag in that small bedroom. Josephine could be very helpful in answering more questions, as long as she had the right answer to this one.

"Ms. Wisniewski, you mentioned your day off, and I assume you are out and about on that day." When she nodded, he asked, "What day of the week is your day off?"

"That's an easy question, detective. My day off is always the same, ever since I started working here. My day off is Monday."

# CHAPTER SEVENTY-TWO

On his way to Chesco to deliver the evidence he'd picked up at Moonglow, Parrott received a text. Never wanting to text and drive, he normally would have pulled over to check messages. But the items he'd collected from the search at Moonglow were burning a metaphorical hole in the trunk of his car, and he was anxious to get them into the evidence room, hopefully before Jerry left for the day.

Jerry's vintage Mustang was still in the parking lot. Parrott hurried to empty his trunk of the bagged items. He loaded everything into the empty box for easy carrying, but he struggled to balance the box as he entered the building and passed through security. When he arrived at the crime lab, he deposited the box on the counter.

Jerry was on a phone call, so Parrott checked his own texts. A message from Tonya popped up. *Dr. Goldstone suggested an ovulation kit. Bought one this morning. Looks like a good time tonight. Fair warning. Love you.*

Parrott didn't know how he felt about "command performance" sex. Wouldn't that set them up for disappointment if Tonya didn't get pregnant this month? On the other hand, how would he know whether the D-aspartic acid was working if he didn't give it the good ol' college try?

Before he could resolve his conflicted feelings, Jerry met him at the counter. "You bringin' me more gifts, Parrott? What is this, Christmas?" He winked.

"Could be," Parrott said. "I'll be singing carols and hanging mistletoe if these items pan out." Jerry's enthusiasm, if not a total match for his own, was enough to make the interaction celebratory. "Have you got a few minutes for me?"

"Come on back to the office. We can log the stuff in. I don't have time to test, but we can log it all in." Jerry grabbed his labels and markers, as well as his iPad and camera. Back in the lab, both

men gloved up, and Jerry put a large piece of white butcher paper on the table.

"Logging is fine. I'm really fired up about one item. Let's save that one for last." He set the shoulder bag under the table for the time being. First, he removed the bag containing the comb. "There's a light-colored hair there, might match up to our victim, but I'm not holding my breath."

Jerry labeled the package, removed the comb, photographed, and entered it onto the list of evidentiary items in the online case folder.

Parrott emptied his pockets of the pacifier, the candy wrapper, and the receipt from the kids' store in Kennett Square. He took each item from its envelope and laid it on the table. "The receipt could be the most important item here. I'm pretty sure it documents the sale of that yellow duck outfit you've got in there."

Jerry's eyebrows rose. "Really? An amazing find if you can prove that." Jerry went through the procedure for each item, labeling, removing, photographing, and logging.

"The pacifier could have our baby's DNA on it. Might be a long shot, but we could try."

"What about the candy wrapper?" Jerry asked.

"Just log it. Hold off testing until later. Let's talk about this box for a minute."

"We already have the box the baby was in and the comparison box from the Baths," Jerry said.

"Yes, and this one came from a closet in Mooney's house. There were several like it. I just want to establish that these are identical. I hope to show all three boxes came from Mooney's."

"Okay, Parrott. Let's see what your last goodie is. You've got me salivating."

Parrott's hand shook a little as he opened the envelope with the shoulder bag inside. "This, my friend, was shoved under the headboard of a bed in the Mooney house. I believe it belonged to Amanda Hoffman."

"You've gotta be kidding me, Parrott, you lucky stiff." Jerry labeled the evidence bag. He placed a new piece of white butcher paper on the tabletop and set the shoulder bag on it. "Shall we see what's inside?"

Parrott held his breath as Jerry removed the contents of the purse and set them on the paper—a lipstick, a ten-dollar bill, some coins, a pair of cheap plastic sunglasses, a bottle of nail polish, a pack of spearmint gum, a small bottle of Tylenol, and a driver's license.

Jerry turned the driver's license over and laid it flat on the table. He peered at it and uttered a loud whistle. "Holy cow, Parrott. Look at the name on the driver's license."

Parrott crossed his fingers mentally as he stared at the Texas ID. The name on the card was Amanda Hoffman.

# CHAPTER SEVENTY-THREE

After finding a loaded gun in T.J.'s gun cabinet, Kate wasn't looking forward to her husband's return home for dinner. She hated to spoil their romantic bonding, but the weapon had brought back all her fears.

Up until a week ago, living in Brandywine Valley had been wholesome and uncomplicated. The baby on her doorstep and the death of a woman on her uncle's neighboring property hung over her like dual rainclouds, thick and humid, and ready to burst. These kinds of things didn't happen here, and not to people she knew.

She wanted to trust T.J., to believe that he had nothing to do with either of the crimes, but she couldn't alibi him out, timewise. He'd been up and out of the house, unavailable when the baby was found. And now, the gun.

Her first impulse had been to remove the bullets from the gun and put them away in the basement, where the other ammunition was locked up. But what if this gun had been used to commit a crime, maybe even the recent murder by the creek? She considered calling Detective Parrott, but held back.

T.J. had to have been the one to put the gun there. The only other people who had been in the house, to her knowledge, had been Detective Parrott and Caro Campbell. Unless, that is, someone else was there while she was staying at Steven's.

Kate fretted all afternoon. *Fret* was a word her mother often used, and Kate didn't, but today it stuck in her head like a mantra: *fret, fret, fret.* She put on a pair of jeans, a light pullover sweater, and a pair of hiking boots, deciding to distract herself by taking Lucy for a walk. The chill in the air and the country smells of earth, animals, and vegetation combined to soothe the anxiety churning inside Kate.

She took a long route, crossing from the Campbell property to the Mooneys'. She passed beeches and maples with spicebush and ferns underneath. She approached the creek at a narrow

bend, where the water rushed over stones freely and fast, creating a lively, but soothing, symphony. The ruins of an old grist mill attracted her attention. She and Catherine and Steven had played there many times as children, ignoring warnings of their parents to steer clear of the often-muddy drop-off into the creek. The rushing waters had called to them like Sirens, tempting them to break the rules, just this once.

The land was beautiful in a wild and exciting way, giving the illusion of privacy in a wide open space. Kate lay back on an inclined slab and closed her eyes, her dog nestled against her side.

She had no idea how much time had elapsed when Lucy nudged her and barked. Kate leaped to her feet, peering into the distance. Lucy took off in the direction from which they'd come. Probably an animal had caught her fancy—a fawn or a rabbit. Soon Lucy circled back to Kate, and they continued to hike the distance back home.

When they arrived at the cottage, the sun had started its descent, and the air had become quite chilly. T.J. would be home any minute, and, while Kate wasn't exactly ready, her walk by the old mill's ruins had given her the courage to confront him about the gun.

T.J. burst into the main room, his cheeks pinked from the cool air, and a gleam in his eyes. From her perspective on the corner of the sofa, he resembled a happy puppy, ready for the next frisky adventure.

Like that puppy, he sniffed the air and looked around before his eyes landed on Kate's form. "What's going on, babe?" he asked. "Why are you sitting here in the dark?" He shrugged out of his denim jacket and hung it on a peg by the door. He flipped on the overhead light.

She waved him over and pointed to the chair across from her. "We need to talk, T.J."

"Uh-oh. I thought things were going great between us." He patted Lucy on the head and sat. The gleam in his eye was gone.

"They were." She covered her face with both hands and rubbed both eyes "After lunch, I cleaned in here. I hadn't gotten around to cleaning the gun cabinet in a long time."

He exhaled and shut his eyes. "And you saw the .38 pistol at the bottom of the cabinet."

"Exactly. And it's loaded." Kate hated the accusatory tone in her voice, so she softened it. "Whose gun is it, T.J.? Where did it come from?"

T.J. leaned back in the chair and closed his eyes for a few seconds. When he opened them, he took a deep breath and exhaled. "I can explain. You don't need to worry."

"How can I not worry? A woman was killed not far from here just a few days ago. To my knowledge, the killer hasn't been found, and there's a loaded gun in our locked cabinet. And I won't even mention the whole abandoned baby deal."

"Okay, Kate. I'll be totally honest with you."

"Does that imply you haven't been totally honest before?" Her patience was fraying at the edges.

"Yes—I mean, no." He looked his wife directly in the eye. "Remember when I left with Lucy? I wrote you the note saying I was going away. And you asked me later why I took Lucy and then left her at the Campbells'--?"

"—And you had surgery to reverse the vasectomy."

"Yes, all that's true, but before I decided to go forward with the surgery, I was confused and upset. You were suddenly treating me like I was a criminal or something, and I couldn't figure out what I had done wrong." He began to pace in the narrow space. "I didn't—don't—want to lose you, and I didn't know what to do.

"So, I took Lucy for a long walk, over by McCorkle's Rock Road. I love that view from the top of Hays Clark Hill, overlooking the twin bridges. It's quiet and secluded. Nobody there but me and Lucy and the ghosts."

Kate thought of her own "thinking walk" with Lucy that afternoon. "I know where you mean. Over by the abandoned railroad."

"Yeah. Nobody goes there anymore. You can't even get there by car."

"We used to hang out there when we were kids. It had such a creepy vibe."

"Still does." He sat again. "Lucy and I walked around, and I couldn't stop thinking about the baby in the box. How you lit up just looking at her. I picked up a dead branch and starting walking,

jabbing at the barren ground." He jabbed the arm of the chair with his fist.

"After a while, my legs needed a rest, so Lucy and I sat on a big, flat rock. I got a good look at the stick I'd been using, wondering where it had come from, since there were no trees around. I examined the bottom and discovered a point. Someone had shaved the end of the branch with a knife."

Kate found herself being drawn into the story, despite wanting to get to the point. "To use as a tool?"

"I thought so. I started poking around the rocks and the scant grasses. I've heard the legends about the Johnston Brothers' outlaw gang. Supposedly their victims are buried there. I came to a place where a big pile of rocks formed a sort of sculpture.

"Lucy started sniffing around the rocks, so I used the point of the branch to pry. The activity helped me take my mind off my problems, so I was all in. I decided to see what was there. Turned out to be that gun."

Kate's intake of breath was audible. "You shouldn't have touched it. You should have left it there and called the police."

"You might be right, but I didn't. I don't know what I was thinking. Only that there are acres and acres of land out here where nobody goes. I wondered how many people have chased their problems into remote areas like this, like me. Hundreds, maybe. I put the gun in my pocket and walked back home. On the way, I decided to have the surgery. I was all worked up about it. I stashed the gun in the cabinet. If I'd been thinking clearly, I would've at least taken out the bullets. I took Lucy to the Campbells', and you know everything else."

Kate leaned across the distance between sofa and chair and took both of T.J.'s hands in hers. "You need to listen to me, T.J. That gun could have been used to commit a crime, and I don't want it in our house."

"Don't get—"

"I mean it, T.J. I want you to call Detective Parrott immediately. You need to give that gun to him."

# CHAPTER SEVENTY-FOUR

After delivering the evidence he'd picked up at Moonglow, Parrott drove back to the station with a pleasant thrumming in his head. He'd never imagined how exciting the word *shoulder bag* could be. Solving difficult cases often amounted to serendipity like this—interviewing the right salesclerk who gave him the right description, so he would recognize the amazing piece of evidence when he happened to look under the right bed at the right time. As his grandmother used to say, "Boy, you were blessed."

Back at the station, he completed paperwork to document all the findings of the day. His rumbling stomach drove him to the break room, where he bought a diet Sprite and three packs of peanut butter crackers from the vending machines.

While he ate, he thought about different scenarios that might result in Hoffman's shoulder bag's being shoved under the bed at Moonglow. Had she put it there herself?

He startled when his cellphone rang, and Kate's name showed on the caller ID.

"Detective," she said in an insistent voice, "can you please come to our house this afternoon? T.J. has something important to tell you."

He didn't mind going back out, but he wondered why T.J. hadn't called, himself. "Is T.J. there now? Maybe he can tell me over the phone."

As soon as those words left Parrott's mouth, he regretted them. It was a lazy officer who took shortcuts during an investigation. Parrott had promised himself long ago that he would never slack on the job, and he shouldn't start doing that now.

"I think you'll want to see for yourself. T.J. needs to show you what he found over by McCorkle's Road." She covered the mouthpiece, and Parrott heard muffled conversation. "Just a minute, he's coming to the phone."

When T.J. said hello, Parrott asked, "What did you find by McCorkle's Road?"

"A gun, a .38 revolver. Loaded with five rounds, one empty chamber."

Because the coroner had speculated that the gunshot wound to the back of Amanda Hoffman's head was from a .38, Parrott lit up. Could this be the gun that killed Amanda Hoffman? He couldn't pass up the chance to find out. "I'll be there in about twenty-five minutes. Don't move it or touch it until I get there."

On the way, Parrott reviewed what he knew and didn't know about the gunshot wound. Powerful enough to have blown most of the victim's face off, the bullet had entered the back of Hoffman's head and exited in the front. No bullet or casing had been found in or near the body. No weapon had been found at the scene.

Not much to go on, unless the handgun or bullets had incriminating fingerprints. Of course, the gun's registration might lead to a person of interest, but that was highly unlikely, as well.

This would be a wild goose chase, except for the fact that Parrott would have another chance to interact with the Baths, both of whom had aroused his curiosity since the baby was found on their porch.

Kate met Parrott at the door, and Lucy licked his hand. T.J. was hunched over his cellphone at the dining table. A half-eaten sandwich and a few potato chips sat on a plate nearby. He shut off the phone and stood when Parrott approached.

"Have a seat, detective?" T.J. asked. "The gun is over there in the gun cabinet, where I set it. You can take it with you when you leave."

Parrott continued to stand. "How about showing me the gun now?" He put on a pair of gloves and set another pair on the table for T.J. He hoped to see how the caretaker would handle the weapon he had allegedly found by accident.

"I'll get it," Kate said, snatching the gloves from the table. "I've got the key right here in my pocket." She used the key to unlock the cabinet and slid her hands into the gloves. "You know, detective, our fingerprints are going to be on this gun. T.J. carried it home from McCorkle's, and I touched it earlier today when I was cleaning the cabinet."

Parrott stared at T.J. He was clearly not as invested in turning over the weapon as Kate was. "Bring it on over here," he said, motioning to Kate. He took the seat opposite T.J. at the small table.

With the gun between them, neither of them touching it, Parrott asked T.J. to tell him exactly how, when, and where he had found the gun, and when he had put it in the cabinet.

"It's like I told Kate. I was depressed and confused last Wednesday, and I took Lucy for a walk down by McCorkle's Road. You know about the rocks, right? There're legends about them from the Revolutionary War."

Parrott nodded. Not having grown up amid the Brandywine topography, he wasn't as familiar with the folklore, but he didn't want to interrupt the narrative.

"Nobody goes there much anymore, so it's a good place to think. The ground is hard and rocky, and nothing grows." T.J. explained all that he'd told Kate—about the tree branch and the unusual rockpile that attracted Lucy's attention. "I decided to use the stick to pry apart the stones. The gun was under a bunch of good-sized stones. I was surprised to find it was loaded—only one empty chamber. I put it in my pocket, brought it back here, locked it in the bottom of the gun cabinet, and figured I'd deal with it later."

"And then what?" Parrott asked.

Kate, who had been standing three feet away, on the other side of the kitchen counter, interrupted. "Then I found it, cleaning the cabinet. T.J. told me what he just told you, and I said we had to call you."

Parrott made sure the hammer block safety was on before removing an evidence bag from his pocket and placing the gun inside. "Good call. Always good to turn over anything suspicious to the police. I'll take this in and run some tests on it."

As he said goodbye and started for the door, carrying the package, Kate's cellphone pinged. She swiped to read the text and hooted with excitement. "It's Steven. Catherine had her baby. It's a girl!"

# CHAPTER SEVENTY-FIVE

Driving back and forth to Chesco was not Parrott's favorite thing, but when the job led him there twice in one day, he could manage. He often joked that his second office was in the driver's seat of his Camry. He did some of his best thinking there.

The .38 pistol found in the rocks might have been buried there before Amanda Hoffman set foot in Pennsylvania, but it wasn't rusted. Chesco might find valuable information linking that gun to its owner, a crime committed using the gun, the person who had used it last—or none of that. Parrott needed to transport the gun and get the ball rolling as soon as possible, regardless. The gun might help solve another case, and another officer might find the gun that would help solve Parrott's. That's how it worked sometimes.

On his way back to Chesco, with the windows down and the chilly afternoon air whipping against his head, Parrott thought about how much progress he'd made in collecting evidence. He now could create a rough timeline of Amanda Hoffman's whereabouts within the last three to four days of her life. She was still pregnant on Friday when she shopped and ate at Kennett Square. She had the baby within the next day or so at an unknown location. Her milk had come in prior to her death and the baby's being left at the Baths'. Either before or after she was shot on the promontory above the creek, someone stashed her shoulder bag under the bed inside the Mooney mansion.

He had his eye on certain people, too, if not as suspects, as persons of interest who had information about the crimes. T.J. Bath was high on the list from the beginning, with his past record, the secrets he'd kept from his wife, his disappearance, and now, finding a gun. Kate's behavior was suspect, too, especially in this last encounter with the gun and the way she kept interrupting. Stuart Mooney and Randy Barton remained of interest. The unidentified man accompanying Hoffman on Friday morning had

dark hair and light eyes. That could be T.J., Mooney, or Barton—or it could be someone else entirely.

The peanut butter crackers had left his system, and hunger churned inside. He pulled a power bar from his glove compartment and tore at the wrapper with his teeth. Since starting the testosterone meds, hunger had been a beast, dogging him every waking hour. Also, eliminating coffee contributed to his feeling of running on empty.The power bar and a swig of water would have to do.

All of this would be worth it if he and Tonya were able to conceive a baby. Which reminded him of her ovulation message. He needed to get home.

The parking lot at Chesco was thinning out, but Jerry's car was still in its spot. Parrott hustled into the evidence lab with the bagged gun from the Baths.

Behind the glassed-in counter, Jerry bent over a microscope, goggles in place and hair sticking out as if he'd run his hands through it a hundred times. Parrott could sympathize, but he hoped whatever had frustrated his friend hadn't come from Parrott's case.

"Back already?" Jerry asked through the glass.

"Yep, I missed you and couldn't stay away." Parrott waved the package with the gun in the air. "More evidence to drop off."

"Just a minute." Jerry finished with his specimen and put it away, as methodically as if he were a jeweler securing the Hope diamond. He came around the side door and invited Parrott into his office.

"Whatcha got?" He pushed the goggles to the top of his head.

Parrott explained how he'd obtained the Colt .38 snub nose in the evidence bag. "I doubt it relates to the Hoffman murder, but merits checking out. No rush on this one."

"Actually, running a gun is a quick process. I can fit it in now, if you want to stick around a few minutes." He tossed Parrott a glove-smock-shoe covering kit and led him into the back section of the lab.

The florescent lights caused Parrott to shade his eyes for a moment. "I don't guess you've had time to get to those other things I dropped off."

"No chance. Swamped like an alligator, but I'll try to get to it tomorrow. The gun should go quickly, though, and hopefully you won't leave empty-handed as far as information goes."

Jerry laid out his butcher paper and withdrew the gun from the evidence bag. He logged it on the evidence form on his clipboard, listing the make and model. He pulled the serial number off the slide.

"Want to make yourself useful, Parrott?" Jerry handed the clipboard over and pointed to the computer on a desk in the corner. "Go to ATF to see if this baby's stolen."

Parrott enjoyed participating in gathering and analyzing information. He keyed in the serial number and waited a few minutes for the software to do its work. The result caused him to sit up straight and whistle. The gun had a short history, and recently had been reported stolen from a Richard Henderson in Sulphur Springs, Texas.

"Amazing," Parrott said. "I never expected this." He dashed back to where Jerry was examining the trigger for fingerprints and DNA. "Hey, this revolver comes from the same city in Texas where our vic is from."

"Fantastic," Jerry said. "I'm getting a bunch of prints here, too." He showed Parrott what he'd lifted from the gun and trigger. Then he opened the barrel. "There's a bullet missing here, and no casing, either." He removed the five bullets. "Hopefully some partials in here."

Jerry did the fingerprint work with remarkable speed and precision. He manually encoded each latent print before loading it into the AFIS system. "I'll get this going now. No telling how long it's going to take."

"The gun may have been handled by multiple people," Parrott said. He thought of T.J. and Kate, to start with, glad he had comparison prints for them both. "Too bad I don't have a bullet or casing from the murder."

"Since the gun's of interest, let's do a firing test," Jerry said. "C'mon back." He took Parrott to a soundproof room with shelves of ammunition and a firing container. Jerry loaded an appropriate bullet into the gun's chamber and fired into the can. The container caught the bullet. Jerry filled out a form and put the bullet and

casing into an envelope with the form. "I can get this to the mobile ATF lab for testing before the end of the day. You should have the results by morning."

"You're a miracle worker, Jerry."

Jerry took a slight bow. "Just doing my job. I'll check back later tonight and email you whatever results I receive."

"And I'll call my contact at the Sulphur Springs PD to let them know we've got their gun." Having this evidence bring him full circle back to Sergeant Davis caused a shiny, warm ball of satisfaction to roll around inside.

A loud gurgle caused both men to laugh. "Is that you or me?" Jerry asked. "I've barely eaten anything today."

"Me, either," Parrott said. "Guess we're both going for that lean and hungry look."

"*Julius Caesar*? Nah. Look where that got poor Cassius. I'm going to clean up and call it a day. Go home and eat a big steak for dinner."

Parrott thought about what was waiting for him at home tonight, way better than eating steak. He crossed his fingers that the D-aspartic acid was doing its job. If not, he'd have to eat crow.

# CHAPTER SEVENTY-SIX

The next morning, after feeding Horace, Parrott checked his email inbox. Nothing had come in from Jerry on the fingerprints, but the report from the firing test showed no matches for the gun with a previous crime. Not surprising since the model was fairly new, and despite being buried under rocks, the weapon was in great shape.

He reviewed the Hoffman file he'd taken from Mooney's desk. The file contained printouts with background information, including photos, physical description, address, parents' names and address, educational background, employment history, church affiliation—all the regular stuff a private detective might provide. Maybe Barton had dug it all up. There was no clue as to what Mooney's interest in the young woman might be. Whatever it was, knowing Mooney kept a file on Hoffman was enough to stir Parrott's imagination, and his appetite to know more.

Parrott held off calling Sergeant Davis at the Sulphur Springs PD, who was an hour earlier. He couldn't wait to tell him about the recovery of the stolen gun and learn about the owner.

Meanwhile, his hunger for food was creating a tornado in his stomach. He scrambled a few eggs and toasted a whole wheat bagel for breakfast.

Horace ate from his bowl and then flew onto Parrott's shoulder while Parrott ate his meal and chased it with a big glass of milk. The cockatiel seemed to be adjusting to the new house now. "Mmmm, egg," the bird squawked.

"I know dogs beg for people food, but I never expected this of you, Horace," Parrott said. He went to the stove to snatch bits of leftover egg from the pan. "Here you go. Thanks for being a good boy in the house."

Horace gobbled the egg from Parrott's fingers and made a beeline for his cage, where he rang the bell. Parrott doubted children would be so easily pleased. Last night, the ovulation test had confirmed Tonya's instincts. They had followed Dr.

Goldstone's directions explicitly. Then they'd stayed up late, talking about their own parents and what responsible parenting looked like.

Parrott pondered where Amanda Hoffman's parents had gone wrong. Presumably, no one set out to be a bad parent or to raise troubled kids, but his line of work had shown him too many heartbreaking examples of both.

The case had kept him awake into the night. The new evidence had presented him with a lengthy to-do list. He was convinced Barton knew way more than he was telling, and Parrott was ready to confront his colleague. Either Barton was dirty or knew who was.

Parrott couldn't approach Barton without Chief Schrik, though. Knowing the chief was an early riser, Parrott texted him. Within five minutes, Schrik called. "You want to bring me up-to-date, Parrott?"

"Right. And if you agree, I think it's time to have a serious chat with Barton." Parrott proceeded to review all the new evidence, starting with fingerprints from Mooney's note that matched fingerprints in Barton's car. "Barton's connected to Mooney—or whoever handled that note."

Parrott provided details about the box, the comb, the receipt, and the shoulder bag found inside the Mooney mansion. Schrik listened without interrupting..

"To top it off, T.J. and Kate Bath turned over a gun—a snub nose .38—that T.J. supposedly found buried under rocks at McCorkle's. Serial number came up as stolen—from guess where? Sulphur Springs, Texas." As he listed each piece of evidence, Parrott became more and more convinced that these things were not coincidences. They formed a pattern that connected Amanda Hoffman to Moonglow. "Barton knows something, and I want to hear what that is. And whose side he's really on."

Horace sang something unintelligible behind him, and Parrott realized he'd been shouting. He lowered his voice. "How 'bout it, chief? Can we question Barton today?"

"Okay, if you're sure you're ready. Because once Barton knows you're onto him, who knows what he'll share with Mooney. And if

you think Moonglow is locked up tight now, you ain't seen nothin once Mooney pulls strings in this community."

"I understand.". Past experience with heater cases involving wealthy and politically connected citizens had taught Parrott a variety of hard-earned lessons. "I'm ready, chief. Ready for a lot of listening and ready for Barton to do a whole lot of talking."

# CHAPTER SEVENTY-SEVEN

After Parrott hung up with Schrik, he put in a call to the Sulphur Springs PD. Fortunately, Sergeant Davis was in. "'Mornin', detective," Davis said. "How're things goin' up there?" Voices jabbered, and a door slammed in the background.

"Moving along. I think you'll be real interested in what fell in my lap yesterday." Parrott's shoulder held the phone to his ear while he washed and dried the frying pan and put it away. "I'll be direct. Somebody related to the case found a Colt .38 snub nose revolver buried under a pile of rocks not too far from where the victim was found."

"No kidding," the sergeant said. "You think it's the weapon?"

"I'm not thinking that far ahead yet, but the serial number says it's stolen from a guy in Sulphur Springs named Richard Henderson. You know who that is?"

"Well, whattya know? I sure do. You're not goin' t'believe this. Richard Henderson manages the local Applebee's. He reported that gun stolen from a small safe at the back of the restaurant. Several months ago, I think." He uttered a dry, crusty sound, half chuckle, half cough. "Henderson was Amanda Hoffman's boss."

Gooseflesh rose on Parrott's arms as the puzzle piece clinked into place. There was a definite connection between Hoffman and the gun hidden in Brandywine Valley.

Although Davis hadn't been the one to interview Henderson or take the stolen handgun report, he promised to go by to talk to the restaurant manager today. "I'll get back to you afterwards." He laugh-coughed again. "That's what I love about this job. These moments when things start to come together. Thanks for letting me know."

Parrott hung up and headed for the station, even more convinced that now was the time to get Barton to come clean. All the evidence so far could be triangulated from Sulphur Springs to the Baths' cottage to Moonglow. Barton's relationship

with Mooney put him right in the middle of the stage, maybe even in a major role.

When he reached his office, Parrott received a group text from Schrik. Barton and he were to meet in Schrik's office at 8:30 to discuss the Hoffman murder. Parrott was eager for the meeting, but he wondered what Barton thought when he saw the text. Parrott imagined, no matter how deeply Barton was involved, the officer would dread the confrontation.

At 8:30 sharp Parrott walked into Schrik's office to find Barton slouching in one of the two guest chairs across from the chief. Barton had a sallow pallor and a thinner face than usual. Either he was ill, or stress was taking a huge toll. Whatever the reason, Parrott pitied the man who had partnered with him on many occasions, a man he'd considered a friend. He closed the door behind him.

Parrott lowered himself into the chair next to Barton and waited for Schrik to start the meeting. The chief consulted an open file in front of him. "We need to talk about this Hoffman case—the murder and the baby abandonment, which I presume are related." He looked from one to another. "I'm not going to bullshit you, Barton. I believe you've had a front row seat to what's been going on at Moonglow, and it's time for you to tell us what you know."

Barton cringed, and closed his eyes, as if shuttering them would keep the chief's demands at bay. "I don't know—"

"Don't tell me you don't know what I'm talking about." Schrik's volume amplified. "We know you've been working for Mooney. For how long, I'm not sure. Don't try to lie about it. We have proof."

Barton crossed his arms and leaned back. "What are you saying? Am I a suspect?"

"You know very well I would have Mirandized you if that were the case. But I'm not playing," Schrik said. "You might be on Mooney's payroll, but your main job is here. We're a three-man team, and I don't need to tell you what that means." Schrik gave both men looks that could melt icebergs, and Parrott shivered, even though he wasn't the true target of the probe. "So, start talking, Barton. Tell us about your connection to Stuart Mooney, and don't leave anything out."

Barton took a deep breath and let it out slowly. Surely, he'd known someday he would have to live in this moment, a mini-judgment day. "Okay. Mooney approached me last spring. My wife had been diagnosed with cancer, and we were devastated. Not just physically and emotionally, but financially. Our insurance plan is good, but apparently not good enough, and we were being hit with astronomical co-pays and drug charges."

"You didn't say anything," Schrik said.

"Sheila didn't want me to. Still doesn't. But it's been a struggle." Barton leaned onto his elbows and sighed. "Maybe Mooney had found out somehow. Who knows the extent of his reach and power? He called my cell one night after work, in mid-May, and set up a meeting. I was curious, but wary.

"We met in the library at Moonglow the next night after I went off duty. He offered me premium scotch, insisting that I taste it. As much as I was determined to stay sharp, I did indulge in a sip, and then a glass. Incredible smoothness, and I rationalized that I was off work and not violating any rules or ethics." Barton spoke in a trance-like monotone. And Parrott, having been in that library, offered that scotch, could identify.

"Mooney was smooth—acting more like a friend than a potential employer—but I'm a cop. I wasn't fooled. What it boiled down to is Mooney had family problems, just like me. Only his couldn't be solved by money. He wanted me to trail his wife and his son."

Schrik sat up straighter. "I'm assuming he told you why."

"He wasn't too specific at that time. He said he wanted to know where they went, who was with them, the usual rich man's paranoia, I thought."

Parrott bristled at the thought of his own portfolio. He vowed he would never fall into the category of having to spy on his loved ones.

Barton stared at his lap, where his hands pressed his thighs. "I made it clear that I wouldn't do anything to compromise my duties here, and he promised that would never happen. The money was too good to pass up. A hundred per hour, plus a two thousand dollar 'signing bonus.' Sheila's chemo drug costs two thousand per month after insurance, so I couldn't turn it down.

"He asked me to keep everything confidential. I told him I would, but as an officer of the law, I couldn't become involved in anything complicit with a crime, and there might come a time when I'd have to talk. He said he understood." Barton paused to wipe his brow. "He was so agreeable that first time. I remember thinking he must be really determined to sew me up."

Schrik pushed the narrative by curling the fingers of one hand in rapid motion, and Barton got the message.

"So, I started spying on Mrs. Mooney certain evenings after I left here. Problem was, Mrs. Mooney is a horse person. She's up at the crack of dawn every morning and out at the stables. Most nights she goes to bed early. What she did in between was when I was working here. So, it took me a while to figure out how and when she could be out doing something Mooney would want to know about. She had a book club once a month and quilting once a week, both in the afternoons. A couple of Saturdays she went to the farmers' market. Sundays she went to church in Chadds Ford, or sometimes into Philadelphia to the church where Steven works. She was always alone. She and Mooney don't go anywhere much together."

Parrott shifted in his seat. He had questions, but kept quiet, since this was Schrik's and Barton's show.

"You get anything on her worth reporting to Mooney?" Schrik asked, as if he had read Parrott's mind.

"Nothing substantial. Only men she interacted with were stable guys, employees on the grounds, husbands of her women friends, guys selling their wares at the farmers' market. And her son. She's not flirtatious or flighty, but she's also not a happy woman. All the money in the world, but she's never smiling or having fun. Seems like she goes through the motions day by day." He shrugged. "I don't think she ever figured out I was following her. She didn't seem like the kind to be doing something underhanded. Never checked her surroundings or anything like that. She left town a little more than two weeks ago, so I thought maybe she had something going in Chicago. But Mooney said she was going to stay with their daughter, who was having a baby."

"How about the son?" Schrik asked. "You tailed him, too?"

"Yeah. Interesting kid. Good-looking, late twenties. Nice set-up in a fancy condo in a posh section of Philly. Single, pretty much a loner. Wears designer clothes, drives a Mercedes SUV. Works at a neighborhood church—not what you'd expect from a trust fund baby."

"Why did Mooney want him tailed?" Schrik asked.

Barton closed his eyes and took in a gallon of air. He expelled it with a whoosh. "He never spelled it out in so many words, but Steven had been active on a dating website. Mooney found out about it—I don't know how—and he was worried. He said Steven was inexperienced when it came to women, and he could be easily taken advantage of."

Barton's body language, from the tensing of his shoulders to the perspiration on his upper lip, told Parrott that watching Steven had been trouble. Parrott was sure Schrik had picked up on the signals, too.

Schrik softened his voice, almost to a whisper. "What did you find out about Steven?"

"It wasn't Steven," Barton said, his voice coming out like sludge over rocks. "It was the girl. Mooney got hold of Steven's password on the dating site. He asked me to put a bug in Steven's condo so he could monitor his son's personal conversations. Easy to do, since Mooney had a key, and I could do it when the kid was at work."

Parrott and Schrik exchanged glances, and Schrik opened his mouth to speak.

"Don't worry. I told him no—that it would violate wire-tapping protocols. Mooney was upset but said okay. He wanted me to step up the tail on Steven. 'I want to know everything he does, everywhere he goes, everyone he talks to. I don't want him to take a piss that you don't know about.'

"I was racking up hours. By that time, Mooney had paid me more than ten thousand dollars, but I was spending it as fast as it came in. Sheila saw how much her illness was costing, and one night she threatened to kill herself, so I wouldn't have to bear such a financial burden. This extra surveillance with Steven seemed like manna from heaven, except for one thing—"

"—That's when you started taking off from work." Schrik pushed his chair back from his desk and gripped the arms, as if he wanted to stand, but thought better of it. "Double dipping is the kind term for it."

Barton nodded. "I was caught between two bosses, two jobs, and not enough time to do either of them well. That last Sunday before Mrs. Mooney left for Chicago, she and Steven went to church and ate lunch in a local restaurant. After the mother took off, Steven went into his condo and came back out with a suitcase. He loaded it into the back of his car and took off, with me following.

"I had no idea where we were going, but once he hit I-81 South, I had a feeling this would be a long trip. Good for building up hours, bad for leaving Sheila and the station. Turned out Steven had hooked up with a girl from out-of-state.

"'Course, Mooney went ballistic and pressured me to stay on the trail and report in every time I learned anything. He promised to reimburse me for gas and meals on the road. Hotels, too, but once we got on I-40 West, Steven drove like a fiend and only stopped for gas and bathroom breaks. He did pull off the highway near Nashville and slept in the car for a few hours. I nodded off, too, but I didn't want to lose him, so I never really got any rest."

By this time, Barton's voice had become dry and hoarse, likely from emotion, rather than physiology. Schrik stood and said, "Parrott, why don't you go get us a couple of bottles of water? But before we do, tell us, Barton, where did you and Steven Mooney end up?"

"Hmmph," Barton said, "after more than twenty-four hours on the road, we ended up in a God-forsaken town in Texas. It's called Sulphur Springs."

# CHAPTER SEVENTY-EIGHT

Before he carried the cold bottles of water back to Schrik's office, Parrott put in a call to Jerry at Chesco. The ring went to voicemail, so he left a message about the gun's being stolen from the place where Amanda Hoffman had worked. "We're closing in on this, Jerry. Hope things are lining up at your end, as well."

Back in Schrik's office, everyone took their same places. Barton's shoulders slumped, and his dark hair looked as if he'd run fingers through it a thousand times. Tension showed on Schrik's face, too, in the set of his jaw and the furrows in his forehead. The three of them had worked closely together for years. Barton's situation impacted them all.

"Okay, let's keep going." Schrik's voice boomed. "Barton, I need to know how you were paid by Mooney, in cash or by check?"

"I know where you're going. Mooney prefers to pay cash, but I've been keeping track of it for Social Security and income tax purposes. Until the dead body turned up on Mooney's property, I didn't think this gig would ever be a problem."

"Except," Schrik said, "you've accepted secondary employment without approval from me. You've missed work and come in late a number of times, and you haven't been aboveboard about the reasons. Sick time can't be used to tail somebody across the country, sorry."

Barton's voice shook. "I understand, and I apologize. I should've cleared everything with you. Maybe I was too proud. I wanted to handle my own problems without involving the department."

"That was a big mistake, Barton, and you should've known better. I'm not without compassion for your problems, but you should have managed things differently. To top it off, our department is in the midst of a murder investigation involving Mooney. You're smack dab in the middle of it—you're no help to us at all, and your dealings with Mooney may be suspicious, as

well." Schrik stared at Barton until the latter looked away. "I'm going to let Parrott talk to you about that."

Not eager to jump into the dressing down of his colleague, Parrott gathered his thoughts. He needed to walk a fine line between letting Barton know how serious his possible involvement with Mooney might become, and not revealing too much about the evidence they had. What they didn't want is for Barton to leak information to the absent Mooney.

Parrott cleared his throat. "You know we've been investigating this murder, and we've uncovered evidence tied to Moonglow. We know you've spent time with Mooney and on his property, and we have your word, but no proof, that you were acting only on his direction to follow Mrs. Mooney and Steven Mooney."

Barton's eyes grew large, and he choked. "So, you're saying I *am* a suspect."

"Not specifically," Parrott said. "However, this would be the best time for you to tell us every single thing you know about Mooney, his wife, his son, his property—even why he's disappeared and purportedly gone to Chicago or Scotland or wherever. If you want us to believe you're innocent of any wrongdoing, now would be the time to tell us everything that could possibly connect you or them to the dead woman."

Barton's head drooped to his chest, and he took a minute or more before speaking. Neither Parrott nor Schrik rushed him. When Barton finally lifted his head, his eyes were moist, and his voice wobbled. "I never thought I'd be on this end of an interrogation, and, man, this is a certain kind of hell. I wish I'd never met Stuart Mooney—that's for sure."

Parrott sensed a stall and pressed Barton by turning his chair to make more direct eye contact. "I'm sure you do. Now talk."

"Okay," Barton said. "I told you I followed Steven Mooney to Sulphur Springs. He met up with Amanda Hoffman there. He checked into a Holiday Inn when he arrived, and she met him in the lobby."

"Wait a minute," Parrott said. "When was this?"

"Ten days before she turned up dead. That was when I called in sick." Barton shifted in his seat. "She had a rolling suitcase with her. They weren't complete strangers. I could tell by their

body language. They might even have hugged. She was obviously pregnant, and that didn't seem to bother Mooney, so I guess he knew about it before.

"Anyway, they sat down in the coffee shop. I positioned myself where I could see her, and I ordered dinner, too. She was a nice-looking girl, talked with a lot of gestures. I couldn't see his face, but it seemed like she was doing all the talking.

"After they ate, Mooney paid the bill, and they walked to the elevator with him pulling her suitcase. I reported to Mooney. He hit the ceiling when he heard the girl was pregnant. He told me not to let them out of my sight, and if they went anywhere close to a city hall where they might get a marriage license, to stop them in their tracks."

"Did they sleep in the same room?" Parrott asked.

Barton cringed. "Yeah, I gave the desk clerk a fifty to find that out. I needed to sleep for a few hours, so I booked a room and set my alarm for four a.m. Checked out and sat in the parking lot, where I could get a good sight on Mooney's SUV. Good thing I did, because the two of them got in the car about five a.m. and started driving. I trailed them all the way back to Nashville, where they spent the night at another Holiday Inn. Again, in the same room, and I got a room, too. The only difference was they stopped so the girl could go to the bathroom. Then on to Philadelphia, to Mooney's condo. I told the senior Mooney I had to get back to the station, and he said, 'That's okay. I'll take over from here.'"

"What do you think he meant by that?" Parrott asked.

"How the hell do I know? I did what he'd asked me to do. If his son wanted to get together with a pregnant woman, it was no sweat off my nuts. If she was of age, and I was sure she was, they weren't breaking any laws. I still thought everything was pretty harmless. A rich kid gets involved with a girl from the wrong side of the tracks. A grade B movie, that's all. I didn't start worrying until the girl turned up dead. Even before you tried to show me the artist drawing, I knew it had to be her."

"But you didn't tell us. You withheld." Parrott shook his head.

Schrik came around the desk and perched on the edge in front of Barton. "Where's Mooney now? Is he coming back here anytime soon?"

"I don't know," Barton said. A high-pitch had crept into his voice. "He ditched me like a day-old bread crust after the girl turned up dead. I'm sure he wants nothing to do with a policeman from West Brandywine right now." Under his breath Barton muttered and dabbed at his forehead and upper lip with a handkerchief. "Took his money with him, too."

Schrik's eyes narrowed. "Is there anything else you haven't told us pertaining to Mooney or this case? If there is, I advise you to tell us now. It will go much worse for you if we find out later that you've withheld other evidence."

Barton closed his eyes and sucked air. "I can't think of anything else. I carted Mooney around in my car a few times. He wanted to get a look at the girl, and he didn't want to use one of his cars that might be recognized."

"So, he didn't mean what he said about taking over from here? He still had you on the payroll?" When Schrik started nit-picking, he was usually ready to take a decisive step.

"Yeah, I was being paid, but nothing like what I got those four days I went to Texas and back. All that stopped with the body by the creek. I got a big hospital bill, and I had to sell my car to pay that and my mortgage."

Schrik in turn sucked in a breath. "Listen, Barton. I have no choice but to suspend you with pay while we investigate this girl's murder. Turn in your badge and gun right now. And you can't use the squad car. I'll ask Parrott to take you home."

Barton bent over as if he'd been stabbed. When he straightened up, without a word, he placed his gun and badge on the chief's desk and tromped out of the office. "I'll go get some things out of my office now. Parrott, I'll meet you there."

"Sorry, but no. Wait outside my door, and Parrott will accompany you."

When he left, Schrik whispered to Parrott. "I'll call the county to send us some help to cover for Barton. We need surveillance on him and any phone calls he makes. You think he's telling the truth?"

Parrott hesitated before replying. "I'm not positive, but for his sake and ours, I hope to God he is."

# CHAPTER SEVENTY-NINE

Parrott had hoped to keep Barton talking in the more casual atmosphere of the car on the way to his house, but Barton stared out the passenger window and remained silent. Parrott couldn't blame him. Barton was a fly caught in a spiderweb. Talking would only make it worse.

When he pulled into Barton's driveway, Parrott struggled to find the right words for this jumbled situation. He felt regret and pity, but also disdain and shame. He reminded himself not to judge. He hoped he'd never have to face the catastrophic illness of his own wife.

Barton yanked on the door handle and muttered thanks. As he exited the car, Parrott called after him. "Give my best to Sheila. You'll both be in my prayers."

The late morning breeze helped Parrott reorient. Instead of going back to the station, Parrott headed to T.J. Bath's cottage. He had questions about the gun. When he arrived, the aromas of cinnamon and almond floated through the open kitchen window.

His knock on the door was perfunctory, since Lucy barked, and Kate had most likely seen him strolling up the walk. Wearing a plaid apron and a puzzled expression, she opened the door. "Anything new?" she asked.

"Same question I was going to ask you. Whatever you're baking smells delicious."

Kate smiled and opened the door wide. "T.J.'s grandmother's biscotti. They sell like hotcakes at the farmer's market this time of year. People stock up for Halloween through New Year's, I guess." She pointed to a chair at the dinette table. "Make yourself comfortable while I pull this batch out of the oven."

"I can't stay. I'm looking for T.J. Any guess where I might find him?"

Kate removed two large cookie sheets from the oven and set them on the stovetop. "He's mowing. Might not hear a text. He's coming home for lunch, though, if you can wait that long."

"About what time will that be?" Parrott asked. "I can circle back."

Sliding a spatula under the pieces of biscotti and using it to transport them to a cooling rack, Kate worked with speed and precision. "Around noon. Anything I can help with?"

"Something unrelated. I've been trying to get in touch with your uncle, Stuart Mooney. Do you, by chance, have a private number for him?"

Kate took off her mitt and wiped both hands on her apron. She cocked an eyebrow. "No, but I have one for Aunt Connie. Let me get it for you." She picked up her cellphone from the kitchen windowsill and scrolled. "You'd better text her first. She doesn't answer calls unless they come from a familiar number." Kate called off the numbers, and Parrott entered them into his phone.

"Thanks," Parrott said, waving his phone and turning to leave. "I'll be back to talk to T.J." He petted Lucy on the top of her soft head and left.

As soon as he got into his Camry, he texted Connie Mooney, asking her to call him regarding the murder investigation. He added another sentence to clarify that this was related to the body found on the Moonglow property. Having never met Mooney's wife, Parrott wasn't even sure she knew about what had happened at Moonglow in her absence.

By then, the sun was well on its way to full spotlight overhead, so it didn't pay for Parrott to go back to the station and return to the Baths' by noon. He drove around Bucolia instead, looking for T.J. The Campbells' farm was over thirty acres, and T.J. might be anywhere. Parrott took a chance and headed toward the outbuilding where he and T.J. had talked that first day. The Polaris was parked there, so Parrott sprinted over the uneven ground.

Luckily, he found T.J., wearing a sweaty T-shirt, jeans, and a baseball cap, lying on the ground next to a large tractor-mower. When he saw Parrott jogging toward him, T.J. rose and wiped his hands on a filthy rag.

Parrott asked T.J. to go with him to McCorkle's. "I'd like to check out the place where you found the gun."

T.J. squinted but didn't question Parrott. "Sure. You want to go right now? I'm at a stopping place, getting ready to go home for lunch."

Parrott appreciated T.J.'s cooperation. He didn't expect to find much in the rocky terrain. Parrott was less interested in the gun than in T.J.'s demeanor when he was forced to talk about the gun.

The two of them rode in Parrott's car to the deserted area. T.J. led the way to the spot where the gun had allegedly been buried. Parrott searched in a wide perimeter for anything that might identify who had hidden the gun or when. He could find neither.

On the way back, Parrott asked T.J. what he knew about the Mooneys.

"Not that much. They're Kate's relatives, you know. They show up for the Campbells' Fourth of July shindig every year, and sometimes we're included in their Christmas celebrations at Moonglow. The old man sends us a case of great scotch every year. Otherwise, we don't see any of them much, except for Steven."

"That the son?"

"Yeah. He and Kate have always been close." T.J. removed his cap and scrubbed at his dark hair. "The daughter, Catherine, lives far away, and she's sort of snooty—not Kate's type."

"What's Steven like?" Parrott asked.

"Quiet. Introverted. Kate says he's got autism or something like that. Nice guy, though."

"He's not married or got a significant other?" Parrott asked.

"Oh, no. Steven's kind of a loner. I've never seen him with anybody, male or female. He and Kate get along real well."

"If he's autistic, I imagine he might be hard to communicate with. Does he have an anger problem?"

"Steven? No. Steven's about the mildest-mannered guy you'd ever hope to meet. Clark Kent-ish, you know?"

It was Parrott's turn to scratch his head. "That how the father is, too? Mild-mannered?"

"Not at all. The few times a year that I see or hear about Stuart Mooney, he's anything but. Maybe nice guys don't fare well in the business world. The older Mooney is as cut-throat as they come. Kate's told me stories, and I've seen with my own eyes how he can act."

"Snooty, like the daughter?" Parrott asked.

"No. Snooty might be okay for someone with billions. But Stuart Mooney's beyond arrogant. He can be downright mean."

"Have you ever seen him being violent or destructive?"

"I haven't, but Kate says he used to belt-whip his kids, especially Steven. I'm happy not to have much contact with Stuart Mooney. Bad dudes like that never change."

# CHAPTER EIGHTY

What can I do for you, detective?" Connie Mooney's telephone voice had the chill of an icicle dropped down the back of a kid's jacket on a snowy day. Perhaps that was her way of keeping strangers at a distance, or maybe she treated her friends and family coldly, too.

Parrott barreled on in his most professional manner, ignoring her frosty tone. "You probably are aware that a woman was murdered last week. Her body was found on your property. Our investigation has revealed connections between the victim and members of your family. We are at a point—"

"Excuse me for interrupting, but I believe you need to talk to my husband about this, not me. I have been in Chicago for the past few weeks. My daughter had a baby, our first grandchild."

"Congratulations to you and your family," Parrott said. "I'm sorry your joy has to be compromised by a murder investigation. I actually do need to speak with your husband, as well as with you and your son, Steven."

"I can't imagine what you would need to talk to me about. I know nothing about a murder. I have absolutely nothing to tell you. And Steven, I'm sure you know Steven doesn't live at Moonglow. I would appreciate it if you leave Steven out of this."

"I will if I can, Mrs. Mooney." Parrott hated misleading the woman, even though his strategy was within the realm of police ethics. He needed to soften her somehow.

"My husband has an attorney in New York named Ethan Price. I suggest you contact him."

"I met Mr. Price, at your home. Your husband stood us both up." Parrott's patience was a thin wire, about to snap. *If only this weren't a heater case.* "Listen, Mrs. Mooney. If your family member had been shot and killed, you would be clamoring for the police to find the perpetrator and bring him to justice. I don't have time to play word games with you. Either you are part of the problem, or you're part of the solution."

A gasp and a long pause spoke volumes. When she spoke, the ice was melting. "I don't mean to be adversarial. I'm fine with being interviewed, although I have no knowledge related to this murder. My husband will be able to tell you the most."

"Do you know how I can reach your husband? I can certainly start with him."

"Why, yes. He's here in Chicago. Celebrating our new granddaughter. He just arrived today. He's out at the moment, but I can have him call you in an hour or so."

Surprised, Parrott asked when the Mooneys would be returning to Brandywine Valley.

"He'll go back tomorrow morning early. I'll stay for another week to help Catherine take care of the baby."

"Is the whole family together then?" Parrott asked.

"No, Steven is in Philadelphia. He couldn't take off from his job." In the background a crying baby intruded into the conversation. "Hello, precious," Mrs. Mooney said. "I'm going to have to help with the feeding. How do you want to proceed?"

Parrott made a quick decision, while the baby continued to whimper. "I expect Mr. Mooney to call me at this number in an hour. I plan on interviewing him first. Maybe I can hold off on talking to you until you return from Chicago. That may depend on how cooperative your husband is. Please make sure he calls me."

"I will, promise," Mrs. Mooney said, the chill in her voice replaced by sugar. Or was it saccharine?

# CHAPTER EIGHTY-ONE

Parrott picked up a ciabatta sandwich, a salad, a side of mac and cheese, and a bottle of lemonade from Wawa on his way back to the station. His stomach swirled with hunger, while his mind swirled with questions. His instincts told him he was close to solving Amanda Hoffman's murder, and he needed to be sharp.

Back in his office, he chowed down while he made a list of questions:

Did Amanda Hoffman stay overnight at Moonglow? Did she have the opportunity to hide her shoulder bag under the bed?

Did Hoffman hide it? Or did she have it with her on the promontory, and her killer hid it there afterwards?

Whose SUV tracks were on the promontory? Kate's? Steven's? Mooney's? Barton's? or T.J.'s?

Was the gun T.J. found used to kill Hoffman?

How did the switchblade fit into the scenario on the promontory?

Why did Stuart Mooney leave town when he had an appointment with Parrott and his attorney?

Before Parrott could add a question about timing, his cellphone rang. Thinking it was Mooney, Parrott startled and stared at the caller ID. It was Jerry.

"Hey, Parrott. You are going to thank me from the bottom of your big ol' heart when you hear what I've got to tell you. First, the gun. Outside was wiped clean, except for T.J. Bath's prints. Inside is where it gets interesting. A number of partials on the bullet casings match up with Amanda Hoffman. Stolen or not, she's the one who loaded the gun."

A hot wave flowed through Parrott's head, neck, and shoulders. "That's great. Anything else?"

"Yeah. Hoffman's prints are all over the place—on the knife, the shoulder bag, the bullets, the baby's outfit—even the candy wrapper. But someone else's prints are there, too. Not as many, but distinctive. We can rule out T.J., Kate, and Barton. Even for

the unknown prints left on the note, on the file folder, and in Barton's car."

"That leaves Steven Mooney." Parrott whispered under his breath. Parrott thanked Jerry from the bottom of his big ol' heart and disconnected. He tried to imagine scenarios in which Steven Mooney would have touched the various items, but not killed Amanda Hoffman. He could think of several, so he tamped down his excitement and postponed drawing conclusions not totally supported by evidence. Interviewing Steven Mooney was becoming more and more critical, and he had to obtain fingerprints one way or another.

Parrott finished his lunch and washed it down with the lemonade. An hour had passed, and he hadn't heard back from Stuart Mooney. Parrott was beginning to think Mooney had given him the slip again, when his cellphone rang, and "restricted" came up.

"You need to talk to me." Mooney said, without identifying himself. Not a question.

"To whom am I speaking?" Parrott asked, even though he recognized the voice.

"Cut the bullshit. You know who this is," Mooney said.

Parrott clenched his teeth and his fist at the same time.. "Okay, Mr. Mooney. I have important information to share with you. I need your help."

"What's the information?" Tension peppered Mooney's voice.

"I can't reveal anything over the phone. Can we meet tomorrow morning at Moonglow?"

"My plane doesn't land until ten a.m. Also, I'm not sure I can get my attorney out there on such short notice."

Parrott wanted to say, "Then you shouldn't have fumbled the meeting everyone showed up for but you." Instead, he said, "I'll plan to meet you there at eleven-thirty, with or without your attorney. I don't have to tell you that time is of the essence."

"Whatever. I told my wife I would cooperate with you. Mostly I just want to get this murder business off my back and off my property. If you can help me do that, I'll cooperate all day long. In fact, I'll sing your praises to all my friends in the township. I'm not without influence, you know."

The lemonade in Parrott's stomach curdled at this not-so-subtle attempt at bribery. "I'll see you tomorrow morning, Mr. Mooney."

"Yes, and one more thing, Parrott. Do I have your word that you won't contact Steven between now and then? Steven is fragile and easily upset."

With both parents working so hard to protect their thirty-something son, Parrott had to wonder whether Steven's autism had caused them to shelter him from life's realities, or whether they knew something that pointed to Steven's guilt. "I'll do my best to honor your wishes, Mr. Mooney."

Their protection of Steven brought a new concern. What if the Mooneys were planning to ship Steven off to Scotland before tomorrow morning?

# CHAPTER EIGHTY-TWO

By the time Parrott ended the conversation with Stuart Mooney, it was one p.m. A lot could happen in the twenty-some-odd hours before Parrott would interview the elder Mooney, and time was not on Parrott's side. Parrott pulled up Steven's address from the Department of Motor Vehicles database and rushed to Chief Schrik's office. He needed to bring the chief up to date on the case, and, more importantly, to request surveillance of Steven Mooney, while he sought a Grand Jury subpoena. He needed to compel the younger Mooney to give testimony in the death of Amanda Hoffman and the abandonment of the baby.

"He needs to be watched, and if he gets anywhere near an airport, bus station, or train station, he needs to be arrested. We can't let him get away, especially to Scotland, where Mooney has lots of connections."

Schrik needed little persuasion. After Barton's account of how Steven Mooney had driven to Sulphur Springs to pick up the pregnant Hoffman woman, the younger Mooney topped the person-of-interest list. "I'll get the ball rolling right away with the county sheriff's office. "You really think they'll send him out of the country?"

"There's something strange about the way the parents are hell-bent on protecting Steven. A grown man, living on his own, working at a church." Parrott rubbed the sides of his head. "I wouldn't put it past them."

"You think he's the murderer?" Schrik asked.

"It's possible—all except for motive. I can't see how Steven benefitted from Hoffman's death. His parents, maybe. They might have been motivated to get rid of the girl, because she wasn't 'Brandywine material.' From what I've seen and heard, Steven is a nice guy. He cared about the girl. Not many guys would take on a woman who was nine months' pregnant with a baby not his own. I wonder if he knew the baby wasn't biologically hers, either."

"You're right," Schrik said. "There are a lot of ifs in this case. I agree with you that Steven might disappear, so I'll call the county now."

Parrott prepared the necessary paperwork and took off for the Chester County Justice Center in West Chester. Dark clouds spread across the sky, creating a veil from the glaring sunlight. He hoped it wouldn't rain. The thirty-minute ride would give him time to collect his thoughts about Steven Mooney. Having never met him, Parrott could only go on second-hand information.

Kate had said Mooney was good-looking and kind, always able to attract girlfriends, but not keep them long. Was that because of the autism, or did Mooney have a mean streak that drove people away after a "honeymoon period"?

Assuming Steven was the companion to Hoffman at Philter Coffee, Caro hadn't recognized him. Not surprising, since Steven had grown up and left the house before the Campbells moved to the adjacent farm, and photos of Steven had been absent from the senior Mooney's publicity spots.

Caro had observed friction between Hoffman and her companion. What if that tension had escalated in the next few days, and, after the birth of the baby, Steven had become violent?

Before he could pursue that line of thought any further, Chief Schrik called, and Parrott picked up on Bluetooth. "FYI, the sheriff has sent two deputies into Philly to babysit our guy. Should be there within thirty minutes."

Parrott thanked him and promised to keep in touch. He was almost at the exit for the justice center. Before he could return to his ruminations, another call came through.

It was Kate. "Detective, can you please come quick? Something's terribly wrong. It's Steven."

Parrott switched lanes and took the exit before he was supposed to. He pulled into a shopping center and parked, leaving his motor running. A flash of lightning and roar of thunder came from the east, and big splats of rain dotted his windshield. "What's the problem?" he asked, not wanting to be diverted from the subpoena.

More lightning and thunder muffled the cellphone reception, but he could tell Kate was crying. "Text…minutes ago…goodbye."

The word "goodbye" echoed in his brain. "You need to speak up. It's raining here, and I can barely hear you."

Kate raised her voice to a shout. "I think Steven is going to commit suicide!"

Parrott's heart revved, and he yelled into the phone. "What makes you think so? And where is he?"

"…Explain when you get here. Not sure where. Just come here, quick. I don't think there's much time."

# CHAPTER EIGHTY-THREE

Parrott hated to abandon his plan for the subpoena, but detective work required flexibility, and what good would a subpoena do if the subject were dead? Also, being called by a close relative for a suicide wellness check gave him an excuse for keeping a close eye on Steven. Now he was acting to save Steven's life.

He made the U-turn and re-entered the highway, using his magnetic roof light. He voice-texted Schrik, saying he was on the way to the Baths'.

A thousand new questions swarmed in his head. Why would Steven Mooney want to commit suicide? He couldn't know that sheriff's deputies were on the way to watch him. Maybe the parents *did* have a plan to spirit him off to Scotland, and he didn't want to go. Or maybe he was riddled with a guilt too heavy to live with.

Then again, Kate could be over-dramatizing the text message she'd received from Steven. Maybe his goodbye meant something innocuous. Parrott couldn't take that chance. If Kate turned out to be right, Steven needed a swift intervention.

Also, without Steven Mooney's testimony, the chances of finding justice for Amanda Hoffman might completely evaporate. The wheel of evidence at this point seemed to revolve around Steven.

In record time, Parrott pulled up to the Bath cottage. Kate flung open the door, gripping her cellphone. Neither T.J. nor Lucy was with her. The rain hadn't arrived this far yet, but the charcoal-colored clouds had followed Parrott.

"We'd better go inside. There's a bad storm coming," Parrott said.

Kate clasped his arm. "Thanks for hurrying. I'm not afraid of rain. I'm afraid for my cousin." She opened the text on her cellphone to show Parrott.

He took the phone from her and read the exchange from start to finish. The first message was from Steven, sent fifty-two minutes ago. *Hi, Kitty.*

Kate didn't reply for three minutes. *Why are you calling me Kitty?*

*Code name. Remember when we were kids?*

*Oh, yeah. I called you* Pup. *Long time ago.*

Steven waited a few minutes to respond. *Wish we could go back. Simpler.*

*What's wrong?* (Kate had obviously picked up on her cousin's mood.)

*Everything is too much. I have to go.*

*What do you mean, Steven? What's too much? Where are you going?*

*Tell everyone I tried to do the right thing.*

*Steven, stop! Where are you? I'll come to you right now.*

*No. Too late, Kitty. Saying goodbye.*

Kate had sent at least ten more messages, but Steven hadn't replied to any of them. Parrott could see why she was so upset. Parrott asked her some rapid-fire questions about Steven's mental state, whether he had ever threatened suicide before, his location when he texted, what method he might use if he were planning a suicide, and where he might have gone to do it. Kate couldn't answer a single one of them with any certainty, but she guessed that he had been at home when he texted an hour ago. She didn't think he would shoot himself or slit his wrists. Maybe not even take pills. He was sort of a neat freak and wouldn't want to leave a mess in his condo.

"Is there any chance there's a tracker on his cellphone?" Parrott asked.

"I doubt it. Not that I wouldn't put it past my uncle to want to know Steven's whereabouts, but Steven is pretty savvy about technology, and he wouldn't stand for that. He needed independence."

The wind had picked up, and the smell of impending rain enveloped the two of them. Parrott dragged her under the porch. Parrott said, "Think hard about this. If you were Steven, where would you have gone after saying goodbye?"

Kate closed her eyes and bit her bottom lip. Thunder rumbled, and raindrops began splashing all around them. "I'm going to guess, and I hope I'm not wrong. The fact that Steven called me Kitty and said he was thinking of simpler times makes me think he's out here. We spent summers running around these parts, climbing, swimming, sometimes disobeying rules.

"One time we decided to swim in the abandoned quarry past McCorkle's Road. We both almost drowned. Nobody told us that once you jumped in, you could never get out, unless someone was there to rescue you. The sides of the quarry are sheer drops. There's no way to climb out, and the water's so cold, a person will go hypothermic in fifteen minutes. Luckily a neighbor on horseback heard our cries and saved us."

Parrott knew from his water safety training and experiences as a lifeguard that drowning was a painful way to die. But drowning was neat and clean. Sometimes the body completely disappeared. That probably wouldn't happen in a self-contained basin like the old quarry, but Parrott was hoping this wouldn't end with a body.

By now both Kate and Parrott were wet from the slanting rain. "Okay, I'll follow your hunch. A few more questions. How would Steven get to the quarry? Is there a road he can take?"

Kate described the route from Strasburg to the New Bolton Center on 926. "Get off at Byrd Road. He'd have to park on the side of the road and walk to the quarry, about a fourth of a mile."

"What kind of car does he drive?"

"Mercedes SUV, black. Maybe three years old." She held an arm over her head to deflect the rain, which was heavier now. "I'll go with you."

"No, I need you to go inside with your cellphone. Keep it charged and on. And, whatever you do, do *not* delete that message string. If you hear from Steven, call me."

Kate didn't argue, but stood there, shivering, her face slick.

Parrott removed his jacket and held it over Kate's head. "Go on inside now." He gave her a gentle push toward the cottage door and darted toward his car.

While he started the engine, he called Schrik for back-up. Parrott had no time to wish Barton weren't out of the picture.

# CHAPTER EIGHTY-FOUR

Parrott took off for Byrd Road, the narrow road leading to the quarry. By now the rain was pounding the windshield, and his wipers slashed across the glass triple fast. Timewise, if Steven had left his condo in Philly soon after texting "goodbye," he should have arrived at the quarry by now, the thunderstorms notwithstanding.

There wasn't much traffic, but the road was curvy and whenever he accelerated, his car slipped on the wet road. He passed McCorkle's Road, where T.J. had shown him the hiding place for the gun. Having heard about Steven's familiarity with the countryside, Parrott guessed Steven might have been the one to hide it there.

Shortly afterward, Parrott came to a sharp bend in the road. As the road straightened out, a shoulder appeared on the right-hand side. Within a hundred yards, a parked car came into view, and Parrott's heart lurched when he identified it as a black Mercedes SUV. *Steven's car.*

Parrott eased his car behind the SUV and killed the motor. The rainclouds continued to gush, but the lightning and thunder had moved on. The cool air hit Parrott's wet shirt and pants, and a shiver ran from his head to his heels.

Parrott rummaged through his trunk. He donned a plastic rain jacket with a hood and traded his loafers for a pair of boots. A thirty-foot rope might come in handy, so he shoved his arm through the coil's center. He locked the car, crossed the road, and hurtled off through the slushy terrain in the direction Kate had given him. He had a quarter-mile dash to the quarry and not a second to waste.

If Steven had left a trail of footprints, the rain had obliterated them, but the rocky ground and a natural path through bushes and brush gave Parrott confidence he was heading in the right direction. As he rushed, the rain lessened to a drizzle, and the sky lightened to a still-gloomy dove gray.

The rain had chased away the animals, but a few insects and birds appeared as Parrott moved eastward. If Kate's estimate had been correct, he should have reached the quarry by now. Disoriented, Parrott wondered whether he should turn back and start in a different direction.

A brushing sound from the vegetation to the east startled him, and he reached for his gun. A moment later a doe peered from around a thick poplar tree. Her eyes met Parrott's, and she dashed across his trail. Parrott put away his gun and kept moving forward on the slick ground. He'd give it another few minutes.

The rain stopped, and the breeze whisked away the humidity. The air smelled earthy and vaguely metallic. Parrott came upon a clearing that opened on his right to a magnificent view—a natural amphitheater surrounded by boulders and hardy vegetation, saplings and brush growing among the blue-gray rocks. The quarry was deep, and its sides dropped straight down with surprising smoothness, as if someone had sculpted them with a precision electric saw. The water inside was deep blue, its depth and temperature a mystery.

Parrott removed his rain jacket, folding it into a small square, and stuffing it in his jacket pocket. Still carrying the coiled rope, he treaded carefully around the edges of the quarry, looking for signs of Steven Mooney. He didn't have to look far.

A black-haired man wearing jeans and a flannel shirt was hunched over, sitting on a rock, his head in his hands. He could have been praying or meditating, but when he heard Parrott's approach, he jumped and crab-walked behind a huge boulder, out of sight.

Parrott called in the loudest, warmest voice he could muster. "Steven, no need to hide. I won't harm you." He clambered across the rocky distance between them, working not to slip on the wet rocks and the muddy earth beneath. Going after someone under these conditions was risky for both the chaser and the chased.

"What do you want?" The cry came from fifty feet or so around the perimeter of the basin.

"Only to talk. I promise." His words were sincere. All the questions about his case had taken a back seat to saving Steven Mooney's life. "Your cousin Kate sent me."

Steven peeked around a rock, meeting Parrott's eyes in the same way as the doe had minutes before. Perhaps he was assessing whether Parrott was predator or protector. "Wh-who are you?"

"My name is Oliver Parrott. I'm a detective. I'd like to talk with you." Parrott climbed to a large, flat rock big enough for five or six people to sit, facing the quarry.

"I don't talk much." Steven sat on the far edge of the rock, a good six or seven feet away from Parrott.

"That's okay. I'll do most of the talking." Parrott set down the coiled rope and turned to get a good look at the younger Mooney. Tall, sturdy, and good-looking in a way that Mooney's father had never been, even in the youthful photos. The eyes, with their gray, distant gaze, the failure to make contact, said a lot.

Parrott allowed those eyes their privacy. He faced forward, directing his speech to the natural world ahead of him. "Your cousin Kate sent me. She's worried about you, and so am I."

"Good person."

"She loves you and doesn't want to lose you. What did you mean when you told her goodbye?"

"Goodbye is g-goodbye."

"Why are you saying goodbye, Steven? You must have a reason." Parrott stole a glance at Steven, who was hunched over his own lap in a sort of upright fetal position.

Steven didn't respond, but he sobbed softly.

"Does it have anything to do with Amanda Hoffman?" Parrott stared straight ahead, though he wanted to watch Mooney's expression.

"Argh." Steven began to wail.

Parrott scooted a few inches closer, hoping to be within reach of grabbing Steven, if necessary. Mooney didn't notice. He was doubled over, racked with loud choking noises.

"It would be good to talk about it," Parrott said. "Good for the soul." He peeked at Steven, whose shoulders shook so hard that Parrott worried the man would fall. "I know you had a relationship with her."

Steven turned to face Parrott and for the first time met his eyes. "I—I l-loved her."

Parrott waited to see if more was forthcoming, but Steven's cries were wordless and almost feral in intensity. Trying to break into the expression of grief, Parrott raised his voice and said, "Steven, I'm so sorry for your loss. I know you loved her. I understand. Now I want you to take a deep breath and hold it for three seconds. One—two—three. Now exhale. Blow it out of your mouth."

Steven cooperated and repeated the process a few times, finally controlling the shaking and sobbing a bit. He still wasn't talking.

Parrott said, "I know you drove Amanda from Sulphur Springs to Philadelphia. Were you with her when she had the baby?"

Calmer now, Steven nodded. "My house."

"She gave birth at your house?" Parrott could imagine how an event like that, shared between a man and a woman, might create a strong emotional bond.

Parrott understood why Hoffman wouldn't have wanted to deliver the baby at a hospital. She had absconded with the baby that didn't belong to her. A hospital would ask too many questions. Steven, however, might not know about the baby's origins.

"Why did you bring Amanda to Pennsylvania?"

"Get married."

"Did you take Amanda and the baby to Moonglow?"

Steven's hands turned into tight knots, and he shivered. "Yeah. They didn't approve. My dad."

Parrott could imagine the form Stuart Mooney's disapproval might have taken. T.J. had said how mean the father had been to his son. "What did he say?"

"No more money."

"He threatened to cut you off if you married Ms. Hoffman?"

Steven nodded. He gripped the edge of the rock as if his life depended on it.

Encouraged by Steven's responses so far, Parrott pushed for more. "So, then what happened?"

"No. I'm not talking anymore."

"Okay, Steven. That's your choice. But I think it would be best for you to tell me the whole story. It would be good to clear your conscience. It's—it's always best to tell the truth." Parrott caught his breath. He hadn't Mirandized the man, and if he confessed, these statements would not be admissible.

Steven grew red in the face and clenched his fists above his head. "You want me to tell the truth? Okay. I'll tell the truth, and then I'll die." He scooted to the edge of the rock and leaned forward. "I killed her."

Before Parrott could stop him, Steven Mooney had pushed off the rock with his legs and leaned forward, spinning into a free-fall over the quarry.

# CHAPTER EIGHTY-FIVE

Steven's leap into the rock quarry sent adrenalin spiking throughout Parrott's whole body. He was jumping in after Steven. He took a deep breath and called 911 from his cellphone. He tethered the thirty-foot rope to the boulder and unrolled it. Then he stripped off his boots, jacket, and gun. All the while, Parrott watched the splash when Steven entered the water, and waited for his head to emerge.

The 911 call didn't go through—not surprising, because reception out here was spotty. He'd leave the phone on the rock in hopes that someone might track it. The same would be true for texts, but he sent a quick 911 text to both Kate and Schrik. Steven's head emerged, and Parrott could tell he was treading water.

The rope fell to a good five feet or so from the surface of the water. He might be able to leap high enough out of the water to grab it, but not if burdened by the weight of Mooney.

Before jumping in, Parrott remembered something from his water safety training. Saving someone from drowning—assuming Steven would allow himself to be saved—was best accomplished without touching the other person. A stick, a pole, or a net would be better than an arm, which the victim might pull underwater, drowning both parties.

He searched for something appropriate, but there were no fence posts or flotation devices, no fallen tree branches. Heart pounding, he rolled up his plastic rain jacket and stuffed it inside the back of his pants like a spear.

Remembering Kate's warning about the water temperature and hypothermia, he used an old trick from his lifeguarding days. He imagined he was in a scorching desert, burning with fever, yearning for relief. He jumped into the frigid water, welcoming the coolness and ready to deal with Steven.

Parrott didn't touch the bottom. Full of algae with nowhere to drain, the water clung to his limbs as he pushed upward . Breaking

the surface, Parrott located Steven several yards away, sputtering and swallowing water.

Apparently, he hadn't weighted himself down with rocks or other heavy objects before jumping, and he was finding that drowning oneself is not that easy. Or maybe Parrott had interrupted Steven's plan, which was good.

The still water was easy for swimming, and Parrott covered the distance between them with a few well-executed strokes. Steven was already turning pale and wearing himself out by struggling.

"You shouldn't have," Steven said.

"I had to. I care about you, and I promised Kate I would help you. Do you know how to float on top of the water?" Parrott demonstrated floating. "Let's both float on top of the water, for a few minutes."

"C-cold." Steven was shivering. "Leave me alone."

"I won't leave you alone, Steven. I can't." Parrott used his legs to tread water as he pulled the rolled-up rain jacket from his waistband in the back. He knotted the two sleeves together to form a circle. If Steven wouldn't cooperate, he would turn the jacket into a floatation device that would enable him to drag Steven through the water.

Parrott examined the sides of the basin for anything that could be used as stairs or lifts. Kate had been right—the quarry sides were a sheer drop. "Steven, you don't have to do this. Please let me help you."

Steven's face contorted into a grimace, and he answered through gritted teeth. "I told you. Leave me alone." He began swallowing water and choking, even as he kicked and swam away from Parrott.

Dragging the rain jacket, Parrott chased after Steven and caught up with him in two strokes. "You give me no choice, man," he said, as he punched Steven in the jaw hard enough to knock him out. He slipped the rain jacket over Steven's head and pulled the body of the jacket under Steven's torso, creating a sling-type contraption. Parrott could swim, towing Steven alongside.

Parrott glided through the water in slow, easy strokes, gazing at the rocks above the quarry for a sign of someone coming to rescue them. Nothing yet.

Despite being unconscious, Steven shivered, and his feet and hands were turning blue.

Parrott was cold, too. He wanted to rub some heat into Steven's extremities, but he needed his hands to keep himself above water.

Parrott could sense he was losing Steven. The water was frigid, and his own toes and fingers were starting to grow numb. Thinking that the banks might reflect the warmth of the afternoon sun, Parrott swam, holding his end of the poncho, dragging Steven to the side where the rope was. The water might have been a degree warmer, but it didn't make a difference.

Parrott eyed the rope. If he let Steven go, he could probably create enough momentum to push himself high enough to latch onto the rope. His survival instinct was kicking in, and he wanted to try, but he couldn't give up on Mooney yet.

Parrott closed his eyes and said a prayer that was part apology, part pleading. His ego as a detective wouldn't let him leave the confessed murderer behind—even if he'd taken a life, and even if he wanted to commit suicide. If Steven died, Parrott would never know the whole story. And he didn't want to return to Brandywine without the full story.

Time was running out. Parrott cocked his head as the clamor and clanging of loud sirens filled the air above them. He hoped it wasn't too late.

# CHAPTER EIGHTY-SIX

Parrott was too far below ground level to be able to tell much about the emergency vehicles, but the wailing of the sirens might have been the sweetest melody he'd ever heard. Figures in black rushed to the edge of the basin, near where Parrott had left his phone and tied the rope.

Steven started to groan, and Parrott feared he might have to punch him again. On the other hand, the man's skin had a bluish pallor, so hypothermia could be setting in. With Steven in tow, Parrott was unable to do much to keep his own blood flow going, so he took turns rubbing one hand or another against his thighs while kicking his legs under water.

The firefighters positioned a huge sling out and over the water, and it was being lowered. A second sling carried a firefighter, dressed in a rubber wet suit. Parrott kicked hard to propel himself and Mooney toward the two lifesaving straps.

"What's his condition?" the firefighter shouted.

The obvious choice was to rescue Mooney first. "Still breathing. Take him. I can keep myself going a while longer."

"Generous of you, but that's not how this works," the wet-suited man replied. "I'll get him hooked up in the first sling, and you'll ride in the second. After the two of you are on the ground, they'll double back for me."

Used to being the rescuer, rather than the rescued, Parrott mumbled a thank you. He could use a warm blanket and whatever else the EMTs might have to help restore his circulation. He identified himself and Mooney and told the firefighter Mooney was suicidal and had confessed to a murder. "He needs to be taken into custody and guarded."

"We know all that already. Chief Schrik's here on the scene. All you need to do right now is help us help you."

Two hours later, Parrott was lying on a gurney in an emergency room cubicle with Tonya by his side.

"We have to stop meeting like this," his wife said.

"I know. It's not good for my sperm count." Parrott chuckled, thinking about last year's hospitalization for fentanyl poisoning. He wiggled his fingers and toes under the warm blankets he was wrapped in. "I feel fine, though."

"That's what you always say." Tonya eyed the IV bag that dripped fluid into Parrott's arm. "Maybe that's the liquid refreshment talking."

"No, I'm serious. I wasn't in the cold water all that long, and I can feel my extremities. What do I need to do to get out of here?"

"The doc wants to keep you for observation at least twelve hours. But, knowing you—"

"—I can't sit around." Parrott held up thumb and forefinger two inches apart. "I'm this close to wrapping up a case."

Tonya sighed and handed Parrott the nurse-call controller and his recovered cell phone. "I brought you clean clothes in case you wanted to sign yourself out against doctor's orders."

Parrott pushed the button on one and called Schrik on the other. Mentally, he was already sitting next to Steven Mooney, asking probing questions.

# CHAPTER EIGHTY-SEVEN

Steven Mooney had been admitted to a room in the same hospital where Parrott was treated, so after Parrott discharged himself, all he had to do was ride the elevator to the sixth floor. The floor station was vacant, so he went directly to room 622. He was pleased to find Sheriff's Deputy Simon seated outside the open door, reading the newspaper.

Parrott thanked the deputy and peeked around him. Mooney was under bed coverings. An electronic alarm system around the bed glowed red and green. His head and arms were wrapped in bandages. All that showed was the man's eyes and mouth, and they were both closed. "How's he doing?"

"Doctors are optimistic. They're raising his body temp slowly. He's probably doing better than he looks." The deputy put his newspaper under his chair. "You can go in."

Eager to talk to Steven Mooney, Parrott knocked on the door and walked in, speaking in a normal volume. "Hello. How are you feeling?"

Mooney opened his eyes and then squinted at Parrott. He groaned. The telemetry and tubes Mooney was hooked up to kept doing their thing, creating a numerical light and sound show. If Mooney was sorry to be alive, he didn't say so.

"Remember me?" Parrott asked. "I'm glad you made it out of the quarry." Parrott pulled a chair to the side of the bed. "We need to continue our conversation about what happened with Amanda Hoffman, but before we go any further, I need to warn you—"

Steven turned his eyes to the wall and grunted. "Call my cousin. If she's here, I'll talk."

"You want me to get Kate over here?" Parrott asked. Under normal circumstances, he probably wouldn't honor such a request, but given Steven's autism, his attempted suicide, and his relationship with Kate, Parrott decided having Kate there might work.

Kate answered the phone right away "I'm in the lobby of the hospital."

Parrott warned her that her role would be merely supportive. While he waited, Parrott looked out the window at the waning sunlight. He also yielded right of way to a nurse's assistant, who checked on Mooney's vitals and made a notation on the computer near the door. "Your dinner will be here shortly—some nice chicken broth with rice, tea, and biscuits. Do you have an appetite?"

Parrott didn't hear the response, but he wanted Mooney to get his strength back. And, actually, chicken broth with rice sounded really delicious to him, too.

When Kate arrived, she acknowledged Parrott and the deputy, but she hastened to Steven's bedside, where she whispered to her cousin without touching him. The only word Parrott could hear was his own name. Steven didn't respond, but his eyes remained on Kate, even when Parrott began talking.

Parrott considered, but then rejected the idea of recording this interview. Kate was there as a witness, and he didn't want to do anything to spook Steven any more than necessary. "Steven Mooney, we have some unfinished conversation. I'm fine with your cousin Kate's being here in the room, because I think you will be more comfortable. But before we start, I need to read you your rights."

Steven didn't react while Parrott Mirandized him, but Kate's eyes opened wide, and she let out a puff of air. She sat in the chair next to the bed. Parrott remained standing. When Parrott asked, "Knowing and understanding your rights as I have explained them, are you willing to answer questions without having a lawyer present?"

Steven closed his eyes and gave a slight nod.

Parrott looked at Kate and then back at Steven. "To be clear, please say the word yes, if you agree to answer questions without a lawyer."

Steven said yes, his only word since Kate had arrived.

Parrott knew he had to proceed carefully. His witness might shut down at any time. Also, he was gambling on Kate's cooperation based on their previous conversations, but blood was thicker than water. "Okay, let's start with what you told me at the

quarry, that you killed Amanda Hoffman. Do you acknowledge that statement now?"

Kate's intake of breath was loud and ragged. "What? You killed her?"

Parrott gave Kate a stern look and raised a hand. Steven replied with a single word, "Yes."

Parrott made his baritone voice as soft as possible. "You also told me you loved Amanda. Is that correct?" When Steven nodded, Parrott continued. "Okay, I'm going to ask you a series of questions regarding the circumstances. I need to hear the truth about what led up to the day that Amanda was killed." He paused to gauge whether Steven was listening and decided he was.

"Let's start with your trip to Sulphur Springs. Was that the first time you met Ms. Hoffman in person?"

Steven grunted. "Yeah. Met online."

Encouraged that Mooney was talking, Parrott went on. "Two questions—did you know she was pregnant, and did you plan to bring her back to Philadelphia?"

"Yes to both. Planned to get married." Steven made eye contact with Kate, whose eyes brimmed with tears, although she remained silent.

"Did you introduce her to your parents? How did they feel about her?"

"Just my dad. Mom in Chicago. He freaked over Amanda's pregnancy." Steven turned to stare at the wall.

"Did your dad's disapproval change your mind about getting married?" Parrott couldn't help feeling sorry for this guy whose dream of happiness had become a nightmare.

Steven shook his head. "No, but decided to wait till after the baby was born."

"You thought things would be better once your parents could see the baby?" Parrott asked.

"Yeah, especially mom."

Parrott could see the logic. Connie Mooney might be sympathetic to Steven's decision, as well as to a newborn. Besides, Stuart Mooney's dossier on Hoffman showed awareness and disapproval of the woman well before he'd met her in person.

"Okay, let's talk about the birth of the baby. Where and when did Amanda give birth?"

"My house. Two and a half days before—"

"—Before Amanda died, correct?" When Steven nodded, Parrott moved forward on conjecture. "Did you then take Amanda and the baby to visit your father at his estate?"

"Yeah."

"Had your father changed his mind about your marriage, now that the baby was born?"

"No. Worse."

Kate touched the edge of the bed. She wiped away tears, but she trembled, perhaps realizing this was the baby she'd later found on her back steps.

Parrott understood, but he shook his head to remind her that this was Steven's story.

"Did your father's disapproval dissuade you from marrying Amanda this time?"

"No!" Steven grabbed at the compresses on his head. At that moment, his dinner tray arrived.

The aroma of chicken broth filled the air, and Parrott's stomach grumbled. Sensing this would be a good time for a break, Parrott called an intermission.

A nurse's aide entered the room. In a sing-song voice she chirped, "Let's get some of those blankets off, so you can eat."

✸ ✸ ✸

While Kate coaxed Steven to eat and drink, Parrott sat quietly in a second chair. Though it was only 5:30, Parrott's body clock screamed midnight. The strain of the quarry had caught up to him, and his energy was depleted. He couldn't stop now, though. The hardest part of the questioning was about to take place, and Parrott had to stay sharp.

With the compresses removed from Steven's head and his right hand, Parrott realized again what a good-looking man Steven was, and how difficult it must have been for him, being on the spectrum, to handle relationships with women who were attracted to him.

Steven pushed his empty soup bowl away, and Parrott pulled up a second chair to the same side of the bed as Kate. He wanted to be at eye level, and he wanted Steven to feel Kate's support while Parrott led him through more agony.

Parrott began by reminding Steven of having received and waived the Miranda warnings and asked if Steven was ready to continue.

He nodded and looked at Kate. "Go on."

Parrott took a deep breath and asked, "Did you take Amanda Hoffman in your SUV to the promontory above Brandywine Creek on the morning she was killed?"

Steven nodded and made a sound like a hiccup.

"Why did you go there early that morning? Wasn't it still dark outside?"

"Get away from my father. He was cruel. Said he'd disown me if I married a woman with a baby. Amanda was upset and wanted to leave right then. I persuaded her to stay the night, but we didn't sleep." He paused to take a few deep breaths. "Didn't want to argue in the house. Thought I could calm her down if we sat out on the grounds. It was quiet and peaceful, dark except for car lights I left on."

"Was the baby with you on the promontory?" Parrott asked. This had been one of the biggest question marks in his hypothetical construction of the scenario.

Steven nodded and hiccupped again. "Sweet baby. On the ground." He looked at Kate and then looked away.

"Were you able to calm Amanda down?" Parrott asked, although he knew the answer.

"No. I said, 'Let's go get married anyway.' I loved her and the baby." A tear spilled from one eye and traveled the length of his face.

"But she didn't want to?" Parrott asked.

"No. She wanted money. She w-wanted money more than I did."

Parrott could imagine how distressing that might be to someone like Steven, to whom money had always been plentiful, but love hadn't. "So, what happened after that?"

"Amanda went nuts. I guess she was crazy all along. She pulled a gun out of her shoulder bag and aimed it at the baby."

"She wanted to kill the baby?" Parrott thought of the Hidalgos' precious Ada and shivered at how close they had come to losing her.

"Yes. She said, 'If the baby is gone, your father will accept us. We'll tell your father we gave it up for adoption.' I couldn't believe she'd kill her own baby."

Parrott glanced at Kate, who was holding both hands over her mouth. Apparently, Steven hadn't known that Amanda was a surrogate. "So, what did you do?"

"Took gun away. I couldn't grab the baby."

"Amanda was holding tightly to the baby?" Parrott asked.

"Yeah. It all happened fast." Steven covered his eyes with his bandaged and unbandaged hands and uttered a low cry. "I had the gun."

"And then?"

"She put the baby down, pulled a knife out of her bag, and opened it. She lifted her arm with the knife and tried to stab the baby's neck." Steven's sobs echoed in the sterile room.

"So, you shot Amanda in the back of the head?" Parrott couldn't imagine how terrifying that had been.

"I had to stop her. I had to save the baby." Steven bent over on the bed, sobbing and shaking, beyond consolation.

Kate was also sobbing, unable to make eye contact with Parrott, but also not attempting to hug or give comfort to Steven.

Parrott gave them time to grieve. That moment on the promontory could never be taken back or erased from memory. Parrott had his explanation now. The rest would be easier.

Once Steven resumed normal breathing, Parrott pushed for more. "What did you do after you shot Amanda?"

"I went ballistic. Pushed Amanda's body off the edge. I grabbed the baby. Took the gun and the shoulder bag. Couldn't find the knife."

"Did you consider calling the police?"

"No. I felt sick, couldn't think. I put the baby in an empty box I had in my trunk. Stuck in some bottles of breast milk Amanda had filled." Steven's voice had transformed to that of a robot.

"Where did you take the baby in the box?" Parrott knew, of course, but needed Steven to say it.

Steven stared at his cousin. "I put her on Kate's back steps. I knew Kate would take good care of her."

"What did you do after that?" Parrott asked.

"Needed to think. Had to get rid of the gun. Wiped it clean and buried it under a pile of rocks over by McCorkle's." He rubbed his face, as if to cleanse it. "Took the shoulder bag back to my father's. Stashed it under a bed where nobody would think to look. I could go back and get it later."

"Did you talk to your father afterwards?" Parrott asked.

"Nah. I'm scared to. More scared to talk to him than to you."

# CHAPTER EIGHTY-EIGHT

Steven Mooney's confession had moved Parrott more than he wanted to admit. Although there was no one to corroborate most of the story, Parrott believed Steven had told the truth. Still, Parrott had arrested him on suspicion of third-degree homicide for a killing committed in the heat of the moment, and manslaughter, as an automatic charge including lesser offenses. The district attorney added misdemeanor charges, because Steven had taken steps to remove, conceal, and alter evidence in a homicide.

Mooney's father, returning from Chicago, declined to meet with his son face-to-face, but swiftly hired a fancy criminal defense law firm. The defense became "defense of others."

Thirty-six hours after his arrest, Steven was arraigned and transferred to a locked mental health facility on the Delaware border, where he would receive intense counseling while the case was pending.

The saddest part was that Hoffman's death was unnecessary. All she'd needed to do if she wanted to get rid of the baby was take her back to Sheltering Palms, where the infant would have been given to her rightful parents, no questions asked.

❖ ❖ ❖

Schrik took Barton off suspension and gave him back his gun and badge. Parrott met with Barton the next day, and Barton apologized for anything and everything he'd done to stand in the way of Parrott's investigation.

"I know I was a jerk, and I let you down. I knew you were onto me, and all I could think of was to stay away from you. You ended up doing twice the work you should have. You deserve better."

Parrott couldn't argue with any of that. Barton's conduct had made the case extra-complicated, but it was a big relief to know that the West Brandywine PD didn't have a dirty cop on its hands.

"Listen, Barton. We've been through a lot together, and we'll probably go through a lot more in the future. As long as we're clearing the air, I have a confession to make."

Barton tilted his head like a St. Bernard waiting for a treat.

"I have your SUV in my garage at home. Now that I don't need it for evidence purposes, I want to give it back to you."

Barton's mouth gaped, and he gripped the arms of his chair. "What? How did that happen?" Before Parrott could explain, Barton said, "Omigosh, that cute little redhead who bought my car was a plant?"

"That's right. If you hadn't been so desperate for money, I'm sure you never would have bought her story."

"Where did the money come from?" Barton asked.

"My bank account. I couldn't let you sell the car. What if it contained important evidence?"

"I'll pay you back somehow," Barton said.

"Absolutely not. Think of it as a get well present for Sheila."

Kate went to visit Steven three times per week while he awaited trial, always loaded with sourdough bread and sweets for her cousin and the staff. She'd met with his team of attorneys several times in preparation for her testimony at trial.

Now that her suspicions of T.J. had been lifted, their communication had improved dramatically. Kate had encouraged him to hire a private investigator to locate his teenage daughter.

"You'd really be open to that?"

"Of course. She might be yearning for a father figure in her life. I could see a lot of good coming out of that."

"You are truly an amazing woman, Kate Bath."

"I'm glad you think so. And I hope you'll think I'll be an amazing mother, too."

T.J. stared at his beautiful wife with tears in his eyes. "Are you saying—?"

Kate nodded and fell into his open arms.

Parrott turned over all the evidence to the prosecutors for the *Commonwealth of Pennsylvania v. Steven Joseph Mooney.* He had the gun, the knife, the shoulder bag, and the receipt from the yellow duck outfit purchase. Although these items supported the charges against Steven in terms of his hiding evidence, they also corroborated his confession.

Sergeant Davis of the Sulphur Springs PD told Parrott the Hoffmans weren't pushing for justice for their wayward daughter. Amanda had gone awry long before she'd met Steven Mooney, and, although they grieved the loss of their only child, they couldn't excuse her behavior. They were especially mortified over Amanda's fleeing from her moral obligations to Sheltering Palms fertility clinic, which amounted in their minds to kidnapping another family's child. Learning that Amanda had threatened the life of the baby had put them over the edge in a different kind of grief—guilt over how they had gone wrong in parenting.

Although the Grand Jury had indicted Steven, and the defense team entered a plea of not guilty, as expected, no one was jumping to set a trial date. Even if the defendant hadn't been the son of a billionaire tycoon, the fact that Steven's actions had saved the life of an innocent baby would make it hard for anyone to convict him of third-degree homicide or manslaughter. Hiding evidence was a different matter, and the prosecutors didn't want to let go of that charge, even though the defense lawyers would undoubtedly drag out Steven's autism and suicidal tendencies.

As far as Parrott was concerned, Steven had suffered enough, and would continue to suffer every time he thought of Amanda Hoffman. Whether Steven could ever have a normal life would remain a mystery.

In the end, Steven pled guilty to interfering with a homicide investigation by hiding evidence. The conditions for this plea deal included continued in-patient specialized psychotherapy in a private facility for trauma and suicidal tendencies, until such a period as his therapists testified his mental health was restored, and the judge would concur and permit him to return to his home and place of employment. Then he would be sentenced to probation and to perform community service for six months. He

would also pay a fine of twenty thousand dollars to be used by Chester County mental health services.

In exchange for meeting these requirements, the misdemeanor would be expunged from Steven's record, but, as he stated in court, he welcomed the chance to "work off" the heavy burden of guilt on his conscience.

❈ ❈ ❈

Parrott's next sperm sample, after being on D-aspartic acid for a month, was encouraging. Dr. Goldstone told him and Tonya to go on a vacation and have some fun. Whether coincidence or conspiracy, Chief Schrik called Parrott in on the same day.

"You did incredible detective work solving the murder and baby abandonment case. I can't promote you or give you a pay raise, but I'd like to give you two weeks off that won't count as vacation time. Why don't you and Tonya go on a trip—see a bit of how the other half lives." The words hadn't tumbled from his mouth for seconds before he broke out into loud guffaws. "What I meant is—*your* half. I mean—"

Happy that he and the chief were able to laugh about such matters now, Parrott chuckled, too. "I know what you mean, and thanks. A vacation might be exactly what the doctor ordered."

When he arrived home from work, Tonya was already poring over brochures she'd picked up at the travel agency. "Where would you like to go, my love?" Parrott asked.

"Oh, Ollie. Right now it's the dry season in Africa. Greater visibility and higher game density near water sources. I'm game if you are."

Hairs stood up on Parrott's arms and the back of his neck. He and Bo had fantasized about visiting the continent of their ancestors, but Parrott had never expected to fulfill that dream. Parrott wrapped his wife in his arms and swayed from side to side. "I'm game," he said, and then he buried his head in her neck and shoulders.

Watching from his cage, Horace chirped, "Perfect ending."

# ACKNOWLEDGEMENTS

Every book has its angels, people who give freely of their time and consideration to assist in the creation of an authentic story, well-told and well-published. I am grateful to the following angels whose expertise and generosity helped conceive, carry, and give birth to MURDER OUTSIDE THE BOX. Steven Siepser, John Moss, and Mamie Duff provided tales and inspiration related to helicopters and the rocky topography in Brandywine Valley. Dr. James Goldstone; Katherine Hughes and Marissa Barnett; and Susan Edmonson, attorney, assisted with details about childbirth, fertility clinics, and related legalities. Katharine Pope of the National Missing and Unidentified Persons System (NamUs), shared details of how Detective Parrott might discover the identity of a woman without a face. Captain Destin Sims of the Galveston Police Department offered many of the procedural details throughout this book and the entire series. Sherri Culver and Howard Rubin provided medical information. Minette Lauren shared her personal experiences with cockatiels like Horace. Phyllis H. Moore rescued me from the ledge by coming up with the book's title. Along with my two writers' critique groups, fellow authors, Karen M. Odden, and Clare Mackintosh, helped extensively with edits. Rebecca Evans designed the spectacular cover and formatting. T.J. Bath made a very generous donation to The Grand 1894 Opera House in order to become a character in this book. And, last, but never least, my husband, alpha reader, consultant, business advisor, and everything else, Edward Richard, helps me navigate this writing journey and fulfill my dreams. I am eternally grateful to each of them and to you. You keep my heart full.

# IF YOU ENJOYED READING THIS BOOK,

please consider rating and giving an honest review and sharing it with other readers.

✝ ✝ ✝

Saralyn is happy to participate in book club or readers' group activities, or speak at meetings or large group events. Contact her at saralyn@saralynrichard.com.

✝ ✝ ✝

For news, contests, surveys, and other fun opportunities, sign up for Saralyn's monthly newsletter.